Basketball on Paper

Other Sports Titles from Potomac Books, Inc.

Pro Basketball Prospectus: 2003 Edition
by John Hollinger

Chris Dortch's College Basketball Forecast: 2003–04 Edition
edited by Chris Dortch

Same Knight, Different Channel: Basketball Legend Bob Knight at West Point and Today
by Jack Isenhour

String Music: Inside the Rise of SEC Basketball
by Chris Dortch

Basketball's Most Wanted: The Top 10 Book of Hoops' Outrageous Dunkers, Incredible Buzzer-Beaters, and Other Oddities
by Floyd Conner

Coaching Matters: Leadership and Tactics of the NFL's Ten Greatest Coaches
by Brad Adler

Basketball on Paper

Rules and Tools for Performance Analysis

DEAN OLIVER

Potomac Books
An imprint of the University of Nebraska Press

Library of Congress Cataloging-in-Publication Data

Oliver, Dean, 1969–
  Basketball on paper : rules and tools for performance analysis / Dean Oliver.— 1st ed.
    p. cm.
Includes bibliographical references and index.
  ISBN 978-1-57488-687-0 (hardcover : alk. paper)
  1. Basketball—United States—Statistical methods.   I. Title.

  GV885.55.O55 2003
  796.323′02′1—dc21

                                        2003012662

ISBN 978-1-57488-688-7 (paperback: alk. paper)

Printed in the United States of America on acid-free paper that meets the American National Standards Institute Z39-48 Standard.

Text design by Pen & Palette Unlimited

First Edition

To Coach Gene Victor and my friends from Caltech.
We made a really good team.

Contents

Acknowledgments

Thanks to Dad for buying me the first Bill James *Baseball Abstract* in 1984. Thanks to Bill James for writing that *Baseball Abstract* and all the other books that inspired so much, then releasing the methods to those of us who follow. Thanks to Dad for buying me *Defensive Basketball.* Thanks to Frank McGuire, Dean Smith, and Clair Bee for their contributions to *Defensive Basketball* and for helping to make coaching such an honorable profession.

Thanks to Coach Gene Victor for making me an assistant coach, valuing my opinion as a precocious college student, and setting me up as a scout with Bertka Views. Thanks to Bill and Solveig Bertka for their guidance and trust while I worked for Bertka Views. Thanks to the Seattle Supersonics organization and to the Charlotte Sting organization for the opportunity to see their needs and for boosting my stock with publishers. Thanks in particular to Yvan Kelly and John Maxwell for being friends on the inside.

I owe an immense debt of gratitude to Doug Steele and Dean Lavergne for providing me with electronic versions of the data used here. They made my life so much easier by doing quality work over a long period of time. I'm sure I owe their wives/girlfriends a few trips to bed-and-breakfasts to make up for the time they've allowed their significant others to spend helping me out.

Thanks to Mohan Sandhu and Jessica Donovan for reading draft chapters and providing comments.

Thanks to Clay Kallam of the Full Court Press *(www.fullcourt.com)* for numerous thought-provoking conversations.

Thanks to Swarna Ghanta for initially and perhaps unintentionally inspiring me to write at all.

I owe an immense debt of gratitude to my very good friend Dave Carta for providing me shelter, wireless Internet, comments on chapters, and a good atmosphere for getting this done. I really can't say thank you enough.

Jefferson Sweeney's complimentary videotape helped out on one of those chapters.

David Berri provided me with inside information on sports economics that helps to make my work a bit deeper. I'm glad the Internet introduced us.

Thanks to ENVIRON International for giving me the time off to make it work.

Thanks to Ross Russell, who designed the cover, and to the basketball that gave its life for that cover.

The Association for Professional Basketball Research, started and stewarded by Robert Bradley, has also been a very valuable resource in developing this book. Bradley's *Compendium of Pro Basketball* is an under-recognized source of a vast amount of NBA information.

Mike Tamada has been a valuable technical reviewer of my work, raising questions about my methods and pointing me in the direction of other people doing related work. Bob Chaikin has also provided useful insight through his years of watching tape and developing his own unique way of evaluating basketball. Thanks to Stuart McKibbin for his insightful research on the Lakers. Thanks also to Nic Antoine for spreading the word and hooking me up with Pete Palmer, whose advice was valuable and whose insight on baseball was used several times in this book. Thanks to Pete for then hooking me up with John Thorn, who, along with Sean Lahman, was integral in putting me in touch with my publisher.

I really appreciate the help of all of you. If no one but you smiles and no one but you thinks a little more upon reading this, I will still be happy. My publisher may not be, but I will.

Abbreviations

Just to make things simpler in the book, I've introduced some abbreviations to shorten equations.

Individual or General Statistics

AST   Assists (if used with TMAST, indicates individual player assists)

BLK   Blocks (if used with TMBLK, indicates individual player blocks)

DQ   Disqualifications (if used with TMDQ, indicates individual player disqualifications)

DREB   Defensive rebounds (if used with TMDREB, indicates individual player defensive rebounds)

DRtg   Points allowed divided by total possessions times 100 (if used with TMDRtg, indicates individual)

EffFG%   Effective field goal percentage (if used with TMEffFG%, indicates individual)

FG%   Field goal percentage (if used with TMFG%, indicates individual)

FG3%   Three-point field goal percentage (if used with TM3FG%, indicates individual)

FG3A   Three-point field goals attempted (if used with TMFG3A, indicates individual player three-point field goals attempted)

FG3M   Three-point field goals made (if used with TMFG3M, indicates individual player three-point field goals made)

FGA   Field goal attempts (if used with TMFGA, indicates individual player field goal attempts)

FGM   Field goals made (if used with TMFGM, indicates individual player field goals made)

Floor%   Scoring possessions divided by possessions (if used with TmFloor%, indicates individual player)

FT%   Free throw percentage (if used with TMFT%, indicates individual)

FTA   Free throw attempts (if used with TMFTA, indicates individual player free throw attempts)

FTM   Free throws made (if used with TMFTM, indicates individual player free throws made)

GS   Games started (if used with TMGS, indicates individual player games started)

L   Losses (if used with TML, indicates individual losses)

MIN	Minutes played (if used with TMMIN, indicates individual player minutes played)
OREB	Offensive rebounds (if used with TMOREB, indicates individual player offensive rebounds)
ORtg	Points produced divided by total possessions times 100 (if used with TMORtg, indicates individual)
PF	Personal fouls (if used with TMPF, indicates individual player personal fouls)
Play%	Play percentage (if used with TMPlay%, indicates individual)
Play	Plays (if used with TMPlay, indicates individual)
Poss	Total possessions (if used with TMPoss, indicates individual player total possessions)
PTS	Points (if used with TMPTS, indicates individual player points)
ScPoss	Scoring possessions (if used with TMScPoss, indicates individual player scoring possessions
STL	Steals (if used with TMSTL, indicates individual player steals)
TOV	Turnovers (if used with TMTOV, indicates individual player turnovers)
TREB	Total rebounds (if used with TMTREB, indicates individual player total rebounds)
W	Wins (if used with TMW, indicates individual wins)
PPG	Points per game (if used with TMPPG, indicates individual)
Win%	Winning percentage (if used with TMWin%, indicates individual winning percentage)
FM	Forced Misses (if used with TMFM, indicates individual forced misses)
FTO	Forced Turnovers (if used with TMFTO, indicates individual forced turnovers)
FFTA	Forced Free Throw Miss
DFGM	Allowed Made Field Goal
DFTM	Allowed Made Free Throw
FMwt	Weight on forced misses relative to defensive rebounds
Stop%	Stops per Possession (if used with TMStop%, indicates individual stops per individual possession)
PtsPerScPoss	Points Produced per Scoring Possession (if used with TMPtsPerScPoss, indicates individual value)

Team Statistics

TMAST	Team Assists
TMBLK	Team Blocks
TMDQ	Team Disqualifications
TMDREB	Team Defensive rebounds
TMDRtg	Team Points allowed divided by total possessions times 100

TMEffFG%	Team Effective field goal percentage
TMFG%	Team Field goal percentage
TMFG3%	Team Three-point field goal percentage
TMFG3A	Team Three-point field goals attempted
TMFG3M	Team Three-point field goals made
TMFGA	Team Field goal attempts
TMFGM	Team Field goals made
TMFloor%	Team Scoring possessions divided by possessions
TMFT%	Team Free throw percentage
TMFTA	Team Free throw attempts
TMFTM	Team Free throws made
TMGS	Team Games started
TML	Team Losses
TMMIN	Team Minutes played
TMOREB	Team Offensive rebounds
TMORtg	Team Points produced divided by total possessions times 100
TMPF	Team Personal fouls
TMPlay%	Team Play percentage
TMPlay	Team Plays
TMPoss	Team Total possessions
TMPTS	Team Points
TMScPoss	Team Scoring possessions
TMSTL	Team Steals
TMTOV	Team Turnovers
TMTREB	Team Total rebounds
TMW	Team Wins
TMPPG	Team Points per game
TMWin%	Team Winning percentage
OR%	Team Offensive Rebounding Percentage
TOV%	Turnovers per Possession
Field%	Field Goals per Possession from the Field (no free throws)
Play%	Play percentage
Play	Plays
TMStop%	Team Stops per Possession
TMPtsPerScPoss	Team Points Produced per Scoring Possession

Defensive Statistics

DAST   Assists by opposing team(s)

DBLK   Blocks by opposing team(s)

DDQ   Disqualifications by opposing team(s)

DDREB   Defensive rebounds by opposing team(s)

DDRtg   Points allowed divided by total possessions times 100 by opposing team(s)

DEffFG%   Effective field goal percentage by opposing team(s)

DFG%   Field goal percentage by opposing team(s)

DFG3%   Three-point field goal percentage by opposing team(s)

DFG3A   Three-point field goals attempted by opposing team(s)

DFG3M   Three-point field goals made by opposing team(s)

DFGA   Field goal attempts by opposing team(s)

DFGM   Field goals made by opposing team(s)

DFloor%   Scoring possessions divided by possessions by opposing team(s)

DFT%   Free throw percentage by opposing team(s)

DFTA   Free throw attempts by opposing team(s)

DFTM   Free throws made by opposing team(s)

DGS   Games started by opposing team(s)

DL   Losses by opposing team(s)

DMIN   Minutes played by opposing team(s)

DOREB   Offensive rebounds by opposing team(s)

DORtg   Points produced divided by total possessions times 100 by opposing team(s)

DPF   Personal fouls by opposing team(s)

DPlay%   Play percentage by opposing team(s)

DPlay   Plays by opposing team(s)

DPoss   Total possessions by opposing team(s)

DPTS   Points by opposing team(s)

DScPoss   Scoring possessions by opposing team(s)

DSTL   Steals by opposing team(s)

DTOV   Turnovers by opposing team(s)

DTREB   Total rebounds by opposing team(s)

DW   Wins by opposing team(s)

DPPG   Points per game by opposing team(s)

DWin%   Winning percentage by opposing team(s)

DOR%	Offensive Rebounding Percentage by opposing team(s)
DTOV%	Turnovers per Possession by opposing team(s)
DStop%	Stops per Possession by opposing team(s)
DPtsPerScPoss	Points Produced per Scoring Possession by opposing team(s)

Team Abbreviations

ATL	Atlanta Hawks
BOS	Boston Celtics
CHA	Charlotte Hornets
CHI	Chicago Bulls
CLE	Cleveland Cavaliers
DAL	Dallas Mavericks
DEN	Denver Nuggets
DET	Detroit Pistons
GSW	Golden State Warriors
HOU	Houston Rockets
IND	Indiana Pacers
LAC	Los Angeles Clippers
LAL	Los Angeles Lakers
MEM	Memphis Grizzlies
MIA	Miami Heat
MIL	Milwaukee Bucks
MIN	Minnesota Timberwolves
NJN	New Jersey Nets
NOR	New Orleans Hornets
NOJ	New Orleans Jazz
NYK	New York Knicks
ORL	Orlando Magic
PIII	Philadelphia 76ers
PHO	Phoenix Suns
POR	Portland Trail Blazers
SAC	Sacramento Kings
SAN	San Antonio Spurs
SDC	San Diego Clippers

SEA	Seattle Supersonics
TOR	Toronto Raptors
UTA	Utah Jazz
VAN	Vancouver Grizzlies
WAB	Washington Bullets
WAS	Washington Wizards

WNBA Team Abbreviations

CHA	Charlotte Sting
CLE	Cleveland Rockers
DET	Detroit Shock
HOU	Houston Comets
IND	Indiana Fever
LAS	Los Angeles Sparks
MIA	Miami Sol
MIN	Minnesota Lynx
NYL	New York Liberty
ORL	Orlando Miracle
PHO	Phoenix Mercury
POR	Portland Fire
SAC	Sacramento Monarchs
SEA	Seattle Storm
UTA	Utah Starzz
WAS	Washington Mystics

Chapter 1

How to Read This Book

One of the most common social introductions is "So what kind of work do you do?" We define ourselves so much by our jobs that the first thing we want to know about the stranger next to us is what job defines them. But what is it that a thirty-second summary of a job can tell the socially correct stranger? Aren't we told by movies like *It's a Wonderful Life* and *City Slickers* that it's our life outside of work that should define us? Wouldn't it be better to ask someone about his wife and kids or about, as Jack Palance suggested with that single intimidating finger raised, the one thing that is most important to him?

That's not why you're here, though, deciding whether to buy this book. You do want the thirty-second summary of my job. Rather than answering with a generic summary, I want to specifically address the different possible readers of the book. Each audience is likely to look for different things, and my suggestions to them on how to read the book can provide a decent overview without stealing the thunder of the chapters.

Coaches, Scouts, and Players

Let's start with what you should not expect in this book. This book does not introduce new offensive structures or defensive schemes. It does not diagram specific plays, describe training regimens, provide shooting drills, or reveal ways to improve your vertical leap. On the bookshelves of your local library or bookstore, you can find several books that cover these topics.

Instead, this book was originally conceived as an aid to coaches in a more general manner. The most obvious specific contribution is through several statistical measures. The book provides formulas for evaluating a team and the contributions of individuals to team success. The formulas arose out of a desire to better describe the goals and structure of the game. For instance,

1

- What goals does a team have? To win now? To win later? To win *this* game? To win a title?

- In what ways does teammate interaction matter? Is teamwork adequately represented in existing stats? What purpose do plays and different offensive sets serve in terms of enhancing teamwork?

- Does defense win championships? Does rebounding win titles? What is the value of a time-out?

- Are there good rules of thumb for applying different game strategies?

- What are good ways to assess the value of individual players? What are the pros and cons of different statistics? How should a coach use statistics in the context of the job?

Most of these are broad questions that a coach considers among the numerous others in their job description. Several of these questions become a lot easier to answer with a clear and logical description of the game of basketball, which is what I was striving for when I started doing this research in 1987.

Along these lines, the book starts off with what I created back in 1987—a way of recording what happens in a game. It's a nontraditional but very straightforward scoring method that illustrates the flow of a game. What comes out of this is a basis for understanding the game that permeates the entire rest of the book. The scoring method itself may not be something that a coach uses in his program—it is certainly not necessary—but it shows a logic in the game that can be used to tie shooting, rebounding, passing, defense, etc., together into a consistent framework of team building. Exactly how they all tie together is the rest of the book.

You'll see a very fundamental tool to evaluate team efficiency, something that some of you have already seen from Frank McGuire or Dean Smith or Clair Bee or any of the other coaches out there who have used it—points per possession statistics. Points per possession statistics—actually represented in this book as points per one hundred possessions—suggest how efficient an offense or defense is in achieving its respective goal, removing the effect of pace. In one of the most prominent aspects of the book, you will also see calculations of *individual* offensive and defensive ratings, reflecting points that players produce and allow per one hundred possessions. If you already use points per possession to evaluate your team, these individual values will make a lot of sense to you immediately. If you don't, these individual calculations will provide you with a theoretically sound basis for combining the many statistics available to you into summary offensive and defensive numbers.

If evaluating players is not all that matters to you—and it shouldn't be the only thing—the framework of the book also provides some illumination of game strategies. You'll see rules of thumb for applying certain defensive strategies and certain player rotations. Like most rules of thumb, they aren't the final word in deciding strategies, but they can give guidance if a decision about strategy is difficult to make.

I began this work in 1987 with the simple premise that a winning *team* is the goal of all the methods I develop. Maybe that means winning in the short term, or maybe it means winning in the long term. Sometimes that is for you to decide. But none of this was constructed for the purpose of fantasy league competition. It was created to compliment the coaching you already do and to provide insights for making that coaching more effective. That's how I hope it gets used.

Fans

Despite what that last section said, this book is *not* a coaching manual. That would be a bit too serious for all of us who grew up with the slogan, "The NBA is fan-tastic!"

Most of the time, all I am is a fan of the game—the NBA, the college game, the WNBA, pretty much any basketball. I wonder about strategic things more than the average fan, but you can just bear with me during those moments. I do care about the MVP, and I like throwing little factoids into the discussion of who is or who should be the MVP. I think the MVP and Rookie of the Year awards aren't much more than popularity contests, but that doesn't mean I can't take sides. And sometimes the work in here lends itself very well to the discussion of these awards. If the MVP and Rookie of the Year awards attempt to reflect a player's contribution to his team's winning percentage, then the numbers in this book have some application to making these selections. If the awards are simply about heart, hairstyles, and how players interact with the media, I can only yell loudly by adding lots of exclamation points to my opinions!!!

You will see a lot of lists in this book. Most efficient offensive and defensive teams in NBA history. Most efficient centers in the NBA. The top offensive and defensive players in the WNBA. The career progressions for players such as Michael Jordan, Reggie Miller, and Lisa Leslie. How many wins various players contributed to their teams. How well various role players filled their roles. Photographers kicked by Dennis Rodman.

You will also see charts in this book. How well Robert Horry plays if he's asked to carry an offense is shown in a chart because it really could take a thousand words to explain. Trends of league efficiency through time just register more quickly with people in a figure than in a list of numbers. What happened when Vince Carter got hurt, came back, then got hurt again in 2002 before the Raptors incredibly made the playoffs—that needs a chart to show how up and down the team was.

I do love talking about basketball. I spent five years at the University of North Carolina and have been bad-mouthing Duke for the seven years since, so I have plenty of experience. But what I like to do normally (not necessarily in the Duke case) is back up what I'm saying with facts. If I'm only spouting out my own opinion, it's just one among thousands of others that can be difficult to pay attention to (unless I add those exclamation points again). So this book adds facts and analysis and a few exclamation points to discussions of various questions of interest to fans.

As you might have guessed by this point, the book does focus most heavily on the NBA. This is primarily due to the availability of a long history of (a) stats, (b) stars, and (c) stupid stories. There is simply a lot to talk about in the NBA. College basketball has been around even longer, but its history is not as well documented in the statistics that I use to help me craft even more stories. The WNBA has been around only a short time but is starting to develop its own character. I've followed it (and its ABL predecessor) fairly carefully and will introduce several topics related to the women's game.

Librarians

You should file this under 796.32 for basketball and under something between 500 and 510 for science.

Contract Negotiators

Understanding the quality of a player is only part of the process of making a contract. And having good statistics is only part of the process of understanding the quality of a player. But logic is a *big*...

Well, maybe not. Making business deals usually involves a fair amount of waiting until the other side is just tired of negotiating. In the world of big-time pro sports, I assume it's the same, having been involved only from the periphery. At the end of a negotiation, both sides emerge with their Colgate smiles to announce the deal and pretend that it is a Small World After All. It's all about the love between a player and his home team. If only CBS Sunday night could get rights to such a heartwarming saga.

There is value in this book to the negotiation of a contract. The value of a player is the substantive core of making that deal. Signing a mediocre player to a top-dollar contract restricts signing other players and can force a coach to make that player a figurehead leader, which can cause trouble with the better players on a team. Underestimating the value of a ballplayer can have the immediate impact of causing that player to go and leave the team stuck with his backups... who may not be so bad, which needs to be considered. Having knowledge of *more* of the different arguments and counterarguments about player value than the guys on the other side of the table is a nice way to win $omething in those talks. Because a player's value to his team is more than just one number, this book looks at a lot of different legitimate ways of valuing players.

Football Players

Hire a tutor.

Fantasy League Players

This book is about winning the *real* game of basketball. Will it help in your fantasy leagues? It might, but what it would be better for is changing the rules of your league so that the fantasy becomes more like reality. The reality of teamwork is not represented in fantasy leagues, but teamwork is seriously considered in this book, and formulas accounting for it in statistics are here, too. The formulas here for individual points produced and individual defensive stops can be applied to a group of fantasy league players. The formulas were not generated with the intention of being used to build a fantasy league, but they can be used that way.

Educators/Parents

I personally learned more math from the backs of baseball, basketball, and football cards than school could teach me by the fourth grade. A late 1980s *Sports Illustrated* editorial supported this kind of learning, with the female author saying that boys who played sports were much better prepared for later math courses than girls who didn't play sports as much. Her point was both to encourage girls' participation in sports and to shock some of those ejucaded types into believing that sports are good educational tools. Argue as you will, but it's undeniable that numbers are a necessary part of sports and that a kid's exposure to them can only help when he or she is exposed to them in class. Every team has its win/loss record to provide a numerical goal. Every basketball player has a shooting percentage, an assist to turnover ratio, and a rebounding average (except for maybe Reggie Theus, who didn't believe in rebounding) to describe their contribution. This book can provide a structure for seeing how those numerical contributions realize the numerical goal.

Soapbox now being put away.

I thank my parents for letting me read *Basketball Digest* instead of a feel-good story like the *Little Red Slipper* (I'm sure *Basketball Digest* thanks my parents, too). Don't get me wrong—sports are not the most important thing in life. But I would like to believe that the lessons of sports—including what I've learned over fifteen years by studying the teamwork and competition of basketball—can apply to life away from the court, away from the field, away from the arena. I'm actually sure that they do apply. Basketball and sports in general just provide a more concrete and often more emotional context to experience life.

Statheads

This book analyzes basketball using statistics to make many points. But what this book doesn't do is try to rank players by one all-inclusive magic number, the Holy Grail of Basketball Statistics. Such a magical ranking number really defeats the purpose of why we talk about basketball. The information we get by talking about the game often breaks the game down into many factors, many arguments, many numbers—not just one vague Quality Index, Tendex Rating, HoopStat Grade, Production Rating, Impact Factor, or IBM Award. To paraphrase some famous guy who wrote a bunch of baseball books: reducing quality to one number has a tendency to end a discussion, rather than open up a world of insight.

Similarly, this book is not about definitively identifying the league MVP. MVP and Hall of Fame votes are not nor will they ever be only about quality of play. They shouldn't be. They are votes because they are popularity contests with quality of play as a contextual constraint. Some statheads nearly lost their heads when Allen Iverson won the 2001 NBA MVP award. Get over it! Iverson played very well, his team did well, and he played with an obvious dedication above and beyond what I have ever seen from a 160-pound weakling. He was very valuable. Maybe Tim Duncan or Shaquille O'Neal was a better player. Who cares? Voters like to spread awards around, and they like to vote based upon relative quality. Shaq didn't play as well in 2001 as he did in 2000. Is it fair to evaluate Shaq against himself? Of course it is! It's a vote! If Iverson won in 2001 because the voters had to use a butterfly ballot from Florida, then maybe you can argue. Then again, the Supreme Court said you should just shut up.

Mathematicians, Statisticians, Economists, Engineers

This book does not include all the formulas and all the complex probability theory that it could have. Much of the work in here could be couched in all those greek symbols that we learned in abstract classes that no one thought were cool. But we are trying to be cool here.

I did use a ton of material from old math classes, statistics classes, engineering classes, science classes, and from economics journals. For example, significance testing (from environmental engineering data analysis) is definitely practical for seeing whether teams play better with or without certain players. Standard deviations and statistical correlations between offensive and defensive performance provide a very valuable tool for assessing winning percentage and, consequently, the value of strategies to different teams. The conservation equations of fluid dynamics and basic mass balances came to mind more than once as I built models of team structure that conserved points scored or wins created.

There is a lot to be said for the tools of math and science in studying sports. I just won't say it very much here.

Finally, an Apology to Football Players

The joke about the football players is unfair (assuming that they actually did understand that it was a joke). In reality, analyzing football is one of the most difficult tasks around. Baseball has been analyzed for years by people such as Bill James, Pete Palmer, Rob Neyer, and thousands of astute people within the Society for American Baseball Research (SABR). They have had the advantages of a slow game where statistics have been well-recorded for a hundred years, where incremental progress toward runs is measured, and, more importantly, a game where the interaction between players is fairly limited. Basketball has none of these advantages, but football is in even worse shape. Football is definitely the most elegantly complex of these big three sports. Successful football coaches are probably legitimate Mensa geniuses because the pattern recognition involved in fully understanding and teaching the game is so intricate. Furthermore, football coaches have to convince their players to do single jobs and to blindly rely upon the performance of their teammates. Many successful football players then get a rap for not thinking because, well, many position players shouldn't be thinking too much on the field (especially offensive players who have plays called for them). If I were to write a book for football players, it would be short: "Know your plays, eat well, work out, and listen to your coach." Of course that is why I'm writing a basketball book.

Chapter 2

Watching a Game: Offensive Score Sheets

Whether you watch college and pro basketball games on TV or just go to local high school games, you have never watched a game quite like you will in this chapter. For one thing, you won't have Tivo to skip commercials. You also won't have a home crowd showering you from all sides with its emotion after each made shot or turnover.

But it is a good game: Game Four of the 1997 NBA Finals. Michael Jordan and his Chicago Bulls are up 2–1 in the Finals playing the underdog Utah Jazz in the Salt Palace. Utah is coming off of a win at home in Game Three, and all games have been won by the home team. Jordan wants to show Karl Malone, who was voted MVP, who really is the most valuable. Malone wants to make up for missing two foul shots at the end of Game One, allowing Jordan to hit his twenty-third career game-winning shot. Utah goes into the game missing sixth man and designated-Jordan-defender Shandon Anderson due to a death in his family, but the Jazz are making no excuses.

The way you'll "watch" the game is through a *score sheet* that follows the passes, the dribbles, the shots, the rebounds, the steals, the fouls—most everything that happens with the ball. By following these most basic elements of offense, the score sheet will highlight the important aspects of the ebb and flow of the game. It will be like a broadcaster's play-by-play transcript of the game.

The score sheet uses a simple shorthand that will become pretty obvious by the middle of the first quarter. Since so many people really tune in to games only in the fourth quarter, the second and third quarters are replayed mostly through that shorthand with brief summaries of the action. Then the fourth quarter is fully described with the accompanying shorthand down to the dramatic end.

The First Quarter

Jump ball: Bulls center Luc Longley against Jazz center Greg Ostertag. In the shorthand for the score sheet, this jump ball is denoted as

Jump 13, 00

with the visiting team's number listed first (Longley's number 13) and the home team's number second (Ostertag's number 00), as is traditional when listing the score.

For this shorthand, you'll see a lot of uniform numbers. Table 2.1 gives the roster of the players and their numbers.

Table 2.1. Chicago and Utah Rosters (starters indicated by asterisks)

Chicago Bulls		Utah Jazz	
Number	Player	Number	Player
33*	Scottie Pippen	32*	Karl Malone
91*	Dennis Rodman	3*	Bryon Russell
13*	Luc Longley	00*	Greg Ostertag
23*	Michael Jordan	14*	Jeff Hornacek
9*	Ron Harper	12*	John Stockton
1	Randy Brown	10	Howard Eisley
35	Jason Caffey	44	Greg Foster
25	Steve Kerr	55	Antoine Carr
7	Toni Kukoc	34	Chris Morris
18	Brian Williams (aka Bison Dele)	31	Adam Keefe
30	Jud Buechler		

You'll get very used to the main characters and their numbers pretty quickly. The first possession of the game starts with the following sequence:

0	UTA	3 12 3 14 12^D $32-_B$ 3^R 14 12^D $3-_Y$

The leading zero at the start of the line is the number of points Utah has at the end of the possession. The team, Utah, is represented here with the three-letter abbreviation UTA. This is followed by the sequence of passes, dribbles, shots, and rebounds making up the possession. This possession indicates that the jump ball ended up in the hands of Bryon Russell, denoted in shorthand above by his number 3 as the first number in the possession. He passes it to John Stockton (12 in shorthand), who gives it back to Russell (3), then over to Hornacek (14), and back to Stockton, who dribbles (12^D, the dribble represented by the superscript D). Maybe it's one of Utah's standard pick and rolls—this system can't represent every detail—but Stockton passes it to Karl Malone (32), who takes a shot from between the foul line and the three-point arc, missing (32_{-B}, the shot symbolized by the horizontal line and the location of the shot represented by the subscript B, as will be diagrammed below). Russell is there to rebound (3^R, the superscript R indicating a rebound), getting it then back out to Hornacek (14) and to Stockton to reset up on the dribble (12^D). Stockton goes back to Russell, who takes a shot from the three-point line straightaway from the hoop, missing (3_{-Y}).

Before continuing with the game, let's explain a little more of the shorthand. First, when using a superscript D to represent dribbling, it is usually reserved for when the dribbling is used to gain significant ground, not just a dribble to get balance or a dribble that doesn't go anywhere beyond where the player is standing. The D is really meant to get a sense of players moving on the court with the ball. So it is possible in this first Utah possession that one of the first several players did dribble even if the D was not shown, but they didn't gain much ground in doing so.

In the shorthand for Malone's shot (32_{-B}), the dash indicates that he missed, and the subscript indicates where he shot it from. The shot location map is shown in figure 2.1. I saw this location map in college and have seen it a few times since, so it is not uncommon in the world of basketball. The floor is broken up into nine primary regions, six within the three-point line and three beyond it. Then there are lay-ups from the left (L) and right (R) sides, as well as dunks (D). The diagram and shorthand do not pin down precisely where a shot came from, but they give sufficient detail for most uses. In this case, they indicate that both Malone's shot

Figure 2.1. Court Division and Labels

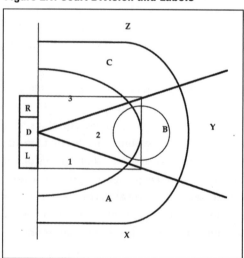

and Russell's ensuing miss came from generally the middle of the floor. These days, there are electronic shot charts out there where scorers can tap the location on the court where a player's shots came from. They are pretty nice, but practically impossible to use in combination with the rest of this system.

Back to the game...

1 CHI	9^R 33^D / 13^D $9^{F00(1)}$X*

The Bulls begin their first possession with Ron Harper getting the rebound of Russell's shot (9^R). He finds Scottie Pippen, who starts dribbling up the court (33^D). He passes across midcourt (/ is used to denote crossing midcourt) to Luc Longley, who dribbles (13^D). Longley passes to Harper again, who is fouled by Ostertag, his first ($9^{F00(1)}$). Harper goes to the line, missing the first (X) and making the second (*).

Again, the score for the team at the *end* of the possession is shown at the left. Chicago is abbreviated CHI, then it is followed by the progression of the possession. This possession introduces the midcourt symbol (/), which is crossed on a pass, a fairly unusual event as you'll see. It also introduces the shorthand for a foul with the big F, followed by the number of the player committing the foul and the number of fouls that player has in parentheses. Finally, it introduces both the missed foul shot (X) and the made foul shot (*).

(When I scored this game, I used only a pen on a lined sheet of paper. The speed of the game made my handwriting a little sloppy, a common problem in games. It definitely took some practice to be able to score a game with this amount of detail.)

0 UTA	$12^{D/}$ 14 00 12^D 3 14 $32–_c$

The Jazz's second possession starts with Stockton dribbling across half-court ($12^{D/}$) before passing to Hornacek. They work it around to several players before Malone takes a shot from the right wing ($32–_c$), missing.

It is more typical for the ball to cross half-court on the dribble than on the pass. Dribbling over half-court is denoted here with / following the D in the superscript, which is the only new notation in this possession.

3 CHI	9RD $23^{D/}$ $13{++}_D$

In the Bulls' second possession, Harper rebounds the Malone miss, dribbling (9RD) before passing to Michael Jordan to bring the ball across half-court ($23^{D/}$). Jordan finds Longley open for a dunk ($13{++}_D$).

New symbols here are the combination of R and D in the superscript on 9— putting together two symbols already described—and the assisted basket. The first few possessions had missed shots, which were symbolized with flat lines. A made shot *without an assist* is denoted by the plus symbol (+), or a flat line crossed vertically. An *assisted* basket gets the second vertical cross, represented here as ++. As with a missed shot, the location of the shot is still denoted in a subscript following the result of the shot.

For those who don't know what exactly defines an assist—join the crowd. No two official scorers will agree on every call. The official definition of an assist is a "pass that leads directly to a score," which is vague enough that the Supreme Court would call the rule unconstitutional and unenforceable. Hall of Famer Oscar Robertson argues that assists weren't so readily awarded during his career in the 1960s as they have been since the 1980s. Supposedly, the scorer used to not be allowed to dribble if an assist were to be awarded, whereas that is not strictly true now. A general guideline I've used in scoring games is to ask the question: "Did the scorer have to do anything *unexpected* to score the basket?" If yes, then there is no assist. If no, give the person who passed it to him an assist.

Back to the game...

2	UTA	$12^{D/}$ 32 14++$_A$
5	CHI	$33^{D/}$ 23^D+$_1$

The above two possessions have Utah scoring their first basket on a jumper from Hornacek off a pass from Malone, then a driving shot from Jordan to bring the score to 5–2 Bulls.

4	UTA	$12^{D/}$ KICK 12 14 32++$_B$

This fourth Utah possession introduces one new item, a kicked ball, which is denoted above with the very obvious "KICK" notation.

This is followed by several possessions shown below with no new notation. The Jazz take their first lead at 9–8 when Malone hits the second of two free throws, then one Jazz possession later, some new notation is introduced.

	5	CHI	$23^{D/}$ 91–$_A$
4		UTA	32^R $12^{D/}$ 3 32 12^D 14–$_X$
	6	CHI	13^R $9^{D/}$ 33 23 33 $13^{F32(1)}$X*
6		UTA	$12^{D/}$ 14 32 3–$_R$ 00^R 12^D 32++$_B$
	8	CHI	$33^{D/}$ 91 23^D 33 23++$_A$
8		UTA	$12^{D/}$ 32++$_2$
	8	CHI	33 / 9^D 23^D–$_3$ 13^R–$_L$ $13^{FR(1)}$ 23 91 33 9 23^D–$_B$
9		UTA	14^R 32^D $12^{D/}$ 3 $32^{DF91(1)}$X*
	8	CHI	$33^{D/}$ 23^D 9 33 23 13 9–$_Y$
11		UTA	3RD / 12 14 <u>32</u> 12++$_R$

In the last possession shown here, Russell grabs a rebound, dribbles, passes across half-court to Stockton, who then goes to Hornacek. Hornacek finds Malone in the post, the underline beneath 32 indicating that Malone is posting up. Malone passes to a cutting Stockton for a lay-up.

The new notation here is the underline representing a player posting up, which can happen and then "unhappen." A player may dribble to get into the post, and he may dribble out of the post area. No notation has been designed to indicate this transience in the post. When an underline shows up under a player's number, it means that the player is in the post at some time during his handling of the ball. Again, the method cannot account for every detail but tries to get many of the important ones.

10	CHI	$33^{D/}$ 91 9 23 9 9 9$\underline{1}$-$_1$ 9^R-$_1$ 9^R+$_L$
11	UTA	$12^{D/}$ 3-$_B$ 00^R-$_2^{ROB}$ <u>TIME 6:00</u> ^{32OB} 00 12^D 3 32 12^D 14^D-$_B$

Back in the game, the Bulls counter the Jazz's score with a lay-up of their own. The next Jazz possession is interrupted for a time-out with 6:00 minutes left in the first quarter (probably NBC taking time for their sponsors).

Also in this last possession is the superscript 32OB, which is an optional notation indicating that number 32 (Malone) inbounded the ball after the time-out. This notation is essential only if he inbounds the ball to someone who scores on the assist so that one knows who to credit the assist to. It is good practice to keep note of the inbounder, but it is rarely necessary.

Right before the time-out in this possession, the superscript ROB indicates that the rebound of Ostertag's shot went out of bounds. Since the possession stayed with Utah, it is evident that the rebound went out of bounds off of a Bull.

The next two possessions introduce a new way for possessions to transition from one team to the other: a turnover. Here is the shorthand, followed by an explanation:

10	CHI	91^R $33^{D/}$ 9 23 $\underline{33}^{BP\ TO}$
11	UTA	3^{STL} 12^D 14^D 3-$_x$

Pippen, number 33, has the ball in the post for the Bulls but makes a bad pass (BP) for the turnover. In this case, Utah's Russell steals the ball (3^{STL}) on the bad pass. The rest of the possession plays out with a Stockton dribble, a Hornacek dribble, and a Russell miss from three-point land. Notice that the crossing of half-court is missing here; I simply forgot to write it down or didn't have time to write it down. It isn't critical to telling the story, and one can guess that it was probably Stockton who dribbled across half-court. Nevertheless, we're sitting on a Russell miss, and someone has to rebound that miss . . .

12	CHI	91^R 33 $9^{D/}$ 33 91 9 $\underline{23}^D$+$_2$

. . . That someone is Rodman, doing what he does best. The Bulls turn this miss into another half-court setup, going to Jordan on the post, where he dribbles into the middle for, using the imagination, a floater from the middle of the lane. That's already six points and one assist for Jordan.

11	UTA	$12^{D/}$ 14 $\underline{32}^D$ $00^{F13(1)}$XX

MVP Karl Malone already has seven points and one assist, so on the ensuing Jazz possession, the Bulls force him to give it up to the less-than-MVP Ostertag, who misses two free throws.

12	CHI	33$^{RD/}$ <u>23</u> 1^{KOB} 13 33^D 23^D $^{F3(1)}$ 23 <u>33</u>$^{TRVL\ TO}$

In the next Bulls' possession, they force us to deal with something new, a ball getting swatted out of bounds. In this case, Randy Brown (number 1), has the ball knocked out of bounds, which we denote with KOB in a superscript. If we have instant replay available, or if TV coverage is good enough, we can also add the number of the player who knocked the ball out of bounds. I didn't see who it was in this case, and TV didn't show it. Finally, Pippen travels, turning the ball back over to the Jazz (<u>33</u>$^{TRVL\ TO}$) to end the possession.

The next few possessions below proceed with nothing out of the ordinary. For instance, Rodman commits another foul (that he protests, as I showed in my handwritten notes), then misses two shots from the field. Rodman actually attempting two shots in two possessions is out of the ordinary, but his missing them is not.

12		UTA	10$^{D/}$ 3−$_x$ 00^R $^{F91(2)}$*X
	12	CHI	33$^{RD/}$ 23 1 <u>33</u>^{D} 91$−_R$
12		UTA	3RD 14$^{D/}$ 10 <u>32</u> 00$−_2$
	12	CHI	13^R 23$^{D/}$ 13 91$−_A$

These are actually the last possessions on which the number 91 shows up during the first quarter, implying that Rodman is about to be yanked, allowing him to kick off his shoes or ride his stationary bike or, at that time, go fight it out with Carmen Electra.

Next, in the era of slow-down basketball, one of the symptoms—or perhaps a cause—is the illegal defense, which makes its first appearance in this Jazz possession:

14		UTA	32^R 14$^{D/}$ <u>32</u> (ILL D WARN) <u>TIME 2:38</u> 32 10^D 14 <u>32</u> 10$^{F1(1)}$**

It is denoted by the rather obvious (ILL D WARN) in the middle of the short-hand. It is probably due to Rodman, but I'm really just picking on him a lot. The Jazz finally rack up more points, their first in quite some time, and maybe it has something to do with Rodman being gone.

14	CHI	33^D 1$^{D/}$ 23^D 13++$_L$

On the other end, Luc Longley answers back with a lay-up off the Jordan-created opportunity. With Rodman off the floor, the two teams are each one for one in scoring opportunities.

The Jazz and Bulls continue to score on the next few possessions as though a terrible burden to scoring has gone away:

16	UTA	$10^{D/}$ $14++_A$
16	CHI	$1^{D/}$ $\underline{23}^{D}+_2$
18	UTA	$10^{D/}$ $14^{D}+_2$
16	CHI	$1^{D/}$ 35 1 $\underline{33}^{D}-_1$

In this last possession above, we get proof that Rodman is out of the game. For the Bulls, number 35 Jason Caffey touches the ball, making five different Bulls not numbered 91 to appear since the last dead ball.

18	UTA	$10^{D/}$ 44 $10^{D}-_C{}^{BK1}$

With this Jazz possession, another new thing happens. Working on his reputation as a good defender, Chicago's Randy Brown blocks the jumper by Utah's Howard Eisley ($10^{D}-_C{}^{BK1}$).

16	CHI	1^R $23^{D/}$ 1 13 $23-_Y$

The Bulls take the rebound downcourt but have to set up again. Ultimately, his Airness takes and misses a three from the top of the arc. Keeping track of game time is next to impossible while writing all this down, but one can speculate that Jordan was taking the three and thinking about getting a two-for-one possession before the end of the quarter.

21	UTA	44^R $10^{D/}$ 32 $14++_Y$

Jordan gave the Jazz one possession, and what they did with it was score on another Hornacek jumper, scoring it from where Jordan missed it.

	16 CHI	23^D / $1-_A$
21	UTA	44^R
		END 1Q

At the end, the Bulls get their second of the two-for-one but can't score on the Brown jumper.

The quarter ends with the Ostertag rebound and the Jazz holding a five-point lead, 21–16.

The Second Quarter: The Bulls Pull Ahead

At this point, the shorthand should be straightforward. The shorthand for the second quarter is presented below without much narrative—to basically fast-forward through the quarter. In summary, the Bulls rely on the strength of their Pippen-led unit to take a lead. Brian Williams notches a couple of hoops and so does Pippen, but the key here is that the Bulls force seven turnovers on twenty-one possessions, leading to three dunks. Predictably, the Jazz call a couple of time-outs during the run to try to stop the Bulls' momentum. In the quarter, the Bulls outscore the Jazz 24–14, reversing the five-point Jazz lead.

The only new shorthand shown in the next sequence of shorthand lines is "OF," which stands for an offensive foul, and "LB," which stands for a lost ball type of turnover.

18	CHI	$25^{D/}$ 7 9 25 $18^{D}+_2$
21	UTA	12^D 32 3 $32^{F25(1)}$ 12^D $32^{OF(2)}$ TO
18	CHI	$25^{D/}$ 33 $18^{F44(1)}$ 25 33 25 9 $33^{D}-_3$ $^{F7(1)}$
23	UTA	$12^{D/}$ 34 55 $12^{D}+_A$
20	CHI	25^D 9 7^D $25++_A$ (The start of a 16–6 run.)
23	UTA	$12^{D/}-_2$
20	CHI	33RD / 25 7 33 9^{BP} TO
23	UTA	$12^{STL\ D/}$ 44 $55-_B$
20	CHI	$7^{RD/}-_2$
23	UTA	55^R $12^{D/}$ 3 12^D 55^D $3-_Z$
22	CHI	33^R $^{F34(1)}$ TIME 8:54 $33^{D/}$ 25 33 25^D 7 $33^{D}+_B$
25	UTA	$12^{D/}$ $55^{D}+_3$
22	CHI	33 $25^{D/}$ 33^D 18 $23-_Z$
25	UTA	44^R LB TO
24	CHI	7^{STL} 25 $18++_D$
25	UTA	12^D 55^{BP} TO (Jazz struggling without Malone.)
26	CHI	33^{STL} 18 $33^{D/}+_D$
27	UTA	12^D TIME UTA 7:19 $^{\#OB}$ / 34 12^D 32 12 $00+_1$
26	CHI	$33^{D/}$ 7 33 25 $18^{F00(2)}$ $33D-_A$
27	UTA	32^R $14^{D/}$ 12 32^{FB} 14 $32-_B$
29	CHI	33RD / 7^D 33 7 33 23 $7++_Z$ (Jordan scores 0 pts in the run.)
27	UTA	$12^{D/\ LB\ TO}$
31	CHI	$25^{STL\ D/}$ $18++_D$ (B. Williams scored 6 points with 2 dunks.)
29	UTA	$12^{D/}$ $14++_A$
34	CHI	23^D $7++_Z$ (Bulls and Jazz play even rest of this quarter.)
31	UTA	$12^{D/}$ TIME UTA 4:53 ^{34OB} 44 12^D 14 $12^{D}+_B$
34	CHI	25^D 33 23 $7^{LB\ TO}$
31	UTA	44^{STL} 14^D $^{FB(2)}$ $12^{D/}$ 44^D $^{OF44(2)}$ TO TIME 4:03
34	CHI	$33^{D/}$ 7^D 25 33 25 23 $25-_Y$
31	UTA	3^R $12^{D/}$ 14^D 32 12^D $32-_C$
36	CHI	23RD / 25 7 25 91 7 33^D $23-_Z$ $33^{R}+_L$ (Pippen scores 6 in Q.)
31	UTA	$12^{D/}$ 14 32^D LB TO
36	CHI	$23^{STL\ D/}$ 25 33 23^D $25-_Z$
33	UTA	3^R $12^{D/}$ 32 12 32^D $^{F91(3)}$ ★★
38	CHI	9 $7^{D/}$ 9 7 $23^{D}+_3$
33	UTA	$12^{D/}$ 3 32 $14-_3$
40	CHI	7^R $9^{D/}$ 33^D $13++_L$
35	UTA	$12^{D/}$ $44++_2$

40	CHI	$33^{D/}$ 13 7_{-x} $13^{R\ F44(3)}$XX
35	UTA	31^{R} $12^{D/}$ 14_{-Y}
40	CHI	7RD $23^{D/}$ 7 23_{-Y}
35	UTA	55^{R} 3_{-Y}
		END 2Q

The Third Quarter: The Jazz Recover

Even before the series, Bulls' coach Phil Jackson had been "discussing" with the press the hard screens that the Jazz guards set. The Jazz responded by mentioning that the Bulls had Dennis Rodman, the league leader in dirty play. There was a subtle war of words behind this series. In the third quarter of this game, the tension between the two teams was clearly heightened.

The Jazz immediately run off seven straight to take the lead in the quarter. The combatants trade baskets for a few possessions until Rodman becomes a true combatant and draws the first technical foul of the quarter. Only a moment later, Pippen and Ostertag get a double technical called on them after Ostertag fouls Pippen hard. After this, another seven fouls get called in the last few minutes of the quarter as the refs try to keep things from getting out of hand. At the end of the quarter, the game is all tied at fifty-six.

New shorthand shown in the following series in this quarter relates only to the technical fouls. These are shown in parentheses, highlighting the guilty party or parties, and then, if free throws are taken, the player shooting the foul shots is listed with a colon and the result of the foul shot.

40	CHI	$23^{D/}$ 9 91 23^{D}_{-3}
35	UTA	$12^{RD/}$ 3 32 12^{D} 32_{-B}
40	CHI	91^{R} $9^{D/}$ 23 13 $33^{BP\ TO}$
37	UTA	$12^{STL\ D/}$ 3 32 $12{+}{+}_{A}$ TIME CHI (Jackson likes early TOs.)
40	CHI	23^{D} 9 33_{-L}
39	UTA	32^{R} $12^{D/}$ $00{+}{+}_{R}$
40	CHI	$33^{D/}$ 23 9 33^{D} $13^{LB\ OB\ TO}$
42	UTA	$12^{D/}$ 14 32 $12{+}{+}_{X}$ (Jazz grab lead back on Stockton trey.)
42	CHI	9^{D} / 91 33 13 33 9 23^{D}_{-2} 23^{R}_{-L} 91^{R} 33^{D} 9 91 $13{+}{+}_{B}$
42	UTA	12^{D} 14 $32^{LB\ OB\ TO}$
42	CHI	$33^{D/}$ 91 33 23 33 91 23^{D}_{-2}
42	UTA	00^{R} $12^{D/}$ 32_{-1}
44	CHI	$9^{RD/}$ 33 23 91 $13{+}{+}_{D}$
42	UTA	$12^{D/}$ 14 32 12^{D}_{-1}
44	CHI	$33^{RD/}-_{Y}$
45	UTA	$14^{RD/}$ $32{+}{+}_{L}$ (TFOUL91 14: *)

44	CHI	25 9 25 18^{KOB} 33^D 25 33–$_B$ (Rodman's T ignites nothing.)
48	UTA	32^R 12$^{D/}$ 14^D–$_2$^{BK33} 32^R 3++$_Z$
46	CHI	25$^{D/}$ 9 25 91 18 33^D+$_2$
48	UTA	12$^{D/}$ 00 12^D 14 <u>32</u> 12^D–$_2$
47	CHI	91^R 33$^{D/}$ ^{F00} (DOUBLE TFOUL 33,00) <u>TIME 5:42</u> *X
50	UTA	00^R 10$^{D/}$ 32++$_B$ (Eisley in for Stockton.)
47	CHI	33^D 9 <u>33</u>^{D} 9–$_Y$
50	UTA	3^R 10$^{D/}$ $^{BP\ OB\ TO}$
48	CHI	1 33^D 9^D 18$^{D\ F00(4)}$ X*
50	UTA	10 3$^{D/}$ 10$^{D\ BP\ TO}$
51	CHI	25^{STL} 33$^{D/}$+$_Y$
50	UTA	10$^{D/}$ 14 32$^{F25(2)}$ 10^D 32^D–$_1$
51	CHI	23$^{RD/\ BP\ TO}$
50	UTA	3$^{D/\ BP\ TO}$
53	CHI	33$^{D/\ F}$ 25 23 <u>18</u>^{FD} 23 25 <u>18</u>^{D} 7 23 <u>18</u>^{D}+$_2$
52	UTA	10$^{D/}$ 3^D 10 3^D 10^D+$_B$
54	CHI	25^D / 18$^{DF32(3)}$ <u>TIME 2:16</u> *X
52	UTA	10$^{RD/\ F33(1)}$ 10^D 14$^{BP\ TO}$
54	CHI	23^D 25$^{D/}$ <u>18</u> 25^D 18–$_R$
54	UTA	44^R 14$^{D/}$ 10 <u>32</u>+$_1$ (Malone scores 6 in 3rd Q.)
56	CHI	33$^{D/}$ 7 33++$_R$
56	UTA	10$^{D/}$ 14 32 10^F 10$^{D\ F7}$**
56	CHI	33$^{D/}$–$_Z$
56	UTA	32^R 10$^{D/}$–$_1$
56	CHI	33^R 23 (All even at the end of third quarter.)
		END 3Q

The Fourth Quarter: Down to the Wire

The fourth quarter will feature the Jazz and the Bulls trading leads six times, the last time coming with under a minute to go. But that is jumping ahead.

58	UTA	12$^{D/}$ 3 <u>32</u>^{D} 12 <u>32</u>++$_1$

The Jazz's first possession starts as usual with John Stockton back in the game after resting at the end of the third. He brings the ball across half-court, passes to Bryon Russell, who finds Karl Malone in the post, where he dribbles and then passes back to Stockton. Stockton reposts Malone, who takes the assist to hit the shot from the left box.

56	CHI	33$^{D/}$ 25 23 25$^{D\ KOB}$ 25–$_Z$

The Bulls start off the fourth with their offensive team on the floor (Kerr in, Rodman out). In this first possession, the Bulls move the ball around the perimeter until it is knocked out of bounds. Steve Kerr takes the inbounds pass and misses a three-pointer from the right side.

58	UTA	34^R $12^{D/}$ 3 $\underline{32^D}-_2$

With a two-point lead, Chris Morris pulls down the Kerr miss (34^R), handing it to Stockton, who heads upcourt to try to repeat the previous possession ($12^{D/}$). This time, Malone misses from the post ($\underline{32^D}-_2$) and . . .

59	CHI	$33^{RD/}$ 23 33^D $7++_Y$

. . . Pippen grabs the rebound, brings it upcourt and gives it to Jordan, who will (not coincidentally) touch the ball on every Bulls' possession of the fourth quarter. In this case, the ball ends up in Toni Kukoc's hands for an open three-pointer at the top, which he bangs home for the 59–58 lead.

58	UTA	$12^{D/}$ $\underline{32}$ $12-_x$

Down by one, Utah sticks with its best two players, especially with Hornacek still off the floor nursing a slight leg injury. Here, Stockton brings it up, posts Malone, who then goes back to Stockton, who misses the three from the left side.

59	CHI	$23^{RD/}$ 7 25 $\underline{23^D}-_1$

Jordan tries to take over. He rebounds the ball, brings it up ($23^{RD/}$), gives it to Kukoc, then to Kerr. Jordan demands the ball in the post, then dribbles around to find a shot from twelve feet on the left side. The Utah crowd gasps. Jordan misses ($\underline{23^D}-_1$).

60	UTA	32^R $12^{D/}$ $32++_A$

The Utah crowd roars as Malone snags the rebound (32^R). "Find Stockton" must be ingrained in every Utah player's mind because they all do it as soon as they get a board. Stockton dribbles up, waiting for Malone, then sets him up for the jumper from the left side to put the Jazz up one ($12^{D/}$ $32++_A$).

61	CHI	$25^{D/}$ 23 25 $\underline{23^{DF3}}$ <u>TIME 9:18</u> 23^D+_D

For the Bulls, it's clear: go to Jordan. Kerr brings it up and does just that. Jordan returns it, then gets it back and tries to take Russell. Russell fouls him, and we go to another stupid beer ad ($\underline{23^{DF3}}$ <u>TIME 9:18</u>). On returning, *Find Jordan* works out with a scary drive through the middle for a dunk (23^D+_D).

63	UTA	$12^{D/}$ 32^D 12^D $3++_Z$

The Utah crowd stirs after the Jordan dunk, but they still have the reliable twosome to counter. Stockton up the court to Malone and back to Stockton. Surprise! Stockton finds Russell on the right wing for a three! Jazz by two.

61	CHI	23^D 25 7 $\underline{18}-_2$

Why is Brian Williams in the game? Kukoc feeds Williams for a good shot in the lane, but Williams tries going with his off-hand (this info is not in the score sheet, but only in unofficial notes also scribbled on the score sheet). He misses badly.

65	UTA	34^R $12^{D/}$ 44 12^D $44{+}{+}_D$ <u>TIME CHI 8:01</u>

Morris rebounds the miss again and finds Stockton. Stockton sets something up for Greg Foster, who shows Brian Williams how to finish with a dunk ($44{+}{+}_D$). Marv Albert tells the TV viewers, "Phil Jackson doesn't like what he sees and calls time-out."

63	CHI	$9^{D/}$ $23^D{+}_B$

The Bulls come out of the time-out with most of their starters. Those starters do what the subs did and defer to Jordan, who hits the second of his six fourth-quarter field goals, this one from the top of the key. Jazz lead goes down to two.

65	UTA	$12^{D/F9}$ 12^D 32 12^D 3^D 34 $3{-}_x$

With the Jazz now facing the Bulls' starting defense, they tighten up. Unable to find a good shot for Malone, Russell tries and misses another three, this time from the left wing.

63	CHI	$33^{RF32(4)}$ $33^{D/}$ $23^D{-}_B$

On the miss by Russell, Pippen pulls down the rebound and Malone thinks he steals it, but he just picks up his fourth foul. The Bulls go to Jordan *again*. Again, Jordan tries the jumper from the top of the key. This time, he misses. The Jazz are still up two.

65	UTA	3^R $12^{D/}$ BPOB TO

Stockton tries to hit Foster cutting to the basket but just passes it out of bounds. Jazz lead stays at two.

65	CHI	$9^{D/}$ 7 <u>13</u> 9 23^D 9 $23^D{+}_C$

The Bulls switch here to having Ron Harper bring the ball up. After a brief post-up for Longley, it is back to Jordan. Jordan dribbles down the right side and makes an impossible runner as he is falling out of bounds ($23^D{+}_C$). Tie game.

65	UTA	$12^{D/}$ 14 32 $12^D{-}_A$ BK9 24-S CK TO

The score is now tied, and the Jazz haven't scored in a few trips up the court. Stockton can find little to set up an offense. He goes to Hornacek, who looks to Malone. With the shot clock running out, Malone passes up the shot and gives it to Stockton. Stockton tries to get his shot from the left wing, throws up a prayer that is blocked by Harper, and the twenty-four-second clock runs out ($12^D{-}_A$ BK9 24-S CK TO). The Delta Center is quiet, but no one is panicking. It's still tied.

67	CHI	$9^{D/}$ 7 33 23 <u>7</u> 33^D $7{-}_x$ 13^{RF44} $23^D{-}_R$ $33^R{+}_L$

The Bulls try to get Kukoc going, posting him and eventually setting up the three-pointer, which he misses. On the Longley rebound, Foster commits a foul.

Jordan dribbles to the baseline but misses. Pippen grabs the rebound and lays it in for a two-point Bulls lead. Everyone can sniff a momentum shift.

66	UTA	12^D <u>TIME UTA 5:22</u> 00 12^D 32 3^D$-_3$ $^{ROB\ 32OB}$ 14^{F23}X*

So the Jazz call a time-out, like every team does when they inhale the aroma of bad momentum. The Jazz return with all their starters, ready to turn the last five minutes into a comeback. If it is going to happen, it starts meekly here. After a miss by Russell and the ball going out of bounds, Hornacek draws a foul on Jordan on the inbounds. The 90-percent-foul-shooting Hornacek misses the first of two, making the fans wonder about nerves. He makes the second (14^{F23}X*), and the Jazz trail by one.

67	CHI	23 9$^{D/}$ 33 <u>23</u>^{D}$-_2$ 91^R 9 23^D <u>33</u>$-_1$ 13^R 91 23 9 23$^{D\ LB\ TO}$

Jordan continues to play—as he would describe it later—like "doo-doo." He misses a shot from the post initially. After the Bulls get the offensive rebound, Pippen plays—as he would describe it later—like "s—" and misses a jumper from the left, but the Bulls get *another* offensive rebound (13^R). Ultimately the ball ends up in Jordan's hands again, and he drives to the hole. Ostertag reaches around to poke the ball away (again I'm using those scribbled notes). Jordan and Jackson and all of Chicago yell "Foul!!!!"...

66	UTA	3^{STL} 12$^{D/}$ 14 12^D 14^{F91} 12^D 3^D$-_B$ 32^R 3 12^D 3$^{D\ OF3}$ <u>TIME CHI 3:20</u>

...And Stockton pushes it upcourt. Give the Bulls credit for actually covering their backcourt while lobbying the officials. The Jazz have to move the ball around before Hornacek draws a foul from Rodman. Russell tries to be a hero on the jumper from the top of the key but misses. Malone is there for the rebound, and the Jazz reset. This time, Russell tries to draw the foul from Pippen but gets called for leaning in. All that work and the Jazz are still down by one with 3:20 to go.

69	CHI	33^D 25 7 23++$_2$

Air Jordan, Air Jordan, Air Jordan. Kukoc finds Jordan cutting to the free throw line. Jordan buries it, and the Bulls are up 69–66.

66	UTA	12$^{D/}$ 32 12^D 32^D$-_A$

MVP, MVP, MVP. Stockton looks to Malone, who dribbles to get himself an off-balance jumper from the left side. Clank. The three-point deficit feels a little bigger.

71	CHI	33^R 23$^{D/}$+$_B$

Pippen grabs the rebound, gives it to The Man. The Man dribbles upcourt, takes and makes shot number five of his six. Five-point lead, 71–66, for the Bulls.

69	UTA	12$^{D/}$ 14^{KOB} 12^D+$_Y$

Down five and having scored one point in the last six minutes, it is do-or-die time for the Jazz. Chicago coach Phil Jackson would call this the biggest play of the game. After the ball gets knocked out of bounds by Rodman, John Stockton (who, as a youngster ten years earlier, was labeled as "too good to not have a nick-name") eyeballs a twenty-four-foot three-pointer. Whoosh.

73 CHI	9^D / $23^{D}+_B$

Swoosh. Jordan makes his sixth and final field goal of the quarter. The Bulls have seventy-three points. The Jazz have sixty-nine.

69	UTA	12^D 14^D-_2

The Jazz comeback does not materialize on this possession with Hornacek missing a frantic runner through the lane.

73 CHI	91^R TIME CHI 1:45 $33^{D/}$ 7 23^D LBTO

Rodman rebounds Hornacek's miss, and, rather than get tied up, he calls the Bulls' second-to-last time-out. Everyone knows who is going to get the call to rescue the Bulls. "Everyone" includes Stockton, who strips Jordan and heads the other way...

70	UTA	$12^{STLD/F23}$ *X

If you were a bug on the floor trying to outrun a gargantuan size thirteen, you'd get an idea of what Stockton was thinking as Jordan trailed him down the court. *Stomp. Wheeeee!* Jordan is whistled for a foul that some would say he did not commit. Stockton escapes with one of two free throws.

73 CHI	33^R 13 $9^{D/}$ 23^D 33 23^D 9 $33-_z$

The Bulls are still comfortable with just over a minute to go, a three-point lead, and, in number 23, the only player ever to single-handedly defeat space aliens in basketball. Here the alien-beater tries to let his teammates do the work, but Pippen bricks a three from the corner.

72	UTA	12^{RF33}**

Still in search of a nickname, Stockton finds a rebound instead. And a foul from the frustrated Pippen. Boring old John makes two. The Bulls lead is one with one minute left.

73 CHI	$33^{D/}$ 23^D-_B

For some reason, Jordan's shots are coming from the top of the key, and they are not falling. Jordan would feel pretty good about so many of them. The Jazz would feel pretty good about so many of them not going in. This one in particular...

74	UTA	12RD / $32++_R$ TIME CHI 0:44.5

...Because Stockton gets *another* rebound, looks upcourt, and, in what ESPN's David Aldridge called "the single gutsiest pass I've ever seen," instinctively throws a perfect touchdown pass to a breaking Malone for the lay-up. And the 74–73 lead.

73	CHI	$7^{D/}$ 25 23^D $25-_Z$

Only 44.5 seconds left. Steve Kerr, who will never do a commercial that recounts the number of times *he* was asked to take the game-winning shot (as Jordan did on TV during this series), leaves a three-pointer short.

76	UTA	14^R TIME UTA 0:26.2 12^D 32 55 32^{F33}* TIME UTA 0:18 *

Hornacek's arm reaches for the rebound, and someone calls for time-out to save Hornacek from losing the ball or getting into a jump-ball situation. The Bulls press the inbounds but cannot prevent Stockton from getting the ball. Stockton passes it upcourt to Malone (12^D 32). Malone looks tentative as he passes to Carr, who passes the hot potato back to Malone. Malone hesitates, then goes to the basket, where he is fouled as he haltingly passes outside. Hornacek tries to keep Pippen from talking to Malone, who stands at the free throw line trying to put the game away. A week after he missed two to lose Game One, Malone makes two. Jazz by three and eighteen seconds on the clock.

73	CHI	$7^{D/}$ 23^D-_Y

As the best one-on-one player in the established galaxy, Jordan pulls up and creates his own good look at the basket. It ain't proof, but his miss makes you think that maybe one guy can't beat the Jazz (at least until the next year).

78	UTA	12RD / 3^D+_D
73	CHI	33
		END

Stockton rebounds *again* and finds Russell, who gives the press a dunk for the front-page picture. With that, the Bulls concede, and the series goes to Game 5.

Although Jordan played poorly in this game, shooting only seven of twenty and committing four turnovers, he would fight through the flu in the next game to score thirty-eight points in one of his classic performances. One of the purposes of presenting this game, however, has been to provide some evidence that great players like Jordan do have poor games on occasion, even in big games. And with the bad game, it is possible that Jordan even cost his team this win.

The Important Lesson of the Score Sheet

The most basic thing to come out of the score sheet is the concept of possessions. In your head, you already have some sense of what this is. In this score sheet, it becomes definitive. In a game, a team alternates possession with its opponent so that, at the end of the game, each team has just about the same number of possessions on which to try to score. Both teams have the same forty-eight minutes (in the NBA, or forty minutes in college, or thirty-two minutes in high school), but

Table 2.2. Per-Game Statistics for the 1990–91 Denver Nuggets

	GM	GA	G%	TM	TA	T%	REB	DREB	TREB	TO	PTS
DEN	47.6	108.1	0.440	21.0	27.6	0.763	18.5	30.9	49.4	16.2	119.9
OPP	49.7	97.1	0.512	29.0	37.4	0.775	15.1	37.4	52.5	18.6	130.8

Table 2.3. Per-Game Statistics for the 1998–99 Miami Heat

	FGM	FGA	FG%	FTM	FTA	FT%	OREB	DREB	TREB	TOV	PTS
MIA	32.3	71.3	0.453	18.6	25.2	0.735	10.1	30.2	40.3	14.9	89.0
OPP	31.3	76.1	0.411	17.2	23.3	0.737	12.4	26.8	39.2	13.5	84.0

they will also have the same number of possessions[1]. For games involving running or trapping teams, that number of possessions will be high—more than one hundred or 110 in the NBA. For walk-it-up teams, that number of possessions will be low—sometimes fewer than eighty. At the end of the season the fast teams will have more possessions than the slow teams, but both will have the same number as their cumulative opponents.

For example, table 2.2 presents the per-game statistics for the 1990–91 Denver Nuggets, who were coached by Paul Westhead and typified his style by running for the sake of running.

And table 2.3 presents the per-game stats for the 1998–99 Miami Heat, one of the slowest teams in history.

How many possessions did these teams use? Since the NBA didn't record possessions during these seasons, we're going to have to make an estimate. That estimate comes from score sheets like the one above. From the Chicago-Utah score sheet, counting the number of lines for each of the teams shows eighty possessions for each. Estimating this number isn't hard using some basic statistics.

It is convenient (and almost correct) to think that there are only three ways for a possession to end: a field goal attempt that is not rebounded by the offense (either a make or a defensive board of a miss), a turnover, or some free throws. We can "count" these events using some basic stats. A field goal attempt that isn't rebounded by the offense is simply FGA − OREB. A turnover is already counted as TOV. Free throws that end possessions are not as well-recorded. Some free throws come in pairs, and the first of the pair cannot end the possession. Some free throws complete three-point plays, which means that the possession is already counted by the FGA − OREB term. Through several score sheets, I have found that about 40 percent of free throw attempts end possessions.[2] In the end then, a good way to approximate possessions from standard statistics is with this formula:

$$\text{Possessions} = \text{FGA} - \text{OREB} + \text{TOV} + 0.4 \times \text{FTA}^{[3]}$$

Table 2.4. Official Statistics for the Chicago–Utah Game

	FGM	FGA	FG%	FTM	FTA	FT%	OREB	DREB	TREB	TOV	PTS
CHI	32	76	0.421	5	12	0.417	10	28	38	8	73
UTA	29	64	0.453	15	21	0.714	5	34	39	14	78

Applying this to Chicago's and Utah's official stats for the scored game (table 2.4) the formula gives 78.8 possessions for Chicago and 81.4 possessions for Utah, which are both pretty close to the actual eighty that they had. When you average Chicago's and Utah's numbers, you get 80.1, which is almost exactly what they each had. Since, on average, teams will have the same number of possessions as their opponents, it is standard to average a team's possession estimate with that of its opponent to get a single value for the game.

Looking back to Denver and Miami, it is now possible to say how many possessions they used. Applying the formula, Denver used 116.9 possessions per game and Miami used 86.4 per game. Most importantly, it's easy to calculate how *efficient* the two teams were with their possessions. Any team can run the ball and shoot quickly just to score a lot of points, which is what Denver did, but that team gives the ball back each time. An efficient offensive team scores more points with its given possessions, not more points overall. Here, despite scoring thirty fewer points per game than Denver, Miami actually was more efficient offensively, scoring 103.2 points per one hundred possessions, which is called an *offensive rating*. Denver's offensive rating was a lowly 102.5 even though they put up all those points. On the defensive end, Denver allowed 113.2 points per hundred possessions—its *defensive rating* was 113.2—one of the worst in history. Miami, on the other hand, prided itself on defense and had a defensive rating of 97.0.

Thinking in terms of possessions and efficiency is the biggest thing that comes out of scoring a game with the score sheet above. Separating pace from estimates of quality allows a lot of useful analysis to be done on teams and players. Throughout the rest of this book, when a team offense is referred to as good, it is because they are efficient, not because they score a lot of points.

Other Coaches Use Points Per Possession

After doing that first score sheet back in 1987, I thought I invented the concept of offensive and defensive ratings or points per possession. When *Basketball Digest* published some of my initial calculations back in 1988, I really thought it was original. Shortly thereafter, I found out that the concept had existed for decades already. I saw it in Frank McGuire's book for coaches called *Defensive Basketball*. Dean Smith, the longtime UNC coach, was McGuire's assistant at the time and used the concept through his tenure in Chapel Hill. Other coaches used the concept as well, including simple formulas to estimate possessions from the basic statistics. In the late 1980s or early 1990s, I actually heard a college broadcaster use the phrase "points per possession."

But the number really still hasn't gotten much use outside of the inner basketball circles. That will likely change soon, if not because of this book (which is personal optimism), then because some NBA insiders have begun keeping the stat and will eventually decide to release it. It is a very simple concept and a very useful one.

Because it is so simple and so useful, I have expanded the concept to be applicable to individual players as well as teams. That calculation, and even the theory, is a bit more complicated than is appropriate for such an early chapter. There is a lot that can be done with just the team numbers for a while.

The Love of Scoring a Game

Scoring a game this way is hard. It involves writing fast, paying close attention, and skipping bathroom breaks. But scoring a game can involve you in the game so much more than casual watching.

The first game I ever scored reflected how involved I was in it through the comments I wrote on the side of the paper, in the exclamation points at certain times of the game, and in how hard I pressed the pen to the paper when something important happened. It was, admittedly, a classic game—Game Four of the 1987 NBA Finals when Magic Johnson hit his "junior junior skyhook" over three Celtics to give the Lakers a 3–1 advantage in the series. Lakers broadcaster Chick Hearn described that play as, "Magic down the middle, hook shot of twelve. Good!" My own scribbling at the end of the game can be seen in figure 2.2.

I was definitely a Lakers fan, as evidenced by the comments at the top, which, for those of the millions of you who can't read my writing, say, "It ain't over 'till Johnny Most cries" and "The refs ARE WEARING GREEN GLASSES." At another point in the game, the network showed the old uneven Boston parquet floor, and I wrote on the side, "Did you see THAT floor?" Early in the fourth quarter,

Figure 2.2. My Score Sheet from Game Four of the 1987 NBA Finals

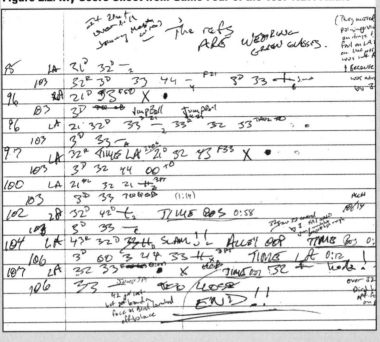

Kevin McHale, who was playing on a broken foot, made a couple of big plays and I disgustedly wrote, "McHale's foot is NOT broken!" I LIKED USING CAPITAL LETTERS, I guess. The famous hook shot is denoted only with "hook!" as I grappled to keep emotion from interfering with my scoring duties.

Even if that score sheet didn't have the analytical value that it turned out to have for me, it would still have great sentimental value. I continue to say to this day that this Lakers–Celtics game was my favorite of all time.

Endnotes

1. Dean Smith and Frank McGuire (and probably many others) have used the concept of possessions as well. Others have also occasionally defined a possession as "uninterrupted control of the ball," which is different from the definition used throughout this book, where a possession continues after an offensive rebound. That alternative definition is what is called a "play" in this book, which is not quite as useful because "plays" are not equal for two teams in a game.

2. In the days when the NBA used a three-to-make-two bonus, the fraction was lower. Since there are no score sheets providing actual possession information from that era, a more theoretical approach has to be taken to get an estimate of that fraction. Basically, we want to adjust the 40 percent used now by the number of times three foul shots were taken in the old days when only two are taken now. This theoretical fraction is estimated from

$$\left[1 - \tfrac{1}{3} P \left(3 \; \text{FTA}\right)\right] \times 0.4$$

where P(3 FTA) is the probability of being in the bonus and actually taking three foul shot attempts and the factor of $\frac{1}{3}$ accounts for one of the three bonus foul shots being above what are awarded now in the bonus. The probability of being in the bonus is estimated by getting the number of fouls per quarter on average (about six) and assuming a Poisson distribution to get the probability of at least five fouls in a quarter (about 70 percent). The probability of three foul shots given that you're in the bonus is just the chance that the guy shooting the shots doesn't make both, which is 1-FT%2. Using a free throw percentage of 75 percent, the theoretical fraction goes from 0.4 to about 0.36. With the rule changes of 2002, it appears that this 0.4 also goes down due to more technical fouls.

3. The technical version of this formula is often used throughout the book, where the field goal attempts that aren't rebounded by the offense are more accurately represented. That formula replaces the OREB term with something a little more complex and, based on my experience, more accurate:

$$\text{Possessions} = \text{FGA} - \frac{\text{OREB}}{\text{OREB} + \text{DDREB}} \times \left(\text{FGA} - \text{FGM}\right) \times 1.07 + \text{TOV} + 0.4 \times \text{FTA}$$

where DDREB represents the defensive rebounds by the opponents.

Chapter 3

The Best Offenses and Defenses (And Some of the Worst, Too)

No one cares about what makes a team average. Anyone can be average. All you have to do to be average is throw together a bunch of guys at random and you get average. It takes work to be good. It takes incompetence to be bad. Good gets you a storyline. Bad gets you a storyline. Greatness gets you a special edition *Sports Illustrated* coffee table book that comes free with your paid subscription. Extreme badness gets you a Golden Raspberry Award.

Average is such a big category that it just takes too long to talk about. Average is to rank 150 out of the three hundred NCAA Division I basketball teams—a long way from making the NCAA Tournament. Average is a 2.0 GPA (or 3.6 at some of those snooty grade-inflated schools). Average is a Toyota Camry.

Average is boring, but you need to know what average is in order to define greatness and to define what is really bad.

Average in the NBA is a .500 record, or forty-one wins in an eighty-two-game season. Teams have historically won as many as seventy-two games and lost as many as seventy-three. That's extreme greatness and extreme badness, respectively.

Average offensive and defensive performance isn't as straightforward to define. Rule changes, talent changes, and possibly even changes in the length of shorts affected the balance between offense and defense. In 1988 when shorts were still short, the offenses were better than in 1998, when shorts were long. It's got to be distracting to a shooter to have so much fabric between his legs.

Yes, even average has its ups and downs (see table 3.1 and box). Figure 3.1 shows how the league average points per hundred possessions rating has changed through the years. In 1974, average was pretty bad relative to average in 1984—that is if you consider better *offense* to be good. The greatest offensive team of 1974 was Milwaukee, with an offensive rating of 102.1. The *average* offensive team of 1984 was the Milwaukee Bucks, with an offensive rating of 107.8,

Table 3.1. Pace Changes, Efficiency Changes, and Rule Changes (Since 1974)

Season	Poss/G	Average Rating	Rule Changes (adapted from the APBR)
1974	107.2	98.6	
1975	104.1	98.6	Time-out requests made at approximately the instant a period expires not to be granted.
1976	105.1	99.3	After any playing court violation, the ball is to be put in play at the sideline. Jump ball to start each quarter eliminated.
1977	105.9	100.6	Elbowing foul revised to include swinging of elbows. Ball moved to half-court after time-out in final 2 minutes of game. 24-second clock reset to 5 seconds after a defensive team causes the ball to go out of bounds. Force-out eliminated.
1978	106.4	102.0	Both coaches must be present if a coach wishes to discuss a rule interpretation with the officials. Baskets scored intentionally into the wrong basket will be disallowed. 24-second clock to be reset to 24 seconds following all violations. Ball entering the basket from below now a violation. Missed free throw tap-in counted as 2 points. Intentional physical contact with officials prohibited.
1979	105.1	105.0	Rolling the ball onto the floor when inbounding now allowed. Technical foul assessed for first illegal defense, 2 technical fouls assessed for subsequent violations. Coach ejected after third zone defense technical. Players and coaches instructed to proceed to dressing rooms at halftime. Hand-checking allowed if it does not impede an opponent's progress.
1980	102.7	106.4	3-point field goal added [23' 9"]. Third official added. Team attempting to bring ball across midcourt before 10-second violation no longer given additional 10 seconds if the defensive team causes the ball to go out of bounds.
1981	101.3	106.7	League returns to 2 officials. Player jewelry prohibited, equipment safety rules defined. 20-second injury time-out eliminated. One 20-second time-out per half added. Red light synchronized to light up when the horn sounds added behind backboard. Game ball changed from brown to orange. 24-second shot not to be reset after technical foul on offensive team.
1982	101.5	106.9	Backcourt foul eliminated. Penalty free throws eliminated. Zone defense rules revised as illegal defense. Ejection of coach following third illegal defense technical removed. Player to report to 8-foot box in front of scorer's table before referee will beckon them into the game. Shattering backboard prohibited. Collapsible rim added.
1983	103.6	104.7	Team allowed to designate player to inbound ball.
1984	102.3	107.6	Fake free throw to induce lane violation prohibited. Basket made simultaneously as illegal defense is called will be allowed and illegal defense call disregarded. Entering spectator stands prohibited.
1985	102.7	107.9	Breakaway foul added for players with a clear path to the basket in the frontcourt if fouled. Game protest rules revised. Overtime period time-outs increased from 2 to 3 regardless of remaining time-outs.
1986	102.8	107.2	
1987	101.5	108.4	
1988	100.1	108.1	
1989	101.3	107.8	Third official added.
1990	99.0	108.1	Tenths of seconds added to game clock.
1991	98.5	107.9	Penalty for flagrant foul increased to 2 free throws and possession. Expiration of time rule [0:00.3 second rule] added.
1992	97.4	108.2	
1993	97.5	108.0	Guidelines for infection control added. Verbal fan interference rule added. Player throwing punch ejected from game and suspended for at least 1 additional game.
1994	95.5	106.3	Flagrant foul rule revised to 5-point system.
1995	93.7	108.3	Taunting prohibited. Hand-checking rules revised to prohibit it from end line in backcourt to free throw line in frontcourt. 3-point field goal line moved in to 22'. Player fouled shooting 3-pointer awarded 3 free throws. "Clear path" rule revised to include backcourt. Player committing 2 flagrant fouls in a game is ejected.

Season	Poss/G	Average Rating	Rule Changes (adapted from the APBR)
1996	92.4	107.7	Player suspended for leaving bench area during fights.
1997	90.8	106.7	Team calling excessive time-outs charged with technical and loses possession.
1998	91.0	105.1	Player not allowed to call time-out if he has both feet in the air or has broken the plane of the sideline or baseline. 3-point field goal line moved back to 23′9″. Player prohibited from using his forearm to impede the progress of a player facing the basket in the frontcourt. No-charge area added under basket.
1999	89.6	102.2	
2000	93.7	104.1	Guidelines adopted to restrict the length of playing shorts to no longer than 1″ above the knee.
2001	92.0	103.0	Delay of game penalty in the final 2 minutes of a game results in a technical foul. On an inbounds play, if there is a 5-second violation or foul before the ball is inbounded, teams are now allowed to substitute. The league also adopted a change giving a player fouled when he has a clear path to the basket 1 free throw and his team possession at midcourt. The old rule gave the player 2 free throws. Instead of 7 time-outs per game, teams will be limited to 6 with a maximum of 3 in the fourth quarter instead of the previous limit of 4. During the last 2 minutes of the fourth period or an overtime period, teams will be allowed 2 time-outs, a reduction from 3. Full time-out reduced from 100 seconds to 60 seconds, except for the first 2 time-outs in each period and the mandatory time-outs in the second and fourth quarters. Unlimited substitutions during 20-second time-outs. Shot clock restored to 14 seconds, instead of 24 seconds, if a defensive violation occurs with 14 seconds or less remaining. Offense can advance ball to halfcourt on 20-second time-out, not just full time-out.
2002	91.3	104.5	Illegal defense eliminated. 3-second restriction for defenders in free throw lane unless a defender is within arm's length of an offensive player. 10-second count to cross midcourt changed to 8 seconds. Reduction in the number of touch fouls by allowing brief contact initiated by a defensive player if it does not impede the progress of the player with the ball.

Figure 3.1. Trends of Pace and Efficiency

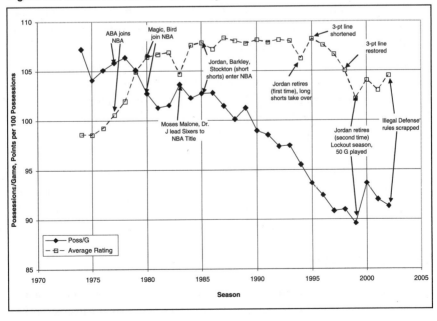

nearly six points higher. If you consider better defense to be good, league defense has gotten much worse. The worst defensive team of 1974 was Portland, with a defensive rating of 103.6. The average defensive team of 1984 was the Utah Jazz, with a defensive rating of 107.9. So either offenses were worse or defenses were better back in the old days. It depends on how you spin it. Does that mean an offense couldn't be great back then? Does that mean that a defense can't be great now?

If kids are learning in high school now what Isaac Newton was the first to figure out three hundred years ago, does that mean that Isaac Newton wasn't very smart? In two hundred years, when they're teaching Einstein's general theory of relativity to high school kids, won't we look dumb? Noooo. We're smart!

And so we evaluate the teams of history against the averages of their times.

The Great Ones

The point in looking at great teams is to find consistencies among those teams, patterns that may suggest how to construct other teams or at least how to predict what teams might be great. For example: Were the great teams star-driven or system driven? Were there any key positions—such as center—that needed a great player in order for the team to have a great offense or defense? Were teams tall or short? Were there any particular coaches who seemed to make good offenses/defenses? As you'll see, each of these questions raises new ones. It's impossible to answer all the questions about great teams this early in the book. But later chapters will return to these lists as they introduce other tools to evaluate teams.

The way that both the great offenses and defenses are listed here is by how much better their team offensive or defensive ratings were relative to the league average in that season. For example, the league average rating in 1974 was 98.6, meaning that the Milwaukee team mentioned above was 3.5 points per hundred possessions better than average offensively and 4.2 points per hundred possessions better than average defensively. It is fair to say from these numbers that those Bucks were a better defensive team than offensive team. By this measure, those Bucks ranked ninety-fourth historically in terms of offense and fifty-seventh in terms of defense.

Finally, you'll see that these lists contain only teams since the 1974 season. Prior to that year, turnovers were not recorded by the NBA, making it impossible to estimate the number of possessions that teams used. This is unfortunate, but the last thirty years still tell a good story.

The Great Offenses

Table 3.2 lists the top twenty-five offenses since 1974. The number-one team was the 2002 Dallas Mavericks—shockingly. Despite Dirk Nowitzki, the team's success

Table 3.2. Top Historical Offenses

Rank	Team	Season	Offensive Rating	League Average	Increment Above League	Players	Comments
1	Dallas Mavericks	2002	112.2	104.5	7.7	Dirk Nowitzki, Steve Nash, Michael Finley	Fewest turnovers ever, great 3-point shooting.
2	Chicago Bulls	1997	114.4	106.7	7.7	Michael Jordan, Scottie Pippen, Toni Kukoc, Dennis Rodman	Won 69 games and title. Very distinct roles. Jordan scored, Pippen controlled ball, Rodman rebounded, Kukoc and Kerr and Harper shot open shots.
3	Utah Jazz	1998	112.7	105.1	7.6	Karl Malone, John Stockton, Jeff Hornacek	Lost in Finals. Hornacek was ideal outside shooting complement to Stockton and Malone, pick and roll.
4	Chicago Bulls	1996	115.2	107.7	7.5	Jordan, Pippen, Kukoc, Rodman	Won 72 games and title. See #2.
5	Denver Nuggets	1982	114.3	106.9	7.5	Alex English, Dan Issel, Kiki Vandeweghe	Highest scoring team in history at 126.5 ppg. Pushed the pace in high altitude. Took and made tons of foul shots by getting inside a lot. Shot few threes.
6	Chicago Bulls	1992	115.5	108.2	7.4	Jordan, Pippen, Horace Grant, B.J. Armstrong	Won 67 games and title. Very well-defined roles.
7	Boston Celtics	1988	115.4	108.1	7.4	Larry Bird, Kevin McHale, Danny Ainge, Robert Parish	Set then record for 3-point shots taken, made, and 3-point percentage, which added to already great post game.
8	Los Angeles Lakers	1987	115.6	108.4	7.3	Magic Johnson, James Worthy, Kareem Abdul-Jabbar, Byron Scott	Won title. Several great players, 3 of which were in their prime, between ages 26 and 28.
9	Utah Jazz	1997	113.6	106.7	7.0	Malone, Stockton, Hornacek	Lost in Finals. See #5.
10	Los Angeles Lakers	1998	111.9	105.0	6.9	Shaquille O'Neal, Eddie Jones, Kobe Bryant, Nick Van Exel	Even early in Kobe Bryant's career, offense was good. It took Phil Jackson to bring good defense.
11	Orlando Magic	1995	115.1	108.3	6.9	Shaquille O'Neal, Penny Hardaway, Nick Anderson, Dennis Scott, Horace Grant	Lost in Finals. Shaq inside, Hardaway, Anderson, and Scott outside. Shaq and Penny healthy.
12	Chicago Bulls	1991	114.7	107.9	6.8	Jordan, Pippen, Grant, Armstrong	Won title. Second year with Phil Jackson and the Triangle Offense. Offense took big leap with Jackson and Triangle.
13	Dallas Mavericks	1987	114.9	108.4	6.6	Mark Aguirre, Rolando Blackman, Derek Harper, Sam Perkins, James Donaldson, Detlef Schrempf	Set then record for 3-point shots taken and made. Little inside game, though Aguirre could score from post.
14	Seattle SuperSonics	1995	114.8	108.3	6.5	Gary Payton, Schrempf, Shawn Kemp	One of many 1995 teams to take advantage of the shorter 3-point line to get a lot of easy points.

(continued next page)

Table 3.2. Top Historical Offenses *(continued)*

Rank	Team	Season	Offensive Rating	League Average	Increment Above League	Players	Comments
15	Indiana Pacers	1999	108.7	102.2	6.5	Reggie Miller, Rik Smits, Jalen Rose, Chris Mullin, Mark Jackson	Numbers somewhat inflated due to lockout year because they supposedly worked out together during lockout.
16	Seattle SuperSonics	1998	111.4	105.0	6.4	Vin Baker, Payton, Schrempf, Dale Ellis	Still shot a lot of threes even though line returns to 23′ 8″, made 39.6%, among the top 10 in history.
17	Los Angeles Lakers	1985	114.1	107.9	6.3	Abdul-Jabbar, Magic, Worthy, Scott	Won title. Best shooting team in history, making 54.5% of their field goals.
18	Phoenix Suns	1995	114.5	108.3	6.2	Charles Barkley, Danny Manning, Dan Majerle, Kevin Johnson	Outstanding passing team.
19	Los Angeles Lakers	1986	113.3	107.2	6.1	Abdul-Jabbar, Worthy, Magic, Scott	See #17.
20	Utah Jazz	1995	114.3	108.3	6.1	Malone, Stockton, Hornacek	See #5.
21	Los Angeles Lakers	1989	113.8	107.8	6.0	Worthy, Magic, Scott, A.C. Green, Mychal Thompson, Michael Cooper	Abdul-Jabbar played limited minutes in last season. 3-point shooting picks up.
22	Los Angeles Lakers	1983	110.5	104.7	5.8	Abdul-Jabbar, Jamaal Wilkes, Magic, Norm Nixon	Lost in Finals. First of many great Magic Johnson–led offenses.
23	Los Angeles Lakers	1990	114.0	108.1	5.8	Magic, Worthy, Scott, Green	Last of many great Magic Johnson–led offenses. Magic retired after this year.
24	Cleveland Cavaliers	1992	113.9	108.2	5.7	Brad Daugherty, Mark Price, Larry Nance, Hot Rod Williams, Craig Ehlo	Had been good offense since Ron Harper left, but now mostly healthy. Still couldn't beat the Bulls.
25	Milwaukee Bucks	2001	108.8	103.0	5.7	Glenn Robinson, Ray Allen, Sam Cassell	Strong jump shooting team without much inside. Allen led 3-point barrage.

during the season, and the fact that the Mavs set a record for fewest turnovers, it didn't really click with anyone that they were watching the most efficient offense in history. Not even when the Mavs shot 58 percent from the field, 52 percent from three-point land, and turned the ball over only eight times in a game against the Clippers on January 26, when they scored 133 points on only ninety-one possessions, a truly amazing performance. The team had some of the top international talent from Germany (Nowitzki), Canada (Steve Nash), Mexico (Eduardo Najera), and China (Zhizhi Wang). Coincidence or not, the players had good basketball skills but were not considered great "athletes" in a league that still values athletes over basketball players (as evidenced further by the five high school players taken in the previous draft).

There are other more familiar teams on the list below the Mavs. The Bulls of the 1990s are on the list four times. Magic Johnson's Lakers are on the list five times. The Stockton-Malone-Hornacek Utah Jazz of the 1990s are on the list four times. There are two Shaquille O'Neal teams, one when he was with the Orlando Magic, one from his second year with the Lakers. The 1982 Denver Nuggets team that scored a record 126.5 points per game is on the list. There is only one Larry Bird team, the 1988 Celtics team that shot the lights out from beyond the three-point arc.

And then there is a Charles Barkley team, a Reggie Miller team, a couple of Gary Payton teams. Chris Mullin and Detlef Schrempf were both on two different great teams. Milwaukee's recent Ray Allen, Glenn Robinson, and Sam Cassell triumvirate posted a great season in 2001 before the infamous collapse of 2002.

So what patterns are there in all these teams?

Were They Star-Driven or System Driven?

Did the teams revolve around some unique offensive system, like the triangle or a motion offense or a fast break? Or did it seem that the presence of certain star players caused them to reach such greatness?

Historic popular analysis of these teams has described them both by their systems and by their stars. The Bulls were known for their triangle offense, brought in by Phil Jackson, and for Michael Jordan. So was it the triangle or Jordan that made them great? My sense—not only in the case of Chicago but for teams in general—is that it was more the talent than the system. The systems catered to the talents and probably helped to make them a little better, but the players were more important.

My justification is a "weight of the evidence" argument, not any one thing specifically. The first line of evidence involves the triangle because it was used with a variety of different talents. First, when Jackson brought the triangle to the Bulls in 1990, the Bulls offense went up from 1.8 above average to 4.1 above average—a

2.3 point improvement—but when Jordan left in 1994, the Bulls offense went from 5.0 above average to 0.1 *below* average—a 5.1 point drop. Basically, the Jordan factor appears to be about twice as important as the triangle in this time period. Later, when Jackson, Jordan, Scottie Pippen, and Dennis Rodman all left, the Bulls continued to play a triangle offense under poor Tim Floyd. Those teams were horrible offensively, the 1999 and 2000 Bulls turning up fifth and fourth on the all-time worst list, respectively (see table 10). No triangle offense could salvage those teams. When Jackson took his triangle offense to the Lakers beginning in 2000, he already had Shaq and Kobe as talents, though Kobe was still only twenty-one. The Lakers of 1999 had an offense that was 5.3 points above average. The triangle-running Lakers of 2000 actually dropped to 3.3 points above average. The Lakers of 2001 and 2002 rebounded to levels near that of 1999. Was it the tri-angle or the maturation of Kobe? It's not obvious. But the fact that Shaq has been on two great offensive teams that didn't use the triangle and on none that did use it is just another piece of evidence to suggest that inherent offensive ability of indi-viduals is a bit more important than the vaunted triangle offense. Just in general, there are a lot of non-triangle offenses on this list, suggesting that it is not a magic system.

In Utah, where the talents of Stockton and Malone were paired for more than fifteen years, you could say that the "system" was the pick-and-roll. Did the pick-and-roll make the offense great, or did the talent make it great? Given that the pick-and-roll is used throughout basketball—it's not so much a system as a tried-and-true play call that forces a weakness in a defense—it's clear that the talent just knew very well how to run the pick-and-roll. The Jazz offense was good with just these two running the pick-and-roll, but they needed the addition of Jeff Hornacek in 1994 for the offense to reach a point where opponents just could not stop it. Hornacek was another good ball handler—having played the point guard position for heavy minutes early in his career—but also had a great outside touch. That third efficient scorer was key to taking the offense to greatness and the Jazz to the brink of titles. An additional note to add, however, is that every Stockton-Malone team that Jerry Sloan coached was better offensively than every one that Frank Layden coached. So maybe Sloan taught the pick-and-roll better...

And what about pace? Does pushing the ball help a team become great? Not in a consistent way. Table 3.3 shows some other statistical indicators for the top twenty-five great offenses, the first one being possessions per game. Doug Moe's Denver Nuggets of 1982 ran a lot to take advantage of their scorers' abilities to get up and down the court and create quickly in the half-court or full court. They were among the runningest teams in history (with Paul Westhead's ill-conceived 1991 Nuggets team being the fastest—see table 3.4). The Nuggets of the early 1980s maintained a frantic pace from 1981 to 1985, but that 1982 team was easily the most efficient. The offense was still very efficient in 1983 (+5.0 over average),

Table 3.3. Other Statistical Indicators of Top Historical Offenses

Rank	Team	Season	Offensive Rating			Possessions/Game			Floor Percentage			Field Percentage			Play Percentage		
			Team Value	League Average	Incr.	Team Value	League Average	Incr.	Team Value	League Average	Incr.	Team Value	League Average	Incr.	Team Value	League Average	Incr.
1	Dallas Mavericks	2002	112.2	104.5	7.7	93.8	91.3	2.4	0.516	0.494	0.022	0.465	0.442	0.023	0.455	0.429	0.026
2	Chicago Bulls	1997	114.4	106.7	7.7	90.2	90.8	-0.6	0.537	0.501	0.036	0.494	0.447	0.047	0.453	0.433	0.020
3	Utah Jazz	1998	112.7	105.0	7.6	89.6	91.0	-1.4	0.544	0.502	0.042	0.476	0.446	0.029	0.474	0.432	0.042
4	Chicago Bulls	1996	115.2	107.7	7.5	91.3	92.4	-1.1	0.540	0.507	0.033	0.495	0.452	0.043	0.456	0.440	0.016
5	Denver Nuggets	1982	114.3	106.9	7.5	110.6	101.5	9.1	0.565	0.532	0.033	0.505	0.481	0.025	0.496	0.460	0.036
6	Chicago Bulls	1992	115.5	108.2	7.4	95.1	97.4	-2.2	0.569	0.527	0.042	0.525	0.476	0.049	0.487	0.452	0.036
7	Boston Celtics	1988	115.4	108.1	7.4	98.4	100.1	-1.7	0.555	0.531	0.025	0.503	0.476	0.027	0.491	0.458	0.033
8	Los Angeles Lakers	1987	115.6	108.4	7.3	101.8	101.5	0.4	0.565	0.533	0.031	0.511	0.478	0.033	0.490	0.459	0.031
9	Utah Jazz	1997	113.6	106.7	7.0	90.7	90.8	-0.1	0.544	0.501	0.043	0.482	0.447	0.035	0.479	0.433	0.046
10	Los Angeles Lakers	1998	111.9	105.0	6.9	94.3	91.0	3.3	0.534	0.502	0.032	0.473	0.446	0.027	0.465	0.432	0.032
11	Orlando Magic	1995	115.1	108.3	6.9	96.3	93.7	2.6	0.549	0.513	0.036	0.498	0.459	0.040	0.472	0.444	0.029
12	Chicago Bulls	1991	114.7	107.9	6.8	96.0	98.5	-2.5	0.563	0.526	0.036	0.518	0.473	0.045	0.484	0.454	0.030
13	Dallas Mavericks	1987	114.9	108.4	6.6	101.5	101.5	0.0	0.557	0.533	0.023	0.498	0.478	0.021	0.479	0.459	0.020
14	Seattle SuperSonics	1995	114.8	108.3	6.5	96.2	93.7	2.5	0.542	0.513	0.029	0.484	0.459	0.025	0.472	0.444	0.028
15	Indiana Pacers	1993	108.7	102.2	6.5	87.1	89.6	-2.5	0.506	0.488	0.018	0.449	0.431	0.018	0.440	0.421	0.019
16	Seattle SuperSonics	1993	111.4	105.0	6.4	90.2	91.0	-0.8	0.518	0.502	0.016	0.464	0.446	0.018	0.453	0.432	0.021
17	Los Angeles Lakers	1985	114.1	107.9	6.3	103.6	102.7	0.9	0.564	0.534	0.030	0.520	0.481	0.039	0.495	0.462	0.033
18	Phoenix Suns	1995	114.5	108.3	6.2	96.7	93.7	3.0	0.535	0.513	0.022	0.480	0.459	0.022	0.467	0.444	0.023
19	Los Angeles Lakers	1986	113.3	107.2	6.1	103.5	102.8	0.7	0.556	0.531	0.025	0.507	0.476	0.030	0.484	0.460	0.024
20	Utah Jazz	1995	114.3	108.3	6.1	93.1	93.7	-0.6	0.549	0.513	0.036	0.487	0.459	0.028	0.486	0.444	0.042
21	Los Angeles Lakers	1989	113.8	107.8	6.0	100.8	101.3	-0.5	0.550	0.527	0.024	0.496	0.473	0.023	0.479	0.453	0.026
22	Los Angeles Lakers	1983	110.5	104.7	5.8	104.1	103.6	0.5	0.553	0.522	0.031	0.514	0.472	0.042	0.476	0.450	0.026
23	Los Angeles Lakers	1990	114.0	108.1	5.8	97.2	99.0	-1.8	0.547	0.528	0.019	0.492	0.474	0.018	0.473	0.456	0.017
24	Cleveland Cavaliers	1992	113.9	108.2	5.7	95.6	97.4	-1.8	0.548	0.527	0.021	0.495	0.476	0.019	0.477	0.452	0.025
25	Milwaukee Bucks	2001	109.5	103.8	5.7	92.0	91.4	0.6	0.507	0.492	0.015	0.460	0.438	0.021	0.444	0.429	0.015

NOTES:
Floor Percentage: Percentage of a team's possessions on which the team scores at least 1 point.
Field Percentage: Percentage of a team's non-foul shot possessions on which the team scores a field goal.
Play Percentage: Percentage of a team's "plays" on which the team scores at least 1 point.

Table 3.4. Fastest Teams in History

Rank	Team	Season	Possessions per Game	League Average	Increment above League	Offensive Rating	Defensive Rating	League Average Rating	Offensive Increment	Defensive Increment	Players
1	Denver Nuggets	1991	114.0	98.5	15.4	105.2	114.7	107.9	-2.7	6.8	Michael Adams, Orlando Woolridge, Reggie Williams, Chris Jackson, Blair Rasmussen
2	Denver Nuggets	1982	110.6	101.5	9.1	114.3	113.9	106.9	7.5	7.0	Alex English, Dan Issel, Kiki Vandeweghe
3	Denver Nuggets	1984	111.1	102.3	8.8	111.3	112.3	107.6	3.7	4.7	English, Issel, Vandeweghe
4	Denver Nuggets	1983	112.4	103.6	8.8	109.7	109.1	104.7	5.0	4.4	English, Issel, Vandeweghe
5	Denver Nuggets	1981	110.0	101.3	8.7	110.8	111.2	106.7	4.1	4.5	English, Issel, Vandeweghe
6	Sacramento Kings	1999	97.6	89.6	8.0	102.7	103.1	102.2	0.5	0.9	Chris Webber, Vlade Divac, Corliss Williamson, Jason Williams, Tariq-Abdul-Wahad
7	Denver Nuggets	1989	108.6	101.3	7.3	108.6	107.1	107.8	0.8	-0.7	English, Fat Lever, Adams, Walter Davis, Danny Schayes
8	Golden State Warriors	1989	108.5	101.3	7.2	107.4	107.7	107.8	-0.4	-0.1	Chris Mullin, Mitch Richmond, Winston Garland, Rod Higgins, Larry Smith
9	Denver Nuggets	1990	106.1	99.0	7.1	108.0	106.7	108.1	-0.1	-1.4	Lever, English, Davis, Adams, Rasmussen
10	Golden State Warriors	1992	104.5	97.4	7.1	113.6	109.9	108.2	5.5	1.7	Mullin, Tim Hardaway, Sarunas Marciulionis
11	Golden State Warriors	1990	106.0	99.0	7.1	109.6	112.6	108.1	1.5	4.5	Mullin, Richmond, Hardaway, Terry Teagle, Higgins
12	Sacramento Kings	2000	99.9	93.7	6.3	105.1	102.1	104.1	1.0	-1.9	Webber, Williams, Divac, Nick Anderson, Peja Stojakovic, Williamson
13	Boston Celtics	1997	96.9	90.8	6.0	103.9	111.4	106.7	-2.8	4.8	Antoine Walker, David Wesley, Rick Fox, Eric Williams, Todd Day
14	San Antonio Spurs	1980	108.7	102.7	6.0	109.8	110.2	106.4	3.4	3.8	George Gervin, Larry Kenon, James Silas, Mark Olberding
15	Denver Nuggets	1988	106.0	100.1	5.9	110.1	106.3	108.1	2.1	-1.8	English, Lever, Adams, Schayes
16	San Antonio Spurs	1984	108.2	102.3	5.9	111.2	111.4	107.6	3.6	3.8	Gervin, Mike Mitchell, Gene Banks, Artis Gilmore
17	Orlando Magic	1990	104.8	99.0	5.8	105.8	114.3	108.1	-2.4	6.2	Terry Catledge, Reggie Theus, Sidney Green, Jerry Reynolds, Otis Smith
18	Golden State Warriors	1991	104.2	98.5	5.7	111.9	110.3	107.9	4.0	2.4	Mullin, Richmond, Hardaway, Higgins
19	Denver Nuggets	1985	108.4	102.7	5.7	110.7	108.4	107.9	2.8	0.5	English, Calvin Natt, Lever, T.R. Dunn, Wayne Cooper
20	Golden State Warriors	1995	99.0	93.7	5.4	106.7	112.2	108.3	-1.5	3.9	Latrell Sprewell, Hardaway, Chris Gatling, Donyell Marshall, Keith Jennings
21	San Antonio Spurs	1977	111.2	105.9	5.3	103.5	103.4	100.6	2.9	2.8	Gervin, Kenon, Billy Paultz, Mike Gale, Allan Bristow
22	Denver Nuggets	1987	106.7	101.5	5.2	109.4	110.2	108.4	1.0	1.8	English, Lever, Bill Hanzlik, Darrell Walker, Dunn
23	San Antonio Spurs	1979	110.2	105.1	5.1	108.2	103.5	105.0	3.2	-1.5	Gervin, Kenon, James Silas, Paultz, Gale
24	Charlotte Hornets	1992	102.3	97.4	4.9	107.1	110.9	108.2	-1.1	2.7	Kendall Gill, Larry Johnson, Muggsy Bogues, Kenny Gattison, Dell Curry
25	San Antonio Spurs	1988	105.0	100.1	4.9	108.2	112.8	108.1	0.1	4.7	Alvin Robertson, Walter Berry, Frank Brickowski, Johnny Dawkins

but the declining skills of thirty-three-year-old Dan Issel and the general lack of a bench began to have an effect after that.

The fastest teams in history, shown in table 3.4, are a mixed bag in terms of efficiency. There are great offenses—the early 1980s Nuggets and the Run-TMC Warriors of 1990 to 1992 (though the M was gone by 1992). There are also bad offenses—the Nuggets of 1992 are a prime example—that seemed to run because "hey, we may be horrible, but at least we'll get a workout trying to improve." (Why is it, by the way, that Denver seems to think that their altitude is a good reason for them to push the pace every year? I know the air is thinner, but aren't all NBA athletes in pretty good shape? The Utah Jazz play at an elevation of about forty-four hundred feet—only eight hundred feet lower than the Nuggets—and they don't have a history of pushing the pace.) There may be an indication that faster teams boasted efficient offenses, but they also had inefficient defenses.

In contrast to those teams, the Jazz and the Bulls of the 1990s tended to like slower paces. The great Showtime Lakers, despite the glorification of their fast break, actually did not push the ball up the court all the time. They could play in the half-court with Kareem Abdul-Jabbar's skyhook and James Worthy, who could score off the wing in the half-court. All those Lakers teams were only slightly above average in pace—that is, until the Slowtime Lakers of 1990 who, without Kareem and with older legs on their stars, still managed to have a great offense by adjusting to shoot three-pointers and to run post-ups inside.

One thing that does seem fairly common about the offenses here is that all teams really did have good inside and outside options. Clearly there should be some interplay between the inside and outside scorers, each forcing the defense to spread out in trying to cover the different options. That is not so much a system but a philosophy of balance, and it makes sense that it's reflected in a list of best offenses.

Table 3.3 incorporates some other statistics that help illustrate the style of these top teams. These statistics can be useful in quickly assessing the style of a team. They reflect the quality of an offense or defense, but in a slightly less complete way than an offensive rating. They all provide slightly different information about *how* the teams got their points. They will be used throughout the book, so it's worthwhile introducing them here.

Floor percentage is the percentage of a team's possessions in which the team scores at least one point. Basically, floor percentage answers the question, "What percentage of a team's times down the floor does it score?" A possession in which a team scores at least one point is known as a *scoring possession*,[1] so floor percentage is just scoring possessions divided by total possessions.

Field percentage is the percentage of a team's non-foul shot possessions in which the team scores a field goal.[2] This value gets at the question: "If we assume no foul will be called (like at the end of a game when refs occasionally swallow their whistles), what chance does this team have to score from the field including the possibility of offensive rebounds and turnovers?"

Play percentage is the percentage of a team's "plays" on which the team scores at least one point. A "play" can be the same thing as a possession in certain situations. For example, if a team runs a play when it comes down the court that leads to an easy lay-up, it is both one play and one possession. But if the team runs a play, misses that lay-up, then gets an offensive rebound and scores, that is still one possession, but two plays.[3]

Teams with high floor percentages and high offensive ratings score very well from two-point land, like the Bulls of the early 1990s and the Lakers of the early 1980s. They have a traditionally good offense that doesn't rely upon the three-pointer to be effective. Teams with low floor percentages and high ratings get their points from three-pointers. The top-ranked Dallas Mavericks team is a good example. The book gets into the topic of risky strategies a bit later, but I will mention right now that this kind of team is generally a bit more unstable and more prone to losing that greatness because the reliability of the three is not as high.

Teams with high field percentages are very efficient from the field. They don't turn the ball over, they get offensive rebounds, and they shoot pretty well (such as the Bulls teams throughout the 1990s). Field percentage doesn't say anything about whether the team gets to the line or not. But teams that have relatively low field percentages and high offensive ratings probably are either making a high percentage of their three-pointers and/or getting to the line a lot, which is what the 1990 Lakers did. Some would say that they got the benefit of a favorable whistle.

Teams with high play percentages and high offensive ratings get many of their points off of first shots, not relying upon offensive rebounders to get their points. An interesting contrast illustrating this is the 1997 Chicago Bulls versus the 1997 Utah Jazz. The Bulls' team had robo-rebounder Dennis Rodman to complement its scorers. The Jazz had, uh, Greg Ostertag, who has been called the Big O, where the O is pronounced "zero." The Bulls scored on only 45 percent of their plays and the Jazz scored on 48 percent, but the two teams both scored on about 54 percent of their possessions and had similar offensive ratings in the end. They just did it in different ways.

Were There Any Key Positions—Such as Center— That Needed a Great Player in Order for the Team to Have a Great Offense or Defense?

There has been the long-standing rule of thumb that a great center is necessary for a great team, but is it necessary for a great offense? This list really suggests that the answer is no. In fact, few of the top offensive teams really featured a center in their offense. The top team that used a center a lot was the Denver Nuggets, which had the 6′9″ mid-range-shooting Dan Issel in the middle. The Celtics of

1988 used post players Robert Parish and Kevin McHale less than any year in the 1990s except for McHale's first year of 1981, and they were at their offensive best. Other than the O'Neal teams and the Lakers teams that had Abdul-Jabbar (and others), most great offenses deemphasized centers.

Point guards don't seem to be vital either, despite being the ones who direct an offense. There are some good ones on this list, including Magic, Stockton, Steve Nash, Gary Payton, Tim Hardaway, and Kevin Johnson. So they do help, but the lack of a classic all-distributing point guard on the Bulls teams, on the Nuggets, on the Celtics, and on the Magic suggests that the ball can be distributed other ways.

On the other hand, there is a correlation between good passing teams and good offensive teams. Teams that have a higher percentage of their field goals accompanied by assists tend to be better offensively. It's not an incredibly strong trend, but only five of the top twenty-five offenses were under the league average in this statistic.

Are There Any Coaches Who Appear with Different Teams on the List?

When a team appears on this list of great offenses several times with the same coach, it may not actually be a reflection of great coaching, but a bit of luck on the coach's part to have good talent for a period of time. However, when a coach builds great offenses on multiple teams, that is at least an indication that the coach knows how to let great talent be a great system. More likely, the coach has some skill that he is passing on to his players to contribute to their greatness.

Table 3.5 shows the coaches associated with the top twenty-five offenses. On this list, the only coach who shows up with different teams is George Karl. Since I've always thought of Karl as a good defensive coach, this surprises me a little. He did get pretty good talent at the two stops. But the fact that no other coach brought similar talent in Seattle to similar heights suggests that Karl gets something extra out of players.

Besides Karl, Phil Jackson and Don Nelson both come close to making the list with two teams. Jackson's 2001 Lakers rank twenty-ninth and Nelson's 1992 Warriors rank twenty-eighth. Whereas Jackson inherited the talent each time (which he does lose a little credit for), Nelson mostly constructed his teams.

Is There Any Correlation between Great Offense and Height?

Are taller teams better? Is there some "optimal" height at which teams seem to be better?

Basketball has three primary physical factors that are traditionally considered important: height, strength, and quickness. The quickness usually refers to quick feet, but I personally think that quick hands are quite important, too.

Table 3.5. Coaches of the Top Twenty-Five Offenses

Rank	Team	Season	Coach
1	Dallas Mavericks	2002	Don Nelson
2	Chicago Bulls	1997	Phil Jackson
3	Utah Jazz	1998	Jerry Sloan
4	Chicago Bulls	1996	Phil Jackson
5	Denver Nuggets	1982	Doug Moe
6	Chicago Bulls	1992	Phil Jackson
7	Boston Celtics	1988	K.C. Jones
8	Los Angeles Lakers	1987	Pat Riley
9	Utah Jazz	1997	Jerry Sloan
10	Los Angeles Lakers	1998	Del Harris
11	Orlando Magic	1995	Brian Hill
12	Chicago Bulls	1991	Phil Jackson
13	Dallas Mavericks	1987	Dick Motta
14	Seattle SuperSonics	1995	George Karl
15	Indiana Pacers	1999	Larry Bird
16	Seattle SuperSonics	1998	George Karl
17	Los Angeles Lakers	1985	Pat Riley
18	Phoenix Suns	1995	Paul Westphal
19	Los Angeles Lakers	1986	Pat Riley
20	Utah Jazz	1995	Jerry Sloan
21	Los Angeles Lakers	1989	Pat Riley
22	Los Angeles Lakers	1983	Pat Riley
23	Los Angeles Lakers	1990	Pat Riley
24	Cleveland Cavaliers	1992	Lenny Wilkens
25	Milwaukee Bucks	2001	George Karl

Unfortunately, the only one of these that can be reasonably measured is height. Maybe you can get strength out of something like

$$\frac{\text{weight} \times (1 - \text{body fat \%})}{\text{height}}$$

But I don't know where to get information on body fat percentage.

What height does for an offensive player is give him room to see and room to shoot. If you can pass over a guy, that's just one additional way to get the ball past a defender. If you don't have to jump to get a clear shot, then you don't have to be as quick. So height should help an offense.

In the numbers, the story isn't perfectly clear but supports this assertion, as shown in table 3.6.

The great offensive teams were generally taller than average. The shortest team was the 1982 Nuggets (with 6′ 9″ Issel being the prominently short one), which was also the fastest. Running probably did help this team create advantages that they didn't get in a half-court offense where height might be more important.

The bottom line is confirmation of traditional lore: height is good, but there are other factors.

Table 3.6. Heights of the Top Twenty-Five Offenses

Rank	Team Name	Season	Height (in.)	League Average Height (in.)	Increment above Average (in.)
1	Dallas Mavericks	2002	79.1	79.0	0.1
2	Chicago Bulls	1997	79.4	78.9	0.5
3	Utah Jazz	1998	78.9	78.9	0.0
4	Chicago Bulls	1996	79.7	79.1	0.7
5	Denver Nuggets	1982	77.4	78.7	-1.2
6	Chicago Bulls	1992	79.3	78.8	0.4
7	Boston Celtics	1988	79.9	79.3	0.7
8	Los Angeles Lakers	1987	80.2	79.3	0.9
9	Utah Jazz	1997	78.9	78.9	0.0
10	Los Angeles Lakers	1998	78.8	78.9	-0.1
11	Orlando Magic	1995	80.4	79.1	1.4
12	Chicago Bulls	1991	79.3	79.0	0.3
13	Dallas Mavericks	1987	80.1	79.3	0.8
14	Seattle SuperSonics	1995	79.3	79.1	0.2
15	Indiana Pacers	1999	79.8	78.9	0.9
16	Seattle SuperSonics	1998	79.2	78.9	0.3
17	Los Angeles Lakers	1985	80.0	78.9	1.1
18	Phoenix Suns	1995	78.4	79.1	-0.7
19	Los Angeles Lakers	1986	80.2	79.1	1.1
20	Utah Jazz	1995	78.9	79.1	-0.2
21	Los Angeles Lakers	1989	80.2	79.0	1.2
22	Los Angeles Lakers	1983	79.4	78.7	0.7
23	Los Angeles Lakers	1990	79.9	78.9	1.0
24	Cleveland Cavaliers	1992	79.5	78.8	0.7
25	Milwaukee Bucks	2001	78.7	78.9	-0.2

NOTE: Average team heights are determined by weighting player heights by minutes played.

What Doesn't Show Up in This List?

Are there any prominent teams not on the list that one would expect to be there? Are there great players who don't show up?

Perhaps the most glaring thing missing from this list is a pre-1982 team. We have stats for eight years worth of teams before then, and you'd think that one of them would be smart enough, brave enough, good enough. Sheesh—the Roswell Rayguns looked pretty good! But I guess they were in the ABA. And I guess they weren't real, except if you live in Nike Town.

Table 3.2 includes nineteen teams from the 1990s or later, six teams from the 1980s, and *none* from the 1970s. It apparently is a lot easier to be great nowadays than it was back in the old days. Is this a vague social commentary on the over-edification of life in the privileged U.S.? Or just a sign of "talent dilution" in the NBA? Those are both bad topics right now. I'll try to stay away.

It really seems that there should be some great offenses from the 1970s in this list. Well, some of you who skipped out on every math class past *if-you-add-four-oranges-to-five-apples-what-do-you-get?* are going to hate me for this next piece of trickery, but you might as well get used to it. My way of accounting for this possible talent dilution is to use—brace yourself—a standard deviation. *Run to the hills and protect the children, it's a math term!* A standard deviation is a measure of how much teams usually deviated from average. If we are saying that offensive teams in the 1990s deviated from average the most, a standard deviation will show that. In fact, that is exactly what figure 3.2 shows. It shows the standard deviation of team offensive (and defensive) ratings through time. Notice that those standard deviations are relatively high in the 1990s. Hmm, could be dilution.

Ignoring dilution, I want to update that table of the best offensive teams for how many standard deviations above average there were. Here is an example: Consider a team that was only 4.4 points per hundred possessions above the league average, but the standard deviation of offensive ratings was only 2.2, as it was in 1978 (as opposed to 3.9 in 1998). That team is 4.4/2.2 = 2.0 standard deviations above average. This can correct for whatever factors may be causing teams to be more different from each other now than they were in the past—dilution, strategy evolution, dilution, etc.

Table 3.7 is the updated list. Look who shoots to the top—the 1982 Nuggets. The usual suspects are still in the top five, only shuffled. But, *in at number six is a team with 'fro's*—the Philadelphia 76ers!!! No Dr. Funk, but they had Dr. J and Dr.

Figure 3.2. Standard Deviations of Team Offensive and Defensive Ratings

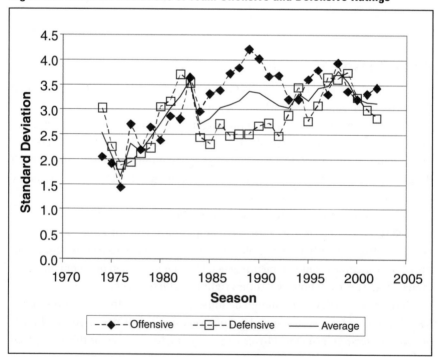

Table 3.7. Top Historical Offenses, by Standard Deviations above Average

Rank	Team	Season	Offensive Rating	League Average	Increment above League	Standard Deviations above Average	Players
1	Denver Nuggets	1982	114.3	106.9	7.5	2.65	Alex English, Dan Issel, Kiki Vandeweghe
2	Chicago Bulls	1997	114.4	106.7	7.7	2.32	Michael Jordan, Scottie Pippen, Toni Kukoc, Dennis Rodman
3	Dallas Mavericks	2002	112.2	104.5	7.7	2.25	Dirk Nowitzki, Steve Nash, Michael Finley
4	Utah Jazz	1997	113.6	106.7	7.0	2.11	Karl Malone, John Stockton, Jeff Hornacek
5	Chicago Bulls	1992	115.5	108.2	7.4	2.00	Jordan, Pippen, Horace Grant, B.J. Armstrong
6	Philadelphia 76ers	1978	106.3	102.0	4.3	1.98	Julius Erving, George McGinnis, Doug Collins, World B. Free, Darryl Dawkins, Henry Bibby
7	Chicago Bulls	1996	115.2	107.7	7.5	1.98	Jordan, Pippen, Kukoc, Rodman
8	Los Angeles Lakers	1987	115.6	108.4	7.3	1.95	Magic Johnson, James Worthy, Kareem Abdul-Jabbar, Byron Scott
9	Houston Rockets	1976	102.1	99.3	2.8	1.93	Calvin Murphy, Mike Newlin, Rudy Tomjanovich
10	Utah Jazz	1998	112.7	105.0	7.6	1.93	Malone, Stockton, Hornacek
11	Indiana Pacers	1999	108.7	102.2	6.5	1.92	Reggie Miller, Rik Smits, Jalen Rose, Chris Mullin
12	Boston Celtics	1988	115.4	108.1	7.4	1.91	Larry Bird, Kevin McHale, Danny Ainge, Robert Parish
13	Orlando Magic	1995	115.1	108.3	6.9	1.91	Shaquille O'Neal, Penny Hardaway, Nick Anderson, Dennis Scott, Horace Grant
14	Los Angeles Lakers	1985	114.1	107.9	6.3	1.88	Abdul-Jabbar, Magic, Worthy, Scott
15	Houston Rockets	1977	105.6	100.6	5.0	1.85	Tomjanovich, Murphy, Moses Malone, Mike Newlin, John Lucas
16	Chicago Bulls	1991	114.7	107.9	6.8	1.84	Jordan, Pippen, Grant, Armstrong
17	Houston Rockets	1979	109.8	105.0	4.9	1.83	Malone, Murphy, Tomjanovich, Rick Barry
18	Seattle SuperSonics	1995	114.8	108.3	6.5	1.82	Gary Payton, Schrempf, Shawn Kemp
19	Los Angeles Lakers	1986	113.3	107.2	6.1	1.81	Abdul-Jabbar, Worthy, Magic, Scott
20	Boston Celtics	1980	110.7	106.4	4.3	1.79	Bird, Cedric Maxwell, Dave Cowens, Nate Archibald, Chris Ford
21	Dallas Mavericks	1987	114.9	108.4	6.6	1.77	Mark Aguirre, Rolando Blackman, Derek Harper, Sam Perkins, James Donaldson, Dotlof Schrompf
22	Los Angeles Lakers	1998	111.9	105.0	6.9	1.75	O'Neal, Eddie Jones, Kobe Bryant, Nick Van Exel
23	Los Angeles Lakers	1980	110.5	106.4	4.1	1.73	Abdul-Jabbar, Jamaal Wilkes, Magic, Norm Nixon
24	Phoenix Suns	1995	114.5	108.3	6.2	1.72	Charles Barkley, Danny Manning, Dan Majerle, Kevin Johnson
25	Milwaukee Bucks	2001	109.5	103.8	5.7	1.72	Glenn Robinson, Ray Allen, Sam Cassell

Dunkenstein. And a player who, by his name alone, had to play in the 1970s—World B. Free.

After Philly, the real offensive dynasty of the 1970s was Calvin Murphy and the Houston Rockets, who show up ninth, fifteenth, and seventeenth for teams between 1976 and 1979. For a short guard, Murphy was a great shooter. He, Rudy Tomjanovich, Moses Malone, and Mike Newlin all scored well for these teams. In 1978, when Houston's team offense was not good, it was because Rudy T, Malone, and Newlin all missed big chunks of time, and their subs just couldn't shoot it into the ocean.

A couple of other interesting entries on the revised list are Bird and Magic's rookie teams. How appropriate that they both made it that year.

So, with these changes to the list, we've definitely added style, but have we added substance? Is there anything new here to change the way we answer the above questions? Not really. With the style came some stars but no obvious systems.

The Great Defenses

Table 3.8 lists the top twenty-five defenses since 1974. If you like teams ranked by how many standard deviations they differed from average, you can look at table 3.9. I'm normally going to be referring to table 3.8, but if I'm making generalizations about what the table is saying, I will definitely try to make sure it applies to table 3.9, too. I should also mention that I personally do not really value one of the two types of rankings over the other. Whereas table 3.9 accounts for how evenly balanced the league is, should you really do this? I have no great philosophical answer for this.

The top two defenses were the Pat Riley Knicks of 1993 and 1994, and they were far and away the best. The distance between the second-ranked defense and the third-ranked defense is as large as the difference between the first-ranked offense and the eighteenth-ranked offense. Riley found a way in those two years to seriously advance his defense. That way was to completely take away the inside. His teams exploited hand check rules and fouled players who got near the basket to prevent lay-ups. After seeing his previous Lakers teams get beat up by the Detroit Pistons Bad Boys, Riley was intent on pushing the envelope in that kind of defense when he got to New York. The Pistons may have closed the go-go 1980s with two sobering championships, but it was these Riley teams that set the tone for the 1990s, causing the rule changes that brought a zone defense to the NBA in 2002.

After the Knicks, there is a fairly wide array of teams that, even without the adjustment for variations of teams within a season, includes teams from the 1970s.

System or Stars?

In the NBA, stars have not often been made by defense alone. Bill Russell is a prominent exception and, unfortunately, the statistics weren't kept in his era to

Table 3.8. Top Historical Defenses

Rank	Team	Season	Defensive Rating	League Average	Relative to League	Players	Comments
1	New York Knicks	1993	99.7	108.0	-8.4	Patrick Ewing, Charles Oakley, John Starks, Charles Smith, Anthony Mason, Doc Rivers, Greg Anthony	Deep team and Pat Riley's best defensive team; changed the league because it roughed people up so much down low. No one shot well or got offensive boards against them.
2	New York Knicks	1994	98.2	106.3	-8.1	Ewing, Oakley, Starks, Mason, Anthony	Lost in Finals. Really the same team as #1, but some injuries to Rivers, Starks, and Smith.
3	San Antonio Spurs	1999	95.0	102.2	-7.2	Tim Duncan, David Robinson, Avery Johnson, Sean Elliott, Mario Elie	Won title in lockout-shortened year. Defensive numbers probably accentuated by lockout, but Twin Towers both outstanding defensive players.
4	Washington Bullets	1975	92.2	98.6	-6.4	Wes Unseld, Elvin Hayes, Phil Chenier, Mike Riordan, Kevin Porter	Lost in Finals. With Unseld and Hayes, you'd think they'd dominate on the boards, but actually forcing turnovers was their best aspect. K.C. Jones coached the '86 Celtics, another great defensive team just outside the top 25.
5	Utah Jazz	1989	101.5	107.8	-6.3	Mark Eaton, John Stockton, Karl Malone, Thurl Bailey, Darrell Griffith	Mark Eaton was a tremendous presence in the middle. Stockton and Malone go from early days of outstanding defense to later days of outstanding offense.
6	Phoenix Suns	1981	100.5	106.7	-6.2	Truck Robinson, Dennis Johnson, Walter Davis, Alvan Adams, Jeff Cook, Johnny High	Forced lots of turnovers, but Coach John MacLeod coupled that with a bunch of guys who forced a lot of missed shots without a legitimate shot blocker.
7	Miami Heat	1997	100.6	106.7	-6.1	Alonzo Mourning, P.J. Brown, Tim Hardaway, Voshon Lenard, Isaac Austin	Riley's second season in Miami, where he played more brutal in-your-face defense with the no-lay-up rule.
8	Philadelphia 76ers	1981	100.6	106.7	-6.1	Dr. J, Darryl Dawkins, Bobby Jones, Caldwell Jones, Steve Mix, Mo Cheeks	Same season as #6. Had legitimate shot blockers stuffing the middle.
9	Cleveland Cavaliers	1998	99.1	105.0	-5.9	Shawn Kemp, Wesley Person, Zydrunas Ilgauskas, Derek Anderson, Cedric Henderson, Brevin Knight	Rack one up for the Czar of the Telestrator. Actually, having a healthy Ilgauskas all season and newly acquired Shawn Kemp to plug in helped a lot.
10	Chicago Bulls	1996	101.7	107.7	-5.9	Michael Jordan, Scottie Pippen, Dennis Rodman, Ron Harper	Won title. One of the worst shot blocking teams in this list, but played tight D all over the perimeter. Only team on both best offense and best defense lists.
11	Los Angeles Lakers	2000	98.3	104.1	-5.8	Shaquille O'Neal, Kobe Bryant, Rick Fox, Ron Harper, Glen Rice	Won title. A second Phil Jackson team featuring tall guards.
12	New Jersey Nets	1983	98.9	104.7	-5.8	Buck Williams, Albert King, Darwin Cook, Darryl Dawkins, Otis Birdsong	Coached by Larry Brown, the team applied a lot of pressure on the perimeter and cleaned up its defensive glass.

(continued next page)

Table 3.8. Top Historical Defenses *(continued)*

Rank	Team	Season	Defensive Rating	League Average	Relative to League	Players	Comments
13	New York Knicks	1997	101.0	106.7	-5.7	Ewing, Oakley, Starks, Allan Houston, Larry Johnson, Charlie Ward	Following Pat Riley's style of defense, Jeff Van Gundy kept the Knicks playing very tight on the perimeter with brutality in the middle.
14	San Antonio Spurs	1998	99.4	105.1	-5.7	Duncan, Robinson, Johnson, Jaren Jackson	Duncan's rookie year and Spurs' first year with Twin Towers. With Robinson alone, the Spurs' best defensive year ranked #36.
15	Seattle SuperSonics	1996	102.1	107.7	-5.6	Shawn Kemp, Gary Payton, Detlef Schrempf, Hersey Hawkins, Sam Perkins	In earlier seasons, the Sonics went for steals at the cost of defending the basket. This year was when they did it all very well.
16	San Antonio Spurs	2000	98.5	104.1	-5.5	Duncan, Robinson, Johnson, Elie	The personnel changes from 1998 to 2001 provide evidence that the Twin Towers are the force behind the defense.
17	Washington Bullets	1983	99.3	104.7	-5.4	Jeff Ruland, Greg Ballard, Rick Mahorn, Frank Johnson	Coached by Gene Shue, this team had the original Bruise Brothers cleaning up the boards, fouling guys hard, and forcing turnovers.
18	Chicago Bulls	1998	99.8	105.1	-5.3	Jordan, Pippen, Rodman, Harper	Won title. See #10.
19	Phoenix Suns	2001	98.0	103.0	-5.1	Jason Kidd, Cliff Robinson, Shawn Marion, Tony Delk, Rodney Rogers	All but Marion were gone by midway through the next season, and the Suns self-destructed.
20	San Antonio Spurs	2001	98.0	103.0	-5.1	Duncan, Robinson, Derek Anderson, Antonio Daniels	See #16. Duncan and Robinson can make any perimeter defenders look good.
21	Atlanta Hawks	1999	97.1	102.2	-5.1	Dikembe Mutombo, Steve Smith, Mookie Blaylock, Grant Long	Mutombo didn't even make First Team All-Defense in one of his best defensive seasons.
22	Phoenix Suns	2000	99.1	104.1	-5.0	Kidd, Robinson, Marion, Rogers, Penny Hardaway	Behind Scott Skiles, this team picked pockets without gambling so much that they allowed easy shots.
23	New Jersey Nets	2002	99.5	104.5	-5.0	Jason Kidd, Kenyon Martin, Keith Van Horn, Todd MacCulloch	Kidd's defense leads very balanced defensive team—much like Phoenix before they let Kidd go.
24	Cleveland Cavaliers	1989	102.9	107.8	-4.9	Brad Daugherty, Mark Price, Ron Harper, Larry Nance, Hot Rod Williams, Mike Sanders	Well-rounded defense that shut down the middle with a couple of shot blockers to back up the mostly straight man-to-man D that Lenny Wilkens liked.
25	Utah Jazz	1988	103.1	108.1	-4.9	Eaton, Malone, Stockton, Bailey, Bobby Hansen	See #5.

Table 3.9. Top Historical Defenses, by Standard Deviations below Average

Rank	Team	Season	Defensive Rating	League Average	Relative to League	Standard Deviations below Average	Players
1	New York Knicks	1993	99.7	108.0	-8.4	-2.88	Patrick Ewing, Charles Oakley, John Starks, Charles Smith, Anthony Mason, Doc Rivers, Greg Anthony
2	Washington Bullets	1975	92.2	98.6	-6.4	-2.86	Wes Unseld, Elvin Hayes, Phil Chenier, Mike Riordan, Kevin Porter
3	Utah Jazz	1989	101.5	107.8	-6.3	-2.49	Mark Eaton, John Stockton, Karl Malone, Thurl Bailey, Darrell Griffith
4	New York Knicks	1994	98.2	106.3	-8.1	-2.35	Ewing, Oakley, Starks, Mason, Anthony
5	Golden State Warriors	1976	95.5	99.3	-3.8	-2.03	Clifford Ray, George T. Johnson, Jamaal Wilkes, Phil Smith, Rick Barry
6	Phoenix Suns	1981	100.5	106.7	-6.2	-1.96	Truck Robinson, Dennis Johnson, Walter Davis, Alvan Adams, Jeff Cook, Johnny High
7	Cleveland Cavaliers	1989	102.9	107.8	-4.9	-1.96	Larry Nance, Hot Rod Williams, Ron Harper, Brad Daugherty, Mark Price, Mike Sanders
8	Utah Jazz	1988	103.1	108.1	-4.9	-1.95	Eaton, Malone, Stockton, Bailey, Bobby Hansen
9	Utah Jazz	1985	103.4	107.9	-4.5	-1.95	Eaton, Griffith, Bailey, Rickey Green, Adrian Dantley
10	San Antonio Spurs	1999	95.0	102.2	-7.2	-1.92	Tim Duncan, David Robinson, Avery Johnson, Sean Elliott, Mario Elie
11	Chicago Bulls	1996	101.7	107.7	-5.9	-1.91	Michael Jordan, Scottie Pippen, Dennis Rodman, Ron Harper
12	Philadelphia 76ers	1981	100.6	106.7	-6.1	-1.91	Dr. J, Darryl Dawkins, Bobby Jones, Caldwell Jones, Steve Mix, Mo Cheeks
13	Phoenix Suns	1978	98.0	102.0	-4.0	-1.89	Gar Heard, Walter Davis, Don Buse, Paul Westphal, Alvan Adams, Ron Lee
14	Utah Jazz	1987	103.7	108.4	-4.6	-1.86	Eaton, Malone, Bailey, Green, Kelly Tripucka, Stockton
15	New York Knicks	1984	103.1	107.6	-4.5	-1.83	Bill Cartwright, Rory Sparrow, Bernard King, Ray Williams, Truck Robinson
16	Milwaukee Bucks	1985	103.6	107.9	-4.2	-1.83	Alton Lister, Sidney Moncrief, Paul Pressey, Terry Cummings, Craig Hodges
17	Seattle SuperSonics	1996	102.1	107.7	-5.6	-1.81	Shawn Kemp, Gary Payton, Detlef Schrempf, Hersey Hawkins, Sam Perkins
18	Los Angeles Lakers	2000	98.3	104.1	-5.8	-1.79	Shaquille O'Neal, Kobe Bryant, Rick Fox, Ron Harper, Glen Rice
19	Denver Nuggets	1977	97.1	100.6	-3.5	-1.78	Bobby Jones, Dan Issel, David Thompson, Ted McClain
20	Houston Rockets	1990	103.4	108.1	-4.7	-1.76	Hakeem Olajuwon, Otis Thorpe, Buck Johnson, Sleepy Floyd
21	New Jersey Nets	2002	99.5	104.5	-5.0	-1.76	Jason Kidd, Kenyon Martin, Keith Van Horn, Todd MacCulloch
22	Detroit Pistons	1990	103.5	108.1	-4.7	-1.74	Isiah Thomas, Bill Laimbeer, Joe Dumars, Dennis Rodman, James Edwards
23	Portland Trail Blazers	1978	98.3	102.0	-3.7	-1.74	Bill Walton, Lionel Hollins, Johnny Davis, Bob Gross, Maurice Lucas
24	Phoenix Suns	2001	98.6	103.8	-5.2	-1.73	Jason Kidd, Cliff Robinson, Shawn Marion, Tony Delk, Rodney Rogers
25	San Antonio Spurs	2001	98.6	103.8	-5.2	-1.72	Duncan, Robinson, Derek Anderson, Antonio Daniels

do a fair evaluation of his teams relative to post-1973 teams. Aside from him, though, defensive stars have generally been given the shaft, having not gotten credit for what they probably did to increase their teams' wins. There is lots more on this later in the book.

When it comes to answering this question, this lack of recognition for defense is a problem. For instance, the ninth-ranked Cleveland Cavaliers had Shawn Kemp anchoring a defense that propelled the team to a surprisingly good season. They had no representatives on any of the All-NBA teams (of any type) that year. But Kemp was a defensive star who clogged the middle and served on two different top defenses. Was that Cleveland team led by a defensive star (versus a system)? I would say that it was, but that is because I personally believe that Kemp has been a defensive star, an opinion I formed not by looking at the records of stardom, which are All-NBA teams or All-Defensive teams. In order to evaluate stardom here, I did look at these two designations.

If you use the All-NBA team as an indicator of stardom, the best offenses had twenty First Team players, eleven Second Team players, and seven Third Team players. The best defenses had only sixteen, ten, and four, respectively. There appeared to be more stars leading the offensive teams than the defensive teams, hinting that system may be more important to defense than to offense.

On the other hand, nearly all of these best defensive teams were led by players on the All-Defensive teams. Plus, with regard to "defensive systems," NBA defenses have not until recently really been allowed to institute much structure. There are degrees of double-teaming, different ways of handling pick-and-rolls, different ways of forcing ball movement, but there really has been just one system—man-to-man defense—with different flavors. Most of the best defensive teams had the ability to play that defense pretty much straight-up without the need to rely on double-teams to a significant degree. The top-ranked Knicks did that and shut down teams from the field. The 1989 Cavaliers also played pretty straight up and just never sent teams to the line, which can result in a lot of free points.

With regard to pace, as with the greatest offensive teams, there are no clear patterns relating pace to defensive efficiency (table 3.10). Though there is no clear trend, the average pace of the best defensive teams is about 0.5 possessions per game slower than average, as opposed to the average pace of the greatest offensive teams, which was 0.3 possessions per game faster than average. There is some reason to believe that pace is an indicator of quality. Quality defense tends to take away easy shots until the pressure of the shot clock forces the offense to take a shot, or, from the offensive perspective, a quality offense can create good shots very quickly and would then use more possessions. The numbers offer only weak support for this. I think the key message, however, is that there are not many cases where setting a fast or slow pace has dictated how efficient a team is. Rather,

Table 3.10. Other Statistical Indicators of Top Historical Defenses

Rank	Team	Season	Offensive Rating			Possessions/Game			Floor Percentage			Field Percentage			Play Percentage		
			Team Value	League Average	Incr.	Team Value	League Average	Incr.	Team Value	League Average	Incr.	Team Value	League Average	Incr.	Team Value	League Average	Incr.
1	New York Knicks	1993	99.7	108.0	-8.3	95.7	97.5	-1.8	0.483	0.524	-0.041	0.412	0.471	-0.059	0.421	0.452	-0.032
2	New York Knicks	1994	98.2	106.3	-8.1	93.2	95.5	-2.3	0.477	0.515	-0.038	0.412	0.463	-0.051	0.414	0.443	-0.029
3	San Antonio Spurs	1999	95.0	102.2	-7.2	89.2	89.6	-0.4	0.459	0.488	-0.028	0.408	0.431	-0.023	0.390	0.421	-0.031
4	Washington Bullets	1975	92.2	98.6	-6.4	105.8	104.1	1.7	0.451	0.483	-0.031	0.410	0.439	-0.028	0.393	0.419	-0.025
5	Utah Jazz	1989	101.5	107.8	-6.3	98.2	101.3	-3.1	0.496	0.527	-0.031	0.438	0.473	-0.036	0.423	0.453	-0.030
6	Phoenix Suns	1981	100.5	106.7	-6.2	104.0	101.3	2.7	0.489	0.520	-0.032	0.440	0.473	-0.033	0.424	0.448	-0.024
7	Miami Heat	1997	100.6	106.7	-6.1	88.8	90.8	-2.0	0.476	0.501	-0.025	0.417	0.447	-0.030	0.413	0.433	-0.020
8	Philadelphia 76ers	1981	100.6	106.7	-6.1	103.1	101.3	1.8	0.490	0.520	-0.030	0.438	0.473	-0.035	0.420	0.448	-0.029
9	Cleveland Cavaliers	1998	99.1	105.0	-5.9	90.6	91.0	-0.4	0.472	0.502	-0.030	0.409	0.446	-0.037	0.411	0.432	-0.021
10	Chicago Bulls	1996	101.7	107.7	-5.9	91.3	92.4	-1.1	0.482	0.507	-0.025	0.428	0.452	-0.025	0.419	0.440	-0.021
11	Los Angeles Lakers	2000	98.3	104.1	-5.8	93.9	93.7	0.2	0.468	0.494	-0.027	0.413	0.441	-0.028	0.408	0.430	-0.023
12	New Jersey Nets	1983	98.9	104.7	-5.8	104.1	103.6	0.5	0.493	0.522	-0.029	0.437	0.472	-0.035	0.430	0.450	-0.020
13	New York Knicks	1997	101.0	106.7	-5.7	91.3	90.8	0.5	0.474	0.501	-0.027	0.405	0.447	-0.042	0.415	0.433	-0.018
14	San Antonio Spurs	1998	99.4	105.0	-5.7	89.1	91.0	-1.9	0.475	0.502	-0.028	0.419	0.446	-0.027	0.409	0.432	-0.024
15	Seattle SuperSonics	1996	102.1	107.7	-5.6	94.8	92.4	2.4	0.479	0.507	-0.028	0.418	0.452	-0.034	0.414	0.440	-0.026
16	San Antonio Spurs	2000	98.6	104.1	-5.5	91.6	93.7	-2.1	0.470	0.494	-0.024	0.422	0.441	-0.019	0.408	0.430	-0.022
17	Washington Bullets	1983	99.3	104.7	-5.4	100.1	103.6	-3.6	0.496	0.522	-0.026	0.450	0.472	-0.021	0.432	0.450	-0.018
18	Chicago Bulls	1998	99.8	105.0	-5.3	89.8	91.0	-1.2	0.478	0.502	-0.024	0.424	0.446	-0.022	0.413	0.432	-0.019
19	Phoenix Suns	2001	98.6	103.8	-5.2	93.2	91.4	1.8	0.470	0.492	-0.022	0.412	0.438	-0.027	0.415	0.429	-0.014
20	San Antonio Spurs	2001	98.6	103.8	-5.2	89.7	91.4	-1.7	0.470	0.492	-0.022	0.422	0.438	-0.016	0.407	0.429	-0.022
21	Atlanta Hawks	1999	97.1	102.2	-5.1	85.9	89.6	-3.7	0.465	0.488	-0.023	0.413	0.431	-0.018	0.401	0.421	-0.020
22	Phoenix Suns	2000	99.0	104.1	-5.0	94.6	93.7	0.9	0.470	0.494	-0.024	0.411	0.441	-0.030	0.407	0.430	-0.023
23	New Jersey Nets	2002	99.5	104.5	-5.0	92.5	91.3	1.2	0.470	0.494	-0.023	0.419	0.442	-0.023	0.408	0.429	-0.020
24	Cleveland Cavaliers	1989	102.9	107.8	-4.9	98.4	101.3	-2.9	0.502	0.527	-0.025	0.459	0.473	-0.014	0.427	0.453	-0.026
25	Utah Jazz	1988	103.1	108.1	-4.9	101.7	100.1	1.6	0.505	0.531	-0.026	0.447	0.476	-0.029	0.432	0.458	-0.025

NOTES:
Floor Percentage: Percentage of a team's possessions on which the team scores at least 1 point.
Field Percentage: Percentage of a team's non-foul shot possessions on which the team scores a field goal.
Play Percentage: Percentage of a team's "plays" on which the team scores at least 1 point.

the cause seems to go the other way. The efficiency of an offense or defense vaguely defines the pace at which a team plays.

To complement the list of fastest teams in table 3.4, table 3.11 shows the slowest teams in NBA history. This list is interesting in that it features a fair numbers of teams led by new coaches. It seems that a slow pace may be a reflection of a coach and a team getting used to each other. However, there also are some common coaches here—Doug Collins, Mike Fratello, Hubie Brown—who just may like it a little slower. And it apparently prepares them for a life in broadcasting.

Are There Key Positions That Have to Be Filled?

This is where I have a bias entering the analysis. When Riley left the Knicks for the Heat, he got Alonzo Mourning to fill the middle for him. That, plus watching the Mark Eaton–led Jazz, the Hakeem Olajuwon–led Rockets, and all the different Mutombo teams has led me to believe that having a shot blocker in the middle is pretty important for a defense. What this list suggests, however, is that this belief is not uniformly true. Many of the best defensive teams actually had fewer blocked shots than average. Even the many teams with good shot blockers didn't necessarily block more than the league average as a *team*.

This goes back to the fact that a lot of these teams featured good straight-up man defenses. They could force bad shots without blocking shots—and all teams were better than average in defensive field goal percentage. Having a shot-blocking presence in the middle does seem to be a trait of many great teams, but the team as a whole does not have to be above average in the shot-blocking department.

Are There Coaches Who Placed Different Teams on the List?

Definitely. Phil Jackson shows up for a Chicago team and a Lakers team. Pat Riley shows up for a Knicks team and a Heat team. Larry Brown shows up for an old Denver team and an old New Jersey team. His recent Philadelphia teams have also been good defensively. Lenny Wilkens had a Cleveland team and an Atlanta team make the lists. His 1979 Sonics team would be twenty-sixth in table 3.10, too, but I stopped at twenty-five teams. K.C. Jones has his Bullets of 1975 on the list, and his Celtics of 1986 almost made the list. Actually, the list of top defensive teams could be considered a list of who's who in coaching (see table 3.12).

Having so many coaches make the lists with different teams does suggest that there may be defensive "systems" that these coaches use. But it seems that many of them just know how to inspire their players to expend the effort on defense and identify the roles necessary to make good defenses. Most of these teams did have players considered to be solid role players, and perhaps it is these coaches who know how to keep role players motivated.

Table 3.11. Slowest Teams in History

Rank	Team	Season	Possessions per Game	League Average	Increment above League	Offensive Rating	W–L Record	Comments
1	Minnesota Timberwolves	1990	91.9	99.0	-7.1	103.6	22-60	Bill Musselman saw the Pistons derail the Lakers with a slow pace and thought that would help the T-Wolves in their first season. They won 22 games, which was better than Charlotte, which won only 19 in their inaugural season.
2	Chicago Bulls	1977	99.7	105.9	-6.2	99.2	44-38	Coached by Ed Badger, the team improved tremendously in his first season, perhaps by slowing the pace.
3	Atlanta Hawks	1984	96.2	102.3	-6.1	105.5	40-42	Mike Fratello's first year as Atlanta's coach. Unlike Badger in Chicago, he didn't improve the team over the previous year.
4	Detroit Pistons	1991	92.5	98.5	-6.0	108.2	50-32	After winning their titles, the Pistons kept getting slower as though it would help even more.
5	New York Knicks	1983	97.6	103.6	-6.0	102.4	44-38	Hubie Brown's first season in New York and he slowed the pace, improving the team 11 games.
6	Houston Rockets	1978	100.6	106.4	-5.8	103.2	28-54	This is one of several teams that seemed to be slow and injury-hampered at the same time. I'm betting that injuries caused the slow pace.
7	Detroit Pistons	1997	85.2	90.8	-5.7	110.6	54-28	Doug Collins's second year with 8-game improvement.
8	Chicago Bulls	1978	100.8	106.4	-5.6	103.1	40-42	Badger's second year, with a decline in record.
9	Utah Jazz	1980	97.2	102.7	-5.6	105.3	24-58	Tom Nissalke's first year in Utah. Slowing it down didn't help. (See #15.)
10	Atlanta Hawks	1982	96.1	101.5	-5.5	105.1	42-40	Kevin Loughery's first year in Atlanta. Team improved 11 games.
11	Chicago Bulls	1976	99.7	105.1	-5.4	96.1	24-58	Dick Motta's last year in Chicago. 23-game decline.
12	Detroit Pistons	1992	92.1	97.4	-5.3	107.5	48-34	Chuck Daly's last year in Detroit. 2-game decline.
13	Minnesota Timberwolves	1991	93.4	98.5	-5.2	106.7	29-53	Bill Musselman's last year in Minnesota. 7-game improvement.
14	Detroit Pistons	1989	96.2	101.3	-5.1	110.8	63-19	Won title by famously slowing down the pace against the Lakers.
15	Houston Rockets	1977	100.8	105.9	-5.0	105.6	49-33	Tom Nissalke's first year in Houston. Slowing it down (and Moses Malone) caused 9-game improvement.
16	San Antonio Spurs	1994	90.6	95.5	-4.9	110.4	55-27	John Lucas coached this team. It improved. It had weird player Dennis Rodman and weird coach Lucas. Lucas left after this season.
17	Dallas Mavericks	1989	96.4	101.3	-4.9	107.4	38-44	Coached by John MacLeod.
18	Chicago Bulls	1987	96.6	101.5	-4.9	108.6	40-42	Doug Collins's first year in Chicago. Improved team 10 games.
19	Portland Trail Blazers	1980	98.0	102.7	-4.7	104.6	38-44	Coached by Jack Ramsay.
20	Atlanta Hawks	1980	98.1	102.7	-4.6	106.6	50-32	Hubie Brown's best NBA season.
21	Miami Heat	1999	85.0	89.6	-4.6	104.7	33-17	The slowest team in the slowest year. Pat Riley had them slowing the pace at all costs.
22	Utah Jazz	1981	96.8	101.3	-4.5	104.6	28-54	Tom Nissalke's last full year in Utah.
23	Chicago Bulls	1975	99.7	104.1	-4.4	98.4	47-35	Motta seemed to slow it down near the end of his run in Chicago to try to compensate for the declining defensive skills of his players.
24	Detroit Pistons	1975	99.7	104.1	-4.4	99.2	40-42	Coached by Ray Scott.
25	New York Knicks	2001	87.7	92.0	-4.3	101.2	48-34	Coached by Jeff Van Gundy.

Table 3.12. Coaches of the Top Twenty-Five Defenses

Coaches of Top Defenses by Increment above Average				Coaches of Top Defenses by Standard Deviations above Average			
Rank	Team	Season	Coach	Rank	Team	Season	Coach
1	NYK	1993	Pat Riley	1	NYK	1993	Pat Riley
2	NYK	1994	Pat Riley	2	WAB	1975	K.C. Jones
3	SAN	1999	Gregg Popovich	3	UTA	1989	Frank Layden (17G), Jerry Sloan (65G)
4	WAB	1975	K.C. Jones	4	NYK	1994	Pat Riley
5	UTA	1989	Frank Layden (17 G), Jerry Sloan (65 G)	5	GSW	1976	Al Attles
6	PHO	1981	John MacLeod	6	PHO	1981	John MacLeod
7	MIA	1997	Pat Riley	7	CLE	1989	Lenny Wilkens
8	PHI	1981	Billy Cunningham	8	UTA	1988	Frank Layden
9	CLE	1998	Mike Fratello	9	UTA	1985	Frank Layden
10	CHI	1996	Phil Jackson	10	SAN	1999	Gregg Popovich
11	LAL	2000	Phil Jackson	11	CHI	1996	Phil Jackson
12	NJN	1983	Larry Brown	12	PHI	1981	Billy Cunningham
13	NYK	1997	Jeff Van Gundy	13	PHO	1978	John MacLeod
14	SAN	1998	Gregg Popovich	14	UTA	1987	Frank Layden
15	SEA	1996	George Karl	15	NYK	1984	Hubie Brown
16	SAN	2000	Gregg Popovich	16	MIL	1985	Don Nelson
17	WAB	1983	Gene Shue	17	SEA	1996	George Karl
18	CHI	1998	Phil Jackson	18	LAL	2000	Phil Jackson
19	PHO	2001	Scott Skiles	19	DEN	1977	Larry Brown
20	SAN	2001	Gregg Popovich	20	HOU	1990	Rudy Tomjanovich
21	ATL	1999	Lenny Wilkens	21	NJN	2002	Byron Scott
22	PHO	2000	Danny Ainge (20G), Scott Skiles (62G)	22	DET	1990	Chuck Daly
23	NJN	2002	Byron Scott	23	POR	1978	Jack Ramsay
24	CLE	1989	Lenny Wilkens	24	PHO	2001	Scott Skiles
25	UTA	1988	Frank Layden	25	SAN	2001	Gregg Popovich

Does It Help to Be Tall?

As with the offense, yes it does. If you want to shut down tall offensive players, presumably tall defenders will help. Interestingly, though, the best defensive teams are on average a little shorter than the best offensive teams (see table 3.13).

Is There Anything Missing from These Lists?

One surprising absence from the list is the 1983 Philadelphia 76ers team, which had three players voted to First Team All-Defense—Bobby Jones, Maurice Cheeks, and Moses Malone. The Sixers also won the title that season, nearly sweeping through the playoffs in doing so. This kind of dominance in winning a title does carry some weight with me. And considering the defensive reputation of the team, an argument can be made that this was a great defensive team. I will

Table 3.13. Heights of the Top Twenty-Five Defenses

Rank	Team Name	Season	Height (in.)	League Average Height (in.)	Increment above Average (in.)
1	New York Knicks	1993	79.3	78.8	0.5
2	New York Knicks	1994	79.3	78.9	0.4
3	San Antonio Spurs	1999	78.9	78.9	0.0
4	Washington Bullets	1975	77.1	78.0	-0.9
5	Utah Jazz	1989	79.9	79.0	0.8
6	Phoenix Suns	1981	78.8	78.6	0.2
7	Miami Heat	1997	78.1	78.9	-0.9
8	Philadelphia 76ers	1981	78.2	78.6	-0.4
9	Cleveland Cavaliers	1998	79.0	78.9	0.2
10	Chicago Bulls	1996	79.7	79.1	0.7
11	Los Angeles Lakers	2000	79.7	78.9	0.8
12	New Jersey Nets	1983	78.5	78.7	-0.2
13	New York Knicks	1997	79.3	78.9	0.4
14	San Antonio Spurs	1998	79.1	78.9	0.2
15	Seattle SuperSonics	1996	79.0	79.1	-0.1
16	San Antonio Spurs	2000	78.4	78.9	-0.5
17	Washington Bullets	1983	78.6	78.7	-0.1
18	Chicago Bulls	1998	79.5	78.9	0.7
19	Phoenix Suns	2001	78.7	78.9	-0.2
20	San Antonio Spurs	2001	79.0	78.9	0.2
21	Atlanta Hawks	1999	79.3	78.9	0.4
22	Phoenix Suns	2000	79.6	78.9	0.7
23	New Jersey Nets	2002	79.4	79.0	0.5
24	Cleveland Cavaliers	1989	79.4	79.0	0.4
25	Utah Jazz	1988	79.9	79.3	0.7

make that argument (and others like it) in a few chapters. For now, this Sixers team ranks between eighty and 120 on these two lists of great defensive teams.

The Worst Teams

That was Greatness. This is Badness. These are your evil stepsisters. These are teams so inept that they shed light on what not to do. "Don't cross the street without looking both ways," and don't go small without looking at the 1982 Denver Nuggets. "Always do your homework when you get home from school," and always do your homework before signing with a Donald Sterling club. I won't spend as much time with these bad teams as I did with the good teams because, of course, "If you can't say something nice, don't say anything at all."

Table 3.14 shows the worst historical offenses. When I first looked at this list, the expansion teams, the Clippers of the late 1980s (whom I saw a fair amount), and the post-Jordan Bulls all made me think that the big thing causing these teams to be so bad was change. Many of these teams had a lot of new players playing together and/or a new coach. Table 3.15 provides some support for this

Table 3.14. Worst Historical Offenses

Rank	Team	Season	Offensive Rating	League Average	Increment Above League	Players	Comments
1	Los Angeles Clippers	1988	97.4	108.1	-10.7	Mike Woodson, Michael Cage, Quentin Dailey, Benoit Benjamin	Somehow won 17 games. Rewarded with #1 draft pick, Danny Manning, as well as Gary Grant and Charles Smith in what was hailed at the time as one of the top drafts ever.
2	Miami Heat	1989	97.8	107.8	-10.0	Kevin Edwards, Rory Sparrow, Grant Long, Rony Seikaly	Expansion year. Glen Rice and Sherman Douglas arrived next year.
3	Vancouver Grizzlies	1996	97.7	107.7	-10.0	Greg Anthony, Bryant Reeves, Blue Edwards	Expansion year, Abdur-Rahim arrived next year.
4	Chicago Bulls	2000	94.2	104.1	-9.9	Elton Brand, Toni Kukoc, Ron Artest	Second year after dismantling.
5	Chicago Bulls	1999	92.4	102.2	-9.9	Toni Kukoc, Ron Harper, Brent Barry, Dickey Simpkins	First year after dismantling. Worst shooting team since 1961. Kukoc is one of two players on both the best and worst offenses.
6	Golden State Warriors	1998	95.8	105.1	-9.3	Latrell Sprewell, Jimmy Jackson, Donyell Marshall, Erick Dampier	Sprewell choked Coach Carlesimo. The rest of their season epitomized it.
7	Miami Heat	1990	99.3	108.1	-8.8	Seikaly, Sherman Douglas, Glen Rice, Edwards	OK, so Rice and Douglas didn't help much as rookies.
8	Dallas Mavericks	1993	99.5	108.0	-8.5	Derek Harper, Jimmy Jackson, Sean Rooks	Hmmm, Jimmy Jackson appears on another horrible offense.
9	Houston Rockets	1983	97.0	104.7	-7.7	Allen Leavell, James Bailey, Elvin Hayes, Calvin Murphy	Murphy and Hayes were old. This team supposedly tanked its last several games in order to get the #1 pick in the draft, which was Ralph Sampson. The draft lottery would start in 1985 as a consequence.
10	New York Knicks	1986	99.5	107.2	-7.7	Patrick Ewing, Pat Cummings, Gerald Wilkins	The first draft lottery brought the Knicks Ewing, but Ewing got hurt and wasn't particularly effective on the offensive end his first year.
11	Detroit Pistons	1981	99.2	106.7	-7.5	John Long, Kent Benson, Phil Hubbard	Not horrible players here, but Long and Benson got hurt a bit. Pistons got Isiah Thomas and Kelly Tripucka in the draft because of this.
12	Denver Nuggets	1992	100.7	108.2	-7.5	Reggie Williams, Dikembe Mutombo, Cadillac Anderson, Mark Macon	They all played most of the games. There just was no offensive talent here. Granted, it was Mutombo's rookie year.
13	New Jersey Nets	1990	100.7	108.1	-7.5	Dennis Hopson, Chris Morris, Sam Bowie, Purvis Short	Back-to-back high draft picks Hopson and Morris never could hit the side of a barn with their shots. Bowie and Short were old.

#	Team	Year				Players	Comment
14	New York Nets	1977	93.3	100.6	-7.3	John Williamson, Nate Archibald, Robert Hawkins, Al Skinner, Jan van Breda Kolff	Williamson, Archibald, and Hawkins were top scorers, but none played more than 52 games.
15	Los Angeles Clippers	1987	101.2	108.4	-7.1	Woodson, Cage, Larry Drew, Benjamin	This series of horrid offensive years is why the Clippers were the butt of jokes well into the 1990s. That and owner Donald Sterling.
16	Los Angeles Clippers	1989	100.8	107.8	-7.0	Ken Norman, Benjamin, Charles Smith, Dailey, Gary Grant	Not getting proper blame is Reggie Williams, who played a little here and was on the #1, #12, and #15 teams, too.
17	San Antonio Spurs	1989	100.9	107.8	-6.9	Willie Anderson, Alvin Robertson, Cadillac Anderson, Vernon Maxwell, Frank Brickowski	The Spurs just really needed David Robinson to get out of the Navy.
18	Los Angeles Clippers	1995	101.5	108.3	-6.8	Loy Vaught, Lamond Murray, Malik Sealy, Pooh Richardson, Terry Dehere	Owner Sterling is why the Clippers fell back to this pitiful level in the 1990s.
19	New Jersey Nets	1988	101.4	108.1	-6.7	Buck Williams, Roy Hinson, John Bagley, Otis Birdsong, Tim McCormick	Two of their big scorers from the previous year disappeared, and Williams had to assume top scorer's role.
20	Memphis Grizzlies	2002	98.2	104.5	-6.3	Pau Gasol, Jason Spazz Williams, Shane Battier, Stromile Swift	Actually the rookies, Gasol and Battier, were the team's best offensive players after Shareef Abdur-Rahim was traded away.
21	Vancouver Grizzlies	1997	100.3	106.7	-6.3	Shareef Abdur-Rahim, Reeves, Anthony Peeler, Greg Anthony	Further proof that even an eventually decent player like Abdur-Rahim doesn't help an offense much at age 21.
22	Chicago Bulls	2002	98.2	104.5	-6.3	A bunch of guys in diapers	Two high school kids, injuries, trades, and the end of Tim Floyd's career.
23	Los Angeles Clippers	2000	97.8	104.1	-6.2	Maurice Taylor, Derek Anderson, Lamar Odom, Tyrone Nesby, Michael Olowokandi	Anderson somehow got a big free agent contract out of this. He showed some ability to create for himself, but no one was efficient.
24	Charlotte Hornets	1990	102.0	108.1	-6.2	Armon Gilliam, Rex Chapman, Dell Curry, Kelly Tripucka, J.R. Reid	Many guys here who actually had decent offensive years, just not this year. Weird that this offense was worse than their expansion year offense the year before.
25	Miami Heat	2002	98.5	104.5	-6.0	Eddie Jones, Alonzo Mourning, Jimmy Jackson, Rod Strickland	Jackson is on 3 different teams of the worst 25. Coach Pat Riley somehow got 36 wins out of the team, making it the most successful of the worst offenses.

Table 3.15. Worst Historical Offenses, Heights, Stability, and Coaches

Rank	Team	Season	Offensive Rating	League Average	Increment above League	Height (in.)	League Average Height (in.)	Increment above Average (in.)	Roster Stability*	Coach (Number of seasons as coach)
1	Los Angeles Clippers	1988	97.4	108.1	-10.7	79.0	79.3	-0.3	0.71	Gene Shue (1, last full)
2	Miami Heat	1989	97.8	107.8	-10.0	78.2	79.0	-0.8	Expansion	Ron Rothstein (1)
3	Vancouver Grizzlies	1996	97.7	107.7	-10.0	78.2	79.1	-0.9	Expansion	Brian Winters (1, last full)
4	Chicago Bulls	2000	94.2	104.1	-9.9	78.7	78.9	-0.2	0.40	Tim Floyd (2)
5	Chicago Bulls	1999	92.4	102.2	-9.9	78.9	78.9	0.0	0.45	Tim Floyd (1)
6	Golden State Warriors	1998	95.8	105.1	-9.3	77.7	78.9	-1.2	0.50	P.J. Carlesimo (1)
7	Miami Heat	1990	99.3	108.1	-8.8	78.5	78.9	-0.4	0.65	Ron Rothstein (2)
8	Dallas Mavericks	1993	99.5	108.0	-8.5	78.7	78.8	-0.1	0.58	Richie Adubato (4), Gar Heard
9	Houston Rockets	1983	97.0	104.7	-7.7	78.7	78.7	0.0	0.49	Del Harris (4, last)
10	New York Knicks	1986	99.5	107.2	-7.7	78.8	79.1	-0.3	0.75	Hubie Brown (4, last full)
11	Detroit Pistons	1981	99.2	106.7	-7.5	78.7	78.6	0.1	0.56	Scotty Robertson (1)
12	Denver Nuggets	1992	100.7	108.2	-7.5	79.6	78.8	0.8	0.57	Paul Westhead (2, last)
13	New Jersey Nets	1990	100.7	108.1	-7.5	79.6	78.9	0.7	0.55	Bill Fitch (1)
14	New York Nets	1977	93.3	100.6	-7.3	78.3	78.2	0.1	ABA Team	Kevin Loughery (4)
15	Los Angeles Clippers	1987	101.2	108.4	-7.1	78.6	79.3	-0.7	0.64	Don Chaney (3, last)
16	Los Angeles Clippers	1989	100.8	107.8	-7.0	79.3	79.0	0.2	0.49	Gene Shue (2), Don Casey
17	San Antonio Spurs	1989	100.9	107.8	-6.9	78.8	79.0	-0.2	0.51	Larry Brown (1)
18	Los Angeles Clippers	1995	101.5	108.3	-6.8	79.2	79.1	0.1	0.44	Bill Fitch (1)
19	New Jersey Nets	1988	101.4	108.1	-6.7	78.6	79.3	-0.6	0.53	Dave Wohl (3), Bob MacKinnon, Willis Reed
20	Memphis Grizzlies	2002	98.2	104.5	-6.3	78.9	79.0	0.0	0.31	Sidney Lowe (2)
21	Vancouver Grizzlies	1997	100.3	106.7	-6.3	78.6	78.9	-0.3	0.42	Brian Winters (2), Stu Jackson
22	Chicago Bulls	2002	98.2	104.5	-6.3	79.0	79.0	0.0	0.53	Tim Floyd (4), Bill Cartwright
23	Los Angeles Clippers	2000	97.8	104.1	-6.2	79.6	78.9	0.7	0.56	Chris Ford (2), Jim Todd
24	Charlotte Hornets	1990	102.0	108.1	-6.2	76.8	78.9	-2.1	0.67	Dick Harter (2), Gene Littles
25	Miami Heat	2002	98.5	104.5	-6.0	78.5	79.0	-0.5	0.44	Pat Riley (7)

* Roster Stability reflects the average number of minutes played by the same people from the previous year to this year.

observation. Jumping to the last two columns of the table, you can see one that shows roster stability (which is under 75 percent for all of these teams), and one that shows how many seasons the coach had been on the job, (which in many cases was only one season). To give some sense of what the roster stability number means, a roster stability of 80 percent implies that one position (or 20 percent of floor time) is completely replaced from one season to the next. Many of these teams are in the 40–60 percent range, meaning that two to three positions on the floor were completely replaced—starters and backups. That is a lot of instability for a team to deal with. Of course, colleges and high schools deal with this kind of instability all the time, but they compete with other teams that also have that kind of instability. (This is why it would pay if some of those top NCAA programs could keep the talent in school.) The only apparent exception in this list, stability-wise, is the 1986 New York Knicks under fourth-year coach Hubie Brown. That team went from a bad season in 1985 (in which Bernard King, a good offensive player, played limited minutes due to injury) to an equally bad season in 1986 (in which King was gone, and in which Patrick Ewing, a good defensive player, played limited minutes due to injury). The team's offensive rating went from 105.0 to 99.5, and its defensive rating went from 109.6 to 105.2. So maybe the overall team didn't change that much, but its best players changed character a lot and had some injuries.

The other listing in table 3.15 is height. As the list of best teams suggested, height helps. Many of these poor offensive teams were shorter than average. But note that most of these teams really are not more than an inch different from the average. That really amazed me as I was going through the calculations of average height. I would have guessed that average heights would have deviated from average by at least an inch or two, but it was more like half an inch. In high school and college, I'm sure that there is a greater deviation in height among teams. The relatively weak correlation I see between height and good offenses (and good defenses) is probably stronger in high school and college leagues—not because each inch is any more important, but because there are more inches separating teams.

Table 3.16 shows the worst defenses. Heading this list are a couple of teams from the lockout season of 1999. Coming out of that lockout, we all knew that plenty of players were out of shape and might not have been as interested in playing as they normally would have been. In comparing this list to the worst offenses, it appears that laziness may affect the defense the most. If defense is effort, as a lot of coaches will tell you, this makes a lot of sense. Table 3.17 adds the height, roster stability, and coaches associated with these teams. There are some similar patterns to those seen among bad offensive teams in that the worst defensive teams are short and tend to have had a lot of roster turnover, both at the player and coaching spots.

Table 3.16. Worst Historical Defenses

Rank	Team	Season	Defensive Rating	League Average	Relative to League	Players	Comments
1	Denver Nuggets	1999	110.4	102.2	8.2	Antonio McDyess, Nick Van Exel, Chauncey Billups, Danny Fortson	Lockout season. Teams shot the lights out against them inside and outside. Did not force turnovers.
2	Los Angeles Clippers	1999	109.7	102.2	7.5	Maurice Taylor, Lamond Murray, Eric Piatkowski, Tyrone Nesby, Michael Olowokandi	Lockout season. Similar to Denver, but forced more turnovers.
3	Denver Nuggets	1998	112.2	105.1	7.1	Dean Garrett, Johnny Newman, Laphonso Ellis, Bobby Jackson, Anthony Goldwire	Different guys than #1—even a different coach, from Bill Hanzlik to Mike D'Antoni—but same problems.
4	Denver Nuggets	1982	113.9	106.9	7.0	Alex English, Dan Issel, Kiki Vandeweghe, T.R. Dunn	Dunn had a reputation as a good defender, but a perimeter stopper does no good if everyone else is just looking for their next shot.
5	San Diego Clippers	1982	113.9	106.9	7.0	Tom Chambers, Michael Brooks, Jerome Whitehead, Joe Bryant	Teams shot almost 53% against these guys. No shot blocker and not particularly quick.
6	Vancouver Grizzlies	1998	112.0	105.1	6.9	Shareef Abdur-Rahim, Bryant Reeves, Blue Edwards, Antonio Daniels, George Lynch, Pete Chilcutt, Lee Mayberry	Slow and immobile on the interior. Particularly bad on the perimeter, where Daniels and Mayberry allowed a lot of threes.
7	Denver Nuggets	1991	114.7	107.9	6.8	Michael Adams, Orlando Woolridge, Reggie Williams, Mahmoud Abdul-Rauf, Blair Rasmussen	Paul Westhead brought his Loyola Marymount philosophy to the NBA, where he seemed to think that allowing teams to score was good. Gave up most points in history.
8	Dallas Mavericks	1993	114.7	108.0	6.7	Terry Davis, Derek Harper, Sean Rooks	Davis and Rooks, both 6' 10" and not overly athletic, manned the middle.
9	Los Angeles Clippers	1998	111.2	105.1	6.2	Lamond Murray, Rodney Rogers, Maurice Taylor, Derrick Martin, Lorenzen Wright	Very similar to the Vancouver 1998 team (at #6), but slightly better on the perimeter.
10	Orlando Magic	1990	114.3	108.1	6.2	Terry Catledge, Reggie Theus, Otis Smith, Nick Anderson	Expansion team.
11	Los Angeles Clippers	2000	110.1	104.1	6.0	Taylor, Derek Anderson, Lamar Odom, Nesby, Olowokandi	Chris Ford coached this team for about half the season after doing the damage in 1999. His Boston teams were average or a little worse.
12	Toronto Raptors	1998	111.0	105.1	6.0	Damon Stoudamire, Doug Christie, John Wallace, Marcus Camby, Oliver Miller	Really poor on the defensive boards.

#	Team	Year				Players	Notes
13	Washington Bullets	1994	112.2	106.3	6.0	Don MacLean, Rex Chapman, Tom Gugliotta, Michael Adams	Notoriously poor defensive players in MacLean, Chapman, and Adams. And they tried Kevin Duckworth in the middle.
14	Vancouver Grizzlies	1999	107.9	102.2	5.7	Abdur-Rahim, Mike Bibby, Felipe Lopez, Cherokee Parks	Third team from that lockout season.
15	San Antonio Spurs	1997	112.3	106.7	5.7	Dominique Wilkins, Vernon Maxwell, Vinny Del Negro, Avery Johnson, Will Perdue	A year later, with Duncan and Robinson, the Spurs were among the greatest defensive teams.
16	Golden State Warriors	1997	112.2	106.7	5.6	Latrell Sprewell, Joe Smith, Chris Mullin, Mark Price	Prior to this season, Sprewell had a reputation as a good defender. By this time, he wanted to be an offensive star.
17	Dallas Mavericks	1981	112.2	106.7	5.5	Tom LaGarde, Jim Spanarkel, Bill Robinzine, Geoff Huston, Brad Davis	Expansion team.
18	Philadelphia 76ers	1996	113.0	107.7	5.3	Jerry Stackhouse, Clarence Weatherspoon, Vernon Maxwell, Derrick Alston	A short team with 6'7" Weatherspoon often manning the middle.
19	Houston Rockets	1978	107.2	102.0	5.2	Calvin Murphy, Moses Malone, John Lucas, Dwight Jones, Kevin Kunnert	Injuries hurt this team. Malone missed 23 games.
20	Chicago Bulls	1986	112.4	107.2	5.2	Orlando Woolridge, Sidney Green, Kyle Macy, George Gervin, Gene Banks	Prominently, Jordan missed most of the season with an injury.
21	Vancouver Grizzlies	1997	111.9	106.7	5.2	Abdur-Rahim, Reeves, Anthony Peeler, Lee Mayberry, Greg Anthony	Opponents dominated the offensive glass against this group.
22	Golden State Warriors	1985	113.0	107.9	5.2	Purvis Short, Sleepy Floyd, Jerome Whitehead, Larry Smith, Lester Conner	They lost Joe Barry Carroll from the previous (and already weak) defense, and he had been their only presence in the middle.
23	Dallas Mavericks	1983	109.8	104.7	5.1	Mark Aguirre, Jay Vincent, Rolando Blackman, Brad Davis, Pat Cummings	A young and fairly small team that would get better.
24	Utah Jazz	1980	111.5	106.4	5.1	Adrian Dantley, Allan Bristow, Ron Boone, Ben Poquette	A few guys known for not being enthusiastic about playing defense. Also the shortest team in the league that year.
25	Portland Trail Blazers	1974	103.7	98.6	5.0	Geoff Petrie, Sidney Wicks, John Johnson, Rick Roberson, Larry Steele	Bill Walton would join this team the next year along with new coach Lenny Wilkens, and they would become average in 1975.

Table 3.17. Worst Historical Defenses, Heights, Stability, and Coaches

Rank	Team	Season	Defensive Rating	League Average	Relative to League	Height (in.)	League Average Height (in.)	Increment above Average (in.)	Roster Stability*	Coach (Number of seasons as coach)
1	Denver Nuggets	1999	110.4	102.2	8.2	77.7	78.9	-1.2	0.33	Mike D'Antoni (1, last)
2	Los Angeles Clippers	1999	109.7	102.2	7.5	78.7	78.9	-0.2	0.76	Chris Ford (1, last full)
3	Denver Nuggets	1998	112.2	105.1	7.1	78.3	78.9	-0.5	0.25	Bill Hanzlik (1, last)
4	Denver Nuggets	1982	113.9	106.9	7.0	77.4	78.7	-1.2	0.98	Doug Moe (1+)
5	San Diego Clippers	1982	113.9	106.9	7.0	78.6	78.7	0.0	0.68	Paul Silas (2)
6	Vancouver Grizzlies	1998	112.0	105.1	6.9	79.7	78.9	0.8	0.66	Brian Hill (1)
7	Denver Nuggets	1991	114.7	107.9	6.8	78.7	79.0	-0.2	0.44	Paul Westhead (1)
8	Dallas Mavericks	1993	114.7	108.0	6.7	78.7	78.8	-0.1	0.58	Richie Adubato (4), Gar Heard
9	Los Angeles Clippers	1998	111.2	105.1	6.2	78.5	78.9	-0.4	0.69	Bill Fitch (4, last)
10	Orlando Magic	1990	114.3	108.1	6.2	78.7	78.9	-0.2	Expansion	Matt Guokas (1)
11	Los Angeles Clippers	2000	110.1	104.1	6.0	79.6	78.9	0.7	0.56	Chris Ford (2), Jim Todd
12	Toronto Raptors	1998	111.0	105.1	6.0	78.0	78.9	-0.9	0.77	Darrell Walker (2), Butch Carter
13	Washington Bullets	1994	112.2	106.3	6.0	78.6	78.9	-0.2	0.68	Wes Unseld (7, last)
14	Vancouver Grizzlies	1999	107.9	102.2	5.7	79.4	78.9	0.5	0.56	Brian Hill (2, last full)
15	San Antonio Spurs	1997	112.3	106.7	5.7	78.2	78.9	-0.7	0.76	Bob Hill (3), Gregg Popovich
16	Golden State Warriors	1997	112.2	106.7	5.6	79.0	78.9	0.1	0.65	Rick Adelman (2, last)
17	Dallas Mavericks	1981	112.2	106.7	5.5	78.3	78.6	-0.3	Expansion	Dick Motta (1)
18	Philadelphia 76ers	1996	113.0	107.7	5.3	78.3	79.1	-0.8	0.48	John Lucas (2, last)
19	Houston Rockets	1978	107.2	102.0	5.2	78.3	78.3	0.0	0.88	Tom Nissalke (2)
20	Chicago Bulls	1986	112.4	107.2	5.2	79.2	79.1	0.1	0.54	Stan Albeck (1, last)
21	Vancouver Grizzlies	1997	111.9	106.7	5.2	78.6	78.9	-0.3	0.42	Brian Winters (2), Stu Jackson
22	Golden State Warriors	1985	113.0	107.9	5.2	78.3	78.9	-0.6	0.67	John Bach (2)
23	Dallas Mavericks	1983	109.8	104.7	5.1	78.3	78.7	-0.4	0.77	Dick Motta (3)
24	Utah Jazz	1980	111.5	106.4	5.1	77.5	78.4	-0.9	0.14	Tom Nissalke (1)
25	Portland Trail Blazers	1974	103.7	98.6	5.0	78.0	77.9	0.1	0.74	Jack McCloskey (2, last)

* Roster Stability reflects the average number of minutes played by the same people from the previous year to this year.

Looking at tables 3.14 and 3.16 together, there is more of what you'd proba-bly call "talent" on the Worst Defense list—Antonio McDyess, Nick Van Exel, Bobby Jackson, Alex English, Dan Issel, Kiki Vandeweghe, Shareef Abdur-Rahim, Moses Malone, Mark Aguirre, Adrian Dantley. On the Worst Offense list, there is Elton Brand (as a rookie), Glen Rice (as a rookie), Patrick Ewing (as a rookie), Dikembe Mutombo (as a rookie), Nate Archibald, Buck Williams, Abdur-Rahim (again, but as a rookie only). It's a shorter list, and the stars seem to be there pri-marily as rookies. Some of you might call Latrell Sprewell a star who actually makes both lists—but he is at best a marginal star. Likewise with Jimmy Jackson, who makes the Worst Offense list with three different teams. That suggests—not confirms—that any offensive evaluation of him as an individual shouldn't show him to be a very good offensive player. Jackson may have had numerous seasons of fifteen-plus points per game, but that did not make his teams good.

Some of these teams were actually decent at certain aspects of the game. The Clippers of 1989, who show up at number sixteen on the Worst Offense list, actu-ally shot close to the league average from the field. But they really didn't take care of the ball, turning the ball over a lot. The Denver defense of 1999 was about aver-age on the defensive boards but forced no turnovers and allowed a high shooting percentage. The 2002 Miami Heat offense had some good players shooting near the league average and committing about the league average number of turn-overs, but Coach Riley had no one that got to the line. Dean Smith said once, "The biggest reason I'm against simply running the ball down and shooting the first shot available is that the defense doesn't have time to foul you." Getting to the line, Coach Smith always said, was one of the best ways to get a score. And those Heat players didn't get there, not because they ran too much, but because they just didn't have the people who forced teams to put them on the line.

After looking at a lot of teams over the years, I have come to realize that teams like these are bad because they don't control four crucial aspects of a game:

1. Shooting percentage from the field.
2. Getting offensive rebounds.
3. Committing turnovers.
4. Going to the foul line a lot and making the shots.

There really is nothing else in the game. These four responsibilities on the offensive side and these four responsibilities on the defensive side are it. (These also come from the formula for floor percentage.) If you aren't shooting from the field, you better be doing a few of the other three things. If you don't have the size to get defensive rebounds, you better force turnovers. If you can't take care of the ball very well, you better get shots up before you turn it over, then go after the boards. When NBC shows halftime stats and they say that New Jersey is "doing everything right" and beating the Lakers in field goal percentage and turnovers but losing on the scoreboard, you can guess that it's because the Nets are not going to the line very often or because they are getting beat on the boards.

Where to Go from Here

So that's it. Those are some good teams and some bad teams, with some of the reasons why they were so good and so bad.

Great *teams* truly are what the individuals of basketball should be striving for. Though great individual stats are fine, it is the success of the team that matters. Of course, the greatness of the above teams was the result of certain individuals more than others. Michael Jordan was a star on those great Bulls teams. He was clearly more responsible than other Bulls for the team's success. But how many of those points did he produce? And how many possessions did he use? How many of those seventy-two wins did he create? How important were his teammates? Answering many of those questions is the goal of the rest of the book.

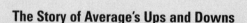

The Story of Average's Ups and Downs

It is actually an interesting story to see how "average" has changed through time. The story is somewhat like fads and fashions that come and go because someone or something is "cool." "Coolness" is definitely a factor in basketball. Michael Jordan's dunking inspired a lot of guys to be like Mike, though often only in their ability to dunk. The emphasis on defense in the late 1980s to early 1990s among the Detroit Pistons, New York Knicks, and Chicago Bulls was copied a lot through the rest of the 1990s and into the new century. Before this, the versatility and passing of Magic Johnson and Larry Bird were imitated. Before that, the dominant center, epitomized by Kareem Abdul-Jabbar or Bill Walton, was viewed as necessary to win a title and drove teams to look desperately for one. Though still viewed as very nice, dominating centers do not appear to be vital anymore.

If the league itself wants to change the style of the game, it cannot just reach out and change what is cool. The NBA tries, of course. They have their advertising campaigns featuring cool Hollywood people. They also try to set the maximum length of shorts to set a fashion statement.

No, the league's power in changing its product lies to a tremendous degree in its ability to change the rules. Rule changes have had significant effects on the pace and efficiency of the game. Whether they had effects on the popularity of the game is difficult to say. Table 3.1 lists the rule changes that have taken place since 1974 along with the pace and efficiency ratings in these years (as also reflected also in figure 3.1 in the main text).

There have been a lot of little rule changes that most people wouldn't notice:

In 1979, players were allowed to roll the ball inbounds. Rolling the ball inbounds to save a losing team time near the end of a game is, in my opinion, a pretty clever idea to take advantage of there not being a rule against it. But the league did formally endorse it in 1979.

Also in 1979, players and coaches were instructed to proceed to the dressing rooms at halftime. I really wonder what inspired this one. Were guys hanging out on the court watching the cheerleaders? Were coaches asking fans for advice? Were they trying to win fans by signing autographs all through halftime?

In 1980, the league went to three officials. In 1981, the league went back to two. In 1989, they decided that three was better again. Throughout all of this, the league resisted the use of instant replay. That changed in 2002. Two examples in the 2002 season stand out as reasons for its implementation. First Cleveland beat New Jersey 100–97 on March 19 when Lamond Murray hit a three-point shot *after* the buzzer—a shot that the referees allowed. Even the play-by-play posted on *NBA.com* shows the end of the game before Murray's shot:

(0:00) [NJN 97-97] Van Horn Jump Shot: Made (27 PTS) Assist: Kidd (10 AST)
(0:00) End Game CLE 100, NJN 97
(0:00) [CLE 100-97] Murray Jump Shot: Made (17 PTS) Assist: Miller (14 AST)

The other incident occurred on April 21 in a playoff game. Charlotte and Orlando were tied with 0.7 seconds remaining when Charlotte's Baron Davis caught and flung an inbounds pass through the basket. It clearly beat the horn but was waved off by referee Bernie Fryer. Fryer said afterwards that he believed it was impossible to "cock to get a three-pointer up to get muscle behind it." Given the nature of the fling-shot, Fryer's point is debatable. But something had to change—either adding replay or amending the rule already on the books that states that the quarter is effectively over with 0.2 seconds left on the clock unless a tip-in off the inbounds pass occurs (the Trent Tucker Rule).

In 1981, player jewelry was banned. Mychal Thompson and Darryl Dawkins were starting to get out of control with their necklaces.

In 1984, in a move to prevent the league from resembling World Wrestling Entertainment in any way, the league forbade players from entering the spectator stands.

In the period between 1979 and 1981, coaches were ejected if their team had three illegal defense technicals called against them.

In 1982, Darryl Dawkins caused another rule change. He used to give his dunks names like Candy Slam and In Your Face Disgrace. But, most prominently, he broke a backboard over Kansas City Kings' player Bill Robinzine, who cowered from the falling glass. In 1982 the league went to breakaway rims and actually *prohibited* breaking the backboard—for whatever good that did relative to the technological improvement.

In 1999 the league finally said enough with the long shorts, mandating that words mean what they say. No "long shorts"! No "jumbo shrimp"! And absolutely no one says (David) "Stern is soft"! So the league said longer shorts were no longer, mandating that the bottom of the shorts be at least one inch above the knee. They didn't say whose knee, though, and we are still waiting for the day when Allen Iverson "forgets" his shorts at home and has to wear Dikembe Mutombo's shorts.

Enough with my shorts fetish and on to the substantive things. The problem is determining what is substantive. Analyzing the effects of rule changes is among the most difficult work that can be done. Each rule change causes coaches to go looking for ways to exploit it. It often takes years for them to find their ways. By that time, the actual effects can be clouded by the "fads" of the league. Following are some of the big changes and how their effects got muted or twisted.

The three-point shot was introduced in 1980. The league average rating the year before was 105.0. Immediately, the league rating went up to 106.4. Teams shot an average of nearly 230 three-pointers, making only about 28 percent of them. Doing the quick calculation, that 28 percent is equivalent to 42 percent from two-point land. But the league was shooting over 48 percent from two-point land before. So the three wasn't the obvious source of increased efficiency. It didn't increase the two-point percentage either, by the way. No, a decline in turnovers that had been seen in previous seasons seemed to be the big reason for the improvement. In the second year of the three-point shot, most NBA teams *stopped* using it! The NBA was *fad-tastic*, enjoying the Magic-Bird rivalry, and the three-point shot was hardly used. It wasn't until 1984 that teams used the shot as much as they had in its initial year, shooting it still at only 27 percent. In that year the league efficiency was 107.5, up 2.5 points with no obvious contribution from the new toy. Eventually, the three-pointer did catch on. By 1988, it was clearly a weapon. The league efficiency peaked at 108.5 that year. From 1980 to 1988, the league may have been slowing down, but the NBA's toy shot had finally become "cool."

With the league getting a lot more physical in the 1990s, especially with the no-lay-up rule of Pat Riley's Knicks, the rule makers in 1995 tried to fix things. They tried to open up the lane by changing what defensive post players could do with their hands—allowing only the forearm in the back—and by shortening the three-point arc. Three-point shooting and overall efficiency did jump in 1995, but the declining trend in pace and efficiency just continued for the next couple years after that.

So, finally, in 2002 the league looked at major changes. They learned that when you change the rules, you don't necessarily get the results you expect. They lightened the rules on defense, allowing teams to play zone with the ironic intention of actually improving offense. Michael Jordan had always complained about how zones would completely stifle offenses, especially with the pressure of the twenty-four-second clock. Well, league efficiency went up as the rule makers had hoped. Maybe it wasn't due to the zone rule as much as it was due to the prohibition of defenders from camping in the lane more than three seconds without guarding someone. This "defensive three-seconds" rule definitely caused an increase in free points through the automatic technical fouls awarded for its violation. Reports from preseason 2002 were that several such fouls were being called per game. During the regular season, the call wasn't made that often, but enough to add a couple of points per game, which is enough to increase league efficiency by 1–2 percent. It is unclear whether any of the groundbreaking rule changes of 2002 actually opened up the lane at all, but the league expressed its happiness with the changes that resulted. It will be interesting to see if it takes a few years for one or two teams to fully exploit the new rules and make Jordan a prophet.

Endnotes

1. Scoring possessions are estimated as

$$FGM + \left[1 - \left(1 - FT\% \right)^2 \right] \times FTA \times 0.4$$

2. Field percentage is estimated from

$$\frac{FGM}{FGA - \frac{OREB}{(OREB + DDREB)} \times (FGA - FGM) \times 1.07 + TOV}$$

3. Plays are estimated by

$$FGA + FTA \times 0.4 + TOV$$

Play % is then Scoring Possessions/Plays.

Chapter 4

Reserve Your Playoff Tickets Now! We Won Three in a Row!

The Lakers of 1972 set a record by winning thirty-three straight games. The Milwaukee Bucks of 1971 won twenty straight. The Bulls of 1996 won eighteen straight.

Now those are winning streaks. They meant something. The three-game winning streak that your local paper highlights, on the other hand, may generate a few more fans at the gate, but does it really tell you if the team is going to be good?

If your local team is Golden State and they win three straight, it might mean that the Warriors at least may be getting better than their typical twenty-win season. If your local team is the Lakers, a three-game win streak is ho-hum.

What a winning streak means does depend on your expectations. Generically, if your team wins 70 percent of its games, it should often win three straight games—about 35 percent of the time. If your team wins 30 percent of its games, it should win three straight only 3 percent of the time.

That *does not* mean that your local .300 team (OK, *my* local .300 team) will rarely win three straight games. "Three percent of the time" means that the Woerriors will only win 3 straight for 3 percent of the (independent) three-game sequences in a season. Given that an NBA season is 82 games long, there are a lot of three-game sequences in a season in which a team could win three games in a row. In fact, if the Warriors come out of the blocks and win three in a row, whoop-de-do, because there is actually about a 90 percent chance that a .300 team will win three in a row *sometime* in the season. That's what I have to tell myself when the paper starts hyping these guys.

So, in order to keep myself from getting let down, I made up some tables that tell me how reasonable it is for the Golden State Warriors to actually win a few games in a row. Knowing that they win actually about 25 percent of their games (not even 30 percent), I look at table 4.1 and see no .250 team column, only .200

Table 4.1. Chance of at Least One Winning Streak of the Shown Length in 82-Game Season

Win Streak	0.200 Team	0.300 Team	0.400 Team	0.500 Team	0.600 Team	0.700 Team	0.800 Team
3	47%	89%	99.50%	100.00%	100.00%	100.00%	100.00%
4	12%	47%	87%	99.39%	100.00%	100.00%	100.00%
5	2.5%	17%	55%	91.6%	99.82%	100.00%	100.00%
6	0.49%	5.5%	27%	70%	97.5%	99.99%	100.00%
7	0.10%	1.6%	12%	45%	88%	99.85%	100.00%
8	0.02%	0.49%	4.8%	25%	72%	98.8%	100.00%
9	0.00%	0.15%	1.9%	13%	53%	95.3%	100.00%
10	0.00%	0.04%	0.76%	6.9%	36%	88%	99.97%
11	0.00%	0.01%	0.30%	3.5%	23%	76%	99.84%
12	0.00%	0.00%	0.12%	1.7%	14%	63%	99.36%
13	0.00%	0.00%	0.05%	0.85%	8.7%	49%	98.1%
14	0.00%	0.00%	0.02%	0.42%	5.3%	37%	95.5%
15	0.00%	0.00%	0.01%	0.21%	3.1%	28%	91.2%

and .300 team columns—nothing is easy for a Warriors fan. A .200 team is going to win three straight games at least once in an eighty-two-game season in about 47 percent of all seasons. Average that with the 89 percent for a .300 team and you get a 68 percent chance that a .250 team is going to win three in a row.[1] That's a pretty high percentage, again proving that the three-game Warriors win streak that the *San Francisco Chronicle* is crowing about is not something for me to get excited about.

My favorite WNBA team is the Charlotte Sting (I've moved around a lot), who play only a thirty-two-game season. In such a short season, it's a little less likely for a .300 team to win three straight—only 56 percent compared to 89 percent in the eighty-two-game season (see table 4.2). Fortunately, the Sting have been pretty

Table 4.2. Chance of at Least One Winning Streak of the Shown Length in 32-Game Season

Win Streak	0.200 Team	0.300 Team	0.400 Team	0.500 Team	0.600 Team	0.700 Team	0.800 Team
3	21%	56%	86%	98.2%	99.93%	100.00%	100.00%
4	4.5%	21%	53%	85%	98.2%	99.97%	100.00%
5	0.89%	6.6%	25%	59%	90%	99.42%	100.00%
6	0.17%	1.9%	10%	35%	72%	96.6%	99.97%
7	0.03%	0.57%	4.2%	18%	52%	89%	99.78%
8	0.01%	0.16%	1.6%	9.3%	35%	77%	98.99%
9	0.00%	0.05%	0.63%	4.6%	22%	63%	96.9%
10	0.00%	0.01%	0.24%	2.2%	13%	48%	92.7%
11	0.00%	0.00%	0.09%	1.1%	7.7%	36%	86%
12	0.00%	0.00%	0.04%	0.51%	4.5%	25%	78%
13	0.00%	0.00%	0.01%	0.24%	2.6%	18%	68%
14	0.00%	0.00%	0.01%	0.12%	1.5%	12%	57%
15	0.00%	0.00%	0.00%	0.05%	0.84%	8.2%	48%

good, definitely not a .300 team. For a team like that, which has won about 60 percent of its games, winning three straight is practically guaranteed. In only .07 percent (100%–99.93%) of all thirty-two-game seasons does a team winning 60 percent of its games not win three straight games at least once. That's why three-game win streaks shouldn't be hyped as much in Charlotte...

Except in 2001. That was an odd year for the Sting. They started off the season 1–10. Their off-season acquisitions from Los Angeles, Allison Feaster and Clarisse Machanguana, were struggling. Their number-two pick in the draft, Kelly Miller, was on the bench. Coach Anne Donovan was doing what coaches do in these situations—trying anything to get her team out of the doldrums, tinkering with lineups, encouraging, yelling, and working hard. And, after that horrid start and Donovan's tinkering, the team did win three in a row, even six in a row. In fact, the Sting went 17–4 the rest of the way and only lost to the WNBA champion Los Angeles Sparks in the Finals.

That truly was an odd team. Teams with a record of 18–14 should not win their games that way. Such streakiness implies a real change in the course of the season. Such streakiness occurs through random chance only about 4 percent of the time. Odds like that are what scientists use to say that oat bran prevents cancer. All those studies of people eating oat bran and getting cancer produce patterns that random chance explains less than 5 percent of the time, allowing them to say that it's probably not random chance and probably oat bran. That kind of statistic doesn't mean absolutely positively that eating oat bran is going to keep you healthy or that the Sting underwent a real change, but it made me look hard at that Sting team for such a change, and it sure made a lot of people switch cereals.

In this basketball case, it looks like Charlotte's defense got a lot better after the bad start, going from a defensive rating of 100.9 in the first eleven games to 88.7 afterward. Tammy Sutton-Brown, a 6′ 4″ rookie center, played in only eight of the first eleven games and started none, but she started all the remaining twenty-one games of the hot streak. Was that Coach Donovan's most important tinker? Maybe. Was it everything? Probably not. Just as eating all those Cheerios ain't gonna help if you're puffing on a Pall Mall in between spoonfuls, Sutton-Brown was, uh, probably just part of a balanced diet.

OK. Enough of the health lesson. Go eat some Froot Loops.

Now, What Season Winning Percentage Does a Streak Imply?

The other particularly strange team that I personally remember well was the 1996–97 Phoenix Suns. Starting the season, they lost their first thirteen straight. Losing that many in a row didn't bode well for them. There were problems. They had traded away Charles Barkley before the season and placed Kevin Johnson on the injured list to start the season. But they still had Michael Finley, one of the best rookies the year before, and Sam Cassell (acquired for Barkley) was taking Kevin Johnson's place. (They also had Robert Horry, though he wasn't as hot a commodity back then before all his playoff success with the Lakers.) To lose thirteen straight seemed a bit extreme for a team with these guys. What were the Suns headed for? History now tells us that they would turn it around and end up 40–42 and become the second NBA team to lose thirteen straight in a season and still make the playoffs (the Chicago Bulls of 1977 were the other team). But what could have been expected from that start?

Clearly, going winless to start the season doesn't mean that the team will go winless throughout the season. Normally, we see a winless team at the start of the season, like the inaugural Miami Heat team that went 0–17, and we guess that they will win between ten and twenty games. But there were higher expectations for that Phoenix Suns team.

Expectations are important here. If expectations were pretty blind to knowledge of the team, that thirteen-game losing streak implied about a 23–59 record, with the odds of different win-loss records stacking up as in table 4.3.[2]

There was only a 2 percent chance that the Suns, if you considered them "any old team," would end up winning the forty games that they did win.

But let's say you were a Suns' believer and a real optimist. You knew that the Suns had some good talent. Before the season, you were pretty sure that the Suns would win at least what they did the season before (only forty-one games) because Barkley was an aging bum who missed ten to fifteen games every year anyway. The Suns picked up some good-looking young talent in Cassell and Horry, plus they still had KJ and Finley. If I could send someone inside your head, pluck every fiber of knowledge you had there and painfully extract all of it, including the key to your bank account—I might find your original odds of what the Suns would do before their thirteen-games loss streak to start the season and put it in table 4.4.

You still gave a little room for the Suns to go down, but you felt, as someone truly tied to that home team, that the team would get better.

Table 4.3. Chances of Winning Various Numbers of Games Given a 13-Game Losing Streak

Wins	Chance	Wins	Chance
8–12	7.9%	41–45	0.5%
12–16	10.8%	45–49	0.1%
16–21	19.4%	49–53	0.0%
21–25	23.9%	53–57	0.0%
25–29	19.4%	57–62	0.0%
29–33	11.3%	62–66	0.0%
33–37	5.0%	66–70	0.0%
37–41	1.7%	70–74	0.0%

**Table 4.4. An Optimist's Original Idea of
Phoenix's Wins in 1997**

Wins	Chance	Wins	Chance
8–12	0.0%	41–45	37.6%
12–16	0.1%	45–49	17.4%
16–21	0.1%	49–53	5.8%
21–25	0.3%	53–57	0.3%
25–29	1.2%	57–62	0.1%
29–33	3.8%	62–66	0.1%
33–37	10.1%	66–70	0.0%
37–41	23.1%	70–74	0.0%

If you really believed this, then that 0–13 start only fazed you a little bit. After that start, you would say, "OK, we just got KJ back. I just know that he can at least make us respectable. Finley and Cassell will play better. Hot Rod Williams will also be back." And you would believe the odds in table 4.5 for the team's ultimate win-loss record.

You'd concede that they probably weren't going to be a winning team. But they wouldn't drop to that twenty-win season that the press was talking about. They could pull out a respectable season with about thirty wins.

Now let's say that the above optimist was the owner of the Suns with expectations well above everyone else's. And let's say that you were actually the coach of the Suns. You were Danny Ainge. You walked into the job at 0–8, lost your first five, and your boss expected you to pull out of the tailspin and win thirty games. That's pressure, but you did it. You actually won forty of your last sixty-nine games. It's contract extension time!

Those were some tough expectations to live up to, but perhaps realistic. It's difficult to set expectations perfectly with the people you work with, but it can be a key aspect of doing the job. In the interest of setting generic expectations, expectations without the benefit of detailed knowledge, tables 4.6 and 4.7 suggest what a winning percentage might be for an NBA or WNBA team, respectively, that wins or loses a certain number of games in a season.

**Table 4.5. An Optimist's Revised Idea of
Phoenix's Win Total after 13-Game Losing
Streak**

Wins	Chance	Wins	Chance
8–12	1.2%	41–45	6.8%
12–16	2.4%	45–49	0.7%
16–21	4.4%	49–53	0.0%
21–25	9.4%	53–57	0.0%
25–29	16.4%	57–62	0.0%
29–33	22.2%	62–66	0.0%
33–37	21.3%	66–70	0.0%
37–41	15.2%	70–74	0.0%

Table 4.6. Chance of Wins, Given Win/Loss Streak in NBA 82-Game Season

Win Range	Win Streak				Loss Streak			
	20 G	15 G	10 G	5 G	5 G	10 G	15 G	20 G
8–12	0%	0%	0%	0%	1%	4%	12%	28%
12–16	0%	0%	0%	0%	1%	5%	16%	29%
16–21	0%	0%	0%	0%	3%	11%	25%	24%
21–25	0%	0%	0%	0%	4%	17%	23%	13%
25–29	0%	0%	0%	1%	6%	22%	14%	5%
29–33	0%	0%	0%	2%	8%	19%	7%	1%
33–37	0%	0%	1%	4%	9%	12%	2%	0%
37–41	0%	0%	2%	7%	9%	6%	1%	0%
41–45	0%	1%	6%	9%	7%	2%	0%	0%
45–49	0%	2%	12%	9%	4%	1%	0%	0%
49–53	1%	7%	19%	8%	2%	0%	0%	0%
53–57	5%	14%	22%	6%	1%	0%	0%	0%
57–62	13%	23%	17%	4%	0%	0%	0%	0%
62–66	24%	25%	11%	3%	0%	0%	0%	0%
66–70	29%	16%	5%	1%	0%	0%	0%	0%
70–74	28%	12%	4%	1%	0%	0%	0%	0%
Expected Wins:	65.9	61.6	55.1	45.6	36.4	26.9	20.4	16.1

Table 4.7. Chance of Wins, Given Win/Loss Streak in WNBA 32-Game Season

Win Range	Win Streak				Loss Streak			
	16 G	12 G	8 G	4 G	4 G	8 G	12 G	16 G
3–5	0%	0%	0%	0%	3%	8%	20%	40%
5–6	0%	0%	0%	0%	3%	8%	18%	25%
6–8	0%	0%	0%	0%	5%	13%	21%	18%
8–10	0%	0%	0%	1%	7%	17%	18%	10%
10–11	0%	0%	0%	3%	10%	18%	12%	5%
11–13	0%	0%	0%	6%	12%	15%	6%	2%
13–14	0%	0%	1%	9%	14%	11%	3%	1%
14–16	0%	0%	3%	12%	14%	6%	1%	0%
16–18	0%	1%	6%	14%	12%	3%	0%	0%
18–19	1%	3%	11%	14%	9%	1%	0%	0%
19–21	2%	6%	15%	12%	6%	0%	0%	0%
21–22	5%	12%	18%	10%	3%	0%	0%	0%
22–24	10%	18%	17%	7%	1%	0%	0%	0%
24–26	18%	21%	13%	5%	0%	0%	0%	0%
26–27	25%	18%	8%	3%	0%	0%	0%	0%
27+	40%	20%	8%	3%	0%	0%	0%	0%
Expected Wins:	26.0	24.5	22.0	18.3	13.7	10.0	7.5	6.0

So, as an example, an NBA team that loses ten straight is probably a 27–55 (.329) team. That team has a 9 percent chance of winning at least thirty-seven, though, in what would be a roller-coaster season (as Toronto had in 2002—see chapter 23). A WNBA team that loses eight straight is probably a 10–22 (.312) team, a winning percentage worse than the NBA team that loses ten straight. So losing eight in a row in a short season implies a worse season record than losing ten straight in a long season.

These, as I will emphasize again, are *average* expectations. Those Suns of 1997 had talent and coincidental injuries that, during the initial losing streak, probably did keep hopes high of turning the team around.

One Last Thing . . .

Winning streaks occasionally come up in the discussion of the greatest teams in history. The 69–13 Lakers of 1972 had a thirty-three-game winning streak, and the 72–10 Bulls of 1996 had only an eighteen-game winning streak. Does that difference in length of winning streaks somehow make up for the three-win difference between the two teams, bringing the Lakers equal to the Bulls?

Cross-generational comparisons of teams are difficult. In this case, you compare records and the Bulls win. You compare streaks and the Lakers win. If you compare playoff success, they end up a draw. When these two teams actually were playing their games, all they wanted to do was win a title. Winning eighteen straight or thirty-three straight wasn't a specific goal. Nor was winning sixty-nine versus seventy-two. They wanted to win a title, knowing that no pundit could ever really take that away. They knew that no one could ever make them compete against history or against the future under realistic conditions. Because no true competition can exist between such great teams, we take polls, we argue, we throw out numbers, we ask computers (kinda like the BCS), and we argue some more. But we can only compare teams of different seasons in some made-up world with made-up rules about how to do so. No one can be proven right or wrong.

In this case, the winning streaks are additional numbers to throw into the argument. Statistically, a Bulls team that won seventy-two of eighty-two games should have had a winning streak longer than eighteen games. The Lakers' thirty-three-game win streak was not unusual, but the Bulls' "short" winning streak was. They should have had at least a twenty-three-game winning streak. Does that mean that the Bulls weren't as good as their record? Or does it just mean that they slacked off when they realized how easy it was to win eighteen games in a row? Both interpretations are fair, but they imply different things about the Bulls' relative strength compared to the Lakers. See? No right or wrong.

Endnotes

1. If you calculate it the more precise way, a .250 team has a 72 percent chance of winning three games in a row at least once in a season. The 68 percent calculated from the table is close enough unless you're some kind of gambler, in which case, you should know better.

2. These chances are based on team records throughout the NBA history. That history gives a general sense of how well teams do that is "blind" to specific knowledge of the details of those teams. For anyone who wants to nitpick, these numbers are based on a smoothed

representation of what NBA teams have done historically. There is a strange blip in the history of NBA teams showing that teams don't win between thirty-three and thirty-seven games as might be expected. I generally don't believe such a blip should exist, so I smoothed it out. If you do believe it, instead of the Suns being expected to win twenty-three games, they were expected to win twenty-two games, not a big difference.

Chapter 5

Teamwork

If Shaquille O'Neal has the ball in the post, guarded single-handedly by Scot Pollard, the responsibility of the defender at the foul line is to double-team him. From Shaquille's perspective, if he sees that defender coming down and leaving Robert Horry free, he can make the pass out to Horry for a wide-open shot.

These sorts of things happen all the time in basketball. Whether it is a standard post-up set or a perimeter passing game, the interaction between teammates to increase the odds of their team's scoring (or to decrease the odds of their opponent scoring) is a fundamental and constant aspect of basketball. A pick-and-roll isolates the teammate interaction to a pair of teammates on the offensive and defensive ends, but it is an essential way for individuals to play off each other's talents. A designed play is nothing more than choreographed teamwork.

When you watch a play evolve, you can identify its most critical part once a team scores. Maybe it wasn't when Shaquille got the ball on the post, but when he cut across the lane just as it opened up. And that was accomplished because Kobe Bryant cleared out, knowing that he would take Doug Christie with him. In a smoothly running offense, each player's role continues throughout to provide fluid opportunities for scoring. There is no measurement of how each cut and each pick increases the odds of a team scoring—not like in baseball, where the bases provide measurable increments toward runs—but the concept is there.

Teamwork is the element of basketball most difficult to capture in any quantitative sense. No other basketball statistical book makes any serious attempt to quantify how teamwork affects the statistics that players put up. Yet there is a huge class of books for coaches that teach plays, illustrate passing drills, and encourage team defense—books *entirely* about taking advantage of teamwork. Teamwork clearly matters, and any basketball statistical book that does not recognize its importance misses a most relevant part of a dynamic game.

That is why this is the first of three chapters that *explicitly* relates teamwork to statistical measures such as assists, rebounds, and field goals. By the end of the third chapter, you will see how I have incorporated the interaction of team-mates—to the degree that there are available statistics to do so—into statistical tools I use for evaluating players. The statistics won't replace a book on how to coach a team and certainly cannot replace the experience of learning/playing the sport with your hands on a basketball. But for a coach whose job revolves around getting players to cooperate, it is important that statistics reflect, to some degree, how well they are doing.

Let Me Count the Ways

Let's just think about the different ways that teammates interact in basketball. On the offensive end, here are a few:

1. A player will pass to a teammate if that teammate has a better chance of scoring, perhaps because a defender previously left to double-team the passer, or because the potential shooter has a mismatch against his defender.

2. Teammates often set picks for one another. Picks offer several small advantages. They can give an offensive player a little space from a defender to either get a shot up more easily or to survey the defense without a defender right on top of him. They can create mismatches by forcing defenses to switch. They can generally create confusion of responsibility on the defensive end.

3. Players will go after a teammate's missed shot, preserving a team's opportunity to score.

4. In a much more subtle act of knowing how to interact on a team, play-ers will simply run through the patterns of an offense. For example, a player standing on the perimeter may cut through the middle of the lane, forcing his defender to stay with him and opening up the per-imeter for the ball handler to create space for himself. In the language of coaches and TV analysts, this is "creating space" or having "good spacing."

5. Finally, players will sometimes provide verbal directions, like notify-ing a teammate that a double-team is coming or directing a teammate to cut through the lane or telling him when to clear out of a low post position.

On the defensive end, teammate interaction is probably even more impor-tant. Here are some examples:

1. In a man-to-man defense, players double-team a scorer who has a higher likelihood of scoring. They also rotate to scorers who have been left open, possibly as a consequence of a double-team.

2. In a zone defense, players recognize a zone of the court that they are responsible for covering and trust that their teammates will cover their own zones.

3. Good defenders will tell each other if a pick is coming on the left or on the right.

4. In rebounding, players block out so that another teammate can get a defensive rebound. Or they may knock a ball free so that another teammate can control it.

That's just a quick list of the aspects of offense and defense in which teammates cooperate. Teammate interaction permeates the game of basketball, and coaches who preach it every day could add details and probably several other generalities to such a list.

A lot of the interactions listed above, however, are not measured by statistics or are measured imperfectly. For example, passing around the perimeter for an open shot before the defense rotates may result in an assist, but the pass before the assist might have been the most important one. Or, if a guy is free under the basket because he went there after his defender double-teamed the ball, his making that cut to the basket deserves some credit on top of the assist and the score, doesn't it?

Picks are not recorded at all, except privately by some teams. Players who are good at picks and shooting get some credit for picks by being more involved in pick-and-roll plays where they end up scoring. But if that same pick-and-roll only sets up the ball handler for an open shot, the pick setter gets no assist and no credit at all. That kind of teamwork is not captured in stats.

Offensive rebounds are recorded, but when an offensive player is fouled by a defender while going after a loose ball, it is not recorded. Dennis Rodman's ability to get offensive rebounds supposedly prevented his defenders from double-teaming others, even though Rodman himself was not a scoring threat. It's hard to say whether his offensive rebounding totals captured the benefit of his tenacity to the team.

Movement away from the ball is recorded by no one I've ever met, but it can be vitally important. Imagine a two-person game where your teammate has a low-post advantage against his defender. It can be very helpful to your teammate if you just draw your man away from that low post. Knowing the places on the court where your defender can't cover you and your teammate is very important to improving your team's chances to score. The same principle applies in a full five-person game. If the threat of Derek Fisher hitting a three-pointer keeps his defender from aggressively double-teaming Shaquille O'Neal, isn't Fisher providing some benefit? Statistics of field goal percentages and assists measure some of the reward for this situation, but how do we isolate the value of movement away from the ball?

"Help defense" is really just equivalent to "defense." No basketball defense operates in a pure man-on-man fashion—there is *always* help. A defense where all five defenders pay attention only to the players they are guarding is not a defense. Four of those five are just standing around guarding a guy without the ball, for one thing. Fundamentally, a defense keeps the ball, not men, from the basket. When a defender leaves his player assignment to block a shot down low, he is defending the ball. Maybe the man on the ball forced his man into the help. Maybe he just screwed up, and the off-the-ball defender made a great play. We can't know that from measurements. But the fact that defenses defend one basketball *first* and five players *second* makes teamwork an inherent part of any defense. Statistics such as blocks, steals, and defensive rebounds get at only small parts of what the defense is doing.

My point is not to paint a depressing picture of the inadequacy of statistics in basketball. (I'll do that in a later chapter on defense.) Rather, I want to illustrate that teamwork is primarily a way of cooperating to increase your team's probability of scoring or to decrease the opponent's probability of scoring (i.e., to increase your team's offensive rating and decrease your team's defensive rating). I'd like to formulate statistics that capture how teamwork accounts for these changes in probability of scoring. The later two chapters on teamwork will detail the challenges I faced in doing so.

Why Baseball Doesn't Help

Bill James has been analyzing baseball for more than twenty years. His research has been tremendously enlightening with regard to the strategy and evaluation of baseball players, but one thing that he has never had to deal with is how teammates really interact to help each other. That is not his fault, but rather the nature of baseball. There isn't much active teamwork in baseball. Rarely does a hitter in baseball consider what a teammate is doing. Most of the time, his teammates are all sitting and chewing gum in the dugout anyway, so you hope he's not thinking about what they're doing. When he has a teammate on base, there are occasional hit-and-run plays called, which are coordinated efforts, but usually the hitter is ignoring the runner in order to deal with the pitcher. But even that hit-and-run doesn't really involve the teammates communicating much with each other. Coaches send in the play, and the players execute their roles without much regard for whether the other guy in the play is actually executing too.

Because teamwork is not a big part of baseball and because baseball measures progress toward scoring through bases, analysis of baseball player contributions is easier than analysis of basketball player contributions. Trying to modify baseball formulas of individual runs created to work in basketball ignores the complex teamwork involved in basketball. Trust me, I tried it, and I've seen a lot of other people who tried it (see box).

Basketball doesn't flow the same way baseball does. It needs a different model, one that captures at least some of the interactions. That's what you'll find in this book.

Approximate Values of Statistics to Teams

There are plenty of methods out there that try to assemble all the individual basketball statistics into one number suggesting the overall value of players. The most basic of these is to add the good statistics and subtract the bad ones, something analogous to baseball's linear weight formula for assessing how many runs an individual produces. This is a standard version:

VALUE = PTS + REB + AST + STL + BLK − TOV − Missed FG − Missed FT

Some formulas also subtract personal fouls. Most formulas have all sorts of different multiplying factors on the different statistics. Maybe assists get multiplied by 0.7 and steals get multiplied by 1.5 because the person who created the formula doesn't believe that assists are as valuable as steals. Maybe offensive rebounds get a weight of 0.8 and defensive rebounds get a weight of 0.5 because someone decided that offensive rebounds are more important. Maybe the multiplying factors change for players at one position relative to players at another position because assists are more important for a point guard than for a power forward. The justifications for the different multiplying factors (or "weights") come from the brains of those who created them in some hope of better matching their personal beliefs or better matching MVP voting or... hell, I don't know what reality these formulas are trying to replicate. All these formulas are just approximate ways of representing someone's opinion about the quality of players. They are "value approximation" methods. They don't tell you anything about strategy. They don't distinguish between a player's offensive and defensive contributions. They don't add up to points scored or points allowed (though one of the methods does estimate individual wins where teammates' values sum to the team win total, which is nice). The NBA has an official award—once called the Schick Award and now called the IBM Award—that is based entirely upon a formula like the one above, but no one really pays much attention to it because no one is sure what it really means.

The way I like to use these methods is to compare them against each other in order to understand the uncertainty in evaluating players. For example, the results of all methods show that Michael Jordan is a great player and Cadillac Anderson is not. But the results of some of these methods say that Dennis Rodman was one of the greatest who ever played, and some of them say he was not much more than the greatest cross-dresser who ever played. This variation in values makes Rodman one of the enigmas of basketball. (The cross-dressing makes him an enigma, too.) It also shows that the methods all place widely varying values on the different statistics. For example, of these methods, I found a few that say that an assist is more valuable than a point scored. I also found one that says that an assist is worth only about 60 percent of the value of a point scored. The uncertainty in the value of an assist, then, is between about 0.6 and 1.4 points.

Looking beyond just assists, I collected information from eleven different methods that I've run across through the years. I threw out one because its weights were almost always on the extreme, and its results were laughable—it had Michael Olowokandi in 1998 (as a rookie) having a greater season than Moses Malone, Gary Payton, Grant Hill, or Clyde Drexler ever had. Having talked to the developer of the method, I unfortunately know that the method was not a joke. It is not worth including here. The others all have some merit and have been used by someone at some time. These methods are described below and summarized in table 5.1.

Manley's Credits

This was the first method I saw, way back in 1988 or so when Martin Manley wrote a book called *Basketball Heaven*. His form is the simplest form, where the weights are all equal to one. The equation at the start of this box is exactly what he used.

Hoopstat Grade

Joshua Trupin and Gerald Secor Couzens wrote a book in the late 1980s called *Hoopstats* that had a different variation. They didn't weight points, but rather weighted field goals made and free throws made. In order to assess the

Table 5.1. Weights Assigned to Different Statistics, Relative to Points

Statistic	Manley Credits	Hoopstat Grade[1]	Steele Value	Heeren Tendex	Bellotti Points Created[2]	Claerbaut Quality Points[1]	Mays Magic Metric[1]	Schaller TPR[3]	Hollinger PER[1]	Berri, Indiv. Wins[1]
PTS	1	1	1	1	1	1	1	1	1	1
AST	1.00	1.39	1.25	1.00	1.08	0.63	0.98	0.90	0.79	0.92
OREB	1.00	1.18	1.00	1.00	0.92	0.63	0.71	0.75	0.85	3.82
DREB	1.00	0.69	1.00	1.00	0.92	0.63	0.71	0.75	0.35	1.71
STL	1.00	1.39	1.25	1.00	0.92	0.63	1.09	1.80	1.20	2.44
BLK	1.00	1.94	1.00	1.00	0.92	0.63	0.87	1.10	0.85	0.86
Missed FG	-1.00	-0.83	-1.00	-1.00	-0.92	-0.63	-0.71	-1.00	-0.85	-1.38
Missed FT	-1.00	0.00	-0.50	-1.00	-0.92	-0.24	-0.55	-0.90	-0.45	-0.79
TOV	-1.00	-1.11	-1.25	-1.00	-0.92	-0.63	-1.09	-1.80	-1.20	-2.77
PF	0.00	0.00	-0.50	0.00	-0.46	0.00	0.00	-0.60	-0.41	-0.46

1. Requires assumption about the average number of free throws made, 2-point field goals made, and 3-point field goals made. Uses approximate current averages.
2. Assumes value of ball possession = 0.92, a value similar to what Bellotti uses.
3. Adds additional 0.5 points for each 3-point shot made.

relative weight of the different statistics to points scored (not made field goals), I assumed a certain proportion of two-point field goals, three-point field goals, and free throws based on what the NBA has seen over the last few years. Those weights are shown in table 5.1.

Steele Value

Doug Steele provides NBA statistics online and uses a number of different weights on various statistics to calculate his value. His weights are also shown below.

Heeren TENDEX

Dave Heeren has written columns about basketball statistics since the 1960s or so and has written a few *Basketball Abstract* books. His form of the equation driving value is pretty much the same as Manley's. He does include a modifier to account for the pace of the game, but that doesn't really change the weights.

Bellotti Points Created

Bob Bellotti wrote a series of books that used an equation very similar to Manley's and Heeren's. Rather than assuming one for all the weights, he insisted that weights be assigned based on the "value of a ball possession," which he said was about 0.92. He also gave a weight to personal fouls.

Claerbaut Quality Points

David Claerbaut wrote a book called *The NBA Analyst* (I seem to be selling a lot of other guys' books here). His system was a bit more convoluted, giving credit to players who shot better than 50 percent from the field and 75 percent from the line. I found a way to reduce it so that it took the same form as all the rest. As you can see from the table, he ends up weighting a lot of the nonscoring statistics relatively less than other methods.

Mays Magic Metric

The Mays Consulting Group has a site on the Internet where they generate the results of their statistic. This one based its weights upon a bunch of equations describing their assumptions. Like the Hoopstat Grade and Quality Points, I had to assume a proportion of different made shots to estimate the weights shown above.

Schaller TPR

Joe Schaller is an Internet writer who does Total Performance Ratings (TPR), stating that this statistic represents "real life value." It again uses an estimated "point value of a ball possession" (analogous to what I call a "play"), which Schaller pegs at 0.9. It has some of the other twists mentioned above, plus a few more. It accounts for team defense, game pace, positional norm, schedule strength, projected improvement or decline, and team wins, though it's not clear how.

Hollinger PER

John Hollinger assembled the book *Pro Basketball Prospectus* after years of writing on the Internet (including time with me at the precursor to *About.com*). The numbers above use his stated value of possession of 1.02, his stated values of rebounding percentages, and so forth. He adjusts for pace and rescales all values to a league average of fifteen. His is also the only one of these measures that includes some accounting for team context, incorporating how frequently a team's baskets are assisted on.

Berri Individual Wins

David Berri is a professor of economics at Cal State Bakersfield. He published a paper in 1999 introducing a method that estimates the number of wins for which players are responsible using a form somewhat like the one above. His weights were rigorously determined from a technical analysis of the data, and the results show teammates' wins summing pretty well to team totals of wins. The weights of his method are the most extreme of all, giving a lot of weight to rebounds, steals, and turnovers. Berri makes adjustments at the end of his calculations to put players in the context of their positions, which helps account for a seeming bias against smaller players. The weights shown in the table are from

1998 data and would change if different years were used, though probably not by a lot.

With ten different rationales for weights and nine different weighting schemes, the ranges of value placed on the different statistics get to be pretty big (see table 5.2). The most uncertain statistic is offensive rebounds, which could be nearly four times as valuable as a point scored or only 60 percent as valuable as a point scored (see table below). But the ranges of nearly all others are about one point. The reason for ranges this big is that the form of the equation presented at the start of this chapter—adding the good statistics and subtracting the bad ones— just doesn't fit basketball. The equation doesn't really mean anything, so how could it fit basketball? In the third chapter of this teamwork section, you will see very different-looking formulas that use standard statistics plus this chapter's concepts of how teammates interact to generate points. There you will see that the formulas do a lot more than sum the good things and subtract the bad.

Table 5.2. Assigned Weights Ranges and Averages

Statistic	Minimum	Maximum	Range	Average
PTS	1	1	0	1
AST	0.63	1.39	0.75	0.99
OREB	0.63	3.82	3.19	1.19
DREB	0.35	1.71	1.36	0.88
STL	0.63	2.44	1.80	1.27
BLK	0.63	1.94	1.31	1.02
Missed FG	-1.38	-0.63	0.75	-0.93
Missed FT	-1.00	0.00	1.00	-0.63
TOV	-2.77	-0.63	2.13	-1.28
PF	-0.60	0.00	0.60	-0.24

Chapter 6

Rebounding Myths and Roles

I listen to the radio a lot when I'm doing research or editing. The other day, an ad for bail bonds came on—*Next time you're in jail, think of us!* I don't end up in jail much, let's just say. So when I heard this ad, I immediately changed the channel to avoid thinking about why I was part of the targeted audience of that station.

Another time a few years ago, the radio ran ads for a vet who had a month-long special of half-price neutering and spaying... and my cat ran away. My dog still sat at my feet and came when I called him. Friends who are cat lovers like to tell me that this event was proof that cats are smarter than dogs.

Such is the life I lead. People love to take full advantage of little stories to teach me lessons. *Cats are smarter than dogs.* Or, *You shouldn't write so much, you'll end up in jail.* They're very funny.

People jump on isolated events as proof of cause and effect, even if they're not just making fun of me. In basketball, there is this one: *Three-point shots are easier for the offense to rebound than two-point shots.* When Bill Walton sees a three-point shot rebounded by the offense, he says this. He's not making fun of me when he says it (at least not that I know of), and he definitely ain't funny. So he must be serious. And, well, he's wrong.

For years, I wondered about this conventional wisdom and never bothered to track it very well. But I did look at statistics for teams that took a lot of three-point shots, and they didn't get many offensive rebounds. They generally rebounded a lot fewer of their own shots than other teams. But that was all I could really say until the Internet came along. Thank Gore for the Internet (or whoever really invented it)! Yes, now that *ESPN.com*, *Sportsline.com*, and *NBA.com* offer play-by-plays online, I have actually been able to look at this. It's a bear to actually deal with all of their ads and how they like to split up the play-by-play into different periods, but I just turn on the radio, prepare myself for jail, and do some research.

So I collected a cross section of play-by-plays, definitely not as many as I'd like to collect but enough to feel pretty comfortable with what I was seeing. I collected them for numerous games between 1999 and 2002 and for various teams to get a reasonable cross section. Over the few thousand missed shots that I tracked, 33 percent of all two-pointers were rebounded by the offense, and 31 percent of all three-pointers were rebounded by the offense. Fewer three-pointers were rebounded by the offense—counter the myth—but it really was about the same. And, frankly, I'm sure just as many dogs as cats ran away during that half-price special.

The primary reason to think that three-point shots would be rebounded more frequently by the offense than two-point shots is that they do create some longer rebounds, ones that go past the defenders blocking out and into an area where the defense's rebounding position is not as good. I would agree that longer rebounds should be rebounded relatively more often by the offense, but I can't check that hunch with the play-by-plays. The reason the numbers don't support three-point shots resulting in more offensive rebounds is twofold. First, long rebounds can come from two-point shots. Mid-range jumpers and almost any shot off the glass can go long, into an area where the defense doesn't have an advantage. Blown dunks definitely can generate long rebounds. Three-point shots don't necessarily have to generate long rebounds either. Second and probably more importantly, of two-point shots, the real close ones lead to a fair number of offensive rebounds because the person shooting the close shot often has good offensive rebounding position. There are lots of sequences in which an offensive player gets inside position on a missed shot, gets the rebound, puts it up, misses, gets another... Lather, rinse, repeat. Or the offensive team gets the rebound because a shooter has good position near the basket and defenders double-team him, leaving another player available for an easy offensive rebound.

Getting offensive rebounds on two-point shots is really no harder than on three-point shots. Strike that one down as a myth.

Where Rebounding Fits

Such myths arise in part because rebounds are relatively poorly understood by basketball people. Some people say that rebounds win championships in spite of clear examples to the contrary: the Lakers of 2002 and the Rockets of 1994 and 1995 won championships without being good rebounding teams. The box in the last chapter showed how analysts have placed widely different weights on both offensive and defensive rebounds in trying to equate them to points. Those analysts say that rebounds might be worth anywhere from 0.6 points to 3.8 points, a huge range. There is even disagreement over how best to get rebounds. Some say you should block out, whereas others say you should just go after the ball.

Rebounding also doesn't necessarily have a defined place in basketball. Some coaching books have one section for offense, one section for defense, and one section for rebounding—as though it is neither offense nor defense. It shouldn't be that way, though. There is offense and there is defense. Period. Rebounding is a *skill* that is associated with both. Just as shooting and establishing a strong pivot foot are offensive skills, offensive rebounding is an offensive skill. Just as moving your feet laterally is a defensive skill, defensive rebounding is a defensive skill. The offensive points per hundred possessions ratings used in this book are improved by offensive rebounding. The defensive points per hundred possessions ratings are improved by defensive rebounding. It's that simple. Offensive rebounding is an offensive skill. Defensive rebounding is a defensive skill.

Rebounding is rarely taught this way, though. Offensive and defensive rebounding seem to be taught together, with all the big men in practice going to one end of the court to work on establishing good position, keeping the ball high, or reading how the ball comes off the backboard. Those may be tactics common to offensive and defensive rebounding, but the two really are different skills and require different mentalities.

On the offensive end, a rebounder has to find space to get around defenders and get close to the basket, where he is frequently poorly guarded due to defensive confusion and inside position. That makes an offensive rebounder a potentially *very* efficient scorer. John Maxwell, public relations director of the Charlotte Sting, did a study on WNBA offensive rebounds supporting this assertion. He found that offensive rebounders improve their field goal percentage from about 41 percent to 48 percent and their points per play from about 0.80 to 0.94. That improved the *team's* points per play from about 0.80 to 0.90. That kind of difference is *huge!* It is the difference between an average offense and a truly great offense. Not only does an offensive rebound preserve a possession, it really does provide an easier opportunity to score.[1] That is important.

In contrast, a defensive rebounder typically starts out with a position advantage, being nearer the basket than offensive players he's trying to keep away. It is at least as important for him to maintain that position as to go after the ball. Maintaining that position keeps an offensive player, even if he does get the board, from being too close to the basket and having a wide-open look. Coaches should teach blocking out as a skill to all players, including guards, because it emphasizes the defensive goal of staying with your man.

As an example of how important converting and defending offensive rebounds can be, just look at the 2002 threepeating® Lakers. Even though their offensive rebounding percentage was only 29 percent compared to their opponents' 28 percent, the Lakers had a large advantage in converting offensive rebounds to points. According to Stuart McKibbin, who tracked a large series of Lakers games, the Lakers scored about 1.1 points per play off of offensive rebounds, relative to 0.95 on other plays (a 20 percent improvement). On the defensive end, they held opponents to only 0.96 points per play off of offensive rebounds, relative to 0.88 on plays that didn't involve an offensive rebound (a 10 percent improvement). Shaq and company (about ⅔ of the scores were Shaq's) were a lot more efficient at turning those offensive rebounds into points than they allowed their opponents to be.

So do you get it? Do you now understand better the importance of rebounding? In my book—and this is my book—offensive rebounding improves offensive ratings and defensive rebounding improves defensive ratings. If you're ever unsure about the value of rebounds, remember that.

Does Rebounding Win Games?

One way that people have looked at the importance of rebounding relative to other stats is by identifying the team that wins the rebounding battle and seeing whether that team wins the ball game. STATS *Basketball Scoreboard* of 1994–95 did the first study I saw on this. It's a simple way of looking at statistics and how well they correlate with winning. Their results (summarized in table 6.1) showed field goal percentage being "the most important," as teams that had the higher field goal percentage won about 79 percent of the games. Defensive rebounding ranked third with a "winning percentage" of 75 percent.[2] Offensive rebounding was way down their list; teams that had more offensive rebounds than their opponents actually won only 49.7 percent of the games.

As STATS pointed out, defensive rebounding ends up so high on the list because it is so highly correlated with field goal percentage. If the Pacers shoot well and the Pistons shoot poorly, the Pacers will have more defensive boards than the Pistons assuming that each team rebounds the same *percentage* of missed shots. And it's that percentage that is interesting, not the total.

So I decided to redo the STATS study with a couple of little modifications to understand better how rebounding fits in with everything else. First of all, I used more recent data—from 1998 to 2002. To make sure that results are similar to theirs, examine table 6.2.

I've shortened the list of statistics and added offensive rebounding percentage and assist-to-turnover ratio. The overall flavor of the STATS list is preserved, though, with field goal percentage at the top, defensive rebounds in at number three, assists still high, and offensive rebounds quite low. In my table, blocks and steals have practically identical win-loss records as those that STATS published.

Table 6.1. Winning Percentage with Statistical Edge over Opponent 1992–1994

Category	Pct
Field Goal Percentage	0.787
Field Goals Made	0.756
Defensive Rebounds	0.750
Assists	0.720
Total Rebounds	0.679
Free Throws Made	0.649
Fewer Personal Fouls	0.647
Free Throws Attempted	0.637
3-pt Field Goal Percentage	0.614
Blocks	0.609
Steals	0.596
Fewer Turnovers	0.586
Free Throw Percentage	0.556
3-pt Field Goals Made	0.520
Offensive Rebounds	0.497
Flagrant Fouls	0.489
Ejections	0.487
Technicals	0.484
Field Goals Attempted	0.455
Disqualifications	0.442
3-pt Field Goals Attempted	0.408

NOTE: From STATS *Basketball Scoreboard* 1994–95, p. 136.

Table 6.2. W–L Record with Statistical Edge over Opponent 1998–2002

Category	Won	Lost	Tied	Pct	STATS Pct.
Field Goal Percentage	4595	1132	33	0.801	0.787
Assists	4007	1414	339	0.725	0.720
Defensive Rebounds	3984	1485	291	0.717	0.750
Assist-to-Turnover Ratio	3991	1717	52	0.697	N/A
Total Rebounds	3526	1959	275	0.636	0.679
Free Throws Made	3453	2022	284	0.624	0.649
Blocks	3182	1930	648	0.609	0.609
Free Throw Attempts	3358	2174	228	0.603	0.637
Fewer Personal Fouls	3256	2094	410	0.601	0.647
Steals	3148	2037	575	0.596	0.596
Fewer Turnovers	3114	2186	460	0.581	0.586
Free Throw Percentage	3224	2459	77	0.566	0.556
Offensive Rebounding Percentage	3205	2513	42	0.560	N/A
Offensive Rebounds	2452	2900	408	0.461	0.497

In general, total defensive rebounds and offensive rebounds are slightly less valuable using the more recent data, but not by much.

This gross comparison of total rebounds says something *simple*, but not something *clear*. As STATS pointed out, the correlation between defensive rebounds and field goal percentage blurs the value of defensive rebounds. What if you look only at games in which field goal percentage is about the same for two teams? Table 6.3 begins to isolate the value of some of the other stats that may be correlated. Field goal percentage and defensive rebounds go to near the bottom

Table 6.3. W–L Record with Statistical Edge over Opponent 1998–2002, FG% Approximately Equal

Category	Won	Lost	Tied	Pct
Free Throws Made	730	284	55	0.709
Assist-to-Turnover Ratio	739	319	11	0.696
Fewer Turnovers	694	282	93	0.693
Free Throw Attempts	691	322	56	0.673
Fewer Personal Fouls	675	307	87	0.672
Steals	646	318	105	0.653
Offensive Rebounds	634	351	84	0.632
Offensive Rebounding Percentage	666	391	12	0.629
Total Rebounds	621	390	58	0.608
Free Throw Percentage	639	416	14	0.604
Assists	593	389	87	0.595
Field Goal Percentage	579	457	33	0.557
Defensive Rebounds	524	461	84	0.529
Blocks	487	447	135	0.519

of the list (with blocks). Free throws and turnovers shoot to the top of the list. Offensive rebounds and offensive rebounding percentage become more relevant than they previously appeared to be, but they are not quite as important as free throws and turnovers. What this implies is that, in games where teams shoot about the same, getting to the line and committing fewer turnovers become generally more important than offensive rebounding.

What happens if you isolate games in which field goal percentage *and* assist-to-turnover ratio are about even? Does this change the relative status of free throws and rebounding? No. Free throws still end up being a deciding factor in 70 to 80 percent of games (table 6.4), in contrast to rebounds, which are the deciding factor in 60 to 65 percent of such games.

Table 6.4. W–L Record with Statistical Edge over Opponent 1998–2002, FG% and AST/TOV Approximately Equal

Category	Won	Lost	Tied	Pct
Free Throws Made	164	44	6	0.780
Free Throw Attempts	153	49	12	0.743
Fewer Personal Fouls	144	57	13	0.703
Total Rebounds	136	69	9	0.657
Offensive Rebounds	130	68	16	0.645
Defensive Rebounds	128	72	14	0.631
Offensive Rebounding Percentage	133	79	2	0.626
Free Throw Percentage	132	78	4	0.626
Fewer Turnovers	108	68	38	0.593
Steals	114	76	24	0.589
Assist-to-Turnover Ratio	109	94	11	0.535
Blocks	97	94	23	0.507
Field Goal Percentage	102	103	9	0.498
Assists	74	109	31	0.418

You could continue this analysis *ad infinitum*. You could even say that offensive rebounds create free throw attempts (though you could be wrong). But doing a thorough analysis gets very complicated. And that simply ain't gonna happen here.

But just look at what statistics are left after removing field goal percentage, assist-to-turnover ratio, and free throw attempts: offensive rebounding percentage, turnovers, steals, and blocks. None of these stats really tells you how well a player creates a good shot for himself, which is such a critical factor in basketball. So to look any deeper is to surely miss the most important aspects of the game.

So, is rebounding important to winning games? Of course. Is it as valuable as shooting, getting to the line, or controlling the ball? In the NBA, it doesn't appear to be so,[3] though, as mentioned above, offensive rebounds do help to improve shooting percentages, something that is hard to factor into this analysis. In high school and college leagues, I would suspect that rebounding may be even more important.

Endnotes

1. Maxwell has proposed a new statistic that multiplies offensive rebounding percentage by a team's points per play following an offensive rebound to get Offensive Rebounding Efficiency. I do not have thorough data for this except for the WNBA teams he studied from 2001. Those numbers are available online at *http://www.fullcourt.com/columns/canyon11202 .html*.

2. STATS actually showed a winning percentage of 76.4 percent. This is because they did not include ties in their calculation of winning percentage.

3. This way of looking at "winningest statistics" by equalizing some out and rechecking team records can be considered loosely similar to the multivariate regression that Professor Dave Berri did in evaluating NBA data. What he did is like taking this technique to the greatest extreme, saying, "But if these three stats are equal, this becomes important, etc." Berri's technique, however, requires a model for how offensive rebounds (and all other stats) create points. In creating such a model, he arrived at the distinctly different conclusion that offensive rebounds were extremely important. Neither Professor Berri nor I have been able to reconcile this difference.

Chapter 7

The Significance of Derrick Coleman's Insignificance

Something that is called "significant" is something that matters. We should care about it and not ignore it. To our parents, cleaning our room was significant—we should do that—but counting all our baseball cards was not—they didn't care if we did that. For basketball coaches who have enough to worry about, it would be helpful to have a tool that tells them when a player substitution is significantly better or significantly worse than another. There is actually a tool for doing just this. "Significance testing" is a tool used to numerically assess whether we should care about certain basketball events. For example, the 2001 Los Angeles Lakers went 45–23 (66 percent) with Kobe Bryant in the lineup but 11–3 (79 percent) without Kobe. Does this mean that the Lakers were better without Kobe? Was this result "significant" enough to say such a counterintuitive thing? Significance testing says no. It very easily could have been a random fluke. I'll illustrate in this chapter how significance testing can tell useful stories about player value, using as an example one of the most publicized cases of how a player's presence hurt his team. That would be when Derrick Coleman was with the (then Charlotte) Hornets between 1999 and 2001.

Brought over from Philadelphia to provide some veteran guidance, Derrick Coleman played power forward on this young Hornets team. But over the course of the three years he was with them, the Hornets were an ordinary 74–80 when he was in the lineup and a rather dominating 54–20 when he sat out. The Hornets were aware of this, their fans were aware of this, *Sports Illustrated* was aware of this (they ran a little blurb), and Coleman must have known about it, too. It may have been a mystery why his presence was so negative, but it was no mystery at the end of the 2001 season that the Hornets found a way to get rid of him.

So What Did Coleman Do to Cause This Kind of Difference?

The first question to ask of Coleman's effect on Charlotte is whether that difference in winning percentage was "significant." It sure *seems* that way with so many games played. But there is a way to say how significant it is. Specifically, there is a way to say what chance there was that such a split occurred just through bad luck.[1] For example, it's pretty obvious that a team like the Lakers of 2002, which won 70 percent of its games, could go 2–2 in a four-game stretch and it wouldn't signal anything to panic about. The team is pretty much the same. Basically, a 2–2 stretch is just a random blip on the record of a team that wins fifty-eight of eighty-two games. But an 8–8 stretch starts to seem different. Or, if the team is not the Lakers but, say, Duke University, which has been winning 90 to 95 percent of its games for the last few years, even a 2–2 stretch may mean something a bit more significant. Significance testing accounts for the number of games in a stretch, how well the team played in those games, and how well they were "supposed" to play.

With regard to Coleman, significance testing says that there was a 0.02 percent chance (or two in ten thousand) that the difference between the Hornets' record with and without him was due to just random chance. *Something* real was different. Tracking down what it was starts with doing significance tests on the team's offensive and defensive ratings. Offensively, the Hornets scored 103.0 points per hundred possessions with Coleman in the lineup. Without him, the Hornets scored 103.9 points per hundred possessions. This kind of difference—103.0 to 103.9—is small and turns out not to be significant, as it could have occurred by pure luck with a 56 percent chance. For reference, if significance testing returns a number greater than 5 percent, it is common to consider the difference in question to be simply the result of luck.[2] In contrast, the Hornets' defensive rating improved from 102.5 to 98.6 without Coleman—a much bigger change and significant at 1.6 percent. The Hornets legitimately did play better on the defensive end when Coleman wasn't on the floor.

A key thing in doing this kind of analysis is to understand that it doesn't reflect purely upon Derrick Coleman. It also reflects upon the player who replaces Coleman in the lineup. If the player replacing Coleman were Tim Duncan and the Hornets played so much better, we'd say, "Duh, why was Coleman playing anyway?" If his replacement is a player (or players) who has been in and out of the NBA, then there is more mystery. Is the sub actually a good player? Were Coleman's teammates playing poorly with him on the floor because Coleman exudes some negative energy? In this case, since this discrepancy in winning percentage grew out of three seasons of the Hornets playing better with Coleman out, there were a lot of different players replacing him in the lineup. Rather than looking at

Table 7.1. Effect of Derrick Coleman's Presence on Charlotte Hornets

Season	Games Played	Minutes/ Game	W–L	Pts per 100 Poss.	
				Off.	Def.
			With Coleman		
1999	37	31.8	15–22	102.2	104.5
2000	78	32.3	44–34	103.5	102.2
2001	39	19.8	15–24	101.1	101.3
Totals	**154**	**29.0**	**74–80**	**103.0**	**102.5**

Season	Games Missed	W–L	Pts per 100 Poss.		Primary Replacements
			Off.	Def.	
		Without Coleman			
1999	13	11–2*	105.3	99.3*	Chucky Brown, Brad Miller, J.R. Reid, Charles Shackleford
2000	8	6–2	104.2	98.3	Chucky Brown, Brad Miller, Eddie Robinson, Todd Fuller
2001	53	37–16*	103.5	98.5	Jamaal Magloire + increased minutes by starters
Totals	**74**	**54–20***	**103.9**	**98.6***	

*Indicates statistically significant difference from Games with Coleman (at 5%).

the seasons as a group, you get a cleaner story by looking at the three seasons individually. Table 7.1 summarizes the three seasons.

In 1999, Coleman missed thirteen of fifty games in a strike-shortened year and was replaced by a committee of journeymen: Chucky Brown, J.R. Reid, Charles Shackleford, and Brad Miller (though Miller has recently come to be viewed as a pretty good player). The Hornets went 11–2 in the games Coleman missed and 15–22 in the games he played. As with the overall three years, the defense in 1999 was significantly better without him, going from 104.5 to 99.3. Were these four players significantly better defensively than Coleman? By reputation, no one has really said so, but the numbers suggest it.

In 2000, Coleman missed only eight of eighty-six total games (including play-offs), the Hornets going 6–2 in those eight games. They went 44–34 in the games Coleman played, the difference between these two records not being statistically significant, mainly because eight games is not a lot of games on which to base an argument. Though the Hornets again did play better defensively when Coleman wasn't there, going from 102.2 to 98.3 in their defensive rating, this difference was not significant at 5 percent (more like 15 percent). Again, his replacement was a committee of non-stars, including Chucky Brown, Brad Miller, Eddie Robinson, and Todd Fuller.

Finally, in 2001, Coleman was replaced in the starting lineup at the beginning of the season by P.J. Brown and was relegated to only twenty minutes per game. Even with fewer minutes, Coleman's apparent negative influence on defense continued. When Coleman was in the lineup, the team defense allowed 101.3 points per hundred possessions and the team went 15–24. When he was out of the lineup, the team defense allowed 98.5 points per hundred possessions and the team went 37–16 (including playoffs). Interestingly, the offense also got better this year with Coleman's absence, going from 101.1 to 103.5. Neither the offensive nor the defensive splits were significant on their own, but the combination of improvements was significant. Unlike previous seasons, the Hornets filled Coleman's missing minutes primarily by increasing the time starters played. Off the bench, Jamaal Magloire also picked up some of Coleman's time.

In every season, the Hornets' offense and defense both improved when Coleman was out, but only the defensive improvement was statistically significant over the long haul and in any individual season. This then focuses the study on a defensive mechanism. What did Coleman do poorly *defensively* that guys like Chucky Brown and Jamaal Magloire did better? (Note that we don't need to talk about things like Coleman's passing or poor shot-making decisions since the numbers don't suggest significant offensive changes.) In order to answer the question of Coleman's defensive shortcoming(s), let me put forth again the four basic aspects of the game that a team must try to control:

1. Shooting percentage from the field.
2. Getting offensive rebounds.
3. Committing turnovers.
4. Going to the foul line a lot and making the shots.

These aspects of the game came up a few chapters ago when I was looking at history's worst teams and trying to identify what they did so wrong. And you'll see them again, so get used to them. With regard to understanding the Coleman Effect, I look to answer the following four related questions:

1. Did opponent field goal percentage go up with Coleman in the lineup?
2. Did opponents rebound a higher proportion of their own misses with Coleman in the lineup?
3. Did teams commit fewer turnovers with Coleman in the lineup?
4. Did teams get to the foul line more often against the Hornets when Coleman was in the lineup? (If teams shoot better from the line against the Hornets with Coleman in the lineup, that would seem to be luck and not something that could be fixed.)

In short, the most important of these four questions seems to be the first one, which addresses the shooting percentage of Hornets' opponents. Over the course of the three seasons, table 7.2 shows how the four above categories broke down with and without Coleman.

Table 7.2. Charlotte's Four Factors with and without Coleman

	DFG% (Q1)	DFG2% (Q1)	DFG3% (Q1)	DOR% (Q2)	DTOV per Poss. (Q3)	DFTA per DFGA (Q4)
With DC	0.443	0.457	0.367	0.274	0.157	0.294
Without DC	0.424	0.440	0.337	0.261	0.158	0.294
Sig:	0.01	0.02	0.09	0.10	0.43	0.48

NOTE: Looking at individual seasons tells a similar story.

In terms of the Hornets forcing turnovers and sending teams to the line, there really was no difference with or without Coleman in the lineup. Opponents did rebound their missed shots slightly better against the Coleman teams, but not enough for us to say convincingly that it made a difference. On the other hand, teams legitimately shot much better against the Hornets from inside the arc when Coleman played and possibly better against them from outside the arc, too. The exact nature of the mechanism is not perfectly clear, but it appears to be several things. If teams shot better only from the outside, it would suggest either that Coleman didn't rotate out very well or that perimeter players had to help him more down low and didn't get back to their own men. If teams shot better only from the inside, it would simply suggest that Coleman couldn't stop his man or didn't provide the same interior help as guys who replaced him did.

As I'll discuss in a later chapter, individual defense is probably the most poorly documented *significant* part of the game. Looking at the effect a player has on his team in and out of the lineup is one of the best current ways to track down issues of individual defense. But using this technique doesn't allow a detailed description of cause.

As a final postscript, when Philadelphia inherited Charlotte's problem, the Coleman Effect showed some indication of carrying over. Though not statistically significant, the Sixers did go 31–32 with Coleman and 14–10 without him. And the difference again seemed to be defense.

Other Players

The Coleman split was perhaps the most prominent case where a team played much better without a player, but there are plenty of other interesting cases where a prominent player missed time and we all made judgments about his value by what happened during that time. This type of test is not a definitive measure of player value, but it provides some interesting indicators.

Michael Jordan, Washington 2002

Before Jordan's second return to the NBA, there were many guesses about what his effect would be on the Wizards' win-loss record. The typical guess was in the thirty-win range, and that was pretty accurate with the Wiz winning thirty-seven. But Jordan could have brought them more victories. In games that Jordan played, the Wizards were 30–30. Without him, they were 7–15. This was significant at 7 percent. The big difference that Jordan brought was not his jump shot, but his defense. With Jordan, the Wizards allowed 102.6 points per hundred possessions. Without him, 106.9. And that was significant at 5 percent. He was doing something to improve the overall team defense. The Wizards did keep their opponents' field goal percentage down with Jordan in there, but the most significant aspect of Jordan's presence was that, hmmm, teams took a lot fewer foul shots when he was around. The effect was especially striking because the Wizards got called for a lot more fouls when Jordan wasn't in the game—23.9 per game versus only 20.6 per game when he was in—and that sent opponents to the line five times more per game, which adds up to a lot of free points. Whether that was Jordan being a leader, or Jordan playing such solid D that he kept his teammates from having to foul, or just Jordan intimidating the referees—that's something the Washington coaching staff could look into.

Steve Francis, Houston 2002

The difference in the Rockets' record was remarkable, 2–21 without him, 26–31 with him. Oscar Torres, Tierre Brown, and Moochie Norris should be ashamed because they were his primary replacements. What did they do so poorly? Offense. The team's offensive ratings declined from 102.6 to 98.7 with these three trying to fill Francis's shoes. In contrast to the Jordan situation, this one was pretty obvious. Francis was known as a tremendous generator of good shots for himself and others. Torres, Brown, and Norris weren't really known for anything except Norris's haircut.

Ron Artest, Chicago-Indiana 2002

Artest began to be hailed as one of the best defensive players in the league in 2002, a stopper of perimeter players. He was very upset that he received not a single vote for Defensive Player of the Year. He didn't even make the Second Team All-Defense. Given the media coverage of his defensive prowess, it was surprising that he didn't make any All-Defense teams. But what effect did he have on his teams' defense? He played for two different teams, and we can at least get a sense of how well each team did with and without him. Chicago's defensive rating in games that he played was 102.0 and a considerably worse 107.7 without him. This was a rather significant difference, supporting the hoopla. But—yes, there is a "but"—when you look at a couple of other splits, he doesn't look as good. First of all, Indiana improved only from 102.6 to 100.9 with Artest in the lineup, an insignificant difference. Second, because Artest was injured at the start of the year in Chicago, we have Bulls games before the trade with and without Artest to compare. Effectively, we're comparing his defense to Trenton Hassell's and Fred Hoiberg's, the biggest recipients of his missing time early on, rather than comparing his defense to Jalen Rose's and Travis Best's, the biggest recipients of his time after the trade. During that period, the Bulls' defense dropped only from 102.6 to 103.6, not to 107.7, and wasn't very significant. Overall, there are some statistical indicators to suggest that Artest is a good defender, but his indicators aren't as strong as those for...

Dikembe Mutombo, Atlanta-Philadelphia 2001

This four-time Defensive Player of the Year was the big prize in the trading deadline exchange of the 2001 season. Philly felt like they needed him to have a chance to win a title (though they still got killed by the Lakers), and Atlanta knew that they couldn't build around him. The trade sent Mutombo to Philadelphia in exchange for Toni Kukoc, Nazr Mohammed, and the injured Theo Ratliff. With Ratliff hurt the rest of 2001, the Hawks really just lost their defensive presence. In that 2001 season, the Hawks without Mutombo and without Ratliff had a defensive rating of 110.0. With Mutombo, their defensive rating was 100.5. You can bet that difference was significant. The Hawks' defense continued to suffer into 2002 with Ratliff remaining on the injured list. Note, however, that there was a price to pay for Mutombo's defense. The offense in Atlanta was significantly worse with him, but only by three points, much smaller than the ten points they picked up on the defensive end by having him there. In Philadelphia, as testimony to the quality of Ratliff's defense, the team defense was almost unchanged by filling Ratliff's slot with Mutombo.

Bruce Bowen, San Antonio 2002

Like Artest, Bowen was considered to be a pretty good man defender, though he didn't do much to stop Kobe Bryant in the playoffs that year. Bowen missed twenty-three games between January and the end of February, during which time the Spurs won only eleven. The announcers in the playoffs liked to point this out as indicative of his value. What is interesting, however, is why he seemed to be valuable. With Bowen, the Spurs' ratings were 108.6 and 99.1 on the offense and defense, respectively. Without him, they went to 101.3 and 101.2—the offense taking the biggest plunge. Only the offensive number is statistically significant at all. Digging a little deeper, though, it becomes apparent that part of the difference was due to schedule. The Spurs played a lot of good teams while Bowen was out. If you compare games only across common opponents with and without Bowen, he appears to be more of a factor. In such games, when Bowen played, the offensive rating was 107.5 and the defensive rating was 97.1. The offensive difference is still significant, but the defensive difference is now approaching significance too. The guys who replaced Bowen were principally Charles C. Smith, Antonio Daniels, and Stephen Jackson. This analysis doesn't speak too highly of them.

Shaquille O'Neal, Los Angeles 2000 to 2002

There were no surprises with O'Neal as there were with Bowen. One of the most dominant big men in history was missed when he was out, and he missed twenty-six games over this period due to injury. In those games, the Lakers went 13–13, in contrast to their .768 winning percentage when Shaq played. The big difference was the offense, which went from 109.1 to 103.9 when he was out, meaning Kobe Bryant couldn't carry the Lakers to much better than average, interestingly. The defense didn't change significantly, going from 101.8 to 102.5. Mark Madsen, Stanislav Medvedenko, and Samaki Walker may have been able to handle the defensive responsibilities, but no one was going to mistake them for threats around the basket.

Allen Iverson, Philadelphia 2000 to 2002

For all the complaints about his bad shots, the Sixers won 62 percent of their games with him and only 48 percent without him. And you know what the difference was? Offense. With Iverson, the Sixers' offense managed to score 103.7 points per hundred possessions. Without him, only 98.2. The defense hardly changed, going from 101.0 to 100.4. But that is roughly five points per game that the Sixers lost on the offensive end without this guy making "bad decisions" on the court. The Sixers as a team did *everything* better when Iverson was out there (except get offensive rebounds). The most significant things they did better with Iverson were to get to the line more and to take/make more threes. What players took his minutes and were to blame for the offensive downfall when he was out? Kevin Ollie, Raja Bell, Speedy Claxton, and, uh, the aforementioned offensive contributor to the Spurs, Bruce Bowen.

Endnotes

1. The basic test used here is the two sample unequal variance student t-test, as one-tailed or two-tailed depending upon the situation. It used the Excel function TTEST(Array1, Array2, Tails, Type), with Tails = 1 or 2 and Type = 3.

2. Strictly, the lower the percentage you set, the more confidence you can have in your assertions. You can say that this offensive difference was significant, but you're just more likely to be wrong. Which never stops Bill Walton.

Chapter 8

Amos Tversky's Basketball Legacy

Y ou may not know who Amos Tversky was, so let me give you some background. Tversky was a psychologist. He didn't help anyone to get over lost loves or to stop feeling guilty about cheating on that lost love who has now come back. If anything, he made people feel more guilty about the way they thought about things. Tversky was known as a cognitive psychologist, someone who tried to understand how people think about and make decisions in the world. Then he showed people why they were wrong to think that way. Really— that is a lot of what he did. Definitely not Dr. Feelgood.

Perhaps the classic example of how Tversky worked was in his posing the following hypothetical example to people[1]:

> Threatened by a superior enemy force, a general faces a dilemma. His intelligence officers say his soldiers will be caught in an ambush in which 600 of them will die unless he leads them to safety by one of two available routes. If he takes route A, 200 soldiers will be saved. If he takes route B, there's a one-third chance that 600 soldiers will be saved and a two-thirds chance that none will be saved. Which route should he take?

Which route do *you* take? Most people opt for route A. Maybe "most people" aren't reading my book, in which case you're a troublesome group of readers. But most people do seem to avoid gambling with lives in this case. That might be consistent with the "risk-averse" behavior that economists like to tell us we exhibit. Now consider another dilemma that Tversky would pose:

> The general again has to choose between two escape routes. But this time his aides tell him that if he takes route A, 400 soldiers will die. If he takes route B, there's a one-third chance that no soldiers will die, and a two-thirds chance that 600 soldiers will die. Which route should he take?

What he found was that most people chose route B. And, as I said, he made people feel guilty about the way they think because, if you look at the first scenario and the second, they are identical. Route A is the same in each and so is route B, so choosing different routes is not exactly logical. If you chose different routes as answers, you are at least "most people" (and you are reading my book! The publishers will like that!).

Tversky took people's perceptions and tested them against reality. In this case, he showed how a different choice of words directed people's decisions in light of the same reality, something that's good to remember when you hear a politician speak.

But the reason Tversky is in this book is because he tested our common perception of hot shooting against basketball reality. The belief in the hot hand is a pretty strong thing among people who have played basketball. We have felt it. We have seen times where it seemed that no matter what defense was played, we could make our shots. If Tversky is going to tell us that we weren't hot, he better have some good proof.

So here is his evidence.

Tversky's Proof

Before I go too far, I should point out that the first author on these hot hand papers was not Tversky, but Thomas Gilovich. So if you don't like the analysis, you can blame Gilovich, too. And the third coauthor, Robert Vallone.

The paper that contained the study is "The Hot Hand in Basketball: On the Misperception of Random Sequences," from *Cognitive Psychology* (an academic journal in which the work is reviewed by other people in the psychology field before being accepted) in 1985. You can tell from the title, "Misperception of Random Sequences," that the authors don't find evidence of hot streaks. The paper is strikingly well-written and doesn't require any real academic training to read it. And it is very fair to the subject, considering a lot of viewpoints of what "hot hand" can mean.

The paper ends up concluding that people's *perceptions* of streaks are stronger than any statistical evidence for them. The statistical evidence comes from these things:

1. *Field goal attempt records of the Philadelphia 76ers from the 1981 season.* The authors looked at whether any of the 1981 Sixers had a higher field goal percentage after having made a basket or after having made two baskets, etc. They found none of the Sixers to have such a pattern. Dr. J improved his shooting percentage from 52 percent to 53 percent after a made shot, and he was the one player who seemed to have even weak indications of hot shooting. Andrew Toney, who was reputed to be a streaky shooter, actually had a slight tendency to shoot better after a miss than after a make. Darryl Dawkins, who is now in this book at least

three times more than I thought he would be, actually showed a clear tendency to shoot better after a miss than after a make. Tversky and company looked at several different ways of interpreting the field goal attempts, including whether streakiness occurred on just certain nights or whether players had longer periods of improved ability that balanced out over time. They didn't find anything other than Dawkins's anti-streak shooting.

2. *Free throw attempt records of the Boston Celtics during the 1981 and 1982 seasons.* As a result of the study of field goal attempts, Gilovich and Tversky proposed two possible reasons that a hot streak wasn't evident—varying defensive pressure and varying shot selection. So they looked at foul shots because there is no defense and the shot is always the same. Again, they found no players who showed a significantly better chance of making their second shot after making their first than if they had missed the first. (Though the authors didn't point this out, their data do show that the Celtics did make a significantly higher percentage of their second free throws than their first, supporting the basketball rule of thumb that it is easier to make the second foul shot than the first.)

3. *Controlled shooting experiments with Cornell's basketball teams.* I don't know about you, but where I went to college, we had little economics experiments where graduate students tortured us for hours playing weird games with us, giving us money in return, then taking it away. For Tversky's hot hand idea, he also experimented with the minds of innocent undergraduates. In this case, Gilovich, who was at Cornell, recruited the school's players to shoot baskets, for which they got paid a certain amount for made shots. (Sounds a lot better than what I had to do.) For each player, these psychologists-cum-basketball analysts made an estimate of the approximate distance at which that player shot 50 percent. Then they had him shoot one hundred shots from that distance—without defense—in order to look for hot streaks or cold streaks. This was generally an improvement over the free throw attempt examination because it wasn't just a series of two foul shots followed by a break, when the hot streak could go away. What the authors saw was the same. Of the twenty-six shooters, only one showed strong indication of streakiness. One player out of twenty-six does not provide much support for the existence of a broad-based hot hand throughout the general basketball-playing populace.

4. *Predictions of shooting ability.* Gilovich made those Cornell basketball players into gamblers. On top of the money he paid for made shots, he

had them bet on whether they would make the next shot. He also assigned an observer to each shooter, and that observer would also bet on whether the shooter would make the next shot (without knowledge of the shooter's bet). It turned out that both the shooter's bet and the observer's bet correlated very well with whether the previous shot went in—a lot better than with the upcoming shot. So most people do see one shot as a cue for the next one—believing in the hot hand in general—but few shooters actually showed a hot hand.

That was Tversky's contribution to basketball—debunking the hot hand. The evidence was reviewed by a lot of smart people before it was published in a very reputable place, but there is more to the story.

Yes, Virginia, There Is a Hot Hand

Dear Editor: I am eight years old. Some of my friends say there is no Hot Hand. Papa says, "If you see it in The Game, it is so." Please tell me the truth, is there a Hot Hand?

— Virginia

Virginia: Your little friends are wrong. They have been affected by the skepticism of a skeptical age. They do not believe except that which they calculate. They think that nothing can be which is not supported by their little numbers. All minds, Virginia, whether they be men's or children's are little. In this great game of ours, man is a mere insect, an ant in his intellect, as compared with the boundless world about him, as measured by the intelligence capable of grasping the whole of truth and knowledge.

Yes, Virginia, there is a Hot Hand. It exists as certainly as love and home court advantage and Michael Jordan exist, and you know that they abound and give to your life its highest beauty and joy. Alas! How dreary would be the world if there were no Hot Hand! It would be as dreary as if there were no Virginias. There would be no childlike faith then, no autographs, no hero worship to make tolerable the excesses of sport. We should have no enjoyment, except in sense and sight. The eternal light with which childhood fills the world would be extinguished.

Not believe in the Hot Hand! You might as well not believe in zone defense! You might get your papa to hire men to count all of the shots of the Philadelphia 76ers, but even if they did not see a streaky shooter, what would that prove? Nobody sees a Hot Hand, but that is no sign that there is none. The most real things in the world are those that neither children nor men can see.

No Hot Hand! Thank God, it lives, and it's on a roll. A thousand years from now, Virginia, nay, ten times ten thousand years from now, it will continue to make glad the hearts of basketball fans. [2]

Skepticism of a Skeptical Age

Amos Tversky's study on whether streak shooters exist was built on the classic skepticism of a scientist. It is a scientist's job to doubt the existence of something unless overwhelming proof can be generated in support of it. In this way, Tversky did not prove that streaks don't exist. He just stated that there was no proof that they do exist.

In our leap to the conclusion that streaks do not exist, we demonstrate our susceptibility to the skepticism of a skeptical age.

But if there is no proof that it exists, there still may be indications. For one thing, it is interesting that the NBA players generally showed an anti-streak tendency, and the college players without defense showed a slight streak tendency. Tversky correctly did not highlight this because it wasn't "statistically significant." But if there are teams out there that can identify trends before they are "statistically significant," those teams can gain a big advantage competitively.

It Exists As Certainly As Home Court Advantage

There is no denying that a home court advantage exists, intuitively or statistically. Tversky wouldn't deny it, I'm sure. But what if there were something with the power of the home court that occasionally took over within shooters? This thing improves their ability to shoot from about 50 percent to about 60 percent. It comes and goes, apparently at the whim of some faceless schedule maker. Maybe some players feel it and others don't. Tversky's tests would not have found this thing.

As a direct analogy, I'm going to use the wins and losses of the Detroit Pistons from 1993 to 2002 as a surrogate for a series of field goal attempts. The Pistons won 48 percent of their games during this period, which is, not coincidentally, close to a typical shooting percentage. The Tversky statistical tests were not set up to look at the details of the Pistons games and suggest that any offered a higher probability of a win than others. But clearly, that wasn't true. On February 20, 2002, for example, when the Pistons had won three in a row and were at home against a weak Wizards team, Tversky's tests couldn't make any prediction other than a 48 percent chance that the Pistons would win. That is because Tversky's tests couldn't see the extra information: the Pistons were playing at home against a weak team. Those statistical tests wouldn't recognize homestands as offering a relatively better chance of winning. Those tests wouldn't see a 2002 team that won 61 percent of its games. Tversky's statistical tests would show none of the real-life understanding that we had as we watched the Pistons for ten years.[3] His tests weren't sophisticated enough to capture how home-court advantage changes the odds of a team winning, so it's not surprising that they wouldn't catch whatever little things we see when a player is hot.

The Tversky paper did suggest that shooters didn't predict their own performance very well. It was that part of the paper that cheated a little bit, though. In fact, four out of twenty-six players were successful in predicting the outcomes of their next shots. Given the test that Tversky and company conducted, four out of twenty-six implies that something was cuing players in to their ability to make their next shot. And it wasn't only the players. The same number of observers—four out of twenty-six—was also able to predict the outcome of the next shot with "statistically significant" results. A truly random situation in which there is no hot hand (or anything else) to tip off what was coming next—a make or a miss—should not have allowed four out of twenty-six shooters and observers to make successful predictions.[4]

If They Did Not See a Streaky Shooter, What Would That Prove?

Tversky and his coauthors admit that there could be other factors that kept them from seeing streaky shooting. They state, for example, that the difficulty of a shot does factor into the likelihood of scoring and, hence, could be considered in assessing whether a hot hand exists. For instance, if a player hits three 20-percent shots in a row, that could be considered "statistically significant" in some way. They never looked at such low-probability shots or how players selected their shots and the variability of difficulty in those selected shots.

If a team does take several low-percentage shots in a row, it is relatively more likely that they will miss them all—and call it a cold streak. Regardless of this study, a team should look to go inside to increase its odds of making a shot or getting fouled. Maybe basketball people would call the missed shots a "cold streak" and psychologists would call it nonsense, but it's hard to dispute the cure.

Making Glad the Heart of Basketball Fans

What I really didn't like about the hot hand study was that it implied that strategy didn't matter. Covering a hot shooter was not a responsible strategy because the pattern of hits and misses is random. It implied that sticking a bunch of kids out there and letting them shoot from designated spots against no defense is about the same as a real game.

Well, that's just not true. Teams do look for matchup advantages where one player will be able to shoot better against the person covering them. Maybe they don't hit three straight when they feel "hot," but only five out of eight. That's still enough to be a useful advantage.

Maybe NBA teams overreact to the perception of a hot hand, which is why NBA players showed a tendency toward anti-streak behavior. The paper's authors do suggest this as a possibility.

I don't imagine that this research is going to change basketball people's belief in the hot hand. Maybe they believe streaks occur more often than they really do. Maybe they aren't very good at recognizing streaks. I can accept either of those possibilities.

But teams will still react to apparent streak shooting because, if streak shooting does exist, it places teams at a competitive disadvantage if they don't acknowledge it. What Tversky's paper made me realize, though, is that it's also to their competitive advantage to recognize streak shooting only as often as it does occur.

Postscript

Amos Tversky died in 1996 of skin cancer. Had he not died, many have said that he would have shared the 2002 Nobel Prize in economics with his longtime collaborator, Daniel Kahneman. Kahneman was awarded the prize for his long series of contributions to understanding human perception in the same way that Tversky's hot hand study did. Had Tversky won that prize, you might say that he'd have won the first Nobel Prize in basketball!

Endnotes

1. This and other citations were frequently developed by Tversky in cooperation with Daniel Kahneman. A list of several is available at *http://www.ac.wwu.edu/~market/tj/logic.html*.

2. With apologies to Francis Church, whose classic Christmas editorial inspired this interlude.

3. I ran a few of Tversky's statistical tests on the Pistons' data sets and saw no indication of streakiness. The probability of a win after a win was not significantly different from the probability of a win after a loss. The serial correlation was not significantly different from zero. And the number of streaks was almost exactly what would be predicted by randomness.

4. The random chance that four out of twenty-six shooters or observers would predict streaks successfully at the 95 percent significance level the authors used is only 4 percent. So there is only about a 4 percent chance that those four just got randomly lucky and did not see something real.

Chapter 9

The Power of Parity

There is a reason you bought this book and are not just scanning your one hundred eighth page while debating its purchase over a mocha at Barnes & Noble. You found some value in it, walked to the counter, pulled out your MasterCard, and said, "Priceless." Good old economics says that you valued this book at least as much as the price my publishers put on it.

Economists say a lot of things about the world, and there is a growing group of economists who say things about sports. They get together at meetings that are paid for by someone else, talk about sports, present papers about sports, and laugh at how good their job is. These are *sports economists*, people I am now proud to call friends. They are also my heroes. When I was in school and reading surveys about the best jobs around, the usual one at the top was actuary. The surveys always had to explain that an actuary is some person who basically determines the odds that insurance companies use to set your rates. Actuaries could tell you how often you'd be involved in an auto accident based on where you drive, the chances that your house would get broken into based on where you live, and the likeliest time for you to die based on everything the computers know about you. Basically, an actuary is a Las Vegas oddsmaker for things you're not allowed to bet on. The reason that is the best job is supposedly because actuaries get paid a lot to do very little. Sports economists neither get paid a lot nor do very little, but their jobs involve exactly what they love—sports, with enough economics thrown in to give their opinions a refreshingly different perspective. That sounds like a fun job.

Sports economists do have a fair amount to say about our sports, but not many people pay attention. They have a lot to say about the stupidity of the public in funding stadiums. Clearly, the public hasn't paid attention to that. Sports economists also have said that baseball's blue-ribbon panel that reviewed the finances of the league's franchises are lying through their teeth about so many franchises losing money. I think the public already knew that. Sports economists have said that big-market teams will be better than small-market teams regardless of a draft that dispenses talent to worse teams and regardless of whether there is free agency or not. That one has been hard to swallow.

But sports economists struggle with the value of sports themselves. What is it that makes a sport like basketball valuable? Each sports economist understands his own passions, but they all feel the need to study how and why the rest of the population values sports. Does star power draw fans to games? Does an increased chance of winning a game draw fans? Does a new publicly funded extravagant stadium with six-dollar hot dogs draw fans?

In answer to all those questions—yes, they probably do help, though I know of no one who has actually looked into the effect of the cost of hot dogs. Another question is whether "competitive balance" draws fans. Does an evenly balanced league help draw fans? What does it take to have an evenly balanced league? How balanced should it be? What does "evenly balanced" even mean?

This chapter is my brief interlude into sports economics, partially as an excuse to look at this competitive balance issue. How strongly teams are drawn to .500 is an aspect of sports that interests me a lot. The natural pull of 0.500 on a team is what the coach of a good team has to fend off every year and is what helps the coach of a bad team every year. That natural pull of competitive balance is something that most people view without question as a valuable thing.

But is competitive balance even necessary? In one extreme, it is pretty obviously so. A league where the same team wins all games for many years is not very interesting. On the other extreme, though, a league with a lot of teams near .500 with a different champion every year has a bit of blandness to it. Two *Sports Illustrated* columnists argued opposing sides of this issue during the 2001 NFL season when the league showed a lot of parity—just as former NFL commissioner Pete Rozelle always wanted. Rozelle's preaching of parity is part of what has so many people believing that parity is good.

Interesting perspectives on this come from sports economists. Sports economists have generally found that greater uncertainty in the outcome of a game does help bring fans out to the park—we like fair fights. But there have also been studies that have looked more closely at this phenomenon to suggest that we actually also want to be pretty confident that the home team is going to win. Some studies have said that we actually prefer games where one team has a 60 to 65 percent chance of winning. That margin would apparently represent the compromise between the boredom of domination and the blandness of parity.

Two other sports economists looked past individual games and tried to gauge how fans' long-term interest in the game wavers with competitive balance.w[1] Over more than ninety years of baseball data, they found something that made sense—fans like single-season surges in imbalance, but they tire of it after three to five years. In other words, fans don't mind a Goliath once in a while, but David better win every few years.

This is interesting for basketball because, in at least one way, the NBA is the least balanced of the major pro sports. It is the prominent professional league that comes closest to a model in which the best team wins every game, the second-best team wins every game except those against the best team, the third-best team wins every game except those against the best and second-best teams, etc.[2] Despite this apparent inequity, fans have continued to flock to NBA games since the early 1980s (though attendance isn't growing as it did through the 1980s). So there are probably other things of interest to NBA fans. For instance, competitive balance may mean that the offense and defense each win about 50 percent of the time, which definitely happens in basketball more than in other sports. Even in looking at team seasonal records, there are other ways of getting a slightly different picture of competitive balance.

One different way is to look at how teams with different records change over the next few seasons. Bad teams should get better, and good teams should get worse. After one year, you end up with the situation in figure 9.1.

The plot shows how team records change given their current record. For example, a team that won 25 percent of its games can be expected to change about 9 percent the next season—*improving* 9 percent. Or looking at the other side of the chart, a team that won 75 percent of its games can be expected to decline 7 to 8 percent the next year. If there were a perfect (statistical) shuffling of teams from one year to the next, you'd see the dots hugging the "line of ultimate

Figure 9.1. The Year After: Good Teams Get Worse, Bad Teams Get Better

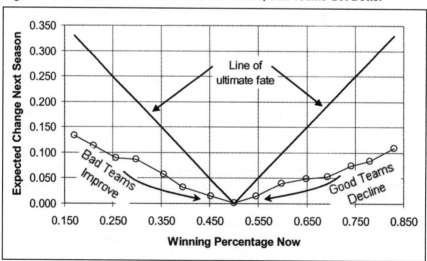

fate," as it is labeled. Teams that won 75 percent of their games would be expected to win 50 percent in the next year, and so would teams that won 10 percent. That kind of parity would be like shuffling all the personnel every year at random.

The figure suggests that it is a little easier for bad teams to climb to .500 than it is for the league to bring a good team down to .500. This makes sense, of course, because, whereas good teams will more likely stand pat with their personnel, bad teams are more likely to literally shuffle personnel around. Table 9.1 echoes the expected change from one season to the next but also shows the chance that teams will improve or decline in one year. This emphasizes the same point— teams get drawn toward .500. But, because the table's data is framed in terms of percentages, you can actually infer a little bit more. Specifically, these probabilities of change suggest that changes in teams' records are not just random. For example, if a team's change from one year to the next were random, you would see that the chance of decline of a .150 team (between 0.10 and 0.20) was about 15 percent. It's not; the historical chance of a .150 team declining is much smaller— about 4 percent. The really bad teams and the really good teams appear to be drawn toward .500 relatively more strongly than random chance would dictate. Maybe this reflects the impact of the draft, with bad teams picking first and good teams picking last. Though the numbers suggest that there is a cause for teams to decline or improve, these numbers don't directly suggest what that cause might be.

Longer-Term Balance

Both the previous figure and table show that competition is drawing teams about a third of the way to .500 in one year. Teams winning 25 percent of their games

Table 9.1. Expected Change and Probability of Change in Winning Percentage over One Year

Current Winning %	Probability of		Expected Change in Winning %
	Improvement	Decline	
10%–20%	96%	4%	13%
15%–25%	86%	14%	11%
20%–30%	79%	19%	9%
25%–35%	73%	25%	9%
30%–40%	63%	35%	6%
35%–45%	58%	39%	3%
40%–50%	54%	42%	1%
45%–55%	49%	48%	0%
50%–60%	44%	53%	-1%
55%–65%	36%	62%	-4%
60%–70%	32%	67%	-5%
65%–75%	32%	67%	-5%
70%–80%	21%	75%	-7%
75%–85%	11%	84%	-8%
80%–90%	0%	100%	-11%

improve about 9 percent of the 25 percent necessary to reach .500, or about a third of the way. But what about after five years? Have all teams been pulled back to .500? Has the deck been completely shuffled? Figure 9.2 looks at the expected change in a team's winning percentage over five years after having a given winning percentage. You can see that bad teams are pretty much at "ultimate fate," or .500, but good teams may not be.

Parity has pulled on the bad teams, but the good teams have resisted. Even ten years down the road, good teams seem to be able to maintain some comfort level between themselves and .500. This is apparently because the classic power-houses of the NBA—Boston, Los Angeles, Chicago, and Philadelphia—have built franchises that stay strong.

This also supports what the sports economists say—that big-market teams will be better than small-market teams. It at least supports the idea that there are big-market teams that stay ahead and a lot of small-market teams that end up lumped together in a pool below them.

Playoff Inequity

One of the more distressing indicators of basketball's inequity (both in the NBA and the WNBA) is its lack of playoff parity. Both leagues have had predictable champions most of the last several seasons. No one was going to knock off the Lakers in 2001 or 2002, and no one was going to beat the Bulls while Jordan played. No one was going to beat the Houston Comets in the WNBA as long as Cynthia Cooper played. The playoffs were more coronations than competitions.

Figure 9.2. Five Years After: Most Teams Approach 0.500

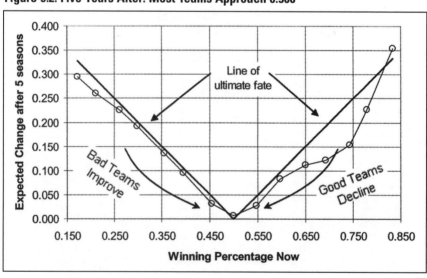

The Lakers championships were particularly strange because, even though they didn't have their conference's best record in 2001 or 2002, they were still Las Vegas' clear favorite to win the title each year. When regular season win-loss records don't capture the strength of a team—suggesting that a team is dogging it during the season—that seriously dilutes the value of regular season games. If the value of regular season competition doesn't matter to teams, why should it matter to fans?

But is it really that bad? Maybe the Lakers did tank games in midseason (losing twice to the horri-Bulls would be support for that), but is it any worse than it's ever been, historically speaking? That is where the economists say no. If you look at competitive balance in the NBA since the 1960s—no matter whether you look at regular season records, turnover in playoff teams, or expected changes in records—there is no obvious trend up or down. The Celtics' win-loss records during their 1960s dynasty suggest that they may have relaxed a little during the regular season, just as the Lakers seem to have been doing during their 2000 mini-dynasty. Michael Jordan gave the league a break when he retired in 1993.

So, no—the NBA overall doesn't appear to have a trend toward competitive imbalance. A few years of the same champion doesn't mean that the league is imbalanced. Those happy-go-lucky sports economists have been saying this for a while about baseball, where fans have complained about the Yankees and Braves always reaching the World Series. Now they get to keep smiling as they say it about basketball.

Endnotes

1. Martin Schmidt and David Berri's paper, "Competitive Balance and Attendance: The Case of Major League Baseball," served as the primary reference for these results on whether competitive balance was beneficial.

2. This is assessed using a Gini coefficient in several papers.

Chapter 10

Teamwork 2:
A Game of Ultimatums

I magine yourself in a situation where someone you don't know was offered a hundred dollars on the condition that they share some fraction of it with you. That player makes an offer of some fraction of the hundred dollars to you— maybe ten dollars, maybe fifty, maybe eighty. If you accept the offer, the deal goes through and you both receive the amount of money defined by the offer. If you refuse the offer, neither of you gets any money, nada, nothing, zippo.

That is the Ultimatum Game, an experiment that continues to confound the economists who study it. In the economist's world, no matter how much money you're offered, it's free money, so you should accept the offer. But would you really accept an offer of five dollars? Or would you rather get nothing in some attempt to punish the person offering the money, the proposer, for not being fair?

Economists study this Ultimatum Game in an attempt to understand how fairness gets factored into economic transactions. They vary the game by chang- ing the total quantity of money or by having the two people compete in some way to determine who is the proposer. The science of game theory, which rests on the idea that people independently try to maximize their own net gain, doesn't very well cover this type of cooperative game. So there are now economists trying to explain it with theories based on the evolution of humans in societies through time. Fundamentally, they say that we always compare ourselves to the people we are in the game with. We demand fairness.

Or at least something close to fairness. In typical Western-type civilizations, *Scientific American* (January 2002) says the average offer in the Ultimatum Game is 45 percent of the money. That is close to 50 percent, which would be pure fair- ness. But it is not quite 50 percent. The player proposing the split offers less than 50 percent apparently because they feel that they have some inherent advantage in being the proposer. Or perhaps they feel they can offer less because they are doing the greater work by making the offer. Whatever the explanation, there are some proposers who offer too little and there are responders who, even though all money is free to them, reject that offer. (Supposedly, "more civilized" Western societies believe that the offers should be more equal than in societies with less established market economies.)

So what does this have to do with basketball? *Scientific American* described the Ultimatum Game as an "abstraction of social interactions." Basketball itself, if every team is a "society," is also essentially an abstraction of social interactions. Whereas the two players of the Ultimatum Game are trying to "win" money from the experimenter, the five players of a basketball team are trying to win a game. Just as the two players of the Ultimatum Game can split that win fifty-fifty but don't, five basketball players can split the credit for their victories evenly but don't. The average Ultimatum Game "team" of two wins one hundred dollars and splits it fifty-five–forty-five. The average basketball team of five loses as much as it wins, and the players are constantly fighting it out for credit/blame. There are Ultimatum Game teams that lose when one player tries to get greedy about credit. In the NBA, that could be any team with Isaiah Rider on it.

Teammates can and do compete among themselves for credit in their team's success. They compete for playing time, and they compete for shots. They ultimately compete for glory—to be the one leading a team to a championship. That competition between teammates does often improve the team. But, just as proposer and responder have to cooperate enough to win the hundred dollars in order to split it between themselves, basketball teammates cannot compete so much against one another that they don't win the game as a team. Allowing your star player to score 70 percent of your points may seem like an optimal theory because he is so much better than his teammates, but does it start infringing upon the fairness that the teammates need to feel is there? More relevantly, is that 70 percent actually better for the team? That's a tough question for coaches blessed (cursed?) with outstanding prospects on a team with mediocre surrounding talent.

Back to economics and game theory for a little insight that may help. There are games in economics, like the Ultimatum Game, that are called "common goods" games. Multiple players contribute various amounts of their own money to a pot that grows in proportion to the size of that pot (the experimenter may double the pot, for example). That pot is then distributed *evenly* to all players regardless of how much they put in. Players are donating money for the common good of all. It turns out that playing this game over and over causes people to be less cooperative. People who put in less money are proportionately better rewarded, so others who originally contributed a lot put in less and less.

And that is where the tip-off is. If basketball teammates start putting in less effort because they feel that a few players are being *unfairly* rewarded, that's when teamwork is breaking down. Good coaches know how to recognize this and how to reward supporting players so that they do continue to put on their shoes and go to work each day. Phil Jackson has made a living out of being able to make great talents cooperate fairly with supporting players. In economics, they have found ways to maintain cooperation in common goods games by alternating these games with ones where "teammates" give money to other players but never receive direct contributions back from those particular players. Greedy players would not get these donations. The economists found a way for teammates to give feedback of reward or punishment among themselves to maintain reasonable cooperation. That is something that Phil Jackson must have developed in a basketball form for his teams.

These economic games highlight the apparent instinct of ours to be fair while building the success of a group. They also illustrate that the credit for group success is understood among players and can at some level be quantified. Quantification of individual credit on a basketball team is one of the main goals of this book as well. I want to engineer the success of a team of individuals, first and foremost. But "engineering," almost by its very nature, means breaking success down into its different components and understanding the value of those components. The previous teamwork chapter built a huge list of the different teamwork "components" in basketball. Subjectively, you can go through and assign a value to each of those components. What I'll be doing in the next teamwork chapter is building a system for assigning that value.

Chapter 11

Basketball's Bell Curve

In 1994, Richard Herrnstein and Charles Murray came out with a book that no one read but everyone talked about called *The Bell Curve*. It was all about the distribution of intelligence in the general populace and what it may mean. This chapter is . . . well . . . less controversial. However, it may be more important.

A bell curve, not *The Bell Curve*, is just a convenient name for a technical statistical thing. That "technical statistical thing" isn't too hard to understand, so I'll explain. What Herrnstein and Murray did to create their bull, err, bell curve was break down roughly how many people in the population have IQs between sixty and seventy, between seventy and eighty, between eighty and ninety, and so forth up to the two-hundred-plus level that I'm sure that they fit into. There are clearly more people in the 100 to 110 "average" range than in the 160 to 170 range, so, if you plot how many people there are in each range, you get a shape kinda like a bell, like the one in figure 11.1. In the case of IQ, the top of the bell represents the average people having IQs around one hundred. The outer parts of the bell, the parts that make it go dingdong, represent the extreme people, the eccentrically smart or exceedingly dumb people—the dingdongs.

This kind of graph is called a statistical distribution—it shows the distribution of people, in this case, having different IQs. The bell shape to the distribution is especially important in basketball, as you'll see.

Rather than slathering on for five hundred pages about what figure 11.1 means, let's transform this plot into something meaningful, i.e., something in basketball. First, strip away "Percentage of People" and make it "Percentage of Games." Then remove "IQ" and replace it with "Points Scored." Then look at the scores for all games over the 2001 and 2002 seasons. What you get is actually two distributions, one for the home teams' points scored and one for the road teams' points scored. Figure 11.2 shows these distributions.

Figure 11.1. Number of People with a Given IQ

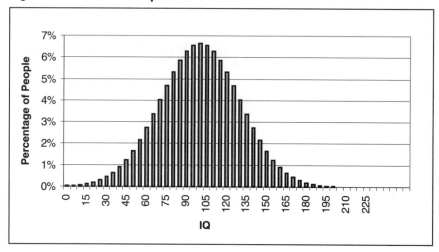

Figure 11.2. Distributions of Home and Road Scores, 2000–2001 and 2001–2002 Seasons

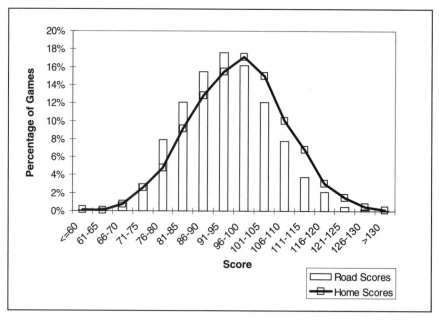

These distributions provide valuable information for translating average score differences into win/loss records. Namely, how much these two distributions overlap (and you can see that they overlap quite a bit) indicates something about how frequently the home or road team wins a game. In other words, you can estimate the home-court advantage based on the above distributions. This comes about because a win by the home team means only that the home team's score is greater than the road team's score. So, if you pick a random point in the home team's point distribution, what is the chance that it is greater than a random point in the road team's point distribution? The answer gives you an estimate of the home-court advantage.

Actually, this is only mostly true. There is actually a little complication that is important for both predictions and for basketball strategy. The complication that arises in basketball (and most sports actually) is that the number of points scored by a team (home or road) is *correlated* to the number of points allowed by that team. Teams often play up or down to their competition. Almost every NBA team does it to

> **Correlation**
> Two values, such as points scored and points allowed, are called *positively correlated* if, as one goes up, the other tends to go up. They are *negatively correlated* if, as one goes up, the other tends to go down.

some degree and some definitely more than others. Correlation also comes about because of "garbage time," which allows a team to get close without changing the winner of the game. What this means to the analogy in the previous paragraph is that if you pick points in the home and road point distribution purely randomly, you are actually going to underestimate the home-court advantage. The correlation causes more overlap of the distributions without actually changing the winning percentage. This correlation is relatively small but not insignificant.

So, using that correlation, what do these distributions of figure 11.2 say? They say, first of all, that the average home team scored 96.7 ppg and allowed 93.5 ppg, for approximately a 3-point home-court advantage during these two seasons. You can see this also in how the home curve is shifted to the right of the road curve. Using this home-court advantage, plus how spread out the distributions are, and the correlation between the two, there is a formula (see Technical Box 1) that estimates a home-court winning percentage of 59.5 percent. The actual home-court winning percentage over these seasons was 59.3 percent. This method, known as the Bell Curve Method, works pretty well.

Predictions of the Bell Curve Method

The home-court advantage is a known thing, though. The preceding calculation isn't a prediction, but a confirmation that the method is accurate. The predictive ability comes when applying the method to individual basketball teams. It suggests whether a team really earned their win-loss record or whether they got lucky or unlucky.

A good recent example of the power of the method to predict is the Houston Rockets team of 2000, which won thirty-four games with the lineup shown on the left of table 11.1.

Table 11.1. Houston Rockets Players in 2000 and 2001

2000 Houston Lineup				2001 Houston Lineup			
Player	G	GS	Min	Player	G	GS	Min
Francis, Steve	77	77	2776	Francis, Steve	80	79	3194
Mobley, Cuttino	81	8	2496	Mobley, Cuttino	79	49	3002
Anderson, Shandon	82	82	2700	Anderson, Shandon	82	82	2396
Williams, Walt	76	66	1859	Williams, Walt	72	31	1583
Olajuwon, Hakeem	44	28	1049	Olajuwon, Hakeem	58	55	1545
Cato, Kelvin	65	32	1581	Cato, Kelvin	35	13	624
Thomas, Kenny	72	29	1797	Thomas, Kenny	74	21	1820
Rogers, Carlos	53	15	1101	Rogers, Carlos	39	0	544
Norris, Moochie	30	0	502	Norris, Moochie	82	6	1654
Bullard, Matt	56	27	1024	Bullard, Matt	61	5	1000
Miller, Anthony	35	14	476	Miller, Anthony	1	0	3
Barkley, Charles	20	18	620	Taylor, Maurice	69	69	1972
Drew, Bryce	72	5	1293	Collier, Jason	23	0	222
Massenburg, Tony	10	0	109	Langhi, Dan	33	0	241
Hamilton, Thomas	22	7	273	Colson, Sean	10	0	30
Curley, Bill	4	0	50				
Gray, Ed	3	0	17				
Gray, Devin	18	2	107				

Going into the 2001 season, the players didn't change much. They lost Charles Barkley, initially to the bar scene in Florida and then to a studio where he discovered his true calling as a talking head. The biggest player change was probably dropping Bryce Drew and picking up Maurice Taylor. Overall, an average of 88 percent of the minutes in each season were played by the same players, a very high rate of roster stability.[1] So the talent was about the same. But it was still quite predictable that this team would improve over their thirty-four wins of the 2000 season. Sure, young Steve Francis was a year older, but the indicator that matters in this chapter is that the Rockets should have won *more than* thirty-four games in 2000. Using the same formula that so accurately estimated the home-court advantage, the Rockets should have won thirty-nine games in 2000. Why? The Rockets of 2000 were outscored by an average of less than one point per game, 99.5 to 100.3, a small disadvantage. They won five games by twenty points or more, showing their ability to win big. But they also got a bit unlucky, losing nineteen games by six points or less and winning only nine decided by this margin. By carrying that same talent and a little maturity into the 2001 season, it was very reasonable to think that they would improve a fair amount. In 2001, the Rockets won forty-five games. Compared to thirty-four wins, this is a huge improvement for a team with the same talent. Compared, however, to the thirty-nine wins they should have had, forty-five wins is a more reasonable six-game improvement.

That Houston team is just one of many cases where a team's season average point differential better reflected its ability than its win-loss record. Over the five years from 1997 to 2003, for teams that deviated from their bell curve projection by more than one standard deviation in expected winning percentage, eighteen of twenty-three changed the next year in the direction of the bell curve projection. There were probably other factors in all cases, but this one—the fact that points scored and allowed can contain more information about a team's actual potential than its win-loss record—is a powerful one. See table 11.2 for a full listing of teams, their point differential, their estimated and actual winning percentages, and whether the prediction of change was correct.[2]

Consistency Can Be Good or Bad

Prediction is one thing. Prediction means that the math behind the numbers provides a good model of what happens in the game. That's important. It's not just some made-up little formula that fits some of the numbers. But the implications of this bell curve method beyond prediction are what make it one of the most important tools in this book.

One of the really valuable parts of the method is that it incorporates the *variability* in a team's scoring. A team that is more variable in how much it scores or how many points it allows is said to have a higher standard deviation or a higher variance (which is the standard deviation squared) and exhibits a

> **Standard Deviation**
>
> Standard deviation is a representation of how wide the bell curve is or how inconsistent a team is in scoring or allowing points. A "variance" is just the standard deviation multiplied by itself.

larger spread in its bell curves. By spreading out the distributions, you increase the amount of overlap of the points scored and points allowed, which reflects how often the team wins. What this means for good teams is that, if they are inconsistent, they win less than they should. What this means for bad teams is that, if they are inconsistent, they win *more* than they should. In other words, being inconsistent brings a team toward .500, toward mediocrity.

As a hypothetical example, a consistent team that averages 106 points offensively and 103 points defensively wins more than an inconsistent team with the same offensive and defensive averages. At the extreme, the ultimate consistent team scores 106 points every game and allows 103 points every game and, of course, wins every game. On the other end, a team that scores 103 points every game and allows 106 points every game loses every game.

As a more realistic example, take a look at the Utah Jazz, one of the most consistent teams through the 1990s. In 1995, the Jazz scored 106.3 points per game and allowed 98.6. The standard deviations of these two numbers were 9.8 and 10.7 points, respectively, meaning that in approximately two-thirds of their games, the Jazz scored between about ninety-six and 116 points and they allowed between eighty-eight and 109 points. Figure 11.3 shows Utah's actual distributions of points

Table 11.2. Bell Curve Projections for Teams Since End of 1997 Season

☺ means a prediction that was correct
✗ means a prediction that was incorrect

Team	Stat	Season 1997	1998	1999	2000	2001	2002
Atlanta	PPG	94.8	95.9	86.3	94.3	91.0	94.0
	DPPG	89.4	92.3	83.4	99.7	96.2	98.3
	CorrGauss%	0.656	0.614	0.607	0.345	0.322	0.383
	Actual Win%	0.683	0.610	0.620	0.341	0.305	0.402
	Expected Change						
Boston	PPG	100.6	95.9	93.0	99.3	94.6	96.4
	DPPG	107.9	98.5	94.9	100.1	96.8	94.1
	CorrGauss%	0.256	0.414	0.450	0.478	0.428	0.574
	Actual Win%	0.183	0.439	0.380	0.427	0.439	0.598
	Expected Change	Up ☺					
Charlotte	PPG	98.9	96.6	92.9	98.4	91.9	93.9
	DPPG	97.0	94.6	93.0	95.8	89.8	92.9
	CorrGauss%	0.566	0.557	0.496	0.578	0.572	0.531
	Actual Win%	0.659	0.622	0.520	0.598	0.561	0.537
	Expected Change	Down ☺	Down ☺				
Chicago	PPG	103.1	96.7	81.9	84.8	87.6	89.5
	DPPG	92.3	89.6	91.4	94.2	96.7	98.0
	CorrGauss%	0.820	0.720	0.258	0.214	0.215	0.255
	Actual Win%	0.841	0.756	0.260	0.207	0.183	0.256
	Expected Change						
Cleveland	PPG	87.5	92.5	86.4	97.0	92.2	95.3
	DPPG	85.6	89.8	88.2	100.5	96.5	98.6
	CorrGauss%	0.560	0.586	0.448	0.392	0.365	0.400
	Actual Win%	0.512	0.573	0.440	0.390	0.366	0.354
	Expected Change						
Dallas	PPG	90.6	91.4	91.6	101.4	100.5	105.2
	DPPG	97.0	97.5	94.0	102.0	96.2	101.0
	CorrGauss%	0.289	0.304	0.417	0.481	0.631	0.629
	Actual Win%	0.293	0.244	0.380	0.488	0.646	0.695
	Expected Change	Up ☺					Down ✗
Denver	PPG	97.8	89.0	93.5	99.0	96.6	92.2
	DPPG	104.1	100.8	100.1	101.1	99.0	98.0
	CorrGauss%	0.299	0.182	0.286	0.436	0.420	0.330
	Actual Win%	0.256	0.134	0.280	0.427	0.488	0.329
	Expected Change	Up ☺			Down ☺		
Detroit	PPG	94.2	94.2	90.4	103.5	95.6	94.3
	DPPG	88.9	92.6	86.9	102.0	97.3	92.2
	CorrGauss%	0.658	0.552	0.598	0.547	0.448	0.566
	Actual Win%	0.659	0.451	0.580	0.512	0.390	0.610
	Expected Change	Up ☺			Up ☺		
Golden St.	PPG	99.6	88.3	88.3	95.5	92.5	97.7
	DPPG	104.4	97.4	90.8	103.8	101.5	103.1
	CorrGauss%	0.379	0.230	0.416	0.274	0.233	0.326
	Actual Win%	0.366	0.232	0.420	0.232	0.207	0.256
	Expected Change						Up ☺
Houston	PPG	100.6	98.8	94.2	99.5	97.2	92.3
	DPPG	96.1	99.5	91.9	100.3	94.9	97.2
	CorrGauss%	0.637	0.481	0.562	0.474	0.579	0.348
	Actual Win%	0.695	0.500	0.620	0.415	0.549	0.341
	Expected Change	Down ☺		Up ☺			

Team	Stat	Season					
		1997	1998	1999	2000	2001	2002
Indiana	PPG	95.4	96.0	94.7	101.3	92.6	96.8
	DPPG	94.4	89.9	90.9	96.7	92.8	96.5
	CorrGauss%	0.530	0.678	0.652	0.639	0.493	0.509
	Actual Win%	0.476	0.707	0.660	0.683	0.500	0.512
	Expected Change						
LA Clippers	PPG	97.2	95.9	90.4	92.0	92.5	95.7
	DPPG	99.5	103.3	99.2	103.5	95.3	96.1
	CorrGauss%	0.422	0.261	0.238	0.170	0.403	0.486
	Actual Win%	0.439	0.207	0.180	0.183	0.378	0.476
	Expected Change		Up **x**				
LA Lakers	PPG	100.0	105.5	99.0	100.8	100.6	101.3
	DPPG	95.7	97.8	96.0	92.3	97.2	94.1
	CorrGauss%	0.631	0.733	0.594	0.758	0.614	0.699
	Actual Win%	0.683	0.744	0.620	0.817	0.683	0.707
	Expected Change				Down ☺	Down **x**	
Memphis	PPG	89.2	96.6	88.9	93.9	91.7	89.9
(Vancouver)	DPPG	99.4	103.9	97.5	99.5	97.5	97.3
	CorrGauss%	0.192	0.248	0.190	0.314	0.327	0.279
	Actual Win%	0.171	0.232	0.160	0.268	0.280	0.280
	Expected Change						
Miami	PPG	94.8	95.0	89.0	94.4	88.9	87.2
	DPPG	89.3	90.0	84.0	91.3	86.6	88.7
	CorrGauss%	0.682	0.652	0.667	0.602	0.585	0.446
	Actual Win%	0.744	0.671	0.660	0.634	0.610	0.439
	Expected Change	Down ☺					
Milwaukee	PPG	95.3	94.5	91.7	101.2	100.7	97.5
	DPPG	97.2	96.4	90.0	101.0	96.9	97.7
	CorrGauss%	0.433	0.437	0.561	0.506	0.627	0.494
	Actual Win%	0.402	0.439	0.560	0.512	0.634	0.500
	Expected Change						
Minnesota	PPG	96.1	101.1	92.9	98.5	97.3	99.3
	DPPG	97.6	100.4	92.6	96.0	96.0	96.0
	CorrGauss%	0.451	0.522	0.512	0.574	0.543	0.594
	Actual Win%	0.488	0.549	0.500	0.610	0.573	0.610
	Expected Change						
New Jersey	PPG	97.2	99.6	91.4	98.0	92.1	96.2
	DPPG	101.8	98.1	95.2	99.0	97.1	92.0
	CorrGauss%	0.350	0.554	0.380	0.468	0.349	0.619
	Actual Win%	0.317	0.524	0.320	0.378	0.317	0.634
	Expected Change				Up **x**		
New York	PPG	95.4	91.6	86.4	92.1	88.7	0.0
	DPPG	92.2	89.1	85.4	90.7	86.1	0.0
	CorrGauss%	0.607	0.577	0.535	0.555	0.576	0.373
	Actual Win%	0.695	0.524	0.540	0.610	0.585	0.366
	Expected Change	Down ☺			Down ☺		
Orlando	PPG	94.1	90.1	89.5	100.1	97.3	100.5
	DPPG	94.5	91.2	86.9	99.4	96.6	98.9
	CorrGauss%	0.490	0.467	0.578	0.519	0.524	0.544
	Actual Win%	0.549	0.500	0.660	0.500	0.524	0.537
	Expected Change	Down ☺		Down ☺			
Philadelphia	PPG	100.2	93.3	89.7	94.8	94.7	91.0
	DPPG	106.7	95.7	87.6	93.4	90.5	89.4
	CorrGauss%	0.301	0.423	0.576	0.547	0.626	0.558
	Actual Win%	0.268	0.378	0.560	0.598	0.683	0.524
	Expected Change					Down ☺	

(continued next page)

Table 11.2. Bell Curve Projections for Teams Since End of 1997 Season
(continued)

Team	Stat	Season					
		1997	1998	1999	2000	2001	2002
Phoenix	PPG	102.8	99.6	95.6	98.9	94.0	95.1
	DPPG	102.2	94.4	93.3	93.7	91.8	95.8
	CorrGauss%	0.519	0.655	0.578	0.650	0.571	0.479
	Actual Win%	0.488	0.683	0.540	0.646	0.622	0.439
	Expected Change						
Portland	PPG	99.0	94.3	94.8	97.5	95.4	96.6
	DPPG	94.8	92.9	88.5	91.0	91.2	93.7
	CorrGauss%	0.610	0.539	0.689	0.719	0.629	0.597
	Actual Win%	0.598	0.561	0.700	0.720	0.610	0.598
	Expected Change						
Sacramento	PPG	96.4	93.1	100.2	105.0	101.7	104.6
	DPPG	99.8	98.7	100.6	102.0	95.9	97.0
	CorrGauss%	0.396	0.344	0.485	0.591	0.678	0.689
	Actual Win%	0.415	0.329	0.540	0.537	0.671	0.744
	Expected Change						Down
San Antonio	PPG	90.5	92.5	92.8	96.2	96.2	96.7
	DPPG	98.3	88.5	84.7	90.2	88.4	90.5
	CorrGauss%	0.249	0.617	0.735	0.678	0.726	0.704
	Actual Win%	0.244	0.683	0.740	0.646	0.707	0.707
	Expected Change		Down x				
Seattle	PPG	100.9	100.6	94.9	99.1	97.3	97.7
	DPPG	93.2	93.4	95.9	98.1	97.3	94.7
	CorrGauss%	0.705	0.710	0.465	0.528	0.501	0.592
	Actual Win%	0.695	0.744	0.500	0.549	0.537	0.549
	Expected Change						
Toronto	PPG	95.5	94.9	91.1	97.2	97.6	91.4
	DPPG	98.6	104.2	92.8	97.3	95.4	91.8
	CorrGauss%	0.413	0.211	0.447	0.495	0.567	0.486
	Actual Win%	0.366	0.195	0.460	0.549	0.573	0.512
	Expected Change						
Utah	PPG	103.1	101.0	93.3	96.5	97.1	96.0
	DPPG	94.3	94.4	86.8	92.0	92.4	95.1
	CorrGauss%	0.776	0.715	0.716	0.634	0.644	0.525
	Actual Win%	0.780	0.756	0.740	0.671	0.646	0.537
	Expected Change						
Washington	PPG	99.4	97.2	91.2	96.6	93.2	92.8
	DPPG	97.7	96.6	93.4	99.9	99.9	94.2
	CorrGauss%	0.554	0.518	0.422	0.395	0.268	0.457
	Actual Win%	0.537	0.512	0.360	0.354	0.232	0.451
	Expected Change						

scored and allowed in that season. Clearly, it's not quite the perfect bell-shaped curve that the other figures showed. That is because eighty-two games are not enough to create such a smooth shape. Nevertheless, a bell curve representation of Utah's scores represents things pretty well. Figure 11.4 shows an example of a bell curve distribution with the 106.3 points per game and 98.6 points per game averages and the standard deviations that Utah had.[3] As you can see, the win-loss record changed to 61–21 in this simulated example, but it effectively is the same.

Figure 11.3. Distribution of Utah Scores, 1995 (W–L: 60–22)

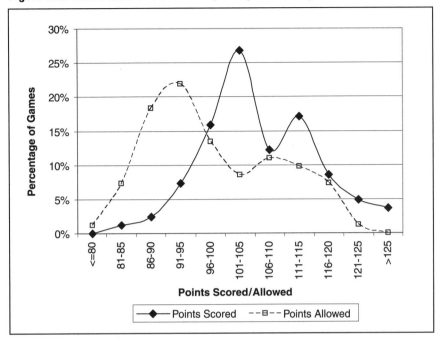

Figure 11.4. Distribution of Simulated Utah Scores, 1995 (W–L: 61–21)

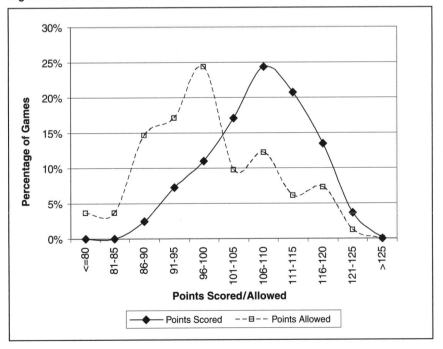

What would happen if the Jazz were even more consistent? What if that pick-and-roll were so precise as to be machine-like? How would the Jazz do? Rather than using the actual standard deviation of ten points, what if the Jazz's standard deviation of points scored and allowed were cut down to four? That's what you see in figure 11.5—two distributions with less overlap but peaks at roughly the same places. The bottom line is that the ultra-consistent Jazz set a record for wins in the season with seventy-nine. That's how much it pays for good teams to be consistent.

Beyond teams, it also pays for individual players to be consistent—the good ones, that is. The really great players in history have been both good and consistent—Magic Johnson, Michael Jordan, Larry Bird, Karl Malone. They've won and they've won consistently. The players whose reputations are a little more controversial are typically ones that have been a bit more inconsistent. Maybe they are erratic in their decision-making—players such as Nick Van Exel, Pistol Pete Maravich, or Allen Iverson. Maybe they just shoot a lot of three-point shots, getting hot and cold—players such as Reggie Miller or Rex Chapman.

High school players who are naturally talented can become inconsistent as a result of the lack of competition. As leaders on their teams, those talented players who relax can then allow opponents to stay closer than they should perhaps. Ideally, these kids face opponents who can challenge them because, though they may be skilled, sometimes they don't really know how to compete or how to

Figure 11.5. Falsely Consistent Utah Scores (79–3)

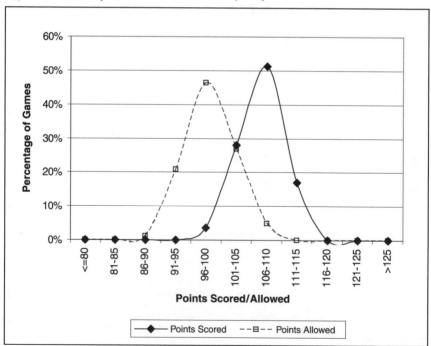

improve their skills. Coaches can still improve the skills of talented players, but it's much harder to do without the reward of beating good competition. Every practice is a drill without the satisfaction of proving much for a talented player. If every game is also not competitive because the player is so good, they might as well be drills. For a coach who has a talented player but doesn't have the competitive schedule to challenge the player, it is important for him to challenge that player in other areas of his game. Recognize the player's weaknesses and build them, even possibly at the cost of a couple of games. If the talent is good enough to get to playoffs where more competitive teams and players are present, that is when you work on the star's ability to compete. But don't focus on having him score a hundred points. It doesn't help him, and it doesn't help the team. (Obviously, I could be saying this about girls' basketball as well. Actually, Lisa Leslie's hundred-point game in high school came to mind before DaJuan Wagner's as I wrote this, because Leslie is the classic dominating high school player, much taller and much more skilled than the others in her league. So even though I used "he" and "him," I could just as easily be using "she" and "her.")

On the other hand, teams that are composed of many young players really *should* look "inconsistent" on paper. The players still have skills to develop and, unless they approach the .500 level, they shouldn't worry so much about hitting that last-second shot to win a close game. They should worry more about taking the right shot or making the right pass—not whether the shot goes in. That is the sort of development that needs to happen before they *compete* to a great degree.

Implications on Strategy

Now let's say you have a competitive, consistent team. You've won a bunch of games, and now you're in the playoffs facing the best teams in the region or in the state. Now you're an underdog. Now you don't want to be consistent because a consistent underdog loses. Now you need to find strategies that are "inconsistent" or "risky," strategies that bring your underdog team closer to being a .500 team against that favorite. Again, this is where having the variability in the bell curve method helps.

What are some "risky" strategies? First and most obviously, a press is a risky strategy because it often gets points off the defense or gives up easy baskets. A second risky strategy is to shoot a lot of threes; one is more likely to get six points or fifty points by shooting twenty three-pointers than by shooting twenty two-pointers. These are pretty obvious risky strategies. Teams often employ them when they are losing at the end of games because they can score a lot of points really quickly with these strategies. They may end up falling much further behind in the end, but they nevertheless have a much better chance with these "risky" strategies of actually winning the game.

A third risky strategy—one most people may not have considered—is to slow the pace down, reducing the number of possessions in a game. This obviously is not done at the end of a game when a team is losing. It's not that kind of "risky" strategy. Rather, the case where this strategy is used is when an underdog gets an early lead on a favorite. What it does is limit the better team from taking full advantage of being better. A good team will win out over a bad team if you play long enough. By cutting a game down to fewer possessions, an underdog is limiting how long the favorite has to prove that it is better. It may be a nail-biter, but the odds are better.

All these strategies fundamentally increase the variability of the difference between points scored and points allowed. Maybe they do it by increasing the variability of points scored (taking a lot of three-pointers does so). Maybe they do it by increasing the variability of points allowed (applying a press can do so). Maybe they do it by removing the correlation between an offense and a defense (that's what a press does by scoring off of turnovers). The slow-down strategy actually works by increasing the variability of both offensive and defensive ratings.[4] After a game in 1997 in which the turtle-slow Cleveland Cavaliers of Mike Fratello beat the favored Chicago Bulls 73–70, I estimated that the Cavaliers improved their odds of winning that game from about 28 percent to 34 percent by slowing the game from ninety-five possessions to seventy-eight possessions. Every 6 percent matters.

Secondary risky strategies can be determined by looking at tactics that cause an opponent to answer with a risky strategy of its own. For instance, a zone often causes an opponent to make more three-point attempts and to slow down the game. I once saw a classic example of a game in which a couple of risky strategies came together to create a victory for an underdog. In 1992, the Florida State Seminoles came into Chapel Hill to play the very strong North Carolina Tar Heels. Florida State grabbed an early lead with Sam Cassell and Charlie Ward hitting early shots, including a couple of three-pointers. With that lead, the Seminoles sat in a zone even though the Tar Heels had good perimeter shooters in Donald Williams and Henrik Rodl. And every time up the court, Florida State put the ball in the hands of Cassell at the perimeter, who dribbled away the shot clock until it got down under fifteen seconds. They scored many of their points off of three-point shots, and they pulled out one of only four wins that opponents notched against the Tar Heels that season. It also made Cassell a star in my book at the time.

Other "risky" strategies that may be considered include:

- Fronting the post in the hopes of getting a steal.
- Releasing your guards after forcing a missed shot in the hopes of getting a long outlet pass.

- Sending your guards to the offensive boards.
- Playing particularly oversized or undersized lineups.

I do not want to imply that these strategies should always be used if you're an underdog. If you are facing a team that has tremendous outside shooters, giving them outside shots, though they may miss a few, is probably not the best idea. Rather, "risky" strategies are ones that you should consider if you don't have clear evidence that one strategy or another is obviously better or not. If you're planning on changing the defense after a time-out but don't have any strong reason to choose one strategy or another, consider whether you are an underdog or favorite (which can depend upon the score and time left in the game), and think of using a risky defense if you're an underdog or a more safe man-to-man if you're the favorite.

Or you can use the rule of thumb that is already pretty well known and is definitely a consequence of the bell curve: At the end of a tight game, go for the win if you're on the road, but go for the tie if you're at home.

Technical Box 1

This box is provided to assist people interested in making the calculations used in this chapter. It provides the formulas and some references for doing the calculations in Microsoft Excel, which has all of the built-in functions necessary to do the calculations.

The basic formula for predicting winning percentage from a team's statistics is

$$\text{Win\%} = \text{NORM}\left[\frac{\text{PPG} - \text{DPPG}}{\sqrt{\text{var(PPG)} + \text{var(DPPG)} - 2\text{cov(PPG,DPPG)}}}\right]$$

where

var(PPG): variance of a team's points scored per game (PPG) throughout a season, which is equivalent to the square of the standard deviation of
  PG [VAR(array) in MS Excel]

var(DPPG): variance of a team's points allowed per game (DPPG) throughout a season, which is equivalent to the square of the standard deviation of

DPPG [VAR(array) in MS Excel]
cov(PPG, DPPG): covariance of PPG and
DPPG [COVAR(array1, array2) in MS Excel]

and NORM [NORMSDIST(value) in MS Excel] is a function that represents how much of a standard bell curve is above a certain value, as shown in figure 11.6.

Figure 11.6. Explanation of NORM Function

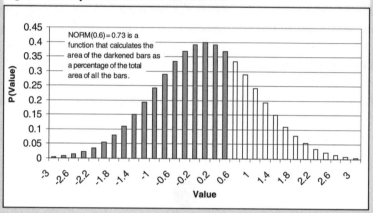

(Not a whole lot of addition, subtraction, multiplication, and division in that formula, huh? Fortunately, all the components are common enough in business that ordinary spreadsheets do carry the functions. That does make this, however, a legitimate "computer" formula. Too many broadcasters like to call the IBM Award a "computer rating." It's only a computer rating if it's too hard to calculate by hand, and the IBM Award is not too hard to calculate by hand. That formula is just basic math. It's not a computer rating, but a fourth-grader rating.)

The values from figure 11.2 serve as a good example of using the formula. In that case, the home teams score an average of 96.7 points per game (PPG) and the road teams allow an average of 93.6 points per game (DPPG). The standard deviation of home points is 11.7 [var(PPG) = 11.7 × 11.7 = 137]. The standard deviation of road points is 11.1 [var(DPPG) = 11.1 × 11.1 = 123]. The covariance between home and road scores is forty-seven. Plugging these into the equation above and using MS Excel gives 0.595 or 59.5 percent.

Technical Box 2

Because possessions are the same for a team and its opponents in a game, offensive ratings and defensive ratings tell the same story as points scored and allowed in terms of who wins a game. Because of that, you can replace PPG and DPPG in the bell curve formula from Technical Box 1 with offensive and defensive ratings to get

$$Win\% = NORM \left[\frac{ORtg - DRtg}{\sqrt{var(ORtg) + var(DRtg) - 2cov(ORtg, DRtg)}} \right]$$

where
var(ORtg):variance of the team offensive rating
var(DRtg):variance of the team defensive rating
cov(ORtg, DRtg):covariance of a team's offensive and defensive ratings.

There is some intuition (and some theory) that helps one take this equation and say that a game of fewer possessions is a game of higher risk. Consider the Mavericks with Dirk Nowitzki, Michael Finley, and Steve Nash against the Chicago Bulls of Ron Mercer and Fred Hoiberg. Who is going to win? The Mavs, right? What if it's a one-minute game, though? There are definitely stretches where worse teams outscore better teams 6–0 or even 8–0. But it's less likely for that worse team to outscore the better team 100–80. That's the intuition.

The theory comes from the denominator of the NORM function above, called the *point spread standard deviation:*

$$\sqrt{var(ORtg) + var(DRtg) - 2cov(ORtg, DRtg)}$$

If this denominator goes up, that is a "riskier" or "higher variance" game. Theoretical statistics has a formula that says that the variance of floor percentage is

$$var(Floor\%) = \frac{Floor\% \times (1 - Floor\%)}{Possessions\ in\ a\ Game}$$

So the variance of floor percentage is higher with fewer possessions. Because offensive and defensive ratings are related to floor percentage through

$$Rtg = Floor\% \times (Pts / ScPoss) \times 100$$

where (Pts/ScPoss) is usually a little bit higher than two, it should be clear that the variance of offensive and defensive ratings also goes up with fewer possessions.

To provide a rough gauge for how risky strategies change winning percentage, figure 11.7 shows winning percentage as a function of that point spread standard deviation for different average point spreads ("Spread = −3" on the figure means that the average point spread is three). The point spread standard deviations shown range across ones I've seen for NBA and college teams. The

Figure 11.7. Effect of Riskier Strategies on Underdog's Winning Percentage

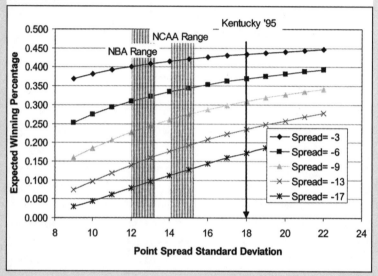

most consistent teams may have standard deviations around nine and the least consistent may have standard deviations around twenty-two. The NBA average is twelve to thirteen, and the college average is around fourteen to fifteen. So, if you're a nine-point underdog, you can increase your chances of winning from 15 percent to over 30 percent by going from a very consistent strategy to a combination of high-risk strategies. That's not something to ignore.

The University of Kentucky under Rick Pitino played a lot of high-risk strategies, pressing and shooting threes. They offset that tendency somewhat with a faster pace to take advantage of their tremendous talent. Their "riskiest" year was 1995, when their overall point spread standard deviation was about eighteen. Despite outscoring opponents by a mammoth eighteen points per game, the team lost five games overall and didn't make it to the Final Four despite a roster that included Tony Delk, Walter McCarty, Rodrick Rhodes, and a young Antoine Walker. In other seasons in Pitino's era, Kentucky played it a bit safer, with point spread standard deviations around fourteen. If Pitino's 1995 club, which was a general "favorite" and not an "underdog," hadn't been such a high variance one, they could have added another 6 percent to their winning percentage. Rather than 28–5, they might have been 30–3 and still alive in the Final Four.

Endnotes

1. This measure of roster stability was introduced to me by Professor David Berri, a sports economist at California State University at Bakersfield.

2. Another way to estimate winning percentages is to adapt Bill James's so-called Pythagorean Formula that he developed for baseball. The equation is

$$\text{Win}\% = \frac{\text{PTS}^z}{\text{PTS}^z + \text{DPTS}^z}$$

where z is 2 in baseball and anywhere from about 8 to 17 in basketball. In the WNBA, John Maxwell of the Charlotte Sting estimated z to be about 9. In the NBA, various estimates exist, from about 11 to 17, depending on when they were estimated. During the higher pace days, the value was higher. That is a disadvantage of the method. The advantage is its simplicity.

3. Figure 11.4 actually shows a statistical simulation of scores using as parameters the averages, standard deviations, and correlation of Utah's 1995 actual results. Other simulations are possible, which is why this is labeled as an "example."

4. That variability is increased because the variance of offensive and defensive ratings is inversely proportional to the number of possessions in a game, according to a binomial model of team scoring possessions. See Technical Box 2.

Chapter 12

The Effect of Bad Referees and Other Short Stories

T he bell curve introduced in the last chapter is a kind of model for how basketball teams behave. It captures a few essential aspects of their behavior and makes a few predictions. In this case, the bell curve captures three things:

1. Teams that score more points than their opponents should have winning records.

2. Teams that are relatively variable in how many points they score and allow will be closer to .500 than teams that are more consistent.

3. Teams that play up or down to their opponents effectively act more consistently than teams that don't and, hence, are further away from .500.

There is no mystery and no subtlety to point number one. Everyone understands that the more you score and the fewer points you allow, the better you'll do. It's a good thing that's in this model; otherwise the bell curve wouldn't work.

Points two and three are more subtle. You hear about players who need to be more consistent or who are good when their heads are in the game—that kind of talk speaks to consistency a bit. The last chapter also pointed out some elements of strategy that are related to being consistent.

But these latter two points actually imply a lot more than what you've seen so far. The inconsistency of teams and how much they play up or down to their opponents also says something about referees and about how good teams really are.

The Effect of Bad Referees

For as long as I can remember, I have simultaneously admired and despised the neutral referee who keeps control of a game. For them not to get caught up in the action, cheering for the underdog, correcting players' errors as a coach would, I admired them. For their inconsistency in calling or not making calls when I thought they should have, I despised them—though I never actually earned a technical foul, either as a player or as a coach. (It was probably because I never mentioned their mothers.)

When I started analyzing basketball in some detail, I was long frustrated in my attempts to understand the ref's role in the game. How do you analyze a neutral contributor to the game? I could look at whether they truly were neutral, whether they called an equal number of fouls on different classes of players or teams; but that approach was flawed because different teams and different players clearly did commit different numbers of fouls. I couldn't come up with a way to identify classes of teams or individuals that "should" receive the same number of fouls.

But when I began using the bell curve model of the game, I realized how to do it. I realized how to strike back at the refs, to let them know how they can change a team's odds of winning or losing if they are doing a bad job. I finally figured out what it means for a ref to do a bad job.

A bad ref is an inconsistent ref. A terrible ref is a biased ref. I was interested only in the bad refs and really hope that the terrible ones are kept from being refs by the professionals who oversee refereeing standards. With cases like Game 6 of the Lakers-Kings Western Conference Finals of 2002, in which horribly biased reffing was perceived by almost all neutral observers, my hopes aren't very high. I'll get back to that.

One of the things that always kept me in good favor with refs was that I told them that they didn't make as many mistakes as the players did. Players miss shots, commit turnovers, pass to the wrong player, hold on to the ball too long, and foul other players. All a ref does is occasionally miss a call or make a call that changes what should have been the outcome of the play, sometimes permitting Kobe Bryant to get away with a takedown and ever so rarely whistling Rasheed Wallace for a foul he surely didn't commit. Everyone in the game is inconsistent, but the players are more inconsistent than the refs.

We know how players' inconsistencies and errors affect the game, but how specifically does a referee error affect the score? A ref's error alters whether a score actually goes up on the scoreboard. This is an assumption for simplicity's sake, but not a bad one. For instance, a ref can miss a charging call and a team gets a score they shouldn't get, or a ref can miss a defensive foul and a team doesn't get a score they should get. With just this simple idea of a ref's inconsistency and without introducing any favoritism into that inconsistency, I can show that, despite the old saying "fouls all balance out in the long run," inconsistency changes the odds of one team winning over another.

The method is simply to simulate two teams that score with a frequency typical of basketball teams, then add in the effect of the officials. For example, I simulated five thousand games between Team A, which scored on 54 percent of their possessions (its floor percentage was 54 percent), and Team B, which scored 50 percent of the time. In each game, I ran through ninety-five possessions for each team, a little faster than today's slow-paced games. On each possession for Team A, they had a 54 percent chance of scoring, and on each possession for Team B, they had a 50 percent chance of scoring. Over the course of a ninety-five-possession game, it should be obvious that Team A is the likely victor. In reality, given no mistakes by referees, I was simulating that Team A had a 70 percent chance of winning. In order to simulate imperfect referees, I figured that reasonable refs made a mistake that affected a score on 5 percent of possessions, a fairly low rate and probably one that Bobby Knight would disagree with (I just hope he doesn't throw a chair at me). So, for the same sequence of possessions and games as before, I input this error rate and found that Team A's winning percentage dropped a measly 1 percent to 69 percent (now I know Bobby Knight is going to throw a chair at me).

So before Coach Knight actually hits me with one of those chairs, I will raise the referee error rate to about 15 percent. He may still think that is too low, but hopefully he'll only slam a phone. In this case, the winning percentage of Team A should still be 70 percent, but their actual winning percentage drops to 65 percent due to referee errors. Over the course of an eighty-two-game NBA season, this means that a team like the 2002 New Jersey Nets, which had a winning percentage of about 65 percent, could blame three or four of their losses on bad reffing. I'm sure they'd start counting with their March 19 loss to Cleveland in which Lamond Murray's shot after the buzzer was allowed. On the other hand, the 2002 New York Knicks, which had a winning percentage of about 35 percent, could thank the refs for three or four of their wins, something I doubt New York fans would ever do.

But there is a kicker. NBA referees are known for giving a few extra calls to the home team and to stars. If they are doing so, they are offsetting the bias they incur by being inconsistent. Let me repeat that: *A ref that shows some bias for home teams and for better players counters the inherent favoritism to weaker teams that results from the refs simply being human.*

Before all you referees that are reading this go out and start telling fans that it's OK that the refs called all those fouls on the Kings in the fourth quarter in their game against the Lakers, let me blow a whistle. In order to offset the bias of neutral inconsistency, it takes only a trivial number of biased calls. Let's say that the Lakers should have won about 70 percent of their games against the Kings at home, which is consistent with the pregame Las Vegas line. A group of neutral refs that makes errors on 15 percent of possessions will bring that winning percentage down to about 65 percent. Referees trying to bring the odds back to 70 percent for the Lakers would have to be biased toward the Lakers on only one of one hundred of all possible calls. Given that there were about two hundred possessions in that game, the refs could have given Kobe the knockdown of Mike Bibby and Vlade Divac's phantom fifth foul on Shaq, but the sixth foul on Scot Pollard and the other three "stunningly incorrect" calls, as Michael Wilbon of the *Washington Post* labeled them, changed the odds heavily in the Lakers' favor. One biased call per hundred is a tiny number, probably something that can occur naturally to a ref who just feels the emotion of a home crowd. One biased call in a hundred is such a small number that a ref consciously trying to rectify the error caused by neutral inconsistency is bound to overcompensate. So don't do it. Just be neutral. We like underdogs anyway.

The Perfect Score

Speaking of underdogs, there is one little weird thing about the bell curve formula that says, "If you're a favorite, don't pile on the underdog." When I say "weird," I mean that I didn't expect it to show up, and I'm not sure if I believe it. Here is the story...

Remember when the Chicago Bulls came off their 72–10 season of 1996 and were crushing every team they played at the start of 1997? No one was seriously talking about them going undefeated, but people were actually saying the word. On a lark, I then started tracking their scores and their expected winning percentage from the bell curve formula following each game (see table 12.1).

The one that caught my eye was that November 13 Miami game. The Bulls blew the Heat out by thirty-two yet only increased their expected winning percentage

Table 12.1. Bulls' First 12 Game Scores and Expected Winning Percentage in 1996

Date	Opponent	Chicago Score	Opponent Score	Expected Win%
11/1/96	BOS	107	98	—
11/2/96	PHI	115	86	0.938
11/5/96	VAN	96	73	0.950
11/6/96	MIA	106	100	0.918
11/8/96	DET	98	80	0.946
11/9/96	BOS	104	92	0.955
11/11/96	PHO	97	79	0.969
11/13/96	MIA	103	71	0.970
11/15/96	CHA	110	87	0.980
11/16/96	ATL	90	69	0.984
11/20/96	PHO	113	99	0.984
11/21/96	DEN	110	92	0.987

from .969 to .970. I started playing a game of what-if. What if the Bulls won 103–72, instead of 103–71? Instead of a winning percentage of .970, the Bulls' winning percentage went up to .972! In other words, according to the bell curve, if the Bulls had won by less, their expected winning percentage would have gone up! I scrambled to make sure I wasn't doing any calculations wrong. I wasn't. So I then kept increasing Miami's score to see what would happen. It turned out that a score of 103–83 created an expected winning percentage of .981—the highest it could be. The perfect score that Chicago could have won by—the one that maximized their expected winning percentage—was 103–83. By actually adding an extra twelve points onto the victory, it only made the Bulls look worse. If they had beaten the Heat by fifty, their expected winning percentage would have dropped to .925.

Remember, I said it was weird, and I'm not sure if I believe it. But it does suggest that there is a degree of beating an opponent that is reasonable, and that going beyond it is bad. I can only make up reasons for this. You're expending too much energy crushing a team that you have already beaten. It makes you overconfident against good opponents if you beat bad ones by that much. Other teams despise you for winning so much, and they get extra prepared.

I don't think this odd result is significant enough for me to say, "Don't pile on an already beaten team," but it never hurts to say so.

Toying With 'Em

In fact, most NBA teams don't "pile on." They do put in scrubs when a game is already decided, which is how I personally got to play college basketball. I was always amazed that garbage time didn't arrive until there was under a minute to play in a forty-point rout, but I was happy for the playing time.

Garbage time makes a good team's statistics look worse than they normally would be (and a bad team's stats look better). A lead by twenty with six minutes to go should become a lead of twenty-four at the end of the (forty-eight-minute) game, if the two teams keep competing at the same level. But more often than not, the point difference ends up being less than twenty. The (expected) winner plays conservatively, just to hold on to the win. They only have to match basket for basket. They run down the shot clock and end up with more bad shots. That is six minutes of time that doesn't reflect their true ability, the kind of ability they'll exhibit against better teams, teams that they'll face in the playoffs.

This aspect of garbage time is at least partially reflected in the bell curve formula—the correlation (or covariance) term in the last chapter. From that formula, you can then find out how good a team is if they don't slack off or play down to their opponents. The formula allows you to remove that correlation, while assuming that the team still would have won the same number of games. That's a way of saying, "The math is hard, so I'm not going to show you the details here." Rather, the details are in this endnote.[1] The results of adjusting offensive and defensive ratings for a team's correlation are called "uncorrelated ratings."

Uncorrelated ratings are interesting in reevaluating those great offenses and defenses of the past. I mentioned in chapter 3 that I thought that the ratings used to rank the best offenses and defenses should be adjusted a little for how good the teams were. That idea came from this concept that better teams do have more opportunities to slack off at the end of blowouts, allowing bad teams to correspondingly look a little better. So table 12.2 adds the credit for the quality of the team into the offensive rating for the best offenses in history.

The Bulls and the Jazz dominate the top five spots of the revised order. But really, the top twenty-five contains mostly the same teams, with only three teams dropping out to be replaced by the 1996 Jazz at number nineteen, the 1986 Celtics at number twenty-four, and the 1991 Blazers at number twenty-five. That 1986 Celtics team went 67–15 and, as a Magic Johnson fan, my memories of those Celtics are etched in pain as I watched how great they were. When I did the research for

Table 12.2. Top 25 Offenses Updated with Uncorrelated Ratings

Team	Season	Standard Offensive Rating	Increment above League	Rank	Uncorrelated Offensive Rating	Increment above League	Rank
Dallas	2002	112.2	7.7	1	112.9	8.3	6
Chicago	1997	114.4	7.7	2	116.9	10.2	1
Utah	1998	112.7	7.6	3	114.2	9.2	2
Chicago	1996	115.2	7.5	4	116.6	8.9	3
Denver	1982	114.3	7.5	5	114.4	7.5	12
Chicago	1992	115.5	7.4	6	116.6	8.4	5
Boston	1988	115.4	7.4	7	116.2	8.2	8
LA Lakers	1987	115.6	7.3	8	116.4	8.1	9
Utah	1997	113.6	7.0	9	115.1	8.4	4
LA Lakers	1998	111.9	6.9	10	112.9	7.8	10
Orlando	1995	115.1	6.9	11	115.6	7.3	14
Chicago	1991	114.7	6.8	12	116.2	8.3	7
Dallas	1987	114.9	6.6	13	115.6	7.3	15
Seattle	1995	114.8	6.5	14	115.6	7.3	13
Indiana	1999	108.7	6.5	15	109.9	7.7	11
Seattle	1998	111.4	6.4	16	112.1	7.0	18
LA Lakers	1985	114.1	6.3	17	115.1	7.2	16
Phoenix	1995	114.5	6.2	18	115.3	7.0	17
LA Lakers	1986	113.3	6.1	19	114.0	6.9	22
Utah	1995	114.3	6.1	20	114.5	6.3	27
LA Lakers	1989	113.8	6.0	21	114.7	6.9	21
LA Lakers	1983	110.5	5.8	22	111.6	6.9	20
LA Lakers	1990	114.0	5.8	23	114.9	6.8	23
Cleveland	1992	113.9	5.7	24	114.2	6.0	31
Milwaukee	2001	108.8	5.7	25	110.1	7.0	28

the original lists of great teams, it surprised me that these Celtics didn't show up on either the great offense or great defense lists. Unfortunately for my painful memories, this adjustment adds them to the list of best offenses and they also jump into the number-ten slot of all-time best defenses (see table 12.3).

There is a lot more shuffling with the defensive teams than with the offensive ones, except at the top, where those Riley-led Knicks clearly exploited defensive rules to a significant advantage. Another five teams also crack the top twenty-five, including the 1997 Bulls at number nine, the 1982 Milwaukee Bucks (with Don Nelson at the helm) at fifteen, the 1991 San Antonio Spurs (with David Robinson and no Tim Duncan) at twenty-one, the 1994 Sonics at twenty-two, and the 2002 Spurs at twenty-three.

The 1983 76ers, who had three players named First Team All-Defense, moved up to thirty-fifth on the list of top defenses, from eighty-fourth. But were they a better defensive team than even that? The adjustment here is for winning percentage in the regular season, not for anything involving playoff performance, and those Sixers nearly swept through the playoffs. I haven't tried to make adjustments for playoffs. Given that the All-Defense awards were made based on regular season performance, it's not clear that there should be an adjustment.

Table 12.3. Top 25 Defenses Updated with Uncorrelated Ratings

Team	Season	Standard Defensive Rating	Relative to League	Rank	Uncorrelated Defensive Rating	Relative to League	Rank
New York	1993	99.7	-8.4	1	99.3	-8.7	1
New York	1994	98.2	-8.1	2	97.6	-8.7	2
San Antonio	1999	95.0	-7.2	3	94.3	-7.9	3
Washington	1975	92.2	-6.4	4	91.6	-7.0	7
Utah	1989	101.5	-6.3	5	101.3	-6.5	12
Phoenix	1981	100.5	-6.2	6	100.0	-6.7	11
Miami	1997	100.6	-6.1	7	99.5	-7.2	6
Philadelphia	1981	100.6	-6.1	8	99.4	-7.3	5
Cleveland	1998	99.1	-5.9	9	98.9	-6.1	17
Chicago	1996	101.7	-5.9	10	100.3	-7.3	4
LA Lakers	2000	98.3	-5.8	11	97.2	-6.9	8
New Jersey	1983	98.9	-5.8	12	98.6	-6.1	18
New York	1997	101.0	-5.7	13	100.4	-6.3	14
San Antonio	1998	99.4	-5.7	14	99.0	-6.0	19
Seattle	1996	102.1	-5.6	15	101.2	-6.5	13
San Antonio	2000	98.5	-5.5	16	98.1	-6.0	20
Washington	1983	99.3	-5.4	17	99.3	-5.4	33
Chicago	1998	99.8	-5.3	18	98.9	-6.2	16
Phoenix	2001	98.0	-5.2	19	98.4	-5.4	32
San Antonio	2001	98.0	-5.2	20	97.9	-5.9	24
Atlanta	1999	97.1	-5.1	21	96.4	-5.9	25
Phoenix	2000	99.1	-5.0	22	98.4	-5.7	27
New Jersey	2002	99.5	-5.0	23	99.3	-5.2	41
Cleveland	1989	102.9	-4.9	24	102.3	-5.5	29
Utah	1988	103.1	-4.9	25	102.6	-5.4	31

Throughout most of this book, you will not see these uncorrelated ratings used very much. They generally tell a similar story to that told by the standard offensive and defensive points per hundred possession ratings. They do shuffle teams around a little bit, but usually not enough to worry about. One situation where it does make a little sense is in looking at . . .

Does Defense Win Championships?

The proverbial "they" say that Defense Wins Championships.

I really don't know who exactly "they" are who claim this, but "they" are wrong. Or at least "they" should step forward and tell me what "they" mean. Because I really can't tell.

Growing up and playing on a few teams (basketball, football, softball, and, of course, dodge ball), I saw lots of games and lots of teams. I won a few championships and played on a few bad teams, too. But in most of the cases where I saw the best teams, it was offense—not defense—that made the teams as good as they were.

There was the basketball team that had a guy who could dunk, who could blow by just about any defender, and who ultimately played college ball. They won our league title because this guy could score. *They* didn't say that defense wins championships. Only "they" did.

On top of that: Who are the players who get recruited for the next level? It sure ain't the guy who sticks to his man like glue but can't buy a wide-open ten footer. It's more likely to be the guy who can break down any defense and has a breakdown about playing defense.

The King of the Court

If you think Michael Jordan is called the greatest basketball player ever because of his defense, then you're probably also wondering about all the fuss over Elvis's death, since you just saw him at the grocery store handing out free samples of Yoohoo. Nike, McDonalds, Gatorade, and Sportsline all paid Jordan because he could hang in the air, do his taxes, then dunk on Shaquille O'Neal—not because he could shut down Steve Smith.

The Fifty Greatest Players

You want more? How about this: Of the fifty greatest players in NBA history (as determined by an NBA blue-ribbon panel in 1996), only three had career scoring averages under fifteen points per game. Of all these players, it is fair to say that only Bill Russell, Dave DeBusschere, and maybe Nate Thurmond made their reputations primarily on defense.

The Recent Champions

But I have heard Defense Wins Championships as much as anyone, and I have at least been partially brainwashed by it. I thought I saw the Bulls winning the 1997 NBA title because they turned up the defensive intensity. I thought I saw the 2001 Lakers turn up their defense in the playoffs.

But I also remember seeing Jordan score thirty-eight points when no defense—not even the flu—could stop him from winning Game 5 of the 1997 Finals. I remember Kobe Bryant tipping in a last-second offensive rebound to beat the Spurs in 2002. I remember no team being able to stop Jordan-Pippen and no team being able to stop Shaq-Kobe.

Given that my memory is horrible, I thought I could be missing something, so I decided to look at this question in more detail. I really tried to find some evidence that Defense Wins Championships.

The Basic Study

Championships are made in the playoffs. Champions win their first-round series, then move on. They win their second-round series, then move on, and so forth. So I decided to look at winners of playoff series and whether they were better defensively than their opponents. If two teams are facing off in an important play-off series, the better defensive team should win—that seems like a reasonable interpretation of the phrase, doesn't it? Well, of the 387 playoff series wins since 1974, 221 (or 57 percent) have been won by the team with the better defensive rating and 240 (62 percent) have been won by the team with the better offensive rating. Offense seems to win.

If They'd Only Apply Themselves

Still trying to prove myself stupid, I figured I'd use the uncorrelated ratings to adjust for good teams that just slack off. As your mom used to tell you, "You could do so much better if you just applied yourself!!" Well, teams *do* apply themselves in the playoffs, so it seems relevant to look at this measure. In fact, it turns out that uncorrelated ratings are better predictors of winners than the standard ratings, but, alas, they still show that the better defensive team wins 59 percent of the time and the better offensive team wins 63 percent of the time.

Really, They Only Got Lazy Defensively

Given the rather dim light this casts on "their" mantra, I pulled out one last desperate trick to try to prove "them" right. The uncorrelated ratings *assume* that teams slack off equally on defense and on offense. I don't know if that is right, but I had no basis to think otherwise. If I change that assumption so that only the defense slacks off in the regular season, then, well, the story still is the same, just less emphatic. With this modification, the better defenses win 61.8 percent of their playoff series, and the better offenses win 62.0 percent of their playoff series.

Just Win, Baby

Maybe I'm still looking at it wrong. Maybe I should just look at the winners of the Finals and see how often they were the most efficient offense or defense. Using standard ratings, the best defense won five titles and the best offense won six. Using uncorrelated ratings, the best defense and the best offense each won seven. Using uncorrelated ratings where only the defense is assumed to slack off in the regular season—ah ha!—the best defense won seven titles and the best offense won only six.

But does that really convince you that Defense Wins Championships?

Endnote

1. The formulas for the "uncorrelated" offensive and defensive ratings, as they are called, are

$$UORtg = ORtg + \frac{(R-1)(ORtg - DRtg)}{2}$$

$$UDRtg = DRtg - \frac{(R-1)(ORtg - DRtg)}{2}$$

where UORtg is the uncorrelated offensive rating, UDRtg is the uncorrelated defensive rating, ORtg and DRtg are the standard offensive and defensive points per hundred possession ratings, and

$$R = \frac{\sqrt{Var(ORtg) + Var(DRtg)}}{\sqrt{Var(ORtg) + Var(DRtg) - 2Cov(ORtg,DRtg)}}$$

Var( ): Statistical variance from game-to-game of the quantity in ( ), which is the standard deviation squared
Cov( ): Statistical covariance between the two quantities in ( )

Chapter 13

Teamwork 3: Distributing Credit among Cooperating Players

Players don't win games, teams do. As a result, players shouldn't look for their own points, they should look to maximize *team* points. Players shouldn't care about stopping their own man if it means that other guys are scoring easily against teammates. Basketball is a team game, where winning *as a team* is all that matters...

Or does it? The Ultimatum Game experiments (see chapter 10) do suggest that something about our humanity forces us to assign uneven credit for team accomplishments. The player offering the money seems to expect a little more than the player accepting the offer. It's not quite a fifty-fifty split. Teammates on a basketball team seem to behave in a similar fashion. A talented player not only wants to win; he wants to be the player leading the team to victory. The player who leads a team to a title enjoys more satisfaction than the player who gets one minute playing defense at the end of the first half of that title game.

As egalitarian as the philosophers would like us to be, we nevertheless instinctively assign individual credit in a team victory. We often name an MVP of a tournament or of a championship series; All-League Teams are compiled. The apparent reason for assigning individual credit is that we all have some need to understand the components of success: What created that championship team? We try to deconstruct a team's success as a hacker tries to deconstruct Microsoft software. Well, maybe not to that degree. Most of us are too lazy to really break down team success (or failure) in any detail. We offer our opinions and arguments, some logical, some purely emotional. We add our votes to those of others.

But basketball consists of an almost endless series of team events that could be broken down to assign credit to individual teammates. It's not just the performance of a championship team that can get broken down. It's every little play that any team runs and every defense that it sets up. That's why Dick Vitale, Billy

Packer, Matt Guokas, and Doug Collins (once he gets fired or quits again) have jobs on TV—to tell us what an outstanding play Joe Point Guard made in recognizing Frankie Forward's coming free on the baseline behind the defense. These former coaches recognize where credit is due in every play, i.e., who was responsible for what and how well they did it.

My original hope for this chapter was to get a few current coaches to actually assign numbers to the credit they mentally assess. For instance, if a point guard passes to that wide-open big guy near the basket, how do you split credit for the two points between the two players? Do you give one point to the passer and one point to the guy who made the shot? Do you give a point and a half to the assist man who saw through his own defender and only a half point to the guy who dunked the ball with no one around him?

I asked a few coaches questions like these using numerous different scenarios involving clear examples of teamwork, hoping to get their opinions and arguments. What I found out is that coaches hate answering these questions on the record, especially if there is "blame" to be assigned. A typical response: "We as a team, coaches included, share in all things. We don't blame any one person for a mistake. We work to correct the mistake." Good attitude, coach. But it doesn't shed any light on what many coaches really do, which is to account for interactions and responsibilities among teammates. So I tried again, simplifying my questions so that they didn't require "blame" or "credit" to be assigned. I asked the following:

> Coaches often look for a player who can distribute the ball to scorers. Coaches also look for scorers. Which is more important? If you have a great distributor and no creative scorers, but another great distributor comes along, what do you do? On the other hand, if you have a great creative scorer and no distributor, but another great scorer comes along, what do you do?

Phrasing the questions this way helped. Coaches did express some preference for having a scorer over a passer. My interpretation of their replies is that they'd assign more credit to a guy who made the basket than to a guy who passed him the ball. An equally correct interpretation is that coaches feel that scorers are in shorter supply than passers. Maybe it is appropriate to say that scoring is more difficult than passing.

That last statement is the basis for my personal Difficulty Theory for Distributing Credit in Basketball: The more difficult the contribution, the more credit it deserves.

- Example 1: On an assist to a big man underneath the basket, the passer gets relatively more credit because most defenses are not going to let a big man get open too often, so a passer seeing that opening deserves relatively more credit.

- Example 2: On a fluke assist to a big man who has no three-point range but makes a wide-open trey because the defense doesn't respect him, the theory gives the passer very little credit because his pass was probably being lightly defended and was virtually guaranteed to be completed, whereas the made shot—even with a defender giving the big man an open look—was quite unlikely.

Another way of viewing these two examples is to consider how much each player's contribution improves the team's expected number of points scored. On any possession in the NBA, the expected number of points to be scored is about one. After a pass to a big man under the hoop, you gotta think that the odds of the team scoring at least two points (maybe three, on a foul) go up. You can see this diagrammatically in figure 13.1, where I've assumed that the big man's dunk is an 85-percent proposition and that he doesn't get fouled after making the shot.

On the other hand, in the second example, after a pass to a poor-shooting big man on the perimeter, you assume that the passer is merely starting the offense, not significantly raising the odds of scoring. That big man's act of taking the shot surprises his defender, who is giving him that shot anyway, and if it goes in, most or all of the credit goes to that big man. This is represented in figure 13.2, where I've assumed that the big man was very unlikely to take the shot and, hence, that the expected value of the possession did not change with the pass to him.

Numerically, it's easy to read one type of "credit" in these two charts. The transition from the first bar to the second bar is the credit given to the passer, 0.7 in the first case and 0.0 in the second. The transition from the second bar to the third is the credit given to the scorer, 0.3 in the first case and 1.0 in the second. If

Figure 13.1. How Expected Points Changes with Pass to Big Man under the Basket

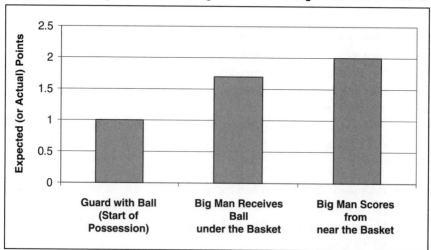

Figure 13.2. How Expected Points Changes with Pass to Big Man far from the Basket

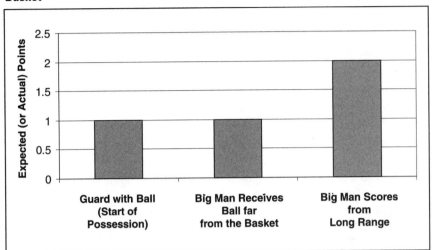

you're going to split the two points of each possession between the two players, it would look like this:

- Case 1: Passer gets 1.4 points and scorer gets 0.6 points.
- Case 2: Passer gets 0.0 points and scorer gets 2.0 points.

That's my Difficulty Theory, in a nutshell. All you have to do is watch every single game, estimate the chance of scoring as a consequence of every dribble, pass, pick, and shot, then add things up.

Or you can make some estimates.

Some Implications of the Difficulty Theory on Player Behavior

This theory is a powerful one. It rewards cooperating players according to the needs of the team. If the team needs more shooters and fewer passers (passes are easier and field goal percentages are low), greater credit goes to players who can shoot. If a defense is pressuring every pass at the cost of easier shots, passers get relatively greater credit for their contribution to a team score. If a player is both a good passer and a good shooter, this theory says that how much he should do of each depends on his teammates' abilities. This interactive weighting dictates that a player's stats should change if his teammates' skills change, in order to optimize the scoring potential of his team. If a player has better shooting teammates around him, it makes more sense to get them the ball. Hence, an assist on a good shooting team tends to be more valuable than one on a poor shooting team.

Don't get confused, though! If you have a poor shooting team, that does not mean that you shouldn't pass the ball. Rather, it means that you need to find ways to get the ball to teammates in better shooting positions, making more of an effort to get the ball to them nearer the basket or in their favorite spots.

This Difficulty Theory also has the benefit of being applicable not only to situations involving an assist to a scorer, but also to other team accomplishments where two or more players cooperate toward that accomplishment. On defense, it takes one player to force his guy to miss a shot and (often) another player to get the defensive rebound. How you distribute credit to those two guys follows the same rule. Who did the harder job? In the NBA, where teams shoot around 45 percent and collect about 70 percent of their opponents' missed shots, it is harder to force guys to miss shots (forcing the miss is successful about 55 percent of the time) than to get the defensive rebounds (again, a team is able to grab the defensive board about 70 percent of the time). So good shot defenders are relatively more important than good defensive rebounders in the NBA. At lower levels, where shooting isn't as good and offensive rebounding is better, this theory shifts relatively more weight toward getting defensive rebounds and dictates that teams should shift emphasis to defensive rebounds in order to improve defense.

Another example of teamwork is when a player gets an offensive rebound that leads to a team score. This is a little different from the previous examples because an offensive rebound does not necessarily mean that a score will occur, nor is an offensive rebound necessary for there to be a team score. An offensive rebound really only increases the odds of a team scoring on a possession—and, according to chapter 6, it might increase the odds quite a bit. Because there isn't as much cause-and-effect with an offensive rebound, assigning credit is more complicated, something I'll discuss for persistent readers below. In general, however, rebounds are more valuable when they are relatively rare. If it is more difficult to get an offensive rebound and also relatively easy to score following a rebound (something that seems to be true), that implies higher value to the offensive rebound. On the other hand, if offensive rebounds are plentiful, but the guys getting them just can't score, that makes the offensive rebounds less valuable.

Two Points Is Two Points Is Two Points

The other important concept in splitting credit among teammates has gone unstated to this point but deserves mention. That concept is that the sum of the parts is neither greater than nor less than the whole. You can't give Kobe Bryant 50 percent of the credit on an assist to Shaq and also give Shaq 80 percent of the credit. Equivalently, you can't say that the value of such a possession is more than the two points that Shaq scored. Kobe and Shaq have to split credit for those two points. You can't give Shaq two points for the basket and Kobe one point for the assist, something that I have heard argued because, as they say, "passing is an important part of the game." Passing is important—assists per field goal shows a correlation with offensive efficiency in chapter 3. I'd rather not give *extra* credit for that, but give relatively more credit to the passers who are making their shooters more efficient.

There are several benefits of constraining credit so that points or wins add up to real totals.[1] The first benefit is that the results "look real." If you create an individual points produced formula that sums to the team total points scored, that implies that you can say a player "produced thirty-four points," rather than saying he "produced forty-five credits," where "credits" are something that don't quite match anything real. Points are something a coach understands, whereas "credits" are not.

The second benefit of this constraint is that it forces value judgments. Most of us like looking at the good things that people do and neglecting some of the bad things, and we tend to cave in to that optimistic nature. Shaq is a great player, so let's give him lots of money! Kevin Garnett is a great player, so let's give him lots of money! Jerry Stackhouse is a great player, so let's give him lots of money! Dikembe Mutombo is a great player, so let's give him lots of money! This constraint says that you need to be careful about assessing who is so "great." It also says that you can't really have a bunch of good players on a team with a bad record. Antawn Jamison may have scored fifty points in back-to-back games in 2001, but he couldn't have been worth more than seventeen wins to the team that season because it won only seventeen games (and only one of his two fifty-point games). And the Warriors still said: "Let's give him lots of money!" Even if Jamison was worth nine wins to the Warriors, that would mean that near–Rookie of the Year Marc Jackson, shooting guard Larry Hughes, point guard Mookie Blaylock, sixth man Bob Sura, center Erick Dampier, and the other sixteen players on the team have to split eight wins. They weren't worth as much as Jamison alone! Having this constraint is like making a budget where you have a fixed amount of money to spend on food, rent, gas, utilities, and entertainment. You gotta find ways to cut. And you can't borrow to do it.

Individual Offensive Ratings and Floor Percentages

I use the difficulty concept to split credit among cooperating teammates, both for offense and for defense. It allows unique assignment of team success to the teammates who cooperated to create that success. In this chapter, I'll present only the formulas for the offensive contributions, contributions splitting the team points and the team scoring possessions to arrive at formulas for *individual* floor percentage and *individual* offensive ratings. (I saved the individual defensive formulas for chapter 17.) Both of these individual offensive statistics are exactly analogous to the team statistics you've seen up to this point:

- *Individual floor percentage* is an individual's scoring possessions divided by his total possessions. It answers the question, "What percentage of the time that a player wants to score does he actually score?" A player like Shaq will do very well here because he shoots well, commits few turnovers, and gets to the line a lot.

- *Individual offensive rating* is the number of points produced by a player per hundred total individual possessions. In other words, "How many points is a player likely to generate when he tries?" Though Shaq may have a high individual floor percentage, his poor foul shooting means that he has a lot of one-point possessions, bringing his offensive rating down a bit. Good three-point shooters like Reggie Miller, who may not have the highest floor percentage, will have higher offensive ratings.

In looking at team numbers, you've actually seen a lot more offensive ratings than floor percentages up to now. In looking at individuals, you will often see both of these measures because they do reflect style differences. How individual players put points on the board is much more variable than how teams as a whole put points on the board.

There are three key elements that go into creating individual floor percentages and ratings. These three elements and their formulas are given below without significant explanation (see Appendix 1).

Individual scoring possessions reflect a player's contributions to a team's scoring possessions. The first contribution is through field goals, sharing credit with those who assisted on the shots:

$$\text{FG Part} = \text{FGM} \times \left(1 - \frac{1}{2} \times \frac{\text{PTS} - \text{FTM}}{2 \times \text{FGA}} \times q_{AST}\right)$$

where

$$q_{AST} = \frac{\text{MIN}}{\text{TMMIN}/5} q_5 + \left(1 - \frac{\text{MIN}}{\text{TMMIN}/5}\right) q_{12}$$

where

$$q_5 = \sum_{i \neq n} \frac{\text{AST}_i}{\sum\limits_{k \neq i} \text{FGM}_k}$$

$$q_{12} = \frac{\dfrac{TMAST}{TMMIN} \times MIN \times 5 - AST}{\dfrac{TMFGM}{TMMIN} \times MIN \times 5 - FGM}$$

(A simplified approximate equation for q_5 is $q_5 \approx 1.14 \times \dfrac{TMAST - AST}{TMFGM}$.)

The second contribution is a player's own assists, which earns him credit based on how easy he made the shots for teammates:

$$AST\ Part = \frac{1}{2} \times \frac{(TMPTS - TMFTM) - (PTS - FTM)}{2 \times (TMFGA - FGA)} \times AST$$

The third contribution is through free throws:

$$FT\ Part = \left[1 - \left(1 - FT\%\right)^2\right] \times 0.4 \times FTA$$

Finally, all of these contributions are aided by offensive rebounds. So you have to remove some credit from the above parts but also add back credit for the player's offensive rebounds, giving this equation:

$$Scoring\ Possessions = \left(FG\ Part + AST\ Part + FT\ Part\right)$$
$$\times \left(1 - \frac{TMOREB}{TMScPoss} \times TMOREB\ weight \times TMPlay\%\right)$$
$$+ OREB \times TMOREB\ weight \times TMPlay\%$$

That "TMOREB weight" is given by

$$TMOREB\ weight = \frac{(1 - TMOR\%) \times TMPlay\%}{(1 - TMOR\%) \times TMPlay\% + TMOR\% \times (1 - TMPlay\%)}$$

and the explanation for why it's there is in Appendix 1.

Individual total possessions is the total number of team possessions that a player can be considered responsible for. This includes scoring possessions, missed field goals that aren't rebounded, missed free throws that aren't rebounded, and turnovers, giving this formula:

$$Possessions = Scoring\ Possessions + Missed\ FG\ Part + Missed\ FT\ Part + TOV$$

The scoring possessions make up the hard part. The others are easy:

$$Missed\ FG\ Part = (FGA - FGM) \times (1 - 1.07 \times TMOR\%)$$

$$Missed\ FT\ Part = (1 - FT\%)^2 \times 0.4 \times FTA$$

Individual points produced is the number of points a player produces through scoring possessions, accounting for three-point shots and how well he does at the foul line. The formula ends up looking a lot like the scoring possession formula, which is ugly:

$$\text{Points Produced} = \left(\text{FG Part} + \text{AST Part} + \text{FT Part}\right)$$

$$\times \left(1 - \frac{\text{TMOR}}{\text{TMScPoss}} \times \text{TMOR weight} \times \text{TMPlay\%}\right) + \text{OR part}$$

The "parts" are different here than for scoring possessions, though. They are different almost exclusively in that they are scaled up by the number of points each scoring possession creates.

$$\text{FG Part} = 2 \times \left(\text{FGM} + \frac{1}{2} \times \text{FG3M}\right) \times \left(1 - \frac{1}{2} \times \frac{\text{PTS} - \text{FTM}}{2 \times \text{FGA}} \times q_{AST}\right)$$

$$\text{AST Part} = 2 \times \frac{\text{TMFGM} - \text{FGM} + \frac{1}{2}\left(\text{TMFG3M} - \text{FG3M}\right)}{\left(\text{TMFGM} - \text{FGM}\right)} \times \frac{1}{2}$$

$$\times \frac{\left(\text{TMPTS} - \text{TMFTM}\right) - \left(\text{PTS} - \text{FTM}\right)}{2 \times \left(\text{TMFGA} - \text{FGA}\right)} \times \text{AST}$$

$$\text{FT Part} = \text{FTM}$$

$$\text{OR part} = \text{OR} \times \text{TMOR weight} \times \text{TMPlay\%}$$

$$\times \frac{\text{TMPTS}}{\text{TMFGM} + [1 - \left(1 - \text{TMFT\%}\right)^2] \times 0.4 \times \text{TMFTA}}$$

That spinning feeling you currently are experiencing is temporary. Or maybe it just becomes so permanent that you don't notice it anymore. For the people who really want to calculate the numbers, those are the offensive formulas that I rely on. The formulas apply different weights to different stats for different players based on the difficulty the players face in recording those stats. For stats that come easily, players get relatively less weight than for stats that are more difficult to post. Notice, as mentioned several chapters ago, that individual floor percentage and individual offensive ratings are not just sums of good statistics and bad statistics. If you really want to understand the details for the formulas, see Appendix 1.

The difficulty concept provides a way to parse out the credit for things that *can be* measured, not just calculated—team floor percentage and team offensive ratings. These are absolutely real things that determine the success of a team. They are not artificial constructions of quality. By breaking them down using the difficulty concept, I wanted to assemble offensive statistics for individuals that were also real—not artificial constructions of statistics that didn't have meaning. The next chapter looks at some of the numbers for individuals and shows how their team offensive success followed.

Endnote

1. There are two ways to constrain credit so that points or wins add up. One way is to do it beforehand—as you give one player credit for 25 percent of a score, you remove that credit from other players. The other way is to assign all credit up front without regard to constraints, then, after summing all points (or wins or whatever real factor you're interested in), scale everyone's credit so that the sum matches the true total. The first way is more difficult, but a better test of the validity of the method. Even though the first way may not exactly replicate team values, if it is close, it says that the method is calibrated to reality. The second way is called "normalization" or, sometimes, "cheating." It usually replicates the team results exactly, but does so by forcing it. In this book, most methods involve distributing credit using the first method. There may be times where the second method is used, but not commonly.

Chapter 14

Individual Floor Percentages and Offensive Ratings

This chapter is about the numbers that are individual floor percentages and offensive ratings—two of the most important stats in this book. They tell *me* a lot about the offensive capabilities of players. Just as a team's offensive rating tells me its ability to produce points per possession, an individual's rating and floor percentage tell me how that person contributes to the team rating. These stats tell me how efficient a player is in creating a score and, because efficiency is what wins games, they tell me a lot about that, too. This chapter should help *you* to see how these stats tell you the same things.

Before jumping into all the numbers, it is important to point out that these two stats are essentially measurements—not artificial ratings of quality. There is no magic floor percentage or rating that is "good" in every league, in the way that a B means "good" in school. Just as a 40-percent field goal percentage may be great in a middle school league and horrible in the NBA, a team that produces eighty-five points per hundred possessions may be good for high school girls and bad in the WNBA. In order to really know what to expect for your high school league, your church league, or your recreational league, it is useful to just calculate team offensive ratings to set an average. From my experience calculating these for some of the lower levels, my sense is that the average ratings for the different age groups look approximately like those in table 14.1.

Table 14.1. Approximate Ranges of Ratings by Level

Level	Boys/Men	Girls/Women
High School	70–120	60–105
Division III College	80–120	70–105
Division II College	85–120	75–105
Division I College	85–120	80–105
Pro	95–115	85–105

I'm more confident in the pro ranges than those for the other levels, where data are somewhat sporadic. The ranges illustrate, though, that as players move up levels, the offensive skills usually get more refined. Individual player variability will, of course, be larger than the team ranges displayed here.

That is a big-picture context for applying the formulas at most any level. The greatest availability of data to illustrate actual numbers is in the NBA. The full history of numbers helps show how good offensive teams are structured, how good the great players can be, how the skills of certain positions can change through time (think of the centers), and how role players can be very useful in making a good offense. Most importantly, the NBA numbers show pretty clearly that these two stats are good predictors of performance. Beyond the NBA, the WNBA now has at least five years of good statistics, which is enough for me to do a little bit of analysis in the attached box.

The NBA Average

The individual ratings and floor percentages for NBA players should be couched by the NBA league averages, which have changed through time. Figure 14.1 shows both the average rating and floor percentage since 1974. That chart gives the kind of perspective that is necessary to evaluate players. A player who scored on 55 percent of his possessions in the 1980s, when the average was about 0.53, was above average—pretty good. A player who had a floor percentage of 0.55 in 2002, when the league average was about 0.49, was a *very* good offensive player. On the other hand, whereas few players until the mid-1980s had offensive ratings much higher than 120, there are many specialist three-point shooters now who can attain ratings that high. The rest of this chapter will give examples of the numbers put up by players of differing styles, while keeping in mind how the league has changed when looking at those numbers.

The 2002 Los Angeles Lakers

With Shaq and Kobe and a bunch of bums, the Lakers' offense turned in an offensive rating of 109.4 in 2002, above the league average of 104.5. Their stars did a great job. But what about the supporting cast? How did they look? The numbers for these Lakers are in table 14.2.

Shaq scored on 59 percent of his total possessions, a truly remarkable number in 2002 and the second best in the league among players producing at least fifteen points per game. His offensive rating of 116 is also quite good, but only fifth in the league. Though Shaq is the best at creating a score, he misses enough foul shots and makes no three-pointers, meaning that his offensive rating is not quite as high. Overall, Shaq produced 24.9 points per game through his various

Figure 14.1. NBA Historical Average Floor Percent and Rating

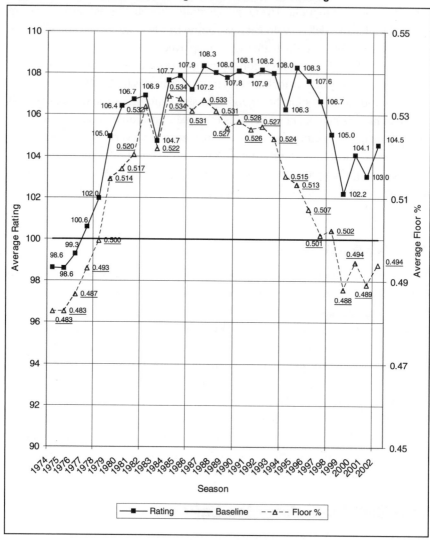

Table 14.2. Lakers' 2002 Individual Floor Percentages and Offensive Ratings

Player	G	Sc. Poss.	Poss.	Floor %	Off. Rtg.	Pts Prod/G	% Tm Poss
Shaquille O'Neal	67	855	1441	0.59	116	24.9	31%
Kobe Bryant	80	949	1766	0.54	112	24.7	30%
Derek Fisher	70	299	633	0.47	114	10.3	17%
Rick Fox	82	327	702	0.47	103	8.8	16%
Robert Horry	81	287	569	0.50	114	8.0	14%
Devean George	82	261	544	0.48	106	7.0	16%
Samaki Walker	69	239	421	0.57	114	7.0	13%
Lindsey Hunter	82	194	463	0.42	98	5.5	15%
Stanislav Medvedenko	71	167	321	0.52	105	4.7	23%
Mitch Richmond	64	113	255	0.44	98	3.9	19%
Mark Madsen	59	106	186	0.57	115	3.6	15%
Brian Shaw	58	84	195	0.43	100	3.4	16%
Mike Penberthy	3	3	3	0.77	156	1.8	15%
Joseph Crispin	6	5	12	0.40	81	1.6	23%
Jelani McCoy	21	14	30	0.47	94	1.4	15%

efforts, lower than his 27.2 scoring average because he received assists on a fair number of his shots.

Kobe was right below him, producing 24.7 points per game, which is barely less than his 25.2 scoring average. Kobe averaged 5.5 assists per game, so he was helping out on a lot of other players' scores. He wasn't nearly as efficient from the floor as Shaq, scoring on only 54 percent of his attempts, but he made up for it partially by making his foul shots and hitting some threes, bringing his offensive rating up to 112. Relative to the league averages of 0.494 and 104.5, Kobe's numbers are still quite high.

Derek Fisher is a great complement to this team. He stands on the perimeter and makes enough jumpers that he himself is efficient. His offensive rating of 114 means that teams cannot ignore him or he'll hurt them. Sure, he plays off the fact that Shaq is down low to draw defenders away, but the threat of him making jumpers reciprocally helps keep defenders off of Shaq. Instead, you should probably double-team and leave some other player open, such as . . .

Vanessa Williams's husband, Rick Fox, hasn't proven himself to be a great offensive player. Like Ron Harper before him, Fox has provided solid defense on a team that didn't need much offensive help. Like Harper before him, Fox was more efficient in a couple of previous years, producing 110 points per hundred possessions in 2001, for example. But he's never been able to be a consistent offensive threat, even with the presence of the big two. Of the top five point producers on this team, Fox is the only one with a below-average offensive rating, implying that defenses should perhaps try to force him to use more possessions (chapter 19 goes beyond this concept to examine how Fox's efficiency changes with responsibility and how it affects team dynamics).

Fifth on the Lakers scoring list is Robert Horry, the player whose shots in the playoffs have doomed opponents since 1994. Horry's offensive numbers resemble those of Fisher: high rating, relatively low floor percentage, and not a lot of points produced per game. Notice the far right column in table 14.2—"% Team Possessions." What this captures is the percentage of the team's possessions a player contributes to when he's in the game. Horry has to do something on only 14 percent of the Lakers' possessions, which is one out of every seven possessions, rather than one out of every five, which is what you'd expect with five guys on the court. Shaq and Kobe carry 61 percent of the team's possessions when they're in the game together, an average load for three guys. That leaves 39 percent for Kobe and Shaq's teammates to handle. That's only 13 percent per guy, so Horry's 14 percent is actually more than his adjusted share. But the fact remains that Horry and Fisher are efficient because they don't have to do too much. When players like Fox, Devean George, and Lindsey Hunter aren't very efficient, that implies to me that they aren't very good offensive players.

Below Horry are a bunch of other Lakers who are perceived as pretty replaceable. Samaki Walker and Mark Madsen posted efficient numbers without carrying a heavy possession load. They are likely benefiting from the presence of Shaq and Kobe. They also might be getting a fair number of garbage minutes.

In general, what I have found is that the kind of offensive structure that the Lakers had in 2002, with the more efficient players also producing relatively more points, is a good one. It is a difficult offense to stop because those who can score efficiently also have the ability to create opportunities well. This is in contrast to...

The 1999 Portland Trail Blazers

I picked this team because it is the last Isaiah Rider team that I can remember. Rider offers a classic example of a player who scored a lot but didn't do it very efficiently. This 1999 team is also nice because the 2000 version didn't have Rider, so I can do a little compare and contrast. The numbers for the 1999 Blazers are in table 14.3.

Rider was indeed the team's leading point *scorer*, but he didn't *produce* the most points per game (taking into account assists and offensive rebounds)—that was Damon Stoudamire. But having these two rather inefficient players at the top of the list was not good for the team. Even though they didn't dominate possessions like Shaq and Kobe did (thank goodness), their leadership produced a team that scored 104.7 points per hundred possessions, above the league average but well below the 107.9 they would score the next year. In 2000, Steve Smith replaced Rider, and Rasheed Wallace took over the scoring lead, giving them the scoring list in table 14.4.

Table 14.3. Trail Blazers' 1999 Individual Floor Percentages and Offensive Ratings

Player	G	Sc. Poss.	Poss.	Floor %	Off. Rtg.	Pts Prod/G	% Tm Poss
Damon Stoudamire	50	329	693	0.47	101	14.1	22%
Isaiah Rider	47	287	620	0.46	99	13.0	24%
Brian Grant	48	284	514	0.55	113	12.1	18%
Arvydas Sabonis	50	292	543	0.54	110	11.9	22%
Rasheed Wallace	49	273	513	0.53	109	11.4	20%
Walt Williams	48	179	375	0.48	111	8.6	19%
Jimmy Jackson	49	196	423	0.46	100	8.6	19%
Greg Anthony	50	137	293	0.47	107	6.3	20%
Stacey Augmon	48	113	209	0.54	108	4.7	13%
John Crotty	3	6	8	0.68	154	4.2	23%
Bonzi Wells	7	14	28	0.50	96	3.8	43%
Kelvin Cato	43	81	162	0.50	99	3.7	16%
Jermaine O'Neal	35	52	101	0.52	102	2.9	17%
Carlos Rogers	2	2	3	0.70	128	1.9	20%
Gary Grant	2	1	1	0.50	107	0.7	10%
Brian Shaw	1	0	2	0.12	25	0.5	20%

Table 14.4. Trail Blazers' 2000 Individual Floor Percentages and Offensive Ratings

Player	G	Sc. Poss.	Poss.	Floor %	Off. Rtg.	Pts Prod/G	% Tm Poss
Rasheed Wallace	81	594	1102	0.54	108	14.8	21%
Steve Smith	82	530	975	0.54	120	14.2	19%
Scottie Pippen	82	513	1047	0.49	106	13.5	20%
Damon Stoudamire	78	476	969	0.49	107	13.3	22%
Arvydas Sabonis	66	357	656	0.54	113	11.2	21%
Bonzi Wells	66	267	534	0.50	103	8.3	24%
Detlef Schrempf	77	296	564	0.52	111	8.2	18%
Brian Grant	63	238	450	0.53	106	7.6	18%
Greg Anthony	82	226	481	0.47	110	6.5	17%
Jermaine O'Neal	70	145	276	0.52	104	4.1	17%
Stacey Augmon	59	108	210	0.51	103	3.7	16%
Gary Grant	3	5	12	0.39	79	3.2	27%
Antonio Harvey	19	20	41	0.48	94	2.1	16%
Joe Kleine	7	5	12	0.42	89	1.5	20%

This may not be an optimal distribution of possessions either, but it is better. Wallace's offensive rating stayed consistently high with more minutes. Smith gave them a very efficient off-guard in place of Rider. Whereas their top two point producers in 1999 combined for a rating of one hundred, their top two point producers in 2000 combined for a rating of 114. That is a big boost, and the resulting team improvement offensively is evidence that such individual offensive ratings "work"— they are good measures of how a team offense will respond to an individual.

After Wallace and Smith, the top point producer was Scottie Pippen, who also joined the club in 2000. Pippen's offensive rating here shows him in his elder days, certainly not at his best, but he frankly was never the most efficient offensive player.

The Bulls, with and without Jordan

It is an interesting comparison to see how the Bulls' offense changed as Jordan went from playing basketball to playing baseball to playing basketball again. The Bulls' team offense went from 112.9 with Jordan leading the scoring in 1993 to 106.0 with Pippen leading the scoring in 1994, a huge drop. But the team's offense started recovering in 1995 with the maturation of Toni Kukoc, the shorter three-point line, and the return of Jordan late in the season. The team offense went up to 109.5. And then there was the monster year of 1996, when the Bulls went 72–10. Their offense leapt to an astounding 115.2. The following subsections show how their individual numbers changed from season to season.

1993

In 1993, Jordan's offensive rating was 119 while he used a huge 33 percent of the team's possessions. Compare that to what Shaq and Kobe did for the Lakers in 2002 and it's better. Pippen's offensive rating was a modest 108, about the league average that year, but he contributed on 25 percent of the team's possessions. B.J. Armstrong and Horace Grant played supreme roles in the supporting cast. (Not all the lesser producing players are shown.) The team's distribution is shown in table 14.5.

1994

In 1994, with Jordan gone, more guys got involved because Pippen couldn't handle the load that Jordan had. Pippen's efficiency numbers didn't change much, except that he tripled the number of three-pointers that he took, raising his offensive rating a little. He essentially diversified his game enough to overcome the fact that defenses now could key on him. Pete Myers—the joke was that he was the new Jordan because he took the off-guard spot—provided almost no offense.

Table 14.5. Select Individual Floor Percentages and Offensive Ratings for the 1993 Bulls

Player	G	Sc. Poss.	Poss.	Floor %	Off. Rtg.	Pts Prod/G	% Tm Poss
Michael Jordan	78	1106	1938	0.57	119	29.7	33%
Scottie Pippen	81	785	1475	0.53	108	19.6	25%
Horace Grant	77	550	926	0.59	118	14.2	18%
B.J. Armstrong	82	450	784	0.57	123	11.7	16%
Scott Williams	71	233	426	0.55	110	6.6	16%
Bill Cartwright	63	187	376	0.50	100	6.0	16%
Stacey King	76	210	394	0.53	107	5.5	19%
Will Perdue	72	182	330	0.55	109	5.0	17%

Table 14.6. Select Individual Floor Percentages and Offensive Ratings for the 1994 Bulls

Player	G	Sc. Poss.	Poss.	Floor %	Off. Rtg.	Pts Prod/G	% Tm Poss
Scottie Pippen	72	759	1426	0.53	109	21.6	27%
Horace Grant	70	557	948	0.59	117	15.8	19%
B.J. Armstrong	82	534	1004	0.53	113	13.8	19%
Toni Kukoc	75	404	840	0.48	100	11.2	24%
Pete Myers	82	335	672	0.50	101	8.3	17%
Steve Kerr	82	307	550	0.56	121	8.1	14%
Luc Longley	27	108	207	0.52	105	8.0	21%
Scott Williams	38	145	272	0.53	105	7.5	22%

Kukoc came in as a twenty-five-year-old rookie. He played only about twenty-five minutes per game but took on 24 percent of the offense when he was in. His offensive rating of one hundred was low, but not atypical for rookies in the NBA.

Notice in table 14.6 that every Bull except Pippen who was there in 1993 was less efficient in 1994, showing how Jordan did make most of his teammates a little better. The overall decline in efficiency of seven points per hundred possessions is very consistent with the replacement of Jordan by a player at the replacement level—with a rating of about ninety-five.

1995

In 1995, Kukoc played a lot better and was the big reason that the team offense improved. Specifically, if you replace Kukoc's 1994 stats with his 1995 stats (table 14.7) in the Bulls' team numbers from 1994, you end up coming very close to the efficiency of the 1995 Bulls, as shown in table 14.8.

Over the nearly two years that Jordan missed, the league changed into a major three-point shooting league. Some Bulls numbers show how floor percentages generally dropped and offensive ratings more or less remained stable. Pippen's floor percentage went from 0.53 to 0.52, but his rating went from 108 to 110. The Bulls' three-point threat of 1993 was Armstrong, whose floor percentage

Table 14.7. Select Individual Floor Percentages and Offensive Ratings for the 1995 Bulls

Player	G	Sc. Poss.	Poss.	Floor %	Off. Rtg.	Pts Prod/G	% Tm Poss
Michael Jordan	17	208	399	0.52	109	25.7	31%
Scottie Pippen	79	793	1523	0.52	110	21.3	26%
Toni Kukoc	81	619	1103	0.56	118	16.1	22%
B.J. Armstrong	82	471	884	0.53	119	12.9	18%
Will Perdue	78	329	592	0.56	111	8.4	19%
Steve Kerr	82	262	463	0.57	129	7.3	13%
Ron Harper	77	258	549	0.47	98	7.0	19%
Luc Longley	55	185	380	0.49	100	6.9	20%
Greg Foster	17	51	98	0.52	104	6.0	17%
Pete Myers	71	183	386	0.47	97	5.3	16%

Table 14.8. Impact of Kukoc's 1995 Improvement on the Bulls

	Sc. Poss.	Poss.	Floor %	Off. Rtg.	Pts Prod
Bulls 1994 Stats	3919	7499	0.52	107	8035
Bulls 1994 Stats, using '95 Kukoc	4134	7761	0.53	110	8500
Bulls Actual 1995	3949	7530	0.52	111	8323

and rating were 0.57 and 123, respectively. By 1995, his numbers were 0.53 and 119. Jordan adapted his game after his baseball career to become more of a perimeter player, too.

1996

With the improved Kukoc, the more confident and proven Pippen, and Jordan, the Bulls 1996 team was going to be good. There was no doubt. But the Bulls ended up being great. Pippen and Kukoc got more efficient but scored less. Dennis Rodman signed up, rebounded a lot, and fit in efficiently. They didn't have an efficient scoring center, but they didn't need one (see table 14.9).

Jordan's return, though, was the key. It's remarkable to realize that he was only *nearly* at his most dominant offensively.

Michael Jordan's Career

Jordan's points per game and scoring titles don't do justice to his impact on the Bulls' success. He posted so many points so efficiently (see table 14.10) that he nearly single-handedly made his team's offenses good. From 1988 to 1997, Jordan's efficiency was near the top in the league for any player producing fifteen or more points per game. He was an extremely rare player in using over 30 percent of his team's possessions, something that neither Magic nor Bird ever did. They never had to.

Table 14.9. Select Individual Floor Percentages and Offensive Ratings for the 1996 Bulls

Player	G	Sc. Poss.	Poss.	Floor %	Off. Rtg.	Pts Prod/G	% Team Poss
Michael Jordan	82	1064	1833	0.58	124	27.6	31%
Scottie Pippen	77	696	1312	0.53	116	19.7	24%
Toni Kukoc	81	487	850	0.57	125	13.1	21%
Luc Longley	62	279	552	0.50	103	9.2	18%
Dennis Rodman	64	278	521	0.53	109	8.9	13%
Ron Harper	80	298	538	0.55	116	7.8	15%
Steve Kerr	82	262	448	0.58	141	7.7	12%
Bill Wennington	71	170	313	0.54	111	4.9	15%

Table 14.10. Michael Jordan's Individual Offensive Efficiency Statistics

Season	G	Sc. Poss.	Poss.	Floor %	Off. Rtg.	Pts Prod/G	% Team Poss	Team Off. Rtg.
1985	82	1106	1921	0.58	118	27.6	30%	108.7
1986	18	179	336	0.53	109	20.4	36%	108.6
1987	82	1336	2355	0.57	117	33.6	36%	108.6
1988	82	1292	2143	0.60	123	32.2	33%	109.0
1989	81	1250	2104	0.59	123	31.9	32%	109.1
1990	82	1226	2092	0.59	123	31.4	32%	112.3
1991	82	1152	1892	0.61	126	29.0	31%	114.7
1992	80	1088	1841	0.59	121	27.9	30%	115.5
1993	78	1106	1938	0.57	119	29.7	33%	112.9
1995	17	208	399	0.52	109	25.7	31%	109.5
1996	82	1064	1833	0.58	124	27.6	31%	115.2
1997	82	1020	1791	0.57	121	26.5	31%	114.4
1998	82	1033	1857	0.56	114	25.8	31%	107.7
2002	60	647	1334	0.49	99	22.0	35%	104.8

Magic Johnson's Career

Magic entered the league on a team that had Kareem Abdul-Jabbar. He had to fit in, unlike Jordan, who had to carry his team as a rookie. And Magic fit in very well, playing multiple positions, using about 23 percent of his team's possessions, and producing 113 points per hundred possessions (see table 14.11). When he had to become the scorer in 1987, he maintained the efficiency and increased his load to 29 percent of the team's possessions. That year's offense was only one of several that he led to greatness.

Table 14.11. Magic Johnson's Individual Offensive Efficiency Statistics

Season	G	Sc. Poss.	Poss.	Floor %	Off. Rtg.	Pts Prod/G	% Team Poss	Team Off. Rtg.
1980	77	755	1357	0.56	113	19.9	23%	110.5
1981	37	430	753	0.57	115	23.3	26%	108.7
1982	78	849	1441	0.59	118	21.9	22%	110.2
1983	79	810	1375	0.59	119	20.7	22%	110.5
1984	67	735	1263	0.58	118	22.3	23%	110.9
1985	77	855	1416	0.60	123	22.7	24%	114.1
1986	72	807	1364	0.59	122	23.1	25%	113.3
1987	80	1066	1768	0.60	124	27.4	29%	115.6
1988	72	814	1418	0.57	118	23.3	26%	113.1
1989	77	956	1631	0.59	125	26.5	27%	113.8
1990	79	933	1609	0.58	126	25.7	27%	114.0
1991	79	859	1505	0.57	124	23.5	26%	112.1
1996	32	248	459	0.54	117	16.8	25%	111.4

Larry Bird's Career

The Legend of Larry is that, as a rookie, he led a team that had no talent to great-ness. The legend is a little exaggerated because the Celtics of 1980 did have talent, but he still deserved the label. As a rookie, Bird's offensive numbers only partially reflect his contribution. As Magic brought energy to the Lakers, Bird brought a positive attitude to the Celtics. That, plus his talents, made for the kind of Hall of Fame career seen in table 14.12.

Reggie Miller's Career

Reggie Miller might have been as good a three-point shooter as Bird. When I first experimented with individual offensive ratings, I tested the measure with Miller and his number was so high that I thought I'd made a mistake. No mistake, though—Reggie has been a great offensive contributor with that deadly outside range. At his peak, Miller created more points per hundred possessions than any of the above three guys, at about 130 (see table 14.13). His peak floor percentage wasn't as high as Jordan's or Magic's, and he didn't dominate an offense like the other guys did. But that 1991 season marked the highest offensive rating I have ever seen for someone using more than 20 percent of his team's possessions. Like Larry, Magic, and Michael, Miller did help one of his teams enough to get them onto the list of history's greatest offenses.

Evaluation Tools

That is how some of the great offensive players in the NBA look on paper. They generated high individual offensive ratings for clubs that were good offensively.

Table 14.12. Larry Bird's Individual Offensive Efficiency Statistics

Season	G	Sc. Poss.	Poss.	Floor %	Off. Rtg.	Pts Prod/G	% Team Poss	Team Off. Rtg.
1980	82	825	1575	0.52	109	21.0	25%	110.7
1981	82	857	1642	0.52	107	21.4	24%	109.7
1982	77	867	1557	0.56	114	23.0	25%	109.8
1983	79	902	1608	0.56	115	23.4	25%	106.9
1984	79	942	1678	0.56	116	24.5	27%	110.9
1985	80	1066	1863	0.57	119	27.8	28%	112.9
1986	82	1004	1811	0.55	117	25.9	28%	111.8
1987	74	959	1691	0.57	121	27.6	27%	113.5
1988	76	992	1746	0.57	122	27.9	29%	115.4
1989	6	52	98	0.53	110	17.9	25%	110.8
1990	75	854	1627	0.52	111	24.1	27%	112.0
1991	60	561	1108	0.51	109	20.0	24%	112.6
1992	45	427	819	0.52	112	20.4	25%	110.8

Table 14.13. Reggie Miller's Individual Offensive Efficiency Statistics

Season	G	Sc. Poss.	Poss.	Floor %	Off. Rtg.	Pts Prod/G	% Team Poss	Team Off. Rtg.
1988	82	360	682	0.53	114	9.5	18%	106.6
1989	74	507	940	0.54	118	15.0	18%	106.8
1990	82	844	1502	0.56	124	22.7	23%	111.5
1991	82	782	1328	0.59	130	21.0	22%	111.7
1992	82	706	1236	0.57	126	18.9	19%	111.7
1993	82	685	1227	0.56	126	18.8	21%	111.9
1994	79	622	1126	0.55	123	17.5	22%	107.8
1995	81	605	1139	0.53	123	17.4	23%	109.6
1996	76	634	1191	0.53	121	18.9	24%	110.8
1997	81	679	1308	0.52	121	19.6	24%	105.8
1998	81	603	1130	0.53	121	16.9	22%	108.4
1999	50	353	691	0.51	119	16.4	21%	108.7
2000	81	572	1124	0.51	118	16.4	19%	108.6
2001	81	598	1202	0.50	115	17.0	20%	102.8
2002	79	499	975	0.51	121	14.9	18%	104.1

Of all those seasons above, the only teams that were below average offensively were the Pacers in the first two years and the last two years of Miller's career. These guys help make good offensive teams.

In general, individual offensive ratings and floor percentages are very good cues as to how well a team will do, a key thing in making these measures useful. The Bulls and the Blazers examples show this, too. But what you often want to do with numbers like these is get a sense for how predictive they are. You want to look at the numbers for a lot of different players, see how they compare, get a sense of the patterns that occur through a player's career, and determine the impact these players have on their teams. That is what I've been doing for the last ten years. I've looked at Dennis Rodman's effect on offenses—he took very few possessions and generally was a bit over the league average efficiency, so his offensive impact was small and positive, like Horace Grant's. I've looked at Allen Iverson—he took a lot of possessions, was only of about average efficiency, and his teams slightly lagged below average offensively. There are hundreds of different individuals whose numbers tell interesting and valuable stories—valuable in signing free agents, making trades, deciding who to play.

I don't have space to go through all the individuals, but I do want to look at a couple classes of individual players that have interested me from the time I created these measures. Specifically, when I first calculated Reggie Miller's very high offensive rating, I was surprised at how high it was. I also calculated offensive ratings for Hakeem Olajuwon, whose offensive rating was only around 110 the same year Miller's was nearly 130. Was there some sort of bias in individual offensive ratings for three-point shooters and against big men? Or was it just that three-point shooters really were more important in generating good team offenses?

To some degree, we've already answered this question back in chapter 3. In that chapter, we saw a lot of great offenses that didn't feature good big men. Kareem Abdul-Jabbar was important on a few good offenses, but the Lakers were good after he left, too. Shaquille O'Neal has been on a couple good offenses, and you saw above that his offensive ratings have also been quite good. Shaq has been a better offensive center than Olajuwon, to make that comparison.

So, in the next couple sections, I want to look at some three-point shooters, some big men, and then at some of those greatest offenses again to show that individual offensive ratings are not biased and that they do provide indications of how an offense will perform.

Three-Point Specialists

Three-point bombers generally are pretty high-risk guys. When they make their shots, they are valuable. When they don't, they get yanked. There are good three-point specialists and there are not-so-good ones. I'll talk about a couple good ones and just one of that other kind.

Steve Kerr, though not even close to being the player who has taken the highest percentage of his shots as three-pointers, is still a classic example of a three-point specialist. His career produced the numbers in table 14.14.

Kerr has usually been on good offensive teams. His outside shooting helps good teams that don't need him to use a lot of possessions. With the Bulls between 1994 and 1998, he had his best years, though he showed signs of his potential in 1992 when he was with Cleveland, whose offense ranked twenty-fourth overall historically. Kerr was a valuable three-point specialist during his prime. Stepping back from the numbers and acknowledging that Kerr would not

Table 14.14. Steve Kerr's Individual Offensive Efficiency Statistics

Season	Tm	G	Sc. Poss	Poss	Floor %	Off. Rtg.	Pts Prod/G	% Team Poss	Team Off. Rtg
1989	PHO	26	26	49	0.52	116	2.2	14%	113.1
1990	CLE	78	234	468	0.50	114	6.9	14%	106.9
1991	CLE	57	127	253	0.50	111	4.9	14%	106.1
1992	CLE	48	141	250	0.56	124	6.5	15%	113.9
1993	CLE	5	8	13	0.58	120	3.1	16%	112.7
1993	ORL	47	63	130	0.48	103	2.9	15%	108.5
1994	CHI	82	307	550	0.56	121	8.1	14%	106.0
1995	CHI	82	262	463	0.57	129	7.3	13%	109.5
1996	CHI	82	262	448	0.58	141	7.7	12%	115.2
1997	CHI	82	250	428	0.58	137	7.2	12%	114.4
1998	CHI	50	146	275	0.53	125	6.8	13%	107.7
1999	SAN	44	79	172	0.46	105	4.1	13%	104.0
2000	SAN	32	32	69	0.47	112	2.4	14%	105.0
2001	SAN	55	73	159	0.46	110	3.2	13%	107.2
2002	POR	65	108	208	0.52	118	3.8	14%	107.4

have survived in the league as a defender makes you realize that his offense must have been quite efficient when he was in the game.

Another good three-point shooter and, surprisingly to me, the player who has taken the highest percentage of his shots from beyond the arc is Brent Barry. Barry has been very efficient when he hasn't had to use a lot of possessions. His 2002 season was his best, as he maintained a 124 rating and increased his offensive role (table 14.5).

Barry, like Kerr, has never been viewed as a great defender. Especially in the last couple years, he has gotten more playing time because his offense makes up for any defensive weaknesses. He and Rashard Lewis, another good three-point shooter, put Seattle near the top of the league offensively in 2002. Of course, Gary Payton, who has never led a Sonics team to a below-average offense, is also part of the equation.

Dennis Scott was another three-point specialist, though not quite as good at his craft as the previous two. His floor percentage was always below 0.50, and his rating never peaked as high. Like Barry and Kerr, Scott was also not known for defense, so when his individual ratings fell in 1997 (table 14.16), he had a hard time finding a job. Though three-point shooters get you a lot of points when they hit one, if they score infrequently, that inconsistency hurts.

Table 14.15. Brent Barry's Individual Offensive Efficiency Statistics

Season	Tm	G	Sc. Poss	Poss	Floor %	Off. Rtg.	Pts Prod/G	% Team Poss	Team Off. Rtg
1996	LAC	79	339	676	0.50	117	10.0	18%	106.5
1997	LAC	59	202	429	0.47	107	7.8	21%	105.1
1998	LAC	41	234	503	0.46	108	13.2	19%	103.3
1998	MIA	17	28	63	0.45	110	4.1	13%	107.6
1999	CHI	37	179	407	0.44	99	10.9	19%	92.4
2000	SEA	80	384	792	0.48	115	11.4	15%	105.6
2001	SEA	67	248	475	0.52	124	8.8	14%	106.4
2002	SEA	81	506	939	0.54	124	14.4	17%	108.9

Table 14.16. Dennis Scott's Individual Offensive Efficiency Statistics

Season	Tm	G	Sc. Poss	Poss	Floor %	Off. Rtg.	Pts Prod/G	% Team Poss	Team Off. Rtg
1991	ORL	82	513	1085	0.47	104	13.8	22%	105.9
1992	ORL	18	142	303	0.47	104	17.5	24%	103.5
1993	ORL	54	340	734	0.46	105	14.3	21%	108.5
1994	ORL	82	421	878	0.48	110	11.8	19%	110.8
1995	ORL	62	288	578	0.50	120	11.2	19%	115.1
1996	ORL	82	528	1084	0.49	118	15.6	19%	112.9
1997	ORL	66	310	694	0.45	107	11.3	17%	105.6
1998	DAL	52	288	670	0.43	99	12.7	20%	100.5
1998	PHO	29	64	139	0.46	109	5.2	15%	107.4
1999	MIN	21	69	140	0.49	115	7.7	14%	101.9
1999	NYK	15	17	50	0.34	81	2.7	14%	98.6
2000	VAN	66	139	310	0.45	109	5.1	13%	102.4

Table 14.17. Brian Taylor's Individual Offensive Efficiency Statistics

Season	Tm	G	Sc. Poss	Poss	Floor %	Off. Rtg.	Pts Prod/G	% Team Poss	Team Off. Rtg
1978	DEN	39	223	449	0.50	100	11.5	16%	103.4
1979	SDC	20	40	89	0.45	92	4.1	19%	107.4
1980	SDC	78	493	939	0.53	114	13.7	16%	106.8
1981	SDC	80	425	721	0.59	124	11.2	15%	107.3
1982	SDC	41	236	424	0.56	117	12.1	16%	106.6

Finally, an interesting guy to look at is the player who took and made the most threes in 1980, when the NBA first introduced the three-point shot. That was Brian Taylor, who clearly made himself a much better player by being able to hit the long shot. When the line was introduced, his offensive rating went up 15 to 20 percent (see table 14.17). But the league didn't quite see the benefit back then. In 1983, everyone stopped using the three—only four players even made twenty-five treys over the whole season—and Taylor didn't even play.

Some Big Men

Whereas there are three-point specialists, there really aren't low-post scoring specialists. Big men have to do it all, and they used to be able to do so. Now, big men are specialists—specialists at rebounding or blocking shots or, these days, fouling Shaq. Teams actually scout the draft for guys who can stop Shaq without fouling so much. That is because Shaq is about all there is for offensive big men, and his numbers are great (table 14.18).

Shaq's floor percentages have been close to the league best since he entered the NBA. If the big guy wants to score, it's tough to stop him. You may be able to hold him to one point through a foul, but he has a 60-percent chance of scoring at least one on you. That's what these numbers say. His individual offensive ratings have led to some very good and occasionally great team offensive ratings.

By contrast, you have Tim Duncan, the other big man with some offensive pop these days (table 14.19). Until 2002, Duncan never posted numbers as good

Table 14.18. Shaquille O'Neal's Individual Offensive Efficiency Statistics

Season	Tm	G	Sc. Poss	Poss	Floor %	Off. Rtg.	Pts Prod/G	% Team Poss	Team Off. Rtg
1993	ORL	81	914	1648	0.55	109	22.1	27%	108.5
1994	ORL	81	1104	1801	0.61	120	26.6	28%	110.8
1995	ORL	79	1070	1770	0.60	118	26.4	31%	115.1
1996	ORL	54	657	1170	0.56	110	23.8	31%	112.9
1997	LAL	51	626	1114	0.56	110	23.9	30%	108.4
1998	LAL	60	769	1321	0.58	113	24.9	31%	111.9
1999	LAL	49	607	1023	0.59	115	24.1	31%	107.6
2000	LAL	79	1118	1892	0.59	115	27.6	31%	107.4
2001	LAL	74	1033	1750	0.59	114	27.0	32%	109.2
2002	LAL	67	855	1441	0.59	116	24.9	31%	109.4

Table 14.19. Tim Duncan's Individual Offensive Efficiency Statistics

Season	Tm	G	Sc. Poss	Poss	Floor %	Off. Rtg.	Pts Prod/G	% Team Poss	Team Off. Rtg
1998	SAN	82	822	1514	0.54	108	19.9	26%	103.9
1999	SAN	50	514	962	0.53	106	20.5	27%	104.0
2000	SAN	74	835	1549	0.54	109	22.8	29%	105.0
2001	SAN	82	895	1676	0.53	106	21.7	28%	107.2
2002	SAN	82	1014	1813	0.56	114	25.3	29%	106.5

as Shaq's and even then, he couldn't carry the team offense to greatness as Shaq has. Duncan is clearly a little behind Shaq, but he is really the next best thing offensively.

Notice that Duncan's Spurs have never quite put up the same offensive ratings as Shaq's Lakers either. The improvement Duncan made in 2002 at age twenty-five is probably the biggest improvement he will make in his efficiency, something that he'll carry through age thirty or so. With better teammates and that individual offensive rating remaining somewhat stable (maybe peaking a couple points higher), he should lead a few offenses to near greatness.

There are other centers out there right now: an old David Robinson, a very old Hakeem Olajuwon, a defensive-minded Dikembe Mutombo, a defensive-minded Ben Wallace, an unfortunately limited Alonzo Mourning, the enigmatic Elden Campbell, and the somewhat comical Vlade Divac. None of these guys are currently doing what Shaq and Duncan are doing on the offensive end, though Robinson once did, as you can see in table 14.20.

His best offensive years were arguably better than Shaq's best offensive years, though that is definitely an argument, not a clear-cut statement. Today, Robinson is still efficient, but hasn't produced twenty points per game since 1998, Duncan's first year. His deference to Duncan on the offensive end has actually been a little strange. The 5 percent drop in his percentage of team possessions in 1999 is not something you see with any of the above superstars.

Table 14.20. David Robinson's Individual Offensive Efficiency Statistics

Season	Tm	G	Sc. Poss	Poss	Floor %	Off. Rtg.	Pts Prod/G	% Team Poss	Team Off. Rtg
1990	SAN	82	938	1606	0.58	116	22.8	26%	107.7
1991	SAN	82	985	1667	0.59	119	24.1	26%	107.8
1992	SAN	68	749	1257	0.60	118	21.9	24%	107.5
1993	SAN	82	945	1681	0.56	113	23.1	26%	109.6
1994	SAN	80	1134	1917	0.59	119	28.6	31%	110.4
1995	SAN	81	1034	1752	0.59	120	25.9	29%	111.7
1996	SAN	82	990	1669	0.59	121	24.5	28%	110.2
1997	SAN	6	50	84	0.60	117	16.4	31%	103.3
1998	SAN	73	755	1326	0.57	114	20.8	29%	103.9
1999	SAN	49	388	688	0.56	111	15.6	24%	104.0
2000	SAN	80	669	1202	0.56	111	16.8	25%	105.0
2001	SAN	80	564	998	0.56	114	14.2	23%	107.2
2002	SAN	78	477	832	0.57	114	12.2	19%	106.5

Table 14.21. Hakeem Olajuwon's Individual Offensive Efficiency Statistics

Season	Tm	G	Sc. Poss	Poss	Floor %	Off. Rtg.	Pts Prod/G	% Team Poss	Team Off. Rtg
1985	HOU	82	831	1447	0.57	113	19.8	23%	107.9
1986	HOU	68	769	1340	0.57	113	22.3	25%	110.1
1987	HOU	75	847	1515	0.56	111	22.4	26%	106.5
1988	HOU	79	859	1557	0.55	110	21.6	26%	107.1
1989	HOU	82	955	1748	0.55	109	23.1	27%	105.7
1990	HOU	82	938	1791	0.52	105	22.8	27%	104.9
1991	HOU	56	560	1038	0.54	109	20.2	25%	107.4
1992	HOU	70	707	1296	0.55	110	20.4	25%	106.2
1993	HOU	82	1008	1793	0.56	114	24.9	28%	109.6
1994	HOU	80	1007	1860	0.54	109	25.4	29%	105.9
1995	HOU	72	917	1698	0.54	110	25.9	30%	109.7
1996	HOU	72	892	1673	0.53	108	25.1	31%	109.3
1997	HOU	78	821	1596	0.51	105	21.6	29%	108.8
1998	HOU	47	379	732	0.52	105	16.4	24%	107.7
1999	HOU	50	432	827	0.52	105	17.4	25%	105.5
2000	HOU	44	219	455	0.48	96	9.9	22%	104.8
2001	HOU	58	337	631	0.53	106	11.6	22%	107.5
2002	TOR	61	215	468	0.46	91	7.0	18%	102.6

Olajuwon was the player that concerned me originally. His individual offensive rating was relatively low, and it troubled me. But it turned out that he didn't ever lead his teams to offensive greatness. The 1993 season, when he led the Rockets to the first of their two championships, was his best individual offensive season and the team's best offensive season (table 14.21).

Of the remaining guys, only Mourning has really been viewed as a primary offensive option. Throughout his career, Mourning's efficiency stats have been a lot like Duncan's—good but not great (table 14.22).

This is all in great contrast to what big men used to do. In 1982, there were nine guys who created fifteen points per game, and the top six were at least as efficient as Shaq or Duncan (see table 14.23).

So, in case you were worried that offensive ratings and floor percentages were biased against big men, you can see that big men can have some very good

Table 14.22. Alonzo Mourning's Individual Offensive Efficiency Statistics

Season	Tm	G	Sc. Poss	Poss	Floor %	Off. Rtg.	Pts Prod/G	% Team Poss	Team Off. Rtg
1993	CHA	78	755	1367	0.55	112	19.6	25%	109.5
1994	CHA	60	593	1092	0.54	110	19.9	27%	108.4
1995	CHA	77	743	1381	0.54	110	19.7	25%	109.6
1996	MIA	70	768	1406	0.55	109	22.0	28%	105.3
1997	MIA	66	614	1152	0.53	106	18.4	27%	106.8
1998	MIA	58	511	929	0.55	109	17.5	26%	107.6
1999	MIA	46	451	830	0.54	107	19.4	27%	104.7
2000	MIA	79	771	1379	0.56	112	19.5	27%	104.5
2001	MIA	13	83	165	0.50	99	12.5	30%	101.9
2002	MIA	75	553	1055	0.52	104	14.6	24%	98.5

Table 14.23. Individual Offensive Efficiency Statistics for Big Men in 1982

Player	Tm	G	Sc. Poss.	Poss.	Floor %	Off. Rtg.	Pts Prod/G	% Tm Poss
Moses Malone	HOU	81	1192	2026	0.59	118	29.5	29%
Kareem Abdul-Jabbar	LAL	76	814	1397	0.58	116	21.3	24%
Dan Issel	DEN	81	840	1402	0.60	123	21.2	25%
Jack Sikma	SEA	82	778	1415	0.55	113	19.4	22%
Robert Parish	BOS	80	742	1324	0.56	112	18.5	25%
Artis Gilmore	CHI	82	685	1110	0.62	124	16.8	19%
Joe Barry Carroll	GSW	76	598	1121	0.53	106	15.7	20%
James Edwards	CLE	77	604	1112	0.54	108	15.6	21%
Alvan Adams	PHO	79	603	1144	0.53	106	15.3	23%

numbers. There are efficient ones, more so in the past, and their numbers have helped create good offenses just as three-point shooters do. But, consistent with the prevailing wisdom, there just aren't many good offensive big men anymore.

The Best Offenses

How did those great offenses from chapter 3 structure their offenses? Are there any patterns in the efficiencies of their best players? That's what this section is about. I won't post all the top offenses, but they are listed in Appendix 2.

We'll start with the 1982 Denver Nuggets in table 14.24. From top to bottom, they had guys with ratings around 110 or better. But at the top were Alex English, Dan Issel, and Kiki Vandeweghe. Those top three were extremely potent throughout their careers, but everyone on these Nuggets got a lot of good opportunities through that fast pace.

What about those surprising 2002 Mavericks (table 14.25)? Dirk Nowitzki was all that he was advertised to be. His 120 rating was the league's highest among those players producing twenty points per game. Reaching this height at age

Table 14.24. Individual Offensive Efficiency Statistics for 1982 Denver Nuggets

Player	G	Sc. Poss.	Poss.	Floor %	Off. Rtg.	Pts Prod/G	% Team Poss
Alex English	82	1009	1734	0.58	118	24.9	25%
Dan Issel	81	840	1402	0.60	123	21.2	25%
Kiki Vandeweghe	82	800	1357	0.59	120	19.9	21%
David Thompson	61	413	778	0.53	108	13.8	27%
Dave Robisch	12	71	123	0.58	120	12.3	21%
Billy McKinney	81	446	781	0.57	115	11.1	17%
T.R. Dunn	82	393	685	0.57	114	9.5	12%
Kenny Higgs	76	343	677	0.51	103	9.2	17%
Glen Gondrezick	80	356	623	0.57	114	8.9	16%
Cedrick Hordges	77	276	539	0.51	100	7.0	17%
John Roche	39	91	175	0.52	114	5.1	15%
David Burns	6	10	23	0.45	89	3.3	19%
James Ray	40	64	147	0.44	87	3.2	24%

Table 14.25. Individual Offensive Efficiency Statistics for 2002 Dallas Mavericks

Player	G	Sc. Poss.	Poss.	Floor %	Off. Rtg.	Pts Prod/G	% Team Poss
Dirk Nowitzki	76	736	1360	0.54	120	21.4	24%
Michael Finley	69	625	1220	0.51	110	19.4	23%
Steve Nash	82	701	1338	0.52	119	19.3	24%
Nick Van Exel	27	163	337	0.48	108	13.5	23%
Juwan Howard	53	347	657	0.53	108	13.3	20%
Raef Lafrentz	27	131	272	0.48	106	10.7	18%
Tim Hardaway	54	227	528	0.43	103	10.1	21%
Adrian Griffin	58	205	377	0.54	115	7.5	14%
Eduardo Najera	62	223	377	0.59	119	7.3	14%
Greg Buckner	44	133	230	0.58	119	6.2	13%
Zhizhi Wang	55	114	241	0.47	110	4.8	21%
Shawn Bradley	53	107	193	0.55	116	4.2	13%
Danny Manning	41	82	165	0.50	101	4.1	15%
Johnny Newman	47	78	159	0.49	109	3.7	11%
Avery Johnson	17	30	60	0.50	102	3.6	20%
Evan Eschmeyer	31	41	80	0.51	102	2.6	14%
Donnell Harvey	18	22	41	0.53	103	2.3	13%
Darrick Martin	3	1	10	0.13	26	0.8	23%
Tariq Abdul-Wahad	4	1	6	0.19	41	0.6	13%

twenty-three suggests greatness considering that Larry, Magic, and Michael didn't reach that rating any earlier than age twenty-five. After Dirk, Michael Finley put up a pretty good year by his standards. He has generally posted ratings around 105 since his rookie year in Phoenix, when he posted a rating of 114. Steve Nash had a great season. He played well in his first two seasons in Phoenix, but it took him two seasons in Dallas before he was able to step up to take more possessions and be efficient with them. Well below them, there were a couple of prominently good role players in Eduardo Najera and Greg Buckner.

The Utah Jazz are on the list for several teams in the 1990s. All of those featured Karl Malone, John Stockton, and Jeff Hornacek. Their individual stats for 1997 (table 14.26) show you why. Their top five regular players all had ratings over 110. If their bench had been better, they might have actually beaten the Bulls.

There were a lot of great Lakers offenses, too. The 1985 version (table 14.27) was incredibly balanced with no one using more than 24 percent of the possessions. Magic distributed and everyone else just hit shots. Kareem was the very efficient big man everyone made him out to be, with a rating of 120.

The rest of the great offenses and their individual ratings appear in the appendix. There is a point that can be made without showing them all. The best offenses all have at least three players at the top who are both well above average in their offensive rating and who use at least 20 percent of their team's possessions. They score efficiently, and they share the ball. The only exception to this appears to be those Bulls teams of the early 1990s, when Jordan was using about

Table 14.26. Individual Offensive Efficiency Statistics for 1997 Utah Jazz

Player	G	Sc. Poss.	Poss.	Floor %	Off. Rtg.	Pts Prod/G	% Team Poss
Karl Malone	82	1040	1771	0.59	119	25.6	31%
John Stockton	82	672	1157	0.58	125	17.6	21%
Jeff Hornacek	82	544	981	0.55	121	14.5	20%
Bryon Russell	81	354	677	0.52	116	9.7	14%
Greg Ostertag	77	288	506	0.57	114	7.5	15%
Antoine Carr	82	271	533	0.51	103	6.7	19%
Shandon Anderson	65	172	365	0.47	99	5.6	18%
Howard Eisley	82	197	424	0.46	98	5.1	21%
Ruben Nembhard	8	17	32	0.54	110	4.4	18%
Adam Keefe	62	128	231	0.56	111	4.1	13%
Chris Morris	73	134	302	0.45	97	4.0	16%
Greg Foster	79	134	280	0.48	98	3.5	16%
Stephen Howard	42	70	123	0.57	112	3.3	19%
Jamie Watson	13	17	35	0.47	99	2.7	15%
Brooks Thompson	2	0	2	0.13	27	0.3	13%

Table 14.27. Individual Offensive Efficiency Statistics for 1985 Los Angeles Lakers

Player	G	Sc. Poss.	Poss.	Floor %	Off. Rtg.	Pts Prod/G	% Team Poss
Magic Johnson	77	855	1416	0.60	123	22.7	24%
Kareem Abdul-Jabbar	79	783	1300	0.60	120	19.8	23%
James Worthy	80	645	1139	0.57	114	16.2	20%
Byron Scott	81	570	1006	0.57	116	14.5	20%
Michael Cooper	82	397	756	0.52	110	10.2	16%
Bob McAdoo	66	311	577	0.54	108	9.4	21%
Mike McGee	76	337	610	0.55	112	8.9	24%
Jamaal Wilkes	42	158	307	0.51	103	7.5	19%
Larry Spriggs	75	257	478	0.54	108	6.9	17%
Kurt Rambis	82	240	435	0.55	110	5.8	13%
Mitch Kupchak	58	150	279	0.54	106	5.1	18%
Ronnie Lester	32	61	125	0.49	97	3.8	21%
Chuck Nevitt	11	8	27	0.29	55	1.4	22%
Earl Jones	2	0	2	0.00	0	0.0	11%

a third of his team's possessions and, well, he used them like no one else in recent memory. For those with long memories, I'll look at Wilt Chamberlain's feats of the 1960s in a few chapters.

A Couple of Bad Teams

Just to give you an idea of what a bad team looks like, I'll pull a couple of interesting ones off the worst offense list. The first is the worst—the 1988 Clippers team that was built around, well, really no one (table 14.28). Michael Cage led the league in rebounding that year, mostly by chasing a lot of his own teammates' missed shots. He unfortunately couldn't sink more than 47 percent of his own shots. Brace yourself, because this is pretty ugly.

Table 14.28. Individual Offensive Efficiency Statistics for 1988 Los Angeles Clippers

Player	G	Sc. Poss.	Poss.	Floor %	Off. Rtg.	Pts Prod/G	% Team Poss
Mike Woodson	80	648	1306	0.50	102	16.7	25%
Michael Cage	72	560	1011	0.55	110	15.4	18%
Benoit Benjamin	66	418	886	0.47	94	12.6	19%
Quintin Dailey	67	407	822	0.49	100	12.2	31%
Larry Drew	74	390	807	0.48	100	10.9	19%
Reggie Williams	35	173	422	0.41	84	10.1	23%
Eric White	17	79	140	0.57	115	9.4	19%
Steve Burtt	19	82	176	0.47	92	8.5	27%
Darnel Valentine	79	323	682	0.47	97	8.3	20%
Ken Norman	66	278	570	0.49	95	8.2	19%
Joe Wolf	42	164	373	0.44	89	7.9	16%

Table 14.29. Individual Offensive Efficiency Statistics for 2000 Chicago Bulls

Player	G	Sc. Poss.	Poss.	Floor %	Off. Rtg.	Pts Prod/G	% Team Poss
Elton Brand	81	782	1491	0.52	105	19.2	27%
Toni Kukoc	24	210	451	0.46	97	18.3	28%
Ron Artest	72	394	878	0.45	95	11.6	21%
Chris Carr	50	209	511	0.41	89	9.1	25%
Rusty Larue	4	17	43	0.40	83	9.0	18%
Fred Hoiberg	31	118	257	0.46	106	8.8	16%
Dedric Willoughby	25	84	202	0.42	96	7.8	21%
Hersey Hawkins	61	203	450	0.45	103	7.6	15%
John Starks	4	13	32	0.42	95	7.6	21%
B.J. Armstrong	27	92	202	0.45	98	7.3	19%
Randy Brown	59	207	503	0.41	84	7.2	17%
Corey Benjamin	48	154	372	0.41	88	6.8	23%
Matt Maloney	51	139	341	0.41	98	6.5	16%
Kornel David	26	76	166	0.46	93	5.9	20%
Chris Anstey	73	212	433	0.49	100	5.9	23%
Khalid Reeves	3	8	20	0.39	84	5.6	22%
Dickey Simpkins	69	175	423	0.41	81	5.0	14%
Will Perdue	67	111	274	0.40	78	3.2	15%
Michael Ruffin	71	107	230	0.47	91	2.9	13%
Lari Ketner	6	4	11	0.37	77	1.4	15%

I also want to highlight the 2000 Chicago Bulls (table 14.29). It was Elton Brand's rookie year. He took 27 percent of his team's possessions and put up an offensive rating right around the league average. Behind him, however, was almost no one who could post a rating of even one hundred. This suggests to me that it really is hard to have a one-man offense, unless you are Michael Jordan.

Finally, there was the 1998 Golden State Warriors (table 14.30). That was the season when the Warriors' slogan was "No More Mr. Nice Guy." Coincidence or not, that was also the season that Latrell Sprewell decided to choke coach P.J. Carlesimo.

Table 14.30. Individual Offensive Efficiency Statistics for 1998 Golden State Warriors

Player	G	Sc. Poss.	Poss.	Floor %	Off. Rtg.	Pts Prod/G	% Team Poss
Latrell Sprewell	14	136	289	0.47	97	20.0	28%
Jimmy Jackson	31	276	614	0.45	94	18.6	26%
Joe Smith	49	384	787	0.49	98	15.8	25%
Donyell Marshall	73	510	1073	0.47	100	14.7	22%
Erick Dampier	82	487	961	0.51	100	11.7	19%
Clarence Weatherspoon	31	164	313	0.53	105	10.6	16%
Jason Caffey	29	153	305	0.50	99	10.4	22%
Tony Delk	74	343	761	0.45	95	9.7	24%
Bimbo Coles	53	223	486	0.46	96	8.8	17%
Brian Shaw	39	136	343	0.40	85	7.5	17%
Muggsy Bogues	59	211	429	0.49	101	7.4	14%
Carl Thomas	10	26	58	0.45	96	5.5	22%
David Vaughn	22	59	135	0.44	86	5.3	22%
B.J. Armstrong	4	9	25	0.38	76	4.7	22%
Todd Fuller	57	109	226	0.48	96	3.8	19%
Brandon Williams	9	16	47	0.33	71	3.7	17%
Adonal Foyle	55	89	212	0.42	82	3.1	17%
Dickey Simpkins	19	31	70	0.44	84	3.1	19%
Felton Spencer	68	94	194	0.48	94	2.7	12%
Gerald Madkins	19	23	49	0.46	103	2.7	11%
Duane Ferrell	50	51	115	0.44	87	2.0	13%
Jeff Grayer	4	3	7	0.43	106	1.8	16%

Sprewell was pretty much alone on an offense that he couldn't carry—not even as well as Elton Brand did in Chicago. Sprewell's best offensive years had been and would later be on teams where he didn't have to carry the offense. And even those years weren't terribly efficient. In this season, Spree played only fourteen games. Given how poorly he was playing, he probably wouldn't have helped if he hadn't been suspended.

Key Messages

That's a look at some representative offensive numbers for players. Individual floor percentages and ratings are the hallmark of a lot of analyses. The analysis of Derrick Coleman in chapter 7 used *team* ratings to get at whether he hurt or helped his team offense. Individual ratings and floor percentages can tell a similar story. That is because they effectively predict things like the Bulls offense getting seven points worse if you replace Jordan with Pete Myers, or the Trail Blazers' offense getting several points better if Isaiah Rider weren't their leading scorer. That's a nice feature. It doesn't tell you about defense, but a hammer ain't gonna help you screw in a nut either.

These statistics can tell you whether a player who is scoring a lot is really doing it like Mike or if he's doing it like Isaiah. The star players will have high ratings and use a high percentage of their team's possessions. The good role players will have high ratings and use a low percentage of their team's possessions. It's a good idea to have your efficient players also scoring the most. That doesn't mean that you can turn efficient Horace Grant into a leading scorer at the same efficiency. Knowing how offensive ratings respond to different responsibilities is a subject for a later chapter. For now, we'll let the numbers swim in your brain a while and get on to something a little easier in the next chapter.

WNBA Statistics

The WNBA was introduced to the world through the promotion of three players—Lisa Leslie, Sheryl Swoopes, and Rebecca Lobo. When the games actually began, Swoopes was pregnant, Leslie played reasonably but her team was poor, and Lobo just didn't play very well. The real stars of the league turned out to be less-promoted players like Cynthia Cooper, Ruthie Bolton-Holifield, and Jennifer Gillom. The WNBA just couldn't know in advance that these players, not the players the league promoted, would be so good. Leslie, Swoopes, and Lobo were well known from their recent college heroics, but no one had really assessed what it took for female college stars to make it at a higher level because there was no higher level. Overseas leagues were far enough away and variable enough in talent that no one really knew.

But now we're starting to know. It became clear fairly early on that the Michael Jordan of the WNBA was Cynthia Cooper (see table 14.31). Cooper dominated the offensive end like no other player since. Until her final season, Cooper was both the most efficient offensive player and the player producing the most

Table 14.31. Cynthia Cooper's Individual Offensive Efficiency Statistics

Season	Tm	G	Sc. Poss	Poss	Floor %	Off. Rtg.	Pts Prod/G	% Tm Poss
1997	HOU	28	264	506	0.52	119	21.6	29%
1998	HOU	30	292	555	0.53	119	22.0	30%
1999	HOU	31	296	561	0.53	119	21.6	29%
2000	HOU	30	241	477	0.50	113	17.9	26%

Table 14.32. WNBA Average Efficiency Statistics

Season	Poss/Game	Floor %	Rating
1997	75.0	0.439	92.3
1998	74.2	0.451	94.8
1999	71.4	0.456	97.1
2000	70.3	0.462	98.2
2001	68.4	0.449	95.9

points in every WNBA season. She was the biggest reason that her team, the Houston Comets, was unbeatable.

Let's put some perspective on these numbers by showing in table 14.32 the average floor percentage and points-per-hundred-possessions rating in the WNBA through time.

When Cooper was producing 119 points per hundred possessions in 1997, the league was producing ninety-two. That twenty-seven-point difference dwarfs anything Jordan ever did in the NBA.

You can see that the WNBA pace has been getting slower, and the efficiency has been getting better. The decline in efficiency in 2001 may be the effect of Cooper retiring, just as there was also a decline in league efficiency when Jordan left the NBA. Why the pace has been slowing is not clear, but it could be for the same reasons as in the NBA—more coaches shouting orders from the sideline, more emphasis on better shots, better ball handling in general. But this is getting away from the players.

After Cooper retired, the next WNBA MVP was Lisa Leslie. I know, I know—Cooper didn't even win the MVP in all her seasons, but that was for the same reason that Jordan didn't win in all his seasons—people like to spread it around a bit. Leslie's 2001 season was a step up for her after she didn't quite live up to the hype early on (table 14.33). Using as high a percentage of her team's offensive possessions as ever, her offensive rating was twelve points over the league average in 2001, easily better than any previous season. The Sparks team was also at

Table 14.33. Lisa Leslie's Individual Offensive Efficiency Statistics

Season	Tm	G	Sc. Poss	Poss	Floor %	Off. Rtg.	Pts Prod/G	% Tm Poss	Team Off. Rtg
1997	LAS	28	219	477	0.46	91	15.6	27%	93.9
1998	LAS	28	253	500	0.51	104	18.5	30%	94.9
1999	LAS	32	220	453	0.49	103	14.5	26%	102.7
2000	LAS	32	259	520	0.50	104	16.8	28%	102.7
2001	LAS	31	275	530	0.52	108	18.4	29%	107.1
2002	LAS	31	251	503	0.50	105	17.1	26%	104.2

Table 14.34. Sheryl Swoopes's Individual Offensive Efficiency Statistics

Season	Tm	G	Sc. Poss	Poss	Floor %	Off. Rtg.	Pts Prod/G	% Tm Poss	Team Off. Rtg
1997	HOU	9	27	48	0.55	118	6.3	21%	99.4
1998	HOU	29	194	406	0.48	105	14.7	24%	105.7
1999	HOU	32	267	522	0.51	110	17.9	27%	105.8
2000	HOU	30	278	517	0.54	115	19.8	28%	109.4
2002	HOU	32	272	553	0.49	108	18.6	30%	99.5

its best, dominating the league as the Comets had with Cooper. Leslie's offense declined a little in 2002, and she didn't repeat as MVP, in part because she didn't play quite as well on the offensive end. But the team did repeat as champs.

Some of those dominating Comets teams did have Sheryl Swoopes helping Cooper out. Swoopes didn't stay pregnant, and when she returned, she was a star, living up to some of the hype (table 14.34). Her offense didn't quite match Cooper's until 2000, when she rightfully won the MVP. Her offensive numbers in 2002 reflect a player who had to do more and couldn't maintain her efficiency. They also could reflect that she was thirty-four years old.

The other player in the WNBA to win an MVP is Yolanda Griffith (table 14.35), Sacramento's very skilled post player. Griffith was one of the former ABL players whose presence in that league was supposed to help it survive. The ABL tried to claim that it had better talent than the WNBA, and Griffith would be one of those players that the ABL would highlight as an example. She definitely has done well in the WNBA, posting offensive numbers that approach Cooper's. Griffith won the MVP as a WNBA rookie in 1999, though you can see that her offensive numbers don't quite match Cooper's.

Aside from these great players, the WNBA also has its good role players, like Crystal Robinson of New York and Latasha Byears of Los Angeles. Robinson's role has been as a hired gun (table 14.36), bombing away from three-point land and

Table 14.35. Yolanda Griffith's Individual Offensive Efficiency Statistics

Season	Tm	G	Sc. Poss	Poss	Floor %	Off. Rtg.	Pts Prod/G	% Tm Poss	Team Off. Rtg
1999	SAC	29	266	446	0.60	117	18.0	24%	100.0
2000	SAC	32	253	442	0.57	115	15.9	24%	103.6
2001	SAC	32	255	444	0.57	116	16.1	24%	100.9
2002	SAC	17	133	238	0.56	117	16.4	24%	96.7

Table 14.36. Crystal Robinson's Individual Offensive Efficiency Statistics

Season	Tm	G	Sc. Poss	Poss	Floor %	Off. Rtg	Pts Prod/G	% Tm Poss	Team Off. Rtg
1999	NYL	31	131	282	0.47	115	10.5	19%	97.2
2000	NYL	27	96	206	0.47	110	8.4	17%	99.1
2001	NYL	32	128	259	0.50	122	9.9	16%	97.6
2002	NYL	32	151	326	0.46	114	11.6	19%	100.6

making a good fraction. Her career-high rating of 122 is as high as you will find among players who played regularly.

Byears became a role player after handling a lot of scoring responsibilities early in her career (table 14.37). By cutting down how often she tried to score—taking more smart shots and not trying to create as much—she improved her scoring efficiency later in her career.

There are also players who score a lot but probably shouldn't be doing so—kind of like the Jerry Stackhouses or Allen Iversons of the WNBA. Chamique Holdsclaw, whom *Sports Illustrated* hinted would be the Michael Jordan of the WNBA when she was still in college, has been the poster child for what happens when bad shooters fire their guns too much. Well, she's getting there, but she started off more like Stackhouse than Jordan (table 14.38).

Table 14.37. Latasha Byears's Individual Offensive Efficiency Statistics

Season	Tm	G	Sc. Poss	Poss	Floor %	Off. Rtg	Pts Prod/G	% Tm Poss	Team Off. Rtg
1997	SAC	28	126	264	0.48	97	9.2	22%	90.4
1998	SAC	30	193	408	0.47	95	12.9	27%	88.4
1999	SAC	32	140	271	0.52	102	8.7	21%	100.0
2000	SAC	32	85	163	0.52	104	5.3	18%	103.6
2001	LAS	32	137	233	0.59	118	8.6	18%	107.1
2002	LAS	26	87	141	0.62	125	6.8	16%	104.2

Table 14.38. Chamique Holdsclaw's Individual Offensive Efficiency Statistics

Season	Tm	G	Sc. Poss	Poss	Floor %	Off. Rtg	Pts Prod/G	% Tm Poss	Team Off. Rtg
1999	WAS	31	248	528	0.47	96	16.3	28%	92.6
2000	WAS	32	260	531	0.49	99	16.5	27%	98.7
2001	WAS	29	229	511	0.45	91	16.0	31%	88.1
2002	WAS	20	174	338	0.52	110	18.6	32%	98.1

That is a taste of the WNBA player efficiency numbers, with a lot more given in chapter 22. It is a young league, and the dominance of individual players like Cooper, Swoopes, and Leslie is not as surprising while the league is still figuring out its style and strategies. At one time in the past, it was very troublesome that the league was promoting players who were less than the best. But I think that state of affairs is changing as the league matures and its ability to self-evaluate becomes better.

Chapter 15

The Holy Grail of Player Ratings

Over the last ten years, many magazines have forecasted a "next Michael Jordan"—with the names including Allen Iverson, Ray Allen, Harold Miner, Vince Carter, Kobe Bryant, and now high-schooler LeBron James. They have, of course, been wrong every time. On July 3, 2002, the *Indianapolis Star* reported on a couple of math guys who supposedly had developed the "Michael Jordan of statistics." Their statistic claimed to measure "the tangibles, intangibles and all other factors that determine a player's value to his team." And they were also wrong.

I'm sure that Wayne Winston and Jeff Sagarin, who jointly developed the statistical method, were thinking that they had found the Holy Grail of Player Ratings when they started working on it. Their concept was powerful yet elementary— if a lineup of Rick Fox, Robert Horry, Derek Fisher, Kobe Bryant, and Shaquille O'Neal produces a net of plus-fifteen points per game, and the same lineup with Mark Madsen replacing Shaq produces plus-five points per game, it means that Shaq is worth ten more points per game than Mark Madsen. If you carry out this analysis with all sorts of lineups, you can figure out the relative values of all players (see Box 1 for details). Other people have thought of this concept, but Winston and Sagarin got hold of the play-by-play data to do it. Despite the concept making sense, the results—as we like to say in this business—don't pass the "laugh test." Winston/Sagarin's results suggested that in 2002, Shaquille O'Neal, commonly viewed as the best player in the league, was only the twentieth best player in the NBA. Their results also suggested that rookie Andrei Kirilenko, not commonly viewed as even being in the league's top fifty, ranked second among NBA players in overall contribution. See? Doesn't pass the laugh test. Or the rolling-of-the-eyes test. Winston and Sagarin acknowledged those embarrassments and were reported to say that they "don't claim their rating is the only tool for evaluating a player's value." Oh well.

The Winston/Sagarin quest for the Holy Grail was a failure because the ideal player rating statistic is just not possible. Winston and Sagarin (who also developed the *USA Today* Sagarin ratings) made a nice attempt but ended up with nothing but a bunch of numbers that they themselves can't explain. When trying to explain Austin Croshere's high rating with the Pacers, Winston said, "They did well when he played, that's all we can say." When that is all that you can say and the NBA coaches can give you ten reasons why Croshere wasn't the best Pacer, not many people are going to have the patience to work with you.

This is not entirely a criticism of Winston and Sagarin (though their demand of a six-figure fee for their software does irk me enough to take a few jabs). Their effort was not unlike that of many others who seek out basketball truth. Every coach, scout, GM, fan, and, uh, basketball writer would like to be able to quantify the true value of the players in the league. As a result, a lot of coaches, scouts, fans, and basketball writers have tried to come up with a measure of absolute value. But when the reality checks come back with several warnings, which they inevitably do, there should be more to back the numbers up than "that's all we can say."

That better not be all you can say! Understanding *why* is as important as understanding *what* or *how much*. If you cannot explain why Kirilenko ranked so much higher than O'Neal, there is great reason to doubt the result. Did Kirilenko shut down opposing scorers? Did he set supremely better picks for the Jazz offense? Is there *any* evidence to support these possibilities? Those are interesting questions, questions whose answers may lead to the conclusion that Winston and Sagarin made a mistake. But they might point to something very interesting and something actually worth the fee they are asking. It is these cases that don't fit common perception that are most important. If Kirilenko truly is better than Shaq, then a team could pull off the greatest trade in history by sending Utah someone of Kirilenko's *perceived* (relatively low) value in return for Kirilenko, whose *real* value is as high as Shaq's perceived (very high) value. But no one is going to do that because Kirilenko's ranking could just be a mistake, and it would cost a team several victories to make such a trade. All of the ratings could be mistakes, but there is no way to determine this. There certainly is no way for the general managers that Winston/Sagarin are targeting to distinguish insightful truths from outright errors.

What about coaches? What would they do with an overall player rating? Would they just put the top-rated guys on the floor and let them do their thing? If players got tired, would coaches simply replace them with the next top-ranked guys? Regardless of position? That would make coaching really easy, wouldn't it? Coaches obviously do play their better players, but they also spend a lot of time fitting talent to a system and fitting a system to the talent. They don't play guys based on pure talent. Player talent is just one of—oh, heck, I don't know, at least eleven factors that affect how a team performs, including:

1. Playing talent
2. Coaching talent
3. Scouting
4. Strategy
5. Strength of schedule
6. Players playing different positions or different roles
7. Chemistry
8. Players playing poorly because they feel underpaid
9. Players playing well in order to get paid better
10. Players playing poorly because they just found out they have another child out of wedlock
11. Coaches coaching well because they are dating the sexy daughter of the owner

OK, I made up a few of those last ones just to get to eleven factors, having pulled the number eleven out of a hat after realizing that the list could be infinite. The point is that an overall player rating is only measuring *performance*, which is the cumulative output of all these factors. Depending on how much of performance is talent, the player rating could be valuable or it could be meaningless. If performance is only 10 percent talent, then taking that talent away from its coaches, its scouts, its system, its mistress, or even paying it differently could entirely change the performance. We as educated basketball watchers believe that performance is more than 10 percent talent, but it is also not 99 percent talent. If performance reflects even 70 percent talent and 30 percent other stuff, an overall player rating based on performance really couldn't distinguish between the true talent levels of Tim Duncan versus Shaquille O'Neal versus Dirk Nowitzki versus Kobe Bryant. The rating might see the overall performance differences, but not the players' true ability differences. So you can't use these overall player ratings to say Who is the Greatest.

So What Would Be Ideal?

Conceptually, there actually is a way to arrive at the ideal player ranking—with an emphasis on "conceptually." If you can simulate a player with all possible combinations of teammates, all possible combinations of coaches, and all possible combinations of strategies against all possible combinations of opposing teams, then you are averaging over all of the eleven different factors—at least the more serious ones. That is a big "if." If you do those simulations for all players who have ever played, then look at the winning percentages of their teams, you have my ideal player rating. That is a bigger "if."

But we don't have to do all those simulations if the world will just listen to me. That's right—if the world would listen to me, there would be no terrorism, there would be colonies on Mars, and, most importantly, there would be a Holy Grail Basketball League. It would be a league in which the NBA's top players are rotated around to different teammates, attempting to get their patchwork teams to win as many games as possible. Does Jason Kidd really help chemistry so much that his teams win no matter who his teammates are? Has Dikembe Mutombo suffered because he's never been surrounded by the offensive talent to compliment his defense? Who has been more responsible for the Lakers' success, Kobe or Shaq? How valuable has Iverson's gunning been relative to the contributions of his current Philadelphia teammates? Is it possible for a pure rebounder (a nice way of saying "nonscorer") like Ben Wallace to be at the top of the ratings? Can Michael Jordan take a ragtag group of players and make them respectable? Wait— that's reality already! Maybe the world is listening to me!

After about twenty games in the Holy Grail season, the best players should begin to separate themselves from others. At that point, I'd propose narrowing down the pool of players to those who have proven to be the best at winning. As the league progresses, better and better players would make up fewer and fewer teams until the final game (or series of games) features the top two players opposing one another with outstanding teammates to decide the title.

Now *that* is my fantasy league.

Back to Reality

Reality leaves us devoid of such a fun and insightful tool for estimating player quality. As a consequence, no matter how smart the person is putting together a player rating, there is always going to be uncertainty in the rating. Right now, with all the different systems out there, there is just a large amount of uncertainty. Those player rating methods that add the good statistics and subtract the bad (see chapter 5) have tremendous variability. The Winston/Sagarin method has obvious flaws in its results. *Sports Illustrated* occasionally tries its hand at player value ratings (see Box 2 for an example) and arrives at "interesting" results. There was a piece of software developed by Bob Chaikin to simulate various player combinations, and it was used for a while by some NBA teams, but it apparently had problems that kept it from widespread and continuous use.

Because of the uncertainty in player ratings, the decision-makers in basketball are going to be very hesitant to spend time and money on something that could *cost* them victories. Maybe with proper use these systems bring extra victories, but the potential for extra losses is huge.

I personally will be taking a stab at something called individual win-loss records in a few chapters. That concept scares me even twelve years after I first implemented it because it approaches an overall player rating. It has the same faults as other player ratings—measuring performance over pure ability. It can't forecast how a player would do if he changed positions or coaches or salary. But it does account for both offense, which was the subject of the last chapter, and defense, which is the other important aspect of a player's contribution. In that way, individual win-loss records are good summaries of offensive and defensive performance. Or, put another way, they place the offensive ratings of the last chapter in the context of individual defense to give some sense of overall impact. Over the long run, that means something.

Do they tell you who the absolute greatest player is? After reading this chapter, you should know better.

Box 1: What the Winston/Sagarin Method Does

What does the WINVAL software of Wayne Winston and Jeff Sagarin actually do? The *Indianapolis Star* article doesn't describe it explicitly, but I can infer quite a lot. Since I didn't ask either of the developers what their system did, I may be wrong. If I'm wrong, I'm inventing a nice new system on the spot that sounds a heck of a lot like theirs.

The Winston/Sagarin system works only by using the scores of games during periods of time that players are on the floor. Winston and Sagarin got access to NBA play-by-play data (apparently through Dallas owner Mark Cuban) and were able to find out exactly what lineups were on the floor for how long and how the score changed during that period of time. For instance, let me make up an imaginary 2002 Mavericks-Pacers game. At the start of the game, the starters in table 15.1 are going against each other.

During this time, the Pacers go up by three points, 22–19. Let's just say that Austin Croshere enters the game for Jeff Foster after about eight minutes. For the

Table 15.1. Starters in Hypothetical Dallas–Indiana Game

Dallas	Indiana
Juwan Howard	Jermaine O'Neal
Dirk Nowitzki	Jeff Foster
Adrian Griffin	Jalen Rose
Michael Finley	Reggie Miller
Steve Nash	Jamal Tinsley

next four minutes, the lineups stay the same, and the Pacers lose one point to the Mavs to lead only 26–24. A first-cut estimate of quality can be done for Croshere versus Foster. That first cut says that Foster's team was plus-three points per eight minutes and Croshere's team was minus-one point per four minutes, or that Foster was $+^3/_8 - (-^1/_4) = +0.625$ points per minute better than Croshere. That is the most basic element behind what Winston and Sagarin did.

Beyond the basics, there are complications. First of all, they actually didn't just look at the score difference over a period of time—they looked at how many points were scored and allowed. Here you'll notice that the Pacers scored twenty-two points in eight minutes of Foster's playing time, but only four points in four minutes of Croshere's playing time. This says to the Winston/Sagarin team that Foster is a better offensive player. On the other hand, the nineteen points allowed by the Pacers in Foster's eight minutes is a lot worse than the five points allowed in Croshere's four minutes. So Foster would look like the better offensive player and the worse defensive player. I'm also guessing that Winston/Sagarin accounted for what team was at home. For instance, if the Pacers were at home here and the average home-court advantage is about four points, that means four points per forty-eight minutes or so, or one point per quarter. The Pacers, just by their home-court advantage, should have outscored the Mavericks by two-thirds of a point in Foster's eight minutes and by one-third of a point in Croshere's four minutes. Credit for that home-court advantage gets removed from each player's contribution. Finally, by looking at all sorts of lineup changes throughout the season, Winston/Sagarin balance how good offensively and defensively each lineup is. This starting lineup of the Mavericks was known to give up a lot of points per minute and to score a lot of points per minute. So an average team would have allowed more than the twenty-four points to them, implying that the Pacers' players did relatively well defensively.[1]

It's a conceptually nice technique that is intuitive. There are definite problems with it, however. The first problem is that it treats that eight-minute span that Foster was in the game as a full game. It sounds obvious, but teams don't compete to win every eight-minute span. The Pacers don't care very much about winning that first eight minutes or any eight minutes as much as they care about winning the forty-eight-minute game. As a result, it is easy to have stretches of games in which the point-spread change during those periods does not reflect true levels of competition. This is a bigger problem in basketball than in other sports because basketball teams definitely do relax, as mentioned in chapter 11. This is also very hard to account for because it can be very hard to tell when a team is just cruising. This also may not be a big problem, at least not as big as a second troubling aspect of such a measure.

A lot of lineups are only together for short periods of time on the floor. For instance, Winston/Sagarin show the Indiana lineups in table 15.2 to be the ten most common.

The rating on the far side is probably (they don't say exactly) the net points per forty-eight minutes produced by that lineup after adjustments for home/road and quality of competition. So the top lineup would lose by an average of fourteen points over a forty-eight-minute game, and the bottom lineup would win by an average of eighteen points. The column representing minutes shows, however, that the best and the worst lineups were on the floor only sixty to seventy minutes each. That amount of time is not enough to establish a true difference. Basically, seventy minutes is about a game and a half. Over a game and a half, an average team like the Pacers could easily outscore opponents by a cumulative eighteen points or could easily be down a cumulative fourteen points, just out of random good or bad luck.[2] That lineup at the top could be just as good as the lineup at the bottom. And, when you look closely, you see that the only difference between those two lineups is replacing Jonathan Bender with Al Harrington. Does anyone really believe that Harrington is even close to thirty-two points better than Bender per forty-eight minutes?

Table 15.2. Ten Most Common Indiana Lineups in 2002

Lineups					Minutes	Rating
Bender	Best	O'Neal	R. Miller	Rose	74	-14.1
B. Miller	Bender	Ollie	O'Neal	R. Miller	65	-13.0
Harrington	O'Neal	R. Miller	Rose	Tinsley	181	-5.5
Foster	Harrington	R. Miller	Rose	Tinsley	72	-5.2
Croshere	O'Neal	R. Miller	Rose	Tinsley	70	-0.6
Foster	O'Neal	R. Miller	Rose	Tinsley	457	3.7
B. Miller	Bender	O'Neal	R. Miller	Tinsley	106	5.6
Artest	B. Miller	O'Neal	R. Miller	Tinsley	349	10.2
Artest	B. Miller	Bender	O'Neal	Tinsley	59	15.3
Best	Harrington	O'Neal	R. Miller	Rose	62	18.1

Somehow, Winston and Sagarin also appear to have made estimates of value that are more extreme than seem reasonable. One of their measures of value is how often a player's team would win if he was surrounded by four average players. It's again a nicely intuitive concept, but they determined that Tim Duncan's 2002 season was worthy of a rating of 89 percent. In other words, a team of Tim Duncan and four average players would win 89 percent of the time, resulting in a record seventy-three wins. That implies, first of all, that Duncan's teammates—David Robinson, Tony Parker, Steve Smith, Malik Rose, etc.—were so much worse than average that they cost the team fifteen games. That seems a bit unbelievable for an NBA Top 50 player, an All-Rookie selection, and a former Olympian. Second, if you believe that Duncan really was this good, it raises some problems. The best team in history, the 1996 Chicago Bulls, won only seventy-two games. Maybe their leader, Michael Jordan, was nowhere near as good as Duncan, but that would be called a minority opinion. If you assume that Jordan was merely as good as Duncan, that means that Pippen and Rodman and the rest of those Bulls were an average team. But the 1994 and 1995 Bulls—without Jordan and Rodman—were both better than average, winning fifty-five and forty-seven games, respectively. The best explanation for this is that Jordan and Duncan were both very good players, but not good enough to take a team of average players to the best record in NBA history.

Box 2: Tyra Banks! Tyra Banks!

This box reprints a column I wrote in February 1997 for The Mining Company, *reflecting upon a player rating technique that* Sports Illustrated *used to evaluate point guards.*

This week's *Sports Illustrated* has Tyra Banks on the cover with her shorts halfway off. I don't know how to compete with that, especially since I probably just sold a bunch more copies just by saying it.

This year, rather than actually complementing their sports coverage with pictures of poorly covered bathing suit models, *Sports Illustrated* chose to devote an entire issue to nothing but bikinis. Their only links to sports were to capture tennis player Steffi Graf and volleyball player Gabrielle Reece in bikinis and—for all you *Playboy* subscribers who get it for the articles—there are actually a few words about Banks' visit to a Laker game.

Given that *Sports Illustrated* took some liberties in their coverage this week, so will I. Unfortunately, I don't have any pictures to make up for this. I don't have any violence either. All I can promise is that I will mention Tyra Banks at least six more times before the end of this article.

So what happened this week? Don Nelson was in the news for trading away the entire Dallas Mavericks team. Given the choice between a cover of Nelson or Tyra Banks, I can see why *SI* went with Banks. As good as Banks looks, Nelson looked equally awful with the trades he made. In particular, his trade with the Nets that sent Jim Jackson, Chris Gatling, Sam Cassell, George McCloud, and Eric Montross for Shawn Bradley, Khalid Reeves, Robert Pack, and Ed O'Bannon was widely viewed as a mistake. Regardless of the ultimate and unpredictable future of these players, if the general populace is so overwhelming in their belief that the Nets won this trade, that indicates that the market value of the Dallas players was much greater than what Nellie got.

In another recent *Sports Illustrated* piece where they actually covered sports, they rated the point guards in the league. Their study showed that cover-boy Terrell Brandon, Cleveland's underpublicized lead guard, is the best in the league this year.

Brandon is indeed a fine point guard, one of the best in the league. He was a worthy All-Star this season and last. He is the primary offensive threat on a relatively meager offensive team. Replacing Brandon with an average point guard brings the Cavaliers down from a decent playoff team to a very average team.

However, the method that *Sports Illustrated* used to rate the point guards is not beyond reproach. What this once-a-year skin magazine did was akin to when a dating agency gives you one of those compatibility tests to see if you have a chance of going out with Tyra Banks. Depending on the questions asked and the pool of candidates, you could end up with Banks or you could end up with someone, well, with great personality.

Specifically, *Sports Illustrated* selected sixteen point guards to rank against one another in nine different categories, weighting assists and turnovers by two, weighting rebounds and blocks by one half, and weighting points, steals, field goal percentage, three point percentage, and free throw percentage by one. I duplicated their study with statistics from two weeks later and got table 15.3, which strongly resembles their results.

Table 15.3. Approximate Point Guard Ratings from *Sports Illustrated*

		Category Weighting									
		Two Points		One Point					1/2 Point		
Rank	Player, Team	AST	TO	PTS	STL	FG%	3PT%	FT%	REB	BLK	Total
1	Brandon, CLV	3	14	14	11	12	14	16	7	15	112.0
2	Stockton, UTA	15	5	4	12	16	16	15	3	4	106.5
3	Payton, SEA	8	11	15	16	15	6	3	12	5	101.5
4	Blaylock, ATL	2	13	10	14	10	13	5	14	12	95.0
5	Anderson, POR	4	16	9	10	7	10	8	13	7	94.0
6	Johnson K., PHO	13	6	8	4	13	15	12	5	3	94.0
7	Hardaway A., ORL	1	12	13	6	9	4	13	15	16	86.5
8	Hardaway T., MIA	9	9	11	9	8	7	9	6	2	84.0
9	Jackson, DEN	16	3	2	2	6	12	11	16	9	83.5
10	Van Exel, LAL	12	10	5	1	4	11	14	4	1	81.5
11	Johnson A., SAS	7	15	3	5	14	2	1	1	10	74.5
12	Kidd, PHO	14	7	1	13	1	3	2	9	13	73.0
13	Stoudamire, TOR	11	2	12	7	2	8	10	8	6	72.0
14	Strickland, WAS	10	4	7	8	11	1	6	10	8	70.0
15	Iverson, PHI	5	1	16	15	3	5	4	11	14	67.5
16	Marbury, MIN	6	8	6	3	5	9	7	2	11	64.5

Table 15.4. *Sports Illustrated* Ratings with Just Six Point Guards

		Category Weighting									
		Two Points		One Point					1/2 Point		
Rank	Player, Team	AST	TO	PTS	STL	FG%	3PT%	FT%	REB	BLK	Total
1	Stockton, UTA	6	1	2	5	6	6	5	2	2	40
2	Payton, SEA	4	3	6	6	5	2	2	5	3	39
3	Brandon, CLV	1	4	5	4	3	5	6	4	6	38
4	Anderson, POR	2	6	3	3	1	4	3	6	4	35
5	Hardaway T., MIA	5	2	4	2	2	3	4	3	1	31
6	Johnson A., SAS	3	5	1	1	4	1	1	1	5	27

A few people have changed positions from the original results, but there are no major differences. Now consider what happens if the candidates are limited only to Anderson, Brandon, Hardaway, Avery Johnson, Payton, and Stockton. Using the exact same methodology, the rankings are shown in table 15.4.

Just by changing the players being evaluated, Brandon drops behind both Stockton and Payton in the rankings of the best players. This is a common trick that lawyers use when they are trying to be slimy.

Of course, the results also can change if you change the weights on the different numbers. Why are assists four times as important as rebounds? Why isn't it three times or six times? Depending on how these values are set, any one of the top five or six point guards can be viewed as "The Best."

Having torn the method to pieces, I should admit that it actually has merit. It isn't very good at identifying the absolute best, but it can separate a class of players that can qualify for that title.

Hmm. I'm forgetting something. Oh, yeah. I have to mention Tyra Banks one more time. That makes sex . . . I mean, six.

Endnotes

1. In actuality, I'm sure that Winston/Sagarin do things in a different *order* than I'm describing. They also have several independent estimates of the value of Foster versus Croshere due to different lineup combinations. They might have each played with O'Neal, Rose, Miller, and Travis Best, for example. In order to handle this, they apply a statistical method that tries to best fit all the data.

2. The minutes played by Pacers lineups are probably low relative to other NBA teams due to the Pacer's trading Jalen Rose and Travis Best, two significant players, midway through the season. That does not change the point here, which is that lineups may not play enough minutes to produce realistic estimates of their quality, but there are probably teams that look better than Indiana.

Chapter 16

Insight on a Box Score

Wake up in the morning, take a shower, and have breakfast over the box scores. It's the perfect way to start a day. At least that does it for me. I can't watch as many games as I'd like, but I keep up with how teams and players are doing by reading the paper or, these days, by getting the story from either the ESPN or Sportsline websites.

The game recap gives you a few things: quotes on what the players and coaches perceived was important, the writer's take on the last two minutes of the game or the stretch of the game when one team made a run, and a quick rundown of leading scorers. Sometimes, they'll add something about Allen Iverson or Kobe Bryant just because it draws a few more readers.

A box score gives you something else. It provides a summary of the entire game. It's a bigger picture than what a game recap typically gives. It cannot show a crucial run that "decided the game," as the popular press likes to say. It cannot show Joe Dumars going three for three in the last minute to seal a victory. It really tries to show the foundation of the game before that last minute or before that last run. It includes information on that last minute, but it doesn't emphasize it. Because it doesn't emphasize much of anything, the box score can be overlooked by people not interested in the whole game. For me, however, the box score is very valuable.

The box score summarizes *one game*, the unit of basketball time that is most important to coaches and players. A team can play great through three quarters then collapse in the fourth to lose. Those first three quarters don't matter. All that matters is the big "L" that goes on a coach's record and into a player's reputation. Because the box score gives a picture of one game, it provides a valuable means of evaluating players and teams over an appropriate time span. No one can truly evaluate a player using just his performance in the last minute of one game. But a full game may be enough. A lot of times, one game is all that a scout can see of a team before making judgments on how to beat that team. Fortunately, one game provides all sorts of plays, all sorts of offenses, and a large variety of player combinations—much of the information necessary to understand a team.

So I'm going to look at a box score and show you how I read it: What do I look for and what does it tell me about what happened in the game? I'll do this primarily from the perspective of the guy reading the paper, then I'll add some of the individual floor percentages and ratings to illustrate what I look for when I do a more careful analysis.

The game I will examine is the Charlotte-Milwaukee playoff game of May 20, 2001. It was Game 7 to decide who went to the Eastern Conference Finals. Baron Davis and Jamal Mashburn were the Hornets stars, while Milwaukee had the trio of Ray Allen, Glenn Robinson, and Sam Cassell. The box score is in table 16.1.

There are a couple of things that jump out at me. First, the third quarter appeared to be when Milwaukee took control, on their way to a 104–95 win. Second, each team played only eight guys, suggesting that they valued this game a lot, as would be expected.

Pace of the Game

The first thing to understand about a game is whether it was won on the offensive or defensive end and, for that, I always look at the pace of the game to get the team's ratings. I typically scan one team's numbers and do the quick calculation of possessions in my head. Using Charlotte's numbers, I get

$$\text{Poss} = \text{FGA} - \text{OR} + \text{TOV} + 0.4 \times \text{FTA}$$
$$= 82 - 14 + 8 + 0.4 \times 28 \approx 87$$

If you use Milwaukee's, you get eighty-eight possessions. Either way, ninety-five points or 104 points divided by eighty-seven or eighty-eight is something greater than one. With the NBA average rating around 105, that would mean that eighty-seven or eighty-eight possessions would produce an average of about ninety-three points. The fact that both teams scored more points than that means that offense told the story of this game. Neither team's defense did a great job stopping the scorers.

This first-cut look is similar to one used by Coach Dean Smith of North Carolina and his predecessor, Frank McGuire. The introductions to their books both say, "A quick glance at three figures (our points per possession, opponent's points per possession, and total possessions) helps the coach to determine any changes he must make." It's not just me who looks at this first. Some of the great coaches in history do, too. It just makes sense for getting an overall feel for the game.

Table 16.1. Box Score for Charlotte–Milwaukee, May 20, 2001

Charlotte

Player	Pos	Min	FGs M	FGs A	3-Ptrs M	3-Ptrs A	FTs M	FTs A	Reb O	Reb D	Reb T	AST	PF	ST	TO	BS	Pts
Mashburn	F	41	7	25	1	2	6	8	1	3	4	9	5	0	1	1	21
Brown	F	39	2	4	0	0	2	2	7	2	9	0	6	0	0	1	6
Campbell	C	33	8	15	0	0	2	2	3	7	10	2	4	1	3	2	18
Davis	G	45	10	16	5	8	4	9	1	1	2	6	4	2	1	2	29
Wesley	G	43	7	17	0	4	1	1	1	1	2	5	5	1	0	0	15
Robinson		17	1	2	0	0	0	0	0	4	4	0	2	0	1	0	2
Magloire		13	1	3	0	0	2	6	1	4	5	1	3	0	0	1	4
Thorpe		9	0	0	0	0	0	0	0	1	1	0	1	0	1	0	0
Coleman		DNP															
Recasner		DNP															
Hawkins		DNP															
Burrell		DNP															
TOTAL		240	36	82	6	14	17	28	14	23	37	23	30	4	8	7	95
			44%		43%		61%		Tm Reb: 9					Total TO: 8		(10 Pts)	

Milwaukee

Player	Pos	Min	FGs M	FGs A	3-Ptrs M	3-Ptrs A	FTs M	FTs A	Reb O	Reb D	Reb T	AST	PF	ST	TO	BS	Pts
Robinson	F	40	10	17	3	5	6	6	1	4	5	1	4	0	1	1	29
Williams	F	27	4	8	0	0	5	6	1	7	8	2	4	0	1	3	13
Johnson	C	37	2	2	0	0	0	1	3	8	11	1	3	0	2	4	4
Allen	G	46	10	18	2	6	6	6	2	4	6	5	4	0	4	2	28
Cassell	G	36	4	12	1	3	8	8	0	3	3	13	3	0	2	1	17
Thomas		29	0	3	0	0	8	8	1	4	5	1	2	0	3	2	8
Hunter		14	1	6	1	3	0	0	0	1	1	2	1	1	0	0	3
Caffey		11	1	2	0	0	0	0	0	3	3	1	2	1	0	0	2
Ham		DNP															
Przybilla		DNP															
Pope		DNP															
Alston		DNP															
TOTAL		240	32	68	7	17	33	35	8	34	42	26	23	2	14	13	104
			47%		41%		94%		Tm R: 7					Total TO: 14		(16 Pts)	

	Period 1	2	3	4	Total
Hornets	26	21	17	31	95
Bucks	23	21	29	31	104

Technicals: None
Disqualifications: Charlotte: Brown, Brown
Officials: Don Vaden, Bennett Salvatore, Steve Javie
Location: Bradley Center
Attendance: 18,717
Time: 2:27

Beyond these numbers, anything else you learn from a box score is gravy. I will always check the pace and the teams' efficiency numbers. I do the following when I am more interested in a specific game and have more time.

What Made the Offenses Good?

In this game, the two teams shot around 45 percent—nothing unusual. They were good because of other things. In Milwaukee's case—and I usually do look at the winners first—they got to the foul line a lot, and they almost never missed. They probably got a little lucky to hit 94 percent. Five of their top six guys all had great days from the line. In terms of turnovers and offensive rebounds, the Bucks also did nothing special. It was their performance at the line that got them the extra offense they needed. Since Charlotte was so far behind after the third quarter, many of these foul shots could have come as a result of late Hornet fouls. But the fact that so many different Bucks made them was critical.

On Charlotte's side of the ball, they generated offense a little differently. They got a lot of shots at the basket by getting a fair number of offensive rebounds and by committing only eight turnovers. The fourteen offensive rebounds compared to the thirty-four defensive rebounds by the Bucks is actually only an average performance on the boards, but it kept the Hornets in it. P.J. Brown was the key here, getting seven offensive boards.

Probably the final thing that made this game an offensive one is that both teams were shooting well from beyond the arc.

Individual Offense/Defense

Because this was an offensive game, I do often look at the top scorers for the two teams. In this case, Milwaukee was led by Robinson and Allen, who both did what the team did—score from the line. They also shot well from the field. Cassell appeared to be a solid complementary player, handing out thirteen assists.

For Charlotte, I would have already noticed Brown's offensive rebounds in looking at the team offensive rebounds. Beyond that, Mashburn and Davis appeared to control the offense. Mashburn had a mixed day, shooting horribly but handing out nine assists. Davis was the overall offensive star, though, shooting well from everywhere but the foul line (which probably hurt).

If the game had been more defensive—or even if just one team had played good defense—I would have looked at individual defense a couple of ways. First, I would have taken what was clear from the team defense—whether it was field goal shooting, foul shooting, turnovers, or stopping offensive rebounds that made the defense good—to look for players who typically do those things. In this case, the defenses were bad, so I wouldn't normally look at it much, but I'll make an exception to give you an example of what you can see. First of all, Milwaukee went to the line a lot, so Charlotte must have fouled people a lot. Indeed, throughout their starting lineup, you see at least four fouls per player. That, especially with the big lead going into the fourth quarter, doesn't really say much, which is typical of box scores. On the Milwaukee defense, the fact that Charlotte committed few turnovers and that Davis had a good game implies that Milwaukee's guards didn't play the greatest defense. On the other hand, Scott Williams and Ervin Johnson both blocked shots to lower Charlotte's field goal percentage, and they both got plenty of defensive boards. It's not clear who matched up with Mashburn so successfully, but that might have been Robinson.

More Detail

That's about as much detail as I'll ever mine from a box score over breakfast. It would actually require a big bowl of cereal to get through so much. But when I do have to analyze a box score, I will calculate a lot of the individual offensive ratings from the game. In this game, you get the numbers in table 16.2.

Table 16.2. Individual and Team Efficiency Statistics

Player	Sc. Poss.	Poss.	Floor %	Off. Rtg.	Pts Prod	% Team Poss
			Charlotte			
Mashburn	11.2	25.0	0.447	94.5	23.6	34%
Brown	4.3	5.7	0.754	159.5	9.1	8%
Campbell	7.8	15.7	0.497	102.8	16.2	26%
Davis	10.6	17.0	0.628	141.5	24.0	21%
Wesley	7.3	14.3	0.510	105.2	15.0	18%
Robinson	0.7	2.4	0.303	60.7	1.5	8%
Magloire	2.5	5.0	0.507	90.6	4.5	21%
Thorpe	0.0	1.0	0.000	0.0	0.0	6%
Totals	**44.5**	**86.1**	**0.517**	**109.0**	**93.9**	
			Milwaukee			
Robinson	9.3	15.8	0.588	137.9	21.8	22%
Williams	6.0	10.2	0.585	122.3	12.4	21%
Johnson	2.3	4.7	0.491	104.5	4.9	7%
Allen	11.3	21.6	0.524	118.8	25.7	26%
Cassell	9.8	18.1	0.542	125.6	22.7	28%
Thomas	3.6	9.0	0.403	98.9	8.9	17%
Hunter	1.4	5.3	0.258	69.6	3.7	21%
Caffey	1.0	1.8	0.558	114.8	2.0	9
Totals	**44.7**	**86.4**	**0.517**	**118.2**	**102.1**	

Poss.	CHA Rating	MIL Rating
86.5	109.9	120.3

Milwaukee was pretty well balanced, with four guys handling more than 20 percent of their team possessions when in the game, all producing more than ten points apiece. Their top three all produced over twenty points apiece, and all did it with ratings over 118. That kind of balance is good to have. It allows you to play guys like Johnson, who don't contribute much offensively. Despite Cassell's four-of-twelve shooting, note that his floor percentage and rating were high as a result of his being a good distributor.

On Charlotte's side, Mashburn's nine assists didn't offset his poor shooting, and his off day hurt the team. His offensive rating of 94.5, combined with his use of 34 percent of the team possessions, was tough on the team offense. Of Charlotte's top four point producers, only one had an offensive rating higher than the opponents' overall offensive rating. That makes it hard to win.

With Mashburn dominating so many possessions, doing it so inefficiently, *and* with so many of his teammates not playing very efficiently either, we can infer that Milwaukee didn't have to dedicate more than straight man-to-man defense to him. And Mash just couldn't take advantage.

Using It While at a Game

One of the things that leapt out when I first looked at the box score was that the third quarter was what killed the Hornets. In that quarter, Mashburn actually hit three of five shots. But the defense fell apart. The Bucks scored thirty-one points on only nineteen possessions in that period. Glenn Robinson, presumably Mashburn's defensive assignment, went only three for seven, but every one of his misses was rebounded by the Bucks. He and Scott Williams pretty much dominated the quarter, going to the line, getting boards, and making shots.

This illustrates how general trends of the game may get only partially reflected in "significant" periods of the game. During this third quarter, Milwaukee was getting to the line a lot, and it helped them. They did it by getting seven offensive rebounds (including team rebounds) on twelve missed shots. Did offensive rebounding win that game for the Bucks? Or was it their shooters, who kept them even throughout the rest of the game? There is no conclusive answer. But at half-time, with the Bucks down by three, you can imagine that Coach George Karl looked at the box, saw only four offensive rebounds, and told his big men to go to the glass. Whether it was that or Williams just being in the right places at the right times, it was an adjustment that got them the lead and the eventual win.

Chapter 17

Individual Defensive Ratings

Baseball represents the epitome of defense. The average major league baseball offense scores four or five times per twenty-seven chances it gets. And you'd think that would be about right, because it is one hitter against nine defenders. Mainly, it is the hitter against a pitcher, but if that hitter puts the ball in play, the pitcher calls on his help defense—which consists of his eight fielders.

There is an analogy to be made here with basketball, especially with man defenses. In a man defense, the defender on the ball is like the pitcher—his main responsibility is the guy trying to put the ball over the fence, err, in the basket. But, if he slips up a little, he has help behind him, and that help is pretty good. There are plenty of good pitchers that rely on their fielders rather than on strike-outs, and there are plenty of good basketball defenders that rely on help defense behind them.

I can take the analogy a little further. When baseball teams put on their Barry Bonds shift, moving all of their infielders to the right of second base to take away his ground balls through the right side of the infield, that's like forcing a young Michael Jordan to shoot a jump shot when he really wanted to drive. When baseball teams bring in a middle reliever to deal specially with one hitter and that middle reliever gets torched, that's like bringing in Ruben Patterson (the self-proclaimed "Kobe-Stopper") to try to stop Kobe Bryant and watching him get posterized a few times.

But one thing that baseball has that basketball doesn't is a tool to evaluate its defenders. I'm thinking mainly of an ERA, an earned run average. An ERA does the nice work of indicating how many earned runs a pitcher gives up per twenty-seven outs he records. Baseball doesn't claim that an ERA is a perfect measure of a pitcher's ability, but it works pretty well. In particular, whereas relief pitcher

ERAs are flawed, starting pitchers with consistently low ERAs are usually among the winningest and most highly valued pitchers. A basketball version of an ERA that shows fewer points allowed per hundred possessions for good defenders is a nice concept. By no coincidence, I'm working on it.

WNBA's Project Defensive Score Sheet

In cooperation with a lot of the WNBA teams' public relations directors, I have a group of volunteers going to games and collecting stats that start to get at a basketball player's points allowed and points stopped. The effort is known as Project Defensive Score Sheet. I'll explain some of the information that this effort is aiming to provide in this section.

The only official defensive statistics that the WNBA (or NBA) collects are defensive rebounds, steals, blocks, and, though some are not defensive, personal fouls. This is a meager collection that does no justice to the value of defense in basketball. The Project Defensive Score Sheet volunteers are collecting additional statistics for individual defenders in order to make up for this, including:

- Forced field goal misses (denoted "FM" for "forced miss"), when a defender forces an offensive player to miss a shot from the field,
- Forced turnovers ("FTO"), when a defender forces an offensive player to commit a turnover,
- Forced free throw misses ("FFTA"), when a defender fouls an offensive player who misses foul shots,
- Allowed field goals ("DFGM"), when a defender allows an offensive player score a field goal over her, and
- Allowed free throws ("DFTM"), when a defender commits a foul that leads to made free throws.

These statistics are without question among the important qualifiers of a player's defense. But they really are just inverses of the offensive statistics that the leagues already record. If Chamique Holdsclaw scores a basket over Tamecka Dixon, Holdsclaw gets an official FGM from the league, and Dixon gets an unofficial DFGM from us. If Holdsclaw misses a driving lay-up when Lisa Leslie comes over to help Dixon, Holdsclaw gets a FGA without an FGM from the league, and Leslie and Dixon both get half an FM from us.

It's not a complicated system, and it's not supposed to be. There are times when an offensive player misses a wide-open shot with no defender around. That is a *team* forced miss. Or, if the offensive player made the shot with no one around, that is a *team* DFGM. Maybe a coach can place responsibility on one player more than another if no one is covering the ball (e.g., a player didn't rotate, or a player double-teamed when she shouldn't have). The volunteers aren't trying to discern all of that.

At the end of a game, the Project Score Sheet volunteers return a sheet like that in table 17.1.

Table 17.1 reflects the tally from the July 11, 2002, Los Angeles Sparks–Seattle Storm matchup. Seattle was a pretty heavy underdog going in but won 79–60, holding the Sparks to 33 percent shooting, as the official box score showed (table 17.2).

Overall, with an estimated seventy-one possessions each, the team ratings in the game were 112 to eighty-five. Relative to the league average rating of ninety-six, the Storm did well on both sides of the ball. But, for the purposes of this chapter, we want to know what Storm players did the job *defensively*.

The way I start looking at this is to see how the opposing Sparks performed as an offense in the general four categories referred to elsewhere in the book (table 17.3).

Table 17.1. Volunteer Score Sheet for July 11, 2002, Sparks–Storm Game

Name	Forced Miss (FM)	BLK	FTO	STL	FTA Miss (FFTA)	DFGM	DFTM
			LA Sparks				
Witherspoon	4	0	0	1	0	1	0
Teasley	4	1	1	0	0	5	0
Leslie	3	6	0	1	0	2.5	0
Milton	4.5	1	0	3	0	9	4
Mabika	6	1	0	1	0	1	0
McCrimmon	4.5	0	0	0	0	1	0
Byears	4.5	0	0	1	0	1	2
Askamp	1.5	0	0	0	0	2.5	0
Desouza	0	0	0	1	0	0	0
Grgin	0	0	0	0	0	1	0
Dixon	0	0	0	0	0	0	0
Team	0	0	1	0	0	6	0
Totals	**32**	**9**	**2**	**8**	**0**	**30**	**6**
			Seattle Storm				
Bird	2.5	1	0	2	0	1.5	0
Barnes	3.5	2	2.5	2	0	3.5	0
Jackson	2	1	1.5	1	1	1.5	5
Vodichkova	3	4	1	1	2	1	4
Lassiter	3.5	0	0.5	1	0	2	4
Edwards	5	0	0	0	0	2	4
Marciniak	0	0	1.5	0	0	0	2
Ragland	3.5	0	1	1	1	0.5	1
Paye	0	0	0	0	0	0	0
Lewis	0	0	0	0	1	0	1
Randall	1	0	0	0	0	1	2
Team	1	0	3	0	0	3	0
Totals	**25**	**8**	**11**	**8**	**5**	**16**	**23**

Table 17.2. Official Box Score from Sparks–Storm Game

LA Sparks

Player	Pos	Min	FGs M	FGs A	3-Ptrs M	3-Ptrs A	FTs M	FTs A	Reb O	Reb D	Reb T	AST	PF	ST	TO	BS	Pts
N. Teasley	G	29	2	3	0	0	0	0	0	2	2	3	3	0	3	1	4
Witherspoon	G	14	0	4	0	2	4	4	0	1	1	0	0	0	0	0	4
M. Mabika	F	36	4	14	3	8	6	6	0	2	2	3	2	1	4	1	17
D. Milton	F	34	2	7	1	2	3	4	3	7	10	1	6	3	4	1	8
L. Leslie	C	37	6	14	1	3	8	11	1	8	9	2	1	1	5	6	21
McCrimmon		22	0	1	0	1	0	0	0	1	1	2	1	1	2	0	0
L. Byears		19	1	5	0	0	1	2	4	2	6	0	2	1	0	0	3
M. Askamp		7	1	1	0	0	0	0	0	0	0	0	0	0	0	0	2
E. DeSouza		1	0	0	0	0	1	2	0	0	0	0	0	1	0	0	1
GrginFonseca		1	0	0	0	0	0	0	0	0	0	0	0	1	0	0	
T. Dixon		DNP															
TOTAL		200	16	49	5	16	23	29	8	23	31	11	15	8	19	9	60
			32.7%		31.3%		79.3%		Tm Rebs: 11				Total TO: 19				

Seattle Storm

Player	Pos	Min	FGs M	FGs A	3-Ptrs M	3-Ptrs A	FTs M	FTs A	Reb O	Reb D	Reb T	AST	PF	ST	TO	BS	Pts
S. Bird	G	33	5	16	3	8	0	1	0	3	3	5	0	2	3	1	13
A. Barnes	G	28	2	6	0	0	0	0	5	3	8	4	3	2	1	2	4
L. Jackson	F	31	8	17	3	4	2	2	0	3	3	2	5	1	2	1	21
A. Lassiter	F	28	3	8	2	5	0	0	0	2	2	5	4	1	2	0	8
K. Vodichkova	C	25	2	7	0	2	2	2	0	3	3	1	4	1	0	4	6
F. Ragland		21	6	9	5	6	2	2	0	0	0	0	1	1	0	0	19
S. Edwards		19	1	4	0	0	0	0	3	3	6	2	2	0	1	0	2
M. Marciniak		6	0	1	0	0	0	0	1	0	1	1	1	0	0	0	0
K. Paye		3	0	0	0	0	0	0	0	0	0	0	0	0	0	0	0
S. Randall		3	1	1	0	0	0	0	0	0	0	1	1	0	1	0	2
T. Lewis		3	2	2	0	0	0	0	0	0	0	0	1	0	0	0	4
TOTAL		200	30	71	13	25	6	7	9	17	26	21	22	8	10	8	79
			42.3%		52.0%		85.7%		Tm Rebs: 11				Total TO: 10				

Line Score	1	2	T
Sparks	23	37	60
Storm	45	34	79

Table 17.3. The Four Factors for the Sparks–Storm Game

Category	Sparks Value	League Average
Field Goal %	16/49 = 33%	42%
Offensive Rebound %	8/(8 + 17) = 32%	32%
Turnovers per Possession	19/70 = 27%	22%
Free Throws	23/29 in 70 poss	14/19 in 69 poss.

The Storm shut down the Sparks' shooting and forced them into a lot of turnovers. They didn't allow any more or any fewer offensive rebounds than normal. They did put the Sparks on the line a lot, so they didn't do well in that aspect.

What this says is that the Storm players forcing turnovers and missed shots were the ones who did the best defensive job. Defensive rebounders were not as important. This then is a prime case for showing the value of the defensive scoresheet results. Defensive rebounds are in the official record, but forced misses and forced turnovers are reflected only partially in blocks and steals, so this volunteer's information provides a lot of insight into the players who made the difference. Let's summarize the Storm players' *total* forced misses and turnovers in table 17.4.

The key turnover-forcing players were Adia Barnes, forcing 4.5 in twenty-eight minutes, and Felicia Ragland, forcing two in twenty-one minutes. Kamila Vodichkova was Seattle's key field goal stopper, preventing seven total shots from going in. Simone Edwards forced five misses in only nineteen minutes, but none of those were blocks, so this unofficial tally is the only one that shows her effort. These players led a pretty balanced defensive effort that stifled the Sparks.

On LA's side, they got hurt defensively by not forcing turnovers and giving up a lot of three-point field goals (table 17.5). The distribution of DFGM shows that Delisha Milton, whose main responsibility was Seattle's Lauren Jackson (as noted in the volunteer's notes), got beaten a lot. She was followed by the overall team, which gave up six uncovered shots, probably due to either bad rotations or transition baskets. On the good side for Milton, she was the only Sparks player who forced many turnovers.

After a game like this, the Seattle coaching staff would probably review these numbers and say, "Good job to all." The Los Angeles staff would look and see that Milton had a rough game guarding Jackson and perhaps think to provide help for her next time. They would also look at those team DFGM and consider ways to

Table 17.4. Total Forced Misses and Forced Turnovers for the Storm

Name	Min	FM	BLK	Total FM	FTO	STL	Total FTO
Bird	33	2.5	1	3.5	0.0	2	2.0
Barnes	28	3.5	2	5.5	2.5	2	4.5
Jackson	31	2.0	1	3.0	1.5	1	2.5
Vodichkova	25	3.0	4	7.0	1.0	1	2.0
Lassiter	28	3.5	0	3.5	0.5	1	1.5
Edwards	19	5.0	0	5.0	0.0	0	0.0
Marciniak	6	0.0	0	0.0	1.5	0	1.5
Ragland	21	3.5	0	3.5	1.0	1	2.0
Paye	3	0.0	0	0.0	0.0	0	0.0
Lewis	3	0.0	0	0.0	0.0	0	0.0
Randall	3	1.0	0	1.0	0.0	0	0.0
Team		1.0	0	1.0	3.0	0	3.0
Totals	**200**	**25**	**8**	**33**	**11**	**8**	**19**

Table 17.5. Total Forced Misses and Forced Turnovers for the Sparks

Name	Min	Total FM	Total FTO	DFGM	DFTM
Witherspoon	14	4.0	1.0	1.0	0
Teasley	29	5.0	1.0	5.0	0
Leslie	37	9.0	1.0	2.5	0
Milton	34	5.5	3.0	9.0	4
Mabika	36	7.0	1.0	1.0	0
McCrimmon	22	4.5	0.0	1.0	0
Byears	19	4.5	1.0	1.0	2
Askamp	7	1.5	0.0	2.5	0
Desouza	1	0.0	1.0	0.0	0
Grgin Fonseca	1	0.0	0.0	1.0	0
Team		0.0	1.0	6.0	0
Totals	200	41	10	30	6

eliminate all those uncovered baskets—whether they were off of fast breaks or off of bad rotations on the perimeter.

Defensive Stops

The kind of detailed evaluation made possible by Project Defensive Score Sheet is nice to do, but it isn't always possible. A lot of times, you really only want to *summarize* the defensive contributions of players. Summaries can give you the quick thumbs-up or thumbs-down to track player contributions. The summary of these statistics is built into something called a "defensive stop" or, ultimately, an individual defensive rating, which is closer to that basketball-like ERA.

What is a defensive stop? A team "stops" its opposition when it gets the ball without allowing a score. That conveniently means that a team's defensive stops plus the number of scoring possessions it allows equals the team's total possessions. The ways that teams stop their opponents are by forcing turnovers or by getting the ball after a missed field goal or missed free throw. Individual defensive stops are just what *players* do to create *team* stops.

The above tally sheet provides most of what you need to calculate individual defensive stops. The only things missing are defensive rebounds from the box score and the formula[1]:

$$\text{Individual Stops} = \text{FTO} + \frac{\text{FFTA}}{10} + \text{FM} \times \text{FMwt} \times (1 - \text{DOR\%}) + \text{DREB} \times (1 - \text{FMwt})$$

The term, FMwt (for "forced miss weight"), is just the weight given to forced misses versus defensive rebounds. Since both of these are necessary to stop a team that misses a shot, the FMwt tells you how important one is versus the other based upon difficulty—as described in the third teamwork chapter. The formula is justified more in Appendix 1 for the offense and is given here for this application:

$$FMwt = \frac{DFG\% \times (1 - DOR\%)}{DFG\% \times (1 - DOR\%) + (1 - DFG\%) \times DOR\%}$$

In this game, because Seattle shut down Los Angeles' shooting as well (DFG% = 33 percent) as they got defensive rebounds (DOR% = 32 percent), the weight on each forced miss, 51 percent, was about the same as on a defensive rebound, 49 percent (though, because forced misses don't always end a possession, their over-all weight gets reduced by the chance that they do end a possession). Normally, the weight is 60 to 65 percent on forcing misses, indicating that it is a harder proposition. In high school basketball and in leagues where a lot of zones are played, teams often allow a higher percentage of offensive rebounds and force a lower field goal percentage, making the importance of defensive rebounds a bit higher. I have seen cases in high school where a team allows less than 40 percent of shots to be made but more than 45 percent of all shots to be rebounded by the offense—such cases are where defensive rebounding needs to be emphasized.

Table 17.6 shows the resulting tabulation of individual defensive stops for the Sparks and Storm.

I've also added columns for the scoring possessions allowed by a player (DScPoss), the total possessions the player faced (DPoss), the stop percentage (Stop %), which is DStops per possession, the percentage of team possessions faced (% Team DPoss), and—the "basketball ERA" we've been going for—the indi-vidual defensive rating (Def. Rtg.).

Most formulas used for the calculations are in Appendix 3. But I did want to explain the defensive rating a bit here. Defensive players, unlike offensive players, have the possibility of being involved in every possession. Every player can guard the ball. You can actually say that all players are guarding the ball in some sense by keeping their men from getting the ball in good scoring position. In that extreme perspective, the team defensive rating is also every individual's defensive rating. With the Project Defensive Score Sheet information on how different indi-viduals do different amounts of defensive work, it would seem a shame to just assign the team defensive rating as each individual's defensive rating. You can use stops and defensive scoring possessions to break down the responsibility for defense among individuals in individual defensive ratings. The way I do it is to translate each individual's stop percentage into a kind of defensive rating, using $100 \times DPtsPerScPoss \times (1 - Stop\%)$, where DPtsPerScPoss is the number of points scored per scoring possession by the opponents, then weight that with the team defensive rating by how much that player was involved in the defense (their % Team Poss. value) to get

$$DRtg = TMDRtg + \%TMDPoss \times \left[100 \times DPtsPerScPoss \times (1 - Stop\%) - TMDRtg\right]$$

Table 17.6. Individual Defensive Stops and Ratings for Sparks–Storm Game

Name	Min	DStops	DScPoss	DPoss	Stop%	% Team DPoss	Def. Rtg.
LA Sparks							
Witherspoon	14	3.2	1.0	4.2	0.76	0.17	102
Teasley	29	4.0	5.0	9.0	0.45	0.18	116
Leslie	37	8.0	2.5	10.5	0.76	0.16	103
Milton	34	8.0	10.8	18.8	0.43	0.32	120
Mabika	36	5.0	1.0	6.0	0.83	0.09	105
McCrimmon	22	2.5	1.0	3.5	0.71	0.09	108
Byears	19	3.8	1.9	5.7	0.67	0.17	106
Askamp	7	0.7	2.5	3.2	0.22	0.26	132
Desouza	1	1.0	0.0	1.0	1.00	0.57	48
Grgin Fonseca	1	0.0	1.0	1.0	0.00	0.57	186
Team	200	1.0	6.0	7.0	0.14	0.02	114
Totals	**200**	**37.2**	**33**	**70**	**0.53**	**0.20**	**112**
Seattle Storm							
Bird	33	4.7	1.5	6.2	0.76	0.11	81
Barnes	28	7.9	3.5	11.4	0.69	0.24	81
Jackson	31	5.1	4.1	9.2	0.55	0.18	87
Vodichkova	25	6.1	3.4	9.5	0.64	0.23	84
Lassiter	28	3.7	3.8	7.5	0.49	0.16	89
Edwards	19	3.2	3.8	7.0	0.46	0.22	93
Marciniak	6	1.5	0.9	2.4	0.63	0.24	84
Ragland	21	3.3	1.2	4.5	0.74	0.13	81
Paye	3	0.0	0.0	0.0	—	0.00	—
Lewis	3	0.1	0.7	0.8	0.13	0.15	102
Randall	3	0.3	1.9	2.2	0.15	0.45	131
Team	200	3.3	3.0	6.3	0.53	0.02	85
Totals	**200**	**39.3**	**28**	**67**	**0.59**	**0.20**	**85**

Here, Delisha Milton got involved in 32 percent of the Sparks' defensive possessions when she was in the game, the most of any starter. Some of this involvement was good (getting defensive boards and forcing turnovers), but some of it was bad (an inability to stop Lauren Jackson, who scored twenty-one points). This summary individual defensive rating of 120 suggests that Milton didn't do a very good job overall defensively. On the other hand, Lisa Leslie's defensive rating of 101 implies that she was relatively more efficient as a defender. Seattle also did not go at her, so she didn't have as many possessions to face as Milton. It actually seems that the Sparks often don't put Leslie on the toughest offensive player on the other team, which might have made sense with Jackson doing so well against Milton.

For the Storm, everyone did reasonably well. Barnes and Sue Bird had the best defensive ratings, though they achieved them in different ways. Barnes stopped a lot of possessions and faced a lot of possessions. Bird allowed very few scores and faced very few possessions. Both *seem* to have done their jobs well, though.

That is the basic mechanism for evaluating individual defense. Since factors like the number of scores allowed and the number of forced misses aren't recorded as official statistics, I have to estimate them in evaluating NBA players and in evaluating all WNBA players until Project Defensive Score Sheet is complete. My estimates of defensive ratings and stop percentage, which are explained in Appendix 3, are definitely approximate. You can see that the estimates in table 17.7 end up a bit different from reality (the numbers in parentheses are the values from the Project Defensive Score Sheet effort).

Some comments:

- Sophia Witherspoon's efforts to force misses are nearly entirely overlooked by the estimates because she blocked no shots. Whereas she actually had 3.2 stops and 1.0 scoring possession, she was estimated to have 1.5 and 3.4—almost backwards. This kind of misrepresentation is particularly likely for good defensive guards.

- Milton's bad day covering Jackson is not captured at all in the estimates because traditional statistics don't include any information on how many

Table 17.7. Estimated (and Actual) Defensive Stops and Possessions for Sparks–Storm Game

Name	Min	DStops	DScPoss	DPoss	Stop%	Def. Rtg.
			LA Sparks			
Witherspoon	14	1.5 (3.2)	3.4 (1.0)	4.9 (4.2)	0.31 (0.76)	123 (102)
Teasley	29	3.6 (4.0)	6.7 (3.0)	10.2 (9.0)	0.35 (0.45)	121 (116)
Leslie	37	9.6 (8.0)	3.5 (7.0)	13.1 (10.5)	0.73 (0.76)	102 (103)
Milton	34	8.7 (8.0)	3.3 (5.0)	12.0 (18.8)	0.73 (0.43)	103 (120)
Mabika	36	5.1 (5.0)	7.6 (4.0)	12.7 (6.0)	0.40 (0.83)	118 (105)
McCrimmon	22	3.2 (2.5)	4.6 (2.5)	7.8 (3.5)	0.41 (0.71)	118 (108)
Byears	19	3.3 (3.8)	3.4 (2.8)	6.7 (5.7)	0.49 (0.67)	114 (106)
Askamp	7	0.6 (0.7)	1.9 (0.7)	2.5 (3.2)	0.23 (0.22)	126 (132)
Desouza	1	1.1 (1.0)	-0.7 (0.0)	0.4 (1.0)	3.07 (1.00)	-10 (48)
Grgin Fonseca	1	0.1 (0.0)	0.3 (0.0)	0.4 (1.0)	0.23 (0.00)	126 (186)
Totals	**200**	**36.7 (37.2)**	**33.9 (27.2)**	**70.7 (69.9)**	**0.52 (0.53)**	**112 (112)**
			Seattle Storm			
Bird	33	6.9 (4.7)	4.7 (1.5)	11.7 (6.2)	0.60 (0.76)	86 (81)
Barnes	28	6.9 (7.9)	3.0 (3.5)	9.9 (11.4)	0.69 (0.69)	81 (81)
Jackson	31	5.9 (5.1)	5.1 (4.1)	11.0 (9.2)	0.54 (0.55)	88 (87)
Vodichkova	25	6.3 (6.1)	2.6 (3.4)	8.8 (9.5)	0.71 (0.64)	81 (84)
Lassiter	28	4.7 (3.7)	5.2 (3.8)	9.9 (7.5)	0.48 (0.49)	91 (89)
Edwards	19	3.3 (3.2)	3.4 (3.8)	6.7 (7.0)	0.50 (0.46)	90 (93)
Marciniak	6	0.6 (1.5)	1.5 (0.9)	2.1 (2.4)	0.28 (0.63)	100 (84)
Ragland	21	3.0 (3.3)	4.4 (1.2)	7.4 (4.5)	0.41 (0.74)	94 (81)
Paye	3	0.3 (0.0)	0.8 (0.0)	1.1 (0.0)	0.27 (—)	100 (85)
Lewis	3	0.3 (0.1)	0.8 (0.7)	1.1 (0.8)	0.29 (0.13)	99 (102)
Randall	3	0.3 (0.3)	0.8 (1.9)	1.1 (2.2)	0.29 (0.15)	99 (131)
Totals	**200**	**38.6 (39.3)**	**32.1 (27.8)**	**70.7 (67.0)**	**0.55 (0.59)**	**85 (85)**

points a player allows. Milton was estimated as having a good day because she did have so many stops, which were actually estimated pretty well.

- The Storm players' estimated defensive ratings are generally more accurate because a lot of players teamed up to slow the Sparks.

- Ragland and Bird both had good days that were not captured by the estimated defensive ratings for the same reasons that Witherspoon wasn't evaluated correctly.

In general, estimating defensive *stops* is relatively accurate and estimating defensive *scoring possessions* is not. Knowing how many field goals and free throws a player gives up is very important, yet this information is absent in the basic defensive statistics recorded by leagues. Without recorded measures of DFGM and DFTM, individual defensive ratings will be very approximate. Using the ERA analogy again, it's like estimating a pitcher's ERA from outs made because no one records how many runs he gives up.

The Data Difficulties

Given the importance of points allowed by players, it is a rather severe problem that leagues are not tracking DFGM and DFTM. Given the importance of forced misses relative to defensive rebounds for estimating defensive stops, it is a rather severe problem that leagues are not tracking which players are forcing 70 to 80 percent of those misses. Given that steals account for only about half of all forced turnovers . . .

You get the point. Current individual defensive statistics are limited, so I could just avoid the question of defensive evaluation for now and force you to buy another book after Project Defensive Score Sheet is a couple of years old. But, out of the generosity of my publisher's heart, I will describe some of the many ways to augment the basic estimates of individual defensive rating with other statistics to help us understand individual defense. (You'll still probably want to buy another book in a couple of years.)

All of those ways involve taking statistics from game-by-game box scores. For instance, there may be no statistics showing the field goals that players allow to their defensive assignments, but box scores do show how NBA centers shot against the Sonics in 2002. With a hodgepodge of players covering that position for the Sonics—Jerome James, Calvin Booth (injured after games early in the season), Predrag Drobnjak, Art Long, Olumide Oyedeji, and Vin Baker—the Sonics knew they had a problem stopping big men. The stats show precisely that in table 17.8, with the big-man positions highlighted.

It is definitely possible to modify the basic estimates of individual defensive rating for the Sonics' big men to account for this 3- to 4-percent increase in field

Table 17.8. Shooting of Opposing Players vs. Sonics in 2002, by Position

Pos	FGM	FGA	FG%	LgAvg.	Significant?*
PG	546	1280	0.427	0.423	
G	125	305	0.410	0.429	
SG	378	876	0.432	0.437	
GF	329	736	0.447	0.437	
SF	307	688	0.446	0.45	
F	326	724	0.450	0.441	
PF	433	910	0.476	0.466	
FC	184	368	0.500	0.469	
C	225	433	0.520	0.478	*

*"Significant?" indicates whether the difference between the actual FG% and the league average is significant at 95%, as generally described in chapter 7.

goal percentage above the league average (though it also must account for the fact that the centers allowed fairly few field goal attempts). The base individual defensive ratings for the Sonics are shown in table 17.9.

Before I present modified defensive ratings to account for the field goal percentage changes, let me discuss the fact that big men tend to get the best defensive ratings using the base technique—as James, Oyedeji, and Radmanovic had the best ratings on the Sonics. Big men—even the Sonics big men—are probably the most important players to a team defense. That explains why you have so many horrible *offensive* centers on the Sonics, err, in the NBA these days—because their defense is presumed to make up for their offense. The offensive *in*ability of different positions generally reflects the defensive *ability* of those positions. In the NBA over the last few years, centers have generally posted offensive ratings two to three points lower than the league average and used only 18 percent of a team's possessions.[2] Teams are paying that premium on the offensive side to get the benefit on the defensive side.

Table 17.9. Base Individual Defensive Ratings for the 2002 Sonics

Player	Position	Min	Stops	Stop%	Def. Rating	Pts Allowed
Gary Payton	PG	3301	583	0.48	107	1307
Brent Barry	SG	3041	603	0.53	104	1176
Rashard Lewis	F	2584	508	0.53	104	1001
Desmond Mason	SF	2420	413	0.46	107	964
Vin Baker	PF	1710	275	0.43	109	688
Vladimir Radmanovic	F	1230	256	0.56	103	470
Predrag Drobnjak	C	1174	203	0.47	107	467
Art Long	FC	989	188	0.51	105	386
Earl Watson	PG	964	177	0.50	106	379
Jerome James	C	949	210	0.60	102	358
Shammond Williams	G	603	99	0.44	108	242
Calvin Booth	C	279	52	0.51	105	109
Olumide Oyedeji	C	221	46	0.57	103	84
Randy Livingston	PG	176	33	0.51	105	69
Ansu Sesay	PF	142	23	0.43	108	57
Antonio Harvey	PF	47	9	0.49	106	19

Table 17.10. 2002 Seattle Team Defensive Rating with and without Various Big Men

Player	With	Without	Difference
Jerome James	104.5	108.2	-3.7
Calvin Booth	111.1	103.6	7.5
Predrag Drobnjak	105.4	106.8	-1.4
Art Long	105.8	105.4	0.4
Vin Baker	106.6	103.8	2.8

The Sonics probably felt like they were paying more than their fare share of the premium. All of their centers struggled a bit defensively (and offensively), and some struggled more than others, that distinction between big men being something that the overall field goal percentage by position did not reflect. If you look at how the team defense performed with and without certain players (table 17.10), you see that James's presence seemed to help the defense, whereas Booth's or Baker's presence did not (though none of the differences are statistically significant at the 95 percent level).

With these kinds of more detailed examinations of box scores, you can actually make modifications to the base individual defensive ratings. Table 17.11 shows the base defensive rating that was shown above. It also shows in the next column over how that rating changes if you incorporate the shooting at the different positions (both the percentage and the number of shots taken). The fourth column shows how the defensive rating changes if you incorporate how the team defense played only in games where the player actually played. The last column shows how individual defensive ratings change if you incorporate both of these factors. I've highlighted in bold some players whose ratings appear to be most

Table 17.11. Individual Defensive Ratings for 2002 Sonics, Modified by Opposing Shooting and Games Missed

Player	Base	FG% By Position	Games with Player Only	Both Modifications
Gary Payton	107	108	107	108
Brent Barry	**104**	**106**	**104**	**106**
Rashard Lewis	104	104	104	104
Desmond Mason	107	108	107	108
Vin Baker	**109**	**110**	**109**	**111**
Vladimir Radmanovic	103	103	103	103
Predrag Drobnjak	107	107	107	107
Art Long	105	106	105	106
Earl Watson	106	107	106	107
Jerome James	**102**	**100**	**101**	**99**
Shammond Williams	**108**	**110**	**110**	**111**
Calvin Booth	**105**	**105**	**110**	**110**
Olumide Oyedeji	103	102	104	103
Randy Livingston	105	107	104	105
Ansu Sesay	108	109	113	113
Antonio Harvey	106	107	110	111

affected by considering these details (excluding players who played very few minutes).

Unfortunately, making these adjustments is neither automatic nor easy, so most of the individual defensive ratings in this book will be the "base" version, unadjusted and approximate.

The Conceptual Difficulties

Accounting for missing data is only one difficulty of evaluating defense, though. Even with improved data through Project Defensive Score Sheet, evaluating individual defense is wrought with conceptual difficulties.

For example, what if Lisa Leslie scores twenty-four points on twenty possessions in a game, but allows twenty-five points on twenty-five possessions? Could you even call her "good" defensively relative to what she did offensively? I see games like this in some of the data we are collecting. The numbers say something but don't necessarily give a value judgment. Sure, Leslie's defensive rating of one hundred is lower than her offensive rating, but she did allow more total points. Did she have a net positive game or a net negative one? I frankly have no conclusive solution to this conceptual problem because—it sounds like a cliché—no single person is a team (I take a stab at addressing this problem in chapter 20).

How would Leslie have had such statistics? Maybe she helped out a lot on other players. Maybe she was facing Yolanda Griffith, who can score very well. This question gets at one of the toughest aspects to handle: matchups. Coaches will often assign their best defensive player to cover the best offensive player on the other team. Joe Dumars had to face Michael Jordan every time Detroit met Chicago. Jordan got his points against Dumars, but it was probably fewer points (or fewer points per possession) than Jordan normally got. Dumars's defensive rating may have been 114 while trying to stop Jordan, whereas most defenders couldn't keep him below a 120 rating. That 114 is, by comparison to league average ratings of 108 or so, not very good. But by comparison to Jordan's average, it is very good. What if all Dumars did was limit Jordan's possessions or limit his shots—not lower his rating? That is still valuable to the team defense, but is even harder to deal with through numbers.

Further, matchups are just a basic part of basketball strategy. Many coaches make changes in personnel just to avoid bad defensive mismatches. A good defender against Shaq (if one exists) may be a horrible defender against a quick outside-shooting replacement. Dumars may be great covering shooting guards but useless on Shaq. Good defensive players are probably only good at the position that they cover. On offense, you can put five guards on the floor, but you can't do that on defense if there is a big guy out there who can catch and shoot on the box over every one of them.

Because of this positional specificity, I see a lot more variation in players' individual defensive ratings as they move through their careers. Whereas I see some consistent patterns with player *offensive* ratings through time—most great players increase their rating and the number of possessions they are responsible for up to age twenty-seven or thirty, then decline—I don't see the same patterns with defensive ratings. Jordan had a very steady rise and fall in his offensive ratings (see chapter 14), but his defensive ratings had a different pattern (table 17.12).

His worst defensive seasons were his first two, then 1990, and then the Wizard season of 2002. Jordan's best defensive years were in 1996 and 1988—not exactly continuous in time. Jordan's ratings do actually, however, show a general improvement at the start of his career and a decline at the end, giving a decent pattern.

Now look at Dikembe Mutombo in table 17.13, one of the most acclaimed defensive players of all time.

Mutombo's worst defensive season was his first, which fits with expectation, but there is no obvious improvement after his second year. He just bounces around

Table 17.12. Michael Jordan's Individual Defensive Efficiency Statistics

Season	Team	Min	Stops	Stop%	Def. Rating	Lg. Avg. Rating	Difference
1985	CHI	3144	689	0.53	107	108	-1
1986	CHI	451	108	0.58	107	107	0
1987	CHI	3281	723	0.55	104	108	-4
1988	CHI	3311	766	0.58	101	108	-7
1989	CHI	3255	772	0.59	103	108	-5
1990	CHI	3197	712	0.55	105	108	-3
1991	CHI	3034	696	0.58	102	108	-6
1992	CHI	3102	687	0.56	102	108	-7
1993	CHI	3067	683	0.58	102	108	-6
1995	CHI	668	138	0.54	103	108	-5
1996	CHI	3090	672	0.57	99	108	-8
1997	CHI	3106	619	0.53	102	107	-5
1998	CHI	3181	616	0.52	100	105	-5
2002	WAS	2092	410	0.53	105	105	0

Table 17.13. Dikembe Mutombo's Individual Defensive Efficiency Statistics

Season	Team	Min	Stops	Stop%	Def. Rating	Lg. Avg. Rating	Difference
1992	DEN	2716	603	0.54	106	108	-2
1993	DEN	3029	755	0.60	102	108	-6
1994	DEN	2853	743	0.65	96	106	-10
1995	DEN	3100	725	0.61	103	108	-5
1996	DEN	2713	687	0.66	101	108	-7
1997	ATL	2973	701	0.65	97	107	-10
1998	ATL	2917	669	0.63	99	105	-6
1999	ATL	1829	423	0.65	92	102	-10
2000	ATL	2984	749	0.66	101	104	-3
2001	ATL	1716	434	0.67	98	104	-5
2001	PHI	875	203	0.62	96	104	-8
2002	PHI	2907	635	0.59	98	105	-7

for reasons that are hard to discern. When he changed teams in the middle of 2001, his defensive rating improved a couple of points. That could very easily be the impact of the coaching change, going from Lon Kruger to noted defensive specialist Larry Brown.

In fact, coaching probably does matter a lot on the defensive end, something that was at least hinted at in chapter 3 by the fact that so many coaches had different teams on the top defense lists. If positional matchups are important, it is coaches who are critical in making decisions about those matchups. A good example is Dumars (table 17.14). Dumars's defensive rating was bad as a rookie and then got better, which is what you'd hope for. Then, around 1993, Detroit's first year without Coach Chuck Daly, his defensive rating got really bad. I doubt that Daly's replacements, Ron Rothstein and Don Chaney, used Dumars at power forward or something crazy like that, but Dumars's defense became much less effective when they were around. In 1996, the Pistons brought in Doug Collins, and Dumars's defensive rating got better again.

One thing to note is that Dumars, though he had a good defensive reputation, had worse than average estimated defensive ratings. This is because Dumars did nothing that registered in the official stat sheet (steals, blocks, or defensive rebounds), which is my main tool for estimating the ratings. Because of that, Dumars is exactly the kind of player whose defensive ratings I trust the least. There are enough players like this that I actually call them "Dumars-like."

Even though I trust them the least, I still do place some value in the estimates of defensive ratings for Dumars-like players. The reason is that Dumars-like players seem to end up on both great and horrible team defenses, as Dumars did himself. The Pistons of 1990 were one of the greatest defenses of all time, placing twenty-second on one list. The Pistons of both 1994 and 1995 were among the worst forty defenses of all time. As good a defensive player as he may have been, Dumars could not keep his teams from being horrible defensively.

Table 17.14. Joe Dumars's Individual Defensive Efficiency Statistics

Season	Team	Min	Stops	Stop%	Def. Rating	Lg. Avg. Rating	Difference
1986	DET	1957	318	0.37	112	107	4
1987	DET	2439	404	0.39	109	108	1
1988	DET	2732	451	0.40	108	108	0
1989	DET	2408	376	0.39	109	108	1
1990	DET	2578	410	0.40	107	108	-1
1991	DET	3046	471	0.40	108	108	0
1992	DET	3192	447	0.37	110	108	2
1993	DET	3094	440	0.37	113	108	5
1994	DET	2591	362	0.36	115	106	9
1995	DET	2544	353	0.36	117	108	9
1996	DET	2193	321	0.40	110	108	2
1997	DET	2923	406	0.39	110	107	3
1998	DET	2326	313	0.37	109	105	4
1999	DET	1116	155	0.38	106	102	4

Table 17.15. Doug Christie's Individual Defensive Efficiency Statistics

Season	Team	Min	Stops	Stop%	Def. Rating	Lg. Avg. Rating	Difference
1993	LAL	332	67	0.50	108	108	0
1994	LAL	1515	299	0.50	108	106	2
1995	NYK	79	15	0.50	104	108	-4
1996	NYK	218	47	0.57	101	108	-7
1996	TOR	818	176	0.56	108	108	1
1997	TOR	3127	645	0.55	106	107	-1
1998	TOR	2939	586	0.52	109	105	4
1999	TOR	1768	348	0.53	103	102	1
2000	TOR	2264	431	0.49	105	104	1
2001	SAC	2939	607	0.53	100	104	-4
2002	SAC	2798	586	0.53	101	105	-4

Another player who is not even fully "Dumars-like" but comes close is Doug Christie, who does more than most Dumars-like defenders to fill up a defensive stat sheet (table 17.15). Christie played on good defensive teams in New York and Sacramento and was rightfully named to a couple of All-Defensive Teams in Sacramento. But he also played with the 1998 Raptors, who were horrible on the defensive end. Christie was still getting steals, but whatever he was doing wasn't enough. He probably wasn't taking part in enough possessions to make a difference—he was a "defensive role player."

Guards who primarily cover men one-on-one and prevent them from getting off shots seem to be defensive role players, not guys who can fundamentally make a good defense. On the other hand, guys like Olajuwon do not end up on bad defensive teams (table 17.16). This is because he was the center of the defense and could impact a lot of possessions, at least until he stopped playing a lot of minutes in 1998.

Table 17.16. Hakeem Olajuwon's Individual Defensive Efficiency Statistics

Season	Team	Min	Stops	Stop%	Def. Rating	Lg. Avg. Rating	Difference	Team Def. Rtg.
1985	HOU	2914	703	0.57	103	108	-5	106
1986	HOU	2467	655	0.62	102	107	-6	108
1987	HOU	2760	743	0.65	99	108	-10	106
1988	HOU	2825	801	0.67	98	108	-10	106
1989	HOU	3024	935	0.73	95	108	-13	105
1990	HOU	3124	972	0.74	93	108	-15	103
1991	HOU	2062	635	0.75	93	108	-15	104
1992	HOU	2636	726	0.69	99	108	-9	108
1993	HOU	3242	905	0.71	96	108	-12	105
1994	HOU	3277	863	0.67	95	106	-11	101
1995	HOU	2853	741	0.66	100	108	-8	107
1996	HOU	2797	705	0.65	101	108	-7	107
1997	HOU	2852	687	0.63	99	107	-8	104
1998	HOU	1633	408	0.66	101	105	-4	109
1999	HOU	1784	447	0.68	96	102	-6	103
2000	HOU	1049	255	0.62	100	104	-4	106
2001	HOU	1545	375	0.65	99	104	-5	105
2002	TOR	1378	348	0.68	96	105	-9	103

Table 17.17. Tim Duncan's Individual Defensive Efficiency Statistics

Season	Team	Min	Stops	Stop%	Def. Rating	Lg. Avg. Rating	Difference	Team Def. Rtg.
1998	SAN	3204	737	0.62	95	105	-10	99
1999	SAN	1963	453	0.62	92	102	-11	95
2000	SAN	2865	679	0.63	94	104	-10	99
2001	SAN	3174	751	0.64	94	104	-10	99
2002	SAN	3329	778	0.62	96	105	-9	100

Table 17.18. David Robinson's Individual Defensive Efficiency Statistics

Season	Team	Min	Stops	Stop%	Def. Rating	Lg. Avg. Rating	Difference	Team Def. Rtg.
1990	SAN	3002	830	0.67	97	108	-11	104
1991	SAN	3095	861	0.68	96	108	-12	103
1992	SAN	2564	751	0.73	94	108	-14	104
1993	SAN	3211	831	0.65	100	108	-8	107
1994	SAN	3241	800	0.66	98	106	-8	105
1995	SAN	3074	803	0.66	99	108	-10	105
1996	SAN	3019	795	0.68	96	108	-11	103
1997	SAN	147	33	0.62	106	107	-1	112
1998	SAN	2457	601	0.66	94	105	-11	99
1999	SAN	1554	408	0.71	88	102	-14	95
2000	SAN	2558	660	0.68	92	104	-12	99
2001	SAN	2371	593	0.67	93	104	-11	99
2002	SAN	2303	556	0.64	95	105	-10	100

Other big guys, like Tim Duncan (table 17.17) and David Robinson (table 17.18) don't end up on bad defensive teams either. They were just too good and too central to defenses to allow the team defense to be bad.

The Great Defensive Teams

Since the Spurs have paired Robinson and Duncan, they have shown up on the list of best defenses several times. Before Duncan arrived, Robinson's Spurs were good defensively, but not great. In 1996, with only Robinson, the Spurs defensive rating was 103.5, 4.2 points better than the league average. In 1998, after the Spurs acquired Duncan, the team defensive rating improved to 99.4, 5.7 points below the league average and good enough to make the top twenty-five defenses.

The difference between the two teams was primarily Duncan, who took minutes formerly used by Vinny Del Negro, Chuck Person, and Sean Elliott, three guards. (I will also note that the team's offensive rating got worse, going from 2.5 points better than average to 1.2 points worse.) The Spurs replaced short guys with tall, and the tall guy was one of the best college defenders ever. It is no surprise that they got better defensively.

The Spurs are one of only a few "legacy defenses," defenses that were great over a period of a few years. The Bulls of the mid-1990s were outstanding for several years. The Knicks of the early 1990s had two consecutive outstanding years.

And the Jazz of the 1980s had defenses show up on the best defense lists. I'm going to take brief looks at the individual defensive players on these teams to try to identify the most important players.

Of these teams, the Bulls teams were the only ones that didn't have a big guy covering the middle, but they had three of history's best non-centers forcing turnovers and missed shots as well as getting defensive boards. Their 1996 team was the best (table 17.19).

Notice the stop percentages for Jordan, Pippen, and Rodman, all at least 0.55. That is very unusual. I could not find another team where three non-centers had averages that high. It's hard enough to find another team where three players *including centers* had stop percentages that high. You saw above that Jordan's stop percentage was regularly that high. Well, so were those of Pippen (table 17.20) and Rodman (table 17.21).

Table 17.19. Individual Defensive Efficiencies for 1996 Chicago Bulls

Player	Min	Stops	Stop%	Def. Rating
Michael Jordan	3090	672	0.57	99
Scottie Pippen	2825	586	0.55	101
Toni Kukoc	2103	379	0.47	104
Dennis Rodman	2088	480	0.61	98
Steve Kerr	1919	304	0.42	106
Ron Harper	1886	375	0.52	102
Luc Longley	1641	317	0.51	102
Bill Wennington	1065	188	0.47	104
Jud Buechler	740	142	0.50	102
Dickey Simpkins	685	120	0.46	104
Randy Brown	671	155	0.61	98
Jason Caffey	545	97	0.47	104
James Edwards	274	45	0.43	105
John Salley	191	45	0.61	98
Jack Haley	7	1	0.44	105

Table 17.20. Scottie Pippen's Individual Defensive Efficiency Statistics

Season	Team	Min	Stops	Stop%	Def. Rating	Lg. Avg. Rating	Difference
1988	CHI	1650	349	0.53	103	108	-5
1989	CHI	2413	524	0.54	105	108	-3
1990	CHI	3148	706	0.56	105	108	-3
1991	CHI	3014	689	0.57	102	108	-6
1992	CHI	3164	684	0.55	102	108	-6
1993	CHI	3123	657	0.55	104	108	-4
1994	CHI	2759	680	0.64	97	106	-9
1995	CHI	3014	749	0.65	98	108	-10
1996	CHI	2825	586	0.55	101	108	-7
1997	CHI	3095	635	0.55	101	107	-5
1998	CHI	1652	334	0.54	99	105	-6
1999	HOU	2011	406	0.55	101	102	-1
2000	POR	2749	571	0.55	99	104	-5
2001	POR	2133	418	0.53	102	104	-2
2002	POR	1996	408	0.55	102	105	-2

Table 17.21. Dennis Rodman's Individual Defensive Efficiency Statistics

Season	Team	Min	Stops	Stop%	Def. Rating	Lg. Avg. Rating	Difference
1987	DET	1155	251	0.52	104	108	-4
1988	DET	2147	479	0.55	103	108	-5
1989	DET	2208	498	0.57	102	108	-6
1990	DET	2377	511	0.55	101	108	-7
1991	DET	2747	619	0.59	101	108	-7
1992	DET	3301	805	0.64	99	108	-9
1993	DET	2410	587	0.63	102	108	-6
1994	SAN	2989	686	0.61	100	106	-6
1995	SAN	1568	390	0.63	100	108	-8
1996	CHI	2088	480	0.61	98	108	-10
1997	CHI	1947	452	0.62	98	107	-9
1998	CHI	2856	634	0.60	97	105	-8
1999	LAL	657	152	0.60	100	102	-2
2000	DAL	389	91	0.59	103	104	-1

That gives me some confidence that the estimated stop percentage, even though I don't have explicit information about the number of scores players give up, is still a reasonable predictor of what will happen. Packaging three guys on the Bulls with numbers that high would suggest that they'd be good defensively. That also is what made it clear that the New Jersey Nets of 2002, by acquiring Jason Kidd (with stop percentages around 0.56) and getting Kenyon Martin (0.57 in his rookie year) back from injury, would be a good defensive team. They actually exceeded expectations a bit by ending up as one of the great defenses.

Moving on to the Knicks, the 1993 and 1994 Pat Riley–coached teams may have been the best ever. But why weren't the 1992 or 1995 versions as good? The 1995 version wasn't as good because the rule changes of 1995 were designed especially to prevent the Knicks from doing what they did so well in 1993 and 1994. And what the Knicks did so well was to hand-check guards and body-check forwards and centers. Statistically, this showed up in much lower opponents' shooting percentages and much higher turnover rates during those two great years (table 17.22).

Effective FG% accounts for the extra value of three-point shots, which, when the arc was shortened in 1995, became a lot easier.

Ewing was the rock in the defense throughout his time with New York. But his defense jumped a lot when Riley took over in 1992, as shown in table 17.23, implying again the value of coaching.

Table 17.22. New York Knicks' Defensive Statistics 1992–1995

Season	Effective FG%	Defensive Rebounding %	Forced Turnovers Per Game	Steals Per Game	Blocks Per Game
1992	47%	71%	15.2	7.7	4.7
1993	44%	72%	16.6	8.3	4.5
1994	45%	71%	17.3	9.2	4.7
1995	47%	71%	15.4	7.2	4.7

Table 17.23. Patrick Ewing's Individual Defensive Efficiency Statistics

Season	Team	Min	Stops	Stop%	Def. Rating	Lg. Avg. Rating	Difference
1986	NYK	1771	414	0.57	102	107	-6
1987	NYK	2206	515	0.57	106	108	-2
1988	NYK	2546	633	0.60	101	108	-7
1989	NYK	2896	734	0.58	103	108	-5
1990	NYK	3165	772	0.60	103	108	-5
1991	NYK	3104	761	0.62	101	108	-6
1992	NYK	3150	773	0.63	98	108	-10
1993	NYK	3003	767	0.65	94	108	-14
1994	NYK	2972	754	0.66	93	106	-14
1995	NYK	2920	708	0.64	98	108	-10
1996	NYK	2783	678	0.64	98	108	-10
1997	NYK	2887	713	0.65	95	107	-11
1998	NYK	848	206	0.66	94	105	-11
1999	NYK	1300	323	0.69	91	102	-11
2000	NYK	2035	465	0.61	97	104	-7
2001	SEA	2107	469	0.59	103	104	-1
2002	ORL	901	211	0.60	101	105	-4

During those two great seasons, Ewing's stop percentage was at about its best. But it was a team effort. Behind Ewing on the 1993 team was a different group of players than on the 1992 team. The 1992 team, which was good defensively, is shown in table 17.24.

Three of the top four guys getting minutes in 1992 were gone in 1993 (table 17.25). And none of them averaged 50 percent as a stop percentage in 1992. In contrast, three of the new guys—Doc Rivers, Greg Anthony, and Charles Smith—all averaged that level. Rivers and Anthony were particularly helpful in increasing the turnover rate, though both seemed to also benefit from Riley's push to pressure guards, as they both had near career highs in stop percentage.

Table 17.24. Individual Defensive Efficiency Statistics for 1992 New York Knicks

Player	Min	Stops	Stop%	Def. Rating
Patrick Ewing	3150	773	0.63	98
Mark Jackson	2461	455	0.48	105
Gerald Wilkins	2344	384	0.42	107
Xavier McDaniel	2344	419	0.46	105
Charles Oakley	2309	473	0.53	103
Anthony Mason	2198	413	0.49	104
John Starks	2118	392	0.48	105
Greg Anthony	1510	263	0.45	106
Kiki Vandeweghe	956	142	0.38	109
Brian Quinnett	190	36	0.48	104
Tim McCormick	108	21	0.49	104
James Donaldson	81	17	0.54	102
Kennard Winchester	64	13	0.52	103
Patrick Eddie	13	2	0.36	110
Carlton McKinney	9	1	0.38	109

Table 17.25. Individual Defensive Efficiency Statistics for 1993 New York Knicks

Player	Min	Stops	Stop%	Def. Rating
Patrick Ewing	3003	767	0.65	94
Anthony Mason	2482	480	0.49	101
John Starks	2477	436	0.45	103
Charles Oakley	2230	497	0.57	98
Charles Smith	2172	436	0.51	100
Doc Rivers	1886	404	0.54	99
Greg Anthony	1699	359	0.54	99
Rolando Blackman	1434	220	0.39	105
Tony Campbell	1062	194	0.46	102
Hubert Davis	815	133	0.41	104
Herb Williams	571	136	0.60	96
Bo Kimble	55	10	0.47	101
Eric Anderson	44	12	0.67	93

One thing that is clear, though, is that the team would not have been great without the performance of the big guy, whose contribution was bigger than everyone's in each season.

The same thing can be said for the Utah Jazz of the 1980s, whose big guy was Mark Eaton. Eaton's contribution came almost entirely in the form of blocking shots, which he did extremely well. His defensive ratings were amazingly good for someone who did only one thing (table 17.26), but that reflects the value of those forced misses.

The other key thing on those Jazz teams was that there were players to get defensive rebounds. Specifically, on the 1989 team that featured Utah's best defense, Karl Malone cleaned up the glass. They also had a young John Stockton taking the ball away a lot, giving a distribution of individual defensive ratings like that in table 17.27.

My sense from looking at teams like these and from individual defensive ratings—though they don't include the number of scores players allow—is that big

Table 17.26. Mark Eaton's Individual Defensive Efficiency Statistics

Season	Team	Min	Stops	Stop%	Def. Rating	Lg. Avg. Rating	Difference
1983	UTA	1528	450	0.66	98	105	-7
1984	UTA	2139	561	0.60	102	108	-5
1985	UTA	2813	810	0.66	97	108	-11
1986	UTA	2551	652	0.59	100	107	-7
1987	UTA	2505	620	0.58	100	108	-8
1988	UTA	2731	639	0.55	101	108	-7
1989	UTA	2914	711	0.60	98	108	-10
1990	UTA	2281	508	0.56	102	108	-6
1991	UTA	2580	566	0.55	103	108	-5
1992	UTA	2023	453	0.56	102	108	-6
1993	UTA	1104	235	0.53	105	108	-3

Table 17.27. Individual Defensive Efficiency Statistics for 1989 Utah Jazz

Player	Min	Stops	Stop%	Def. Rating
John Stockton	3171	665	0.51	101
Karl Malone	3126	728	0.57	99
Mark Eaton	2914	711	0.60	98
Thurl Bailey	2777	502	0.44	104
Darrell Griffith	2382	441	0.45	104
Mike Brown	1051	207	0.48	102
Bob Hansen	964	179	0.46	104
Marc Iavaroni	796	136	0.42	105
Jim Les	781	136	0.43	105
Eric Leckner	779	160	0.50	102
Jim Farmer	412	65	0.39	106
Jose Ortiz	327	56	0.42	105
Bart Kofoed	176	30	0.42	105
Scott Roth	72	16	0.55	99
Eric White	2	0	0.29	110

guys are the key to D. Height forces offensive guys to take tough shots. Length forces guys to make tougher passes. Height doesn't guarantee a good defensive player because tall guys can be lazy (see Derrick Coleman chapter). But most active little guys just can't quite be the defenders that the top big men are.

The exceptions to this occur at lower levels of basketball, where the quick players can pressure poor ball handlers into a lot of turnovers before they even get a shot at the basket. But if basketball is a half-court game, then big men become much more important.

Project Defensive Score Sheet Wrap-Up

The efforts of Project Defensive Score Sheet volunteers are filing into my office on a regular basis. Evaluating what the data say is going to take a little while. For the purpose of analyzing specific games and WNBA players throughout a season, the data will be invaluable. But I'd like to use it to also form better estimates of the defensive scoring possessions and defensive ratings for all players regardless of league. There are decades of statistical information about NBA players that may indicate things about individual defense that no one has figured out. Doing the research to figure that out is the effort that is going to take time.

Hopefully, this project will also evolve to include volunteers for the NBA, too. Just coordinating the project for the WNBA has been complicated, involving numerous people with varying backgrounds and organizations with varying abilities to accommodate us. For a bigger league, the coordination effort would be even greater.

At competitive college and high school levels, in-house efforts to collect this kind of information already occur to some degree. For coaches who want a little more specific guidance in evaluating the defensive performance of players, I'd recommend that they collect these stats. Simply forcing a staff member to watch the defense so explicitly provides a unique perspective on what players do. For that perspective alone, it is valuable.

Endnotes

1. The weight on forced missed free throws (FFTA) is based on a 75-percent free throw percentage. The weight goes from one-tenth to one-fifth if the free throw percentage is only 50 percent. Forcing missed free throws, in any case, is a relatively small part of defensive stops except when fouling a player like Shaquille O'Neal who has as hard a time scoring from the line as from the field.

2. Pete Palmer recommended this based upon similar ways of evaluating the defensive value of different baseball positions. This is why, for example, shortstops and catchers don't have to hit as well to be in the lineup or, even more extreme, why pitchers can hit so poorly and still be valuable.

Chapter 18

Should I Firebomb Billy Donovan's House?

Someone actually asked me, "Should I firebomb Billy Donovan's house?" It was a frustrated University of Florida basketball fan who, though he clearly didn't have any intentions of carrying out the act, really wanted to know whether his coach was doing a good job. He thought Donovan was doing a horrible job but didn't really know where Donovan stood as a coach relative to other coaches out there.

Some background: Donovan was a player and assistant coach under Rick Pitino. Donovan began as a men's basketball head coach at Florida in 1996 and showed instant success recruiting players. He brought in acknowledged high school talents right away and raised the expectations of fans. In Donovan's first two seasons, he saw little success on the floor as both teams ended up below .500. In Donovan's third season, the team began winning, going 22–9 and 10–6 in the Southeastern Conference, making the Sweet Sixteen in the NCAA tournament. The very next season, Donovan led his Gators to the Final Four, beating the North Carolina Tar Heels before losing to Michigan State in the title game. No one wanted to firebomb his house then.

The next couple of years, with equivalent or better talent, Donovan's Gators exited the NCAA tournament in the first or second round—not what fans thought should happen after the previous success. Fans began to say that Donovan was a great recruiter but a poor coach. Fans began to wonder about his ability to "coach."

That's why we're here—to evaluate what a coach does. What fans are thinking is that a coach should manage talent to win. What Florida fans were thinking was that Donovan didn't manage the great talent he recruited well enough to win the games he "should" win.

But coaching, especially at levels below the NBA or the WNBA, is about more than just winning. Every coach wants to win and every player wants to win, but one of the difficult things about being a coach at an amateur level is deciding the degree to which you want to win games versus everything else you want to do as a coach. Donovan, for example, is also held responsible for graduating players. (Though the following doesn't tell a complete story, Florida's website states, "Thirteen of the 14 seniors who have suited up to play for coach Donovan have graduated from the University of Florida.") Coaches also want to send players to the next level of basketball, something Donovan has done more often than any of his predecessors at Florida.

Donovan works in a competitive NCAA men's program. For coaches at lower levels, some of the balancing between winning and other goals is even harder. At some levels, just distributing playing time to all players is a very high priority. A lot of programs want to win but also state that they want everyone to "have fun" playing, too. And then there are questions of fairness. How fair should a coach be? Should a coach play a more senior player even if he's not quite as good as a more junior one? If a starting player gets injured and the replacement is as good or better than the original player—or even if the team starts playing better with that replacement—how do you decide whether to reinsert the injured player when he's healthy again? That is a tough question even when winning is all that matters.

These questions are all part of a coaching philosophy that each coach has to decide for himself. A coach's philosophy is an important thing in order for him and his program to be a success. And, as legendary coach John Wooden said, "Success is a peace of mind which comes as a direct result of knowing that you did the best you could to be the best you are capable of becoming." Or, as Morgan Wootten said in his classic coaching manual, *Coaching Basketball Successfully*, about choosing a philosophy, "What do you emphasize—winning a basketball game or winning in life?" It is Wootten's book that I have used as a reference for many things nonstatistical in basketball. The following words in Wootten's book are what make this chapter so hard to write: "A trap every coach must avoid falling into is evaluating the success of the program in terms of wins and losses. . . . [I]f you and the players evaluate performance strictly on winning and losing, the team will not reach its potential." I couldn't agree more.

But, as Dr. Joseph Palmieri wrote in *Coaching Basketball,* "The 'win at any cost' philosophy is educational suicide and cannot be defended or advocated, but winning is, and always will be, one of the primary goals of any basketball coach. A coach who can't win might not be adequately carrying out his duties." That part of coaching—the part that, on its own, is "educational suicide"—is the only part into which I can contribute unique insight.

And, before I do so, I do want to emphasize the place of the work in this book. It is a complement to coaching—not a replacement and not even a big part. I do feel that the quantitative evaluation of strategies, teams, and players can be used by a coach, but knowing all these things by heart does not make a good coach. They can help a coach be a better one. Coaches do a lot of analysis in their heads without this book. They read players and patterns on the floor. Too many scientists dismiss the decisions of nonscientists (an accurate description of many coaches) as arbitrary or subjective. But a lot of nonscientists are making decisions based on thorough but subjective contemplation of things they see. Sometimes they do so because there is no good scientific way to put all the factors together, which is when some scientists ignore some factors as irrelevant, just as some coaches ignore statistics as irrelevant. Some coaches, like some scientists, are not very good. They are horribly irrational sometimes. I have tried throughout this book to provide a scientific approach to factors that *do* matter to coaches. One of those factors is how other people perceive their performance, which brings me back to the point of this chapter.

Dealing with Expectations

The way that people evaluate a coach's ability to coax success out of players is to compare actual success to expectation. If people expect a team to win a lot of games and the team doesn't, the coach is usually the one who gets blamed. If there is no *immediate* expectation of success but of future success, there has to be some progress toward that future success or the coach will be held responsible. Even if a coach comes in without facing expectations but recruits well enough or talks big enough to raise them, the team had better meet those expectations.

Pulling out some of my references from sports economics again, there are several papers that study coaching impact by comparing actual win-loss records to expectations. Many of these papers say that certain measurable player statistics should predict a team's winning percentage—they set the expectation. To the degree that they don't predict a team's winning percentage—i.e., the team goes above or below expectations—that is a measure of coaching ability. For example, let's say that Professor Joe Sportshaq believes that a team will be better than .500 in proportion to the difference between a team's field goal percentage and their opponents' field goal percentage. Specifically, Sportshaq's model for predicting NBA team winning percentage is

$$\text{Expected Win\%} = (\text{FG\%} - \text{DFG\%}) \times 5 + 0.500$$

That sounds like a pretty decent model, especially since, as mentioned in chapter 6, winning the field goal percentage battle in a game is correlated very

Table 18.1. Coaches Winning More than Expected as Based on Field Goal Percentage Forecast

Rank	Coach	Expected Win%	Actual Win %	Actual – Expected	Impact/Year
1	Paul Westphal	0.517	0.627	0.110	2.1%
2	Phil Jackson	0.641	0.744	0.103	1.0%
3	Chuck Daly	0.459	0.556	0.097	2.1%
4	Lenny Wilkens	0.499	0.586	0.088	0.8%
5	Rick Adelman	0.498	0.578	0.080	0.9%
6	John Calipari	0.316	0.391	0.076	3.4%
7	Larry Bird	0.613	0.687	0.074	2.8%
8	Del Harris	0.578	0.650	0.071	1.6%
9	Dick Motta	0.266	0.333	0.068	2.2%
10	Rick Pitino	0.356	0.411	0.056	1.8%

NOTE: Minimum 165 games coached.

well with winning the game itself. Looking back to 1992, a few coaches have consistently guided their teams to winning percentages above those predicted by this formula (table 18.1).

By this method, renowned coaches such as Phil Jackson, Chuck Daly, and Lenny Wilkens do in fact turn up as some of the best. Paul Westphal's name at the top of the list is something of a surprise, but most of the names seem reasonable. If the results seem reasonable, it's tempting to say that the end (results) justify the means (the method).

At the bottom of the list (table 18.2) are a few recognizable names and a few current coaches.

Again, the fact that this list contains coaches who don't have the greatest reputations implies that Professor Sportshaq's method may have some value.

Sports economists have used this type of technique to assess primarily baseball managers and have come up with the same qualitative "It seems to make sense" ratings. In one paper, a couple of sports economists actually used this type of rating system to develop a manager "learning curve"—an equation that suggested how manager efficiency should change through time and as a result of

Table 18.2. Coaches Losing More than Expected as Based on Field Goal Percentage Forecast

Rank	Coach	Expected Win%	Actual Win %	Actual – Expected	Impact/Year
1	Sidney Lowe	0.399	0.264	-0.135	-3.7%
2	Jim Lynam	0.511	0.401	-0.110	-3.1%
3	Brian Winters	0.305	0.196	-0.109	-4.9%
4	Don Chaney	0.443	0.337	-0.106	-3.1%
5	Wes Unseld	0.362	0.289	-0.073	-2.4%
6	Tim Floyd	0.275	0.205	-0.070	-2.4%
7	John Lucas	0.478	0.424	-0.054	-1.1%
8	Bob Hill	0.645	0.592	-0.052	-1.2%
9	Alvin Gentry	0.509	0.458	-0.051	-1.2%
10	Bernie Bickerstaff	0.508	0.459	-0.049	-1.3%

NOTE: Minimum 165 games coached.

changing teams. Their results said that manager efficiency increases, then plateaus and possibly declines through time (if they stay around until they're senile)—a result that makes some sense. The economists also said that managerial efficiency declines if a manager changes teams, something that also makes some sense.

Hopefully, no general managers with quick trigger fingers are reading this, because I don't quite believe this kind of coaching evaluation tool. For one thing, the results depend on the model. Sportshaq's model is just one of many that forecasts a winning percentage as a function of other statistics. Chapter 11 presented another method, the bell curve model, that could be used just as easily. Table 18.3 shows the top ten "best" coaches (since 1992) using the bell curve.

Westphal is still at the top, and four coaches that appear here also appear on the previous list of top coaches. But Jeff Van Gundy at number four on this list is a big change. By the other model, Van Gundy is thirty-sixth, and his "expected" winning percentage is higher than his actual winning percentage. So, depending on what model of expectation you have, Van Gundy was either a below-average coach or one of the best in the league. The same goes for Rick Pitino, who was on the list of best coaches above but actually shows up seventh on the list of worst coaches using the bell curve model (table 18.4).

These methods aren't very consistent either in assessing what percentage of a team's success a coach may be responsible for. If you have a model that doesn't predict win-loss records very well, it looks like the coach is more important. Sportshaq's model says the best and worst coaches could be responsible for about 3 to 5 percent of a team's annual win-loss record, but the bell curve model says that coaches could be responsible for 1 to 2 percent.

What also seems particularly strange is the use of *current* season statistics to define expectations. Why should the current season field goal percentage or points scored be a measure of expectation? Some of the papers using this approach admit that the model of win-loss record is not one of expectation but of

Table 18.3. Coaches Winning More than Expected as Based on Bell Curve Forecast

Rank	Coach	Expected Win%	Actual Win %	Actual − Expected	Impact/Year
1	Paul Westphal	0.590	0.627	0.037	0.7%
2	Del Harris	0.614	0.650	0.036	0.8%
3	Larry Bird	0.657	0.687	0.030	1.2%
4	Jeff Van Gundy	0.562	0.590	0.028	0.5%
5	Bob Weiss	0.411	0.439	0.028	0.9%
6	Dave Cowens	0.444	0.472	0.028	0.8%
7	Phil Jackson	0.717	0.744	0.027	0.3%
8	Pat Riley	0.612	0.634	0.023	0.2%
9	Scott Skiles	0.572	0.595	0.023	1.0%
10	Paul Silas	0.553	0.573	0.020	0.6%

NOTE: Minimum 165 games coached.

Table 18.4. Coaches Losing More than Expected as Based on Bell Curve Forecast

Rank	Coach	Expected Win%	Actual Win %	Actual − Expected	Impact/Year
1	Wes Unseld	0.343	0.289	-0.054	-1.8%
2	John Calipari	0.444	0.391	-0.053	-2.4%
3	Brian Winters	0.237	0.196	-0.042	-1.9%
4	Jim Lynam	0.440	0.401	-0.039	-1.1%
5	Alvin Gentry	0.497	0.458	-0.039	-0.9%
6	P.J. Carlesimo	0.449	0.415	-0.035	-0.9%
7	Rick Pitino	0.444	0.411	-0.033	-1.1%
8	Tim Floyd	0.228	0.205	-0.023	-0.8%
9	Sidney Lowe	0.286	0.264	-0.022	-0.6%
10	Bill Fitch	0.361	0.339	-0.021	-0.4%

NOTE: Minimum 165 games coached.

skill. A better measure of expectation may involve something from the previous season.

Using Parity Charts for Expectation

An alternative measure of expectation is the prior season's record. That record sets an expectation that a coach may have to live up to. But a better measure of expectation comes from those charts in chapter 9 showing the expected change in winning percentage given the prior season's winning percentage. A coach who takes over a team that wins about 20 percent of its games would normally be expected to increase the winning percentage by about 11 percent. Doing less than that is something of a failure.

This method of looking at coaching success is also fraught with problems, but let me show the results first. Table 18.5 shows the best coaches according to this technique (also since 1992), and table 18.6 shows the worst.

Here, I've ranked the results by the last column, which indicates the chance that the coach would have posted his actual winning percentage (or better)

Table 18.5. Coaches Winning More than Expected as Based on Pull of Parity

Rank	Coach	Expected Win%	Actual Win%	Actual − Expected	Impact Per Year	Chance of Actual Win % by Luck
1	Phil Jackson	0.590	0.744	0.154	1.5%	1.8E-14
2	Jerry Sloan	0.554	0.672	0.118	1.1%	7.06E-13
3	George Karl	0.548	0.659	0.112	1.1%	4.21E-11
4	Pat Riley	0.535	0.634	0.099	0.9%	2.04E-09
5	Lenny Wilkens	0.511	0.586	0.075	0.7%	5.17E-06
6	Gregg Popovich	0.534	0.631	0.098	1.8%	2.11E-05
7	Del Harris	0.543	0.650	0.107	2.5%	2.66E-05
8	Paul Westphal	0.531	0.627	0.095	1.8%	4.39E-05
9	Rick Adelman	0.507	0.578	0.071	0.8%	9.16E-05
10	Larry Bird	0.561	0.687	0.125	4.8%	0.000115

NOTES: Minimum 165 games coached.
The notation 2.11E-05 means 0.0000211 or 2.11×10-5.

Table 18.6. Coaches Losing More than Expected as Based on Pull of Parity

Rank	Coach	Expected Win%	Actual Win%	Actual − Expected	Impact Per Year	Chance of Actual Win % by Luck
1	Tim Floyd	0.321	0.205	-0.115	-4.0%	1.000
2	Sidney Lowe	0.350	0.264	-0.086	-2.4%	0.999
3	Wes Unseld	0.362	0.289	-0.074	-2.5%	0.994
4	Bill Fitch	0.388	0.339	-0.048	-1.0%	0.981
5	Don Chaney	0.386	0.337	-0.050	-1.5%	0.962
6	Dick Motta	0.385	0.333	-0.051	-1.6%	0.962
7	Darrell Walker	0.384	0.331	-0.052	-2.5%	0.931
8	Garry St. Jean	0.409	0.382	-0.027	-0.5%	0.887
9	John Calipari	0.414	0.391	-0.022	-1.0%	0.754
10	Jim Lynam	0.418	0.401	-0.018	-0.5%	0.748

Note: Minimum 165 games coached.

through sheer luck, given the expectations. So, the chance that Larry Bird would have won 68.7 percent of his ball games in the 214 games he coached if he really were an average coach who couldn't make his team exceed expectations (of 56.1 percent) is 0.000115, or about one in ten thousand. The chance that Sidney Lowe would have won 26.4 percent or more of his 299 games just by sheer luck as an average coach is 99.9 percent. An average coach would likely have won more. This way of looking at coaching success provides a way of weighting both how far above expectations the coach was and how long he did it.

Again, the results "make some sense." I subjectively agree with them more than I do with the other lists. I do have a problem with Larry Brown not showing up as a top coach on any of these lists. I do feel better about this last technique because, unlike the other techniques, Brown is recognized as a positive influence on his teams (and was ranked eleventh), adding about 1 percent per year to a team's winning percentage. I also like this last method because it treats coaches who are good at making bad teams average equally with coaches who keep great teams great. Sometimes, a coach may be able to make a bad team good quickly but not make that team great, and this method would see that coach as average.

But the method is also flawed in assessing Tim Floyd to be as bad as he's listed. He walked into his job with the Chicago Bulls, who had a prior record of 62–20, and was faced with an "expected" winning percentage of 0.678 or fifty-six wins. But with the Bulls' top talent departing, that figure was very unrealistic, and no one really expected the Bulls to even win thirty games. If you remove that first season, Floyd looks pretty close to being an average coach. Likewise, Phil Jackson's rating was significantly aided by the reacquisition of Michael Jordan before the 1996 season. Winning seventy-two games on top of an "expectation" of forty-five wins is a lot bigger than winning seventy-two games on top of an expectation of sixty wins, which is more reasonable with Jordan's return. This all gets at . . .

The Ideal Expectation

Ideally I could sit down with all the prognosticator predictions of the last ten years, average their forecasted wins, and get a better measure of "expectation" for all the coaches. Prognosticators do their best to make expectations based on talent. When teams exceed those talent expectations, their coaches get Coach of the Year votes from the prognosticators. Basically, prognosticators subtract their own assessments of talent from the actual performances to get their coaching ratings.

The danger of subtracting "talent" from performance to get a coaching rating is that it assumes that everything besides talent can be controlled by a coach. *Everything* is a really big category. Everything includes (you've seen part of this list before):

1. Scouting
2. Play calling
3. Time-out strategy (see box for information on the value of a time-out)
4. Practice strategy
5. Strength of schedule
6. Players playing different positions or different roles
7. Players' familiarity with one another's tendencies (chemistry?)
8. Players playing poorly because they feel underpaid
9. Nutrition and strength training
10. Possession by evil spirits
11. Biorhythms

Of these things, coaches don't have a lot of control over scouting ability, player familiarity with each other, evil spirits, or biorhythms (unless you're Phil Jackson). Coaches will get more credit than perhaps they deserve when they inherit good scouts or players who are just coming to understand where they like to get the ball. Coaches who inherit players possessed by demons, such as Dennis Rodman, well, they just have to preach the Tao of Jackson.

Fundamentally, though, to evaluate coaches, you need some measure of talent separate from performance, one that accounts for changing talent levels as players get hurt, get old, get tired of playing baseball, or get pregnant. As they say in some sports economics papers, accounting for such things is "outside the scope of this investigation." For now, we'll just have to leave it to the coaches' bosses to do thorough subjective contemplation of the things they see their coaches do.

So . . . About That Molotov Cocktail?

No, you still shouldn't firebomb Donovan's house!

I did try to evaluate Coach Donovan numerically. With limited college statistics available, I couldn't do a complete job. I could evaluate his performance relative to the bell curve predictions. Using that technique, Donovan gets mixed marks. Against the SEC, Donovan hasn't looked particularly good (table 18.7).

But against his overall schedule (table 18.8), he hasn't done badly.

The results generally show that Donovan isn't a net positive coach, struggling particularly in the 2002 season, which was when the "firebomb" question was posed to me. But this really means only that his teams are blowing out a lot of easy teams, then losing the close ones. Is that a measure of his coaching? It is certainly one that I have heard a complaint about.

But I can't really do a specific evaluation of what the expectations are for an NCAA team. Clearly, the subjective expectation has been that Florida should have done better. But that expectation has been based on over-hyped talent—Brett Nelson and Teddy Dupay being good examples. Maybe these two players' lack of development is Donovan's fault. Maybe they would have been superstars in another program. If that's true, then maybe you should find the matches.

But give him a little time so we can be sure.

Table 18.7. Billy Donovan's Coaching Performance Against the SEC

Season	Bell Curve	Actual	Performance
1999	10.6-7.4 (0.589)	11-7 (0.611)	0.022
2000	13.7-4.3 (0.759)	13-5 (0.722)	-0.037
2001	14.3-3.7 (0.795)	13-5 (0.722)	-0.073
2002	12.8-5.2 (0.710)	11-7 (0.611)	-0.099

Table 18.8. Billy Donovan's Coaching Performance Against All Opponents

Season	Bell Curve	Actual	Performance
1999	23.0-11.0 (0.676)	24-10 (0.706)	0.030
2000	28.2-7.8 (0.784)	28-8 (0.784)	0.000
2001	23.5-7.5 (0.757)	24-7 (0.774)	0.01
2002	24.7-7.3 (0.772)	22-10 (0.688)	-0.084

The Value of a Time-Out

What is the value of a time-out? That is such a hard question that it can't really be answered as it is phrased. I think it's actually a lot easier to ask specific questions about time-out usage, especially as they are used questionably. For example,

- If a player is falling out of bounds with the ball, should he call a time-out to save the possession?
- If the other team is making a run, should a team call a time-out to interrupt it?

These two questions set the stage for miniature case studies, where intuition lends some pretty good insight:

1. If a player is falling out of bounds and calls a time-out when the team is winning by twelve with ten seconds to go, the value of the time-out is nil. The team is going to win anyway.

2. If the player calls the time-out when falling out of bounds and the team is tied with ten seconds to go, the value of the time-out is large. The chances of that possession changing the outcome of the game are large.

3. If a team is up by twelve with three minutes to go when the opponent goes on a 10–0 run to cut it to two points with forty seconds to go, the value of *still having* a time-out is high. The value of calling a time-out before it got that close would also potentially have been high (to put in good ball handlers, to put in good foul shooters, to install a stall offense).

4. If a team is up by twenty-two points with three minutes to go before a 10–0 run brings it to a twelve-point lead with forty seconds to go, the value of either using a time-out or having time-outs left is relatively small. The team is still likely to win. I would think you would want to save the time-out until it was an eighteen-point run or so.

In general, then, I think that having time-outs available (not necessarily using them) is most valuable when the odds of winning the game can change the most. This situation occurs at the end of close games, of course, but also early in a game if someone starts to open up a big lead. If a player is just falling out of bounds early in a game with the score tied, they probably should not call a time-out. (If you're coaching at a lower level, where teaching may be as important as winning, calling a time-out to teach the players—regardless of how it impacts the current game—is valuable.)

I watched North Carolina coach Dean Smith for many years, and the way he used time-outs always made me nervous. He would almost always save his time-outs for the end of a game, even if the opponent was making a run earlier. I'd love to go back, now that I understand time-out policy a little better, and watch Smith's use of them.

In fact, I recently happened to see the replay of the UNC-Michigan NCAA Final of 1993 on ESPN Classic, and Smith was absolutely brilliant in time-out strategy during that game. Not only did he use his own time-outs well, but...

With 15:16 to go in the second half, Smith called for a surprise double-team on Michigan's inbounds pass after a routine made basket, double-teaming the player to receive the pass and forcing him to call time-out. The game was still close, about a three-point difference, and the two teams had been fighting for control the whole game. At this point in the game, Michigan was taking the inbounds pass for granted. With the surprise pressure, Smith (or the scouts who had noticed Michigan's tendency to take inbounds passes for granted, as commentator Billy Packer pointed out) made sure that the Wolverines would have one fewer time-out to use if the game remained close at the end.

And as the game approached the end, the game was indeed close. Down by two points with about ten seconds to go, Michigan's Chris Webber called the infamous time-out his team didn't have left. That most certainly changed the odds of winning the game a lot.

Chapter 19

The Problem with Scorers

All right—what does figure 19.1 look like to you?

Figure 19.1.

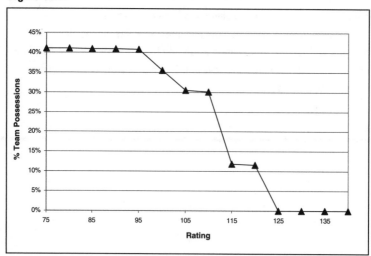

Stock market after 2000? Sex drive as a function of age?

Uh, no. That is actually Allen Iverson at age twenty-six.

And figure 19.2—do you know what this is?

"Looks kinda similar. This one must be the stock market. No, wait! It's Pauly Shore's acting career!"

Good guesses, but no. This is a profile of 2001 and 2002 Jerry Stackhouse, specifically of his offense. I call these "offensive skill curves," plots of how efficient

Figure 19.2.

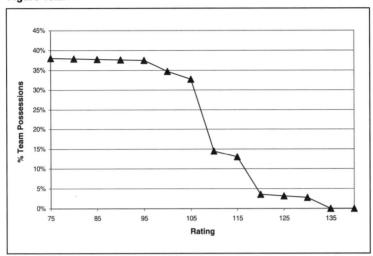

a player is (along the bottom) and what percentage of a team's possessions he can use to still maintain that efficiency (along the side). They show you the basics of a player's offense. These two players are "scorers" who use a high percentage of a team's offense but aren't the most efficient players doing so. Both Iverson and Stackhouse use 32 to 35 percent of their team's possessions and you can see that, with 33 percent of team possessions used, they both have offensive ratings between 100 and 105, about average in the NBA in the single-digit years. If someone convinces them to take fewer possessions, dropping down to a standard 20 percent, they do get more efficient, with ratings going up to about 108 for Stackhouse and about 112 for Iverson. At that point, they are producing a lot fewer points but are doing it more efficiently.

That is the theory behind these curves. Players like Iverson and Stackhouse take a fair amount of bad shots. If they were to restrict themselves to taking smarter shots, how much would their efficiency improve? Conceptually, each player has a skill curve that is a function of his own ability (which is a function of his age) and possibly also a function of his teammates' ability. Generally, the only way for players to improve their rating is to take smarter and smarter—hence, fewer and fewer—shots (and passes). This means that the curve must go down— fewer possessions in order to get higher ratings. At some point, though, even taking only the smartest shots, a player can be only so efficient. Based on these concepts, I've always envisioned generic skill curves that decrease continuously with increasing rating. I've imagined curves that look something like those in figure 19.3.

The curve could be a straight line like the one in the middle, or it could be curved up or down like the two dashed lines. But the key word has been "imag-

Figure 19.3. Generic Skill Curve

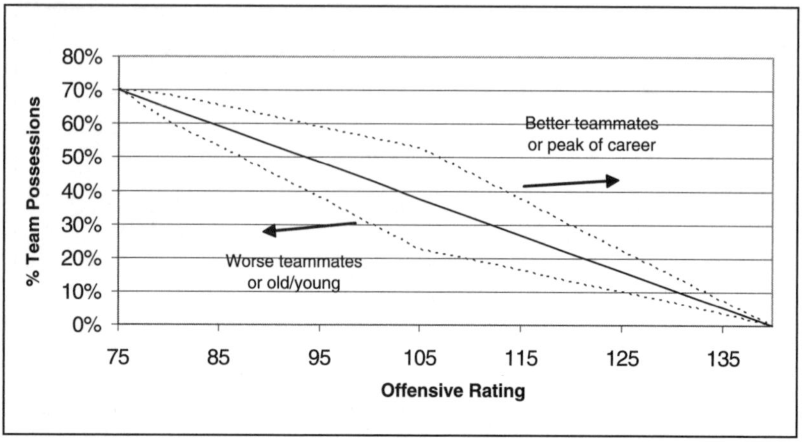

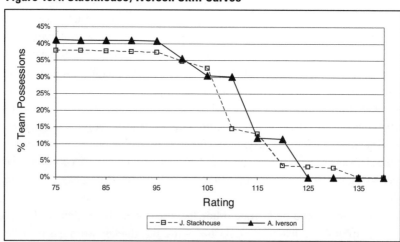

ined," as in "fantasized" or "dreamed." Because actually getting curves that look as smooth as this is about as hard as finding Pauly Shore these days.

Generating these curves means interpreting the statistics of players who refuse to be nice to the scientist. Guys like Stackhouse and Iverson just refuse to have games in which they use less than 20 percent of their team's possessions. Their coaches beg and plead for more unselfish play—not even on my behalf— and they don't listen. I'm left without a lot of data to say what would happen if they used fewer possessions. I try to stretch info from when they take 24 or 25 percent of their team's possessions. I end up with the bumpy, jagged curves you see in figure 19.4 (putting them side by side for you).

Because they are a little lumpy and a little blurry, I think of skill curves kind of like sonograms—you know, those movies that doctors take of kids while they're

Figure 19.4. Stackhouse/Iverson Skill Curves

still in the womb. Most of us look at them and can't tell head from butt until it just clicks. But you get fascinated by the pictures, looking for arms and legs, trying to get a sense of personality by—I dunno—how much the baby is moving or whether its hand is either waving at you or flipping you off. People gawk and say, "Oooh, there's his little thing! How cuuute!" Just for the record, skill curves don't have "things." Don't bother looking for them.

Females of the basketball species do have different curves than males. Uh, I guess that's true in more ways than one. You've seen a couple males. Now here's a female in figure 19.5 (and, no, you can't see her "things" either).

That is Ticha Penicheiro, alongside the curves for Iverson and Stackhouse. Penicheiro was the point guard for the Sacramento Monarchs. She was flashy, she was an All-Star, but her curve indicates that she wasn't very efficient. An NBA player with this kind of curve would not last in the league, much less be an All-Star. I think it is simply a coincidence that Ticha's curve ended up a lot smoother than those of the guys.

The fact that the league average offensive efficiencies in the WNBA are lower than those in the NBA means that skill curves do coincidentally allow you to see differences in male and female skill curves—kinda like a sonogram without the "thing." That doesn't mean it's always easy. Figure 19.6 shows another skill curve alongside those of Iverson and Stackhouse. Is it a man or a woman?

That rather extraordinary curve belongs to Cynthia Cooper (using numbers from 1998 and 1999). She may look more like a man on paper, but she's just hot in my book. Just to further substantiate that she *was* the Michael Jordan of the WNBA, figure 19.7 has Jordan's curve for the seasons of 1996 and 1997—very similar, but (weirdly) not as smooth.

Figure 19.5. Stackhouse/Iverson/Penicheiro Skill Curves

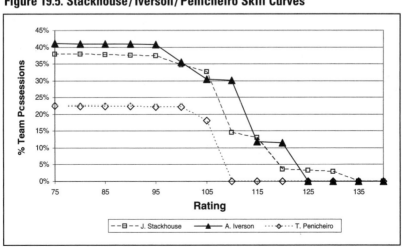

Figure 19.6. Stackhouse/Iverson/Anonymous Skill Curves

Figure 19.7. Stackhouse/Iverson/Jordan Skill Curves

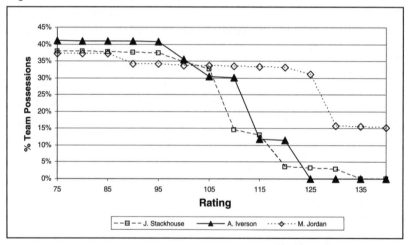

Both Jordan and Cooper bring their curves much farther out to the right than Iverson and Stackhouse. They can be efficient with more possessions than the mere mortal, or even the mere Iversons and Stackhouses.

Iverson and Stackhouse do frustrate a lot of people with how much they control the ball. Even with Stackhouse's attempt to be more unselfish in 2002, his load of the offense only dropped from 34 percent to 32 percent (he did cut back his shooting even more, from 35 percent to 31 percent of total shots). This is a problem for coaches, a lot of whom have been raised with the thought that more equal distribution of the ball is better, especially when their stars aren't very efficient. Coaches want more even distribution of the ball, but should they? With stars using such a high percentage of a team's possessions, they allow other players to

Figure 19.8. Iverson/Snow Skill Curves

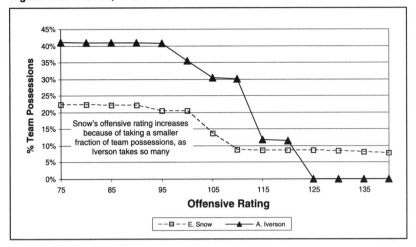

use fewer possessions, raising their offensive ratings. For example, if Iverson used 35 percent of the team's possessions, that leaves about 65 percent for the other four guys, or about 16 to 17 percent apiece. This helps a player like Eric Snow, the 76ers' point guard, improve his rating several points from where he'd be if he had to use 20+ percent of Philly's possessions, as shown in figure 19.8.

If Snow had to be a very active player in the offense, using more than 20 percent of the possessions—not even close to Iverson's current load—he'd be much less efficient. Remember, chapter 7 showed how much better Philly's offense has been with Iverson than without him. They have lots of guys who do reasonably well if they use 15 to 20 percent of the possessions, but not if they use more than 20 percent. That is the problem with *nonscorers*.

(I actually did want to title this chapter "The Problem with Everyone," but I think that desire came in part from the natural bitterness that temporarily sets in on an author after writing a couple hundred pages:

> All work and no play makes Jack a dull boy. All work and no play makes Jack a dull boy. All work and no play makes Jack a dull boy. All work and no play makes Jack a dull boy. All work and no play makes Jack a dull boy. All work and no play makes Jack a dull boy. All work and no play makes Jack a dull boy. All work and no play makes Jack a dull boy. All work and no play makes Jack a dull boy. All work and no play makes Jack a dull boy. All work and no play makes Jack a dull boy. All work and no play makes Jack a dull boy. All work and no play makes Jack a dull boy. All work and no play makes Jack a dull boy. All work and no play makes Jack a dull boy.

I always wanted to do that.)

In the chapter where I first showed some of the players' individual ratings, I talked about how the Lakers' top two players, Shaq and Kobe, carry the rest of the team. They each use about 30 percent of the team's possessions, allowing players like Fisher and Horry to sit back and take only the shots that they want. The skill

Figure 19.9. Shaq/Kobe Skill Curves

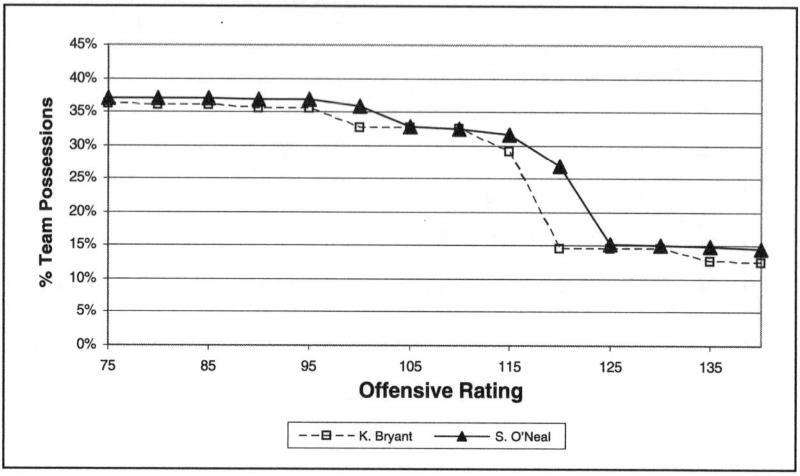

curves for Shaq and Kobe (figure 19.9) are both very strong, going out far to the right, meaning that they can maintain high efficiency at heavy loads. (Something I also will point out is that the curves fairly well reproduce what players actually did. Shaq actually used 31 percent of the Lakers' possessions in 2002, which projects to a 115–118 rating on the curve. In reality, his rating was about 116. Kobe's 30 percent usage of possessions projects to about a 113 rating, when he actually had a 112 rating.)

Because Shaq and Kobe were so strong, they allowed players like Fisher and Horry to use a lot fewer possessions (16 percent and 14 percent, respectively), which puts them at much higher efficiencies on their skill curves (Figure 19.10).

Figure 19.10. Fisher/Horry Skill Curves

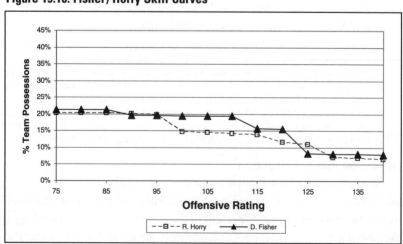

If Fisher and Horry were forced to generate more offense, their curves say that they probably wouldn't be able to do it very efficiently. If either guy had to generate 20 percent of his team's offense, his rating would drop maybe twenty points. "Maybe" is a key word. These two guys are good examples of uncertain players. They both have a lot of flat areas in their curves, which are regions of highest uncertainty. Maybe Fisher's curve to the left of the 105 rating actually should climb higher. Maybe he can use more possessions and stay relatively efficient. But there were so few games where Fisher did use 20+ percent of the possessions that it is hard to say. Plus, when he did, he was sometimes good and sometimes bad.

Constructing these skill curves is very difficult. It took me years to get to a point where I was happy enough with them to present them. This is because of situations like Fisher's. He had so few games where he used a lot of possessions—how could I estimate what he *would* do? This is especially difficult when trying to estimate over the long haul. In specific games, Fisher did have high possessions and high efficiency ratings. Maybe he was facing a poor defense. Maybe he was given a lot of good shots because the opposing coach didn't think that he could beat them. This latter situation is not a long-term outcome, and I don't want to weight those games very much unless they happen frequently.

So, like sonograms, skill curves are neat to look at, but you probably don't want to know the details about how to make them. Generally, they come from looking at box scores and the general trends that players show when using a lot of possessions. How much better do players seem to get if they use fewer possessions? If they seem to get worse when they use fewer possessions, I say, "That's not right." It's just not a sustainable trend. If a player is getting worse when he uses fewer possessions, that is because some teams have found ways to frustrate the player into fewer shots and poorer shots, not because the player is actually getting worse. Effectively, I force the curves to be declining. The details of how I do that would scare someone who doesn't know formal statistics. They would scare someone who did know formal statistics for different reasons. That's why, for now, I just want to show the skill curves and let people gawk at them like they are sonograms. The concept that possession rates and efficiency ratings play off each other in different fashions for different players is a useful one, and I want that concept to stand unobstructed by the details of how we got there. Maybe I'll write a math book later that explains the details.

Optimizing Offense

A big part of the reason I always wanted offensive skill curves was to be able to take a stab at optimizing offense. There are so many armchair coaches out there who think that a team would be so much better if whatshisname shot more and

Table 19.1. Approximate Lakers Starting Lineup and Possession Distribution

Player	% Tm Poss	Off. Rtg.
Bryant	30%	114
O'Neal	30%	117
Fisher	16%	115
Horry	14%	114
Fox	10%	108
Totals	**100%**	**114**

so-and-so shot less. Skill curves can be used to look at this issue—something I hinted at already, but I now want to give a brief example. We'll use the Lakers offense since we've talked about it a bit.

The Lakers lineup of Shaq, Kobe, Fisher, Horry, and Rick Fox produced a rating of about 114, which comes from the distribution of possessions shown in table 19.1.

That is a very good offense. When the Lakers are putting their best players on the floor, theirs is a tough offense to stop. But some people complain that it is just a Kobe and Shaq show, so what would happen if they cut down their usage of the ball a bit, say to 25 percent per player? Using skill curves for the five players that appear in table 19.2, I redistributed possessions as in table 19.3, just giving more possessions to Fisher, Horry, and Fox.

The Lakers offense would decline substantially. A seven-point drop would be huge.

Of course, I could have redistributed the possessions the wrong way. It's probably reasonable to say that, rather than Fisher and Horry, Fox would actually pick up more of the offense, having done so in Boston before going to the Lakers.

Table 19.2. Skill Curves for Lakers

Off. Rtg.	Percent of Team Possessions Used				
	K. Bryant	S. O'Neal	D. Fisher	R. Horry	R. Fox
75	36.1%	37.1%	21.4%	20.3%	20.8%
80	36.1%	37.0%	21.3%	20.3%	20.8%
85	36.0%	37.0%	21.3%	20.2%	20.7%
90	35.5%	36.9%	19.6%	20.2%	20.7%
95	35.5%	36.8%	19.6%	19.8%	20.7%
100	32.7%	35.9%	19.5%	14.7%	18.3%
105	32.6%	32.8%	19.4%	14.5%	17.6%
110	32.5%	32.6%	19.4%	14.2%	7.5%
115	29.2%	31.6%	15.8%	13.9%	7.4%
120	14.6%	27.0%	15.6%	11.7%	7.4%
125	14.6%	15.2%	8.3%	11.0%	7.3%
130	14.5%	15.0%	8.2%	7.0%	7.3%
135	12.8%	14.8%	8.1%	6.9%	7.2%
140	12.5%	14.6%	7.9%	6.7%	7.2%

Table 19.3. Lakers Possession Distribution if Fisher, Horry, and Fox Given More Responsibility

Player	% Tm Poss	Off. Rtg.
Bryant	25%	116
O'Neal	25%	121
Fisher	20%	90
Horry	17%	93
Fox	13%	107
Totals	**100%**	**107**

Table 19.4. Lakers Possession Distribution with Fox Picking Up Slack

Player	% Tm Poss	Off. Rtg.
Bryant	25%	116
O'Neal	25%	121
Fisher	17%	113
Horry	15%	100
Fox	18%	102
Totals	**100%**	**112**

Giving more possessions to Fox allows Fisher and Horry to maintain their high ratings, in which case the team offensive rating drops to only 112 (table 19.4).

The offense stays pretty close to where it was originally. Fox, though he was the least efficient of the original five at the levels of possessions used, can maintain his efficiency through higher possession rates. His value to the original offense may not have been high, but he serves as a good buffer if Kobe or Shaq can't shoulder their usual load.

You get the point. You could play with the numbers to see whether there is a more optimal distribution of possession rates among these five or, with the curves for all Lakers players, you could see what the Lakers should do if Shaq or Kobe is out. It's a very interesting little optimization project, one that would make for a different kind of fantasy basketball league, I'd think.

Of course, coaches do this kind of optimization in their heads without doing any calculations. Could these curves help them? Possibly. Coaches don't all have uniform opinions of players, and these curves could provide a little supporting or dissenting information to consider when they have questions.

Chapter 20

Individual Win–Loss Records

The concept is simple—how many wins and losses is this guy going to give me? That is the bottom line, the ultimate question that you can ask about a player's worth.

But whereas the concept is simple, the answer is not. "Well, it depends on how much he plays and..."

"OK, so tell me how many wins and losses he creates per minute."

"But it depends on who he plays with and whether you're going to sign this other guy."

"You can get your parking validated at the front desk. Have a good day."

Individual win–loss records are nice because the concept seems so simple. Individual win–loss records are evil because determining them is so complex. When I was nineteen years old and starting to work on all these things, I was naïve enough to believe that individual wins and losses per minute could be determined and could be transferable from one team to the next. I thought that trade evaluation would be easy.

Nearly fifteen years later, I have come to find that individual wins and losses can be determined but aren't so easily transferable. Part of the problem is that it is difficult to say whether an *individual* player can "win" at a *team* game like basketball. Broadcasters like to say that Kobe Bryant won a game by himself or that Julius Erving took over a game, but no coach will ever say that any individual wins a game on his own. Even Wilt Chamberlain's hundred-point performance in 1962, which may have been the greatest individual single-game performance in NBA history, couldn't stand on its own to win the game for Philadelphia; the opposing New York Knicks scored 147, so Philly needed the extra sixty-nine points thrown in by other guys.

Because there is no such thing as a true individual win or loss, all we can do is create some statistics that *look like* individual wins and losses. There is then no great way to calibrate those statistics, improve them, or verify them. Without those reality checks to indicate what the method does wrong, there is no good way for us to say what form of an individual win–loss record "works."

I have historically calculated a few different types of individual win–loss records, though I now mostly use only two. I'll talk about those two below and finish up by summarizing other possible ways of getting at individual win–loss records.

Game-by-Game Wins and Losses

If a *team* has a higher offensive rating than defensive rating in a game, it wins the game. That's a basic fact. So, if a player has a higher individual offensive rating than individual defensive rating in a game, we can call that an individual win. That is the premise of "game-by-game" wins and losses.

Game-by-game wins and losses are one of my personal favorite statistics to look at. I'll show you why by looking at some of the results. First, table 20.1 shows the game-by-game win–loss records for a great team, the 1996 Chicago Bulls. Everyone knows this team. They went 72–10 and were led by Air Jordan. Jordan dominated the offense. He had some help, but he was the bona fide leader of the offense.

Now, table 20.2 shows a good but not great team: the 2002 New Jersey Nets. They went 52–30 and were led by Jason Kidd, but the scoring was fairly evenly distributed. You could argue that the team was pretty much all role players.

Table 20.1. Game-by-Game Win–Loss Records for 1996 Chicago Bulls

Player	W–L (%)
Michael Jordan	70-12 (0.854)
Steve Kerr	63-19 (0.768)
Toni Kukoc	56-25 (0.691)
Scottie Pippen	55-22 (0.714)
Ron Harper	52-28 (0.650)
Dennis Rodman	37-27 (0.578)
Jud Buechler	34-33 (0.507)
Randy Brown	33-31 (0.516)
Luc Longley	30-32 (0.484)
Bill Wennington	29-40 (0.420)
Dickey Simpkins	28-25 (0.528)
Jason Caffey	27-26 (0.509)
James Edwards	10-17 (0.370)
John Salley	7-9 (0.438)
Jack Haley	0-1 (0.000)

Table 20.2. Game-by-Game Win–Loss Records for 2002 New Jersey Nets

Player	W–L (%)
Jason Kidd	47–35 (0.573)
Kerry Kittles	47–35 (0.573)
Lucious Harris	46–28 (0.622)
Aaron Williams	44–38 (0.537)
Todd MacCulloch	41–21 (0.661)
Keith Van Horn	41–40 (0.506)
Richard Jefferson	37–42 (0.468)
Jason Collier	36–41 (0.468)
Kenyon Martin	36–37 (0.493)
Anthony Johnson	15–15 (0.500)
Donny Marshall	10–8 (0.556)
Brandon Armstrong	9–21 (0.300)
Derrick Dial	8–16 (0.333)
Brian Scalabrine	5–17 (0.227)
Steve Goodrich	3–4 (0.429)
Reggie Slater	1–1 (0.500)

Table 20.3. Game-by-Game Win–Loss Records for 1994 Denver Nuggets

Player	W–L (%)
Dikembe Mutombo	50–32 (0.610)
Bison Dele	47–33 (0.588)
LaPhonso Ellis	45–34 (0.570)
Bryant Stith	44–38 (0.537)
Mahmoud Abdul–Rauf	40–40 (0.500)
Reggie Williams	36–46 (0.439)
Tom Hammonds	31–37 (0.456)
Robert Pack	27–39 (0.409)
Rodney Rogers	26–53 (0.329)
Mark Randall	10–17 (0.370)
Kevin Brooks	9–21 (0.300)
Darnell Mee	9–24 (0.273)
Marcus Liberty	1–2 (0.333)
Roy Marble	1–4 (0.200)
Adonis Jordan	1–5 (0.167)
Mark Macon	1–6 (0.143)
Jim Farmer	0–4 (0.000)

Table 20.3 shows an average team: the 1994 Denver Nuggets. They went 42–40 but were the first number-eight playoff seed to defeat a number-one seed. The image of Dikembe Mutombo gripping the ball with both hands while lying on the floor at the end of that upset is one that the NBA likes to show to torture Sonics fans. Five guys played heavy minutes on the team: Mutombo, Bryant Stith, LaPhonso Ellis, Reggie Williams, and Mahmoud Abdul-Rauf. Off the bench, Brian Williams (who would become Bison Dele), Rodney Rogers, and Robert Pack all put in about twenty minutes per game. Abdul-Rauf led the team in scoring and might have been considered the leader of the team by doing so and by being relatively veteran.

Table 20.4. Game-by-Game Win–Loss Records for 1994 Dallas Mavericks

Player	W–L (%)
Tim Legler	42–37 (0.532)
Popeye Jones	41–39 (0.513)
Fat Lever	34–47 (0.420)
Doug Smith	29–50 (0.367)
Lucious Harris	22–54 (0.289)
Sean Rooks	17–30 (0.362)
Donald Hodge	16–24 (0.400)
Jim Jackson	16–66 (0.195)
Greg Dreiling	15–29 (0.341)
Jamal Mashburn	14–65 (0.177)
Lorenzo Williams	12–20 (0.375)
Tony Campbell	11–30 (0.268)
Darren Morningstar	9–12 (0.429)
Randy White	7–11 (0.389)
Derek Harper	5–23 (0.179)
Terry Davis	5–10 (0.333)
Morlon Wiley	2–9 (0.182)
Chucky Brown	1–0 (1.000)

And table 20.4 shows a bad team: the 1994 Dallas Mavericks, who went 13–69. Jimmy Jackson and rookie Jamal Mashburn were the leaders of the offense here.

What's obvious about these records is that they don't measure absolute quality. Steve Kerr was not a better player than Scottie Pippen. And if Tim Legler was the best player on those Mavericks, that couldn't have been a good sign.

That last statement, in itself, says something. Legler's *role* on that team was to shoot threes and not make mistakes. He generally did those things. And, frankly, that's what his game-by-game record says—he filled his role decently. He wasn't asked to score a lot or rebound a lot. He just went out there and did what he was good at. His role wasn't very important, even if he did it well. On the other hand, Jackson and Mashburn's roles involved scoring and being the leaders of that Dallas team, and they didn't do those things very well. That's why the team suffered. They dominated the possessions. They scored points. They were the players that the other guys looked to. They were the leaders of this team, but they were too young and too inefficient to lead effectively. Their roles were important, but both filled their roles poorly enough to drag the team down to their own individual win–loss records.

So game-by-game records suggest how well players carry out their roles. It's a soft-science kind of description, but it seems right. If you have a bunch of players who perform their roles well, you will have a winning team, whether or not it has one scorer, like the Bulls did (or two, if you include Pippen), or several, like the Nets did. To some degree, that meshing of players willing to play specific roles can be considered "chemistry"—an elusive term that also falls under the classification of soft science.

Naturally, some players are going to be asked to take on different roles in their careers. This measure cannot predict how a player will perform in a new role, but it can show how well a player fills his new role as he grows.

Let's look at Michael Finley, a player who has been a scorer for most of his career. Since Dirk Nowitzki joined him in Dallas in 1999, though, he has had to learn to defer to Nowitzki. Table 20.5 presents how Finley's game-by-game record has progressed.

Finley was the leader of the Mavs in 1999, and the team record mimicked his to a substantial degree. Nowitzki was a rookie then, getting limited playing time because he just wasn't very good yet. By 2000, Nowitzki was the second-leading scorer on the Mavs, with numbers that looked a fair amount like Finley's (though his offensive rating was already higher, 111 to 106). The team's record was now a little better than Finley's (and actually similar to Nowitzki's—see table 20.6). In 2001, the Mavs began the full transition from Finley's team to Nowitzki's team. The team's win–loss record easily exceeded Finley's and was pretty close to the average of Finley's and Nowitzki's (shown below). In 2002, Nowitzki was the legitimate leader of the offense, with Finley and Steve Nash playing important but supporting roles. Nowitzki's win–loss percentage actually *declined* as he took on the larger role of full leader, but the team's overall record ended up almost the same as Nowitzki's, which was its best in history. Finley's individual record also improved in 2002 as he better recognized his role as a supporting player in the great Mavs offense.

One player whose role never changed was Jordan. His role was to do anything to win, if you can consider that a role. He was an outstanding scorer, and he did it a lot. He was also a leader, and his team's records—shown alongside his win–loss record in table 20.7—reflect how well he led.

Table 20.5. Michael Finley's Game-by-Game Win–Loss Records

Season	Team	Player	W–L (%)	Team W–L (%)
1999	DAL	Michael Finley	23–27 (0.460)	19–31 (0.380)
2000	DAL	Michael Finley	35–47 (0.427)	40–42 (0.488)
2001	DAL	Michael Finley	39–43 (0.476)	53–29 (0.646)
2002	DAL	Michael Finley	36–33 (0.522)	45–24 (0.652)

Table 20.6. Dirk Nowitzki's Game-by-Game Win–Loss Records

Season	Team	Player	W–L (%)	Team W–L (%)
1999	DAL	Dirk Nowitzki	14–33 (0.298)	17–30 (0.362)
2000	DAL	Dirk Nowitzki	39–43 (0.476)	40–42 (0.488)
2001	DAL	Dirk Nowitzki	61–21 (0.744)	53–29 (0.646)
2002	DAL	Dirk Nowitzki	54–22 (0.711)	53–23 (0.697)

Table 20.7. Michael Jordan's Game-by-Game Win–Loss Records

Season	Team	Player	W–L (%)	Team W–L (%)
1992	CHI	Michael Jordan	65–15 (0.813)	67–13 (0.838)
1993	CHI	Michael Jordan	59–19 (0.756)	56–22 (0.718)
1995	CHI	Michael Jordan	12–5 (0.706)	13–4 (0.765)
1996	CHI	Michael Jordan	70–12 (0.854)	72–10 (0.878)
1997	CHI	Michael Jordan	63–19 (0.768)	69–13 (0.841)
1998	CHI	Michael Jordan	58–24 (0.707)	62–20 (0.756)

NOTE: The APBR is collecting box scores from before 1992, but they are not yet available for this book.

There was rarely much difference between Jordan's win–loss record and his team's, which seems like a good sign for a leader.

Using only statistics, it's actually hard to identify the leader of a team. Is it the player producing the most points? Using the most possessions? The oldest? I will admit that there is not a clear definition. I do tend to think of players who use the most possessions as leaders—not just those who use the highest percentage of possessions while in the game, but those who use the most overall or on a per-game basis. But sometimes, you look at teams and that definition doesn't quite fit. It's a definition I'm using operationally for now, though.

In light of the leadership question, David Robinson is an interesting player to consider. Robinson was a great player, but there were continual questions about whether he could win the big games, whether he could take the big shots, whether he could be the leader. When Tim Duncan arrived to join Robinson, he may not have had all of Robinson's shot-making ability, but he was a leader and would take those tough shots. Again, it's a soft-science argument, but Robinson's win–loss record is more different from his team's win–loss record than I would expect of so great a player. Whereas Jordan's win–loss record almost always tracked perfectly with his team's record, Robinson's has exceeded his team's in every season and often by a lot (table 20.8).

Table 20.8. David Robinson's Game-by-Game Win–Loss Records

Season	Team	Player	W–L (%)	Team W–L (%)
1992	SAN	David Robinson	56–12 (0.824)	42–26 (0.618)
1993	SAN	David Robinson	60–22 (0.732)	49–33 (0.598)
1994	SAN	David Robinson	65–15 (0.813)	54–26 (0.675)
1995	SAN	David Robinson	68–13 (0.840)	61–20 (0.753)
1996	SAN	David Robinson	73–9 (0.890)	59–23 (0.720)
1997	SAN	David Robinson	4–2 (0.667)	3–3 (0.500)
1998	SAN	David Robinson	60–13 (0.822)	50–23 (0.685)
1999	SAN	David Robinson	37–12 (0.755)	36–13 (0.735)
2000	SAN	David Robinson	49–13 (0.790)	41–21 (0.661)
2001	SAN	David Robinson	60–19 (0.759)	56–23 (0.709)
2002	SAN	David Robinson	58–19 (0.753)	54–23 (0.701)

NOTE: The APBR is collecting box scores from before 1992, but they are not yet available for this book.

Robinson was doing well, but he wasn't carrying his team. Whereas Nowitzki's win–loss percentage came down as he assumed a greater leadership position with the Mavs—and the team matched his record—Robinson's win–loss record remained above the team's throughout the time that the team needed him to carry them. Robinson always took the smart shot, but maybe not the big shot. If he'd created more, his offensive rating would have come down, but the team might have won more. It's an odd argument, and they are odd numbers. Don't get me wrong—Robinson is perhaps one of the ten best players ever, but so many other great players, players who haven't been subject to the nagging questions about leadership, have win–loss records that match their team totals.

Karl Malone's win–loss record matched his team's win–loss record quite well (table 20.9).

It matched better than John Stockton's (table 20.10), whose responsibility as a team leader might have been slightly less than Malone's.

Or how about Tim Duncan (table 20.11)? How has the Spurs' team record paralleled his own?

The Spurs' record is definitely closer to Duncan's than it ever has been to Robinson's. I really don't know if this is fair to David Robinson, but what this says to

Table 20.9. Karl Malone's Game-by-Game Win–Loss Records

Season	Team	Player	W–L (%)	Team W–L (%)
1992	UTA	Karl Malone	57–24 (0.704)	54–27 (0.667)
1993	UTA	Karl Malone	61–21 (0.744)	47–35 (0.573)
1994	UTA	Karl Malone	54–28 (0.659)	53–29 (0.646)
1995	UTA	Karl Malone	58–24 (0.707)	60–22 (0.732)
1996	UTA	Karl Malone	59–23 (0.720)	55–27 (0.671)
1997	UTA	Karl Malone	61–21 (0.744)	64–18 (0.780)
1998	UTA	Karl Malone	61–20 (0.753)	61–20 (0.753)
1999	UTA	Karl Malone	37–12 (0.755)	36–13 (0.735)
2000	UTA	Karl Malone	46–18 (0.719)	45–19 (0.703)
2001	UTA	Karl Malone	56–24 (0.700)	51–29 (0.638)
2002	UTA	Karl Malone	45–35 (0.563)	43–37 (0.538)

Table 20.10. John Stockton's Game-by-Game Win–Loss Records

Season	Team	Player	W–L (%)	Team W–L (%)
1992	UTA	John Stockton	60–22 (0.732)	55–27 (0.671)
1993	UTA	John Stockton	50–32 (0.610)	47–35 (0.573)
1994	UTA	John Stockton	63–19 (0.768)	53–29 (0.646)
1995	UTA	John Stockton	64–18 (0.780)	60–22 (0.732)
1996	UTA	John Stockton	55–27 (0.671)	55–27 (0.671)
1997	UTA	John Stockton	60–22 (0.732)	64–18 (0.780)
1998	UTA	John Stockton	40–24 (0.625)	51–13 (0.797)
1999	UTA	John Stockton	35–15 (0.700)	37–13 (0.740)
2000	UTA	John Stockton	45–19 (0.703)	45–19 (0.703)
2001	UTA	John Stockton	58–23 (0.716)	52–29 (0.642)
2002	UTA	John Stockton	53–29 (0.646)	44–38 (0.537)

Table 20.11. Tim Duncan's Game-by-Game Win–Loss Records

Season	Team	Player	W–L (%)	Team W–L (%)
1998	SAN	Tim Duncan	55–27 (0.671)	56–26 (0.683)
1999	SAN	Tim Duncan	41–9 (0.820)	37–13 (0.740)
2000	SAN	Tim Duncan	35–20 (0.636)	37–18 (0.673)
2001	SAN	Tim Duncan	55–26 (0.679)	57–24 (0.704)
2002	SAN	Tim Duncan	63–18 (0.778)	57–24 (0.704)

me is that a team *can be* as good as its best player and probably *should be* as good as its best player. But that best player sometimes has to take the tough shot, or do whatever it was that Robinson didn't do—that thing that no one can quite put their finger on.

Moving past the question of Robinson's place in history (a question I address for other players in the next chapter), there definitely seems to be a trend of teams having win–loss records matching those of their leader. And that is useful. It's useful in assessing what might happen if players leave. For example, when Jordan retired after 1993, the leadership of the Bulls fell to Scottie Pippen. Pippen had established a game-by-game win–loss rate of about 50–30 as a kind of secondary leader, so you would have expected the Bulls to win fifty games. In fact, Pippen improved a little (for the unpredictable reasons that players do change), but the projection of fifty wins was still a good one. Pippen's actual game-by-game record in the first year of Jordan's absence was 52–20, better than his previous records, but not greatly different. And the Bulls went 51–21 in those games. When Pippen went down with injuries for ten games, the dominant possession user became Toni Kukoc (see chapter 13), who used 24 percent of team possessions and was being groomed to lead the offense with Pippen. But Kukoc was a rookie, so he wasn't very efficient, and his game-by-game record was 31–44—winning about 40 percent of his games. So, when Pippen was gone and Kukoc was in charge, the Bulls won four of ten, about what would be expected.

Using the same logic, what would happen if Kobe Bryant were left without Shaq? People speculate that Kobe wants his own team to lead, and this statistic, in combination with the fact that he now co-leads the team, provides a straightforward estimate of how he'd do. Table 20.12 illustrates what the Lakers have done with Shaq.

The team has very much paralleled his record. Table 20.13 shows how Kobe's record has looked.

Kobe's individual win–loss record has gotten a lot better since he was an eighteen-year-old rookie, but it's never quite matched the team's record. That reflects Shaq being the leader and being better than Kobe to this point. Kobe's winning percentage is sitting around .600 to .700, suggesting that a Kobe-led team would win between forty-nine and fifty-six games, not quite as successful as

Table 20.12. Shaquille O'Neal's Game-by-Game Win–Loss Records

Season	Team	Player	W–L (%)	Team W–L (%)
1997	LAL	Shaquille O'Neal	37–14 (0.725)	38–13 (0.745)
1998	LAL	Shaquille O'Neal	43–17 (0.717)	46–14 (0.767)
1999	LAL	Shaquille O'Neal	36–13 (0.735)	31–18 (0.633)
2000	LAL	Shaquille O'Neal	66–13 (0.835)	66–13 (0.835)
2001	LAL	Shaquille O'Neal	54–20 (0.730)	51–23 (0.689)
2002	LAL	Shaquille O'Neal	51–16 (0.761)	51–16 (0.761)

Table 20.13. Kobe Bryant's Game-by-Game Win–Loss Records

Season	Team	Player	W–L (%)	Team W–L (%)
1997	LAL	Kobe Bryant	26–44 (0.371)	48–23 (0.676)
1998	LAL	Kobe Bryant	38–41 (0.481)	58–21 (0.734)
1999	LAL	Kobe Bryant	30–20 (0.600)	31–19 (0.620)
2000	LAL	Kobe Bryant	34–14 (0.708)	43–5 (0.896)
2001	LAL	Kobe Bryant	41–25 (0.621)	44–22 (0.667)
2002	LAL	Kobe Bryant	46–32 (0.590)	54–24 (0.692)

a Shaq-led team, but still good, especially given the talent of the rest of the Lakers. In fact, the Lakers have won only thirteen of twenty-five games (52 percent) since the start of the 2000 season during times when Kobe has had to take over for Shaq. That suggests that the Kobe-led Lakers might not be as good as expected, but I'd still put more faith in the 60- to 70-percent forecast at this point.

More research needs to be done with this statistic. At present, it is a curious number, one that appears to say how well a player fulfills his role, regardless of how valuable that role is to the team. But the potential power for prediction (how well would the Lakers do with Kobe and no Shaq?) or the power for understanding the past (how good was Oscar Robertson, who clearly led his team?) is huge. When more box scores become available in the future, this statistic will become more readily available and more readily interpretable.

Individual Bell Curve Records

The closest thing to the ideal individual win–loss measure outlined at the start of this chapter is this, individual bell curve records (also see "individual net points," as outlined in the box). Individual bell curve records aim to show roughly how many wins and losses players produce for their team. When you sum these individual win–loss records for all teammates, you end up pretty close to the team total, giving the measure a sense of reality.

As with the game-by-game records, it's easiest to get a feel for them by first looking at a few. Table 20.14 shows the 1996 Bulls again.

Table 20.14. Bell Curve Win–Loss Records for the 1996 Chicago Bulls

Player	W–L (%)
Michael Jordan	16.1–0.5 (0.972)
Scottie Pippen	11.9–1.6 (0.885)
Toni Kukoc	7.7–0.4 (0.951)
Luc Longley	3.8–3.4 (0.524)
Steve Kerr	5.2–0.0 (0.997)
Ron Harper	7.2–1.0 (0.879)
Dennis Rodman	6.8–1.6 (0.806)
Bill Wennington	2.7–1.1 (0.717)
Jack Haley	0.0–0.0 (0.012)
John Salley	0.2–0.5 (0.248)
Jud Buechler	2.0–0.5 (0.799)
Dickey Simpkins	1.1–1.4 (0.432)
James Edwards	0.0–0.9 (0.049)
Jason Caffey	0.4–1.5 (0.201)
Randy Brown	1.3–1.1 (0.529)

The numbers here suggest that Jordan on his own contributed a net fifteen to sixteen wins to the team, which was net sixty-two. That means that if you surrounded him with average teammates, the team would have won fifty games or so—about what the Bulls did in the previous two years without him. But Jordan had two other Hall of Famers and some very good role players on his team, so they won seventy-two. Recall chapter 15 and the discussion of Sagarin/Winston method of evaluating players. Their method said that Tim Duncan's 2002 performance was so good that, with average teammates, his team would have won seventy-three games, essentially the same as this Bulls team. Jordan was probably as good as Duncan, if not better, and wasn't surrounded by average teammates. As I said above, there is no way to truly check individual win–loss results, but there clearly is a major discrepancy between the Sagarin/Winston method and this one. I can't say that mine is absolutely correct, but . . .

Here's why Sagarin/Winston's number seems so implausible: If Duncan were responsible for fifty games—three times as many as my method said Jordan was responsible for—and he "won" every single one of them, that would leave thirty-two games that his teammates were responsible for. If they were average, they'd win sixteen, giving the team a total of sixty-six victories, still below seventy-one. Duncan would somehow have to be responsible for sixty games, "winning" all sixty, and then his teammates would chip in with eleven wins and eleven losses. Exactly how could one player be responsible for sixty games in a season? I don't think it's possible. Instead, table 20.15 shows what I calculated as the win distribution for those 2002 Spurs.

Duncan was good. No, he was outstanding. But I can't see a way to get my estimate anywhere near 60–0.

Table 20.15. Bell Curve Win–Loss Records for the 2002 San Antonio Spurs

Player	W–L (%)
Tim Duncan	16.2–1.2 (0.929)
David Robinson	10.3–0.7 (0.937)
Steve Smith	6.7–2.2 (0.757)
Antonio Daniels	5.1–1.8 (0.741)
Malik Rose	4.3–2.9 (0.603)
Tony Parker	3.8–5.5 (0.405)
Terry Porter	3.1–1.2 (0.713)
Danny Ferry	2.0–0.2 (0.895)
Charles C. Smith	2.0–2.7 (0.423)
Bruce Bowen	1.7–4.8 (0.259)
Mark Bryant	0.6–0.2 (0.763)
Jason Hart	0.2–0.1 (0.757)
Amal McCaskill	0.1–0.5 (0.146)
Stephen Jackson	0.1–0.9 (0.081)
Cherokee Parks	0.1–0.8 (0.086)

So where do these bell curve win–losses come from? They are actually easier to calculate than the game-by-game records. If you have a player's season offensive rating and defensive rating, that player's winning percentage is determined using the bell curve formula:

$$\text{Win\%} = \text{NORM}\left[\frac{\text{ORtg} - \text{DRtg}}{\sqrt{11^2 + 11^2 - 2 \times 40}}\right] = \text{NORM}\left[\frac{\text{ORtg} - \text{DRtg}}{12.7}\right]$$

where the factors of eleven and forty are average NBA team values of standard deviation and covariance, and NORM is the Microsoft Excel function NORMSDIST(). Don't worry—there is an easier way to calculate this winning percentage. Specifically, Bill James's baseball work uses a formula for individual winning percentage that looks like this:

$$\text{Win\%} = \frac{\text{ORtg}^2}{\text{ORtg}^2 + \text{DRtg}^2}$$

You can use this kind of formula for basketball, too, which is called a Pythagorean-like formula. But you do have to change the exponent from two to another number that depends on what league you're looking at. In the NBA in the 1980s, the exponent was about sixteen or seventeen. In the NBA in the 1990s and since, a value of thirteen to fourteen is a little more accurate. In the WNBA, an exponent of about nine to ten works (and I usually use this form in the WNBA with an exponent of 9.1 over the bell curve form). In college and other levels, it's more difficult to assess an appropriate value for the exponent because of varying levels of competition, but it should be between six and ten, I believe. In general, the fewer possessions there are in the game (or the shorter the game—thirty-two minutes in high school versus forty-eight minutes in the NBA, for example), the smaller the exponent is. I often use this "Pythagorean-like" formula in place of the bell curve formula because it is easier to calculate. I usually use an exponent of 16.5 for NBA players because I found it to be accurate in the 1980s, when I first started calculating it. Using something as low as thirteen for NBA players is still fine and doesn't make a big difference. Here are the 1996 Bulls using this simpler equation with an exponent of 16.5 (and showing an extra decimal point on the offensive and defensive ratings for people to calculate more precisely [see table 20.16]).

The method also estimates the number of "games" a player is responsible for. It does so using a weighted average of the following four components:

1. Percentage of team offensive possessions contributed to.
2. Percentage of team defensive stops made.
3. Percentage of team minutes played.
4. Percentage of games started.

I weight each of the first two by a factor of three each and the last two by a factor of one each. The rationale is that offense and defense are *the* elements of the game. Minutes played and games started are both factors that already are partially reflected in the first two components, but they both provide just a little bit of extra information that I don't want to exclude. Specifically, starters usually have importance early in games, which is when most games really are decided, despite the saying that the last two minutes are the only ones that count. Minutes played is a modifier to account for guys who are on the court a lot for their individual defense but, like Joe Dumars, may not have registered a lot of statistics in the process.[1]

This estimate of how many games a player is responsible for is not arbitrary, but also not fixed in any sense. You could estimate it any number of reasonable

Table 20.16. Bell Curve and Pythagorean Win–Loss Records for 1996 Chicago Bulls

Player	Offensive Rtg.	Defensive Rtg.	Bell Curve W–L (%)	Pythagorean W–L (%)
Michael Jordan	123.6	99.4	16.1–0.5 (0.972)	16.1–0.4 (0.973)
Scottie Pippen	115.8	100.5	11.9–1.6 (0.885)	12.3–1.2 (0.912)
Toni Kukoc	124.7	103.6	7.7–0.4 (0.951)	7.7–0.4 (0.955)
Luc Longley	102.9	102.1	3.8–3.4 (0.524)	3.8–3.4 (0.531)
Steve Kerr	140.8	106.0	5.2–0.0 (0.997)	5.2–0.0 (0.991)
Ron Harper	116.4	101.5	7.2–1.0 (0.879)	7.4–0.8 (0.906)
Dennis Rodman	109.0	98.0	6.8–1.6 (0.806)	7.2–1.2 (0.852)
Bill Wennington	111.3	104.0	2.7–1.1 (0.717)	2.9–0.9 (0.754)
Jack Haley	76.6	105.2	0.0–0.0 (0.012)	0.0–0.0 (0.005)
John Salley	89.0	97.7	0.2–0.5 (0.248)	0.1–0.6 (0.177)
Jud Buechler	113.0	102.3	2.0–0.5 (0.799)	2.1–0.4 (0.837)
Dickey Simpkins	102.0	104.2	1.1–1.4 (0.432)	1.1–1.5 (0.413)
James Edwards	84.4	105.4	0.0–0.9 (0.049)	0.0–0.9 (0.025)
Jason Caffey	93.1	103.7	0.4–1.5 (0.201)	0.3–1.6 (0.143)
Randy Brown	98.9	98.0	1.3–1.1 (0.529)	1.3–1.1 (0.538)

ways, which is what I tried to do, and then I merged them. Note that I cannot come up with any reasonable way that gives a player responsibility for sixty of eighty-two games. Top players may be responsible for about a fourth of team games. Subjectively, I can see this going about as high as a third of team games, but that is pushing it.

The bell curve win–loss records for individuals provide a sense of overall value of players. Jordan contributed a lot of games and a lot of wins. Dennis Rodman was a net positive on the Bulls in 1996, going 6.8–1.6, but his impact was smaller, making a difference probably in half as many games as Jordan. Although Rodman's value is one of the more uncertain things in basketball, I am not uncomfortable asserting that he was valuable but to a limited degree, as his win–loss record implies. In his three years with the Bulls, he missed a lot of games, and the Bulls hardly missed him, going 165–34 (83 percent) with him and 38–9 (81 percent) without him. If the guys replacing him were Toni Kukoc, Dickie Simpkins, John Salley, Bill Wennington, Brian Williams, Jud Buechler, and Jason Caffey—no Hall of Famers—this kind of difference implies that Rodman's overall role was small, even if he filled it well.

What I like less about this method is that it's not straightforward when it comes to making predictions. It doesn't meet the ideal described at the start of this chapter because the win–loss records are fairly context sensitive. Would all of the Bulls' role players have had the same records elsewhere? No. Ron Harper could not have contributed a 7–1 record through a mostly defensive contribution on any team that needed offense. Harper's bell curve record would have been worse on most teams.

Another example of context sensitivity is Allen Iverson. Because he plays for Larry Brown, a very good defensive coach, Iverson's offensive rating is higher than the team's defensive rating, making his high rate of shooting bad shots still valuable. Would he be valuable on a team that desperately needs defense? Yes, but less so. He would still allow teammates to take better shots, but his 101 rating would be a losing offense on an average defensive team. You can see in table 20.17 that Iverson's offensive rating hasn't changed much through time, but his defensive rating got a lot better when Brown took over as coach in 1998.

Table 20.17. Allen Iverson's Bell Curve Win–Loss Records

Season	Off. Rtg.	Def. Rtg.	W–L (%)
1997	104	112	3.7–11.2 (0.251)
1998	109	106	8.7–6.3 (0.582)
1999	105	99	6.8–3.2 (0.684)
2000	102	102	7.0–7.5 (0.480)
2001	106	100	11.0–4.8 (0.698)
2002	101	100	7.7–6.7 (0.534)

That improvement in defense made Iverson a net winning player, or at least a .500 player. If Brown hadn't signed on, would the defense have improved enough to make Iverson's offense valuable? I have doubts.

Other Possible Ways

I know of two other methods for estimating individual wins for players. Note that neither method can estimate individual losses, which further emphasizes the unreality of the concept of associating wins and losses with individuals.

The first alternative way to generate individual wins is a scientific approach proposed by David Berri, a sports economist. Berri generated a statistical model explaining how *team* wins are related to all the measured *team* statistics like offensive rebounds, assists, blocks, etc. That model explains the win data very well, saying that a team adds about 0.058 wins with each offensive rebound, 0.014 wins with each assist, and so forth. Berri then extends the team model to individual players (adding a little bit of complexity to try to account for individual defense). In the end, his model says that multiplying a player's statistics by some weights gives an overall estimate of the number of wins that the player generated. I mentioned Berri's work back in chapter 5 along with other methods that calculate value based on the same kind of weight system. The unique aspect of Berri's method is that he does follow scientific rigor in estimating weights on statistics and how they influence wins. Well, actually there is another unique aspect—how much it ends up valuing offensive rebounds. Chapter 5 showed that his results ended up weighting offensive rebounds nearly four times as much as a point scored! This creates individual win counts that show players like Rodman at the very top. I don't have Berri's numbers for the 1996 season, but his 1998 results show Rodman as creating twenty-one wins, tops in the league by two full wins. In contrast, the bell curve method shows Rodman generated 8.3 wins and 2.4 losses.

Let me get away from basketball for a moment. Berri is a sports economist, and one of the reasons he developed his method was to do, duh, economics. You see, every person in the workforce has a problem evaluating how well they are doing their job and how well their employees are doing. After we finally get out of school and don't have to worry about report cards, a lot of people actually wish they had report cards again just to get a sense of how well they are doing. The benefit that Berri claims you find in basketball and other sports is that there are effectively report cards for the workers—their stats. But there are too many stats without a grade point average to summarize things. Berri wanted a GPA for players, something that summarizes their relative performance. By having something like that, he could study how worker-athletes respond to changes in their workplace. How do workers respond to changes in management (coaching)? How do workers respond to changes in pay (a new contract)? How do workers respond when they know they are being more carefully watched (the last year before free agency)? Are there differences in pay for equal quality workers due to factors like race?

All of these are important social questions—not just basketball questions. They deserve a good measure to allow their study using sports. I personally don't think that Berri's measure is a great one, and I'd be concerned that any studies he does of important social questions would get brushed aside because his measure of quality is questionable.

Now back to basketball.

Finally, Sean Smith developed a technique that he called "win shares," naming it after Bill James's technique that he introduced in his recent *Historical Baseball Abstract*. Smith's method, which (like James's method) is quite new, introduces the concept of a margin—that level of team points below which no team would ever win. He sets that level at 60 percent of the league average for points scored. By setting a margin, every point beyond that margin wins games, he says. Each team then wins a certain number of games, and they may need different numbers of points to get those wins. So he determines how many points above the margin equate to a win, then parses them out based upon a Tendex-like statistic. Though I have some immediate reservations about the method and I have not had time to fully review it, I think it has some promise. The results Smith produces do pass the laugh test—you don't immediately laugh them away when you see them. For example, Smith's top season ever was Shaq's 2000 MVP year, for which Smith estimated twenty-seven wins. Although I estimated a bell curve record of only 16–1 for Shaq that season, a record of 27–0 doesn't seem horribly out of line. It would mean that his teammates had to produce another forty wins and fifteen losses, which is not trivial and is actually comparable to Kobe's game-by-game win–loss record. The results are sane enough to be worthy of a second look, but not in this book.

Both of these methods, as I mentioned in general with respect to individual win–loss records, are difficult to validate. They have reasonable approaches, as I think my own methods have as well. But being unable to validate any of these methods causes lots of controversy, especially when people really want the Holy Grail statistic. It is not scientifically appropriate to criticize any of the above methods by saying, "Michael Jordan isn't ranked the best in their system, so it can't be right." But with all the methods seeming reasonable, it is hard to evaluate their dramatically different results in other ways. Hopefully, someone in the near future will figure out a way to allow validation of individual win–loss records. Otherwise, it is just a popularity contest, and scientists aren't very good at those.

Postscript

These individual win–loss records are interesting summaries of player contribution. They get at what we all want to know—the overall value of players. In such a team game, that value seems inherently to be a function of team context. I think that fact limits the usefulness of the summaries a bit. But I do look at them and will present numbers in the next two chapters for several prominent NBA and WNBA players.

Individual Net Points

Individual wins make sense when looking at an overall season. In a game context, however, a more typical question is how many net points a player contributed. If a team wins a game by nine points, can't we come up with a way to distribute that plus-nine points among the winning teammates?

As with individual wins and losses, the answer is, "Of course, but..."

As with individual wins and losses, the "but" leads to "there is no good way to confirm what is right." Sitting in the stands with Spike Lee, we perceive that a player who scores a lot has a lot of net positive points. But with the game-by-game individual win–loss concept from above (which you should *never* discuss when sitting next to Spike), a player with a higher offensive rating than defensive rating seems to have net positive points, regardless of how many he scores. Because neither perspective can be considered right (even though the concept of net points is so conveniently simple), I want to do *something* to generate it. Besides, I use the concept in chapter 23, so I better give you a definition.

Let's take the case of sitting next to Spike. But instead of having Spike at a Knicks game, let's consider a slightly different scenario. In this hypothetical scenario, the Knicks get fed up with Latrell Sprewell (that's not so hypothetical) and trade him to his hometown team of Milwaukee for Anthony Mason and three hundred thousand cases of beer. The Bucks, fearing that the troublesome Sprewell and the sudden local beer shortage will hurt attendance, request that the Knicks also give them Spike Lee. Knicks General Manager Scott Layden, knowing that a bunch of New York fans with that much beer might actually get drunk enough to like him, goes along with the trade, leaving Spike befuddled but suddenly inspired to write a new screenplay about how the evils of alcohol turn an entire city against one of its favorite sons.

Sorry. That last paragraph serves as mere theater, allowing me to keep the Spike Lee reference and still use the Milwaukee-Charlotte box score from chapter 16 to generate individual net points. So pretend that Spike was at that game, that Sprewell got suspended for the game due to an incident involving poker chips, a monkey, and car keys, and then we'll get to the facts.

You and Spike just witnessed Ray Allen, Sam Cassell, and Glenn Robinson going off against the Hornets, leading the Bucks to a 104–95 win. Each player produced a ton of points, a ton being about twenty in the world of 2001 basketball. Enhancing the table from chapter 16, table 20.18 has some of the Bucks players' relevant offensive and defensive numbers.

This table shows how many points each player produced, and, if we could only come up with how many points they allowed, we'd have net points. But as you no doubt recall, chapter 17 introduced the depressing topic of defense and included a little section called "Conceptual Difficulties" that presented this exact dilemma. Some critic is going to pan me for this, but I will quote myself from that chapter:

> For example, what if Lisa Leslie scores twenty-four points on twenty possessions in a game, but allows twenty-five points on twenty-five possessions? Could you even call her "good" defensively relative to what she did offensively? I see games like this in some of the data we are collecting. The numbers say something but don't necessarily give a value judgment. Sure, Leslie's defensive rating of one hundred is lower than her offensive rating, but she did allow more total points. Did she have a net positive game or a net negative one?
>
> — Dean Oliver, Chapter 17

The chapter goes on to say that there is no good solution to this problem. I did have some faint hope after writing that chapter that by this chapter I would

Table 20.18. Individual Efficiency Statistics for Milwaukee Bucks

Player	Min	Poss.	Off. Rtg.	Pts Prod	Def. Rtg.
Robinson	40	15.8	138	21.8	114
Williams	27	10.2	122	12.4	102
Johnson	37	4.7	105	4.9	104
Allen	46	21.6	119	25.7	113
Cassell	36	18.1	126	22.7	115
Thomas	29	9.0	99	8.9	110
Hunter	14	5.3	70	3.7	109
Caffey	11	1.8	115	2.0	99
Totals	**240**	**86.4**	**118.2**	**102**	**109.9**

have had an epiphany. Didn't happen. What you're going to get here is an average answer—literally. My best answer for determining the net points that a player contributes in a game is the average of the two possible perspectives of defining net points. The first was the efficiency version, and the other was, well, the Spike Lee version:

1. The first method says that a player's net point total is defined by the difference between the player's offensive and defensive ratings and the number of possessions the player uses on the offensive end.

$$\text{Net Points} = \frac{(\text{ORtg} - \text{DRtg}) \times \text{Poss}}{100}$$

2. The second method says that a player's net point total is defined by how many points the player produces minus approximately how many he would give up, assuming his defensive rating and the expected number of possessions he would face while in the game:

$$\text{Net Points} = \text{PtsProd} - \text{DRtg} \times \frac{\text{TmPoss} \times \text{MIN}}{\text{TmMIN} \times 100}$$

where the fraction at the end of the formula is an estimate of how many (individual) possessions the player faces while in a game.

These two versions represent pretty different things. The first one represents efficiency. A player whose offensive rating is lower than his defensive rating will have a negative value of net points, even if he produces forty points. If Jerry Stackhouse scored forty points but went thirteen for fifty from the field doing it, this version would likely give him a negative total of net points. On the other hand, Stackhouse would probably have a positive value of net points using the second method because those forty points would be balanced against the amount of time he was on the court. If he was on the court for forty minutes, his team may have faced eighty possessions and, hence, Stackhouse himself would only face about a fifth of those (sixteen), and a defensive rating of even 120 would mean he allowed only about nineteen points. Averaging these two estimates is a way of handling both concepts. And that average turns out to be pretty useful when looking at trends of individual versus team performance over a season, as chapter 23 does.

But let's get back to this game. Can't keep Spike Lee waiting. Adding the different versions of net points to table 20.18 produces table 20.19.

Spike's take on things would be the second version, showing Ray Allen and Sam Cassell leading the way. You can just nod your head and smile, while noting

Table 20.19. Individual Net Points Statistics for Milwaukee Bucks

Player	Min	Poss.	Off. Rtg.	Pts Prod	Def. Rtg	Net v 1	Net v 2	Net Avg
Robinson	40	15.8	138	21.8	114	3.7	5.3	4.5
Williams	27	10.2	122	12.4	102	2.1	2.5	2.3
Johnson	37	4.7	105	4.9	104	0.0	-8.9	-4.4
Allen	46	21.6	119	25.7	113	1.2	6.9	4.0
Cassell	36	18.1	126	22.7	115	2.0	7.9	4.9
Thomas	29	9.0	99	8.9	110	-1.0	-2.6	-1.8
Hunter	14	5.3	70	3.7	109	-2.1	-1.8	-2.0
Caffey	11	1.8	115	2.0	99	0.3	-1.9	-0.8
Totals	240	86.4	118.2	102	109.9	6.2	7.4	6.8

privately that actually Robinson was most efficient and contributed about the same number of net points.

Overall, the Bucks won by nine points on the scoreboard. Both of these methods are supposed to yield a sum over all teammates that is close to plus-nine, but both fall a little short in this game, coming up with a team total of about plus-seven. That small error is entirely due to the conceptual problem that no player is a team.

In the end, individual net point totals are useful in summarizing player contributions in a game. As chapter 23 will show, trends in how individuals contribute net points to a team are comparable to team trends in net points, allowing subjective comparisons of what players are really driving a team, positively or negatively.

Endnote

1. For many players, games started is not an easily available statistic. As a consequence, I have frequently left it out of the estimates of individual "games."

Chapter 21

Player Evaluation Files: The Great Ones

Most of the people who have read Bill James's books on baseball were primarily interested in the evaluation of players. How much credit players should get for the success or failure of their teams is not only important to the players—it's also important to fans. I don't have enough room in this book to address every possible debate about basketball player quality. Nor do I have the Holy Grail statistic (which probably doesn't exist) to rank all the NBA players in history from number one to number 3,042 or WNBA players from number two to number 392 (with number one clearly being Cynthia Cooper). But I have some tools that add dimension to the debates. In some cases, I can only use those tools to raise more questions, but in others, I think I have a pretty good handle on whether Joe beats Jack.

But is there really ever any conclusive answer to who the best player is? Has anyone ever walked away from a debate saying, "Y'know, Jim was right about Joe being better than Jack"? People usually argue until their dying day for their favorite players, and then they influence their kids enough to ensure that their kids argue for the same player. Like politics and religion, sports heroes run in the family and come out of weird innate values that people have. No chapter in a book like this is going to change that.

And perhaps it shouldn't. Bill James keeps writing books about baseball's greatest players (at least three or four already) because people always want a new opinion, not an absolute answer. I think James legitimately tries to develop ratings that are "absolute," but every time he comes out with a new set of ratings, people will pay money to look for their favorite player and see how James's rating of him changed. If James kept saying the same things because he'd found the ultimate rating technique, people would start buying new books looking for other people with different opinions. All James has to do is change the order of his rankings in order to get a new book published. It's a horrible racket. Naturally, I don't think that's why he does so many different versions of player rankings. In fact, he probably doesn't like doing it. He completely rewrote his most recent book because he changed his mind about how to rank players midway through it.

I don't want to write eight books on evaluating players. As you can probably see from a few earlier chapters, overall ranking of players is not the highest priority of this book. For the purpose of coaching a team—an activity that goes forward in time—I don't see the value in looking back to assess the difference between the twenty-first and the twenty-eighth top-ranked players in history. Even if number twenty-one and number twenty-eight are contemporary players who are available on the free agent market, if twenty-one is a forward and twenty-eight is a point guard and I need a point guard, I'm going after twenty-eight over twenty-one. Individual player ratings aren't accurate enough to be trusted in a case where the need is so obvious. Maybe I could trade number twenty-one for someone better, but that's second-order thinking. In a world where player value is uncertain, the first-order thought—take care of your need with the best player available—is the thought that you should obey. If player value were much simpler and clearer, like the values of pieces and positions in a chess game, *then* you could think about second-order things, which is what chess is about.

So what you see below are a lot of first-order discussions about player value. I've broken those first-order discussions into two chapters. The first chapter discusses some of the NBA's greatest players and what they did so well. It definitely doesn't discuss all of the greatest players, but some of them have interesting stories to be told. For instance, Magic Johnson and Larry Bird were noted for making teammates better, but did they really do so? Bill Russell versus Wilt Chamberlain was the rivalry that probably inspired the phrase "defense wins championships," but was Russell so much better defensively? John Stockton and Karl Malone played together for a long time, so how should we split the credit for the Jazz's success between the two? Those discussions are in this chapter. The second chapter examines some of the less frequently discussed players. For instance, what has been the value of "freaks," players too short or too skinny to fit the mold of a classic basketball player? How valuable can shooting specialists like Reggie Miller or defensive specialists like Bruce Bowen be to a team? The second chapter also looks at a few players who couldn't live up to the "potential" they were labeled with, then at players who played for a long time but maybe never played at an exceptional level. And, finally, this second chapter looks at some of the highest-profile WNBA players, though "high profile" women players don't have nearly as high a profile as their male counterparts. How good are they, and how has that changed over the brief history of their league?

For both the questions being debated and some of the answers, let me give credit to members of the Association of Professional Basketball Research (APBR).

It takes the guts of Mike Goodman to put out his overall historical ratings of players (with Vlade Divac rated higher than Willis Reed) and then get hammered for them. It takes the wisdom of people such as Bijan Bayne, David Bender, Robert Bradley, Chuck Durante, John Grasso, Al Hoffman, Bob Kuska, and Mike Tamada to generate useful insight out of the hammering. They have significantly contributed to my thoughts on the topics I discuss below.

Magic, Bird, and Jordan

These are only three of many candidates for the title of greatest player in history. They are, however, the only ones in the modern statistical era for whom I can do reasonable statistical comparisons. Although a claim can be made for Shaquille O'Neal's candidacy here, I've chosen to discuss him later along with Kobe Bryant, who has teamed with Shaq for all three of his championships.

Numbers alone will never tell the full story of what Magic Johnson, Larry Bird, and Michael Jordan brought to the game. They were good, and the way they were good inspired other players to be like them. Numbers don't really capture the inspiration they provided. What numbers do provide, however, is a nice summary of thoughts that can be manipulated with rules—rules that, amazingly, have been generally agreed to. For example, if one MVP is good (the "thought," in this case), then 1+1+1+1+1+1 = 6 MVPs must be better (addition being the "rule"). We don't have to go into the details of each and every one of those MVP seasons to say that a player who wins six MVPs is probably better than one who wins only one. A pretty good summary of the info is 6 > 1. It isn't the whole story, but the details would have to be extremely convincing to change our conclusion. That's what I look for in the numbers—points that would be hard to refute without a significant amount of research.

Table 21.1 provides a summary of Magic Johnson's numbers.

Table 21.1. Magic Johnson's Career Summary Statistics

Season	Tm	G	Floor %	Off. Rtg.	Pts Prod/G	% Tm Poss	Stop %	Def. Rtg.	W–L (%)
1980	LAL	77	0.56	113	19.9	22%	0.55	101	10.4–2.3 (0.819)
1981	LAL	37	0.57	115	23.3	26%	0.62	98	6.4–0.7 (0.899)
1982	LAL	78	0.59	118	21.8	22%	0.56	102	12.4–1.5 (0.895)
1983	LAL	79	0.59	119	20.6	22%	0.54	103	11.9–1.4 (0.895)
1984	LAL	67	0.58	118	22.3	23%	0.53	105	10.2–1.7 (0.855)
1985	LAL	77	0.60	122	22.3	23%	0.47	106	11.2–1.3 (0.898)
1986	LAL	72	0.59	121	22.9	25%	0.47	106	10.4–1.3 (0.886)
1987	LAL	80	0.60	123	27.1	29%	0.49	106	13.2–1.3 (0.909)
1988	LAL	72	0.57	117	23.1	26%	0.48	107	9.9–2.5 (0.797)
1989	LAL	77	0.58	123	26.0	27%	0.52	105	13.2–1.0 (0.928)
1990	LAL	79	0.58	124	25.1	27%	0.50	106	13.2–1.1 (0.924)
1991	LAL	79	0.57	122	23.1	26%	0.50	104	12.8–1.1 (0.920)
1996	LAL	32	0.54	114	16.3	25%	0.48	107	3.1–1.2 (0.717)
13–Yr Totals		**906**	**0.58**	**120**	**22.9**	**25%**	**0.52**	**104**	**139–19 (0.882)**

An offensive rating of 120 and a defensive rating of 104 over a career in which the average rating was about 108—that's impressive. You won't see many players throughout the rest of this chapter with numbers even close. Those who saw Magic play may balk at the good (not great) defensive rating because Magic did not have the greatest defensive reputation. I am actually fairly comfortable with the number, though. What made Magic a good defender was his height. His height allowed him to get defensive rebounds, to get steals from shorter guards who had a hard time passing over or around him, and to cover multiple different positions reasonably well, a flexibility that a coach loves. All of those abilities show up in his good defensive number. On the offensive end, Magic produced about twenty-three points per game and used about a quarter of the Lakers' possessions. His career progression of offensive ratings shows how he was able to step up his offense around 1986 when Kareem Abdul-Jabbar slowed down. Through Magic's thirteen-year career, he generated a net win–loss record of 139–19. That is nearly eleven wins per season and only about one loss or, per eighty-two games, about 12.5–1.7. Or you could point out that, in 1987, Magic posted thirteen wins and one loss, while the crosstown Clippers posted twelve wins and seventy losses.

Larry Bird also had a thirteen-year career. It's probably not fair to present two all-time greats so early in the chapter because their numbers are so similar that you might think "ho-hum." But Bird's statistics, for the record, are not ho-hum (table 21.2).

Magic's offense was slightly better. Bird's defense was slightly better. Magic's net winning percentage was higher. Bird had more wins. In Magic's best seasons, his win–loss record was about 13.2–1.2. In Bird's best seasons, his win–loss record was about 14.8–1.5. If I needed a forward, I'd go with Bird, and if I needed a point guard, I'd go with Magic. If forced to choose, I probably would go with Magic.

Something to add here is a look at whether these two guys really did make their teammates better, since they were probably the players most prominently mentioned as doing so. It turns out to be a mixed story. Some players definitely

Table 21.2. Larry Bird's Career Summary Statistics

Season	Tm	G	Floor %	Off. Rtg.	Pts Prod/G	% Tm Poss	Stop %	Def. Rtg.	W–L (%)
1980	BOS	82	0.52	109	20.9	25%	0.59	98	11.6–2.9 (0.798)
1981	BOS	82	0.52	107	21.4	24%	0.59	99	11.8–4.1 (0.740)
1982	BOS	77	0.56	114	23.0	25%	0.59	99	12.7–1.9 (0.868)
1983	BOS	79	0.56	115	23.3	25%	0.59	98	13.3–1.4 (0.905)
1984	BOS	79	0.56	115	24.5	27%	0.57	101	13.4–1.9 (0.874)
1985	BOS	80	0.57	119	27.6	28%	0.56	103	14.9–1.7 (0.897)
1986	BOS	82	0.55	117	25.8	28%	0.57	99	14.6–1.3 (0.916)
1987	BOS	74	0.57	120	27.4	27%	0.55	104	13.9–1.5 (0.903)
1988	BOS	76	0.57	121	27.6	29%	0.54	106	13.6–2.0 (0.874)
1989	BOS	6	0.53	109	17.9	25%	0.52	107	0.5–0.4 (0.566)
1990	BOS	75	0.52	110	23.9	27%	0.54	105	9.9–5.0 (0.666)
1991	BOS	60	0.51	108	19.9	24%	0.56	103	7.1–3.8 (0.649)
1992	BOS	45	0.52	112	20.3	25%	0.54	104	5.7–2.3 (0.716)
13–Yr Totals		**897**	**0.55**	**114**	**23.9**	**26%**	**0.57**	**101**	**143–30 (0.825)**

seemed to play better with these guys, but many didn't seem impacted. Nate "Tiny" Archibald is an example of a player who definitely played better with Bird. He had a mediocre year in 1979 with an offensive rating of one hundred, but with Bird joining him in 1980, his rating shot up to 114 and then stayed high. I have tried to estimate Archibald's ratings before 1979 (using a turnover rate of 21 percent per possession, as he showed later), and they appear to be consistent with the one hundred rating (though he was probably better in 1973 and earlier). Archibald's numbers in table 21.3 show the sharp increase in 1980 with Bird's arrival. The increase was due in part to him not having to take as large a role in the offense (as chapter 19 would suggest).

No other players showed nearly as significant an improvement as Archibald did with Bird's arrival in Boston. Cedric Maxwell (table 21.4) had almost no change in his efficiency and showed continuously good ratings even after he left the Celtics in the mid-1980s. Maxwell appears to have been a rather underrated player, also.

Chris Ford showed an improvement in his rating from 1979 to 1980, but not his floor percentage. That was due to him taking advantage of the three-point line that was new in Bird's rookie year. Lesser players like Rick Robey and Jeff Judkins showed minimal improvements. Dave Cowens showed almost no change.

Table 21.3. Nate Archibald's Career Summary Statistics

Season	Tm	G	Floor %	Off. Rtg.	Pts Prod/G	% Tm Poss	Stop %	Def. Rtg.	W–L (%)
1974	KCO	35	0.50	102	18.9	18%	0.43	102	2.6–2.8 (0.481)
1975	KCO	82	0.48	99	26.0	24%	0.44	100	7.2–8.1 (0.472)
1976	KCK	78	0.49	99	25.1	22%	0.42	102	5.6–9.0 (0.384)
1977	NYN	34	0.49	99	21.3	21%	0.44	101	2.3–3.4 (0.408)
1979	BOS	69	0.50	100	11.8	22%	0.40	109	1.6–5.2 (0.232)
1980	BOS	80	0.56	114	16.3	19%	0.41	105	8.0–2.7 (0.748)
1981	BOS	80	0.55	111	15.6	19%	0.38	107	6.3–4.1 (0.606)
1982	BOS	68	0.55	111	14.6	20%	0.36	109	4.7–3.3 (0.587)
1983	BOS	66	0.52	104	12.1	20%	0.35	108	2.5–4.0 (0.382)
1984	MIL	46	0.51	101	7.9	17%	0.40	107	1.2–2.5 (0.322)
10–Yr Totals		**638**	**0.54**	**108**	**17.2**	**19%**	**0.40**	**105**	**24–22 (0.526)**

Table 21.4. Cedric Maxwell's Career Summary Statistics

Season	Tm	G	Floor %	Off. Rtg.	Pts Prod/G	% Tm Poss	Stop %	Def. Rtg.	W–L (%)
1978	DOS	72	0.55	109	7.5	18%	0.59	97	4.4–0.9 (0.832)
1979	BOS	80	0.60	121	19.0	19%	0.51	105	11.3–1.3 (0.899)
1980	BOS	80	0.61	123	16.7	18%	0.49	102	10.5–0.5 (0.952)
1981	BOS	81	0.61	123	15.0	17%	0.46	104	9.7–0.7 (0.936)
1982	BOS	78	0.60	119	14.7	18%	0.45	105	8.6–1.3 (0.872)
1983	BOS	79	0.56	113	12.2	17%	0.44	104	6.3–2.1 (0.756)
1984	BOS	80	0.56	113	12.6	17%	0.43	107	6.3–2.9 (0.683)
1985	BOS	57	0.59	121	11.1	17%	0.41	109	4.5–1.0 (0.823)
1986	LAC	76	0.56	114	15.1	19%	0.44	112	5.5–4.5 (0.549)
1987	LAC	35	0.58	116	14.4	18%	0.41	114	2.5–1.8 (0.579)
1987	HOU	46	0.62	125	7.5	16%	0.42	108	2.7–0.3 (0.906)
1988	HOU	71	0.56	113	4.2	15%	0.44	107	2.0–1.0 (0.673)
11–Yr Totals		**835**	**0.58**	**118**	**12.8**	**18%**	**0.46**	**106**	**74–18 (0.804)**

Table 21.5. Robert Parish's Career Summary Statistics

Season	Tm	G	Floor %	Off. Rtg.	Pts Prod/G	% Tm Poss	Stop %	Def. Rtg.	W–L (%)
1977	GSW	77	0.51	102	9.1	17%	0.63	95	4.7–1.8 (0.719)
1978	GSW	82	0.48	94	12.0	24%	0.62	95	4.7–5.0 (0.488)
1979	GSW	76	0.51	100	16.3	24%	0.68	94	8.6–4.0 (0.684)
1980	GSW	72	0.51	101	16.2	26%	0.59	102	5.3–5.5 (0.488)
1981	BOS	82	0.57	113	17.3	26%	0.64	96	11.0–1.1 (0.908)
1982	BOS	80	0.56	112	18.5	25%	0.60	99	10.6–2.0 (0.839)
1983	BOS	78	0.58	114	17.8	23%	0.59	98	10.5–1.2 (0.899)
1984	BOS	80	0.57	115	17.6	21%	0.53	102	10.5–2.0 (0.841)
1985	BOS	79	0.57	114	16.8	19%	0.51	105	9.4–2.8 (0.769)
1986	BOS	81	0.56	112	15.4	21%	0.54	100	9.3–2.0 (0.824)
1987	BOS	80	0.56	113	16.8	19%	0.53	104	9.6–3.4 (0.740)
1988	BOS	74	0.57	114	13.2	18%	0.52	107	6.9–2.9 (0.704)
1989	BOS	80	0.59	118	18.1	21%	0.55	106	11.0–2.1 (0.838)
1990	BOS	79	0.58	116	14.6	20%	0.51	106	8.1–2.3 (0.780)
1991	BOS	81	0.60	122	14.1	19%	0.57	103	9.9–0.8 (0.927)
1992	BOS	79	0.56	113	13.2	20%	0.56	104	8.0–2.3 (0.777)
1993	BOS	79	0.57	113	12.1	20%	0.58	104	7.5–2.3 (0.762)
1994	BOS	74	0.53	105	11.0	20%	0.54	106	4.1–4.5 (0.478)
1995	CHA	81	0.47	94	4.9	16%	0.54	104	1.2–4.2 (0.216)
1996	CHA	74	0.52	106	4.1	14%	0.55	108	1.8–2.5 (0.416)
1997	CHI	43	0.51	103	3.7	20%	0.49	104	0.8–0.9 (0.485)
21–Yr Totals		**1611**	**0.55**	**111**	**13.7**	**21%**	**0.57**	**102**	**149–54 (0.735)**

Note: Assumes a 21% turnover per possession rate for 1977 season.

After Bird's rookie year, Robert Parish joined the Celtics from Golden State, and he showed a significant improvement in his performance (table 21.5). His offensive rating went from 101 with Golden State to 113 with Boston in 1981. Parish was admittedly still young and might have improved some if he had stayed with Golden State, but the jump he showed in Boston was large enough and consistent enough that it appears to be the Bird effect.

Dennis Johnson, a prominent Boston acquisition in 1984, showed almost no change in his offensive rating and floor percentage that season. His rating went from 106 to 107, and he used 2 percent fewer possessions (table 21.6). When Bird missed most of the 1989 season, Johnson was near the end of his career, and his

Table 21.6. Dennis Johnson's Career Summary Statistics

Season	Tm	G	Floor %	Off. Rtg.	Pts Prod/G	% Tm Poss	Stop %	Def. Rtg.	W–L (%)
1977	SEA	81	0.52	101	9.2	16%	0.54	97	4.4–2.6 (0.625)
1978	SEA	81	0.52	103	12.9	21%	0.49	99	5.7–3.5 (0.623)
1979	SEA	80	0.51	103	15.8	21%	0.48	101	6.5–4.8 (0.578)
1980	SEA	81	0.51	104	18.8	24%	0.49	102	7.4–5.6 (0.568)
1981	PHO	79	0.53	108	18.5	24%	0.48	100	8.3–3.3 (0.716)
1982	PHO	80	0.53	108	19.3	23%	0.44	104	7.8–4.8 (0.618)
1983	PHO	77	0.52	106	14.8	20%	0.46	102	6.4–3.8 (0.626)
1984	BOS	80	0.52	107	13.7	18%	0.44	106	5.4–4.8 (0.529)
1985	BOS	80	0.53	109	17.0	20%	0.42	109	5.6–5.6 (0.500)
1986	BOS	78	0.53	107	16.2	21%	0.44	104	6.3–4.7 (0.571)
1987	BOS	79	0.52	106	15.3	19%	0.41	109	4.4–6.8 (0.392)
1988	BOS	77	0.53	108	15.0	20%	0.41	111	4.2–6.3 (0.402)
1989	BOS	72	0.51	103	11.7	17%	0.43	111	2.3–6.5 (0.259)
1990	BOS	75	0.54	109	9.4	15%	0.44	109	3.6–3.8 (0.491)
14–Yr Totals		**1100**	**0.52**	**106**	**14.9**	**20%**	**0.45**	**105**	**74–64 (0.535)**

Note: Assumes 22% turnover per possession rate in 1977.

rating did drop about five points before bouncing back up in his last season, suggesting that losing Bird's presence late in his career did hurt.

Magic's effect is a little more difficult to see. Kareem Abdul-Jabbar posted ratings of 113 and 115 before Magic joined the Lakers in 1980, then wasn't below 116 until he started getting phased out of the offense in 1987. It's not as though this increase was due to Kareem reaching his peak age—he was thirty-two when Magic arrived and should have been on the decline. It's the absence of a decline that makes his improvement seem related to Magic's arrival. Table 21.7 shows Kareem's stats back to 1974, with his pre-1978 statistics estimated using a turnover rate of 17 percent (which is based upon his rates later).

Jamaal Wilkes was also positively affected by the presence of Magic. Shown in table 21.8 are Wilkes's summary stats with a 17 percent turnover rate prior to 1978 (also estimated based on his later rates). Although Wilkes's offensive rating didn't jump in 1980 when Magic first arrived, his numbers are high enough above the rest of his career during that 1981–1983 period to suggest a positive influence.

Finally, there is Bob McAdoo, who served with enough different teams to provide a good history of his efficiency before joining the Lakers. As with Wilkes, the

Table 21.7. Kareem Abdul-Jabbar's Career Summary Statistics

Season	Tm	G	Floor %	Off. Rtg.	Pts Prod/G	% Tm Poss	Stop %	Def. Rtg.	W–L (%)
1974	MIL	81	0.54	108	25.9	25%	0.65	89	16.9–1.1 (0.937)
1975	MIL	65	0.52	103	27.9	30%	0.65	92	12.3–3.0 (0.805)
1976	LAL	82	0.54	108	27.0	27%	0.73	90	17.4–1.5 (0.920)
1977	LAL	82	0.57	114	24.5	27%	0.67	92	15.4–0.7 (0.955)
1978	LAL	62	0.56	113	24.2	27%	0.67	94	11.4–0.8 (0.935)
1979	LAL	80	0.57	115	23.4	23%	0.61	98	14.1–1.5 (0.904)
1980	LAL	82	0.59	118	23.1	24%	0.58	100	13.8–1.2 (0.918)
1981	LAL	80	0.59	118	23.6	25%	0.55	101	13.1–1.3 (0.907)
1982	LAL	76	0.58	116	21.3	24%	0.52	104	10.5–2.1 (0.832)
1983	LAL	79	0.59	118	19.1	23%	0.51	104	10.1–1.5 (0.873)
1984	LAL	80	0.58	115	19.2	24%	0.49	106	8.9–3.0 (0.748)
1985	LAL	79	0.60	120	19.7	23%	0.51	104	10.8–1.3 (0.889)
1986	LAL	79	0.58	117	21.1	25%	0.48	106	10.0–2.2 (0.822)
1987	LAL	78	0.57	114	16.0	21%	0.47	107	7.4–3.0 (0.710)
1988	LAL	80	0.54	108	13.0	20%	0.48	107	5.4–4.4 (0.552)
1989	LAL	74	0.52	104	9.4	19%	0.48	107	2.8–4.1 (0.406)
16–Yr Totals		1239	0.58	115	21.1	23%	0.58	99	118–26 (0.817)

Table 21.8. Jamaal Wilkes's Career Summary Statistics

Season	Tm	G	Floor %	Off. Rtg.	Pts Prod/G	% Team Poss	Stop %	Def. Rtg.	W–L (%)
1975	GSW	82	0.48	97	13.8	21%	0.52	97	5.2–5.5 (0.486)
1976	GSW	82	0.49	98	16.6	23%	0.53	94	7.5–4.5 (0.628)
1977	GSW	76	0.51	103	16.7	21%	0.52	99	7.1–4.1 (0.631)
1978	LAL	51	0.50	99	13.6	21%	0.55	99	3.5–3.2 (0.523)
1979	LAL	82	0.52	104	17.7	22%	0.50	103	6.9–5.8 (0.546)
1980	LAL	82	0.51	104	18.5	22%	0.45	105	5.8–7.1 (0.450)
1981	LAL	81	0.55	110	20.1	23%	0.43	106	8.1–4.7 (0.630)
1982	LAL	82	0.56	112	18.4	22%	0.39	109	7.0–4.5 (0.609)
1983	LAL	80	0.57	114	17.4	22%	0.38	109	6.6–3.6 (0.646)
1985	LAL	42	0.51	103	7.5	19%	0.38	110	0.8–2.0 (0.295)
1986	LAC	13	0.47	97	6.0	19%	0.40	114	0.1–0.7 (0.098)

Table 21.9. Bob McAdoo's Career Summary Statistics

Season	Tm	G	Floor %	Off. Rtg.	Pts Prod/G	% Team Poss	Stop %	Def. Rtg.	W–L (%)
1974	BUF	74	0.55	111	27.6	25%	0.61	95	14.2–1.8 (0.887)
1975	BUF	82	0.53	107	31.3	30%	0.59	95	16.0–3.2 (0.833)
1976	BUF	78	0.51	103	29.4	30%	0.58	96	12.6–5.2 (0.707)
1977	BUF	20	0.50	99	22.6	27%	0.58	98	2.0–1.9 (0.515)
1977	NYK	52	0.53	106	24.4	26%	0.59	97	8.0–2.3 (0.775)
1978	NYK	79	0.53	106	25.0	26%	0.57	99	11.1–4.4 (0.714)
1979	NYK	40	0.55	107	24.1	26%	0.53	103	5.0–2.8 (0.636)
1979	BOS	20	0.51	100	18.3	26%	0.48	106	1.0–2.0 (0.325)
1980	DET	58	0.49	98	19.9	25%	0.49	108	2.3–7.6 (0.234)
1981	DET	6	0.42	82	12.4	26%	0.57	101	0.1–0.8 (0.071)
1981	NJN	10	0.51	103	8.2	24%	0.53	104	0.3–0.4 (0.466)
1982	LAL	41	0.52	104	8.7	22%	0.49	105	1.5–1.7 (0.462)
1983	LAL	47	0.56	111	12.8	24%	0.52	103	3.6–1.3 (0.736)
1985	LAL	66	0.54	108	9.4	21%	0.47	106	3.0–2.4 (0.553)
1986	PHI	29	0.50	101	9.2	21%	0.42	108	0.7–1.8 (0.276)

turnover rate for early seasons in McAdoo's career is estimated at 17 percent based on his later seasons (table 21.9).

Aside from McAdoo's 1974 season, his two most efficient seasons were in 1983 and 1985 at ages thirty-one and thirty-three with Magic distributing the ball. Magic made old guys young again, it appears.

Michael Jordan didn't have to make his teammates better, though I don't doubt that he did. Previous chapters showed how Steve Kerr and Ron Harper both had higher ratings when playing alongside Jordan, for example. Even disregarding any complementary effects, Jordan's individual numbers (table 21.10) stand on their own, and they look even better than those of Magic and Bird.

Until his return to the Wizards in 2002, both Jordan's win–loss record and his winning percentage were better than Magic's and Bird's. His win–loss record of 2002 actually is worse than it should be if you adjust for how much the team defense improved when Jordan played, but I haven't done so here. Having looked at Jordan's numbers extensively already in this book, I don't have much more to

Table 21.10. Michael Jordan's Career Summary Statistics

Season	Tm	G	Floor %	Off. Rtg.	Pts Prod/G	% Tm Poss	Stop %	Def. Rtg.	W–L (%)
1985	CHI	82	0.58	118	27.6	30%	0.53	107	13.4–3.2 (0.808)
1986	CHI	18	0.53	109	20.4	36%	0.58	107	1.5–1.2 (0.563)
1987	CHI	82	0.57	117	33.5	36%	0.55	104	16.0–3.2 (0.834)
1988	CHI	82	0.60	123	32.1	33%	0.58	101	17.8–0.8 (0.955)
1989	CHI	81	0.59	122	31.6	32%	0.59	103	17.1–1.2 (0.932)
1990	CHI	82	0.58	122	31.2	32%	0.55	105	16.2–1.6 (0.908)
1991	CHI	82	0.61	125	28.8	31%	0.58	102	16.1–0.5 (0.968)
1992	CHI	80	0.59	121	27.7	30%	0.56	102	15.4–1.1 (0.934)
1993	CHI	78	0.57	119	29.4	33%	0.58	102	15.5–1.7 (0.900)
1995	CHI	17	0.52	108	25.3	31%	0.54	103	2.3–1.2 (0.663)
1996	CHI	82	0.58	122	27.2	31%	0.57	99	15.9–0.6 (0.964)
1997	CHI	82	0.57	120	26.1	31%	0.53	102	14.8–1.3 (0.922)
1998	CHI	82	0.56	113	25.6	31%	0.52	100	14.1–2.4 (0.854)
2002	WAS	60	0.49	99	22.0	35%	0.53	106	3.3–8.3 (0.286)
14-Yr Totals		**990**	**0.57**	**119**	**28.5**	**32%**	**0.56**	**103**	**180–28 (0.864)**

say here other than that he was probably the best player to have played (since statistics became more available in 1978).

Dennis Rodman

First, given the colorful nature of Rodman's career, it seems fitting that the Rodman file should have a theme song:

Just sit right back and you'll hear a tale,
A tale of a fateful trip
That started right at courtside
And ended with a kick.

The victim was a photo-man.
The guilty had hair of blue.
They met one day in a painful way,
As I'll describe to you.
This story's all too true.

The rebound headed out of bounds
Next we were shocked to see
Rodman tripped on the cameraman
Then kicked him in the knee.
They said it was his knee.

The kick earned Rodman a big fat fine
And a civil lawsuit, too,
From Eugene Amos,
The Commish'ner, too.
A psychiatrist . . . and his couch.

The mood is set
So if you can
We'll take a scan
Through the Rodman file.

Probably the player of modern times whose value has been most debated, Rodman was the most extreme role player in the NBA for five or six years. Rodman was asked to get rebounds and play defense. Everything else he did—the book signings in a wedding dress, the technical fouls, the cameraman assaults—those were inevitable examples of Dennis being Dennis. They were definitely distractions, and no one knows how to quantify that.

On the court, some have said that Rodman was both the greatest rebounder and greatest defender in history. The rebounding claim may be true. Rodman won the 1993 rebounding title by 4.4 per game, a feat bettered only by Bill Russell in 1959. Rodman rebounded about 25 percent of total rebounds available (10 percent would be expected with ten players on the court), slightly more than Russell or Chamberlain typically got. On defense, Rodman was legitimately good, especially early in his career when he guarded a variety of different players using his good foot speed and active arms. But Rodman also developed a reputation with the referees for flopping and for playing dirty (subtly grabbing players' bodies in places where the refs wouldn't normally look, to put it nicely)—and the underlying incidents raised questions about his ability. Rodman also seemed to be less effective as a man defender after he decided to become a rebounding machine.

That gets at the whole Dennis Rodman story, which won't ever be a Sunday night family movie but will likely be told on film sometime. Rodman's career started rather anonymously, exploding in 1987 when he claimed that Larry Bird won the MVP "because he's white." Rodman didn't become any better at that point, but people immediately knew who he was. Rodman apologized to Bird, and Bird didn't accept the apology. The following season, he played poorly as Rodman's Pistons beat the Celtics in the playoffs. More attention was focused on Rodman with a *Sports Illustrated* story and numerous short television profiles. With all the attention—good and bad—something happened to Rodman. He retreated a little bit from the player he had been becoming and became something else. Before the 1988 playoff matchup, Rodman averaged 20 percent of the team possessions on the offensive end and had ratings of 108 and 112. He ran up and down the court, finishing on the fast break and around the basket. His man defense was already good, and he got noticed for it in the 1988 finals. But after that point, Rodman backed off on his offense, using only 15 percent of team possessions in 1989. It seemed that Rodman intentionally focused his game. In 1991, right after winning back-to-back titles, Rodman seemed to start becoming the robo-rebounder that people would remember him as. At that time, his percentage of the offense dropped to 13 percent. The 1992 season was similar, but Rodman's rebound tally increased, and he won the first of seven straight rebounding titles.

Then, with Chuck Daly retiring as Pistons coach after 1992, Rodman went "out of control" in 1993. He led the league with 18.3 rebounds per game, but he further shunned standard offense (only 12 percent of team possessions) at a time when the Pistons could have used his help. The team defense fell apart, and it's difficult to say whether Rodman's failing attitude had anything to do with it. Rodman's net win–loss record went from a career best of 12.9–0.6 (.957) in 1992 to a near worst 6.2–3.6 (.635) in 1993. So, with the Pistons franchise beginning to come undone after a very successful run, Rodman was traded to San Antonio before the 1994 season.

In two years in San Antonio, Rodman was at his best and his worst. He played very well when Coach John Lucas allowed him to do whatever he wanted and be whomever he wanted in 1994. Then came the start of the 1995 season when Lucas resigned, Bob Hill was hired, and Rodman was deciding whether to play, working out on his own before joining the Spurs in December. The Spurs went 40–9 with him the rest of the way and were a modest 22–11 without him over the season, including a month where he was injured. When Rodman played, his on-court performance was very good. In 1995, as in 1994, his floor percentage and offensive rating were both very high, and his defensive rating remained at the one-hundred level. His net winning percentage was about .900 (table 21.11).

But the Spurs were tiring of his distractions—a word they used often. One of their big complaints was that Rodman wouldn't join the team huddle at time-outs, but as Dave Berri pointed out to me, what did Rodman need to hear in the huddle? A play wasn't going to be called for him, and he knew his job was to play defense and get rebounds. That doesn't justify Rodman's behavior; he was not behaving as a professional—another common Spurs' phrase—but he was helping the team win. The Spurs probably could have found a way to work with him, even if he wasn't in the huddle. Instead, they let the distraction distract them from winning, and they shipped Rodman off to Chicago for Will Perdue. Perdue, though he was coming off his best year in Chicago, had a win–loss record of only 4.8–2.0 in a full season, whereas Rodman had a win–loss record of 5.9–0.4 in just forty-nine games. The Spurs apparently were willing to sacrifice a few wins just to avoid distractions.

That trade hurt the Spurs a lot more than it helped the Bulls. The Bulls probably would have won three straight titles even without Rodman, who contributed only six to eight wins and one to three losses per year in Chicago (also recall that the Bulls won 81 percent of their games without him during that three-year stretch). But the Spurs fell behind the Sonics in the hunt for the West and lost to the Jazz in the second round of the playoffs in 1996. San Antonio tried to put a good spin on it all. Coach Hill said, "You've got to have talent, that's a given. But the biggest challenge is to get talented people with character." And, of Rodman's replacement, Charles Smith, Hill said, "He fit in with everybody else so well. He's very mature, very bright, and he's a professional."

Throughout his career (see table 21.11), Rodman made a net positive contribution, if there was any doubt. I used to wonder whether he hurt his value by

Table 21.11. Dennis Rodman's Career Summary Statistics

Season	Tm	G	Floor %	Off. Rtg.	Pts Prod/G	% Tm Poss	Stop %	Def. Rtg.	W–L (%)
1987	DET	77	0.55	108	6.6	19%	0.52	104	3.0–1.9 (0.616)
1988	DET	82	0.57	112	12.0	20%	0.55	103	7.2–2.2 (0.763)
1989	DET	82	0.60	119	9.8	15%	0.57	102	8.1–0.7 (0.918)
1990	DET	82	0.63	125	9.6	13%	0.55	101	8.7–0.3 (0.969)
1991	DET	82	0.58	115	9.4	13%	0.59	101	9.3–1.3 (0.878)
1992	DET	82	0.59	121	12.0	13%	0.64	99	12.9–0.6 (0.957)
1993	DET	62	0.53	107	10.0	12%	0.63	102	6.2–3.6 (0.635)
1994	SAN	79	0.57	115	7.9	10%	0.61	100	9.7–1.2 (0.888)
1995	SAN	49	0.59	119	10.2	14%	0.63	100	5.9–0.4 (0.935)
1996	CHI	64	0.53	107	8.7	13%	0.61	98	6.1–1.9 (0.765)
1997	CHI	55	0.54	109	9.2	13%	0.62	98	6.1–1.4 (0.809)
1998	CHI	80	0.52	105	7.8	11%	0.60	97	7.7–2.7 (0.743)
1999	LAL	23	0.46	90	4.0	8%	0.60	100	0.8–3.0 (0.207)
2000	DAL	12	0.49	101	5.5	9%	0.59	103	0.6–0.8 (0.447)
14–Yr Totals		**911**	**0.57**	**114**	**9.2**	**13%**	**0.59**	**100**	**92–22 (0.808)**

ignoring his offense after 1988. But I'm pretty convinced now that it helped make him better. He decided to be a single-minded rebounder, and by being so good at it, he became a player with an extremely high winning percentage, though he probably contributed to fewer games overall. In essence, he became an 8–2 type of player rather than a 10–4 type of player. Fewer wins, but even fewer losses.

Charles Barkley

Early in his career, Charles Barkley was so quick on the post that he could beat triple teams, going through them by faking going around them, or going around them by using the threat of going through them. He never looked 6′ 4″ because he so easily got to the basket and finished with either the soft lay-up or an amazingly easy-looking dunk. But Barkley was so good that he was criticized for not being a good teammate, something that haunted him throughout his career, especially with his lack of an NBA championship.

Statistically, Barkley's offense was relentless (table 21.12). Aside from Reggie Miller, Barkley's individual season offensive ratings are the highest I've seen for players scoring twenty-plus points per game. In 1990, he posted a rating of 128 while producing twenty-six points per game, a dominating year. For four straight years, Barkley had floor percentage values over 0.60 and offensive ratings over 120. A few other great players had long periods with ratings that high, but I believe that only Kevin McHale was able to keep up floor percentages that high for so long.

On the other end of the court, Barkley was frequently criticized for his defense. He didn't always get back on defense, and he sometimes didn't seem to care. Barkley's numbers actually reflect this. His defensive rating fluctuated a lot through his career, getting as low as one hundred and as high as 109, averaging

Table 21.12. Charles Barkley's Career Summary Statistics

Season	Tm	G	Floor %	Off. Rtg.	Pts Prod/G	% Tm Poss	Stop %	Def. Rtg.	W–L (%)
1985	PHI	82	0.57	114	14.0	20%	0.54	105	7.9–2.5 (0.762)
1986	PHI	80	0.56	111	20.3	24%	0.62	100	11.9–2.8 (0.807)
1987	PHI	68	0.58	119	24.1	25%	0.58	104	11.9–1.7 (0.873)
1988	PHI	80	0.62	125	26.9	27%	0.51	108	14.4–1.3 (0.915)
1989	PHI	79	0.62	127	25.9	25%	0.53	109	14.1–1.1 (0.924)
1990	PHI	79	0.63	128	25.0	25%	0.54	105	14.4–0.6 (0.958)
1991	PHI	67	0.60	122	26.7	29%	0.52	107	11.4–1.4 (0.892)
1992	PHI	75	0.59	118	22.8	26%	0.55	106	12.0–2.4 (0.832)
1993	PHO	76	0.58	119	25.0	27%	0.58	103	13.4–1.4 (0.906)
1994	PHO	65	0.55	112	21.0	26%	0.57	103	8.9–2.8 (0.758)
1995	PHO	68	0.56	117	22.2	27%	0.60	105	10.3–2.2 (0.827)
1996	PHO	71	0.55	115	22.6	27%	0.60	105	10.5–3.2 (0.768)
1997	HOU	53	0.55	115	20.2	24%	0.61	100	8.7–1.1 (0.883)
1998	HOU	68	0.56	115	16.1	22%	0.58	104	8.4–2.2 (0.790)
1999	HOU	42	0.56	113	17.9	24%	0.58	100	6.2–1.1 (0.845)
2000	HOU	20	0.54	109	15.3	23%	0.52	105	1.8–1.0 (0.632)
16–Yr Totals		**1073**	**0.58**	**119**	**22.1**	**25%**	**0.57**	**105**	**166–29 (0.851)**

out at 105. In 1993 and 1994, when he saw an opportunity to win a title, Barkley cared and the Phoenix defense actually missed him when he was out (107 rating with him and 110 without him). In 1995, after missing out twice on a title, Barkley seemed to be relaxing in the regular season, and Phoenix's team defense was worse with him than without him (112 versus 107). Though I am still gathering the numbers for his days in Philadelphia, I wouldn't doubt that the Sixers played better without Barkley in his last couple of years there when he wanted out.

Overall, Barkley was truly one of the greats, despite the bad publicity. In the late 1980s, some of that bad publicity led me to investigate questions about his ability. It was during those investigations that I developed the concept of an individual floor percentage. Because I developed that technique then and it did show that Barkley was not a "loser," as I foolishly had begun to classify him, I actually started rooting for Barkley. When John Paxson hit that three-pointer at the end of Game 6 to win the 1993 NBA title for the Bulls over Barkley's Suns, I pretty much knew that he would never win one. The only way he was going to win it was to do it then and to do it against Jordan. Oh, how that might have changed the 1990s.

John Stockton and Karl Malone

When I first began serious work on basketball back in the summer of 1987, I wrote every NBA team to request material that would help my research. The Utah Jazz organization was, along with Cleveland, the most cooperative. They sent me game-by-game records of how the team had done with and without individual players. I pored through what they sent, searching for patterns, not quite sure what I was looking for. What eventually struck me was how well the Jazz did with John Stockton getting a lot of minutes. I hadn't yet developed the individual floor percentage method, but upon its development in 1988, I ran it on Stockton pretty quickly after trying it on Barkley. The method wasn't quite as refined then as it is now, but it indicated that Stockton had the highest floor percentage in the league in 1988 (table 21.13). That was, as some might remember, Stockton's breakthrough season. He was called the player too good to not have a nickname. He was named Second Team All-NBA. He outplayed Magic Johnson in the 1988 Western Conference Semifinals as the Jazz took the Lakers to seven games before the Lakers managed to gut it out. I can't say that the Jazz "fell" to the Lakers because there was no knockout in that series.

That's about as much as I can write about Stockton without mentioning Karl Malone, his teammate for more than seventeen years. There has never been a pair of players that played so well together for so long. As a result, it's hard to say how good either one of them would have been without the other. You can try. Stockton had one year without Malone—his rookie season when his rating was a decent 104. But that really says almost nothing. Rookie years are mediocre indicators of

Table 21.13. John Stockton's Career Summary Statistics

Season	Tm	G	Floor %	Off. Rtg.	Pts Prod/G	% Tm Poss	Stop %	Def. Rtg.	W–L (%)
1985	UTA	82	0.52	104	7.2	18%	0.48	104	2.9–2.9 (0.500)
1986	UTA	82	0.55	112	10.2	18%	0.52	103	6.1–1.9 (0.765)
1987	UTA	82	0.57	115	10.5	19%	0.53	102	6.6–1.2 (0.845)
1988	UTA	82	0.61	124	18.9	21%	0.52	102	11.8–0.5 (0.956)
1989	UTA	82	0.59	121	21.3	22%	0.51	101	13.2–0.8 (0.942)
1990	UTA	78	0.59	122	22.0	24%	0.49	105	11.9–1.3 (0.901)
1991	UTA	82	0.57	119	21.6	24%	0.52	104	12.6–1.8 (0.874)
1992	UTA	82	0.56	119	20.2	23%	0.53	104	12.2–1.6 (0.883)
1993	UTA	82	0.56	117	18.7	23%	0.49	107	9.9–2.8 (0.779)
1994	UTA	82	0.58	119	18.6	22%	0.50	104	11.5–1.5 (0.883)
1995	UTA	82	0.58	122	18.4	22%	0.52	105	11.5–1.1 (0.912)
1996	UTA	82	0.57	122	17.4	21%	0.46	108	10.5–1.6 (0.866)
1997	UTA	82	0.58	122	17.0	21%	0.49	105	10.9–1.1 (0.907)
1998	UTA	64	0.57	120	14.1	22%	0.47	107	6.7–1.1 (0.854)
1999	UTA	50	0.55	113	12.8	22%	0.53	98	8.8–1.2 (0.881)
2000	UTA	82	0.56	118	14.0	22%	0.52	102	9.4–1.2 (0.888)
2001	UTA	82	0.56	120	14.2	22%	0.51	103	9.3–0.9 (0.910)
2002	UTA	82	0.57	120	15.3	22%	0.51	106	10.2–1.6 (0.867)
18–Yr Totals		**1422**	**0.57**	**119**	**16.3**	**22%**	**0.50**	**104**	**176–26 (0.870)**

future success. Malone's rookie year offensive rating was ninety-two, well below his career rating of 113. They both needed a year to adjust to the NBA, but they quickly discovered that they could run the pick-and-roll and get out on a fast break and make them work. That intuitive sense of where a teammate is going to be and how he is going to react in concert with your own reactions—it is perhaps my favorite aspect of team sports, and they had that. I'm sure they found it remarkable, too, not just a by-product of practicing together for a long time. Some of it was practice, but some of it was that mythical wavelength that they shared.

Because the two players' careers are so intertwined, splitting up credit between them seems like a horrible thing to do. Maybe they both should have the same number of individual wins and losses. That should be the Stockton-Malone Theorem: Two players so good that they are together and winning for fifteen years in a row must share the identical individual win–loss record. It seems only right.

But, alas, the cruel numbers generated different win–loss records for the two. Stockton was 176–26, for an 87 percent winning percentage. Malone was 215–54, for an 80 percent winning percentage (table 21.14). Malone had more net wins per season, but Stockton had a higher winning percentage. I really don't know whether winning percentage or net wins is a better measure of the player and, in this case, maybe that is a good thing.

Kobe and Shaq

You have to wonder how good Kobe would be if he'd gone to college. You have to wonder, if he had gone to college and established himself there as the next Jordan, would he have been the number-one pick in the draft for some struggling

Table 21.14. Karl Malone's Career Summary Statistics

Season	Tm	G	Floor %	Off. Rtg.	Pts Prod/G	% Tm Poss	Stop %	Def. Rtg.	W–L (%)
1986	UTA	81	0.48	92	14.5	24%	0.56	102	2.7–9.2 (0.226)
1987	UTA	82	0.53	104	19.8	25%	0.53	102	7.7–6.1 (0.559)
1988	UTA	82	0.54	107	25.0	28%	0.55	101	11.2–5.3 (0.679)
1989	UTA	80	0.57	115	26.6	29%	0.57	99	14.6–1.7 (0.894)
1990	UTA	82	0.58	117	27.6	31%	0.56	102	14.9–2.0 (0.881)
1991	UTA	82	0.58	116	26.8	29%	0.56	102	14.8–2.4 (0.862)
1992	UTA	81	0.58	118	25.6	29%	0.56	103	14.1–1.8 (0.886)
1993	UTA	82	0.60	119	25.1	28%	0.58	103	14.5–1.6 (0.898)
1994	UTA	82	0.56	111	23.8	27%	0.60	100	13.8–3.4 (0.802)
1995	UTA	82	0.57	114	24.1	29%	0.61	101	13.9–2.7 (0.838)
1996	UTA	82	0.58	116	23.7	29%	0.60	102	14.2–2.2 (0.866)
1997	UTA	82	0.59	118	25.3	31%	0.58	101	14.6–1.6 (0.900)
1998	UTA	81	0.58	117	25.0	31%	0.58	102	14.5–1.9 (0.886)
1999	UTA	49	0.55	111	22.5	30%	0.59	96	13.9–1.7 (0.891)
2000	UTA	82	0.56	114	23.5	31%	0.57	100	13.6–2.1 (0.865)
2001	UTA	81	0.55	112	21.9	29%	0.57	101	12.2–2.7 (0.817)
2002	UTA	80	0.52	107	21.3	28%	0.58	102	10.0–5.6 (0.640)
17–Yr Totals		1353	0.56	113	23.7	29%	0.57	101	215–54 (0.799)

franchise that he could carry on his shoulders? You have to wonder, if that had happened *and* Kobe decided to come out after his sophomore season *and* the Bulls got the number-one draft pick (as they did), would people have screamed *conspiracy?* But most importantly, with the whispers about Kobe wanting his own team independent of Shaquille O'Neal, would all of that have made Kobe happy? He has three rings on his fingers, yet the rumors persist that he wants his own team.

In his first season, Kobe struggled with erratic shots and turnovers, not uncommon for rookies. His offensive rating of one hundred wasn't horrible, but it humbled him a little to not be great (table 21.15). Upon looking at these numbers, though, you have to wonder again: What would his freshman college stats have looked like? Would they have been great? Would his offensive rating have been 110, 115, 120?

As a sophomore, err, second-year NBA pro, Kobe improved a lot. His offensive rating jumped up to 109 as he maintained 26 percent of the team possessions—a tremendous sign of future success. That kind of performance on its own is All-Star material, though Kobe was only getting twenty-five minutes per game.

More fantasy: Would Kobe have improved a lot as a college sophomore? Or would he have dominated so much as a frosh that he couldn't improve much as a

Table 21.15. Kobe Bryant's Career Summary Statistics

Season	Tm	G	Floor %	Off. Rtg.	Pts Prod/G	% Tm Poss	Stop %	Def. Rtg.	W–L (%)
1997	LAL	71	0.45	100	7.1	24%	0.48	105	1.6–3.2 (0.339)
1998	LAL	79	0.51	109	14.4	26%	0.44	106	5.4–3.8 (0.588)
1999	LAL	50	0.51	105	18.8	25%	0.50	104	7.7–6.6 (0.537)
2000	LAL	66	0.53	108	21.1	26%	0.54	98	9.4–2.5 (0.788)
2001	LAL	68	0.53	112	26.8	31%	0.50	105	9.9–4.2 (0.704)
2002	LAL	80	0.54	112	24.7	30%	0.49	103	11.6–3.8 (0.754)
6–Yr Totals		414	0.52	109	18.8	28%	0.49	103	46–24 (0.655)

sophomore? Doubtful. Vince Carter, a similar player, improved over all three of his college seasons.

In his third season (fantasy: "In his rookie season with the Bulls"), Kobe posted a 105 rating on the offensive end. That was worse than his second year, but mostly the decline was due to the lockout-induced back-to-back games that had significant effects on the quality of play throughout the NBA.

In his fourth season (fantasy: "With Phil Jackson returning to the Bulls to coach the new Michael Jordan"), Kobe's defense showed significant improvements under the guidance of new Lakers coach Phil Jackson. The Lakers were at their most dominant that season, going 67–15. They went 12–4 without Kobe, though, suggesting that he was not a *necessary* piece of the puzzle.

In his fifth season (fantasy: "Guiding the up-and-coming Bulls with a Jordanesque thirty-three-points-per-game average"), Kobe reached a new level. Shaq tried to make Kobe feel more important than that 12–4 record implied by trying to get him a scoring title. But late in the season with Allen Iverson far ahead in the scoring race, Shaq's scoring average overtook Kobe's in the Lakers' late push for home-court advantage in the playoffs. Kobe's offensive rating of 112 and use of 31 percent of the team's possessions were both extremely impressive. He helped the Lakers pretty easily win another title. Again, however, the Lakers were a successful 11–3 without Kobe.

So the fantasy is definitely different from reality. No Bulls team that Kobe would have rebuilt would do so well without him. And so we hear the whispers that Kobe wants his own team.

That means that Kobe's basketball ball-and-chain is Shaq. Magic, Bird, and Jordan made their teammates better, but Shaq somehow makes Kobe worse. There is some precedent for such a situation. Scottie Pippen did apparently improve when Jordan retired for a year and a half, maintaining the improvement when Jordan came back. So maybe Shaq should do the same. But Pippen didn't win a title while Jordan was out. What would Kobe be trying to prove if Shaq retired? That he could win a title without Shaq? And how would Shaq feel about that, since he never would have won a title without Kobe?

These two could fight for their share of credit for the success of the Lakers. It's potentially a very ugly situation. Coach Jackson has historically shown that he can allow his players to fight for credit without tearing the team apart. For now, as I suggested in the previous chapter, Shaq gets more credit (table 21.16). In an era where floor percentages average around 0.49, Shaq has maintained his at 0.59. That 59 percent chance of a score on 31 percent of a team's possessions makes it very difficult for other teams to beat the Lakers.

Table 21.16. Shaquille O'Neal's Career Summary Statistics

Season	Tm	G	Floor %	Off. Rtg.	Pts Prod/G	% Tm Poss	Stop %	Def. Rtg.	W–L (%)
1993	ORL	81	0.55	108	22.0	27%	0.64	100	12.0–4.5 (0.729)
1994	ORL	81	0.61	119	26.4	28%	0.58	103	15.5–1.6 (0.904)
1995	ORL	79	0.60	117	26.2	30%	0.57	104	13.2–2.5 (0.839)
1996	ORL	54	0.56	109	23.5	31%	0.58	103	7.0–3.6 (0.660)
1997	LAL	51	0.56	109	23.6	30%	0.63	99	8.3–2.3 (0.783)
1998	LAL	60	0.58	112	24.6	31%	0.58	101	9.7–2.1 (0.820)
1999	LAL	49	0.59	115	23.9	31%	0.56	102	12.9–2.3 (0.848)
2000	LAL	79	0.59	112	26.7	31%	0.62	95	15.6–1.5 (0.913)
2001	LAL	74	0.59	114	27.0	31%	0.60	101	13.7–2.4 (0.853)
2002	LAL	67	0.59	116	24.9	31%	0.57	100	11.7–1.3 (0.897)
10-Yr Totals		**675**	**0.59**	**113**	**25.0**	**30%**	**0.60**	**101**	**120–24 (0.832)**

Patrick Ewing and Hakeem Olajuwon

These two somewhat maligned centers met in the 1994 NBA Finals, and one of them had to lose—Ewing, as it turned out. Both were overshadowed through most of their careers, though Olajuwon got his due while Jordan played baseball during 1994 and 1995. The lack of dominance shown by these two players while Magic, Bird, and Michael reigned was what really changed people's minds about centers being necessary for success in the NBA.

In fact, both Ewing and Olajuwon ended up as victims of the evolving complex defenses of the NBA. Increasing double-teams on post players really took away the ease of their low-post moves. The position of center, which had been stylized by Wilt Chamberlain, Kareem Abdul-Jabbar, Bill Walton, and others as something of a finesse position, became the brutish position that Shaquille O'Neal epitomizes today. That is not to say that Shaq doesn't have offensive moves. In fact, his moves are what allow him to get away with what he does in the post. He does back players in, but he has enough quickness to also give defenders the impression that he can go around them. Ewing and Olajuwon, in contrast, are carryovers from the older times, guys with spin moves, turnarounds, and moderate range jump shots. These kinds of moves allowed big men to get close to the basket for easier shots in years gone by, but by the 1990s these moves served primarily to gain space as defenders had their bodies all over low-post scorers. As a result, these two centers ended up being relatively less efficient scorers than many of their predecessors, with offensive ratings hovering at about the league average.

On the other hand, the advantage that centers have always had is that their position in the defense—guarding the back line right next to the basket, threatening little guys who get close to the basket—gives them a very important role, one that Ewing and Olajuwon have carried out in Hall of Fame fashion. Ewing and Olajuwon were two of the best defenders of their times, shutting down the middle with more than blocked shots. They consciously changed shots and kept perimeter players out of the middle. There have been other centers who have done these things as well or better—players like Mark Eaton, Adonal Foyle, Tree Rollins, Charles Jones, and Ben Wallace—but teams have been hesitant to play them because their offense has been so weak. So even the "average" offense of Ewing and Olajuwon made them valuable by allowing them to be on the court so long. Teams will sacrifice offense at center for the benefit of defense. If they don't have to make that sacrifice—if they have guys like Ewing and Olajuwon who are better offensively than the average center—it makes those centers much more valuable.

This is also evident in a study done by Kevin Pelton, a business student at the University of Washington. Pelton looked back to the mid-1980s at teams and their leading scorers to see whether there was a winning trend among teams with leading scorers at certain positions. What he found was convincing evidence that teams whose leading scorer is a power forward or center win the most. Table 21.17 reproduces his findings.

Center-led teams particularly stand out. These include Ewing's teams, Olajuwon's teams, Shaq's teams, Alonzo Mourning's teams, and David Robinson's teams. These teams didn't win because of their offense. The average offensive rating of these center-led teams was pretty much exactly the league average. But the defensive rating was a couple points better than average. Teams that don't have a high-scoring center have to find ways to make up points, either with high-scoring surrounding players or with smaller, more offense-minded guys substituting for the low-scoring big man.

This doesn't imply that high-scoring centers are necessary for winning. The Lakers, the Celtics, and the Bulls (especially the Bulls) all proved that's not true. It

Table 21.17. Winning Percentage with Leading Scorer at Below Position

Year	PG	SG	SF	PF	C
1987	0.793	0.364	0.610	0.497	0.512
1988	0.659	0.461	0.532	0.454	0.500
1989	0.512	0.463	0.474	0.593	0.500
1990	0.667	0.496	0.446	0.479	0.488
1991	0.434	0.558	0.468	0.503	0.516
1992	0.337	0.514	0.494	0.520	0.556
1993	0.366	0.466	0.471	0.622	0.632
1994	0.409	0.442	0.368	0.568	0.594
1995	0.490	0.476	0.446	0.546	0.646
1996	0.536	0.476	0.507	0.439	0.598
1997	0.524	0.478	0.435	0.468	0.656
1998	0.524	0.460	0.329	0.604	0.622
1999	0.470	0.533	0.400	0.489	0.633
2000	0.461	0.522	0.308	0.528	0.726
2001	0.442	0.476	0.503	0.522	0.683
Totals	**0.479**	**0.490**	**0.449**	**0.526**	**0.587**

Table 21.18. Patrick Ewing's Career Summary Statistics

Season	Tm	G	Floor %	Off. Rtg.	Pts Prod/G	% Tm Poss	Stop %	Def. Rtg.	W–L (%)
1986	NYK	50	0.49	99	18.5	26%	0.57	102	3.7–5.2 (0.414)
1987	NYK	63	0.51	101	19.4	27%	0.57	106	4.0–7.5 (0.350)
1988	NYK	82	0.54	108	18.0	26%	0.60	101	9.3–3.9 (0.705)
1989	NYK	80	0.57	114	20.6	23%	0.58	103	11.4–2.6 (0.815)
1990	NYK	82	0.57	115	25.2	28%	0.60	103	14.0–2.8 (0.833)
1991	NYK	81	0.54	107	24.0	30%	0.62	101	11.5–5.6 (0.675)
1992	NYK	82	0.56	112	21.2	25%	0.63	98	13.9–2.3 (0.860)
1993	NYK	81	0.52	105	21.2	28%	0.65	94	12.5–3.3 (0.790)
1994	NYK	79	0.53	108	22.0	28%	0.66	93	13.9–1.9 (0.878)
1995	NYK	79	0.52	105	21.3	29%	0.64	98	11.0–4.8 (0.695)
1996	NYK	76	0.49	100	20.7	30%	0.64	98	8.5–6.8 (0.553)
1997	NYK	78	0.51	104	20.4	28%	0.65	95	11.6–3.8 (0.755)
1998	NYK	26	0.52	103	18.0	29%	0.66	94	3.5–1.2 (0.747)
1999	NYK	38	0.48	95	15.8	27%	0.69	91	4.2–2.7 (0.604)
2000	NYK	62	0.49	98	14.2	24%	0.61	97	5.3–4.4 (0.546)
2001	SEA	79	0.47	93	9.5	20%	0.59	102	2.3–7.2 (0.239)
2002	ORL	65	0.48	97	5.8	22%	0.60	102	1.3–2.5 (0.341)
17–Yr Totals		1183	0.53	105	18.9	27%	0.62	99	142–69 (0.674)

Table 21.19. Hakeem Olajuwon's Career Summary Statistics

Season	Tm	G	Floor %	Off. Rtg.	Pts Prod/G	% Tm Poss	Stop %	Def. Rtg.	W–L (%)
1985	HOU	82	0.57	112	19.8	23%	0.57	103	10.9–3.1 (0.781)
1986	HOU	68	0.57	113	22.2	25%	0.62	102	10.4–2.4 (0.811)
1987	HOU	75	0.56	111	22.4	26%	0.65	99	12.3–2.5 (0.831)
1988	HOU	79	0.55	109	21.6	26%	0.67	98	12.4–2.8 (0.816)
1989	HOU	82	0.55	108	23.1	27%	0.73	95	14.7–2.5 (0.856)
1990	HOU	82	0.52	104	22.8	27%	0.74	93	14.3–3.5 (0.805)
1991	HOU	56	0.54	108	20.1	25%	0.75	93	10.0–1.3 (0.882)
1992	HOU	70	0.54	110	20.3	25%	0.69	99	11.4–2.8 (0.801)
1993	HOU	82	0.56	113	24.7	28%	0.71	96	16.7–1.7 (0.909)
1994	HOU	80	0.54	108	25.1	29%	0.67	95	15.3–2.7 (0.852)
1995	HOU	72	0.54	108	25.4	30%	0.66	100	12.0–4.4 (0.734)
1996	HOU	72	0.53	106	24.6	31%	0.65	101	10.7–5.2 (0.674)
1997	HOU	78	0.51	104	21.2	29%	0.63	99	10.0–5.4 (0.649)
1998	HOU	47	0.51	104	16.1	24%	0.66	101	4.8–3.5 (0.579)
1999	HOU	50	0.52	105	17.3	25%	0.68	96	7.1–2.3 (0.753)
2000	HOU	44	0.48	95	9.8	22%	0.62	100	1.7–3.4 (0.329)
2001	HOU	58	0.53	106	11.6	22%	0.65	98	5.5–2.0 (0.738)
2002	TOR	61	0.46	91	7.0	18%	0.68	96	2.3–4.2 (0.350)
18–Yr Totals		1238	0.54	108	20.4	26%	0.67	98	183–56 (0.766)

just means that if you have an average efficiency center (league-wise) who also plays good defense, that gives you a lot better shot at winning than an average efficiency off-guard who also plays good defense.

I've said enough. Ewing's and Olajuwon's numbers appear in tables 21.18 and 21.19, respectively. Their win–loss records do a pretty good job reflecting their overall contributions, which were positive and substantial.

Allen Iverson

No player who has won the NBA MVP award has not been elected into the Basketball Hall of Fame. None that are eligible, at least. You have to wonder whether Allen Iverson will be an exception.

Allen Iverson won the MVP in 2001, and every person who could calculate protested wildly. Shaquille O'Neal, Tim Duncan, and Chris Webber all posted numbers as good or better. They and several other players won verbal votes of support for the award. People pointed out that Iverson's Sixers also won Coach of the Year, Defensive Player of the Year, and Sixth Man of the Year, yet they didn't win the championship—so why should Iverson get the MVP? He shot far worse than Dominique Wilkins ever shot for the Hawks, and Wilkins's good credentials were never good enough for an MVP (table 21.20).

In reality, Iverson won the MVP for his heart, persevering through injuries and scoring so many points for a small guy. He was, well, a freak, and he might have won the award for the freakish reasons that Spud Webb won the slam dunk championship in 1986.

No, Iverson was not the normal MVP. Iverson was a little like former Bullets' center Wes Unseld, who won the MVP in his rookie year of 1969 and then never even made an All-NBA Team again. Just as Iverson scored a lot of points for a short guy, Unseld grabbed a ton of rebounds for a short 6'7" center. Just as Iverson was the "heart" of a surprisingly good Sixers team, Unseld was the supposed "heart" of those Bullets that surprised everyone by jumping from a 36–46 record to a 57–25 record. NBA observers in both seasons were looking for ways to explain such dramatically unexpected *team* results. Those observers with votes decided to reward the "freakish" stars of those teams, short guys who could do things most people their height couldn't. Not coincidentally, those observers with votes also gave the Coach of the Year award to the respective coaches of both teams.

History usually forgets the questions surrounding awards after enough time has passed. Unseld was elected to the Hall of Fame despite few NBA accolades beyond those from his rookie year. He never even led the league in rebounding.

Table 21.20. Dominique Wilkins's Career Summary Statistics

Season	Tm	G	Floor %	Off. Rtg.	Pts Prod/G	% Tm Poss	Stop %	Def. Rtg.	W–L (%)
1983	ATL	82	0.52	104	16.3	23%	0.45	105	5.6–5.9 (0.487)
1984	ATL	81	0.53	108	20.4	26%	0.49	106	7.7–6.4 (0.547)
1985	ATL	81	0.52	105	25.2	31%	0.48	107	6.9–8.6 (0.443)
1986	ATL	78	0.55	111	28.0	31%	0.48	105	10.6–5.1 (0.675)
1987	ATL	79	0.56	115	26.7	30%	0.45	107	11.2–3.6 (0.755)
1988	ATL	78	0.54	112	27.8	33%	0.44	109	8.9–6.4 (0.585)
1989	ATL	80	0.55	114	24.2	28%	0.45	108	9.5–4.6 (0.675)
1990	ATL	80	0.57	118	24.5	29%	0.46	112	10.0–4.3 (0.697)
1991	ATL	81	0.55	116	24.6	27%	0.49	109	10.9–4.2 (0.721)
1992	ATL	42	0.54	113	25.6	29%	0.44	110	4.5–3.2 (0.582)
1993	ATL	71	0.55	118	26.8	30%	0.42	112	8.8–4.1 (0.681)
1994	ATL	49	0.51	109	21.7	29%	0.51	105	5.1–3.0 (0.626)
1994	LAC	25	0.52	110	25.2	29%	0.42	111	2.2–2.4 (0.477)
1995	BOS	77	0.49	106	16.6	25%	0.42	113	3.3–7.5 (0.308)
1997	SAN	63	0.50	107	17.0	28%	0.44	114	2.7–6.7 (0.288)
1999	ORL	27	0.45	92	4.8	30%	0.48	100	0.6–1.5 (0.280)
15–Yr Totals		1074	0.54	111	22.8	29%	0.46	108	108–78 (0.583)

Table 21.21. Allen Iverson's Career Summary Statistics

Season	Tm	G	Floor %	Off. Rtg.	Pts Prod/G	% Tm Poss	Stop %	Def. Rtg.	W–L (%)
1997	PHI	76	0.48	102	23.6	29%	0.45	112	3.1–11.8 (0.208)
1998	PHI	80	0.52	108	21.4	27%	0.47	106	8.1–6.7 (0.550)
1999	PHI	48	0.50	105	25.1	31%	0.50	99	11.1–5.4 (0.672)
2000	PHI	70	0.49	101	25.9	33%	0.47	102	6.7–7.8 (0.463)
2001	PHI	71	0.50	106	28.5	34%	0.53	99	11.4–4.6 (0.710)
2002	PHI	60	0.48	101	29.2	36%	0.54	100	7.7–6.8 (0.533)
6–Yr Totals		405	0.50	104	25.4	31%	0.49	104	48–43 (0.527)

Iverson actually has more qualifications, including three scoring titles and a couple of All-NBA Teams. Questions will persist about his value—that's part of the reason he was a primary subject of chapter 19, "The Problem with Scorers." Iverson is the classic example of a player who scores a lot, but not very efficiently. His benefits to a team's win–loss record sometimes just aren't very clear. For right now, my numbers (table 21.21) suggest that he has been slightly better than a .500 contributor. He has made the Sixers better but not great. On teams that really didn't have a lot of scorers, he made life easier for his teammates, something the numbers in the table don't completely account for. But until AI puts together a season with an offensive rating over 110 or delivers a title to his team, I can see why there are doubts about his greatness.

Wilt Chamberlain and Bill Russell

It is with great hesitation that I discuss players from the distant past. For the distant past is always an era of better days and better people, like Wilt Chamberlain and Bill Russell. May James Naismith save my soul.

When I was a kid, Chamberlain's feats were already the stuff of legend. He scored one hundred points in a single game. He averaged fifty points per game over a full season. He had fifty-five rebounds in one game. He had seventy-five blocked shots over three games. He blocked shots so hard that shooters worried about getting their arms broken. These were stories that I heard about the Big Dipper. As a kid, these stories were as mythologically intimidating to me as the five Chinese brothers who could swallow oceans and withstand fire. Chamberlain was a freak of nature, a Goliath, and, to some, an evil one.

Bill Russell, on the other hand, was the fierce team player at the back of the Celtics defense. Nothing, they told me, characterized Russell better than the fact that he won. In Russell's thirteen years, the Celtics won eleven NBA championships. That was all that needed to be said.

In discussions over whether Chamberlain or Russell was the better player, Chamberlain supporters commonly point to his individual numbers, and Russell supporters highlight his team numbers. But the individual numbers are part of the team numbers, and the team numbers contain the individual numbers. It's hard to see one without seeing at least part of the other. Neither the individual nor the team statistics were collected completely in the 1960s when these two were active. That means that debating the merits of the two is not only complicated by the difficulty of distinguishing individual performance from team performance, but also by incomplete statistical pictures of both kinds of performance. What I am doing in this section, however, is providing estimates of some of the missing team statistics from the 1960s. Those more complete team statistics start telling a clearer story about the individuals, a story that, not coincidentally, seems to fit with the anecdotal information you can find in history books.

Let me start with the estimation of the team statistics and get it out of the way. Turnovers and offensive rebounds are the key statistics missing from NBA team records prior to 1974. That's why there are no pre-1974 teams in the chapter 3 survey of best offenses and defenses. But there is a record of turnovers and offensive rebounds for teams over the thirty or so years since then. That record can be used to estimate what happened before. For example, straightforward averages of these two numbers over time are 17.1 turnovers per game and 13.8 offensive rebounds per game. If you just assume those values for Chamberlain's and Russell's teams, you can do most of the rest of the study below and get about the same results as I get. But I actually went a little beyond a simple average to account for other information as well. For example, in 2002, there were about fourteen turnovers per team per game, and in 1974, there were about twenty-one, so there probably were even a few more in 1964. I accounted for that trend. I even went beyond that to consider how more missed field goals might impact offensive rebounds, how more assists might mean more turnovers, and so forth. For those who have heard of "multiple regression," that is the tool I used to consider the fact that turnovers and offensive rebounds are related to all sorts of different statistics. For those who don't know about multiple regression, let me just call it a sophisticated statistical technique. The details of the process appear in Appendix 4.

The results of the estimation are the backbone of my analyses of Chamberlain and Russell. Those estimates are good enough to allow calculation of possessions for teams in the 1960s using the simple version of the possession formula

$$\text{Possessions} = \text{FGA} - \text{OREB} + \text{TOV} + 0.4 \times \text{FTA}$$

Possessions are the tool for assessing how good offenses and defenses were. Table 21.22 shows the relevant per-game statistics for estimating possessions as well as the per-game possession estimates themselves.

From the table, it appears that the Celtics ran at a higher pace than the teams Chamberlain played on. The possession rates of 120 to 130 per game are thirty to forty possessions higher than the rates seen in NBA games of around 2000. Note that Chamberlain's 1965 team is actually the weighted average of the San Francisco

Table 21.22. Rates of Team Statistics per Game for Russell and Chamberlain

Season	Russell's Team (Celtics)					Chamberlain's Team				
	FGA	FTA	OREB	TOV	Poss.	FGA	FTA	OREB	TOV	Poss.
1957	101.8	36.7	20.6	28.2	124.1					
1958	107.8	35.9	22.6	27.7	127.2					
1959	112.7	35.6	23.7	27.1	130.3					
1960	119.6	33.6	25.2	26.0	133.8	115.7	35.8	25.4	26.9	131.5
1961	117.7	35.5	25.3	26.0	132.5	112.4	39.3	25.2	27.0	130.0
1962	113.9	33.9	23.3	24.7	128.8	111.6	40.1	24.2	26.2	129.6
1963	109.7	34.7	22.3	25.0	126.3	105.6	35.0	22.0	25.2	122.8
1964	109.6	31.1	22.1	24.5	124.5	97.2	35.3	20.9	26.8	117.2
1965	107.6	32.3	21.9	24.5	123.1	101.8	36.6	21.1	25.0	120.3
1966	104.6	34.5	21.2	24.3	121.5	102.4	39.3	22.6	26.2	121.7
1967	102.8	36.6	20.6	24.0	120.8	100.0	42.1	21.9	25.3	120.3
1968	102.1	36.4	21.0	23.9	119.6	102.6	40.7	23.0	25.2	121.2
1969	101.4	32.4	19.9	23.3	117.8	92.9	38.5	19.7	24.7	113.3
1970						97.0	32.2	17.1	21.5	114.2
1971						95.8	33.1	17.4	21.5	113.2
1972						97.4	34.5	18.2	21.1	114.2
1973						95.4	27.6	16.7	20.7	110.5

Note: Offensive rebounds and turnovers are estimated values.

Warriors, for whom he played thirty-eight games, and the Philadelphia 76ers, for whom he played thirty-five games.

Possession rates from table 21.22 get put together with records of points scored and allowed to produce table 21.23, which shows the Celtics and Chamberlain's teams' points per hundred possessions ratings.

Russell's Celtics teams were outstanding defensively, as good as about nine points per hundred possessions better than the league average. Teams were scoring only about eighty-five points per hundred possessions against Russell's teams when the league average was ninety to ninety-five. Chamberlain's teams were better offensively, almost always better than Russell's teams and as good as about

Table 21.23. Team Offensive and Defensive Ratings for Russell and Chamberlain

Season	Lg. Avg. Rtg.	Russell's Team (Celtics)				Chamberlain's Team			
		Off. Rtg.	Diff.	Def. Rtg.	Diff.	Off. Rtg.	Diff.	Def. Rtg.	Diff.
1957	83.7	85.1	1.4	80.8	-2.9				
1958	85.8	86.4	0.6	82.0	-3.8				
1959	87.6	89.3	1.7	84.3	-3.3				
1960	90.7	93.0	2.3	86.8	-3.9	90.2	-0.5	88.5	-2.2
1961	92.4	90.3	-2.1	86.1	-6.4	93.1	0.6	92.4	-0.1
1962	94.3	94.0	-0.4	86.8	-7.5	96.8	2.4	94.7	0.3
1963	95.6	94.1	-1.5	88.4	-7.2	96.5	0.9	98.2	2.6
1964	93.7	90.8	-2.9	84.4	-9.2	91.9	-1.8	87.5	-6.1
1965	93.1	91.6	-1.5	84.9	-8.3	90.7	-2.4	93.4	0.4
1966	93.1	92.8	-0.3	88.7	-4.3	96.5	3.4	92.6	-0.4
1967	97.3	98.8	1.5	92.1	-5.2	104.1	6.8	96.3	-1.0
1968	97.7	97.1	-0.6	93.7	-4.0	101.2	3.5	94.1	-3.6
1969	96.1	94.2	-1.8	89.5	-6.6	99.0	3.0	95.4	-0.7
1970	100.1					99.6	-0.5	97.9	-2.2
1971	97.8					101.4	3.6	98.6	0.9
1972	98.1					106.0	7.9	95.2	-2.9
1973	96.9					101.1	4.3	93.4	-3.5

eight points better per hundred possessions than the league average. Because Russell's teams won so often through the 1960s—and frequently beat Chamberlain teams—it's easy to see where the phrase "defense wins championships" might have come from. But if Russell's teams were that much better than average defensively, it was unfair to really make that generalization.

It's comforting that Russell, the man with the defensive reputation, led several teams to outstanding defensive ratings, and that Chamberlain, the man with the offensive reputation, led several teams to outstanding offensive ratings. That gives me the confidence that these numbers are in the ballpark. Further, if you use the straight historical averages of turnovers and offensive rebounds, rather than the estimates I used, Russell's teams still look good defensively, and Chamberlain's still look good offensively. These results are pretty robust.

Those are the team numbers, but what information do they contain about the individual abilities of Chamberlain and Russell?

Russell is the easier story, so we'll start there. The biggest question is how much responsibility Russell should get for his team's success. One way to look at this is by observing how much the Celtics changed with and without him. Before Russell showed up, the Celtics were coming off of a 39–33 season in which they lost in the first round of the playoffs. In his first season, they improved by five games and won their first title. Russell took them from good to great. The big difference was the defense, which went from a defensive rating 2.8 points worse than average to one 2.9 points better than average. That 5.7-point improvement was only partially offset by a 1.8-point decrease in the offensive rating. Russell was never acclaimed for his offense, so this offensive drop is not a surprise. The fact that the Celtics' offensive rating was only about average throughout his career in Boston also supports this assessment of Russell's offensive impact.

At the end of Russell's career, the drop-off in team defense was equally dramatic, going from a defensive rating of about ninety (6.6 points better than average) with Russell to about ninety-nine (not even a point better than average). The team went from 48–34 and a title to 34–48 and out of the playoffs. Thinking that such a decline might have been a fluke, I looked to see how the second year without Russell went. Though the Celtics were better at 44–38, the defense was still nowhere near where it had been with Russell—only 1.9 points better than average. By the end of Russell's career, if the estimated points allowed per hundred possessions stats above are accurate, there were seven Russell teams that would jump ahead of the twenty-fifth-rated defense of chapter 3. And not a single Celtics defense since.

During Russell's tenure, the Celtics D averaged six points better than average, consistent with the changes in the defense when he joined the team and when he left. He certainly had help, though. K.C. Jones and Tom "Satch" Sanders were acclaimed defenders who reportedly could stop opposing guards and forwards before they got to Russell. However, the Celtics' defensive ratings did not change dramatically as these two players entered and exited the Boston lineup as it did with Russell.

The Celtics' routinely outstanding defensive ratings during Russell's tenure and the dramatic changes in their defensive ratings with and without Russell only reinforce the likelihood that Russell was the greatest defender in NBA history. His offense was probably ordinary or worse than average, based on the average performance of the Celtics offenses, but if he could make *the entire team defense* five to six points better than average, that is an impact on the order of Jordan's during his prime, which we know from the data above to have generated win–loss records of about 16–1.

Chamberlain's legacy is much more difficult to assess, in part because it has already been built up over the years on statistics that are of questionable value. The big ones are the 50.4 points per game he scored throughout 1962 and his hundred-point game on March 2, 1962. Those statistics stand as intimidating markers of his greatness. But they are also incredibly flawed. Point totals can come as a result of just a lot of shots and a lot of turnovers. Wilt most certainly dominated not only points scored but also shots and turnovers for those early Warriors teams. I want to more closely examine Wilt's high-scoring seasons to see if they involved only high point totals or high point totals with high efficiency.

First of all, let's put the fifty-points-per-game season in perspective with today's NBA, because fifty points per game is just a gaudy number. Thirty-five points per game is a big number, but not gaudy. Yet if you adjust fifty points per game by the difference in pace between 1962 (126 possessions per game) and 2002 (91 possessions per game), it becomes only thirty-five points per game. Whereas I cannot see Shaquille O'Neal or Allen Iverson going for fifty points per game in a season, I can possibly see them getting 35 points per game. For Shaq or Iverson to reach that level, they would probably have to use a few more possessions per game. They'd have to take a few more shots and control the ball even more. That is probably what Wilt did, too.

One of the proposed reasons for Wilt dominating the Warriors' offense so much in 1962 is that he had poor teammates who couldn't contribute to the offense. Wilt's teammates in 1962, though, consisted of two Hall of Famers, Paul Arizin and Tom Gola, as well as Guy Rodgers, a potential Hall of Famer. Arizin was at the end of his career but still productive. Gola was an All-Star who left the Warriors after that season and had two more All-Star seasons with the Knicks afterward. Rodgers, the point guard feeding Wilt so many assists (though probably not called a "point" guard at the time), was in the fifth season of a twelve-year career that featured four All-Star appearances. Though the Warriors didn't have

Hall of Famers coming off the bench as the Celtics did, it does appear that Wilt had some decent teammates who could have helped more in the offense.

It appears that a big part of the reason that Wilt was taking so many shots was because of *someone's* desire to increase his point total. Wayne Lynch's account of Chamberlain in his book, *Season of the 76ers,* indicates that Warriors owner Eddie Gottlieb wanted Chamberlain to score as many points as possible, apparently even at the cost of winning. Corroborating this is a story from Wilt's own book, *Wilt,* in which he talks about management pressure on Rodgers to pass the ball:

> Coach McGuire starts out by telling Guy Rodgers, "You have one job on this team and one job only—get the ball to Wilt."
>
> Guy asks him, "When I sit down to negotiate my contract next year with Mr. Gottlieb, and he says he won't give me a raise because I didn't score enough points, will you be sitting there with me to tell him why?"
>
> "You bet your ass I will," Coach McGuire told him.
>
> Well, Guy's scoring average dropped from 12 points a game to eight—but I understand that he got a raise next season.

If the Warriors truly were more concerned about Wilt's individual point total than about winning, that raises questions of integrity beyond what I can consider here. At the very least, it really shrinks the value of both Wilt's individual and the Warriors' team statistics. Wilt's 50.4 points per game (or even the pace-adjusted value of thirty-five points per game) was inflated artificially, and the team's win–loss record of 49–31 was deflated artificially.

Even if an owner were pushing aside the goal of winning, not many NBA players today can score thirty-five points per game. What Wilt was doing was still a remarkable feat, just not as superhuman as it initially seems. Wilt was doing what Jordan did in 1987 with the Bulls, taking a large share of the team load and decreasing his own efficiency at the same time. (Jordan's offensive rating fell to 117 from his rookie season value of 118 when he should have been improving.) What surprised me, though, was that Wilt didn't even take on as large a load as Jordan, it appears. Jordan took 39 percent of his team's shots while on the court, and Wilt took 35 percent. Jordan scored 43 percent of his team's points while on the floor, and Wilt scored 40 percent. Jordan didn't score fifty points per game as Wilt did for two reasons—the pace was slower in 1987 than in 1962, and Jordan played forty minutes per game compared to the 48.5 that Wilt played.

That Jordan season serves as a good reference point for Wilt's 1962 season because they both took on such large loads. If Jordan's individual offensive rating was 117, about eight points higher than his team's offensive rating, it seems like a reasonable first cut to add eight points onto the Warriors' team offensive rating of ninety-seven to estimate Wilt's individual rating at approximately 105, about ten points higher than the league average that year. In trying to cross-check this number, I assumed that roughly a third of Wilt's boards were offensive, and I made various estimates of how many turnovers Wilt committed. The most turnovers I'd ever seen from a center was about 360 in an eighty-two-game season by Artis Gilmore, around 4.5 per game. Using that rate for Wilt implies an offensive rating of about 109, a bit higher than the 105 figure. But Gilmore averaged 4.5 turnovers per game in only thirty-seven minutes per game, whereas Wilt played 48.5 minutes per game. Scaling up, Wilt could have averaged about 5.5 turnovers per game. At that rate, Wilt's offensive rating was 105, exactly the number arrived at using the simple estimate. Further, with this turnover rate, Wilt was using about 33 percent of the Warriors' possessions, a number that appears sensible relative to Jordan's 36 percent of the Bulls' possessions (that is, if Wilt produced about 3 percent fewer points, he probably also used 3 percent fewer possessions.) If he actually turned the ball over only 4.5 times per game, he would have been using 32 percent of the team's possessions.

So in 1962, Wilt had a rating of about 105 and a floor percentage of about 0.56. It's possible that the values were as low as 100/0.53 and as high as 110/0.58. I'd be surprised if his actual numbers were outside this range. Stepping back, these numbers aren't as gaudy as the fifty-points-per-game figure that the *Guinness Book of World Records* shows. A 105 rating, from an absolute perspective, is remarkably pedestrian. It means that he did not score every time he touched the ball or even close to it. Allen Iverson in his 2001 MVP year had an offensive rating of about 105. Given that the league rating was only about 95 in 1962, not 104 as in 2001, that 105 rating is more comparable in difficulty to Jordan's 117 rating in 1987, when the league average was 108. Clearly, that speaks well of Chamberlain's offensive skills, regardless of whether he posted them because someone desired a show or because his teammates just couldn't score.

Wilt's offensive rating was clearly depressed when he was trying to score so many points, even if you use basic statistics such as field goal percentage to show it. As soon as Wilt stopped scoring thirty points per game, his field goal percentage went from 54 percent to 68 percent. In his first seven seasons, when he consistently took 29+ percent of his team's shots, his field goal percentage was about 51 percent. Beginning in 1967, when he started taking 20 percent or fewer of his team's shots, his field goal percentage increased to about 62 percent. That 11-percent increase in field goal percentage alone probably boosted his offensive rating twenty or so points. In 1967, when Wilt won his first championship, he wasn't the top scorer he'd once been, but he was very effective, helping the offense to one of history's best seasons. Could he have done it without Hal Greer, Billy Cunningham, and the rest of his Sixers teammates? Probably not. But Wilt's willingness to cut back in order to help make the team so good was important (something I wonder about with Iverson).

Chamberlain was a great offensive player by any measure. What I think I've found is that he wasn't superhuman. His gaudy point totals were a product of a faster-paced era, his forty-eight minutes per game of playing time, and an offensive philosophy that put the ball in his hands to score points even at the cost, perhaps, of winning games. In the end, his point totals combined with his offensive ratings only lower his greatness to that of approximately Michael Jordan, which ain't bad.

Defensively, Chamberlain does not appear to have been as good as Russell, but his defense seemed to get better through time. The evidence for this primarily comes from the team defensive ratings. Table 21.23 shows that a lot of Wilt's early teams were only average defensively, whereas his later teams tended to be quite good defensively. Also, as Chamberlain moved from team to team, it seemed that his effect on the defense became stronger later in his tenure with each team. For instance, when Wilt joined the Warriors in 1960, the defense improved by only 1.0 points. When he joined the Sixers in 1965, their defense ended up more than two points better than the previous season, but with Wilt joining in midseason, there doesn't seem to have been an immediate improvement in defense in midseason. When Wilt jumped to the Lakers in 1969, the Lakers defense improved about 1.3 points. Correspondingly, the Sixers defense declined by about three points. Finally, when Wilt retired, the Lakers defense declined by about 2.5 points. This overall defensive improvement would also be consistent with Wilt reducing how much effort he expended on the offensive end. None of the apparent improvements Wilt made in team defenses seem to be as large as those Russell made when he came and went with the Celtics.

This defensive assessment doesn't quite fit with the unofficial counts of blocked shots posted by Wilt. There have been reports of seventy-five blocks in three games and multiple games of fifteen blocks. Those counts would suggest a defensive monster of immense proportion. How could anyone have scored near the basket with him there? How could they have posted even average offensive ratings? I'm really not sure. Something just doesn't fit. Maybe Wilt's blocks all went right back to the offensive team. Maybe opponents ran the fast break every time they could to beat Wilt back, and he dominated only in the half-court. In the modern era, it's pretty unusual for a player blocking three shots per game to be part of a bad defensive team. There isn't much record of players blocking even five shots per game and none with fifteen blocks per game.

Though I can't fully reconcile Chamberlain's defensive reputation with the numbers, I think I understand his overall effect better now. His team numbers and his own numbers suggest that he was a talented individual asked to do too much on the offensive end early in his career—either because his teammates weren't up to the task or because an owner wanted to showcase his star. That situation possibly led to a nonoptimal use of his offensive skills, with Wilt pouring in points without a lot of concern for efficiency. His natural ability ended up making all those points very efficient, though Jordan's 1987 season was probably better than any of Wilt's. As he matured and began playing with different coaches,

Chamberlain toned down his scoring, took smarter shots, and became more effi-cient—efficient to a very high level. With Wilt not having to expend so much ener-gy on the offensive end (and with the overall league pace slowing), his defense also seemed to improve. In his best seasons, Wilt probably posted about twenty wins and one loss.

In comparing Chamberlain to Russell, most people like to ask the hypothet-ical question: "If you had ten guys in a gym to pick teams from, which of the two would you take first?" If the rest of the guys were gym rats with lousy jumpers, Wilt probably is the better choice because of his combination of offensive and defen-sive skills. But if the rest of the guys were NBA stars, it is hard to ignore Russell's five- to six-point effect on team defense.

Chapter 22

Player Evaluation Files: Freaks, Specialists, and Women

To a significant degree, the previous chapter was just a popularity contest because great players are like pretty women—you'd be happy to take any of them to the dance. Most coaches aren't blessed with great players (no further comment on pretty women). A coach's challenge is to make less-than-great players work together well enough to have a successful or even great team. It is possible. This chapter pulls out the files of the players that coaches usually get stuck with. Some of these players may have one single great skill. Some of them may have great potential. Some of them were good for a long time but perhaps were never "great." And then, I will speak about women again, not just the great ones but the ones whom the WNBA has heavily marketed as the league has grown from its infancy into its toddler years.

Shooting Specialists—Reggie Miller and Chris Mullin

Reggie Miller and Chris Mullin have been criticized as one-dimensional shooters, but they were undoubtedly fine marksmen. How valuable was that single dimension to the teams they played on, especially in light of the observation that shooting is the most important aspect of the game (see chapter 6)? If these two weren't valuable, no other shot makers could be.

Two aspects of their playing styles counterbalance their great shooting a little. First, they weren't great defenders, though Miller worked on his D tremendously and became a solid defender on the teams of the mid- to late 1990s. Second, as shooters, they didn't create as many shots as "scorers." They knew their shots and they made them, but they didn't create a whole lot for themselves.

The results are the numbers in tables 22.1 and 22.2.

Table 22.1. Reggie Miller's Career Summary Statistics

Season	Tm	G	Floor %	Off. Rtg.	Pts Prod/G	% Tm Poss	Stop %	Def. Rtg.	W–L (%)
1988	IND	82	0.53	113	9.4	18%	0.39	111	4.0–2.8 (0.588)
1989	IND	74	0.54	118	14.9	18%	0.43	112	6.6–3.2 (0.676)
1990	IND	82	0.56	123	22.5	23%	0.41	113	10.5–3.0 (0.777)
1991	IND	82	0.59	129	20.9	22%	0.40	114	10.7–1.5 (0.879)
1992	IND	82	0.57	125	18.7	19%	0.41	113	9.6–2.2 (0.812)
1993	IND	82	0.56	125	18.7	21%	0.42	112	10.2–1.8 (0.849)
1994	IND	79	0.55	123	17.4	22%	0.45	106	10.0–1.0 (0.905)
1995	IND	81	0.53	122	17.2	23%	0.44	108	9.7–1.4 (0.871)
1996	IND	76	0.53	120	18.7	24%	0.43	110	8.9–2.5 (0.782)
1997	IND	81	0.52	120	19.3	24%	0.44	108	10.5–2.1 (0.833)
1998	IND	81	0.53	120	16.7	22%	0.42	105	10.0–1.3 (0.881)
1999	IND	50	0.51	118	16.2	21%	0.41	108	5.5–1.6 (0.771)
2000	IND	81	0.51	117	16.2	19%	0.42	107	9.0–2.5 (0.785)
2001	IND	81	0.50	115	17.0	20%	0.43	106	9.6–3.2 (0.750)
2002	IND	79	0.51	121	14.9	18%	0.42	109	9.2–1.9 (0.831)
15–Yr Totals		1173	0.54	121	17.3	21%	0.42	110	134–32 (0.807)

Table 22.2. Chris Mullin's Career Summary Statistics

Season	Tm	G	Floor %	Off. Rtg.	Pts Prod/G	% Tm Poss	Stop %	Def. Rtg.	W–L (%)
1986	GSW	55	0.54	112	12.8	21%	0.43	112	2.8–3.0 (0.485)
1987	GSW	82	0.55	113	13.9	20%	0.42	113	4.9–4.6 (0.518)
1988	GSW	60	0.54	114	19.1	23%	0.45	113	4.9–4.2 (0.535)
1989	GSW	82	0.55	114	25.2	26%	0.46	107	10.3–4.1 (0.717)
1990	GSW	78	0.56	120	23.6	24%	0.45	113	9.3–3.5 (0.724)
1991	GSW	82	0.57	120	23.9	23%	0.46	110	11.3–3.3 (0.772)
1992	GSW	81	0.56	117	23.3	22%	0.46	110	10.2–4.2 (0.707)
1993	GSW	46	0.53	112	22.5	23%	0.45	111	4.6–3.9 (0.538)
1994	GSW	62	0.52	110	15.8	20%	0.48	111	4.5–5.2 (0.461)
1995	GSW	25	0.49	108	18.0	23%	0.47	112	1.4–2.5 (0.366)
1996	GSW	55	0.52	113	12.5	19%	0.47	111	3.7–2.9 (0.564)
1997	GSW	79	0.54	116	13.6	18%	0.49	112	7.0–3.9 (0.642)
1998	IND	82	0.50	113	10.1	18%	0.51	101	7.3–1.5 (0.826)
1999	IND	50	0.50	116	8.9	18%	0.52	104	4.0–0.8 (0.827)
2000	IND	47	0.45	111	4.6	17%	0.52	103	1.7–0.6 (0.738)
2001	GSW	20	0.41	98	5.3	15%	0.48	108	0.3–1.1 (0.211)
16–Yr Totals		986	0.54	115	16.8	22%	0.47	110	88–49 (0.640)

Miller in particular was very valuable. Miller's career numbers reflect a 9.4–2.2 record per eighty-two games, a very good figure, but not equivalent to the 14.9–2.3 that Jordan averaged. Miller has been remarkably consistent through the years in terms of his win–loss record, posting between nine and eleven wins and between one and three losses pretty much every season since his third in the league. Consistency is definitely a sign of greatness.

Mullin had some very good years, his top being in 1991 when his win–loss record was 11.3–3.3. His offensive ratings never got as high as Miller's—only 120 compared to Miller's 129. He was a good player, and his peak seasons reflect a good player at his best, but he didn't show the sustained greatness.

The last thing I want to do with these scorers is make a relative comparison with Dennis Rodman. One might look at Reggie Miller as the best pure-shooting role player who ever played. He shot so well that it was all he really had to do to be an All-Star and a member of several U.S. teams. He wasn't, however, the kind of do-it-all person that Jordan, Bird, Magic, or many centers were. In that capacity, he added about 9.6 wins and 2.3 losses per eighty-two games. For perspective, consider Dennis Rodman. Rodman was perhaps the best pure non-shooting role player who ever played. He was effectively the anti-Reggie, doing things that Reggie didn't and not doing things that Reggie did. In that capacity, he added 8.3 wins and 2.0 losses per eighty-two games. As a purely subjective judgment, it doesn't seem bad to me that these two opposite-style extreme players end up with similar win–loss records. Some might argue that Rodman should look better than Miller. I'm certainly not convinced, but I do hope that people can agree that neither of them, though both very good players, contributed as much as the ultra-superstars in the previous chapter.

Defensive Specialists

The man defender who can shut down his own man is a convenient player for a coach. You just stick him out there with a defensive assignment, and you don't have to worry about things. There is no complex coordination of rotation assignments or forcing dribblers to go one way into help defense. In a defense where all players can guard their man alone, defense is simple and good. Passing to men left open through a double-team just doesn't happen as often in an offense built around straight man defense. But if one or two players cannot cover their men, it can neutralize the benefit of everyone else on that defense. Opposing teams get the ball to the player with the mismatch and let him go, knowing that help defense probably won't come.

That's why straight man defenders who don't also help other players to force the ends of possessions can be either valuable or not valuable. And those are the players I'm looking at here. Joe Dumars was the player examined in chapter 17 as the classic great man defender who put up no defensive stats to suggest how good he was. Though I'm not convinced that the current statistics will ever character-ize this type of player perfectly, I do think they reflect some of this mixed benefit that they provide. The numbers generally show that if these man defenders are on a good defense, they look good. If they're not, they don't.

Until Dumars's offense grew to a high level, his value was generally marginal (table 22.3). His stop percentage was continuously low, but, in guarding the toughest defensive assignments during Detroit's best years between 1987 and 1992, he did some valuable defensive work. Until we can determine how valuable that was, which will happen when more box scores are available, his value was questionable. At this point, a lot of the responsibility for the success of those

Table 22.3. Joe Dumars's Career Summary Statistics

Season	Tm	G	Floor %	Off. Rtg.	Pts Prod/G	% Tm Poss	Stop %	Def. Rtg.	W–L (%)
1986	DET	82	0.54	109	10.3	18%	0.37	112	2.9–4.2 (0.411)
1987	DET	79	0.53	107	12.1	17%	0.39	109	3.8–4.9 (0.435)
1988	DET	82	0.54	109	14.3	19%	0.40	108	5.4–5.0 (0.519)
1989	DET	69	0.55	114	17.2	22%	0.39	109	6.2–3.2 (0.659)
1990	DET	75	0.56	116	17.2	22%	0.40	107	7.8–2.6 (0.748)
1991	DET	80	0.56	115	19.7	24%	0.40	108	8.8–3.9 (0.695)
1992	DET	82	0.53	112	19.0	23%	0.37	110	7.1–5.7 (0.555)
1993	DET	77	0.54	117	21.0	23%	0.37	113	7.7–4.8 (0.619)
1994	DET	69	0.50	109	18.6	23%	0.36	115	3.4–7.1 (0.321)
1995	DET	67	0.47	103	17.8	24%	0.36	117	1.3–9.0 (0.128)
1996	DET	67	0.50	115	11.6	17%	0.40	110	5.1–2.6 (0.666)
1997	DET	79	0.50	116	14.0	19%	0.39	110	7.3–3.3 (0.692)
1998	DET	72	0.48	114	12.1	18%	0.37	109	5.1–2.9 (0.637)
1999	DET	38	0.46	112	10.6	18%	0.38	106	2.7–1.2 (0.688)
14–Yr Totals		1018	0.52	112	15.6	21%	0.38	110	75–60 (0.553)

Table 22.4. Bill Laimbeer's Career Summary Statistics

Season	Tm	G	Floor %	Off. Rtg.	Pts Prod/G	% Tm Poss	Stop %	Def. Rtg.	W–L (%)
1981	CLE	81	0.56	112	10.8	15%	0.50	107	6.0–3.6 (0.630)
1982	CLE	50	0.54	110	7.3	18%	0.50	110	1.9–1.8 (0.512)
1982	DET	30	0.57	115	13.2	17%	0.53	104	3.1–0.7 (0.811)
1983	DET	82	0.56	113	14.5	17%	0.54	103	9.1–2.6 (0.779)
1984	DET	82	0.60	122	16.8	18%	0.51	106	10.7–1.2 (0.899)
1985	DET	82	0.58	117	16.7	19%	0.53	105	10.2–2.1 (0.828)
1986	DET	82	0.57	115	16.2	18%	0.54	105	9.9–2.5 (0.796)
1987	DET	82	0.58	118	14.9	17%	0.56	103	10.7–1.3 (0.893)
1988	DET	82	0.55	113	13.2	16%	0.56	102	9.4–2.5 (0.792)
1989	DET	81	0.55	113	12.9	17%	0.59	101	9.5–1.8 (0.843)
1990	DET	81	0.56	118	11.7	15%	0.58	100	10.1–0.8 (0.926)
1991	DET	82	0.54	114	10.8	15%	0.54	103	8.4–2.0 (0.806)
1992	DET	81	0.51	106	9.2	16%	0.51	104	4.9–3.9 (0.558)
1993	DET	79	0.57	118	8.2	15%	0.50	108	5.8–1.6 (0.789)
1994	DET	11	0.54	111	8.7	18%	0.51	109	0.6–0.5 (0.562)
14–Yr Totals		1068	0.56	115	12.7	17%	0.54	104	110–29 (0.793)

Pistons teams goes to the big guys like Rodman and Laimbeer. Laimbeer's numbers were surprisingly good, as shown in table 22.4.

T.R. Dunn was a man defender who hung around the league for fourteen years, posting single-digit scoring averages (table 22.5). Guys who stick around that long must be offering something besides their points. In this case, Dunn's value as a defender was questionable as he served on a lot of bad defenses, including the 1982 Nuggets, which was one of the worst. But Dunn did register more steals and blocks than Dumars by creating more stops. Also, Dunn didn't hurt the team offensively, being a smart role player who didn't make many mistakes and who finished when he had his shot. He didn't make any Denver offenses good, but he was a piece that fit into a team that had many players who could shoot well. His overall winning percentage throughout his career was over .500, though he contributed a win–loss record of only 3.9–2.6 per eighty-two games.

Table 22.5. T.R. Dunn's Career Summary Statistics

Season	Tm	G	Floor %	Off. Rtg.	Pts Prod/G	% Tm Poss	Stop %	Def. Rtg.	W–L (%)
1978	POR	63	0.49	98	4.0	15%	0.52	97	1.6–1.4 (0.534)
1979	POR	80	0.52	105	7.9	15%	0.48	103	3.8–3.0 (0.556)
1980	POR	82	0.51	102	7.3	16%	0.51	104	3.2–3.9 (0.447)
1981	DEN	82	0.52	104	5.2	13%	0.47	109	1.7–3.4 (0.328)
1982	DEN	82	0.57	114	9.5	12%	0.49	112	5.3–3.9 (0.576)
1983	DEN	82	0.55	111	9.1	11%	0.49	108	5.5–3.7 (0.596)
1984	DEN	80	0.56	113	7.6	9%	0.51	110	5.5–3.7 (0.601)
1985	DEN	81	0.58	117	6.4	9%	0.47	108	5.4–1.8 (0.747)
1986	DEN	82	0.56	113	6.1	8%	0.49	105	5.7–2.0 (0.744)
1987	DEN	81	0.55	110	4.2	7%	0.45	110	2.8–3.0 (0.478)
1988	DEN	82	0.60	121	3.1	6%	0.48	106	4.0–0.6 (0.874)
1989	PHO	34	0.58	116	1.8	7%	0.43	108	0.7–0.2 (0.755)
1990	DEN	65	0.56	112	2.3	9%	0.51	105	1.5–0.6 (0.711)
1991	DEN	17	0.56	117	3.8	11%	0.43	115	0.4–0.3 (0.560)
14–Yr Totals		**993**	**0.55**	**110**	**6.0**	**10%**	**0.49**	**107**	**47–31 (0.598)**

Table 22.6. Bill Hanzlik's Career Summary Statistics

Season	Tm	G	Floor %	Off. Rtg.	Pts Prod/G	% Tm Poss	Stop %	Def. Rtg.	W–L (%)
1981	SEA	74	0.53	107	5.6	15%	0.45	106	2.4–2.1 (0.532)
1982	SEA	81	0.53	107	6.6	12%	0.46	104	4.0–2.6 (0.603)
1983	DEN	82	0.49	98	7.3	17%	0.45	109	1.1–4.9 (0.181)
1984	DEN	80	0.53	108	6.7	15%	0.44	112	2.0–3.4 (0.378)
1985	DEN	80	0.52	103	8.4	17%	0.44	109	2.0–4.3 (0.319)
1986	DEN	79	0.53	108	13.0	22%	0.47	106	4.7–3.8 (0.552)
1987	DEN	73	0.52	108	13.3	20%	0.44	111	3.3–4.9 (0.407)
1988	DEN	77	0.47	96	5.2	14%	0.46	107	0.9–3.8 (0.198)
1989	DEN	41	0.49	99	5.3	14%	0.43	109	0.5–1.9 (0.226)
1990	DEN	81	0.52	106	6.6	14%	0.47	107	2.7–3.1 (0.466)
10–Yr Totals		**748**	**0.52**	**105**	**7.9**	**16%**	**0.45**	**108**	**24–35 (0.406)**

A good contrast to Dunn is his former teammate Bill Hanzlik, who fit a similar mold. Hanzlik was also a nonscoring defender, though taller than Dunn. Hanzlik didn't survive quite as long as Dunn because, though he could score more *frequently* than Dunn, he couldn't maintain a high offensive rating. By being a slightly worse defender, too, he was actually hurting teams (table 22.6).

Michael Cooper and Maurice Cheeks were two other players with solid defensive reputations in the 1980s. They both played for very successful teams, the Lakers and the Sixers. Cheeks had a greater offensive role than Cooper, though both acted as point guards. Again, as primarily man defenders, their numbers don't look as great as their reputations would suggest (tables 22.7 and 22.8). But both do come out looking good, especially Cheeks. Whether he deserves Hall of Fame membership for such a good win–loss record is a subject for another book.

In the modern era, Gary Payton has been known as The Glove for being able to shut down opposing scorers. This was true in the mid-1990s, but his defense has definitely declined. The voters for the NBA All-Defense Team disagree, having named him to the First Team All-Defense from 1994 through 2002. But not only do my numbers in table 22.9 suggest a decline, any numbers you look at suggest likewise. The Sonics team defense was below average from 1999 to 2002. Point

Table 22.7. Michael Cooper's Career Summary Statistics

Season	Tm	G	Floor %	Off. Rtg.	Pts Prod/G	% Tm Poss	Stop %	Def. Rtg.	W–L (%)
1979	LAL	3	0.39	79	1.4	33%	0.59	99	0.0–0.0 (0.058)
1980	LAL	82	0.53	108	9.1	16%	0.43	106	3.9–3.2 (0.546)
1981	LAL	81	0.53	106	10.4	14%	0.46	105	5.0–4.3 (0.538)
1982	LAL	76	0.54	109	11.6	17%	0.47	106	5.0–3.5 (0.594)
1983	LAL	82	0.56	114	8.7	13%	0.47	105	5.7–1.9 (0.750)
1984	LAL	82	0.56	118	10.7	14%	0.47	107	7.0–1.7 (0.800)
1985	LAL	82	0.52	109	10.0	16%	0.45	107	4.7–3.5 (0.572)
1986	LAL	82	0.53	113	10.7	16%	0.45	107	5.8–2.6 (0.691)
1987	LAL	82	0.53	116	11.0	16%	0.43	108	6.0–2.3 (0.727)
1988	LAL	61	0.48	106	9.9	15%	0.45	108	2.9–3.7 (0.435)
1989	LAL	80	0.51	114	8.0	14%	0.44	108	4.4–2.3 (0.663)
1990	LAL	80	0.47	103	6.9	15%	0.45	108	2.3–4.4 (0.340)
12–Yr Totals		873	0.53	111	9.7	15%	0.45	107	53–33 (0.612)

Table 22.8. Maurice Cheeks's Career Summary Statistics

Season	Tm	G	Floor %	Off. Rtg.	Pts Prod/G	% Tm Poss	Stop %	Def. Rtg.	W–L (%)
1979	PHI	82	0.51	101	9.6	15%	0.50	100	4.8–4.1 (0.540)
1980	PHI	79	0.55	111	13.1	16%	0.50	101	7.9–2.1 (0.787)
1981	PHI	81	0.57	114	11.5	16%	0.53	99	8.2–1.0 (0.887)
1982	PHI	79	0.57	115	13.8	18%	0.53	102	8.7–1.6 (0.843)
1983	PHI	79	0.58	117	13.9	18%	0.50	101	8.8–1.0 (0.900)
1984	PHI	75	0.57	114	13.6	17%	0.48	105	7.3–2.3 (0.761)
1985	PHI	78	0.61	124	13.9	16%	0.46	108	8.8–1.0 (0.896)
1986	PHI	82	0.59	119	17.4	18%	0.45	107	10.3–2.2 (0.826)
1987	PHI	68	0.58	117	17.0	19%	0.47	108	7.9–2.6 (0.753)
1988	PHI	79	0.58	118	15.5	18%	0.46	110	8.2–3.1 (0.724)
1989	PHI	71	0.57	115	13.6	18%	0.42	113	5.0–3.7 (0.574)
1990	SAN	50	0.56	114	12.2	15%	0.43	107	4.4–1.8 (0.708)
1990	NYK	31	0.63	129	8.8	14%	0.46	108	2.5–0.1 (0.949)
1991	NYK	76	0.56	113	9.1	14%	0.48	107	5.3–2.5 (0.679)
1992	ATL	56	0.55	111	5.5	13%	0.49	108	2.2–1.6 (0.571)
1993	NJN	35	0.56	114	4.4	13%	0.49	105	1.4–0.4 (0.759)
15–Yr Totals		1101	0.57	115	12.6	17%	0.48	105	102–31 (0.764)

Table 22.9. Gary Payton's Career Summary Statistics

Season	Tm	G	Floor %	Off. Rtg.	Pts Prod/G	% Tm Poss	Stop %	Def. Rtg.	W–L (%)
1991	SEA	82	0.51	103	9.7	17%	0.49	108	3.1–5.8 (0.350)
1992	SEA	81	0.52	104	11.5	18%	0.46	109	3.5–6.4 (0.351)
1993	SEA	82	0.56	112	14.0	20%	0.49	105	7.7–3.0 (0.718)
1994	SEA	82	0.55	110	16.7	22%	0.48	103	8.7–3.5 (0.714)
1995	SEA	82	0.56	116	20.7	24%	0.48	107	10.2–3.4 (0.752)
1996	SEA	81	0.52	109	19.9	24%	0.53	102	10.2–4.1 (0.713)
1997	SEA	82	0.53	111	21.5	26%	0.52	103	11.2–3.9 (0.743)
1998	SEA	82	0.53	111	20.7	26%	0.51	103	11.2–3.6 (0.757)
1999	SEA	50	0.51	100	22.4	28%	0.51	106	5.7–4.2 (0.578)
2000	SEA	82	0.52	111	24.5	27%	0.51	104	11.6–5.0 (0.700)
2001	SEA	79	0.52	111	24.0	28%	0.47	107	9.5–5.8 (0.620)
2002	SEA	82	0.54	114	23.9	28%	0.48	108	10.7–5.1 (0.680)
12–Yr Totals		947	0.53	111	19.0	24%	0.49	105	103–54 (0.658)

guards have generally shot about the same or a little better against the Sonics than against the rest of the league. Doug Steele, who has collected statistics for me, also has been tracking how Payton's defensive assignments have done relative to their own average performance levels since 1996. He found Payton to be among the best in the league at his position in 1996 and 1997, but he fell off in 1998 and even more in 1999 so that he now rests at about average defensively. 'Nuff said.

Payton has done a lot more than play defense in his career. He's also been a fine point producer. That shows up clearly in his stats as he has regularly posted ten-plus win seasons since 1995.

Then there is Bruce Bowen (table 22.10), who was named to a couple of Second Teams All-Defense. Bowen is another specialist like T.R. Dunn, stopping the highest scoring off-guards and small forwards but contributing little himself on the offensive end. He was first acknowledged for his defense in 2001 while in Miami. But Pat Riley didn't see enough value in his defense to keep him, allowing him to leave for nothing. Bowen ended up in San Antonio, where his role was the same—defensive guy. As in Miami, where he had other scorers around him, his defense was good, but not good enough to make up for a hesitant and off-the-mark shooting touch. Though Bowen's career defensive rating is a very good 102, it's not good enough to make up for a career offensive rating of ninety-seven. (As noted in chapter 7, San Antonio actually played significantly better *offense* in 2002 with Bowen than without him, a highly unexpected result. Perhaps Bowen's defense turns defensive stops into offensive scores a lot more often than normal. Or it could just be a weird fluke, which seems more likely at this point. Other Bowen teams have not shown any significant differences either offensively or defensively when he is in the lineup.)

So if I've been critical of these guys, what players really were great defensively? My system likes players who can both cover man-to-man and help teammates on defense. Centers, by being in the middle of the defense, almost automatically have to help, so if they can also shut down their men, they look pretty good. Dikembe Mutombo, for example, has been tremendous in his career. When he's been traded, there has always been a clear decline in his former team's defense and a corresponding improvement in his new team's defense. His excellent career defensive rating of ninety-nine reflects this (table 22.11).

Besides centers, there are perimeter players who have shown multifaceted ability on defense. Jordan (career defensive rating: 103), Rodman (one hundred),

Table 22.10. Bruce Bowen's Career Summary Statistics

Season	Tm	G	Floor %	Off. Rtg.	Pts Prod/G	% Tm Poss	Stop %	Def. Rtg.	W–L (%)
1997	MIA	1	0.00	0	0.0	0%	1.00	60	—
1998	BOS	61	0.50	103	5.8	14%	0.51	104	2.1–2.7 (0.442)
1999	BOS	30	0.38	80	2.6	10%	0.47	104	0.1–1.5 (0.032)
2000	PHI	42	0.46	91	1.5	11%	0.44	104	0.2–0.8 (0.165)
2000	MIA	27	0.44	103	4.6	11%	0.46	104	0.8–1.0 (0.468)
2001	MIA	82	0.42	97	7.3	13%	0.49	100	3.6–5.4 (0.397)
2002	SAN	59	0.42	94	6.9	14%	0.47	102	1.7–4.8 (0.261)
6–Yr Totals		**302**	**0.44**	**97**	**5.4**	**13%**	**0.48**	**102**	**8–16 (0.343)**

Table 22.11. Dikembe Mutombo's Career Summary Statistics

Season	Tm	G	Floor %	Off. Rtg.	Pts Prod/G	% Tm Poss	Stop %	Def. Rtg.	W–L (%)
1992	DEN	71	0.53	103	17.0	21%	0.54	106	5.1–7.1 (0.417)
1993	DEN	82	0.56	110	14.5	17%	0.60	102	9.7–3.4 (0.741)
1994	DEN	82	0.55	108	12.3	16%	0.65	96	10.3–2.3 (0.818)
1995	DEN	82	0.56	112	12.3	15%	0.61	103	9.8–3.2 (0.755)
1996	DEN	74	0.55	109	11.6	15%	0.66	101	8.7–3.1 (0.740)
1997	ATL	80	0.56	111	13.4	18%	0.65	97	11.6–1.6 (0.877)
1998	ATL	82	0.57	114	13.2	18%	0.63	99	11.3–1.6 (0.875)
1999	ATL	50	0.58	114	11.4	15%	0.64	92	7.3–0.3 (0.960)
2000	ATL	82	0.58	116	12.0	15%	0.66	101	11.4–1.5 (0.883)
2001	ATL	49	0.52	105	10.1	14%	0.67	98	5.2–2.1 (0.708)
2001	PHI	26	0.57	115	12.6	17%	0.63	95	3.5–0.2 (0.937)
2002	PHI	80	0.55	111	11.6	15%	0.59	98	10.3–1.8 (0.851)
11–Yr Totals		**840**	**0.56**	**110**	**12.8**	**17%**	**0.63**	**99**	**104–28 (0.786)**

Bird (early in his career with ratings around one hundred, and he always had quick hands), Karl Malone (101), John Stockton (career steals leader, career rating 104), their Jazz coach Jerry Sloan (ratings around ninety-two, about seven points better than the league average), Jason Kidd (102), and Bobby Jones (100) all qualify. These are guys who could guard a man and help out successfully on other players, a valuable combination of abilities that is more difficult for non-centers.

The Promises

There have been so many players with so much talent who have wasted it. They promised to give us so much more than they delivered. Chris Washburn was the most stark example during my impressionable years—a kid leaving North Carolina State after a single troubled season. Unlike the modern NBA, where really young kids are given a bit more time to develop, Washburn entered the league in 1986 as the surprise number-two pick in the draft and was expected to produce immediately. Whether it was pressure or lack of structure or lack of precedent, Washburn wasn't ready for the NBA. His performance on the court was not very good, not even for a rookie. Teammates recognized his talent but also sensed that he was distracted by so many other things that he was going to waste his talent. The big distraction for him was a drug problem, which, when discovered, promptly cost him his career. That career lasted not even two unproductive seasons (table 22.12)

Could Washburn have succeeded with a different organization or with a different coach? Maybe, but there really was no sign in his numbers of his supposed talent.

Table 22.12. Chris Washburn's Career Summary Statistics

Season	Tm	G	Floor %	Off. Rtg.	Pts Prod/G	% Tm Poss	Stop %	Def. Rtg.	W–L (%)
1987	GSW	35	0.40	78	3.9	22%	0.45	111	0.0–1.6 (0.004)
1988	GSW	8	0.46	92	4.2	20%	0.38	115	0.0–0.3 (0.032)
1988	ATL	29	0.51	100	2.0	17%	0.54	105	0.2–0.5 (0.345)
2–Yr Totals		**72**	**0.44**	**84**	**3.2**	**20%**	**0.47**	**110**	**0.3–2.4 (0.099)**

Table 22.13. Cedric Ceballos's Career Summary Statistics

Season	Tm	G	Floor %	Off. Rtg.	Pts Prod/G	% Tm Poss	Stop %	Def. Rtg.	W–L (%)
1991	PHO	63	0.52	104	7.5	30%	0.42	109	1.2–2.3 (0.353)
1992	PHO	64	0.52	104	6.7	28%	0.43	108	1.2–2.2 (0.364)
1993	PHO	74	0.60	120	11.8	22%	0.48	107	5.9–1.1 (0.840)
1994	PHO	53	0.57	115	16.8	24%	0.46	108	5.2–2.0 (0.719)
1995	LAL	58	0.53	111	19.2	25%	0.47	110	4.8–4.4 (0.521)
1996	LAL	78	0.56	116	18.9	25%	0.47	107	9.1–2.9 (0.761)
1997	LAL	8	0.44	94	10.3	17%	0.48	105	0.2–0.9 (0.181)
1997	PHO	42	0.51	105	13.9	25%	0.50	108	2.1–3.2 (0.391)
1998	PHO	35	0.53	109	8.6	23%	0.53	101	2.1–0.7 (0.740)
1998	DAL	12	0.50	103	15.8	27%	0.49	106	0.7–1.1 (0.394)
1999	DAL	13	0.46	96	11.6	24%	0.51	104	0.4–1.2 (0.262)
2000	DAL	69	0.49	104	15.6	26%	0.49	107	3.7–5.9 (0.383)
2001	DET	13	0.43	99	5.1	21%	0.51	102	0.3–0.4 (0.395)
2001	MIA	27	0.48	103	6.2	23%	0.52	99	1.1–0.7 (0.611)
11–Yr Totals		**609**	**0.53**	**110**	**12.9**	**25%**	**0.48**	**107**	**38–29 (0.567)**

By contrast, the 1993 Phoenix Suns had three young players with great promise: Cedric Ceballos, Richard Dumas, and Oliver Miller. Of these, Dumas and Miller never lived up to some very early promise. Ceballos himself had a couple of "incidents" in his career involving coaches and unscheduled water skiing, but he proved to be at least an average NBA starter. His career is shown on paper in table 22.13.

Dumas was a slasher who dominated the Long Beach summer league games to the point that observers stated he was the best to ever play there. During his first year in Phoenix for the nearly champion Suns, he played a valuable scoring role off the bench. He was efficient, he was productive, and then he got busted for drugs (table 22.14). He was forced to sit out 1994 in rehab, returning in 1995 to earn relatively few minutes. After a rookie season with a bell curve win–loss record of 4.0–2.0, his career ended after 1996 with relatively poor numbers.

Miller came out of Arkansas as a center with great hands, good shooting touch, and good passing skills on the post. At 6'9", he was undersized vertically, but at 290 pounds, he was oversized horizontally. The horizontal issue ended up limiting his minutes in the NBA. His stop percentage was over 60 percent his first three seasons in the league (table 22.15), but then it fluctuated at lower levels as his weight ballooned. In his second season in the pros, he showed promise with an offensive rating of 108 and a defensive rating of 101. Miller was last seen playing for a good ABA team.

Do you remember Walter Berry? At St. John's, he was a unanimous selection for Player of the Year, and he won the Wooden Award his junior year. But he was

Table 22.14. Richard Dumas's Career Summary Statistics

Season	Tm	G	Floor %	Off. Rtg.	Pts Prod/G	% Tm Poss	Stop %	Def. Rtg.	W–L (%)
1993	PHO	48	0.55	111	14.3	23%	0.52	105	4.0–2.0 (0.670)
1995	PHO	15	0.52	104	5.1	22%	0.50	110	0.2–0.5 (0.323)
1996	PHI	39	0.49	98	6.1	17%	0.48	112	0.4–2.6 (0.125)
3–Yr Totals		**102**	**0.53**	**107**	**9.8**	**21%**	**0.51**	**108**	**4.6–5.1 (0.478)**

Table 22.15. Oliver Miller's Career Summary Statistics

Season	Tm	G	Floor %	Off. Rtg.	Pts Prod/G	% Tm Poss	Stop %	Def. Rtg.	W–L (%)
1993	PHO	56	0.48	97	6.4	17%	0.60	102	1.6–3.0 (0.353)
1994	PHO	69	0.54	108	9.8	17%	0.63	101	5.8–2.3 (0.718)
1995	DET	64	0.53	106	8.8	18%	0.61	107	3.4–3.7 (0.476)
1996	TOR	76	0.51	102	12.8	19%	0.56	108	3.6–7.5 (0.323)
1997	DAL	42	0.46	91	5.1	15%	0.63	103	0.6–2.9 (0.177)
1997	TOR	19	0.56	113	6.0	17%	0.57	105	1.0–0.3 (0.742)
1998	TOR	64	0.48	95	7.6	16%	0.52	109	0.9–5.7 (0.135)
1999	SAC	4	0.41	84	2.9	20%	0.35	109	0.0–0.1 (0.024)
2000	PHO	51	0.53	106	6.4	14%	0.62	95	3.5–0.8 (0.806)
8–Yr Totals		**445**	**0.51**	**102**	**8.4**	**17%**	**0.59**	**104**	**20–26 (0.435)**

selfish, unpopular, didn't like to practice, and didn't play much defense. Consider this 1988 *Sporting News* quote about Berry: "Walter Berry, who isn't in good stead with Spurs management, also isn't particularly popular with the public. He recently conducted a camp in San Antonio in which only four kids attended the first week."

The Spurs hired Larry Brown that summer to take over the team, and one of his tasks was deciding what to do with Berry, who had a good year in 1988 (table 22.16) but was haunted by the selfishness label. Brown was a coach known to emphasize fundamentals, and Berry reportedly said that he wasn't a "fundamental player," so Brown fundamentally shipped him off to New Jersey. Berry lasted not even half a season there before getting shipped to Houston, then shipped out of the country. Berry played very well overseas for a long time, which seems to have been where the NBA wanted him.

Another promising player who failed in the NBA was Ralph Sampson, but he failed for reasons other than attitude, weight, or drugs. Sampson was a three-time First Team All-American in college at Virginia and the number one pick of the Houston Rockets in 1983. At 7′ 4″ with great offensive skills, how could he miss? It turned out that he could miss by being too thin and too fragile. He started off fine, winning Rookie of the Year honors. He had an offensive rating of 104 as a rookie and a net win–loss record of 7.0–6.9 (table 22.17). He looked to be on his way to a solid career.

But then Houston got "lucky"—they won the rights to the number-one pick in the draft, whom everyone knew would be Akeem Olajuwon, another center. Also available was one Michael Jordan, but even the Rockets, with their franchise

Table 22.16. Walter Berry's Career Summary Statistics

Season	Tm	G	Floor %	Off. Rtg.	Pts Prod/G	% Tm Poss	Stop %	Def. Rtg.	W–L (%)
1987	POR	7	0.81	166	1.6	16%	0.64	101	0.1–0.0 (1.000)
1987	SAN	56	0.53	105	15.8	25%	0.42	112	2.0–5.0 (0.289)
1988	SAN	73	0.55	109	15.3	25%	0.43	113	3.1–5.5 (0.359)
1989	NJN	29	0.49	98	8.1	21%	0.44	110	0.4–1.9 (0.161)
1989	HOU	40	0.56	111	8.3	18%	0.47	106	2.1–1.0 (0.673)
Totals		**205**	**0.54**	**107**	**12.6**	**23%**	**0.44**	**111**	**8–13 (0.363)**

Table 22.17. Ralph Sampson's Career Summary Statistics

Season	Tm	G	Floor %	Off. Rtg.	Pts Prod/G	% Tm Poss	Stop %	Def. Rtg.	W–L (%)
1984	HOU	82	0.52	104	19.6	26%	0.58	104	7.0–6.9 (0.505)
1985	HOU	82	0.52	102	20.5	25%	0.54	104	6.9–8.1 (0.461)
1986	HOU	79	0.51	101	18.6	24%	0.55	104	5.5–8.2 (0.403)
1987	HOU	43	0.50	99	14.8	23%	0.56	102	2.5–3.9 (0.389)
1988	HOU	19	0.48	96	15.7	21%	0.50	105	0.7–2.3 (0.242)
1988	GSW	29	0.46	92	15.6	24%	0.54	109	0.5–4.3 (0.096)
1989	GSW	61	0.48	96	6.8	18%	0.51	105	1.1–3.4 (0.247)
1990	SAC	26	0.37	74	4.2	18%	0.56	106	0.0–1.8 (0.005)
1991	SAC	25	0.39	78	3.7	17%	0.58	104	0.0–1.5 (0.020)
1992	WAS	10	0.36	72	2.7	17%	0.55	105	0.0–0.4 (0.004)
9–Yr Totals		**456**	**0.50**	**99**	**14.9**	**24%**	**0.56**	**104**	**24–41 (0.374)**

center drafted the year before, couldn't pass on the rights to Olajuwon. And so the Twin Towers era began. Olajuwon was perceived at the time as having the back-to-the-basket game that required him to play center, whereas Sampson could play facing the basket, so Sampson was moved to power forward. The team definitely played better with the Twin Towers, going from twenty-eight wins in Sampson's rookie year to forty-eight wins in Olajuwon's rookie year, but Sampson himself didn't show signs of improvement. He showed signs of transition. His offensive rating slightly declined to 102, and moving away from the center position cost him a bit of defensive effectiveness because he occasionally had to guard quicker people.

Sampson's decline continued very slowly in 1986, though the Rockets as a team got better. People seemed to know by then that it was Olajuwon's team, not Sampson's. Sampson's offensive rating dropped to 101, and his share of the offense dropped to 24 percent, but the Rockets won fifty-one games and reached the NBA Finals. Sampson's big redemption was hitting the off-balance prayer to beat the Lakers in the Western Conference Finals after Olajuwon had fouled out.

Then came the disastrous 1987 season when two Rockets were expelled from the league for drugs (this must be the Don't Do Drugs chapter) and Sampson's knees began giving out. It would take several years for the Rockets to recover, and Sampson never would. Sampson's career numbers go downhill more dramatically than anyone else I've seen. After his promising start, it was hard to watch him as he declined. It's almost as hard to look at the numbers.

Finally, I can't let this section go by without revisiting Derrick Coleman. I wrote a whole chapter on him and how his Charlotte teams just didn't seem to fare as well with him in the lineup as with him sitting out. Coleman was also a number-one draft pick, but through most of his career, Coleman's teams did seem to play better defense with him out of the lineup than with him in it. There are three exceptions: 1992, 1996, and 1997 (I don't have records for his 1991 season). Those three seasons are interesting because they were the three worst *team* defenses he played on, as shown in table 22.18.

Table 22.18. Team Defensive Ratings for Derrick Coleman

Season	With Coleman	Overall	Difference
1992	110.0	111.0	-1.1
1993	105.8	105.2	0.6
1994	105.2	104.9	0.3
1995	110.1	108.6	1.5
1996	111.8	113.0	-1.1
1997	110.0	111.5	-1.4
1998	106.4	105.4	1.0
1999	104.5	102.4	2.1
2000	102.0	101.5	0.6
2001	101.3	99.9	1.4
2002	101.9	100.3	1.6

Table 22.19. Derrick Coleman's Career Summary Statistics

Season	Tm	G	Floor %	Off. Rtg.	Pts Prod/G	% Tm Poss	Stop %	Def. Rtg.	W–L (%)
1991	NJN	74	0.53	106	17.9	23%	0.52	106	6.1–5.9 (0.506)
1992	NJN	65	0.54	110	18.9	25%	0.51	108	5.9–4.7 (0.556)
1993	NJN	76	0.53	109	20.4	26%	0.58	102	10.1–3.8 (0.728)
1994	NJN	77	0.54	110	19.9	25%	0.57	102	10.0–3.5 (0.740)
1995	NJN	56	0.52	106	19.9	26%	0.54	107	4.8–5.5 (0.465)
1996	PHI	11	0.43	89	11.1	24%	0.52	110	0.1–1.3 (0.050)
1997	PHI	57	0.50	103	17.8	24%	0.53	108	3.4–6.5 (0.347)
1998	PHI	59	0.49	102	17.0	25%	0.55	104	4.3–5.8 (0.424)
1999	CHA	37	0.47	96	13.2	23%	0.57	101	2.9–6.1 (0.322)
2000	CHA	74	0.49	103	15.5	24%	0.57	100	6.5–4.5 (0.590)
2001	CHA	34	0.45	96	7.9	22%	0.55	100	1.1–1.9 (0.368)
2002	PHI	58	0.51	106	14.5	21%	0.52	102	5.8–3.3 (0.636)
12–Yr Totals		678	0.51	105	17.2	24%	0.55	104	61–53 (0.535)

So, on a real bad defense, Coleman was fairly valuable, but on good to average defenses, he was a liability. That implies that at least Coleman wasn't the worst defender in the league. A defensive rating of about 106 may fit the pattern. My defensive rating formulas suggest a better number, about 104. If 106 is more accurate, Coleman was slightly worse than a .500 player. As it stands, he looks slightly better than .500 (table 22.19), not all you want out of a number-one pick.

The Freaks

"Freak" is such a horrible term, but so appropriate for certain players in NBA history. Circus freaks were people who were on display for some characteristic so odd that we'd pay to see it. Basketball freaks, such as Manute Bol, Muggsy Bogues, Gheorghe Muresan, and Spud Webb, were players who were on display on NBA hardwood for people to gawk at. Each player's diminutive or gargantuan size was at least as important as his skills. But what were their skills? How good were they? Were they good enough to be in the league, or were they just sideshows?

Bol and Bogues entered the league with the same franchise—the Washington Bullets—and actually played a season together in 1988. Bol, at 7′7″, had already been in Washington two years before the franchise drafted the 5′3″ Bogues out of Wake Forest. After the Bogues pick, the Washington brass had to defend it to the press, insisting that they believed in Bogues's talent and weren't just trying to draw fans to a freak show. But a freak show would have actually helped those Bullets, who, before Bol or Bogues joined the team, were called the "NBA's color-less monument to mediocrity." Having Bol and Bogues around at least meant that the team was interesting, though not any more successful. In 1988, the one year Bol and Bogues played together, the Bullets posted another colorless 38–44 record before leaving Bogues unprotected in the expansion draft. In that year, the two posted the numbers in table 22.20, both with losing records, both with limited impact.

Bogues was taken in the expansion draft by Charlotte. This made sense because, even though Bogues's win–loss record was poor, he showed enough potential to have had a lot of trade value, something Washington didn't recognize, protecting Steve Colter over him. It was a surprising decision at the time, but it seemed that the Bullets had had enough of the freak show because they also let Bol go during that off-season.

Bogues had a fairly productive career, especially during his nine years in Charlotte as a starter whom the Hornets never could quite kick out of the lineup. They always seemed to want to—his jump shot was poor, he couldn't penetrate and be a threat, and opposing guards could easily shoot over him—but his ability to lead a break and to avoid turnovers kept him in the lineup. His teammates also really enjoyed having him around. Bogues was never an All-Star, but he was cer-tainly an inspiration because he proved that someone only 5′3″ could be a legiti-mate NBA starter. His career numbers showed a net winning record (table 22.21), averaging 5.0–3.9 over eighty-two games. He was a lot more than a sideshow.

Bol didn't find a home as Bogues did, despite his record-setting seasons for blocked shots. Bol was so thin that he had a hard time covering powerful players on the post. When you watch games from the 1980s on ESPN Classic, all players look thinner and smaller than modern players, but Bol still stands out, with legs and arms so thin that they look like insect appendages. Bol's coaches tried but couldn't put weight on him, and they had a hard time finding a role for him in the offense. Don Nelson—master of the gimmick—turned him into a three-point shooter in Golden State, primarily to keep him out of the middle where he clogged the lane. After two seasons in the Bay Area, Bol played three in Philadelphia, then

Table 22.20. Summary Statistics for Bogues and Bol in 1988

Player	G	Min/G	Floor %	Off. Rtg.	Pts Prod/G	% Tm Poss	Stop %	Def. Rtg.	W–L (%)
Bogues	79	21	0.49	99	6.7	16%	0.49	106	1.9–4.5 (0.293)
Bol	77	15	0.49	97	2.5	8%	0.61	101	1.6–2.6 (0.378)

Table 22.21. Muggsy Bogues's Career Summary Statistics

Season	Tm	G	Floor %	Off. Rtg.	Pts Prod/G	% Tm Poss	Stop %	Def. Rtg.	W–L (%)
1988	WAB	79	0.49	99	6.7	16%	0.49	106	1.9–4.5 (0.293)
1989	CHA	79	0.53	107	8.3	17%	0.46	111	2.5–4.4 (0.367)
1990	CHA	81	0.57	115	12.9	16%	0.45	110	6.6–3.8 (0.631)
1991	CHA	81	0.56	113	10.0	15%	0.46	111	4.9–3.8 (0.564)
1992	CHA	82	0.55	111	11.9	15%	0.44	112	4.8–5.4 (0.471)
1993	CHA	81	0.55	111	12.8	16%	0.46	110	5.9–4.9 (0.546)
1994	CHA	77	0.55	111	14.3	18%	0.45	110	5.6–4.9 (0.533)
1995	CHA	78	0.56	114	13.6	19%	0.45	108	7.0–3.2 (0.686)
1996	CHA	6	0.48	99	4.1	17%	0.36	117	0.0–0.2 (0.078)
1997	CHA	65	0.52	113	9.9	16%	0.45	111	4.0–3.0 (0.574)
1998	CHA	2	0.52	110	3.5	21%	0.67	98	4.5–0.9 (0.835)
1998	GSW	59	0.49	100	7.2	14%	0.43	108	0.0–0.1 (0.258)
1999	GSW	36	0.52	105	5.8	15%	0.51	101	1.7–1.0 (0.628)
2000	TOR	80	0.53	112	5.9	13%	0.43	108	3.6–2.0 (0.635)
2001	TOR	3	0.17	36	0.8	10%	0.52	103	0.0–0.1 (0.000)
14–Yr Totals		**889**	**0.54**	**110**	**10.1**	**16%**	**0.46**	**109**	**53–42 (0.556)**

Table 22.22. Manute Bol's Career Summary Statistics

Season	Tm	G	Floor %	Off. Rtg.	Pts Prod/G	% Tm Poss	Stop %	Def. Rtg.	W–L (%)
1986	WAB	80	0.49	95	4.1	8%	0.63	99	2.9–4.7 (0.378)
1987	WAB	82	0.47	94	3.1	8%	0.61	101	1.5–4.2 (0.270)
1988	WAB	77	0.49	97	2.5	8%	0.61	101	1.6–2.6 (0.378)
1989	GSW	80	0.42	88	4.2	10%	0.58	102	0.8–5.6 (0.131)
1990	GSW	75	0.37	75	2.2	8%	0.57	108	0.0–4.6 (0.005)
1991	PHI	82	0.40	80	2.2	7%	0.62	103	0.2–5.2 (0.039)
1992	PHI	71	0.41	81	1.9	7%	0.56	106	0.1–4.1 (0.027)
1993	PHI	58	0.38	81	2.3	10%	0.58	106	0.1–3.0 (0.026)
1994	MIA	8	0.09	18	0.3	11%	0.53	105	0.0–0.2 (0.000)
1994	PHI	4	0.51	103	1.5	6%	0.62	103	0.1–0.1 (0.502)
1994	WAB	2	1.00	200	0.2	2%	0.57	107	0.0–0.0 (1.000)
1995	GSW	5	0.54	134	2.2	5%	0.50	111	0.2–0.0 (0.967)
10–Yr Totals		**624**	**0.43**	**87**	**2.8**	**8%**	**0.60**	**103**	**8–34 (0.181)**

got lost in the shuffle in his ninth year and has hardly been seen since. In the end, his numbers show in table 22.22 how bad his offense was and the fact that his defense didn't consist of much more than blocking shots.

Before Bogues entered the league, Spud Webb was a 5′6″ point guard who had won the NBA's slam dunk contest. I wondered at the time whether winning this "sideshow" contest at the All-Star Game hurt or helped Webb's legitimacy as a player, because Webb showed some promise as a point guard. In Atlanta, he earned fifteen minutes per game behind the incumbent Doc Rivers his first four years, then went up to twenty-five minutes per game in 1990 when Rivers was hurt. Even the following year with Rivers back, Webb got nearly thirty minutes per game. But, after four straight fifty-win seasons from 1986 to 1989, the Hawks faltered to forty-one and forty-three wins as Webb got more time. The Hawks were in transition—Dominique Wilkins was getting older—so they moved Webb to Sacramento for Travis Mays.

In Sacramento, Webb was a starter for four years. He played decently, but no one thought he was the solution. The team won between twenty-five and

Table 22.23. Spud Webb's Career Summary Statistics

Season	Tm	G	Floor %	Off. Rtg.	Pts Prod/G	% Tm Poss	Stop %	Def. Rtg.	W–L (%)
1986	ATL	79	0.54	109	8.8	25%	0.50	105	3.5–2.2 (0.615)
1987	ATL	33	0.51	104	8.2	24%	0.51	104	1.2–1.3 (0.481)
1988	ATL	82	0.52	104	7.0	20%	0.47	108	2.2–3.4 (0.385)
1989	ATL	81	0.53	107	5.0	15%	0.47	108	2.1–2.3 (0.478)
1990	ATL	82	0.56	114	10.7	18%	0.43	113	4.5–4.0 (0.530)
1991	ATL	75	0.53	113	13.9	20%	0.44	111	5.1–3.9 (0.566)
1992	SAC	77	0.49	105	16.7	22%	0.42	112	3.4–7.8 (0.303)
1993	SAC	69	0.51	107	15.6	21%	0.42	112	3.3–6.1 (0.349)
1994	SAC	79	0.52	110	13.6	19%	0.42	111	4.6–5.4 (0.459)
1995	SAC	76	0.50	109	12.6	19%	0.40	110	4.1–5.1 (0.446)
1996	ATL	51	0.54	116	6.3	18%	0.40	112	1.9–1.1 (0.632)
1996	MIN	26	0.46	103	10.7	21%	0.42	113	0.6–2.0 (0.230)
1998	ORL	4	0.36	73	3.3	29%	0.38	109	0.0–0.1 (0.003)
12–Yr Totals		**814**	**0.52**	**108**	**10.9**	**20%**	**0.44**	**110**	**36–45 (0.448)**

thirty-nine games in those four years, which was less successful than the thirty-one to fifty wins per season that Charlotte was putting up at the same time under Bogues's leadership. Bogues was also putting up offensive ratings between 111 and 114, whereas Webb was posting ratings between 105 and 110 (table 22.23).

In the end, Webb didn't post quite the resume that Bogues did. His offensive ratings didn't peak as high, though he did use a higher percentage of his team's possessions. Bogues, though not a great defender, pressured ball handlers incessantly and just filled his role a little better than Webb. If game-by-game records are good indicators of how well a player filled his role, Bogues's record of 272–276 looks better than Webb's 160–221 (both going back only through the 1992 season).

The last two players I want to bring up here were both giants. One of them even played a giant in a movie—the movie that essentially ended his career. That would be Gheorghe Muresan, the 7′7″ Bulgarian who played for the Bullets until he tore a tendon in his ankle while filming a scene for the movie *My Giant*. Muresan was actually a pretty good center. He put up offensive ratings as high as 114, and, though he wasn't very mobile, he was a big deterrent in the middle. His career really looks now like it could have been better and longer (table 22.24).

The other giant was Utah's Mark Eaton. Eaton was twice named Defensive Player of the Year, blocking shots and thoroughly shutting down opponents in the middle of the Utah defense. Between 1985 and 1989, the Jazz defense was among history's best. Eaton's defensive rating was around ninety-nine during this period,

Table 22.24. Gheorghe Muresan's Career Summary Statistics

Season	Tm	G	Floor %	Off. Rtg.	Pts Prod/G	% Tm Poss	Stop %	Def. Rtg.	W–L (%)
1994	WAB	54	0.52	104	5.2	21%	0.61	105	1.4–1.8 (0.442)
1995	WAB	73	0.56	111	9.5	19%	0.58	107	4.8–2.9 (0.625)
1996	WAB	76	0.57	114	13.7	21%	0.61	102	8.6–1.9 (0.818)
1997	WAB	73	0.56	110	9.4	17%	0.57	102	5.6–2.0 (0.736)
1999	NJN	1	0.00	0	0.0	87%	0.25	114	0.0–0.0 (0.000)
2000	NJN	30	0.50	98	3.5	20%	0.48	107	0.3–0.8 (0.252)
6–Yr Totals		**307**	**0.56**	**111**	**9.1**	**19%**	**0.59**	**104**	**21–9 (0.687)**

Table 22.25. Mark Eaton's Career Summary Statistics

Season	Tm	G	Floor %	Off. Rtg.	Pts Prod/G	% Tm Poss	Stop %	Def. Rtg.	W–L (%)
1983	UTA	81	0.41	81	4.8	14%	0.66	98	0.6–6.0 (0.092)
1984	UTA	82	0.51	100	6.3	11%	0.60	102	3.6–4.7 (0.431)
1985	UTA	82	0.47	94	10.2	14%	0.66	97	5.0–7.0 (0.415)
1986	UTA	80	0.48	94	8.7	13%	0.59	100	3.3–6.8 (0.328)
1987	UTA	79	0.47	92	8.5	13%	0.58	100	2.6–7.2 (0.266)
1988	UTA	82	0.47	93	7.7	12%	0.55	101	2.8–7.1 (0.283)
1989	UTA	82	0.50	99	7.1	10%	0.60	98	5.7–4.8 (0.541)
1990	UTA	82	0.56	111	5.4	9%	0.56	102	5.8–2.0 (0.745)
1991	UTA	80	0.55	108	5.7	8%	0.55	103	5.9–2.8 (0.677)
1992	UTA	81	0.52	103	4.0	8%	0.56	102	3.5–3.2 (0.520)
1993	UTA	64	0.53	107	3.0	8%	0.53	105	1.9–1.7 (0.538)
11–Yr Totals		**875**	**0.49**	**97**	**6.6**	**11%**	**0.59**	**100**	**41–53 (0.433)**

about nine points better than the league average. But his offensive rating was around ninety-five, about thirteen points worse than the league average. When a player like Eaton is responsible for shutting down so many shots on the defensive end but is doing little on the offensive end (and not doing it well), should he look like a good player or a bad one?

That is a tough question. My straight numbers say that Eaton was a net negative, something that just intuitively seems wrong to me (table 22.25).

Having some doubts about such a negative result, I'd like to cross-check it in other ways, but that's actually tough to do. The first and most obvious way to do this is to look at how the team did without him. Unfortunately, Eaton really didn't miss much time during his career. The only season that he did miss much time was his last, which was statistically pretty different from the period when he was Defensive Player of the Year. In that season, the Jazz were 34–30 with Eaton and a much better 13–5 without him. The team offensive rating was 110.5 with him and 110.2 without him, essentially the same. The team defensive rating was 108.7 with him and a much better 104.7 without him. Weird. It's not as though the players who took Eaton's minutes when he missed games were defensive studs. David Benoit, Ike Austin, and Mike Brown got the most significant increases in minutes, and their defensive ratings were 107, 107, and 108, respectively.

Trying to infer Eaton's effect by how the team changed at the start and end of his career is also difficult. When Eaton joined the Jazz in 1983, the Jazz team defensive rating did improve from 111.7 to 105.1, a very large improvement. How much of this was due to Eaton is not clear. Eaton only played twenty minutes per game, and, perhaps equally relevantly, defensively deficient forward Adrian Dantley played only twenty-two of the team's eighty-two games after playing forty minutes per game in eighty-one games the previous season. Dantley was such a bad defender that the worst two Jazz defensive seasons between 1983 and 1989 (1984 and 1986) were also the only two seasons that Dantley played at least two thousand minutes (table 22.26).

Table 22.26. Adrian Dantley's Career Summary Statistics

Season	Tm	G	Floor %	Off. Rtg.	Pts Prod/G	% Tm Poss	Stop %	Def. Rtg.	W–L (%)
1977	BUF	77	0.56	115	19.2	17%	0.46	103	9.6–2.1 (0.818)
1978	IND	23	0.59	118	25.1	23%	0.51	101	3.8–0.4 (0.908)
1978	LAL	56	0.57	115	19.3	21%	0.45	103	6.9–1.3 (0.841)
1979	LAL	60	0.54	111	16.7	23%	0.44	105	5.3–2.3 (0.696)
1980	UTA	68	0.58	119	25.2	27%	0.46	111	9.2–3.5 (0.726)
1981	UTA	80	0.59	119	28.4	28%	0.42	111	11.6–4.4 (0.727)
1982	UTA	81	0.60	121	28.6	28%	0.39	114	10.5–4.4 (0.705)
1983	UTA	22	0.60	124	28.3	25%	0.38	109	3.3–0.5 (0.879)
1984	UTA	79	0.61	125	28.3	27%	0.37	112	11.4–1.8 (0.862)
1985	UTA	55	0.58	117	24.6	27%	0.41	107	7.0–1.9 (0.789)
1986	UTA	76	0.60	121	26.8	29%	0.38	109	10.3–2.1 (0.829)
1987	DET	81	0.59	121	19.1	22%	0.40	109	9.0–2.0 (0.820)
1988	DET	69	0.60	124	18.3	23%	0.38	109	7.7–1.0 (0.882)
1989	DET	42	0.59	122	16.7	22%	0.41	108	4.6–0.7 (0.860)
1989	DAL	31	0.54	108	19.2	26%	0.38	112	1.8–2.9 (0.376)
1990	DAL	45	0.56	112	14.1	22%	0.37	111	2.7–2.4 (0.525)
1991	MIL	10	0.51	102	5.7	22%	0.38	111	0.1–0.4 (0.240)
15–Yr Totals		**955**	**0.59**	**119**	**22.5**	**25%**	**0.41**	**109**	**105–32 (0.767)**

In 1983, when Dantley was out, Eaton got some of his minutes and would certainly have improved the defense from horrible to at least good. But it appears that the offense also got worse, as would be expected, and the team won at about the same rate as with Dantley. The Jazz did make a net improvement from pre-Eaton 1982 to post-Dantley 1987. But most of this improvement came in 1984, when both Eaton and Dantley were playing. In that season, the team went from 30–52 to 45–37, a level they would approximately hold until 1988 when Stockton and Malone were becoming stars.

So it remains a bit unclear how prominent Eaton's overall contribution was to the Jazz. The statistics and the reputation agree that he was a very good defensive player. The statistics also suggest his overall contribution was less than a .500 record, but that just seems strange for a Defensive Player of the Year. Even one with as little offense as Eaton.

Some Forgotten Players

Shawn Kemp, Terry Cummings, Jack Sikma, Gus Williams, Terry Porter, and Derek Harper are just some of the players who were good or even great at times, but never developed legacies. I'm sure you can think of some I've forgotten. Many of these players hung on long enough to post astounding career numbers. Why don't we remember these players? Should we remember them?

Kemp is not truly forgotten, but what seems to be forgotten is how good he once was. Weight problems and drug problems, if they had occurred before he was so good, would have put him in the "Promises" section above, rather than here. But Kemp did make six straight All-Star teams and was named to the postseason All-NBA Second Team three times before the drugs and the cheeseburgers. He

Table 22.27. Shawn Kemp's Career Summary Statistics

Season	Tm	G	Floor %	Off. Rtg.	Pts Prod/G	% Tm Poss	Stop %	Def. Rtg.	W–L (%)
1990	SEA	81	0.51	103	6.4	22%	0.59	105	2.4–3.0 (0.443)
1991	SEA	81	0.55	109	14.8	23%	0.53	106	6.5–4.7 (0.579)
1992	SEA	64	0.56	113	15.5	24%	0.61	103	7.3–1.9 (0.792)
1993	SEA	78	0.55	110	17.7	24%	0.61	100	10.0–2.9 (0.777)
1994	SEA	79	0.56	112	17.9	25%	0.65	96	11.8–1.4 (0.896)
1995	SEA	82	0.57	114	18.2	25%	0.60	102	10.8–2.3 (0.823)
1996	SEA	79	0.55	110	18.9	26%	0.64	97	11.5–2.0 (0.853)
1997	SEA	81	0.53	108	18.0	26%	0.61	99	10.4–3.4 (0.752)
1998	CLE	80	0.49	98	17.5	27%	0.60	96	7.9–6.2 (0.561)
1999	CLE	42	0.54	109	19.8	29%	0.58	99	9.9–2.6 (0.789)
2000	CLE	82	0.47	96	17.2	30%	0.60	100	4.9–8.4 (0.368)
2001	POR	68	0.44	90	6.4	24%	0.59	99	1.3–3.9 (0.244)
2002	POR	75	0.48	98	5.9	20%	0.56	103	1.7–3.1 (0.350)
13–Yr Totals		**972**	**0.53**	**106**	**14.9**	**25%**	**0.60**	**100**	**96–46 (0.677)**

was the key big man on several very good Seattle teams and, if the Sonics hadn't run into the unbeata-Bulls of 1996 in the Finals, he would have had an NBA title on his resume and perhaps a Finals MVP.

At his best, which was between 1994 and 1996 (table 22.27), Kemp was indeed a fine player. He was the most consistent scorer on the team, with floor percentages around 0.55 and ratings around 112. He was producing 25 percent of the offense, too. But Seattle felt the need to have a more true center, though there really weren't a lot of them to be had. They went out and got Jim McIlvaine in the free-agent market and paid him more than Kemp was making. McIlvaine wasn't even a .500 player and at best was a specialist who blocked shots. Kemp had already established himself as a solid defender, though at times he was vulnerable to foul trouble. The McIlvaine signing proved to be a good example of how paying a player too much can hurt a team, even if the salary cap isn't an issue, because it caused a rift as Kemp became more discontented about his contract. Seattle then shipped him out for everyone's supposed good.

Kemp went on to play out his career at a much lower level. It is not clear how history will view him. Not having any college career to help him get into the Hall of Fame, his candidacy will be based entirely on what he did in the NBA. A thorough comparison to other Hall of Famers is beyond what I can do here, but my sense is that the black marks against Kemp—the weight problems, the drug problems, the profile of Kemp's many out-of-wedlock children—sufficiently diminish his statistics (which continue to look worse the longer he hangs on) enough that he will have trouble making the Hall.

Terry Cummings was not really a player on my radar screen of interesting players until a rather heated debate about his ability arose within the APBR. Cummings almost scored twenty thousand points in his career. He almost collected ten thousand rebounds. He had almost eight consecutive twenty-points-per-game seasons. He almost made it to the NBA Finals. He almost did a lot of

Table 22.28. Terry Cummings's Career Summary Statistics

Season	Tm	G	Floor %	Off. Rtg.	Pts Prod/G	% Tm Poss	Stop %	Def. Rtg.	W–L (%)
1983	SDC	70	0.57	113	22.2	25%	0.53	106	8.7–3.7 (0.699)
1984	SDC	81	0.56	112	21.6	26%	0.48	111	7.2–6.7 (0.521)
1985	MIL	79	0.56	112	21.9	27%	0.55	101	11.1–2.7 (0.804)
1986	MIL	82	0.53	104	18.7	26%	0.54	101	8.1–4.9 (0.622)
1987	MIL	82	0.55	109	19.5	25%	0.55	103	9.4–4.1 (0.695)
1988	MIL	76	0.53	105	19.4	26%	0.48	107	5.2–7.3 (0.418)
1989	MIL	80	0.53	108	21.7	28%	0.49	106	7.8–6.1 (0.561)
1990	SAN	81	0.54	109	21.0	27%	0.51	104	9.1–4.6 (0.664)
1991	SAN	67	0.53	107	16.6	23%	0.48	104	5.6–4.0 (0.581)
1992	SAN	70	0.55	110	16.2	24%	0.49	104	6.6–3.1 (0.677)
1993	SAN	8	0.48	94	3.5	20%	0.47	108	0.0–0.3 (0.142)
1994	SAN	59	0.51	100	7.5	21%	0.50	105	1.7–3.1 (0.363)
1995	SAN	76	0.50	100	7.0	21%	0.53	104	2.0–3.5 (0.360)
1996	MIL	81	0.53	106	8.1	19%	0.52	109	3.0–4.6 (0.391)
1997	SEA	45	0.52	105	7.7	21%	0.52	103	2.0–1.5 (0.575)
1998	PHI	44	0.54	108	5.1	17%	0.50	105	1.5–1.1 (0.583)
1998	NYK	30	0.49	98	7.2	23%	0.56	99	1.2–1.2 (0.484)
1999	GSW	50	0.51	101	8.6	23%	0.57	99	4.4–3.2 (0.576)
2000	GSW	22	0.48	98	8.1	23%	0.51	107	0.4–1.4 (0.236)
18–Yr Totals		1183	0.54	108	15.5	25%	0.52	105	95–67 (0.586)

things, but he didn't quite get them done. On the positive side, Cummings played a long time, won Rookie of the Year over Dominique Wilkins and James Worthy, and appeared on both a postseason All-NBA Second Team and Third Team. At no time during his long career, however, did I personally think of Cummings as an all-time great. That was a common sentiment in the APBR discussion as well.

Looking at Cummings's statistics now (table 22.28), I can see the reason for that sentiment. Despite his long career, Cummings's peak stats really weren't as good as, say, Kemp's. After his first three years, which were oddly his best offensively, his offensive rating never went over 110, not a very high bar when the average rating in the 1980s was 108. Cummings didn't do an extraordinary amount defensively either, especially if his position was considered to be power forward. His selections as Rookie of the Year in 1983 and for the Second Team All-NBA in 1985 appear justified, but the rest of his career doesn't stand out.

Jack Sikma had an early highlight in his career, finding himself as the starting center in the NBA Finals his first two seasons in the league. Early success—like that of Cummings—can set a player up for high expectations. Sikma, though, was not the biggest star on those early teams, so expectations for him may not have been so high. Sikma effectively played a role on those early Sonics—a big role, but not a full leadership role. Still, after such initial team success, Sikma was well known by fans, and when they didn't see him in any more NBA Finals and when his All-Star seasons ended six years before his career ended, there was a sense of, "Why is he still in the league?"

Before then, though, Sikma was a legitimately good player. Like Scottie Pippen, Sikma improved his game a lot when he had to carry his team for a little while. That improvement came in 1981 as Gus Williams, the team's top scorer the

Table 22.29. Jack Sikma's Career Summary Statistics

Season	Tm	G	Floor %	Off. Rtg.	Pts Prod/G	% Tm Poss	Stop %	Def. Rtg.	W–L (%)
1978	SEA	82	0.50	100	10.7	18%	0.55	96	5.5–3.7 (0.599)
1979	SEA	82	0.51	104	15.9	20%	0.59	97	9.5–3.7 (0.720)
1980	SEA	82	0.53	107	14.5	19%	0.58	98	9.1–3.0 (0.751)
1981	SEA	82	0.52	106	18.0	23%	0.56	101	8.8–5.1 (0.634)
1982	SEA	82	0.55	113	19.4	22%	0.62	97	13.0–1.7 (0.886)
1983	SEA	75	0.54	111	18.2	22%	0.59	99	10.1–2.0 (0.833)
1984	SEA	82	0.55	112	19.1	22%	0.56	104	10.5–3.7 (0.739)
1985	SEA	68	0.55	113	18.4	22%	0.58	104	9.1–2.5 (0.782)
1986	SEA	80	0.53	108	17.0	22%	0.55	103	8.4–4.6 (0.648)
1987	MIL	82	0.53	109	13.2	19%	0.58	101	8.1–3.1 (0.722)
1988	MIL	82	0.56	115	16.3	20%	0.52	105	9.8–2.9 (0.774)
1989	MIL	80	0.52	115	13.7	18%	0.53	105	8.4–2.3 (0.785)
1990	MIL	71	0.49	107	13.8	20%	0.51	107	5.1–4.5 (0.526)
1991	MIL	77	0.48	103	10.2	20%	0.52	105	3.5–4.8 (0.425)
14–Yr Totals		1107	0.53	109	15.6	21%	0.56	101	119–48 (0.714)

previous three years, sat out in a contract dispute. That season, which wasn't successful in the win column, forced Sikma to use a much higher percentage of the offense (23 percent) than he had in the past (table 22.29). His offensive rating stayed about the same, proving that he could do more on the offensive end than he had before. So when Williams returned in 1982, Sikma was more confident, and his offensive rating shot up to 113 while he still maintained 22 percent of the offense.

Sikma continued to be a good player for many years, but his defense couldn't hold together a team defense that collapsed in 1984, with a transition from Lonnie Shelton to Tom Chambers at small forward. Chambers was not a good straight man defender like Shelton and needed help behind him. Sikma hadn't had to provide that much help before, and he didn't do the team defense things—making steals and blocks—that often make such help most beneficial. So Sikma could have been doing as good a job with his own man as before, but he didn't have the the kind of skills that helped his team as its perimeter defense worsened.

In comparing Sikma with Cummings and Kemp, it appears that Sikma did about as much as Kemp to help his team win. Sikma's win–loss record ended up with about twenty more wins than Kemp's, but they had similar peaks, and Kemp's decline after he left Seattle was simply greater than Sikma's. In their first eight years, Sikma's average win–loss record per eighty-two games was 9.8–3.3, and Kemp's was 9.3–2.8, almost identical.

Sometimes I do like to adjust offensive ratings by how much responsibility a player takes in the offense. Though the curves of chapter 19 don't always show it, I look at each additional percentage of the offense as equivalent to a point on the offensive rating. It's a rule of thumb, so-called because thumbs are big and clumsy but also useful. If you adjust offensive ratings up for these three players based on the percentage of team possessions above 20 percent, you get table 22.30.

Table 22.30. Quick Adjustment for Percentage of Team Possessions

Player	Off. Rtg.	% Tm Poss	Effective Off. Rtg.	Def. Rtg.	Net Difference
Kemp	106	25%	112	100	12
Cummings	108	25%	113	105	8
Sikma	109	21%	110	101	8

If you think that the percentage of the team offense is this important, then Kemp was quite a bit more valuable than Cummings and Sikma. In my mind, it's clear only that Cummings's career is the least impressive of the three. Kemp and Sikma could very well have been considered comparable to one another.

Moving on to a guard, Gus Williams was the point scorer on those early Sikma teams. His holdout in 1981 was considered a big factor in Seattle's twenty-two-game drop-off that season, but how big was it? Well, Williams was a good player, but not one whose absence should have been worth twenty-two games. Williams's record was an impressive 10.8–2.5 in 1980. If his replacement went 0–13.3, that's only an eleven-win decline, and his replacements—Vinnie Johnson, primarily, with some time going to Downtown Freddie Brown—weren't *that* bad. Nevertheless, with Seattle's big-time drop-off, Williams got his money.

Seattle fans still love Gus, who scored a lot of points and helped bring them their only title, but his career, with statistics shown in table 22.31, was just that of a good player whose success with the team came about because of a coach having good (not great) talent that he put together in the right away. In light of the modern-day game, where stars and only stars seem to win championships, that 1979 Sonics title team may have been the most recent one to not have a definite Hall of Famer leading the way.

Derek Harper and Terry Porter both had long and esteemed careers at point guard, joining with some other good players to post successful seasons. Both reached the NBA Finals but couldn't help their teams pull out a victory. Porter reached the Finals in the prime of his career with Portland, whereas Harper toiled

Table 22.31. Gus Williams's Career Summary Statistics

Season	Tm	G	Floor %	Off. Rtg.	Pts Prod/G	% Tm Poss	Stop %	Def. Rtg.	W–L (%)
1976	GSW	77	0.50	100	11.6	20%	0.52	95	5.1–2.6 (0.659)
1977	GSW	82	0.53	106	9.7	15%	0.49	100	5.2–2.4 (0.688)
1978	SEA	79	0.51	103	17.1	23%	0.52	97	7.7–3.9 (0.668)
1979	SEA	76	0.54	108	18.1	26%	0.51	100	8.1–2.6 (0.755)
1980	SEA	82	0.56	113	21.1	24%	0.49	102	10.8–2.5 (0.813)
1982	SEA	80	0.55	110	23.2	28%	0.47	103	9.9–3.9 (0.718)
1983	SEA	80	0.54	108	20.9	26%	0.47	104	8.2–4.6 (0.640)
1984	SEA	80	0.53	106	20.1	26%	0.47	108	5.9–7.5 (0.442)
1985	WAB	79	0.50	101	20.9	26%	0.46	106	5.1–8.6 (0.375)
1986	WAB	77	0.49	100	14.4	23%	0.40	108	2.6–6.9 (0.273)
1987	ATL	33	0.45	91	5.6	21%	0.41	108	0.2–1.7 (0.094)
12–Yr Totals		**825**	**0.53**	**106**	**17.2**	**25%**	**0.48**	**103**	**69–47 (0.594)**

for years with the Mavericks while they were still called an expansion team before he found the Finals in New York in 1994 at age thirty-two. Both rolled through their careers at levels just below stardom. Porter did make two All-Star teams at least. Harper always just missed out.

Though their reputations were somewhat similar, Porter was the better player. He was the number-two scorer on those great Blazers teams (two NBA Finals appearances) of the late 1980s to early 1990s. Harper was number three behind Mark Aguirre and Rolando Blackman on the good Mavericks (one Western Conference Finals appearance) of the mid- to late 1980s. Porter's teams were more successful than Harper's, and Porter was a bigger part of them. It did seem that Porter was just slightly ahead of Harper on everything. If you look at their floor percentages through the first eight years of their careers (shown below), Porter averaged 0.55 and Harper averaged 0.54. Porter's offensive rating was 117, and Harper's was 113. Porter's defensive rating was 107, and Harper's was 109.

Harper's one advantage over Porter was that he was named to the Second Team All-Defense in 1987 and 1990, whereas Porter was never named to any post-season teams. But even that Harper advantage is somewhat muted. As noted above, Porter's defensive rating was actually better than Harper's because Porter's Blazers teams were better defensively than Harper's Mavericks in *every* season. Subjectively, I think that Harper's ball-hawking defense was better than the numbers give him credit for. But being a point guard, it was hard for him to make a huge difference with his defense, which is why the numbers show Dallas's defense to have been so poor.

In the end, the numbers, though close on a lot of little fronts, show Porter to be a pretty productive player (table 22.32) and Harper to be only slightly above average (table 22.33).

Table 22.32. Terry Porter's Career Summary Statistics

Season	Tm	G	Floor %	Off. Rtg.	Pts Prod/G	% Tm Poss	Stop %	Def. Rtg.	W–L (%)
1986	POR	79	0.52	107	7.3	20%	0.46	108	2.3–2.8 (0.450)
1987	POR	80	0.55	112	15.7	19%	0.47	108	6.8–4.3 (0.611)
1988	POR	82	0.57	118	17.4	19%	0.47	107	9.6–2.6 (0.790)
1989	POR	81	0.55	115	19.4	20%	0.44	109	8.5–4.1 (0.675)
1990	POR	80	0.56	120	19.2	22%	0.47	105	10.3–1.4 (0.883)
1991	POR	81	0.58	125	17.7	21%	0.49	104	10.6–0.6 (0.949)
1992	POR	82	0.54	118	17.7	21%	0.46	106	9.3–2.1 (0.819)
1993	POR	81	0.52	114	17.5	21%	0.43	108	8.1–3.4 (0.700)
1994	POR	77	0.49	109	13.3	22%	0.44	108	4.8–3.8 (0.555)
1995	POR	35	0.48	107	9.3	20%	0.45	108	1.5–1.6 (0.471)
1996	MIN	82	0.50	107	10.5	20%	0.46	111	3.1–5.4 (0.367)
1997	MIN	82	0.47	104	7.5	20%	0.45	109	2.2–4.1 (0.342)
1998	MIN	82	0.51	116	9.3	19%	0.44	109	4.7–2.2 (0.685)
1999	MIA	50	0.51	113	9.9	18%	0.49	100	7.3–1.4 (0.839)
2000	SAN	68	0.50	113	9.3	18%	0.47	101	5.0–1.1 (0.816)
2001	SAN	80	0.48	112	7.5	17%	0.48	100	5.1–1.2 (0.811)
2002	SAN	72	0.47	108	6.1	17%	0.50	101	3.1–1.2 (0.715)
17–Yr Totals		**1274**	**0.53**	**114**	**12.9**	**20%**	**0.47**	**106**	**102–43 (0.702)**

Table 22.33. Derek Harper's Career Summary Statistics

Season	Tm	G	Floor %	Off. Rtg.	Pts Prod/G	% Tm Poss	Stop %	Def. Rtg.	W–L (%)
1984	DAL	82	0.49	97	6.5	16%	0.47	109	1.2–5.3 (0.178)
1985	DAL	82	0.55	112	10.1	16%	0.51	107	5.7–3.2 (0.645)
1986	DAL	79	0.57	116	13.1	19%	0.49	109	6.4–2.8 (0.695)
1987	DAL	77	0.58	120	17.1	20%	0.47	108	8.8–1.9 (0.819)
1988	DAL	82	0.55	114	18.0	21%	0.46	108	8.8–4.0 (0.687)
1989	DAL	81	0.52	112	17.7	22%	0.47	109	7.7–5.2 (0.596)
1990	DAL	82	0.54	114	18.7	23%	0.48	107	9.5–3.7 (0.720)
1991	DAL	77	0.53	112	20.1	25%	0.45	111	6.9–6.1 (0.530)
1992	DAL	65	0.51	106	17.6	24%	0.43	112	3.0–7.0 (0.297)
1993	DAL	62	0.50	108	17.8	23%	0.38	117	2.2–6.7 (0.247)
1994	DAL	28	0.43	93	11.2	19%	0.43	111	0.3–3.3 (0.075)
1994	NYK	54	0.50	106	9.0	18%	0.50	99	3.7–1.5 (0.716)
1995	NYK	80	0.49	108	11.9	17%	0.42	107	5.1–4.8 (0.515)
1996	NYK	82	0.48	105	13.5	19%	0.46	106	5.4–5.9 (0.476)
1997	DAL	75	0.48	102	10.2	18%	0.43	111	2.1–6.3 (0.247)
1998	ORL	66	0.46	100	8.5	18%	0.43	107	1.9–4.6 (0.293)
1999	LAL	45	0.48	107	7.6	15%	0.42	108	2.9–3.4 (0.464)
16–Yr Totals		**1199**	**0.52**	**110**	**13.7**	**20%**	**0.46**	**109**	**81–76 (0.518)**

Women of the WNBA

The WNBA is an evolving league. But will it evolve enough to survive? It's not really a question of whether the women are as good as the men or what the quality of the league's basketball is. It's a matter of finding enough people interested in the WNBA to develop a niche. Baseball found its niche, and that's a slow sport with owners and players who hate us! Uh, that's not my point. Some people think baseball is a horrible sport, but there are enough people who love it that it thrives (though the owners say otherwise). Baseball carved out its niche in the United States long ago, before there were numerous other pro sports to compete for attention. In the United States today, many sports are trying to build their own base of fans that will allow them to survive the diverse pro sports jungle. Not only is women's hoops looking to establish a footing in the market, but so are men's soccer, women's soccer, beach volleyball, X-Games galore, and probably team handball and ultimate frisbee in years to come. All these sports are looking for a sizeable enough chunk of the public to care about what they do so that their participants can make a good living. As interesting as the economics of such survival sounds to me, I leave its study to my sports econ friends. My interest lies in the players who make up those evolving leagues. Guys like George Mikan and Bob Cousy helped the NBA survive, and guys like Russell/Chamberlain, Bird/Magic, and Jordan made it grow. The WNBA is still in the survival stage. Here are its Mikans and Cousys.

Unlike the old NBA, the WNBA was promoted heavily upon its founding. Some of the promotion was done to ensure the WNBA victory over its elder league, the American Basketball League (ABL), which already had a season under its belt by the time the WNBA started. The WNBA's early promotional efforts are useful in retrospect to show how talent can be very easily misperceived in the early days of a league. In particular, the WNBA initially promoted Lisa Leslie, Sheryl Swoopes, and Rebecca Lobo as its marquee stars. Swoopes, when healthy, has lived up to the marquee label. Leslie struggled at first but has certainly become a superstar. And Lobo never lived up to the hype, before or after the injuries that have severely limited her playing time. But the WNBA simply missed Cynthia Cooper, who would become easily its best player.

I've already discussed Cooper a fair amount in other chapters, but it's fair to emphasize again how thoroughly she dominated the WNBA (table 22.34). As Mikan led the Lakers to five titles in his first six years, Cooper led the Comets to four straight titles in her only four years in the league. With or without Sheryl Swoopes, she won titles. She lost only three playoff games in four years. She was thirty-four when she played her first WNBA game and thirty-seven when she quit. And since she quit, Houston hasn't won another championship, even with Swoopes. That's the short story.

In contrast to Cooper is Lobo. Still fresh in fans' memories from her role with the undefeated UConn women's team of 1995, Lobo was allocated to the franchise nearest her college market—the New York Liberty, which was also conveniently a big market. Those responsible for allocating the talent and for valuing Lobo so highly apparently forgot about the fact that she didn't play much or perform very well for the gold-medal-winning 1996 Olympic team.

Lobo didn't start off particularly well in the WNBA, trailing Sophia Witherspoon on the scoring list for the Liberty. At the end of the season she was named to the Second Team All-WNBA (over Witherspoon) in an election that seemed more related to her heavy promotion than to her performance (gotta wonder whether any old All-NBA Teams had similar issues). Admittedly, the Liberty did well as a team, losing to the Comets in the Finals. But they won with balance and a team defense that was headed by Teresa Weatherspoon. Lobo's contribution was a less than .500 record (table 22.35). Lobo showed definite signs of improvement in her second year as she took a smaller role (and didn't have the pressure of the heavy promotion), but injuries seem to have halted that progression.

Weatherspoon—aka T-Spoon—was just the kind of player to wreak havoc in the earliest days of the WNBA. Ball handlers were sloppy when the league started (a turnover rate of 25 percent per possession), and T-Spoon could make them pay

Table 22.34. Cynthia Cooper's Career Summary Statistics

Season	Tm	G	Floor %	Off. Rtg.	Pts Prod/G	% Tm Poss	Stop %	Def. Rtg.	W–L (%)
1997	HOU	28	0.52	119	21.6	29%	0.54	92	5.7–0.1 (0.985)
1998	HOU	30	0.53	119	22.0	30%	0.51	91	6.0–0.1 (0.985)
1999	HOU	31	0.53	119	21.6	29%	0.47	97	6.0–0.2 (0.962)
2000	HOU	30	0.50	113	17.9	26%	0.47	96	5.2–0.5 (0.908)
4–Yr Totals		**119**	**0.52**	**118**	**20.7**	**28%**	**0.50**	**94**	**22.8–0.9 (0.961)**

Table 22.35. Rebecca Lobo's Career Summary Statistics

Season	Tm	G	Floor %	Off. Rtg.	Pts Prod/G	% Tm Poss	Stop %	Def. Rtg.	W–L (%)
1997	NYL	28	0.41	85	12.0	23%	0.59	87	2.2–2.8 (0.436)
1998	NYL	29	0.49	101	11.0	21%	0.56	91	3.2–1.3 (0.715)
1999	NYL	1	0.18	39	0.5	71%	0.28	105	0.0–0.0 (0.000)
2001	NYL	16	0.30	61	1.0	18%	0.53	97	0.0–0.4 (0.015)
2002	HOU	21	0.43	97	1.9	19%	0.51	94	0.3–0.3 (0.577)
5–Yr Totals		**95**	**0.44**	**91**	**7.5**	**22%**	**0.60**	**90**	**5.7–4.7 (0.547)**

for it. Because of such high turnover rates early on, guards could dominate the defense of the early WNBA. This is in contrast to the NBA (turnover rate of about 16 percent) and the contemporary WNBA (21 percent), where bigger players seem to be more important defensively. Consistent with this declining turnover trend is the fact that Weatherspoon's defense has not been as dominant since her first two years, when she won the Defensive Player of the Year award. She has recently started showing her age as the Liberty defense has become not really even better than average (table 22.36).

In actuality, guards' defensive effectiveness in the WNBA has not died out completely. In the 2001 season, Debbie Black won the Defensive Player of the Year award doing basically what T-Spoon did—swiping the ball. She was known for such a style of play coming out of the ABL, where she averaged more than four steals per game in her first season. Interestingly, though the ABL claimed it had better talent than the WNBA in the days when the ABL could still muster a fight, the ABL stars—Black included—have not become the stars of the WNBA. Black's defensive rating of eighty-six in 2001 was great, but she certainly is not an overall star (table 22.37).

One exception among former ABL players is Yolanda Griffith, the WNBA's MVP in her first season after coming over from the ABL. Griffith is a power forward who plays defense and can score inside. Her arrival with the Sacramento Monarchs

Table 22.36. Teresa Weatherspoon's Career Summary Statistics

Season	Tm	G	Floor %	Off. Rtg.	Pts Prod/G	% Tm Poss	Stop %	Def. Rtg.	W–L (%)
1997	NYL	28	0.46	94	9.0	16%	0.66	85	3.2–1.2 (0.720)
1998	NYL	29	0.42	89	9.1	17%	0.68	86	3.0–2.2 (0.568)
1999	NYL	31	0.46	102	9.3	16%	0.58	93	3.5–1.4 (0.712)
2000	NYL	32	0.48	102	8.9	15%	0.57	93	3.5–1.5 (0.693)
2001	NYL	32	0.48	102	9.3	18%	0.56	96	3.0–1.7 (0.631)
2002	NYL	32	0.43	97	7.2	15%	0.50	99	1.9–2.2 (0.453)
6–Yr Totals		**184**	**0.46**	**98**	**8.8**	**16%**	**0.59**	**92**	**18.0–10.4 (0.633)**

Table 22.37. Debbie Black's Career Summary Statistics

Season	Tm	G	Floor %	Off. Rtg.	Pts Prod/G	% Tm Poss	Stop %	Def. Rtg.	W–L (%)
1999	UTA	32	0.45	94	7.1	13%	0.57	101	1.5–3.0 (0.336)
2000	MIA	32	0.43	91	5.5	14%	0.61	92	1.8–1.9 (0.488)
2001	MIA	32	0.46	95	7.1	16%	0.66	87	3.1–1.4 (0.685)
2002	MIA	32	0.52	115	7.4	14%	0.60	96	3.4–0.7 (0.835)
4–Yr Totals		**128**	**0.47**	**98**	**6.8**	**14%**	**0.61**	**94**	**9.8–7.0 (0.584)**

Table 22.38. Yolanda Griffith's Career Summary Statistics

Season	Tm	G	Floor %	Off. Rtg.	Pts Prod/G	% Tm Poss	Stop %	Def. Rtg.	W–L (%)
1999	SAC	29	0.60	117	18.0	24%	0.74	87	5.7–0.4 (0.939)
2000	SAC	32	0.57	115	15.9	24%	0.75	88	6.0–0.5 (0.922)
2001	SAC	32	0.57	116	16.1	24%	0.69	88	5.8–0.5 (0.924)
2002	SAC	17	0.56	117	16.4	24%	0.57	101	2.5–0.6 (0.798)
4–Yr Totals		**110**	**0.58**	**116**	**16.6**	**24%**	**0.71**	**90**	**20.0–2.0 (0.910)**

transformed them from an 8–22 laughingstock to a 19–13 team that went to the playoffs. She has kept the team in the playoffs since. By one measure, individual winning percentage, she has been the best player in the WNBA (table 22.38).

On Griffith's team, there have been two other players of interest—Ruthie Bolton (formerly Bolton-Holifield, but I seem to have chosen only players who don't hyphenate for this review, so she qualifies) and Ticha Penicheiro. Bolton has been the designated marksman, the outside shooter who is a little slow on defense. She made a splash during the inaugural WNBA season by finishing second to Cooper in the scoring race. Her absence during most of 1998 helped cause the Monarchs' poor 8–22 season (table 22.39).

Penicheiro is a flashy point guard who wasn't much more than flash when she entered the league. Lacking much of a shot, Penicheiro made her mark (and multiple All-Star teams) with no-look passes and great court vision. The fact that she looks very good in a tank top (as the WNBA likes to show in its promotions) hasn't hurt either. Her game gets people turning their heads on the court, and her looks get them turning their heads off the court, as some like to say. Penicheiro's game actually has come a long way as she has cut down her turnovers significantly and improved her shooting. Efficiency-wise, she was well below average at first but has become at least average on the offensive end (table 22.40).

Another player who has shown steady improvement in her game is Mwadi Mabika of the Los Angeles Sparks. Mabika played in the league's first-ever game and had the Sparks' best offensive and defensive ratings in a loss to the Liberty. Though she wouldn't follow up that performance consistently throughout the inaugural season, it caught my eye at the time. In writing about the game, I called it the "first little evidence of a basketball star." Five years later, she is a star, making the First Team All-WNBA, and her numbers show why (table 22.41).

Table 22.39. Ruthie Bolton's Career Summary Statistics

Season	Tm	G	Floor %	Off. Rtg.	Pts Prod/G	% Tm Poss	Stop %	Def. Rtg.	W–L (%)
1997	SAC	23	0.45	105	17.4	25%	0.59	97	3.2–1.6 (0.672)
1998	SAC	5	0.42	86	10.3	25%	0.45	100	0.1–0.5 (0.205)
1999	SAC	31	0.47	109	12.9	20%	0.46	99	3.2–1.3 (0.715)
2000	SAC	29	0.46	104	12.3	22%	0.45	101	2.4–1.8 (0.570)
2001	SAC	31	0.42	100	7.2	22%	0.53	95	1.8–1.2 (0.607)
2002	SAC	32	0.45	104	10.0	25%	0.57	100	2.3–1.7 (0.587)
6–Yr Totals		**151**	**0.45**	**104**	**11.6**	**23%**	**0.52**	**99**	**13.1–8.0 (0.621)**

Table 22.40. Ticha Penicheiro's Career Summary Statistics

Season	Tm	G	Floor %	Off. Rtg.	Pts Prod/G	% Tm Poss	Stop %	Def. Rtg.	W–L (%)
1998	SAC	30	0.41	83	9.0	17%	0.59	94	1.3–3.9 (0.249)
1999	SAC	32	0.41	84	10.2	19%	0.56	94	1.4–4.1 (0.258)
2000	SAC	30	0.50	103	10.0	18%	0.56	96	3.0–1.6 (0.653)
2001	SAC	23	0.46	99	9.2	16%	0.56	94	2.1–1.3 (0.628)
2002	SAC	24	0.49	113	13.1	19%	0.64	97	3.5–0.9 (0.795)
5–Yr Totals		139	0.45	95	10.2	18%	0.58	95	11.3–11.7 (0.491)

Table 22.41. Mwadi Mabika's Career Summary Statistics

Season	Tm	G	Floor %	Off. Rtg.	Pts Prod/G	% Tm Poss	Stop %	Def. Rtg.	W–L (%)
1997	LAS	21	0.42	86	5.9	23%	0.60	90	0.7–1.0 (0.414)
1998	LAS	29	0.41	92	7.9	19%	0.56	95	1.5–2.0 (0.432)
1999	LAS	32	0.45	100	11.4	21%	0.56	97	2.8–2.0 (0.584)
2000	LAS	32	0.47	110	12.2	21%	0.63	89	4.4–0.7 (0.869)
2001	LAS	28	0.48	113	11.1	19%	0.57	95	3.4–0.7 (0.834)
2002	LAS	32	0.50	116	16.2	24%	0.53	96	4.6–0.9 (0.844)
6–Yr Totals		174	0.46	106	11.1	21%	0.57	94	17.4–7.2 (0.707)

Chamique Holdsclaw made only the Second Team All-WNBA in 2002. But she did win two Bud Light awards. Bud Light sponsors two WNBA awards, oddly named Peak Performer awards. They aren't, fortunately, given to the player who drinks the most Bud Light or who wins a quarters tournament. They are given simply to the leading scorer and leading rebounder, which happened in both cases to be Holdsclaw. Holdsclaw has yet to live up to the All-World forecasts she garnered in college, but she is a good player who had a great season in 2002 (table 22.42).

Now we return to the marquee players, Leslie and Swoopes. Leslie has won the last two WNBA titles with the Sparks and an MVP award. Swoopes has two MVPs, two Defensive Player of the Year awards, and four titles from when Cooper was around. Though it hasn't been played up much, the two do have something of an evolving rivalry. Leslie won her MVP when Swoopes was out with an injury. She also won a title while Swoopes was out. But when Swoopes returned in 2002, though she won the MVP again, she didn't lead her Comets to a title. A rivalry may be taking shape here (see tables 22.43 and 22.44).

...but the new kid on the block is Indiana's Tamika Catchings, daughter of former NBA player Harvey Catchings (maybe she is tired of being described that way). In her rookie year of 2002, Catchings took the league by, uh, Fever (since Sue

Table 22.42. Chamique Holdsclaw's Career Summary Statistics

Season	Tm	G	Floor %	Off. Rtg.	Pts Prod/G	% Tm Poss	Stop %	Def. Rtg.	W–L (%)
1999	WAS	31	0.47	96	16.3	28%	0.60	96	3.3–3.3 (0.501)
2000	WAS	32	0.49	99	16.5	27%	0.59	98	3.6–3.3 (0.524)
2001	WAS	29	0.45	91	16.0	31%	0.65	91	3.2–3.1 (0.505)
2002	WAS	20	0.52	110	18.6	32%	0.73	90	3.8–0.6 (0.865)
4–Yr Totals		112	0.48	98	16.7	29%	0.63	94	13.9–10.3 (0.575)

Table 22.43. Lisa Leslie's Career Summary Statistics

Season	Tm	G	Floor %	Off. Rtg.	Pts Prod/G	% Tm Poss	Stop %	Def. Rtg.	W–L (%)
1997	LAS	28	0.46	91	15.6	27%	0.71	85	3.7–1.9 (0.657)
1998	LAS	28	0.51	104	18.5	30%	0.73	88	5.0–1.1 (0.818)
1999	LAS	32	0.49	103	14.5	26%	0.66	92	4.1–1.6 (0.724)
2000	LAS	32	0.50	104	16.8	28%	0.69	87	5.4–1.1 (0.837)
2001	LAS	31	0.52	108	18.4	29%	0.68	90	5.5–1.1 (0.836)
2002	LAS	31	0.50	105	17.1	26%	0.75	87	5.7–1.0 (0.857)
6–Yr Totals		182	0.50	103	16.8	28%	0.70	88	29.5–7.7 (0.792)

Table 22.44. Sheryl Swoopes's Career Summary Statistics

Season	Tm	G	Floor %	Off. Rtg.	Pts Prod/G	% Tm Poss	Stop %	Def. Rtg.	W–L (%)
1997	HOU	9	0.55	118	6.3	21%	0.54	92	0.6–0.1 (0.905)
1998	HOU	29	0.48	105	14.7	24%	0.65	85	4.6–0.7 (0.868)
1999	HOU	32	0.51	110	17.9	27%	0.68	88	6.2–0.8 (0.888)
2000	HOU	30	0.54	115	19.8	28%	0.70	86	6.5–0.4 (0.935)
2002	HOU	32	0.49	108	18.6	30%	0.70	86	6.5–0.8 (0.890)
5–Yr Totals		132	0.51	110	17.0	27%	0.67	86	24.4–2.8 (0.897)

Bird took it by Storm). She was easily the Rookie of the Year and probably could have won every award (except those Bud Light awards) if voters didn't have a general prejudice against rookies. She was a truly outstanding player who will help the league survive. If the WNBA is going to do more than survive, though, Catchings may need someone who can compete with her. Maybe that's Holdsclaw or Swoopes or Leslie. It's a little early to say, but Catchings's rookie numbers (table 22.45) were exceptional enough to make you wonder whether she'll get too good—so good that no one can match her.

Table 22.45. Tamika Catchings's Career Summary Statistics

Season	Tm	G	Floor %	Off. Rtg.	Pts Prod/G	% Tm Poss	Stop %	Def. Rtg.	W–L (%)
2002	IND	32	0.51	121	19.4	27%	0.75	91	7.1–0.5 (0.932)

Chapter 23

Basic Tools to Evaluate a Team

Lenny Wilkens has been a coach for so long and for so many teams that he probably doesn't need much help evaluating his team at season's end. He's seen it all. He's won a title. He's had some bad teams. He's turned out some good players. He's had some disappointments. He still ends most seasons feeling frustrated, as most coaches do when they don't win a championship. But only occasionally does he live through a season like the one he had with Toronto in 2002. That Raptors season was one roller-coaster ride that, despite the team's valiant end in the playoffs, made every fan and every media member wonder what was going on. It must have flustered Coach Wilkens, too.

What happened that season? In brief, the Raptors were supposed to win the Central Division or at least finish second. They started off reasonably well, then went on a thirteen-game losing streak, found themselves out of the playoff hunt, then miraculously put together a nine-game winning streak at the end of the season which, with Milwaukee's incredible fold-job and with the Raptors having a tie-breaker against Indiana, landed them in the playoffs as the seventh seed in the Eastern Conference, even without their best player. Whew! That 2002 season was one of the most unique I have witnessed, especially for a team with an ordinary win-loss record of 42–40. Because it was such an unusual season for the team, I wanted to study it using a lot of the tools provided in this book to give you a feel for how they can help us better understand teams.

The Team

I start with the team because it is the *team* that wins and loses, not individuals. I have not emphasized this enough throughout the book: Understand the team first and its players second (assuming the goal is winning, not improvement of players, which is more common at lower levels). When Coach Wilkens ended the 2002 season with his head spinning, his first job was to understand that team. Given that the Raptors of 2001 came within minutes of reaching the Eastern Conference Finals, his goal for them in 2002 (and definitely the goal of others) was probably for them to be Eastern Conference finalists, if not better. In that light, finishing at 42–40 and as seventh seed in the weak East was a disappointment. It wasn't as though they entered the season with any worse talent either, having actually picked up (an admittedly old) Hakeem Olajuwon over the summer.

With the season being a disappointment, was it the team's offense or the defense or both that let them down? Looking at team offense and defense, it is clear that the Raptors' decline from a 47–35 record in 2001 was primarily due to a drop on the offensive end (see figure 23.1)

The offense, which was better than average by nearly three points in 2001, dropped to two points below average in 2002. The defense actually improved. That focuses the rest of the discussion on offense and the reasons for the decline. (All team and individual statistics for the 2002 season are also shown in tables at the end of this chapter.)

Looking at the four areas of the game that define an offense (see chapter 3 or chapter 7), what declined? Table 23.1 shows that the declines occurred primarily in how many turnovers the team committed (increasing from 14 percent of team possessions to 16 percent) and in how often they got to the foul line (28 free throw attempts per hundred field goal attempts in 2001 compared to twenty-six in 2002).

Figure 23.1. Raptors Offensive and Defensive Ratings, 2001 and 2002

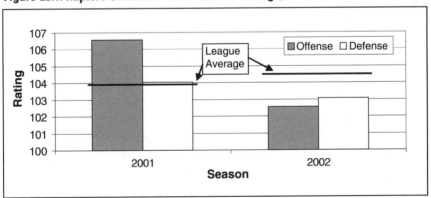

Table 23.1. Toronto's Four Offensive Factors in 2001 and 2002

Season	FG%	OREB%	TOV%	FTA/FGA
2001	43.7%	31%	14%	0.28
2002	43.4%	31%	16%	0.26

Those trends are ones to keep in mind as we start breaking the team down into its individual players.

But there is more to the story of the Toronto Raptors than a constant decline from 2001. Figures 23.2 and 23.3 illustrate the team's offensive and defensive ratings through the season as well as its net points. The second chart showing cumulative net points particularly reveals how the first half of the season was relatively productive but was then followed by a huge decline and a subsequent recovery.

That incredible change in the second half of the season, like the two areas where the team declined overall, provides hints as to the most important players on the team.

Figure 23.2. Raptors Ratings, Moving 5-Game Averages

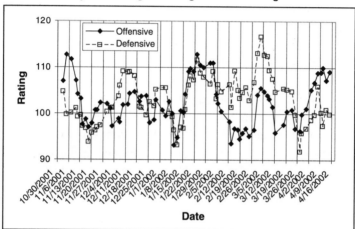

Figure 23.3. Raptors Net Points

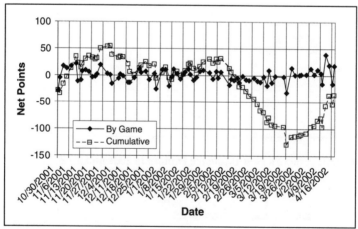

Players

Again, once I understood that the *team's* problem was offense, not defense, it told me what to look for in the players. Once I understood that the team had major streaks, it told me to look for players who seemed to spur those streaks. Team first, players second. This is the second section, so here are the players. As mentioned above, the player and team season statistics for 2002 are shown at the end of this chapter.

Vince Carter

Carter was a big reason for the team's offensive decline, probably more so than his absence. By that, I mean that Carter's offensive efficiency slid so much in 2002 that when he missed twenty-two games, the team didn't miss him quite as much as they might have if he had been performing as he had in 2001. Table 23.2 shows Carter's career numbers, and you can see that his 2002 offensive rating was well below where it had been.

Some of Carter's decline was injury-related. The first record of injury I can find is from a December 12 game against San Antonio in which he bruised his right calf. His offensive rating coming into that game was about 112, which, perhaps not coincidentally, was the highest value he'd reach all season. His season rating declined steadily from that point until he went on the injured list after the February 7 game. Figure 23.4 shows a peak in Carter's offensive performance right around December 11 that he would never duplicate through the rest of the season.

But even before that December 12 game, Carter wasn't quite the same as he had been in 2001. Maybe it was the new rules allowing zones, but Carter wasn't shooting as well from two-point land, only 43 percent compared to his previous 48 percent. He was taking more three-pointers, which was also reducing how often he got to the line (his FTA/FGA figure went down from 0.30 to 0.28, an aspect of his game that got a lot worse after the injuries). He also was committing more turnovers, another key decline observed in the team numbers. Even at the start of the season, Carter was taking some heat from the media for not doing the same things that Kobe Bryant does. Those critics were vague in their criticisms—they said Carter was "not taking over the game" or something like that.

Table 23.2. Vince Carter's Career Summary Statistics

Season	Tm	G	Floor %	Off. Rtg.	Pts Prod/G	% Tm Poss	Stop %	Def. Rtg.	W–L (%)
1999	TOR	50	0.52	106	17.0	25%	0.50	104	4.6–3.5 (0.568)
2000	TOR	82	0.53	111	23.2	28%	0.49	105	10.4–4.9 (0.681)
2001	TOR	75	0.53	114	25.0	29%	0.49	104	11.3–3.3 (0.775)
2002	TOR	60	0.49	107	23.0	29%	0.47	105	6.4–5.3 (0.547)
4–Yr Totals		267	0.52	110	22.5	28%	0.49	105	33–17 (0.659)

Figure 23.4. Vince Carter's Ratings, Moving 5-Game Averages

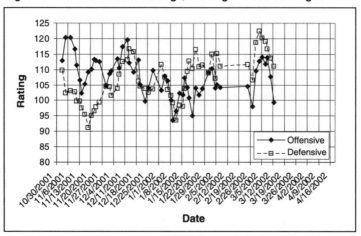

From the numbers—which show more three-point attempts, less success inside, and fewer attempts from the line—it just looks like Carter wasn't as aggressive. Teams had found a way to take away the inside from him, and it was not clear whether Carter could overcome the adjustment and return to his 2001 offensive levels again. Maybe there was reason to believe his declines in 2002 would be temporary, but it wasn't obvious in the numbers.

So part of the overall team decline in offense was due to Carter. But the huge team decline in the second half of the season was due mainly to Carter being gone, not playing worse. Figure 23.5 shows the net points that Carter produced (as defined in chapter 20) through time. That chart has a flat line starting in early February, which was when Carter went out and when the huge decline in the team net point chart began. The chart also shows the end of Carter's season in mid-March, which was exactly when the huge *increase* in the team net point totals began.

Looking at both of those odd periods together, using the significance testing of chapter 7, it's clear that the Raptors didn't really miss Carter—their stats were about the same with him and without him. Their offensive rating declined about two points, their defensive rating improved about three points, and they ended up winning more often without him than with him, but none of these changes were statistically significant. Basically, the team's huge plunge that began when he went out in February was offset by its huge resurgence that began when he went out in March.

So what was it that the *other* players were doing in those two periods that made the team flip-flop? Remember, this is a unique team. A weird team. A team that befuddled even wise old Lenny Wilkens. That's because a lot of things happened to the Raptors that season—not just Carter missing games.

Figure 23.5. Vince Carter's Net Points

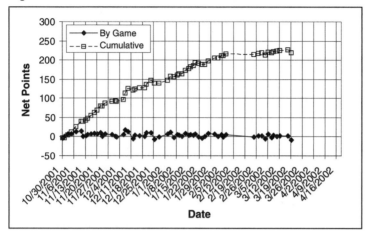

When Carter went out the first time, the team behaved mostly as expected. The offense declined, and the defense stayed about the same—consistent with the subtraction of Carter's individual skills. In the seven games that he missed, the offense had only a single game in which it scored more than a point per possession. (The team was also missing Jerome Williams, a role player with a 113 offensive rating.)

What happened when Carter returned to the sinking ship? That was less predictable. The team kept sinking, losing six more games. The offense was at about the league average (106), but the defense got horrible. The Raptors' defensive rating of 117 over this stretch was worse than could be blamed solely on Carter. No, it was apparently an overall failure of the defense. The team gave up 50 percent shooting in all but one of those six games, and the points were coming primarily from opposing point guards, shooting guards, and small forwards. All of Toronto's perimeter defense was struggling.

Whatever it was, this problem went away when Carter called it a season beginning with the March 22 game against Cleveland. Over the rest of the campaign, the Raptors' defense was awesome, posting an average rating of ninety-eight, much better than it had been the first time Carter sat out. The defense found a way to create more turnovers and force opponents into worse shooting percentages. From a blasphemously subjective perspective, one could say the Raptors found a defensive chemistry after Carter left. Frankly, the team legitimately changed when Carter told them he wouldn't be back. They reestablished roles that were more optimal for the team. In terms of statistical significance, this change may not have been reflected in the nine-game winning streak, but it was reflected in the defensive improvement and strongly reflected in the lack of offensive decline. Whereas the team's offense declined about twelve points in Carter's first eight games away (a very statistically significant decline), the offense was essentially unaffected after Carter's last game on March 19. Other players really stepped up at that point.

Morris Peterson

Mo-Pete was the big beneficiary of Carter's absence. His game changed after Carter left that second time. He became more aggressive. He took responsibility for a higher percentage of the offense (22 percent versus 20 percent), he began producing six points per game more, and his offensive rating went from about 103 to about 111. Just as Scottie Pippen became a better player when Michael Jordan left the Bulls in 1993, as Jack Sikma became a better player when Gus Williams sat out on the Sonics in 1981, it appears that Peterson became a better player when Carter got hurt.

Peterson's cumulative net point total showed a downward trend in February and an upward trend in mid-March, corresponding perfectly with the team roller-coaster ride (figures 23.6 and 23.7). Such a correspondence is usually an indicator of a team relying on a player. Peterson's improvement at the end of the season was a positive indicator of his future.

Antonio Davis

Davis was the other Raptor who stepped up during Carter's absence, the more senior leader who became the leader only after Carter went down. Remember how the game-by-game win-loss records for apparent leaders of teams seem to mimic the team's actual win-loss record? Well, the Raptors went 12–2 after Carter went out in March, and Davis's game-by-game record was a nearly parallel 11–3, the best on the club during the time. He was apparently leading the team. Before Carter went down for good, Davis was producing only about fourteen

Figure 23.6. Morris Peterson's Ratings, Moving 5-Game Averages

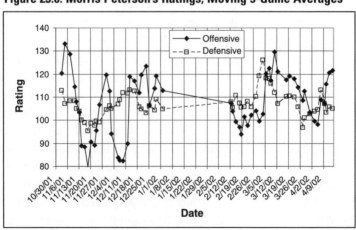

Figure 23.7. Morris Peterson's Net Points

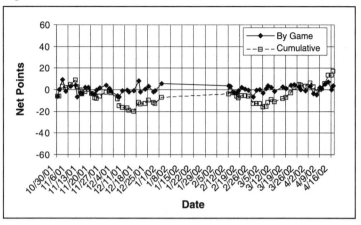

points per game. Afterward, he was creating about eighteen. Before Carter went down, Davis's defensive rating was about 105. Afterward, it was about ninety-eight. It was no coincidence that Davis's cumulative net points curve also reflected the team pattern (figures 23.8 and 23.9).

Davis and Peterson were the most important guys on this team not named Carter. Their ability to step up after Carter went down implied that if Toronto was going to be good in 2003 with Carter back, these two needed to play well. This was particularly true if Carter's individual offensive decline was relatively permanent (see Late Editing Note at end of chapter).

Alvin Williams

Unlike Davis and Peterson, Alvin Williams was mostly just along for the ride at the end of the season and appeared to be less important to the success of the

Figure 23.8. Antonio Davis's Ratings, Moving 5-Game Averages

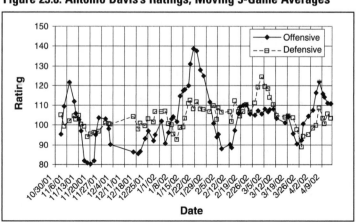

Figure 23.9. Antonio Davis's Net Points

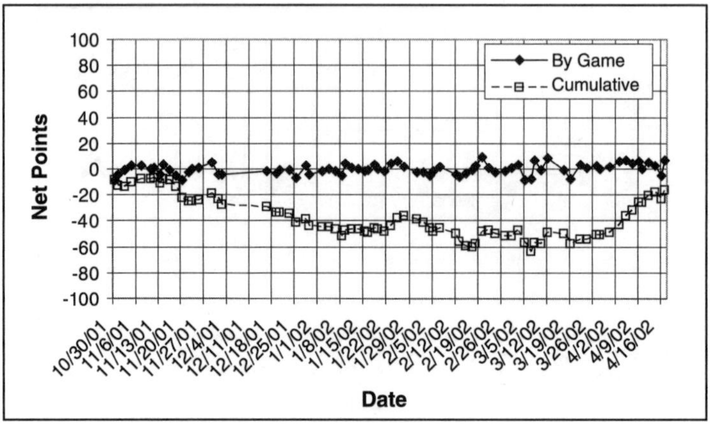

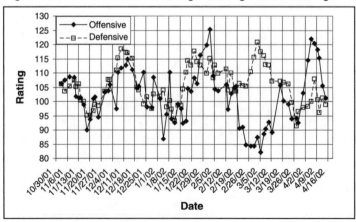

team. Williams did play better during that late run, but his impact on the team's net point total was more muted, as you can see by comparing his net points pattern to that of the other guys (figures 23.10 and 23.11). Williams, like Carter, also showed a general offensive decline from 2001, and he showed it in the same ways—worse shooting inside the arc, fewer free throw attempts, and more turnovers. Based on these stats, Coach Wilkens needed to find a way to open up the inside for his guards.

Jerome Williams

A valuable addition to the defense of this team, the Junkyard Dog arrived in mid-2001 as a role player who did a good job. Like Alvin, Jerome's net point curve more flattened out than rose when the team's hot streak began at the end of the season (figures 23.12 and 23.13). But unlike Alvin, his net point contribution

Figure 23.10. Alvin Williams's Ratings, Moving 5-Game Averages

Figure 23.11. Alvin Williams's Net Points

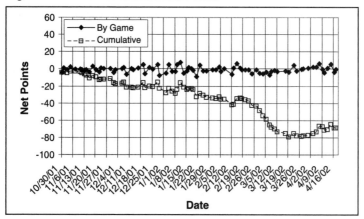

Figure 23.12. Jerome Williams's Ratings, Moving 5-Game Averages

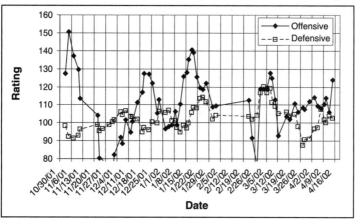

Figure 23.13. Jerome Williams's Net Points

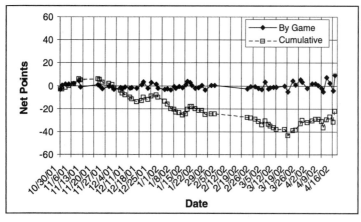

never went very far negative, and it was only negative because he just didn't contribute a lot of points to the offense. He used 16 percent of the team's possessions, and he used them with a pretty good offensive rating, something like a poor man's Horace Grant.

Keon Clark

Toronto ended up letting Clark go as a free agent at the end of the 2002 season, apparently because they felt that his asking price was too high, not that he wasn't valuable. Clark's 2002 season epitomized his career: mixed. You look at it one way—his basic defensive stats—and he looked pretty good. You look at it another way—his inability to shore up the defense during the thirteen-game slide—and he looked ineffective (figures 23.14 and 23.15).

Figure 23.14. Keon Clark's Ratings, Moving 5-Game Averages

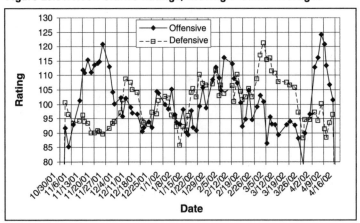

Figure 23.15. Keon Clark's Net Points

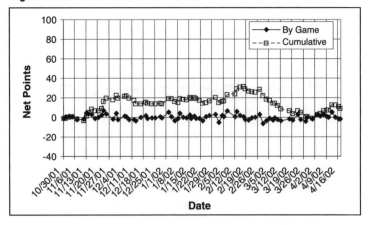

Table 23.3. Keon Clark's Career Summary Statistics

Season	Tm	G	Floor %	Off. Rtg.	Pts Prod/G	% Tm Poss	Stop %	Def. Rtg.	W–L (%)
1999	DEN	28	0.49	96	3.6	14%	0.55	107	1.5–6.5 (0.189)
2000	DEN	81	0.53	105	8.2	17%	0.57	103	8.8–6.5 (0.577)
2001	DEN	35	0.47	93	6.8	18%	0.55	104	2.6–11.9 (0.180)
2001	TOR	46	0.56	110	8.3	19%	0.63	99	9.4–2.3 (0.807)
2002	TOR	81	0.51	102	10.6	21%	0.60	100	5.4–4.1 (0.568)
4–Yr Totals		271	0.52	103	8.3	19%	0.58	102	28–31 (0.471)

Offensively, Clark's rating bounced around a lot in his career. Inconsistency is what he was about. When he came to the Raptors in 2001, Wilkens gave him more freedom on the offensive end and he responded well, posting a rating of 110. But his 2002 season was not an improvement, with his rating declining to 102, as seen in his career numbers in table 23.3.

With Carter returning for 2002, it didn't appear that Clark would have to take as large an offensive role and could be a generally smart role player. However, whether it was his asking price or some other factor, the Raptors didn't see Clark's defense as being valuable enough to re-sign him.

Chris Childs

Childs's departure from Toronto in the off-season was not as surprising as Clark's. Childs had lost the point guard slot to Alvin Williams and didn't play particularly well in reserve. Aside from his second season in the league, when he played surprisingly well with the Nets, Childs rarely had an offensive rating over one hundred. His defense was decent, but not something to cry about losing (figures 23.16 and 23.17).

Figure 23.16. Chris Childs's Ratings, Moving 5-Game Averages

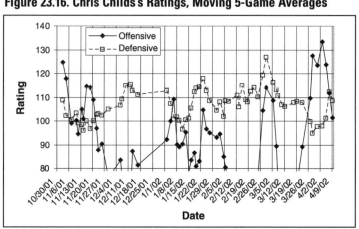

Figure 23.17. Chris Childs's Net Points

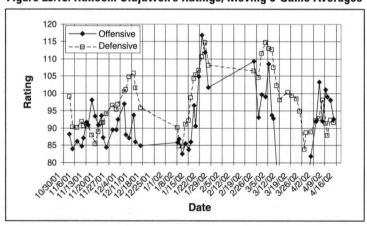

Hakeem Olajuwon

His offensive rating was a career low ninety-one in 2002. His percentage of the team offense was a career low 18 percent. His defense, which had been his calling since he arrived in America, still contributed positively, but it was hard to get him on the court if he was just clogging the middle of the offense (figures 23.18 and 23.19). Back injuries pretty much forced Olajuwon to call it quits, but he might have had another decent season in him. With his defense and the departure of Clark, another defensive stopper, it would have helped the 2003 Raptors if Olajuwon had been available and had an offensive season with a rating of even 102 or 103.

Figure 23.18. Hakeem Olajuwon's Ratings, Moving 5-Game Averages

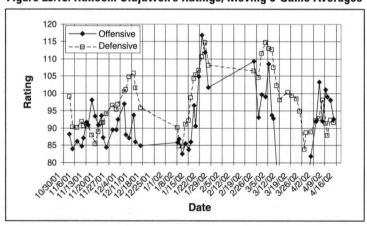

Figure 23.19. Hakeem Olajuwon's Net Points

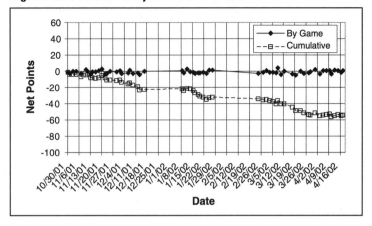

Chapter End Note

Though most of the analysis above emphasized the team offense because that is what dramatically changed in 2002, the defense should not be completely ignored. The defense improved about two points from 2001, and that two points kept them in the playoff hunt. That two-point improvement did not apparently come from players left over from 2001. You can see in table 23.4 that all these players had minimal changes in their stop percentages and defensive ratings.

Rather, the team defensive improvement was probably due to the acquisition of Olajuwon, who was always a tremendous defensive presence. His thirteen hundred minutes came with a defensive rating of ninety-six, much better than the defensive ratings of any other Raptors and better than that of the departed Charles Oakley (103). Having Jerome Williams for a full season over Corliss Williamson also helped.

Going into 2003, the Raptors' defense was not likely to be any better. Its main contributors were the thirty-eight-year-old Olajuwon, the departed Keon Clark, and the twenty-nine-year-old Jerome Williams. The defense was going to be a problem, but not one that couldn't be overcome by an offense that returned a healthy (and possibly 2001-level) Carter and a probably improved Peterson.

One last thing I looked for in Toronto's statistics was whether there were any obvious statistical indicators suggesting strategy. The interesting one was that they performed much better when they pushed the pace. It helped both their offense and defense, suggesting that they were good at turning turnovers into points. That kind of knowledge can help a team if they know it. Or it can hurt them if opponents know it.

Table 23.4. Raptors' Individual Defensive Ratings in 2001 and 2002

Player	Season	G	Min	Stop %	Def. Rtg.
Vince Carter	2001	75	2979	0.48	106
	2002	60	2385	0.47	105
Chris Childs	2001	26	550	0.49	105
	2002	69	1576	0.46	106
Keon Clark	2001	46	968	0.62	100
	2002	81	2185	0.60	100
Dell Curry	2001	71	956	0.43	108
	2002	56	886	0.41	108
Antonio Davis	2001	78	2729	0.53	104
	2002	77	2977	0.51	104
Eric Montross	2001	12	81	0.64	99
	2002	49	656	0.52	103
Tracy Murray	2001	38	453	0.42	109
	2002	40	473	0.42	107
Mamadou Ndiaye	2001	3	10	0.38	110
	2002	5	46	0.43	107
Morris Peterson	2001	80	1809	0.46	107
	2002	63	1989	0.44	107
Michael Stewart	2001	26	123	0.49	105
	2002	11	93	0.57	101
Alvin Williams	2001	82	2394	0.49	106
	2002	82	2927	0.48	105
Jerome Williams	2001	26	378	0.59	101
	2002	68	1641	0.55	102

Finally, I should emphasize that this kind of statistical report is a complement to educated observation, not a replacement for it. In scouting teams, I would often study their statistics before seeing them in order to frame questions about what I was seeing. Knowing that seeing a single game can lead to a distorted truth about players—one game can be a player's best or worst—I used statistics to provide a better average through time, and, if that average is quite different from what I saw on the court, I would ask why. Why did a player whose offense looked so statistically efficient play so poorly? Did his numbers for that game reflect that he played poorly, or did the stats continue to suggest efficiency? If they continued to suggest efficiency, what was I missing in that player's game when I saw him? Or what were the statistics missing that I saw in his game? This kind of report is supposed to provide some insight, to make more concrete what a coach/scout observes, but also to raise questions. Sometimes asking those questions is what provides the most important insight.

Late Editing Note: 2003 Update

Having written the above before the start of the 2002–2003 season, I can now actually do some follow-up assessment of the Raptors. As of this writing, their record is bad, 23–49. The drop has been primarily due to defense—the losses of Olajuwon and Clark did hurt. The offense was two points per hundred possessions below average in 2002, and it's been about three points below average in 2003—not dramatically different. The defense was about 1.5 points per hundred possessions better than average in 2002, but has been over three points worse than average in 2003.

Unlike in 2002, though, the Raptors have definitely missed Vince Carter. Carter has sat out thirty-three games, during which the team has gone 6–27. The team's offensive rating has been 103.0 with him (in a league averaging about 104.3, making them about the same as in 2002), but only 99.4 without him, a big drop that makes sense given his skills. The team's defensive rating has been 107.0 with him but 108.9 without him, a smaller drop that isn't significant. The improvement in the team offense when Carter plays doesn't mean, however, that Carter has returned to his former self. His numbers have rebounded a bit from the 2002 season to an offensive rating of 112 and 27 percent of his team's possessions (close to the 114 and 29 percent he posted in 2001).

Neither Morris Peterson nor Antonio Davis has been able to step up their games to make up for Carter's absence. Whatever spark they had over the last few weeks of the 2002 season wasn't there in 2003. Both have been markedly less efficient (Peterson's offensive rating has been 101 and Davis's has been ninety-nine), and Alvin Williams's slight improvement hasn't made up for it.

Right now, Lenny Wilkens is expected to be let go. Expectations for team success were set a couple of years ago, and his teams haven't lived up to them, even though the team decline in 2003 was somewhat predictable.

Summary Statistics for 2002 Toronto Raptors

This section contains the basic stats that I review when looking at a team. I looked at them extensively in preparing the above summaries, but due to the unique circumstances surrounding the Raptors, I also looked at much more.

There was no significant difference between their actual record and the bell curve projection in table 23.5. Hence, there was no immediate reason to expect major changes in their win-loss record in the following season.

Looking at the four measures of ability to convert possessions shown in table 23.6, with league averages of 104.5, 0.49, 0.43, and 0.44, the team was very average in most departments. They were slightly worse than average offensively and slightly better than average defensively.

Table 23.5. Raptors' Winning Percentage Relative to Bell Curve Projection

	Win	Loss	Win%
Actual	42	40	0.512
Bell Curve	40	42	0.486

Table 23.6. Raptors' Efficiency Statistics

	Rating	Floor%	Play%	Field%
Offensive	102.6	0.49	0.41	0.44
Defensive	103.1	0.49	0.42	0.43

The team's pace was 89.1 possessions per game, with the average being 91.3, so they were a little slow.

The four basic factors associated with making an offense or defense work are in table 23.7 and show a primary weakness in getting to the line.

And, finally, tables 23.8 through 23.12 contain all the individual stats.

Table 23.7. Raptors' Four Factors

	FG%	OREB%	TOV%	FTA/FGA
Offense	0.434	0.314	0.161	0.255
Defense	0.441	0.299	0.171	0.315

Table 23.8. Raptors' Individual Statistics – I

Player	G	GS	MPG	FG%	3PT%	FT%	RPG	APG	STL	BLK	PPG
Vince Carter	60	60	39.8	0.428	0.387	0.798	5.2	4.0	94	43	24.7
Antonio Davis	77	77	38.7	0.426	0.000	0.818	9.6	2.0	54	83	14.5
Morris Peterson	63	56	31.6	0.438	0.365	0.751	3.5	2.4	73	11	14.0
Alvin Williams	82	82	35.7	0.415	0.321	0.736	3.4	5.7	135	26	11.8
Keon Clark	81	31	27.0	0.490	0.000	0.674	7.4	1.1	58	122	11.3
Jerome Williams	68	32	24.1	0.490	—	0.676	5.7	1.1	78	25	7.6
Hakeem Olajuwon	61	37	22.6	0.464	0.000	0.560	6.0	1.1	74	90	7.1
Dell Curry	56	4	15.8	0.406	0.344	0.892	1.4	1.1	22	6	6.4
Tracy Murray	40	3	11.8	0.411	0.385	0.810	1.3	0.5	11	8	5.7
Chris Childs	69	4	22.8	0.328	0.275	0.817	2.2	5.1	56	5	4.1
Mamadou Ndiaye	5	0	9.2	0.600	—	0.800	2.2	0.0	0	2	4.0
Derrick Dial	7	0	7.1	0.423	0.250	0.833	1.6	0.6	2	0	4.0
Jermaine Jackson	24	0	11.7	0.476	0.500	0.667	1.1	2.4	9	1	2.4
Eric Montross	49	24	13.4	0.402	0.000	0.323	2.9	0.3	12	23	2.4
Michael Stewart	11	0	8.5	0.348	—	0.545	2.3	0.3	4	3	2.0
Carlos Arroyo	17	0	5.6	0.448	—	0.667	0.7	1.2	6	0	1.8
Michael Bradley	26	0	4.5	0.520	0.000	0.500	0.9	0.1	0	6	1.2
Team	82		240.9	0.434	0.349	0.739	42.1	21.7	688	454	91.4
Opponents	82		240.9	0.441	0.346	0.752	41.9	19.9	628	383	91.8

Table 23.9. Raptors' Individual Statistics – II

Player	G	FGM	FGA	FG%	3PM	3PA	FTM	FTA	FT%	PTS	PPG
Vince Carter	60	559	1307	0.428	121	313	245	307	0.798	1484	24.7
Antonio Davis	77	410	963	0.426	0	1	293	358	0.818	1113	14.5
Morris Peterson	63	336	768	0.438	84	230	127	169	0.751	883	14.0
Alvin Williams	82	403	971	0.415	62	193	103	140	0.736	971	11.8
Keon Clark	81	380	775	0.490	0	5	155	230	0.674	915	11.3
Jerome Williams	68	190	388	0.490	0	0	138	204	0.676	518	7.6
Hakeem Olajuwon	61	194	418	0.464	0	2	47	84	0.560	435	7.1
Dell Curry	56	141	347	0.406	45	131	33	37	0.892	360	6.4
Tracy Murray	40	85	207	0.411	40	104	17	21	0.810	227	5.7
Chris Childs	69	97	296	0.328	33	120	58	71	0.817	285	4.1
Mamadou Ndiaye	5	6	10	0.600	0	0	8	10	0.800	20	4.0
Derrick Dial	7	11	26	0.423	1	4	5	6	0.833	28	4.0
Jermaine Jackson	24	20	42	0.476	1	2	16	24	0.667	57	2.4
Eric Montross	49	53	132	0.402	0	1	10	31	0.323	116	2.4
Michael Stewart	11	8	23	0.348	0	0	6	11	0.545	22	2.0
Carlos Arroyo	17	13	29	0.448	0	0	4	6	0.667	30	1.8
Michael Bradley	26	13	25	0.520	0	2	4	8	0.500	30	1.2
Team	82	2919	6727	0.434	387	1108	1269	1717	0.739	7494	91.4
Opponents	82	2820	6390	0.441	377	1089	1513	2011	0.752	7530	91.8

Table 23.10. Raptors' Individual Statistics – III

Player	G	MIN	OFF. REBS	DEF REBS	TOT REBS	AST	PF	DQ	TO	PTS	HI
Vince Carter	60	2385	138	175	313	239	191	4	154	1484	43
Antonio Davis	77	2977	254	486	740	155	225	3	159	1113	29
Morris Peterson	63	1989	91	132	223	153	174	2	86	883	29
Alvin Williams	82	2927	58	223	281	468	191	1	150	971	28
Keon Clark	81	2185	182	421	603	88	258	4	140	915	26
Jerome Williams	68	1641	165	221	386	75	153	0	68	518	22
Hakeem Olajuwon	61	1378	98	268	366	66	147	0	98	435	16
Dell Curry	56	886	23	58	81	61	50	0	41	360	18
Tracy Murray	40	473	18	35	53	19	38	0	25	227	16
Chris Childs	69	1576	18	136	154	351	177	3	123	285	14
Mamadou Ndiaye	5	46	6	5	11	0	6	0	1	20	8
Derrick Dial	7	50	2	9	11	4	1	0	3	28	9
Jermaine Jackson	24	280	3	24	27	57	24	0	14	57	10
Eric Montross	49	656	36	104	140	16	92	1	25	116	10
Michael Stewart	11	93	12	13	25	3	22	0	4	22	7
Carlos Arroyo	17	96	3	9	12	21	12	0	12	30	6
Michael Bradley	26	117	7	17	24	3	10	0	6	30	6
Team	82	19755	1114	2336	3450	1779	1771	18	1174	7494	116
Upponents	82	19755	995	2437	3432	1629	1613	10	1250	7530	122

Table 23.11. Raptors' Individual Statistics – IV

Player	Scor. Poss./G	Poss. Per G	Floor Pct.	RTG.	Points Prod./G	% Tm Poss.	Def. Stops		Def. Rtg.
							Per G	Stop%	
Vince Carter	10.5	21.5	0.49	107	23.0	0.29	6.9	0.47	105
Antonio Davis	7.2	14.1	0.51	104	14.7	0.20	7.3	0.51	104
Morris Peterson	5.9	11.9	0.50	109	13.0	0.20	5.1	0.44	107
Alvin Williams	6.0	12.5	0.48	103	12.8	0.19	6.3	0.48	105
Keon Clark	5.3	10.4	0.51	102	10.6	0.21	5.9	0.60	100
Jerome Williams	4.0	7.1	0.57	113	8.0	0.16	4.9	0.55	102
Hakeem Olajuwon	3.5	7.7	0.46	91	7.0	0.18	5.7	0.68	96
Dell Curry	2.5	5.7	0.44	101	5.8	0.20	2.4	0.41	108
Tracy Murray	2.0	4.7	0.43	103	4.8	0.21	1.9	0.42	107
Chris Childs	2.7	6.4	0.42	94	6.0	0.15	3.8	0.46	106
Mamadou Ndiaye	1.9	2.6	0.71	145	3.8	0.15	1.5	0.43	107
Derrick Dial	1.7	3.6	0.48	101	3.6	0.27	1.4	0.55	102
Jermaine Jackson	1.6	2.8	0.56	114	3.2	0.13	1.9	0.44	107
Eric Montross	1.2	2.9	0.42	83	2.5	0.12	2.6	0.52	103
Michael Stewart	1.2	2.6	0.47	93	2.4	0.16	1.8	0.57	101
Carlos Arroyo	1.1	2.4	0.44	89	2.2	0.23	1.1	0.53	103
Michael Bradley	0.6	1.1	0.50	97	1.1	0.14	0.8	0.47	105
Team	43	88	0.49	103	91		45	0.51	104

Table 23.12. Raptors' Individual Statistics – V

Player	Net Win%	Net W	Net L	Game-by-Game		
				Win%	Wins	Losses
Vince Carter	0.547	6.4	5.3	0.517	31	29
Antonio Davis	0.518	6.6	6.1	0.519	40	37
Morris Peterson	0.576	4.8	3.5	0.524	33	30
Alvin Williams	0.420	5.1	7.1	0.451	37	45
Keon Clark	0.568	5.4	4.1	0.444	36	45
Jerome Williams	0.806	5.2	1.3	0.552	37	30
Hakeem Olajuwon	0.350	2.3	4.2	0.443	27	34
Dell Curry	0.298	0.9	2.1	0.364	20	35
Tracy Murray	0.360	0.6	1.1	0.289	11	27
Chris Childs	0.164	0.8	4.2	0.319	22	47
Mamadou Ndiaye	0.999	0.1	0.0	0.800	4	1
Derrick Dial	0.464	0.1	0.1	0.333	2	4
Jermaine Jackson	0.716	0.6	0.2	0.650	13	7
Eric Montross	0.059	0.2	2.4	0.286	12	30
Michael Stewart	0.265	0.1	0.2	0.222	2	7
Carlos Arroyo	0.148	0.1	0.3	0.429	6	8
Michael Bradley	0.265	0.1	0.3	0.647	11	6
Team	0.480	39.3	42.7	0.449	344	422

Chapter 24

Weather Forecasts

Every morning you turn on the local news and wait for someone with way too much makeup on to tell you what the weather is going to be in the thirty feet between your doorway and the car, then in the fifty feet between your car and your office, which is probably different. Rain or shine? Hot or cold? Sweater or jacket?

But most weather forecasts are just a form of entertainment. The weather gives people something to talk about. It's a little bit of information that can start chitchat among people who happen to be at the same intersection of low-pressure fronts. And weather forecasters are usually entertaining people who find ways to keep a prediction of rain from being, well, dry. Actually, you can usually tell who the TV weather guy is just from his looks because he is the one dressed most like a clown. Big yellow blazer, spiky hair, or no hair at all—depends on the day, it seems.

I didn't develop the stuff in this book to make weather forecasts and look like a clown. But there is definitely an element of forecasting to the work I've done here. In fact, all the methods in this book have been developed with an eye to the future. The future doesn't mean predicting games—another form of entertainment that can make you look like a clown—but understanding how players will behave if they join a new team or why underdogs will start taking riskier strategies. Predicting the future often means understanding things well enough to be able to change the future. That's what a coach or a scout is supposed to do. They should better anticipate opponents' strategies in a game or better envision how a player at a local high school is going to fit within a college system (or whether that kid is even going to college). They anticipate enough to make a difference.

I hope I've provided some concepts to aid in making forecasts and, more importantly, making a difference. Let me simply condense those concepts from the rest of the book below.

- *In trying to understand basketball, get to know the team first and players second.* If you can understand a team's characteristics, you know what to look for in player characteristics. The structure of this book—with early chapters dedicated to team issues and later chapters dedicated to player concepts—was meant to emphasize this point.

- *Record team possessions to evaluate efficiency.* If you record possessions as that unit of time between when your team gains control of the ball and when your opponent gains control, both teams will have the same number of possessions in each game (plus or minus two), just as they have the same thirty-two minutes, forty minutes, or forty-eight minutes. Counting possessions allows you to use a unique measurement tool for evaluating offense and defense—points per possession, or points per hundred possession ratings as used herein. Also, keep in mind that offensive rebounds are *offensive* contributions and defensive rebounds are *defensive* contributions. Basketball isn't a game of offense, defense, and rebounding. There is only offense and defense. Frank McGuire used possessions. Dean Smith wrote about them in his book. Many programs across the country have used this concept. The NBA tracks possessions behind the scenes. It just makes sense.

- *Understand what a winning streak means.* Don't get caught up in the hype of a short winning streak (though you can use it for motivation). Short losing streaks don't necessarily imply that a team needs to be shaken up; they could just be random fluctuations. Longer winning or losing streaks imply a real change in a team, and you can use those streaks to identify what might have changed and make changes for the future.

- *There are four factors of an offense or defense that define its efficiency: shooting percentage, turnover rate, offensive rebounding percentage, and getting to the foul line.* Striving to control those factors leads to a more successful team.

- *Shooting percentage is a very important statistic.* In the NBA, the team that shoots the best wins the most. Shooting and stopping the opponents' shooters are the bottom lines. This does not mean that the skill of shooting is absolutely most important. It means that shooting skill is important, and the selection of good shots (through passing or well-run plays) is mutually important. At levels below the NBA, where ball handling is very important, shooting may not be as crucial—you can't shoot if you can't get the ball past half court. But shooting is a fundamental aspect of Naismith's original game that remains important.

- *Teamwork is a way of coordinating teammates' interactions to increase a team's chances of scoring or to decrease an opponent's chance of scoring.* If a team needs more passing in order to score (it's a "harder" job on your team), good passers should be rewarded more. If a team needs defensive rebounding, those players who make more effort to get the defensive boards should get relatively more reward. Teamwork means applying the skills of different teammates to strengthen their collective weaknesses without weakening the strengths.

- *Teammates will fight for credit over the success of a team, and that is healthy as long as players don't get disproportionate credit for easier jobs.* I have built a model of basketball decision-making in this book that gives more credit for accomplishing difficult but necessary tasks. If a player is a good shooter, he should generally shoot more—until the defense keys on him enough to make him a worse shooter.

- *Don't get caught up in streaky shooting.* Studies don't show a lot of support for the existence of the "hot hand" or for people's ability to recognize when a player is hot.

- *If a team is favored, it should play safer strategies than if it is an underdog.* It's a rule of thumb, not an absolute rule. If a team's skills are best suited to risky strategies, it shouldn't abandon them. It would be good, however, to build a team that can play both high-risk strategies and low-risk strategies because almost every team is an underdog sometimes and a favorite other times.

- *Know when to compete and what you're competing for.* If you're a young team looking to improve in the long run, don't compete as hard to win each game as you compete to simply improve. Don't worry as much about whether that potential game-winning shot goes in; worry about how well the team worked to create that last shot. A good wide-open shot that doesn't go in may be better in the long run than a bad off-balance shot that miraculously does go in. If a team is already good and talented, it's more important to think about competing to win each game. That's when making that good shot is as important as setting it up.

- *Compete to win, but don't try to crush an opponent once you've won.* It's common sports courtesy, of course. But there are indications that not running up the score against your opponent makes you a better team, too.

- *Neutral referees who simply make occasional mistakes can end up favoring underdogs.* But even a slight bias by referees toward favorites can easily counteract the underdog's "advantage" to the point of overwhelming it.

- *Defense probably doesn't win championships.* No more than offense does, at least. This saying may have come out of the Chamberlain-Russell era when Russell's Celtics were better defensively than Chamberlain's teams were offensively, making a comparison between the two players somewhat unfair. However, if there is a temptation for teams to slack off during the regular season and pick it up in the playoffs, then this saying may hold some truth. Particularly, if teams slack off only on the defensive end—not on offense—then it's possible that defense may win championships after all.

- *Individuals who make up a team produce points, and they use possessions.* Players who score a lot of points can also use precious possessions doing so. You want your highest scorers to also be efficient in producing points. It makes for a better offense and a team that wins more.

- *There is no Holy Grail of player statistics.* All individual statistics are highly influenced by the context in which they are generated. A player's teammates make him better or worse. A player's coach can do the same. Changing a player's environment can easily change that player's performance. A player's talent level changes only with age, experience, injury, and state of mind, but what you see on the court is the product of talent and context. The tools of this book are mostly measurements or pseudo-measurements of *performance* (not talent). As measurements, they are tools that are useful for answering questions about quality or about talent or about how a player will fit in some system, but they aren't answers themselves.

- *Individual defense is poorly measured right now and may never be perfectly measured.* There is an effort under way within the WNBA to help improve our understanding of individual defense. From even existing information, it appears that traditional ideas about good defenders aren't necessarily right. In particular, good ball defenders like Joe Dumars who don't cause the end of possessions (they perhaps deny the ball to good scorers) are useful to a defense when the rest of the defense can force the end of a possession. Their skill is not valuable if the rest of the defense can't stop opponents. Big men in the middle are inherently best at both stopping their own man and stopping other offensive players who go to the middle. As a result, big men are apparently the most important defenders. Smaller players can be relatively more important in leagues where ball handling is weak enough that even setting up shots in the half-court is difficult. But, in a league like the NBA where half-court offense is the norm, teams are willing to pay an offensive premium for big men who play good defense. Having a center whose offensive rating is at the league average is then an advantage. Having a good offensive center like Shaq is a huge advantage.

- *Coaching is often evaluated based on expectations.* Beating expectations by only a couple of wins per year (over eighty-two games) seems to separate the good coaches from the mediocre. Coaches achieve this success by coaxing greater performances out of similarly skilled players. An explicit measurement of the degree to which coaches are able to do this is not yet available, but such a measure may be significant (it may show that coaches generate more than a couple of wins per year).

- *Given equal defense, an individual who increases his/her responsibility in an offense will become less efficient.* This decrease in efficiency happens as a player takes more difficult shots or makes more difficult passes. Players who can maintain even an average efficiency with a large responsibility on the offensive end can help their teammates by lowering their teammates' responsibilities, making them more efficient role players. The tendency of a player's offensive efficiency to fluctuate with changing offensive loads is unique and can be estimated.

- *Although individuals cannot win games on their own, they play roles in achieving team success.* Players are forced to take on roles of various importance within a team framework where the ball can be distributed to players at different rates. You can evaluate a player's overall contribution either by how well he performs his role or by how important that role is. A team with all role players performing their roles well will win games. Most teams need a leader, however, who carry a team on his back—that role being the most important. A team record can very well reflect the ability of its leader to carry the team.

Several of these concepts are not basketball-specific. Concepts like teamwork, competition, the effect of supposedly neutral forces, and the value of people with different roles all have analogies beyond basketball and beyond sports. I haven't emphasized this because I don't want to give the impression that Basketball Is Life, the rest being details. Basketball is *not* life. It is a game with aspects that look a lot like other parts of life—to me, anyway. But that is because basketball is my passion and my expertise. By being so passionate about this game, I've learned things that are relevant to other passions in my life—football, science, politics, working, girls—not necessarily in that order.

To the coaches out there so passionate about their craft—I hope these concepts help you persevere through all the challenges you face. It's a tough profession.

To the basketball fans, the scientists, the teachers, the parents, and the football players who are passionate about what they do—I hope that you found my work thought-provoking enough to inspire you in your craft.

Appendix 1

Calculation of Individual Offensive Ratings and Floor Percentages

Chapter 13 describes the concepts behind distributing credit to teammates cooperating to produce points and scoring possessions for their teams. Specifically, it provided the concepts and formulas for individual offensive ratings and floor percentages. This appendix gets into a little more of the details of why those formulas are constructed the way they are.

To refresh your memory: individual offensive ratings and floor percentages are constructed from the following three statistics:

- Individual scoring possessions, which represents the credit an individual gets for the times his/her team scores at least one point

- Individual possessions, which represents the credit an individual gets for the times his/her team ends a possession and gives it back to the opponents

- Individual points produced, which represents the credit an individual receives for the points that his/her team generates on the offensive end

Each of these statistics incorporates the difficulty concept, which generally gives more credit to the player performing the more difficult role in meeting a team objective. Difficulty is often defined by the probability of achieving that role, with the lower probability meaning greater difficulty and more credit.

Those are the generalities. Here are the details.

Individual Scoring Possessions

A team scores through field goals and free throws—nothing else. On field goals, individuals either score them, assist on them, or get offensive rebounds that sometimes leads to them. On free throws, no assists are ever awarded (something that seems a little unfair), so credit needs to be split only between the foul shooter and players who get offensive rebounds that lead to foul shots.

For field goals, the most critical splitting of credit is that between the shooter and the assistant. How difficult is a shot for an individual? His or her field goal

343

percentage is an indication of that. How difficult is the assist to that player? Without measured stats, the best we can say is that the difficulty of the assist is probably proportional to the ease of a shot. Thus, for splitting the credit of a player's field goals between him and all the players who assisted those field goals, I use this equation:

$$\text{FG Part} = \text{FGM} \times \left(1 - \frac{1}{2} \times \frac{\text{PTS} - \text{FTM}}{2 \times \text{FGA}} \times q_{AST}\right)$$

This equation gives a player credit for his field goals (FGM) but subtracts credit proportional to his effective field goal percentage $\left(\dfrac{\text{PTS} - \text{FTM}}{2 \times \text{FGA}}\right)$ and the percentage of his shots that are assisted on (q_{AST}). The factor of one-half is used to split credit between the two players—the assistant, who has no measure of failure, and the shooter, whose missed field goals are a measure of failure.[1]

So what percentage of a player's shots are assisted on? What is q_{AST}? (This paragraph is for readers who want to earn lots of credit for accomplishing a difficult task.) Obviously, guards who record more assists than big men probably have fewer of their shots assisted on. Aside from that bit of obvious wisdom, there isn't a lot to go on. I developed a rather brutally complicated formula that I use to estimate the percentage of a player's shots that are assisted, denoted as q. You can tell how complicated the formula is by the fact that the following formula is the *simplified* version:

$$q = \frac{\text{MIN}}{\text{TMMIN}/5} q_5 + \left(1 - \frac{\text{MIN}}{\text{TMMIN}/5}\right) q_{12}$$

where

$$q_5 = 1.14 \times \frac{\text{TMAST} - \text{AST}}{\text{TMFGM}}$$

$$q_{12} = \frac{\dfrac{\text{TMAST}}{\text{TMMIN}} \times \text{MIN} \times 5 - \text{AST}}{\dfrac{\text{TMFGM}}{\text{TMMIN}} \times \text{MIN} \times 5 - \text{FGM}}$$

The equation for q is made up of two approximations, q_5 and q_{12}, each weighted by how many minutes a player is on the floor. If a player is on the floor a lot, $q5$ is more appropriate because it was developed based on the probability of a player having a field goal assisted on, assuming that the same five players play together (hence the number five on q_5) throughout a game.[2] If a player is on the floor fairly infrequently, q_{12} works better (the twelve meaning it's good for the twelfth man) because it was based upon an assumption of fairly even distribution of assists per minute.

Whew. OK. That was the painful paragraph. Now, stepping back from the details for a reality check: You may ask why a player with a good effective field goal percentage should get more credit taken away from his shots than a bad shooter. It goes back to the example early in the chapter. It is often more difficult for a passer to get a ball to a good shooter than to a poor one. So a high-percentage shooter should thank his assistants relatively more, giving more credit back to them.

If you take away credit from a shooter for his assisted field goals, you also give credit to him when he is making the assist. This is the assist part, which is

$$\text{AST Part} = \frac{1}{2} \times \frac{(\text{TMPTS} - \text{TMFTM}) - (\text{PTS} - \text{FTM})}{2 \times (\text{TMFGA} - \text{FGA})} \times \text{AST}$$

The factor of one-half is used to account for the same lack of a statistic to measure failure of assists. Also, if you're taking away credit from shooters based on their effective field goal percentage, you give credit to assistants based on the effective field goal percentage that they create.

Before we start talking about offensive rebounds, let's consider free throws, which are easy. A player's scoring possessions off of foul shots is identical to the team formula:

$$\text{FT Part} = \left[1 - \left(1 - \text{FT\%} \right)^2 \right] \times 0.4 \times \text{FTA}$$

The part in brackets is just the fraction of free throw possessions on which the player makes at least one foul shot.

The basics of a player's scoring possessions consist simply of adding the field goal part and the free throw part together. Offensive rebounds, however, work by starting a new play that can lead to some of these field goals or free throws. So I take that total and subtract partial credit, giving it to offensive rebounders. The credit that goes to offensive rebounders is based on the relative difficulty of their task (the team's offensive rebounding percentage, TMOR%) to scoring on a play (the team play percentage, TMPlay%). Because an offensive rebound does not guarantee a score, the relative difficulty gets adjusted to reflect the chance that a score will happen off of that offensive rebound—the TMPlay% again. The credit given to a player getting an offensive rebound is then his offensive rebounds (OR) times the weight on offensive rebounds due to its relative difficulty (TMOR weight) and the TmPlay%:

$$\text{OR part} = \text{OR} \times \text{TMOR weight} \times \text{TMPlay\%}$$

So, when a team scores off an offensive rebound, what is the relative difficulty of an offensive rebound (where the TMOR% is 0.3) versus the difficulty of scoring on a play (where the TMPlay% is 0.45)? I get at the difficulty by looking back at the Ultimatum Game, which suggests that teammates *compete* somewhat for credit. That *competition* between roles suggests that you can pit the two roles—offensive rebounding and scoring—against one another and assign a relative weight to them based on how often they "beat" each other. The absolute difficulty that offensive rebounders overcome is 70 percent (1—TMOR%), and the difficulty that the scorers overcome is 55 percent (1—TMPlay%). Making the analogy of a 70 percent team competing against a 55 percent team, the winning percentage of that 70 percent team is going to be (borrowing from Bill James)

$$\frac{0.70 \times (1 - 0.55)}{0.70 \times (1 - 0.55) + (1 - 0.70) \times 0.55} = 0.66$$

The weight on an offensive rebound in this case is 0.66, and the weight on scoring would be 0.34. The formula for the offensive rebounding weight is then

$$\text{TMOREB weight} = \frac{(1 - \text{TMOR}\%) \times \text{TMPlay}\%}{(1 - \text{TMOR}\%) \times \text{TMPlay}\% + \text{TMOR}\% \times (1 - \text{TMPlay}\%)}$$

The range on this offensive rebound weight for NBA teams in 2002 was from 0.57 for Golden State, which shot poorly but got lots of rebounds, to 0.70 for Detroit, which shot reasonably well but got few offensive rebounds despite the presence of league rebound leader Ben Wallace. What this implies is that an offensive rebound was about 20 percent more valuable for Detroit than it was for Golden State. Because of how poorly the Warriors finished plays, they basically needed six offensive rebounds to help their offense as much as five Pistons offensive rebounds helped their offense.

That is the credit given to each offensive rebound, meaning that the credit taken away from the field goal and free throw producers is the sum of all credits given to offensive rebounders. This makes the final formula for scoring possessions:

$$\text{Scoring Possessions} = \left(\text{FG Part} + \text{AST Part} + \text{FT Part}\right)$$
$$\times \left(1 - \frac{\text{TMOR}}{\text{TMScPoss}} \times \text{TMOR weight} \times \text{TMPlay}\%\right) + \text{OR part}$$

Some of you will remember that offensive rebounds do increase a team's offensive rating about 15 percent. It may then be tempting to adjust the offensive rebound component for this. However, John Maxwell, who did the study, also reported that nearly all of this improvement in efficiency was in the offensive rebounder's own ability to score, not in helping his teammates. Because of this, the improvement already shows up in the offensive rebounder's increased field goals or free throws without a simultaneous increase in his individual possessions.

Individual Total Possessions

The scoring possession formula was the hard one. The formulas for total possessions and points produced are relatively easy. If they have hard parts, they're the same parts that are hard in the scoring possession formula.

An individual racks up a total possession when he ends the team possession, which can happen through one of four ways:

1. A scoring possession,
2. A missed field goal that is rebounded by the defense,
3. A missed foul shot that is rebounded by the defense, or
4. A turnover

So an individual's total possessions will be

Possessions = Scoring Possessions + Missed FG Part + Missed FT Part + TOV

You know scoring possessions from the previous section. The league records individual turnovers (since 1978), so the fourth term is particularly easy. The second and third terms are the only ones that require any explanation.

The possessions that end due to a player's missed field goals are just those field goals he misses multiplied by the percentage of shots not rebounded by the offense:

Missed FG Part = (FGA − FGM) × (1 − 1.07 × TMOR%)

The factor of 1.07 comes from the technical version of the team possessions formula, where it makes the estimates a bit more accurate. There is no adjustment for players who anecdotally have a higher percentage of their missed field goals rebounded by their own team. Supposedly, Allen Iverson and Dominique Wilkins, who took a lot of their team's shots and missed a fair amount, had role players who knew to go to the offensive glass and rebounded a higher percentage of their misses than might be expected. I don't know if it's even true, so I don't assume it is.

For the possessions that end on a missed foul shot, I assume simply that none are rebounded by the offense and the formula is

Missed FT Part = (1 − FT%)^2 × 0.4 × FTA

Changing this assumption doesn't make a big difference. It might help Shaq a little, but not many other players.

And that's it for the individual possession formula.

Individual Points Produced

The formula for points produced is very similar to the one for scoring possessions, but it accounts for the number of points generated on each scoring possession. It has the same structure:

$$\text{Points Produced} = \left(\text{FG Part} + \text{AST Part} + \text{FT Part}\right)$$
$$\times \left(1 - \frac{\text{TMOR}}{\text{TMScPoss}} \times \text{TMOR weight} \times \text{TMPlay\%}\right) + \text{OR part}$$

but this time the parts have slightly different looks to them.

The field goal part now accounts for three-point shots made by the player:

$$\text{FG Part} = 2 \times \left(\text{FGM} + \frac{1}{2} \times \text{FG3M}\right) \times \left(1 - \frac{1}{2} \times \frac{\text{PTS} - \text{FTM}}{2 \times \text{FGA}} \times q_{AST}\right)$$

All that changes from the scoring possession formula is replacing FGM by the points generated by all field goals, which is

$$2 \times \left(\text{FGM} + \frac{1}{2} \times \text{FG3M}\right)$$

The assist part is also modified only for how many points each assist creates:

$$\text{AST Part} = 2 \times \frac{\text{TMFGM} - \text{FGM} + \frac{1}{2}(\text{TMFG3M} - \text{FG3M})}{(\text{TMFGM} - \text{FGM})} \times \frac{1}{2}$$
$$\times \frac{(\text{TMPTS} - \text{TMFTM}) - (\text{PTS} - \text{FTM})}{2 \times (\text{TMFGA} - \text{FGA})} \times \text{AST}$$

The first part of this equation is an estimate of how many points were created per assists to two-point shooters and to three-point shooters.

The free throw part of the points produced formula is trivial: FT Part = FTM. At this point, the NBA doesn't give assists on two-shot fouls, so no credit from free throws gets taken and given to assistants. You could argue that some free throws occur after an assisted basket on a three-point play and therefore some credit should be taken away. It is a legitimate argument, but such assists are probably not a big factor.

The very last thing is the offensive rebound part. Again, the only difference from the scoring possession formula is a multiplication by the expected number of points on a scoring possession. For simplicity (Don't laugh! I know that almost nothing in this appendix has been "simple"), I assume that the expected number of points scored on a scoring possession is the same on all offensive rebounds. The offensive rebound part is then:

$$\text{OR part} = \text{OR} \times \text{TMOR weight} \times \text{TMPlay\%}$$

$$\times \frac{\text{TMPTS}}{\text{TMFGM} + [1 - (1 - \text{TMFT\%})^2] \times 0.4 \times \text{TMFTA}}$$

That's it. These are the offensive formulas I rely on for individuals, formulas that in turn rely upon the difficulty concept for distributing credit in cooperative actions. Over the fifteen years or so that I've been calculating these values, the formulas have evolved and they will continue to evolve. But the results are generally robust. The biggest change I made was the addition of offensive rebounds, which I did not include for years because they didn't definitely contribute a scoring possession. After adding them as a probabilistic contributor to scoring possessions, players who got a lot of offensive rebounds like Dennis Rodman received more credit and looked like better offensive players. Aside from that, improvements in the estimation of the difficulty of different actions have made only slight changes in the numerical results.

Endnotes

1. It turns out that this assumption implies that 75 to 80 percent of all passes that potentially could be assists reach the shooter successfully.

2. The more complicated form of the equation for q_5 is

$$q_5 = \sum_{\substack{i \neq n}} \frac{\text{AST}_i}{\sum_{\substack{k \neq i}} \text{FGM}_k}$$

where n represents the player for whom q_5 is being calculated. Basically, this sums the chances of each player assisting other players. It's an ugly formula, but it works pretty well. The simplified form in the text approximates this more complicated version fairly well.

Appendix 2

Individual Floor Percentages and Offensive Ratings for History's Great Offenses

In order to present a broader spectrum of teams, the greatest teams listed in tables A2.1 through A2.25 are from the list using standard deviations above average (table 3.7 in chapter 3).

Table A2.1. 1982 Denver Nuggets

Player	G	Sc. Poss.	Poss.	Floor %	Off. Rtg.	Pts Prod/G	% Tm Poss
Alex English	82	1009	1734	0.58	118	24.9	25%
Dan Issel	81	840	1402	0.60	123	21.2	25%
Kiki Vandeweghe	82	800	1357	0.59	120	19.9	21%
David Thompson	61	413	778	0.53	108	13.8	27%
Dave Robisch	12	71	123	0.58	120	12.3	21%
Billy McKinney	81	446	781	0.57	115	11.1	17%
T.R. Dunn	82	393	685	0.57	114	9.5	12%
Kenny Higgs	76	343	677	0.51	103	9.2	17%
Glen Gondrezick	80	356	623	0.57	114	8.9	16%
Cedrick Hordges	77	276	539	0.51	100	7.0	17%
John Roche	39	91	175	0.52	114	5.1	15%
David Burns	6	10	23	0.45	89	3.3	19%
James Ray	40	64	147	0.44	87	3.2	24%

Table A2.2. 1997 Chicago Bulls

Player	G	Sc. Poss.	Poss.	Floor %	Off. Rtg.	Pts Prod/G	% Tm Poss
Michael Jordan	82	1020	1791	0.57	121	26.5	31%
Scottie Pippen	82	749	1416	0.53	115	19.9	24%
Toni Kukoc	57	365	657	0.56	119	13.7	22%
Luc Longley	59	279	555	0.50	103	9.7	20%
Dennis Rodman	55	252	467	0.54	111	9.5	13%
Jason Caffey	75	278	496	0.56	112	7.4	19%
Brian Williams	9	32	66	0.48	98	7.2	26%
Steve Kerr	82	250	428	0.58	137	7.2	12%
Ron Harper	76	220	414	0.53	120	6.6	13%
Randy Brown	72	179	360	0.50	102	5.1	18%
Bill Wennington	61	129	234	0.55	113	4.3	16%
Robert Parish	43	79	153	0.52	104	3.7	20%
Dickey Simpkins	48	56	130	0.43	87	2.4	18%
Jud Buechler	76	75	166	0.45	101	2.2	13%
Matt Steigenga	2	2	6	0.317	61.5	1.8	26%

Table A2.3. 2002 Dallas Mavericks

Player	G	Sc. Poss.	Poss.	Floor %	Off. Rtg.	Pts Prod/G	% Tm Poss
Dirk Nowitzki	76	736	1360	0.54	120	21.4	24%
Michael Finley	69	625	1220	0.51	110	19.4	23%
Steve Nash	82	701	1338	0.52	119	19.3	24%
Nick Van Exel	27	163	337	0.48	108	13.5	23%
Juwan Howard	53	347	657	0.53	108	13.3	20%
Raef Lafrentz	27	131	272	0.48	106	10.7	18%
Tim Hardaway	54	227	528	0.43	103	10.1	21%
Adrian Griffin	58	205	377	0.54	115	7.5	14%
Eduardo Najera	62	223	377	0.59	119	7.3	14%
Greg Buckner	44	133	230	0.58	119	6.2	13%
Zhizhi Wang	55	114	241	0.47	110	4.8	21%
Shawn Bradley	53	107	193	0.55	116	4.2	13%
Danny Manning	41	82	165	0.50	101	4.1	15%
Johnny Newman	47	78	159	0.49	109	3.7	11%
Avery Johnson	17	30	60	0.50	102	3.6	20%
Evan Eschmeyer	31	41	80	0.51	102	2.6	14%
Donnell Harvey	18	22	41	0.53	103	2.3	13%
Darrick Martin	3	1	10	0.13	26	0.8	23%
Tariq Abdul-Wahad	4	1	6	0.19	41	0.6	13%
Charlie Bell	2	0	0			0.0	0%

Table A2.4. 1997 Utah Jazz

Player	G	Sc. Poss.	Poss.	Floor %	Off. Rtg.	Pts Prod/G	% Tm Poss
Karl Malone	82	1040	1771	0.59	119	25.6	31%
John Stockton	82	672	1157	0.58	125	17.6	21%
Jeff Hornacek	82	544	981	0.55	121	14.5	20%
Bryon Russell	81	354	677	0.52	116	9.7	14%
Greg Ostertag	77	288	506	0.57	114	7.5	15%
Antoine Carr	82	271	533	0.51	103	6.7	19%
Shandon Anderson	65	172	365	0.47	99	5.6	18%
Howard Eisley	82	197	424	0.46	98	5.1	21%
Ruben Nembhard	8	17	32	0.54	110	4.4	18%
Adam Keefe	62	128	231	0.56	111	4.1	13%
Chris Morris	73	134	302	0.45	97	4.0	16%
Greg Foster	79	134	280	0.48	98	3.5	16%
Stephen Howard	42	70	123	0.57	112	3.3	19%
Jamie Watson	13	17	35	0.47	99	2.7	15%
Brooks Thompson	2	0	2	0.13	27	0.3	13%

Table A2.5. 1992 Chicago Bulls

Player	G	Sc. Poss.	Poss.	Floor %	Off. Rtg.	Pts Prod/G	% Tm Poss
Michael Jordan	80	1088	1841	0.59	121	27.9	30%
Scottie Pippen	82	887	1569	0.56	114	21.9	25%
Horace Grant	81	605	920	0.66	132	15.0	16%
B.J. Armstrong	82	374	696	0.54	112	9.5	19%
Bill Cartwright	64	259	493	0.53	104	8.0	17%
John Paxson	79	273	461	0.59	121	7.1	12%
Stacey King	79	262	473	0.55	112	6.7	19%
Will Perdue	77	192	352	0.54	107	4.9	18%
Cliff Levingston	79	176	302	0.58	115	4.4	15%
Scott Williams	63	128	222	0.58	114	4.0	16%
Craig Hodges	56	94	209	0.45	105	3.9	19%
Bob Hansen	66	85	175	0.48	99	2.6	12%
Mark Randall	15	14	27	0.50	100	1.8	21%
Rory Sparrow	4	2	8	0.22	56	1.1	23%

Table A2.6. 1978 Philadelphia 76ers

Player	G	Sc. Poss.	Poss.	Floor %	Off. Rtg.	Pts Prod/G	% Tm Poss
George McGinnis	78	805	1566	0.51	102	20.5	28%
Julius Erving	74	718	1342	0.53	109	19.7	25%
Doug Collins	79	711	1332	0.53	108	18.2	22%
World B. Free	76	600	1111	0.54	107	15.7	24%
Henry Bibby	82	433	826	0.52	105	10.6	15%
Darryl Dawkins	70	371	656	0.57	112	10.5	17%
Steve Mix	82	368	673	0.55	110	9.1	17%
Joe Bryant	81	260	533	0.49	98	6.4	19%
Caldwell Jones	80	248	504	0.49	97	6.1	14%
Harvey Catchings	61	111	226	0.49	96	3.6	14%
Ted McClain	29	47	104	0.46	91	3.3	16%
Mike Dunleavy	4	5	10	0.46	95	2.4	27%
Glenn Mosley	6	6	17	0.36	68	1.9	37%
Wilson Washington	14	9	26	0.33	64	1.2	31%

Table A2.7. 1996 Chicago Bulls

Player	G	Sc. Poss.	Poss.	Floor %	Off. Rtg.	Pts Prod/G	% Tm Poss
Michael Jordan	82	1064	1833	0.58	124	27.6	31%
Scottie Pippen	77	696	1312	0.53	116	19.7	24%
Toni Kukoc	81	487	850	0.57	125	13.1	21%
Luc Longley	62	279	552	0.50	103	9.2	18%
Dennis Rodman	64	278	521	0.53	109	8.9	13%
Ron Harper	80	298	538	0.55	116	7.8	15%
Steve Kerr	82	262	448	0.58	141	7.7	12%
Bill Wennington	71	170	313	0.54	111	4.9	15%
Jack Haley	1	2	6	0.40	77	4.6	45%
Dickey Simpkins	60	117	229	0.51	102	3.9	18%
Jud Buechler	74	117	236	0.50	113	3.6	17%
James Edwards	28	48	112	0.42	84	3.4	22%
Jason Caffey	57	96	203	0.47	93	3.3	20%
John Salley	17	25	56	0.45	89	2.9	16%
Randy Brown	68	99	202	0.49	99	2.9	16%

Table A2.8. 1987 Los Angeles Lakers

Player	G	Sc. Poss.	Poss.	Floor %	Off. Rtg.	Pts Prod/G	% Tm Poss
Magic Johnson	80	1066	1768	0.603	123.9	27.4	29%
James Worthy	82	728	1258	0.578	116.1	17.8	21%
Kareem Abdul-Jabbar	78	627	1099	0.571	114.0	16.1	21%
Byron Scott	82	603	1116	0.540	114.9	15.6	19%
Michael Cooper	82	416	782	0.532	116.9	11.1	16%
A.C. Green	79	421	701	0.601	121.6	10.8	15%
Mychal Thompson	33	154	303	0.509	102.1	9.4	21%
Kurt Rambis	78	244	446	0.546	110.2	6.3	14%
Billy Thompson	59	166	307	0.543	107.9	5.6	19%
Wes Matthews	50	112	226	0.497	100.8	4.6	20%
Adrian Branch	32	66	122	0.544	110.0	4.2	26%
Frank Brickowski	37	74	128	0.581	115.2	4.0	15%
Mike Smrek	35	36	75	0.478	94.3	2.0	15%

Table A2.9. 1976 Houston Rockets

Not available because of lack of individual turnover statistics.

Table A2.10. 1998 Utah Jazz

Player	G	Sc. Poss.	Poss.	Floor %	Off. Rtg.	Pts Prod/G	% Tm Poss
Karl Malone	81	1010	1728	0.58	118	25.2	31%
John Stockton	64	437	758	0.58	122	14.5	22%
Jeff Hornacek	80	528	942	0.56	120	14.2	21%
Howard Eisley	82	326	677	0.48	104	8.6	21%
Bryon Russell	82	316	598	0.53	116	8.4	15%
Adam Keefe	80	317	518	0.61	125	8.1	14%
Shandon Anderson	82	307	556	0.55	112	7.6	19%
Greg Foster	78	211	433	0.49	99	5.5	16%
Antoine Carr	66	173	337	0.51	104	5.3	17%
Greg Ostertag	63	172	342	0.50	98	5.3	14%
Chris Morris	54	102	216	0.47	101	4.0	22%
Jacque Vaughn	45	81	190	0.43	86	3.7	24%
William Cunningham	6	5	8	0.58	118	1.5	11%
Troy Hudson	8	6	12	0.49	99	1.5	29%

Table A2.11. 1999 Indiana Pacers (Fifty-Game Season)

Player	G	Sc. Poss.	Poss.	Floor %	Off. Rtg.	Pts Prod/G	% Tm Poss
Reggie Miller	50	353	691	0.51	119	16.4	21%
Rik Smits	49	318	618	0.51	105	13.2	27%
Mark Jackson	49	243	475	0.51	112	10.9	19%
Jalen Rose	49	249	528	0.47	98	10.6	24%
Antonio Davis	49	235	419	0.56	112	9.6	18%
Chris Mullin	50	194	389	0.50	117	9.1	18%
Dale Davis	50	212	360	0.59	118	8.5	15%
Travis Best	49	178	365	0.49	106	7.9	19%
Derrick McKey	13	33	65	0.50	104	5.2	15%
Sam Perkins	48	99	206	0.48	110	4.7	15%
Austin Croshere	27	40	93	0.43	96	3.3	21%
Al Harrington	21	27	65	0.41	82	2.5	23%
Fred Hoiberg	12	9	22	0.40	89	1.6	14%
Mark Pope	4	1	7	0.21	43	0.8	15%

Table A2.12. 1988 Boston Celtics

Player	G	Sc. Poss.	Poss.	Floor %	Off. Rtg.	Pts Prod/G	% Tm Poss
Larry Bird	76	992	1746	0.57	122	27.9	29%
Kevin McHale	64	646	1040	0.62	126	20.5	21%
Danny Ainge	81	581	1076	0.54	121	16.0	17%
Dennis Johnson	77	569	1074	0.53	110	15.3	20%
Robert Parish	74	489	860	0.57	114	13.3	18%
Jim Paxson	28	109	203	0.54	111	8.1	19%
Fred Roberts	74	222	409	0.54	110	6.1	19%
Darren Daye	47	142	261	0.54	108	6.0	20%
Jerry Sichting	24	55	95	0.58	118	4.7	13%
Dirk Minniefield	61	134	273	0.49	101	4.5	15%
Reggie Lewis	49	103	206	0.50	100	4.2	25%
Brad Lohaus	70	142	287	0.50	102	4.2	20%
Mark Acres	79	163	288	0.57	113	4.1	12%
Artis Gilmore	47	90	166	0.54	104	3.7	16%
Conner Henry	10	16	37	0.440	98.0	3.6	22%
Greg Kite	13	12	32	0.368	73.1	1.8	18%

Table A2.13. 1995 Orlando Magic

Player	G	Sc. Poss.	Poss.	Floor %	Off. Rtg.	Pts Prod/G	% Tm Poss
Shaquille O'Neal	79	1070	1770	0.60	118	26.4	31%
Anfernee Hardaway	77	794	1416	0.56	119	21.9	25%
Nick Anderson	76	500	956	0.52	119	15.0	19%
Horace Grant	74	476	763	0.62	126	13.0	14%
Dennis Scott	62	288	578	0.50	120	11.2	19%
Donald Royal	70	338	616	0.55	111	9.8	17%
Brian Shaw	78	306	685	0.45	97	8.6	19%
Anthony Bowie	77	219	428	0.51	107	6.0	17%
Anthony Avent	71	145	291	0.50	100	4.1	14%
Jeff Turner	49	83	172	0.48	111	3.9	15%
Brooks Thompson	38	52	124	0.42	97	3.2	25%
Tree Rollins	51	37	75	0.49	99	1.5	8%

Table A2.14. 1985 Los Angeles Lakers

Player	G	Sc. Poss.	Poss.	Floor %	Off. Rtg.	Pts Prod/G	% Tm Poss
Magic Johnson	77	855	1416	0.60	123	22.7	24%
Kareem Abdul-Jabbar	79	783	1300	0.60	120	19.8	23%
James Worthy	80	645	1139	0.57	114	16.2	20%
Byron Scott	81	570	1006	0.57	116	14.5	20%
Michael Cooper	82	397	756	0.52	110	10.2	16%
Bob McAdoo	66	311	577	0.54	108	9.4	21%
Mike McGee	76	337	610	0.55	112	8.9	24%
Jamaal Wilkes	42	158	307	0.51	103	7.5	19%
Larry Spriggs	75	257	478	0.54	108	6.9	17%
Kurt Rambis	82	240	435	0.55	110	5.8	13%
Mitch Kupchak	58	150	279	0.54	106	5.1	18%
Ronnie Lester	32	61	125	0.49	97	3.8	21%
Chuck Nevitt	11	8	27	0.29	55	1.4	22%
Earl Jones	2	0	2	0.00	0	0.0	11%

Table A2.15. 1977 Houston Rockets

Not available because of lack of individual turnover statistics.

Table A2.16. 1991 Chicago Bulls

Player	G	Sc. Poss.	Poss.	Floor %	Off. Rtg.	Pts Prod/G	% Tm Poss
Michael Jordan	82	1152	1892	0.61	126	29.0	31%
Scottie Pippen	82	759	1351	0.56	114	18.7	22%
Horace Grant	78	521	831	0.63	125	13.4	16%
Bill Cartwright	79	386	714	0.54	108	9.8	16%
B.J. Armstrong	82	361	675	0.53	111	9.1	20%
John Paxson	82	332	565	0.59	124	8.5	14%
Stacey King	76	210	419	0.50	100	5.5	18%
Will Perdue	74	175	330	0.53	105	4.7	17%
Craig Hodges	73	150	310	0.49	110	4.7	18%
Dennis Hopson	61	141	292	0.48	96	4.6	20%
Cliff Levingston	78	173	325	0.53	106	4.4	16%
Scott Williams	51	67	123	0.54	109	2.6	18%

Table A2.17. 1979 Houston Rockets

Player	G	Sc. Poss.	Poss.	Floor %	Off. Rtg.	Pts Prod/G	% Tm Poss
Moses Malone	82	1022	1750	0.58	117	24.9	24%
Calvin Murphy	82	755	1389	0.54	111	18.8	22%
Rudy Tomjanovich	74	627	1132	0.55	111	17.0	20%
Rick Barry	80	563	1097	0.51	105	14.4	20%
Robert Reid	82	450	834	0.54	108	10.9	17%
Mike Newlin	76	394	757	0.52	107	10.6	19%
Mike Dunleavy	74	321	584	0.55	112	8.9	18%
Dwight Jones	81	231	470	0.49	98	5.7	18%
Slick Watts	61	164	323	0.51	100	5.3	14%
Alonzo Bradley	34	48	98	0.49	96	2.8	19%
Jacky Dorsey	20	26	47	0.54	106	2.5	20%
Tom Barker	5	4	6	0.55	116	1.5	19%
E.C. Coleman	6	4	6	0.78	159	1.5	7%

Table A2.18. 1995 Seattle Supersonics

Player	G	Sc. Poss.	Poss.	Floor %	Off. Rtg.	Pts Prod/G	% Tm Poss
Gary Payton	82	836	1478	0.57	118	21.3	25%
Detlef Schrempf	82	698	1189	0.59	127	18.4	21%
Shawn Kemp	82	742	1310	0.57	115	18.3	25%
Kendall Gill	73	451	898	0.50	107	13.2	21%
Sam Perkins	82	415	754	0.55	126	11.5	16%
Vincent Askew	71	335	593	0.56	118	9.9	17%
Sarunas Marciulionis	66	265	525	0.50	106	8.5	22%
Nate McMillan	80	275	555	0.49	109	7.6	13%
Ervin Johnson	64	116	242	0.48	96	3.6	13%
Byron Houston	39	57	116	0.49	103	3.1	23%
Bill Cartwright	29	39	86	0.46	91	2.7	10%
Dontonio Wingfield	20	22	51	0.42	89	2.3	32%
Steve Scheffler	18	19	29	0.65	134	2.2	14%

Table A2.19. 1986 Los Angeles Lakers

Player	G	Sc. Poss.	Poss.	Floor %	Off. Rtg.	Pts Prod/G	% Tm Poss
Magic Johnson	72	807	1364	0.59	122	23.1	25%
Kareem Abdul-Jabbar	79	831	1421	0.59	118	21.2	25%
James Worthy	75	668	1119	0.60	120	17.9	21%
Byron Scott	76	504	928	0.54	111	13.5	20%
Michael Cooper	82	410	777	0.53	114	10.8	16%
Maurice Lucas	77	388	740	0.52	106	10.2	20%
Mike Mcgee	71	249	511	0.49	103	7.4	20%
Petur Gudmundsson	8	30	53	0.56	111	7.4	19%
A.C. Green	82	274	498	0.55	108	6.6	15%
Kurt Rambis	74	227	398	0.57	114	6.1	12%
Mitch Kupchak	55	160	312	0.51	103	5.8	19%
Larry Spriggs	43	107	230	0.47	94	5.0	23%
Ronnie Lester	27	41	101	0.41	83	3.1	21%
Chuck Nevitt	4	6	16	0.36	72	2.9	31%

Table A2.20. 1980 Boston Celtics

Player	G	Sc. Poss.	Poss.	Floor %	Off. Rtg.	Pts Prod/G	% Tm Poss
Larry Bird	82	825	1575	0.52	109	21.0	25%
Cedric Maxwell	80	662	1085	0.61	124	16.8	19%
Nate Archibald	80	643	1148	0.56	115	16.5	19%
Dave Cowens	66	461	891	0.52	104	14.1	20%
Rick Robey	82	457	837	0.55	109	11.1	21%
Chris Ford	73	368	713	0.52	111	10.9	16%
M.L. Carr	82	432	833	0.52	105	10.7	20%
Pete Maravich	26	122	238	0.51	106	9.7	25%
Gerald Henderson	76	238	472	0.50	101	6.3	21%
Jeff Judkins	65	152	288	0.53	110	4.9	20%
Eric Fernsten	56	90	164	0.55	108	3.2	18%
Don Chaney	60	87	198	0.44	89	2.9	18%

Table A2.21. 1987 Dallas Mavericks

Player	G	Sc. Poss.	Poss.	Floor %	Off. Rtg.	Pts Prod/G	% Tm Poss
Mark Aguirre	80	922	1663	0.55	114	23.7	30%
Rolando Blackman	80	757	1341	0.56	117	19.6	23%
Derek Harper	77	637	1101	0.58	121	17.4	21%
Sam Perkins	80	561	1013	0.55	114	14.5	18%
James Donaldson	82	456	705	0.65	132	11.4	11%
Detlef Schrempf	81	362	668	0.54	113	9.3	19%
Brad Davis	82	320	587	0.55	117	8.3	18%
Roy Tarpley	75	296	572	0.52	103	7.9	19%
Al Wood	54	166	323	0.51	106	6.3	23%
Bill Wennington	58	88	177	0.50	100	3.0	15%
Dennis Nutt	25	25	51	0.50	113	2.3	27%
Uwe Blab	30	30	68	0.44	85	1.9	20%
Myron Jackson	8	6	16	0.40	85	1.7	34%

Table A2.22. 1998 Los Angeles Lakers

Player	G	Sc. Poss.	Poss.	Floor %	Off. Rtg.	Pts Prod/G	% Tm Poss
Shaquille O'Neal	60	769	1321	0.58	113	24.9	31%
Eddie Jones	80	559	1055	0.53	117	15.5	19%
Nick Van Exel	64	426	819	0.52	118	15.2	20%
Kobe Bryant	79	538	1048	0.51	110	14.6	26%
Rick Fox	82	449	926	0.48	105	11.9	18%
Elden Campbell	81	398	748	0.53	106	9.8	22%
Robert Horry	72	307	558	0.55	114	8.8	13%
Derek Fisher	82	277	541	0.51	110	7.2	16%
Corle Blount	70	144	256	0.56	112	4.1	13%
Mario Bennett	45	88	153	0.58	115	3.9	22%
Sean Rooks	41	80	141	0.57	112	3.8	17%
Jon Barry	49	56	122	0.46	109	2.7	17%

Table A2.23. 1980 Los Angeles Lakers

Player	G	Sc. Poss.	Poss.	Floor %	Off. Rtg.	Pts Prod/G	% Tm Poss
Kareem Abdul-Jabbar	82	944	1609	0.59	118	23.1	24%
Magic Johnson	77	755	1357	0.56	113	19.9	23%
Norm Nixon	82	765	1439	0.53	107	18.7	21%
Jamaal Wilkes	82	755	1467	0.51	104	18.5	22%
Jim Chones	82	429	861	0.50	100	10.5	17%
Spencer Haywood	76	359	694	0.52	104	9.5	21%
Michael Cooper	82	371	695	0.53	108	9.1	16%
Mark Landsberger	23	92	168	0.55	106	7.8	21%
Ron Boone	6	18	48	0.37	76	6.1	21%
Kenny Carr	5	8	23	0.35	72	3.3	19%
Don Ford	52	77	149	0.52	104	3.0	12%
Brad Holland	38	48	100	0.48	100	2.6	24%
Ollie Mack	27	29	59	0.50	97	2.1	18%
Martin Byrnes	32	31	69	0.45	91	2.0	17%
Butch Lee	11	10	22	0.424	87.0	1.8	34%

Table A2.24. 1995 Phoenix Suns

Player	G	Sc. Poss.	Poss.	Floor %	Off. Rtg.	Pts Prod/G	% Tm Poss
Charles Barkley	68	730	1294	0.56	119	22.6	27%
Kevin Johnson	47	401	699	0.57	119	17.7	26%
Danny Manning	46	387	709	0.55	110	17.0	23%
Dan Majerle	82	551	1069	0.52	119	15.5	17%
A.C. Green	82	443	776	0.57	120	11.3	14%
Elliot Perry	82	421	779	0.54	114	10.8	20%
Wesley Person	78	309	614	0.50	116	9.1	17%
Wayman Tisdale	65	288	556	0.52	105	9.0	22%
Danny Ainge	74	254	491	0.52	119	7.9	18%
Richard Dumas	15	39	74	0.53	105	5.2	22%
Danny Schayes	69	160	309	0.52	105	4.7	19%
Trevor Ruffin	49	91	216	0.42	98	4.3	34%
Joe Kleine	75	145	280	0.52	107	4.0	14%
Aaron Swinson	9	11	21	0.50	103	2.4	21%
Antonio Lang	12	6	15	0.385	78.2	1.0	14%

Table A2.25. 2001 Milwaukee Bucks

Player	G	Sc. Poss.	Poss.	Floor %	Off. Rtg.	Pts Prod/G	% Tm Poss
Ray Allen	82	747	1429	0.52	119	20.8	24%
Glenn Robinson	76	741	1506	0.49	103	20.5	28%
Sam Cassell	76	706	1344	0.53	111	19.6	26%
Tim Thomas	76	397	818	0.49	109	11.7	21%
Lindsey Hunter	82	332	741	0.45	108	9.7	19%
Jason Caffey	70	261	478	0.55	109	7.5	17%
Scott Williams	66	195	369	0.53	109	6.1	15%
Darvin Ham	29	68	133	0.51	104	4.8	13%
Ervin Johnson	82	179	297	0.60	122	4.4	8%
Jerome Kersey	22	36	69	0.52	102	3.2	15%
Mark Pope	63	86	161	0.53	111	2.8	9%
Rafer Alston	37	47	105	0.45	98	2.8	19%
Michael Redd	6	7	18	0.38	74	2.3	28%
Joel Przybilla	33	21	52	0.40	81	1.3	10%

Appendix 3

Individual Defensive Formulas

The premise of individual defense is that players force "stops," preventing the other team from scoring. A team "stop" occurs when a team gets the ball back without the opponent scoring, so an individual stop is when a player contributes to such a play. An individual can do that by forcing a missed shot that then gets rebounded by his team, by getting a defensive rebound, by forcing a turnover, or by fouling a player who misses both foul shots, the second of which is then rebounded by the defense. Estimating stops is rather straightforward. I will explain that first and then get to the more conceptually difficult job of converting stops into individual defensive points allowed per hundred possession ratings.

Individual Defensive Stops

As mentioned in chapter 17, the biggest difficulty in estimating stops is that the official statistics don't record them all. Official statistics don't track how many missed shots a player forces, how many turnovers a player forces, or what happens when a player commits a foul (i.e., whether the fouled player makes the shots, whether he misses and the ball is rebounded by the defense, etc.). So we have to estimate these things using the statistics that are available.

In particular, defensive stops can be broken down into two categories: approximate defensive stops and really approximate defensive stops. The approximate stops are easier. They use the defensive stats that are recorded—steals, blocks, and defensive rebounds—to identify some fraction of the stops a player is responsible for. This part is given by the formula:

$$\text{Stops}_1 = \text{STL} + \text{BLK} \times \text{FMwt} \times (1 - 1.07 \times \text{DOR\%}) + \text{DREB} \times (1 - \text{FMwt})$$

where FMwt represents the difficulty of forcing a missed shot versus the difficulty of getting a defensive rebound (following the same logic as the offensive rebounding weight used in the individual scoring possession formula):

$$\text{FMwt} = \frac{\text{DFG\%} \times (1 - \text{DOR\%})}{\text{DFG\%} \times (1 - \text{DOR\%}) + (1 - \text{DFG\%}) \times \text{DOR\%}}$$

So this first part is just the number of forced turnovers through steals, the number of a player's blocks that lead to a team stop, and the number of a player's defensive rebounds, with weights given to blocks and defensive rebounds based on difficulty. Since forcing a missed shot is typically harder than getting a defensive board (about 55 percent versus 70 percent in the NBA), blocks receive more weight. That may be different in lower levels of basketball, and this formula would automatically account for it.

The very approximate part of defensive stops comes when estimating how many forced turnovers and forced misses a player has that aren't captured by steals and blocks. This part of the equation relies on team statistics and assumes (out of necessity) that all teammates are equally good (per minute) at forcing turnovers and misses. The formula is

$$\text{Stops}_2 = \left[\frac{(\text{TMDFGA} - \text{TMDFGM} - \text{TMBLK})}{\text{TMMIN}} \times \text{FMwt} \times (1 - 1.07 \times \text{DOR\%}) + \frac{(\text{TMDTO} - \text{TMSTL})}{\text{TMMIN}} \right]$$
$$\times \text{MIN} + \frac{\text{PF}}{\text{TMPF}} \times 0.4 \times \text{TMDFTA} \times (1 - \text{TMDFT\%})^2$$

All that stuff in the square brackets estimates the forced misses and forced turnovers by each teammate per minute. It gives appropriate credit for the forced misses as indicated by the FMwt and by the chance that a forced miss will be rebounded. What's in the square brackets is multiplied by a player's total minutes, MIN, to get at each individual's total. This is the part of the formula that can most be improved through Project Defensive Score Sheet. Tracking actual forced misses and forced turnovers dramatically improves this estimate. Some players are clearly better at forcing bad shots and forcing turnovers than others, and this estimate cannot account for that. In chapter 17, I illustrated one way to improve this portion of the equation

$$\frac{(\text{TMDFGA} - \text{TMDFGM} - \text{TMBLK})}{\text{TMMIN}}$$

That improvement used the position-specific field-goals-allowed data. Whereas the above formula estimated that all Sonics forced 0.17 misses (nonblocks) per minute, the position-specific information suggested that point guards such as Gary Payton forced 0.21 misses (non-blocks) per minute and centers such as Jerome James forced only 0.08 misses (non-blocks) per minute (because many of the misses centers forced were through blocks).

The final part of the formula is just an estimate of how often a player causes an opponent to go to the foul line and score. It basically splits up opposing teams' made free throws by how many fouls a player commits. It also has some inaccuracy but is not as big a part of the overall estimate of defensive stops as forced misses and forced turnovers.

The resulting formula for individual stops is, of course, the sum of the parts:

$$Stops = Stops_1 + Stops_2$$

When working from a Project Defensive Score Sheet tabulation, the count of individual defensive stops is simpler:

$$Stops = FTO + STL + \frac{FFTA}{10} + (FM + BLK) \times FMwt \times (1 - DOR\%) + DREB \times (1 - FMwt)$$

With an individual's total defensive stops, their stop percentage is just

$$Stop\% = \frac{Stops \times TMMIN}{TMPOSS \times MIN}$$

If a player has eight stops, playing forty minutes in a forty-eight-minute game (giving TMMIN $= 5 \times 48 = 240$) in which the team had ninety possessions, that gives a stop% of 0.53. This assumes that the number of possessions the player faces is proportional to how many the team faces, which is a somewhat questionable assumption that is addressed more as we talk about individual defensive ratings.

Individual Defensive Ratings

Fundamentally, individual defensive ratings try to get at how many points a player allows per hundred possessions. Individual stops address only a part of that. Frustratingly, basketball doesn't track how many points a player allows in any way. That is what makes individual defensive ratings as approximate as any statistic in this book. Fortunately, the reason that no one tracks how many points a player allows is because each score a team allows can commonly be attributed to many individuals—each score that a team allows is in many ways a *team* score. So by ascribing team scores approximately equally to teammates, the formula may not be making such a big error.

At least that's how I like to rationalize it all.

In reality, I do have to make an assumption about how many scoring possessions an individual allows. I can do it either of two ways. The first way is to assume that all teammates allow the same number of scoring possessions per minute. The second way is to assume that all teammates face the same number of total possessions per minute. Neither is right, but I have generally grown more comfortable interpreting the second way. Hopefully, Project Defensive Score Sheet will improve upon them both. (My hope is that if I keep mentioning this project, it will become more official.)

The basic theory behind individual defensive ratings is that a player's defense impacts each possession to a limited degree, providing a base defensive rating, but that a player is more prominent in those possessions where he directly allows a score or contributes a stop, providing a modification to the base defensive rating. The formula reflecting this theory is

$$DRtg = TMDRtg + \%TMDPoss \times [100 \times DPtsPerScPoss \times (1 - Stop\%) - TMDRtg]$$

With the detailed results from Project Defensive Score Sheet, the values of %TMDPoss and Stop% could be found directly, as they were in chapter 17, whereas they are normally estimated very approximately. Specifically, the number of individual stops a player has plus the number of scoring possessions he allows equals the number of defensive possessions he faces:

$$DPoss = Stops + DScPoss$$

Unless defensive scoring possessions are tabulated as

$$DScPoss = DFGM + 0.45 \times (FFTA + DFTM) \times \left[1 - \left(1 - \frac{DFTM}{FFTA + DFTM} \right) \right]^2$$

(I've found through limited experience that 0.45 is better than 0.4 in the free throw part) individual defensive scoring possessions are just not known. So we typically know only an individual's stops and have to estimate either defensive scoring possessions or defensive possessions. In estimating values from team statistics, I choose to estimate defensive possessions assuming that each player sees one-fifth of all team possessions

$$DPoss = 0.2 \times \frac{TMPoss}{TMMIN} \times MIN$$

This means that %TMDPoss = 0.2 all the time, and the formula for individual defensive rating becomes

$$DRtg = TMDRtg + 0.2 \times [100 \times DPtsPerScPoss \times (1 - Stop\%) - TMDRtg]$$

where the Stop% is estimated as shown above. If using a Project Defensive Score Sheet tabulation, a player's stop% is

$$Stop\% = \frac{Stops}{Stops + DScPoss}$$

Those are the defensive formulas that drive my evaluations of player defense. Until measurements of field goals allowed and free throws allowed are available, all these estimates are quite approximate. Even if those stats were available, it does appear to be true that defensive ability is strongly a function of defensive system, which is dictated by a coach. In this case, it can be difficult to transfer defensive evaluations from one team to another. And that is why players like Joe Dumars and Doug Christie can end up on both great defenses and horrible defenses.

Appendix 4

Team Statistic Historical Regression

The chapter 21 review of Wilt Chamberlain and Bill Russell relied upon some estimates of the number of turnovers and offensive rebounds that their respective teams posted in the 1960s. Those estimates were based upon a technique called multivariate linear regression, which basically assumed that the number of turnovers a team had in a season can be estimated as

$$\overline{TOV} = a_0 + a_{Seas} \text{ Seas} + a_G \text{ G} + a_{FGA} \text{ FGA} + a_{FTA} \text{ FTA} + a_{REB} \text{ REB} + a_{PF} \text{ PF} + a_{DQ} \text{ DQ}$$
$$+ a_{FGM} \text{ FGM} + a_{FTM} \text{ FTM} + a_{PTS} \text{ PTS} + a_{AST} \text{ AST}$$

and the number of offensive rebounds a team had can be estimated as

$$\overline{OREB} = b_0 + b_{Seas} \text{ Seas} + b_G \text{ G} + t_{FGA} \text{ FGA} + b_{FTA} \text{ FTA} + b_{REB} \text{ REB} + b_{PF} \text{ PF} + b_{DQ} \text{ DQ}$$
$$+ b_{FGM} \text{ FGM} + b_{FTM} \text{ FTM} + b_{PTS} \text{ PTS} + b_{AST} \text{ AST}$$

The multivariate regression (which is available in Microsoft Excel under the Tools menu and Data Analysis package) automatically looks for the best values of the a's and b's in the above equations to make the estimates, $\overline{TOV}$ and $\overline{OREB}$, as accurate as possible given the data available. The data available for making these estimates is all the NBA team statistics since 1974, when turnovers and offensive rebounds were first recorded. The mathematical process that occurs behind the scenes to estimate the a's and b's for teams since 1974 is not something I'm going to explain here (doing that would be too much like the tests I took in college). But I can tell you that the result is not only the a's and b's, but also how well the formulas actually estimate the known data. Do they miss by an average of one hundred turnovers per team per season (about one per game) or by an average of three hundred? If the formulas actually do a good job explaining the turnovers and offensive rebounds since 1974, the assumption is then that the formulas also describe what happened prior to 1974.

In the end, the formulas are reasonably accurate. How you define "accurate" is not even perfectly defined. On average, the predictions are right—the average error is pretty close to zero. Or you could say that most of the errors in estimating turnovers are plus or minus one hundred per team per season (the standard error is about one hundred or, in estimating offensive rebounds, it is seventy-four). Another way to look at things is to say how what percentage of the variation in turnovers and offensive rebounds is explained by the formulas. In each case, it's about 80 percent (81 percent for the turnovers and 80 percent for the offensive rebounds). I would call this "not bad." For those familiar with regression, the Excel package outputs the summaries of accuracy shown in table A4.1.

The resulting values of *a*'s and *b*'s are summarized in tables A4.2 and A4.3 along with their standard errors and p-values, which indicate how reliable the values are. Smaller p-values indicate that the numbers are, using the language of the Derrick Coleman chapter, "significant." When p-values are greater than about 0.05, most people don't consider the corresponding *a* or *b* value to be reliably different from zero. When a p-value is less than 0.05, that doesn't mean that the *a* or *b* value is correct, it just means that there probably is some dependence on that statistic.

For example, the first table shows that turnovers are directly proportional to assists. Each assist implies about 0.0803 turnovers, after accounting for the effect of everything else. Or, with regard to offensive rebounds, the very small p-values for FGA and FTA imply that they are important in estimating offensive rebounds—not a big surprise. On the other hand, fouling out, made field goals,

Table A4.1. Regression Summary Statistics

	Turnovers	OREB
Multiple R	0.90	0.90
R Square	0.81	0.80
Adjusted R Square	0.81	0.80
Standard Error	97	74
Observations	710	710

Table A4.2. Parameter Estimates for Turnover Regression

Parameter	Value	Std. Error	p-value	Significant?
a_0	35170	2004	2.3E-57	*
a_{Seas}	-17.6	1.002	1.7E-57	*
a_G	11.7	1.60	6.0E-13	*
a_{FGA}	-0.0615	0.0227	6.8E-03	*
a_{FTA}	0.373	0.0525	3.1E-12	*
a_{REB}	0.144	0.0252	1.6E-08	*
a_{PF}	0.180	0.0333	8.8E-08	*
a_{DQ}	0.91	0.481	5.8E-02	
a_{FGM}	-0.0666	0.0832	4.2E-01	
a_{FTM}	-0.3676	0.0734	7.0E-07	*
a_{PTS}	-0.0373	0.0377	3.2E-01	
a_{AST}	0.0803	0.0308	9.3E-03	*

*The notation 1.1E-08 means 0.000000011 or 1.1×10^{-8}.

Table A4.3. Parameter Estimates for Offensive Rebound Regression

Parameter	Value	Std. Error	p-value	Significant?
b_0	-8852	1532	1.1E-08	*
b_{Seas}	4.43	0.766	1.1E-08	*
b_G	-11.5	1.22	5.0E-20	*
b_{FGA}	0.217	0.0173	1.0E-32	*
b_{FTA}	0.447	0.0401	1.3E-26	*
b_{REB}	0.174	0.0192	1.7E-18	*
b_{PF}	0.0099	0.0255	7.0E-01	
b_{DQ}	0.81	0.367	2.8E-02	*
b_{FGM}	0.1551	0.0636	1.5E-02	*
b_{FTM}	-0.3119	0.0561	3.8E-08	*
b_{PTS}	-0.104	0.0288	3.2E-04	*
b_{AST}	-0.085	0.0235	3.2E-04	*

*The notation 1.1E-08 means 0.000000011 or 1.1×10^{-8}.

and points don't seem to have any relationship to turnovers, and personal fouls don't seem to have any relationship to offensive rebounds. (Strictly, I should have done collinearity tests and eliminated insignificant variables, but I didn't feel it was necessary for the discussions being made in chapter 21.)

I use this technique in chapter 21 to attempt to fill in some missing team statistics in the days before offensive rebounds and turnovers were recorded. I think it serves a generally valuable service in this case because the results don't have to be overly accurate and because I am not taking overly seriously the values of a's and b's. However, this kind of regression technique is commonly used much more seriously in other fields of study and even in basketball. David Berri's technique for evaluating player value uses this technique, and I am somewhat more dubious of its reliability in such cases.

I was taught that math and science were objective when I was a kid. But as I have gone on to study real problems in the world, I have found that, even though the math may be exact, how you ask the question or set up the solution is where some subjectivity is introduced.

Glossary

Assist: As judged by official scorers, an assist is awarded to a player making a pass to a teammate leading directly to a made field goal.

Bell curve winning percentage: Winning percentage estimated from a team's average values of points scored and allowed, as well as the variability of points scored and allowed. Bell curve percentages can also be calculated with a team's offensive and defensive ratings.

Block out: A technique employed by a player to prevent opposing players from getting near the basket to get a rebound. Synonym: box out.

Board: A rebound.

Box: See "post."

Covariance: A statistic that represents how two sets of numbers change together.

Defensive rating: Points allowed (by a team or individual) per hundred possessions.

Defensive stop: A stop occurs when a defense regains the ball without allowing the opponent a scoring possession.

Field goal: When a player makes a basket during regular play (not as a result of a foul).

Field percentage: The percentage of times a team scores a basket on possessions where no free throws are awarded. Illustrates how well teams score without drawing fouls.

Floor percentage: The fraction of a team's or individual's possessions on which there is a scoring possession.

Free throw: When a player makes a basket from the foul line (or free throw line) after a foul is committed.

Garbage time: That period near the end of certain games when the victorious team is evident and second-string players are in the game.

Man-to-man defense: A type of defense where each player on the defense is primarily responsible for preventing a single opposing player from scoring. This is in contrast to a zone defense.

Offensive rating: Points scored (by a team) or produced (by an individual) per hundred possessions.

Percentage of team possessions: A representation of how often an individual uses a team possession. With five players on the court, an average value of the percentage of team possessions would be one-fifth or 20 percent.

Pick-and-roll: A type of play where one offensive player sets a pick on the defender covering the ball handler, then moves away (the "roll") to try to make the defender confused about who to cover.

Play: The technical definition of a play in this book is the period between when one team gains control of the ball and when they lose control of the ball, either when the opposing team gains control or when a shot goes up. For example, if a team misses a shot, gets the rebound, and then makes the follow-up, that is two plays and only one possession.

Play percentage: The fraction of a team's plays (see Play) on which it produces a scoring possession.

Points per hundred possessions rating: See "rating."

Points produced: In a team context, points produced is the same thing as points scored. In an individual context, points produced represents the number of points an individual generates through various offensive contributions, including assists, field goals, free throws, and offensive rebounds.

Possession: The period of time between when one team gains control of the ball and when the opposing team gains control of the ball. Contrast with play.

Post: The post is a vaguely defined area within five to ten feet of the basket where offensive players (usually big men) try to establish position so that, when they get the ball, they can score. "Posting up" is when a player is trying to establish such position. Synonyms: box, block.

Pythagorean winning percentage: Winning percentage estimated from a team's average values of points scored and allowed.

Rating: In this book, a rating is typically meant to convey how many points are scored or allowed per hundred possessions. Points scored (or produced) per hundred possessions is an "offensive rating." Points allowed per hundred possessions is a "defensive rating."

Scoring possession: A scoring possession occurs when a team scores at least one point. An individual scoring possession is awarded to an individual when contributing to a team scoring possession (or a partial scoring possession is awarded when multiple individuals contribute).

Standard deviation: A statistic that represents how varied a group of numbers are.

Stop: See "defensive stop."

Uncorrelated ratings: Points per hundred possession ratings that are adjusted by how much teams play up or down to their opponents. Teams that do not play up or down to opponents will have the same uncorrelated ratings as regular ratings. Also see "rating."

Variance: The standard deviation multiplied by itself. Another way to represent how much variation exists in a group of numbers.

Zone defense: A type of defense where each defender is primarily responsible for preventing any player in a given zone of the court from scoring.

References

This book was constructed from research in a lot of different fields, including traditional basketball coaching, sports economics, and statistics. Listed below are some of the prominent articles, books, and other documents that provided me data or made me think over the years.

Berri, David. 1999. "Who Is 'Most Valuable'? Measuring the Player's Production of Wins in the National Basketball Association." *Managerial and Decision Economics*, v. 20, pp. 411–420.

Berri, David. "Mixing the Princes and the Paupers and Other Determinants of Worker Productivity in the National Basketball Association." In review.

Bradley, Robert. 1999. *Compendium of Professional Basketball.* Xaler Press, Tempe, AZ.

Douchant, Mike. 1995. *Encyclopedia of College Basketball.* Visible Ink Press, Detroit, MI.

Gilovich, Thomas; Vallone, Robert; and Tversky, Amos. 1985. "The Hot Hand in Basketball: On the Misperception of Random Sequences." *Cognitive Psychology*, v. 17, pp. 295–314.

James, Bill. 1985 (or many other years). *Baseball Abstract.* Ballantine Books, New York, NY.

Krause, Jerry, and Pim, Ralph (editors). 2002. *Coaching Basketball.* Contemporary Books.

McGuire, Frank. 1959. *Defensive Basketball.* Prentice Hall, Inc. Englewood Cliffs, NJ.

Porter, Philip K., and Scully, Gerald W. 1982 "Measuring Managerial Efficiency: The Case of Baseball." *Southern Economic Journal,* v. 48, pp. 642–650.

Quirk, James, and Fort, Rodney. 1992. *Pay Dirt.* Princeton University Press, Princeton, NJ.

Sachare, Alex (editor). 1994. *Official NBA Basketball Encyclopedia,* Second Edition. Villard Books, New York, NY.

Schmidt, Martin, and Berri, David. 2001. "Competitive Balance and Attendance: The Case of Major League Baseball." *Journal of Sports Economics,* v. 2, no. 2, pp. 145–167.

Scully, Gerald W. 1994. "Managerial Efficiency and Survivability in Professional Team Sports." *Managerial and Decision Economics,* v. 15, no. 5, pp. 403–411.

Staw, B. M. and H. Hoang. 1995. "Sunk costs in the NBA: Why Draft Order Affects Playing Time and Survival in Professional Basketball." *Administrative Science Quarterly,* v. 40, no. 3, pp. 474–494.

The TI-55 Calculator Handbook. (That's how I learned statistics.)

Wootten, Morgan. 1992. *Coaching Basketball Successfully.* Leisure Press, Champaign, IL.

Index

Entries in *italics* refer to figures or tables.

About the Author

Dean Oliver is currently an assistant coach with the Washington Wizards and has worked in analytical roles with the Seattle Supersonics, Sacramento Kings, and Denver Nuggets. He has taught basketball analytics for many years and has been a frequent contributor to international sports analytics journals and conferences. He lives in Washington DC.